RED HANDS

Also by Christopher Golden

The Pandora Room

Ararat

Dead Ringers

Sons of Anarchy: BRATVA

Snowblind

Baltimore, or, The Steadfast Tin Soldier and the Vampire (with Mike Mignola)

Joe Golem and the Drowning City (with Mike Mignola)

Father Gaetano's Puppet Catechism (with Mike Mignola)

The Boys Are Back in Town

Wildwood Road

The Ferryman

Strangewood

Straight On 'til Morning

Soulless

The Myth Hunters: Book One of The Veil

The Borderkind: Book Two of The Veil

The Lost Ones: Book Three of The Veil

The Ocean Dark (as Jack Rogan)

The Shadow Saga

Of Saints and Shadows

Angel Souls and Devil Hearts

Of Masques and Martyrs

The Gathering Dark

Walking Nightmares

The Graves of Saints

King of Hell

RED HNDS

Christopher Golden

ST. MARTIN'S PRESS
NEW YORK

First published in the United States by St. Martin's Press, an imprint of St. Martin's Publishing Group

RED HANDS. Copyright © 2020 by Christopher Golden. All rights reserved. Printed in the United States of America. For information, address St. Martin's Publishing Group, 120 Broadway, New York, NY 10271.

www.stmartins.com

The Library of Congress Cataloging-in-Publication Data is available upon request.

ISBN 978-1-250-24630-1 (hardcover)
ISBN 978-1-250-24631-8 (ebook)

Our books may be purchased in bulk for promotional, educational, or business use. Please contact your local bookseller or the Macmillan Corporate and Premium Sales Department at 1-800-221-7945, extension 5442, or by email at MacmillanSpecialMarkets@macmillan.com.

First Edition: 2020

10 9 8 7 6 5 4 3 2 1

For James A. Moore

RED HANDS

1

Later, Maeve Sinclair will think of the girl with the pink balloon, and her heart will ache with a sting unlike anything she's felt before. She'll feel that sting forever, or for as long a forever as the world is willing to give her. In her mind's eye, the little girl's hand will always clutch the balloon string so fiercely, and Maeve knows it's because the girl lost her balloon at the Fourth of July parade the year before. When you're three years old, that's the sort of thing that can scar you, and little Callie Ellroy was three last year when she watched her Mickey Mouse balloon sail into the blue and vanish forever.

It's not Mickey this year, just an ordinary pink balloon, even a bit underinflated, as if Callie didn't want to invest quite as much of her now-four-year-old adoration this time around. Yet she holds the string so tightly and smiles so brightly, showing all her crooked teeth and every ounce of the joy bursting within her, that Maeve is sure the little girl can't help but love that balloon. A little deflated or not. Plain, ordinary, boring balloon or not. Her sneakers are the same pink as the balloon, and though Maeve can't hear the words she speaks when she tugs her mother's arm and points at her sneakers, the pantomime is enough to communicate just how much delight she's taken from this moment of pink epiphany.

Maeve has watched Callie Ellroy grow. She can remember the

moment five years ago when Biz Ellroy—short for Elizabeth—had rushed up to her, beaming, and shared the news that she was pregnant with the little bean that would become Callie. Biz had even picked out her name already.

At twenty-nine, the memory makes Maeve feel unsettlingly adult. She'd been standing in nearly the same spot where she stands today, watching a troupe of clowns toss candy from the back of an antique fire truck while the Conway High School marching band blatted on trumpets and thundered on drums in a rough approximation of "Yankee Doodle Dandy." But she'd been twenty-four then, still young enough that older people hesitated to take her seriously. Now she's on the verge of thirty, unmarried, no children, steadily employed but not in love with her job, and looking for a change.

Maeve gets a little shiver as she watches Biz holding Callie's hand. The same antique fire engine goes by, probably the same clowns on the back, throwing the same stale candy. Only Maeve figures the fire engine is a little more antique now than it was then, and aren't they all, really?

Time is fucking merciless, Maeve thinks. It doesn't ever slow down for you, even when you need it to. Even when, for instance, you still live in your hometown and can never escape the certainty that there's another life for you out there, somewhere. Maeve wants to work to improve people's lives, but after four years studying global health and public policy at George Washington University, dipping her toe in the water of half a dozen D.C. internships, she felt lost. She came back to Jericho Falls and got a job working for CareNH, a White Mountains political action committee. The money sucks, but she loves New Hampshire. She loves her parents and her brother and sister. Over the past year, she's foolishly allowed an old flame to reignite, and that makes it harder to leave and all the more important that she does.

The new job's in Boston. A nonprofit called Liquid Dreams, which she thinks is a stupid name, but she admires the hell out of the company's mission, fighting for clean drinking water in the United States and around the globe, and fighting against corporations trying to monopolize control of the water supply. It's a fight worth having, and so what if her job is as an events coordinator and not impacting the company's political efforts? She'll be serving that admirable goal, and that's what matters to her.

It's time to leave Jericho Falls. She just has to tell her family. And she has to tell her . . . Nathan. Her Nathan. She guesses he's her boyfriend, but that seems too concrete a word for the tentative way they dance around each other. Or, more accurately, the way she dances around him. Maeve is sure he'll want to carry on seeing her, even if it means a long-distance relationship. Three hours in the car doesn't seem that long to begin with, but Maeve already knows it's going to wear on them, and the truth is she never really thought of her thing with Nathan as long-term, just like she never thought she'd stay home for seven years after college. Both things just sort of happened. She wonders if she ought to leave both of them behind—Jericho Falls and her relationship. Nathan's sweet and a comfort to be around, but so were the plush animals in her childhood bedroom.

Today's parade feels like an ending of sorts, and maybe a beginning, too. The mayor rolls by, sitting in the back of an old Cadillac convertible with his leathery wife, who's never quite learned how to apply her makeup. Maeve feels a rush of love for the old doll and for her town, because in other places the mayor's wife might've been replaced by a younger, blonder version, but in Jericho Falls, she looks just the way you'd expect her to look. The future is going to catch up to her town soon, and though Maeve yearns to be a part of the rush of the real world, it saddens her to think of Jericho Falls changing. She thinks, momentarily, that the mayor's wife should ditch him for a younger, more attractive husband and then run for mayor herself. If the future has to come to Jericho Falls, Maeve wants it to arrive in heels.

All these thoughts spin through her head while she glances around the crowd. Her dad, Ted, munches an ice cream sandwich from a street vendor. He's with Rue Crooker, maybe his best and oldest friend, so close that when the kids were little they called her Auntie Rue. Maeve's brother, Logan, is over beside their mom, on the other side of the street, which is a good illustration of their lives since Ellen

Sinclair finally had enough of her husband's alcoholism and changed the locks on the house. None of it has been as ugly as Maeve feared, but it hasn't been pretty, either. Her dad's had a rough time with addiction, but he's kicked the pills at least, and he's trying, which is maybe why Ellen and Ted can stand across the street from each other and offer a smile and subdued wave.

Maeve likes that. They'll always be family, thanks to the three children they share, so it's nice if they can manage not to hate each other. The youngest member of Maeve's family finally arrives, her twenty-one-year-old sister, Rose, who grins nervously as she approaches their mother and Logan while holding hands with her girlfriend in public for the very first time.

This is the Sinclair family today, doing their best to reenact a tradition begun decades earlier. The Jericho Falls Fourth of July parade, held at 11:00 A.M. on the actual goddamn Fourth of July, no matter the weather and no matter the stink some locals put up because they like the parade but they want to be on vacation somewhere nicer, somewhere with a great fireworks display, on the actual holiday. Other cities and towns cave to the pressure, celebrate a few days before or even after the Fourth, but not Jericho Falls. Fuck that. It's another thing that makes Maeve proud of her town.

She'll dwell on all of this later. She'll turn it over in her head, wondering if there was something she could have done differently, anything that might have changed the outcome. If she had been paying more attention to her family, or the parade, or the crowd instead of being lost inside her head and worrying about breaking the news of her new job and impending departure to her mom, would she have been able to save lives?

Would she have been able to save herself?

Of course, she'll never know.

The car comes from Kingsbury Road, which is perpendicular to Main Street. Over the squeal of a coterie of kilted bagpipers she hears another sound, someone's music turned up obnoxiously loud, a 1970s pop confection blaring from car speakers, and she scowls at how inconsiderate people can be. This moment ought to be about the parade, about the town celebrating its history and its future and the very nature of Jericho Falls as a safe place, a nice place to live in a world where such places grow rarer by the day.

Biz Ellroy drops her bag of popcorn into the road. Somehow there's a tiny lull in the bleating music, and in that lull Maeve can hear little Callie cry out, "Oh no, Mummy!" as mother and daughter release each other's hands. Callie hops off the curb as Biz reaches for the fallen red-and-white striped bag, trying to rescue whatever she can, which is understandable when a little bag of popcorn costs six bucks. In that same lull, in the same sliver of a moment between bagpipe bleats, Maeve hears the roar of a car engine.

It's a parade. No engines are roaring. Some are groaning, some are putt-putt-putting, as floats and antique cars and baton twirlers inch up Main Street. A big old Ford pickup truck tows a flatbed carrying a bunch of Little League players and a float that's supposed to look like a miniature Fenway Park. The kids swing their bats at imaginary pitches while the pickup truck lurches and groans in its deep, pickup truck voice. But this other engine roars, and its roar is not coming from the parade, not from in front of Maeve and her family but behind them, over Maeve's right shoulder. She's about to turn and search for the source of that roar when she sees Biz drop her popcorn and Callie pull away from her mom and both of them go for the bag with that "Oh no, Mummy!"

Callie's fist is tightly closed on the string of that pink balloon. You'd damn well better believe it.

Biz picks up the popcorn bag. Smiling, she takes a couple of kernels out and tosses them at her wild-haired little girl with the big blue eyes, and she steps back onto the curb, beckoning for Callie to follow.

The engine roars. People shout warnings and scream in panic, and some of them run or dive or hurl themselves out of the way as a sparkling silver BMW careens from Kingsbury Road onto Main Street, 1970s pop music crying from the open windows, not slowing for the people who can't get out of the way in time. Not slowing for Mrs. Kestler, who taught Maeve science in middle school, or Geoff Strahan, whose brutal father trained him from birth to be a major-league baseball player, only to have him go to law school, come home to open his practice, and coach Little League.

Not slowing for other people, some of whose faces Maeve knows and some she doesn't.

Not slowing for her sister, Rose, whose girlfriend, Priya, is knocked over in the rush to flee. Rose helps Priya to her feet, but it's too late for them to run. Maeve's father discards his ice cream sandwich as he breaks through the crowd. He's screaming. Maeve is sure he won't reach them in time, but somehow he does, hands outstretched. Ted shoves his youngest child and her girlfriend out of the way, the effort halting his own momentum, leaving him stranded for the last vital second before the BMW's grille will make contact. Ted jumps as high as he can, avoiding the impact of the front end, but he hits the hood, the windshield, goes up and over the car and smashes down onto the pavement in its wake.

The car roars onward. Maeve screams for her father, runs toward where he has fallen.

People are running. Screaming. The bagpipers have ceased, but up and down Main Street, there are still high school musicians playing horrible screeching noises on instruments most of them will never touch again after graduation, and which some of them will never touch again after today . . . after this Fourth of July with its sweet-smelling breeze and glorious blue sky and the promise of a perfect night of barbecue and baseball ahead.

But at least those kids will be alive.

Maeve kneels by her father, sees his blood and doesn't want to touch him, afraid to hurt him further. He's breathing, and this is good. He is alive. She looks up, tracking the car's trajectory. Across the street, she sees Kristie Burns, her best friend since the seventh grade, mirroring her expression. The BMW slews sideways, skidding on clothing and blood, bumping over someone's legs, then seems to leap toward the curb as it takes aim at more spectators. Or maybe the driver is just trying to get around the Ford pickup and the Little League float. Kristie Burns is in its path, and as Maeve watches, it appears that she has locked eyes with the driver, who maybe guns the engine or maybe not, but in the last moment Kristie staggers backward three steps and falls on her ass and the BMW leaps the curb and strikes a fire hydrant, saving Kristie's life. The collision is no symphony of tearing metal but a single whump and a kind of grinding whine as the car's engine begins to realize it's going to die.

Water pours out from under the crumpled BMW hood and pools beneath the car, spreading into the road, beginning to wash away a bit of the blood that has been spilled. So many people are shouting. Police sirens wail, but they could just as easily be a part of the parade as the signal that it has ended, that people are dead.

Maeve spots something overhead, drifting in the air. Little Callie Ellroy's pink balloon.

She spins, searching the crowd, scanning the bodies in the bloodied road, and her gaze lands on Biz, on her knees on the asphalt, mouth open in a silent scream, eyes full of tears, holding a single pink sneaker in both hands.

In that moment, the driver's door on the BMW swings open wide. A bare foot stretches out and touches the pool of water spreading from the shattered hydrant.

And the day gets so much worse.

The driver slips from behind the wheel and staggers to his dirty feet. He's wearing blue cotton pajama pants and a T-shirt that looks as if it must have been white before all the bloodstains. He's been shot at least twice, maybe three times if the reason he's staggering is a third bullet wound in his left leg. The first two are to his torso—one blood-stain has its locus at his right shoulder, the other about four inches to the left of his heart. He's dying, Maeve knows. One look is all it takes to see the shadow of death looming over him. But the driver limps away from the car, wild eyes scanning the buildings beyond the crowd. He begins to stumble toward the brick post office building, or maybe toward the alley between the post office and the bookstore café. There's a parking lot behind them, and beyond that a hill slopes through a maze of short streets and then to the river.

He doesn't make it to the river. He doesn't even make it to the post office. People shout. Others are still screaming, trying to help the people he'd struck with his car, some of whom are beyond help. Distant sirens grow not so distant, more urgent, as if now that their purpose has turned dire, the sound reflects that. Most of the people who'd been on the sidewalk around Kristie Burns when the car plowed toward her have scattered out of the way, leaving only a few to help Kristie to her feet as the BMW ticks and steams and floods hydrant water from under its hood.

As the driver stagger-marches to the sidewalk, these last few scramble out of his way, maybe because he's just done something totally insane, or because someone shot him and the bright red stains on his white T-shirt continue to spread. As he steps onto the sidewalk, a barrel-chested guy with a beard emerges from the frantic, grieving, stunned crowd.

"Mother. Fucker." The bearded guy says it just like that, as if it's two words. His hands are fisted at his sides, and the rage on his face is made all the more terrifying by the tears streaming down his cheeks. He isn't just furious, he's broken, and he's going to break the driver to make them a matched set.

The bearded guy raising his fists triggers others to move toward the driver. One of them is Tim Mak, who brought Maeve to his junior prom when she was only a sophomore and then promptly abandoned her to be with his friends. Tim's changed a lot in the intervening years, slimmer and more handsome, much better taste in clothes. But in this moment, he looks fierce in a way Maeve would never have imagined he might be. He looks dangerous.

It's Tim who reaches the driver first. Blocks his path with a "Where the fuck do you think you're going?" as the sirens grow louder. Police. Ambulances. Floats and other parade vehicles are inching out of the way, making room for the arrival of first responders. Tim Mak puts out a hand to stop the driver, with Kristie Burns looking on from a few feet away, still visibly shaken by her close call.

Tim plants a hand, fingers splayed, on the driver's bloodied T-shirt. The driver reaches out and grabs Tim by the face, shoves him backward. As Tim takes one step back, Maeve is sure she sees the imprint of the driver's hand flare red on Tim's skin before it fades. But something's happened. Tim retches, gagging, jerking his body. He coughs and tries to lift shaking hands to his mouth, even as black-red fluid streams from both nostrils and his left eye.

Maeve doesn't feel as if she's inside her own body anymore. She's frozen, jaw hanging open, forgetting to breathe as she watches Tim Mak collapse into a heap of shuddering limbs, and then go still. Kristie stares for a second at Tim's unmoving form and snaps out of her shock—or maybe immerses herself even more deeply into the maelstrom of emotions that burst across her features.

"You crazy fucking prick!" Kristie shouts. "What did you just do to him?"

It's possible she doesn't manage to get those last few words out, that Maeve's brain fills them in because she expects them. Kristie rushes at the driver while she's screaming, lunging for his throat. He knocks one of her hands away and grabs a fistful of her wild red hair, twists her around to drive her out of his path. Kristie tries to fight. Still clutching her hair in one hand, he grabs her wrist with the other and shoves her off the curb. She sprawls in the street, convulsing, and then she, too, goes still.

Maeve's brother, Logan, starts across the street without a word. One second he's with the rest of the family, and then he's in motion. He doesn't get far before Mom rushes forward, wraps her arms around Logan's chest, and halts him in his tracks with a torrent of angry, fearful words. Rose is holding her girlfriend, Priya, who is sobbing and shaking. Maeve's mother starts comforting those around her, telling everyone to keep back, to go home, to make way for the emergency vehicles.

As if Kristie hasn't just died in the street. As if Ted Sinclair isn't bleeding on the pavement.

Maeve has forgotten how to breathe. It's chaos all around, and her heart is slamming in her chest. Across the street, as the water from the hydrant spreads farther, pooling around the mangled body of a girl in an American flag tank top, several other people rush at the BMW driver. Some are smart enough to run the other direction, but these three men take it upon themselves to stop him, maybe thinking they'll make him pay for what he's done.

An icy chill runs up Maeve's spine. Hot tears course down her face. She shifts a few feet, trying to get a look at Kristie's eyes, hoping to see a spark of life but knowing in her heart there's not a glimmer. She thinks of a hundred summer days like this one, spent at the lake, out on Jack Spencer's boat. She thinks of watching scary movies during sleepovers, Kristie's eighth-grade determination to get her first kiss, playing soccer together and laughing as they realized neither of them were very good. All those memories lie dead on Main Street.

When the sirens and the shouts are abruptly drowned out by the roar of a black helicopter sweeping overhead, Maeve barely notices. In her subconscious, she accepts its presence, and a little flicker of awareness recognizes that it means something, that black helicopter, slicing the air, lifting and turning as it searches for a place to land.

One by one, the three men trying to stop the BMW driver reel away from him, bodies racked with seizure, coughing and gasping, black-red mucus streaming from noses and eyes. From her knees, bereft, alone, and feeling invisible, Maeve thinks she sees their skin flare red or flush pink where the driver touches them.

Instead of continuing toward the alley, the driver turns toward the crowd. Bloody and stumbling but somehow more focused, his lips curled in a sneer that says he's made up his mind about something ugly, he lunges toward a group of people clustered too closely together for all of them to elude him. A middle-aged woman with a glorious mane of coiled black hair is nearest and cannot escape the hand he reaches toward her. His fingers close on her bare upper arm. She pulls free, but she's already dying. Her skin is dark, but even so, Maeve is sure she can see the momentary handprint left behind.

She can't watch it anymore. Far off to her left, the dispersing crowd has knocked over a popcorn vendor's cart, and there is popcorn blowing all over the road and onto the grass and sidewalk. Scattered kernels blow like tiny tumbleweeds onto the pooling water under the BMW and float as if set adrift to race in a child's dream. Maeve focuses on the popcorn, entirely losing track of the sounds around her. They blend into one larger noise, beneath all of which is the whine of helicopter rotors powering down, somewhere south along Main Street.

The first police car arrives. There's an ambulance behind it. She sees them out of the corner of her eye, unwilling to tear her gaze from the popcorn regatta floating in the hydrant water. Until several kernels float up to and bump up against the dead girl in her American flag tank top.

Maeve flinches and rises to her feet. Her family's otherwise occupied as she walks half a dozen paces and picks up a baseball bat that has fallen from the hands of one of the kids on the Little League float. The kids are long gone, having fled their miniature Fenway, and that's for the best.

It's possible she hears Logan call out her name as she begins to run, but Maeve doesn't slow down. She doesn't turn or hesitate. The BMW driver is a pale, middle-aged, ordinary man with sallow cheeks and dark circles beneath his eyes. He's got a fistful of a young father's T-shirt in his left hand, rucking it up to expose the guy's tattooed back, reaching out his right hand to touch that tattoo. The young father has a curly-haired toddler in his arms, and practically throws the little girl at his wife as the seizures rack his body and he falls.

That's the last one, though. The last one the driver touches.

Maeve steps up and swings the bat with all the strength and training of her varsity softball days. The driver turns toward her just as the bat is about to connect. When the blow lands, the aluminum bat rings true, as if she's hit a homer, but the sound is accompanied by the crack of bone. His eyes are wide as he staggers backward, sways a bit, and then falls toward her, bouncing once as he hits the pavement. His neck is twisted to one side, and she can see the indentation on his forehead where the bat did its damage.

When he tries to rise, ordinary blood running from his nose, she hits him again, this time in the back of the head. But he's been shot at least three times, been punched and shoved and kicked, and now he's taken an aluminum bat to the skull, so he isn't quite done yet.

The driver is on the pavement. The puddle of water stretching out from the hydrant beneath the BMW reaches him, flowing around him. He skids himself forward in the water, dragging his chest and face and then lurches one more time to his feet, head hanging askew, reaching for her throat.

Maeve grabs his wrist with her free hand, twists his arm away. He falls to the ground, but she's still holding on, barely noticing him, staring instead at her fingers clenched around his wrist. Instinct had done it. She's reacted faster than she could think, had grabbed him to avoid him doing the same to her, and though he's on the ground now, it's only after he convulses once and then dies, his gaze going flat and dull as doll's eyes, that she manages to release her hold on him.

A scream cuts through the buzzing in her head. Her mother's voice. The scream is her name, and she turns as her mother races toward her. Logan and Rose had been deemed more important, more in need of attention, as has always been the case. Her whole life, they've thought of her as more capable, less in need of their love and comfort. Now Maeve is listening to her own heartbeat, waiting for the cough and the seizures to come. She's going to die like the others, she is certain.

But the seizures don't come. Maeve shudders. Shock had dried up her tears, but now with her relief, they return. Her hands shake, but she feels good, she feels fine. Better than fine. Somewhere behind her, Kristie Burns lies dead. So many people are dead. Biz Ellroy is lying on the grass across the road, cradling a pink sneaker in her arms. The pink balloon is long gone. But the BMW driver is dead and Maeve is still alive and she feels herself about to shatter inside, fractured by a dozen conflicting emotions.

"Maeve, oh my God," her mom says.

That voice—the voice of safety and reassurance, of comfort and warmth—is the root of her childhood. As often as she fought with her mother through middle and high school and has dismissed so much of her advice since then, in this moment she's a little girl again and when she looks up and their eyes meet, her mother sees how much Maeve needs her.

"Oh, my baby," Ellen Sinclair says, "that was so . . . You were so brave."

Maeve cracks. A sob racks her body and she tries to speak, but no words will come. She laughs at her inability to summon language. She knows this is all part of the shock, but oh God, she wants to go home. She wants to check on her dad. He can't have gone through all the things he's endured just to die now, like this.

Her mom takes her hands, squeezes them, pulls her into an embrace. Maeve leans into her, leans on her the way she always has, even when she didn't realize how much of her emotional weight her mother carried for her. Ellen kisses her girl's forehead. Maeve lays her head on her mother's shoulder, eyes open, and she sees her brother rushing to join them.

Police push through the crowd, hurrying over to the bodies of the people the driver touched. She spots Auntie Rue, a no-nonsense woman with a sleeve of purple tattoos and half her skull shaved. Rue snaps instructions at the officers, barking orders about quarantine and disease. She isn't a cop, just a citizen, and doesn't look like the kind of person the police would ordinarily listen to, but she speaks with authority, and suddenly they're wary. They're right to be.

Logan joins the hug. Maeve reaches up to touch his face, meets his eyes, so grateful for his kindness. As she touches him, she feels her mother jerk in her arms. At first she can't make sense of it, but Logan steps back, his expression contorting in horror. He lifts one hand to cover his mouth, to stifle a cry, as their mother slips from Maeve's arms and hits the pavement. Convulsing again, and then again, Ellen Sinclair rolls over, and Maeve sees the vile black-red sludge issuing from the corner of her mouth and dripping from her nose. Dark sores appear on her skin.

"Mom?" Maeve whispers as a vast hollow place fissures open within her, an empty chamber where emotion should be. She cries out this time. "Mom?" But there is no answer.

When Maeve's sister shouts, though, it isn't for her mother. Rose shouts her brother's name. Maeve glances up and sees Logan in the midst of a shaking fit that sprays that hideous sludge from his mouth. His eyes are squeezed tightly shut, but squibs of that sludge are being forced out through his lashes. There's a hint, a little red afterimage, the imprint of Maeve's hand on Logan's cheek, but when she blinks it's gone, and so is he.

Logan is dead before he hits the pavement.

Her sister stares at her, stares at her hands.

Maeve sways from side to side, not knowing what to do, or where to run, or what she's become. She glances at her father, who has propped himself up on one hand, wincing in pain but alive. The BMW driver, the man she'd killed, the man whose hands she'd avoided but whose skin she'd been touching while the last flicker of life left his body. The small-town cops pushing people back from the bodies, from the crime scene, have paused and watch her with the same stunned wariness as the rest. Auntie Rue takes a step toward her. Maeve stares at her hands.

A second black helicopter buzzes overhead. The remaining bystanders have been staring at her, but they glance up, tracking the helicopter, and as one they all hear the voices barking commands. People begin to clear a path. Through the crowd, she sees three figures in yellow hazmat suits accompanied by armed men in black body armor. All of them wear air filtration masks like they're afraid of contamination. Of contagion.

She turns toward her father. He must see the decision in her eyes, because he shakes his head.

"Maeve, no," he says, clutching his ribs, wincing in pain, blood on his face.

But Maeve has never been good at doing what she's told. She sees those hazmat suits, the guns and the body armor, and she thinks of the bullet holes in the man she killed, the man who killed so many, and she can't stay here.

So she runs.

People who saw her mother and brother die get out of her way. People who did not are already in motion, clearing a path for the black helicopter's team. The police who saw Logan and Mom die don't try to follow her until Rue shouts at them that they can't let her leave, but by then, Maeve has broken into a run. She bolts through the crowd, across the park, away from Main Street, away from the river. She races through backyards on Kingsbury Road, and then she's into the woods she'd spent most of her childhood wandering. Maeve knows every path, even the ones that are so narrow and overgrown they hardly look like trails at all.

She glances up. Sunlight streams through breaks in the canopy of the woods, and in those breaks she can see the mountains ahead. Her heart races, and she doesn't allow herself to think of anything except reaching the foothills, getting lost up there. She won't be able to hide forever, but she needs time to think.

Her hands itch. Her fingers feel strangely cold.

She thinks of her mom and of Logan, and her breath hitches in her chest. Tears stream down her face as she runs. All she wants to do is scream, to lie down on the trail and curl up and wait for all of this to catch up to her, to punish her.

Branches whip past her face. Maeve ducks and stumbles, then turns off the trail. She wonders if this is what madness feels like. If this is what it feels like to be a killer.

In the distance, she hears the buzz of a black helicopter, and she plunges into deeper woods, always staying on course for the mountains.

She thinks of Callie Ellroy's pink balloon and feels the icy cold of her fingers, and a terrible knowledge stabs at her—she can never touch anyone again.

Not ever.

Z

Rue Crooker stood in the middle of a street rapidly emptying of spectators, surrounded by broken, bloody bodies and the loved ones grieving over them. Armed men and women in black body armor wove between abandoned floats and spread out to encircle the scene while a woman in civilian clothes strode through, glancing left and right to survey the carnage. People in hazmat suits rushed by her, heading for the crashed BMW. The body-armored security detail approached the car with weapons leveled, as if they expected to be attacked from within.

One of them paused by the corpse of the BMW driver—the man who'd killed and injured so many—and went to nudge the body with the toe of his boot. A muffled bark from one of the hazmat suits made him freeze and back away. Whoever the driver had been, the person in the hazmat suit knew him. Recognized him. Had expected to find him here.

Of course they had. How else could a squad of Blackcoats show up so fast?

She went to Ted, went down on one knee beside him. "Hey, no," she said as he tried to rise. "You need to stay right here."

His eyes were glazed with pain and grief. He glanced over at the bodies of his ex-wife and his son, then cringed and looked away, unprepared. Five feet away, his daughter Rose wept in the embrace of her girlfriend. Ted cast a pleading glance up at Rue.

"Maeve," he said.

"I know," Rue replied, though she didn't, really. How could she possibly guess what part of this horror had carved itself deepest? "Just wait. You need doctors to look you over."

Ted seemed to agree, or maybe he was just numb.

Rue's heart thumped like it wanted to break free. Flushed with heat, somehow she felt cold inside. *So this is shock*, she thought, observing the whole, wretched tableau that spread around her. Several of those struck by the car were still alive and in dire need of medical attention. Ted seemed in remarkably good condition. He had jumped right before the car hit him, which Rue thought might have saved his life. At the very least, it had saved him from a broken leg or two.

Sirens wailed. Police officers hurried through the remnants of the crowd. Several EMTs were on-site, moving from victim to victim, searching for those who were not already beyond their help. Someone shouted for an ambulance. Others called to the Blackcoats for aid but received no reply. The young civilian woman also seemed deaf to these cries. Even the hazmat team paid no attention to the people who'd been struck by the BMW, but Rue had expected that. They weren't here for the broken, bleeding ones—they had come because of the man behind the wheel.

"Ted, just keep still," she said. "Help is coming. I'll make sure of it."

He groaned and nodded, squeezing his eyes closed. There were tears on his face, but Rue thought they had sprung from grief instead of physical pain. She turned away, let him have his privacy.

She went to Rose and her girlfriend, Priya. Touched Rose on the shoulder. "Stay with your dad."

Sniffling, Rose nodded, still in Priya's embrace.

The hazmat team surrounded the dead driver. The civilian woman began to shout orders, apparently in command, and the Blackcoats closed in, beginning to surround the people who had been touched by the driver or by Maeve Sinclair. Rue whipped out her phone, tapped the screen, and began to record.

"Excuse me!" she shouted. "Excuse me, what are you doing? Who are you? How did you get here so quickly?"

The woman in charge raised a hand to halt the Blackcoat security team. The hazmat crew had already yanked out a body bag and started to transfer the driver into it without a single crime scene photo having been taken, without even a police officer approving their actions. They didn't stop what they were doing, but whatever menace the Blackcoats had intended toward those mourning their dead had halted or at least paused.

"I'm going to ask again!" Rue said. "What do you think you're doing?"

Popcorn containers and other parade debris blew along the pavement. A stroller had been left behind in the hurried exodus of onlookers. Someone had snatched up their baby and just run, and Rue didn't blame them at all. She probably should have run as well, but she wasn't wired that way. At the age of fifty-four, neither her knees nor her demeanor were inclined to do much running.

"Put that phone away. It's illegal to record during a crisis like this," the young woman said, not taking a step.

Her whole team seemed to be frozen. More sirens blared. Local police started to shout to one another. An ambulance drove up onto the lawn of a house on the corner of Kingsbury. Another black helicopter buzzed overhead and seemed to hover a thousand feet above the BMW. The woman put a hand to her ear, frowning, and Rue realized that though she might appear to be giving the orders, she was getting them from somewhere else.

Rue kept recording. She took a step closer. One of the Blackcoats turned his weapon on her.

"The phone. Now," the woman said.

"Fuck you. If you're any kind of law enforcement, which I doubt, there's nothing illegal about me filming. And since you've got a private security detail with no badges or identification, I'd say you've got even less authority over me."

The woman whirled her hand in the air and turned her back on Rue. On that signal, the entire response team began to behave as if Rue had turned invisible. The confidence in that disregard broke through the numbness and shock and made Rue afraid all over again. She wasn't a concern—less trouble than a mosquito—which meant these people had a lot of power or had much larger worries, or both. *Probably both.*

"Attention, all civilians!" the woman shouted. "I'm sorry for your loss and your pain, but please stand away from the deceased. I repeat, you must step back from the bodies. I know you don't want to be parted from your loved ones, but each of them must be temporarily quarantined. This will be a brief quarantine, and I promise they will be returned to you as quickly as we're able to process and release them."

Rue kept recording, but hardly anyone moved. Some of them understood immediately, horror dawning on their faces as they recalled the way the driver had touched these people, only to have them collapse in painful seizures and die. Others were too numb to put it together.

A police lieutenant jogged over to the woman and quietly demanded to know what she was up to, who she was. Basically the same questions Rue had been asking. The woman flashed some kind of ID, and Rue watched the cop blink in surprise and nod, backing away, hands raised as if in apology for interrupting. *So whoever the fuck she is, she does have* some *authority behind her.*

A Blackcoat called to her. "Vargas." So now the woman had a name, which helped give Rue someone to hate. Vargas had a head of tight curls, dyed red, and Rue might've found her attractive under other circumstances. But not today.

Ignored, Rue glanced around at the people who had died after being touched by the BMW driver, or by Maeve Sinclair, who'd run off in the chaos. She refused to look at the bodies of Ellen and Logan Sinclair, but she did glance back at Ted. Stubborn as he was, and despite his own fifty-three years, Ted had managed to get to one knee and was trying to rise, one arm across his ribs, his face etched with pain. There were scrapes and bloody bruises on his arms and right cheek, but still he struggled to stand. Rose pulled away from Priya, reached for her father, and the two of them held one another, both shaking. Over Rose's shoulder, Rue could see Ted's eyes, which were flat and dull. Empty.

Bereft. That was the word. Of course he was bereft. Ted had slid into shock. Maeve had run off, vanished up into the woods of Mount Champney, the tallest peak along the Mekwi Range. Rue Crooker and Ted Sinclair had met years earlier but had become best friends their sophomore year in high school, thanks to a Siouxsie and the Banshees concert and their shared crush on a freckle-faced freshman girl neither of them would ever get to kiss. Now they were both divorced from their respective wives. Rue felt like her divorce had left her happier, but the same couldn't be said for Ted.

Ted broke away from Rose and started limping toward the bodies of his wife and son.

"Sir!" a Blackcoat shouted. "I'm going to have to ask you to back away."

Confused faces stared at the soldier, then at Vargas. Rue had thought her a civilian, but that seemed unlikely now if she were the one giving the orders. Whoever these people were, however, they weren't completely wrong. The locals were grieving and horrified. Her friends and neighbors would need answers that Rue knew weren't forthcoming. She saw a bearded man stand, both of his huge fists clenched, sweat stains on his *Red Sox Nation* T-shirt. He started toward the soldier.

"Wait!" Rue said, lowering her phone. She let the hand holding it dangle at her side, but didn't stop the recording. Even if the only video was of the pavement, at least it would pick up the audio. "Please . . . listen. They're right. You saw how these people died. This is some kind of contagion. Back away from the dead and don't touch them until medical personnel have cleared them. Everyone, please just stand back, but don't go anywhere. All of you will have to be checked out, too."

Ted stared at Rue. She had seen him so drunk he couldn't raise his head, and so high he couldn't remember his own birthday, but she'd never seem him like this. He looked utterly lost.

"They died in, like, two seconds," the huge-fisted man growled. "If I got infected by that, I'd already be lyin' in the goddamn road."

He had a point, but they couldn't take any chances. Not with something so deadly. Rue began to reply, to plead with them to follow instructions, when she felt a cool shadow blot out the Fourth of July sun. She turned to see a towering black-armored soldier behind her, with Vargas standing beside him.

"Clear the area," Vargas said, copper eyes glinting.

Rue glared. "I'm trying to help you."

"I don't recall asking—"

"These people don't know you. They need to be comforted, and they need medical attention. They need to be quarantined. We need to be sure they—"

"I don't know who you think 'we' might be," Vargas said, giving her the disdainful once-over that Rue's hair and tattoos prompted all too frequently. "But 'we' isn't you. We'll be quarantining the remains. Everyone else can go home and wait for the bodies to be released."

Something snapped in Rue. The caul of shock that had hung over her tore away, her thoughts clearing. "You want them to go home? They were just exposed to what looks to me like the deadliest germ in the world, and I've seen some deadly fucking germs. Nothing kills on contact like that. Nothing. You want to send these people home, you're either monumentally stupid or you already know they're not infected. I'm going to guess the latter, since you people buzzed in here about a minute and a half after the dead guy in the Beemer. I get the idea you know exactly who this is and what just happened here."

Rue pointed to Ted. "My friend just lost half his family and got hit by a goddamned car. Maybe you want to explain to him why that happened? Oh, and also . . . who the fuck *are* you?"

Vargas stepped in so close that Rue could smell her tropical-scented body wash. The woman had gone unsettlingly still.

"You seem to know what you're talking about," Vargas said, studying her more critically than before. "You don't look like a scientist."

Rue couldn't decide whether to laugh or knock her on her ass. Instead, her spine stiffened. "Dr. Rue Crooker. I'm a biologist at Boston

University, and you're pushing folks around in my hometown when they've just seen people die in front of them. So maybe dial it back, *Vargas*."

The smaller woman blinked, perhaps startled that Rue knew her name. It wasn't much, but it was all she had.

"I think we'll have to quarantine you, too, Dr. Crooker," Vargas said, gesturing to two of the Blackcoats.

Rue had never put her phone away, never stopped the recording. Now she picked it up and held it between herself and Vargas, making sure the other woman knew she was on camera.

"I don't think we'll be doing that today."

Which was when Ted took a few shuffling steps toward Vargas. With every second that passed, the bruising and swelling of his injuries seemed worse. "Take a look around," he said. "You think we're going to let Dr. Crooker go anywhere with you?"

Behind him, his daughter Rose broke a little further, her face contorted with loneliness and shock. "Dad?"

"No," he said. "You girls stay back."

Rue glanced across the street, between buildings, at the woods and the mountains beyond. Maeve had taken off in that direction. Finding her was going to be vital, but first this situation had to be contained.

The bearded man in the Red Sox Nation T-shirt stepped up beside Ted. "You see how many cameras are on you?"

Vargas blinked and for the first time seemed to notice there were at least half a dozen people with their phones out, recording what had been unfolding. Most seemed to be bystanders who had stayed behind to help the injured but were unencumbered now that more EMTs and police had shown up. One was a middle-aged woman who stood protectively over a dead man. Tears streamed down her face, but the look of determination in her eyes was unmistakable.

"People aren't stupid," Ted said, wiping at his eyes. "This might be a small town, but it's a Fourth of July parade in America, and you come in here in your black helicopters and talking contagion. There's going to be half a dozen news trucks here in half an hour or less. Now tell us what just happened, goddamn it. We deserve an answer."

Vargas glanced from Ted to Rue and then turned toward the police lieutenant who'd backed down from her before. The man had been clearing the intersection, shouting for people to remove the floats that were blocking more emergency vehicles from arriving. Now he turned, said something to a pair of EMTs who were hustling a gurney toward their ambulance, bearing a man who'd been struck by the BMW and badly injured.

"Lieutenant," Vargas called.

But as the policeman started toward her, another voice interrupted them, and the lieutenant almost collapsed with relief. Chief Kaminski had arrived.

"Ma'am, I'm Len Kaminski, chief of police. Obviously, we've got a lot on our hands here," the chief said, waving at his officers to go back to what they'd been doing. "I'm told you wanted us to stay out of your business."

"That's changed," Vargas said. "Place all these people under arrest for interfering with a federal investigation."

Voices erupted all around her, but to Rue, all that noise suddenly seemed little more than a distant buzz. Tiny details resolved into sharp contrast. The last two letters on Kaminski's badge had been worn away, as if the chief had scraped up against something. He had a little scar under his left eye and a few wiry white hairs in his otherwise dark eyebrows. His nostrils flared in disgust as he glanced around at the people with their phones out, and for half a moment, his gray eyes rested on Rue. Then he looked at Vargas.

"Lady, this is New Hampshire. *Live Free or Die* is our state motto. You come in here in the midst of the ugliest, most heartbreaking thing that's ever happened in this town, no identification, and tell me to arrest people who just suffered loss and horror like this? You're either that arrogant or that stupid, and I don't really care which. Any idiot can see this is some kind of government bullshit gone haywire. You want to cover up the mess you made, you'll have to do it with your own people, and face the media shitstorm that comes your way. I guess what I'm saying is, go fuck yourself."

People in the crowd—Rue guessed people who hadn't just watched their friends or spouses die—clapped and cheered. More phones had come out during this mini-speech, while Vargas's fury visibly simmered.

"This whole town is about to be quarantined," Vargas sneered as if the words were punishment.

"You were ready to send everyone home a minute ago," Rue replied. "You know that whatever this is, none of us has it."

Vargas responded with the most venomous smile Rue had ever seen. "Can't be too careful, Dr. Crooker. If you want to make sure none of you get infected, I suggest you stop making my job more difficult."

Rue flinched, wondering if she'd heard right. Not the words—those were clear enough—but the tone. Then she noticed the way the Blackcoats had shifted, several of them moving into position near Vargas, as if guarding her. Chief Kaminski noticed, too, and cast a nervous glance toward Rue, as if warning her to heed Vargas's words. Their eyes met, Rue saw the policeman's fear, and that was when she knew she'd heard Vargas's threat exactly as it had been intended.

She thought about Ted Sinclair's daughter, off in the woods, terrified and alone and maybe worse, and knew she ought to say something. Whatever this threat was, the dead people in the street were testament enough to how dangerous it could be. But someone would tell Vargas soon enough, or there'd be cell phone footage of what happened when Maeve hit the driver with that baseball bat, and then these helicopters and the soldiers in their gleaming body armor would be all over the mountainside hunting for her.

Rue thought it would be a good idea if somebody else found her first.

3

For the longest time, there were zero thoughts in Maeve's head. Pain drove her, grief pumping her blood and keeping her legs moving. Eyes wide, searching the shadows between trees as if the forest might reveal itself to be part of a dream, she ran along familiar trails. Her feet remembered them, knew how to navigate the rocks and roots that jutted from the ground. She diverted onto a narrow side trail she knew most hikers avoided because of its steep incline and inhospitable terrain. Her escape turned from a run to a climb, knees rising, hands grasping edges of rock, head ducking beneath branches, until at last she hauled herself up onto a smooth ridge where the trail became a bit easier.

Only then did she pause, heart thundering, salt from her tears drying on her lips. An ocean of pain had dragged her under and threatened to drown her, but now she washed up onto this mountain ledge for just a moment. Long enough to begin to catch her breath. Long enough for conscious thought to return and reality to set in.

Mom's dead.

Logan . . . Logan's dead.

Her body seemed to fold in on itself, shoulders caving inward as if she were some sort of bird, eager to wrap herself in protective wings. She hugged herself, taking deep rasping breaths. She studied her trembling fingers, expecting to find them dappled with blood. But they were just her fingers, just her hands.

Over the sound of her heartbeat, she could hear the wind picking up, rustling the branches of trees all around her. Shafts of sunlight streamed through the lattice of those interlocking branches. God, it was beautiful.

So beautiful it hurt.

Emotion surged inside her, so powerful that she couldn't hold it in. Maeve threw her head back and screamed at the sky, the trees, the mountain, and her own goddamned hands, these things that no longer felt a part of her. While the echo of her scream danced up and down the climbing trail, she thought of Medusa, the gorgon of Greek myth, whose hair was a nest of deadly serpents and whose gaze could turn human beings to stone.

"Logan," she whispered. "I'm sorry."

She remembered the way he had always picked the worst possible times to smile at her, when she was in a rage or brokenhearted or wallowing in a moment of self-doubt. The times when she didn't want to see anyone, didn't want anyone to try to make her feel better. Logan would never try to comfort her with words or to cheer her up when she had been working hard at radiating disdain and dismay. But in her lowest moments, he'd always had that smile that said he understood. That he was there for her if she needed him.

Maeve covered her mouth with both hands to keep from screaming out her grief again.

While they'd been growing up, the Sinclair kids had heard one constant refrain from their dad. One day, he'd told them, their parents would be gone and the only people they'd really be able to count on would be one another. Friends and colleagues and mates would come and go, he had assured them, but they needed to nurture their familial bond. Maeve had loved Logan, but for several years she had been promising herself that she'd make a greater effort to know and understand him. To be a better sister.

Instead . . .

I killed him. Grief thrust its fist inside her chest, clutched at her heart, and squeezed. Her breath hitched, and she hugged herself even tighter, her face contorting. She whispered his name so quietly that even her own ears could not hear, and then she mouthed other words, just her lips moving, unable to give voice to them.

Mom. What did I do? God, what did I do?

Her legs gave out. Somehow she found herself sitting between two slanted rocks, hip aching from an impact she hadn't felt, elbow raw from a scrape her mind hadn't noticed. Desperately alone, primal, lost in a way she had never conceived, she unleashed the scream she'd been trying to hold back, this one longer and louder, tearing her throat ragged.

As it echoed and she listened to her heart continue to beat—against all odds, because she should be dead now, shouldn't she?—a sudden, sober voice surfaced inside her mind. *What if they hear you?*

"Logan," she whispered, thinking for a moment—for a single, lunatic, superstitious second—that this must be the ghost of her brother haunting her, helping her, staying with her the way their father had always urged.

But it wasn't Logan. Just her own voice, a calm sliver of her subconscious, smashing through the grief and the images that had burned into her mind—that single balloon, the BMW, that one sneaker, the blood—oh God, the blood—the car hitting her dad, him smashing into the windshield. The driver, reaching for the next person and the next. The baseball bat. Mom and Logan hugging her. Coughing. Falling. Black tears in their eyes.

"Hush," she said to that stern voice in her head.

Just me, she thought.

But as she rose to her feet, steadied herself, and began climbing the trail again, she couldn't shake the doubt that had taken root, because that voice didn't sound like her. It didn't feel as if it had come from her.

Maeve laughed softly, and the laugh became a sob, because she realized she might be going just a little bit crazy. *Really, who could blame me?*

Still, that stern voice had gotten its way. Grief still enveloped her—she was drowning in it, floating in it, but she had to swim if she wanted to live. Maybe she didn't deserve to live, not after what she'd done. Would Dad and Rose hate her now? Would they want her to live or want her to die?

She could still feel the tingle in her fingertips of the touch that had killed two of the people she loved the most in the world, could still smell the sickness that erupted out of them. She'd poisoned them, destroyed them, and after seeing what happened to the BMW driver, she knew the same thing might happen to anyone she touched.

But she wanted to live.

So she picked up her pace and watched her footing, and her mind skipped forward to the next step and the next, and what she would need to do to hide and survive on the mountain. And she *would* need to hide, because they'd come after her—of that much, she was certain. That black helicopter had shown up so fast, it had to have been chasing the man in the BMW. Which meant that the moment they put all the pieces together, they'd be after her, too. They were going to kill her, or at least capture her, punish her. All the choices she had been on the verge of making in her life had just been obliterated. Her future had been rewritten. From now on, all she could do was think one step ahead, one hour ahead.

She had killed, but oh, lord, how she wanted to live.

4

At a quarter past noon, Walker pulled his battered old Jeep Wrangler up to the curb in front of his ex-wife's house and killed the engine. The radio went silent, and he missed the music immediately. He had no particular love for 1980s pop, but it filled his head and blotted out the regrets and self-recrimination that tended to flood the hollow places in his mind when he came here. His ex's house, yeah, but once upon a time it had been *their* house. The Walker family home. He and Amanda and Charlie had lived there together, at least during the periods when work hadn't dragged Walker across the country or across the ocean.

He missed Amanda, but more than that, he missed the family they'd been. The family he'd taken for granted. In the gray light of an overcast early July day, the place seemed to breathe as if it were a dusty old museum dedicated to a better life.

"Shit," he whispered, smiling as he chided himself. "This is what unemployment does."

With a soft laugh, he got out of the car and started up the walk. He wasn't actually unemployed, but for the past nine months, he might as well have been. Walker had fucked up on the job, at least the way his employers viewed it. His personal opinion differed. He had taken a difficult and potentially deadly decision out of their hands by eliminating their opportunity to study an ancient bacteria that might've killed millions. They'd wanted to research it, find a way to counteract it, just in case some enemy turned it into a weapon, and maybe turn it into a weapon for themselves. Walker had nearly died after being infected by it, and he had been unwilling to give them the benefit of the doubt.

Them being the United States Department of Defense. His employers never called themselves that, of course. Since he had worked for them, that special division had gone through half a dozen official titles, a whole alphabet soup of names that were all smoke screens to cover the truth—that they were part of DARPA and thus the DoD.

Having the bosses pissed at him all these months had been difficult. On the upside, however, he'd been able to spend a lot more time with his son, Charlie, who was fast careening toward his thirteenth birthday. The kid would be starting the seventh grade in less than two months, and that seemed inconceivable to Walker. People always talked about how the passage of time gathered momentum, and it had proven painfully, excruciatingly true. He felt as if he'd barely blinked, like Charlie had jumped into the pool during his first swim lesson years ago and emerged as this lanky, mop-headed kid on the verge of becoming a teenager. He told himself it was simply the nature of things, but he knew that feeling of accelerated time had been exacerbated by the fact that his work had kept him away from home so often, not to mention the small matter of his divorce.

The best he could do was try to make up for some of that lost time here and there before Charlie turned old enough to lose interest in hanging out with his father.

As Walker strode up the front path, a light rain began to fall. The air hung thick with humidity, the temperature hovering around eighty-five degrees, typical enough for northern Virginia on the Fourth of July. Once they were near the peak of Old Rag Mountain, the breeze would cool them down. Overnight, it would turn chilly up near the tree line. Walker breathed a bit easier just thinking about it.

He steeled himself to ring the bell, to see Amanda and the past she represented, but the front door opened before he even reached the stoop. She stood on the threshold with a smile on her face, wearing jean shorts and a burnt-orange tank top, hair in a ponytail, no shoes, a woman ready to have the house to herself and a strawberry margarita in her hand.

"It can't be Ben Walker at my door," she said. "On time? Unheard of."

Walker had been on the receiving end of barbed attacks and acid wit from Amanda a thousand times, mostly deserved, and he knew what her razor-edge sarcasm sounded like. This wasn't it. Whatever history they shared, today Amanda had decided they could both live with the changes time had wrought.

He smiled. "Sometimes I amaze even myself."

Walker wanted to tell her she looked fantastic, that dressed the way she was, her skin tanned a lovely bronze, her hair back, she didn't look a day older than when they'd met. It would've been honest and sweet and true, but he knew it would come out awkward, and he worried that Amanda would take it the wrong way, as if he were trying to rekindle something now that he had time to be around more and she had broken off with the artist she'd been dating for the past couple of years. He remembered the way she liked him to run his fingers along the soft skin at the small of her back, and knew it would be best for him to keep his mouth shut.

"Not much of a day for hiking," she said, looking at the sky, blinking away a raindrop that struck her face.

"This'll be here and gone pretty quick," Walker replied. "Plus, most of our hiking will be tomorrow. This afternoon's just about getting up there and making camp, catching a few fish, building a fire. Burning some marshmallows."

Amanda smiled. "Sounds perfect."

A moment passed. Then another. Suddenly the easy comfort between them fell away, lost between the old familiarity and the things they no longer knew about one another. Taking the conversation further, talking about work or family or their romantic lives, would be a step too far, and they had not quite managed to become real friends again. Maybe they never would.

"Charlie, you ready?" Amanda called back through the house. She gave a small shrug. "You want to wait inside?"

Walker smiled. If it was uncomfortable out here, how much more uncomfortable would it be in the house they had once shared? He would notice every change, but also everything familiar.

"I'm sure he'll be out in a second," he said.

Amanda looked relieved. She leaned against the doorframe, and regret suffused him in a way he rarely allowed. Walker had become expert at walling off such emotions, but this time it sneaked up on him.

"How are you?" he asked. "Really."

"I'm doing all right," she said. "Stressed about work, as always. Trying to keep our boy good and kind. He's starting the seventh grade, which can be rough. Kids get mean around then, or maybe the mean shit just starts to hurt a little more when you're that age."

"He is a good kid," Walker said. "He really is. And that's all you."

Amanda feigned modesty. "Not *all*. But maybe most."

Walker remembered loving her. It was a nice moment. Then the familiar clump of impossibly heavy footfalls thumped down the stairs behind her, and Charlie appeared, enormous pack on his back, Washington Nationals cap on his head, at least two inches taller than he'd been during April vacation that year.

"Time to head out!" he said happily. He bent over a bit to support the weight of his pack as he pointed a finger at the Jeep parked by the curb. "But I get to pick the music."

His mother didn't have to ask him for a kiss. Charlie gave her a peck on the cheek, told her he loved her without hesitation, then came out onto the stoop as if he were a soldier presenting himself for inspection.

"I have Oreos in my bag," he announced.

"Then I think we have everything," Walker said. He glanced at Amanda. "Thanks for this. Enjoy your quiet time. Have an extra margarita for me."

"Oh, I will."

She watched them march down the front path to the Jeep, but by the time they had climbed in and Walker had started the car, he noticed she had gone back inside, the door tightly shut. A strange relief washed over him as Charlie buckled his seat belt and connected his phone to the car so he could play the weird combination of rap and country that tended to infiltrate his playlists.

"Are there really Oreos in your pack?" Walker asked.

"I'd never lie about the important things," Charlie replied gravely.

A country song began to play—one of a thousand tunes about whiskey—and the utter normalcy and contentment of the moment set Walker at ease in a way he hadn't ever expected to achieve again.

In his front pocket, his phone began to vibrate.

He stiffened, thought about letting it go to voice mail. For months, his employers had given him nothing but research jobs or training sessions for new hires. It was a holiday, and he had scheduled vacation days following the Fourth of July. Nobody should be calling him right now. His phone should not have been vibrating.

"Dad?" Charlie asked. "Is that your phone?"

Walker huffed quietly and reached into his pocket, sliding out his phone. The number was unfamiliar, but it was a Washington, D.C., area code. His thumb hovered over the screen, hesitating one last moment, and then abruptly the phone went silent. He stared at the screen.

A gust of wind rattled the Jeep and the rain picked up, spattering the windshield.

"Come on," Charlie said. "Let's get going."

Fuck them, Walker thought. He didn't like not knowing what the call had been for, but he and Charlie had planned this hiking trip for months. He put the Jeep in gear, and then the phone began to vibrate again.

"Ignore it," Charlie said. "They don't own you, Dad."

But for someone to call, not leave a message, and call back immediately . . . that worried Walker. One foot on the brake, engine idling, he answered the phone.

"Who's this?"

"Dr. Walker, this is Alena Boudreau. I hope you remember me. That'll make this go more smoothly."

An image of the woman swam up from his memories. Early seventies, fit, beautiful, with an air of drive and command that cowed most of the people she encountered. The first time he'd met her, in General Wagner's office, she'd reminded Walker of British actress Helen Mirren. Her grandson, David, also worked for DARPA. Years ago, they'd done some work that he wished he'd read at that time—it might have saved him a lot of pain and terror in Guatemala later.

"I remember you, Ms. Boudreau."

"Director Boudreau now," she replied, her voice sounding tinny and distant on the phone, almost like a computer voice. "As of today, I'm running something called the Global Science Research Coalition. The SRC's objectives will be familiar to you."

Walker frowned. What the hell did this have to do with him? He glanced at Charlie, saw the way his son had begun to rip at the skin on his fingertips, a nervous habit he'd developed over the past year. Charlie's face held no emotion, a numb mask, impatient but somehow still hopeful.

"Yeah, listen, congratulations on the new job," Walker said, phone to his ear, turned away to watch the rain falling outside the driver's window. "It's a holiday, Director. I'm literally just pulling onto the road for a camping trip with my son."

"I'm sorry," Alena said. "I should've been clearer. I'm running the SRC now, and you, Dr. Walker, have been traded to my team."

"I work for General Henry Wagner—"

"General Wagner has had a no-good, very bad day. He's not in charge of shit right now. The SRC was born today, they gave me the reins, and they did that in the middle of a crisis."

Walker didn't want to ask. He knew he shouldn't. The rain picked up, pounding the roof of the Jeep. He glanced at Charlie, who had begun to shake his head, his lips pressed into a white line of anger. Back on the front stoop of the house, Amanda had stepped out to see what had gone wrong, to find out why they had only pulled a few feet up the road.

"According to the GPS tracking in front of me, Dr. Walker, you're about forty minutes' drive from Davison Army Airfield. I'll meet you there in three-quarters of an hour."

"Director Boudreau—"

"Alena is fine, Walker. We're going to be working together, after all."

"I don't work for you. Even if I did, I'm on vacation."

In the passenger seat, Charlie began to mutter a stream of colorful cusswords.

"Wake up, Walker," Alena said. "Meet the new boss, not as dim as the old boss. You're needed, and I expect you to be there in forty-five minutes. I will see you there. Might as well just bring your camping gear. You may need it."

The line went dead. She had hung up.

Father and son were quiet there in the car, engine idling, rain pattering the glass and hood. Walker expected Charlie to ask for an explanation, but the boy had grown up now, nearly thirteen, and he was smart enough to read the situation.

"Charlie . . . ," Walker began.

"This is bullshit." He sneered the last word. Walker didn't think he'd ever heard his son swear prior to the last two minutes, but he wasn't about to admonish him.

"Yeah, it is," Walker said. "I'm sorry, kid. They wouldn't call me in like this if they didn't really need me."

Charlie winced, then blinked away the hurt in his eyes. "*Oh*, well, they really need you." He huffed, just the same way Walker always did, then popped open the passenger door. He climbed out, dragging his backpack with him. One hand on the open door, Charlie ducked his head to fix his father with a look of blazing recrimination.

"I guess it's a good thing I don't," Charlie said.

He slammed the door, turned, and marched back toward his house. Walker rolled the window down and called after him, but Charlie did not turn around or even slow his step. Instead, the boy picked up speed and ran toward the house. His mother greeted him at the door. She didn't even ask, made no gesture in Walker's direction. Instead, she just closed the door.

Walker didn't hesitate for more than a second or two. There were a lot of questions in his mind about what had happened to General

Wagner and how Walker himself had come to work for Alena Boudreau, but it was clear she was the one giving the orders.

Heart heavy, he hit the gas and aimed for Davison.

The worst part about all of it was that although Charlie's words had stung, and although Walker hated having to cancel their trip, he was also curious and buzzing with anticipation. He'd been so long in the doghouse he had wondered if they would ever trust him again. Now they had a use for him. Now they needed him.

So does Charlie, he thought.

But he kept his foot on the gas.

Davison Army Airfield looked as if it hadn't changed in decades. Squat buildings, one runway, another stretch of tarmac where half a dozen combat helicopters sat idle, waiting to be called into use. The first time Walker had found himself at Davison, it had reminded him of a dozen airfields the army had thrown up in a matter of days or weeks in hostile territory. The Green Zone in Iraq had one like it, and Walker found some comfort in that, as if it meant this place stood ready for anything, able to shift into action at a moment's notice.

A guard checked him in at the gate, told him where to park. They were expecting him. The skies were gray and a light rain fell, wind blowing hard enough that it seemed to come from everywhere and nowhere. A sleek silver plane sat on the tarmac, something he hadn't seen before, sparkling new but somehow reminding him of the propeller planes in old newsreels, the first transcontinental flights. This one had no propellers. And he had a feeling it would get him wherever he was going a hell of a lot faster than the ones in the newsreels.

Nobody came out to greet him. A couple of soldiers stood outside a small hangar, sneaking a shared cigarette. The windows of the two-story control tower were opaque in the wan light. It was the Fourth of July, and he wondered if most of the airfield staff had been given the day to celebrate or if they had other duties to attend to.

Fortunately, Walker didn't need a welcome party. He stood in the rain for a few moments, studying the black Mercedes that idled next to the plane. Its headlights were on, mostly lost in the gloom, but he couldn't hear its engine over the noise of the jet. He started across the wet tarmac, cocked his head to try to get a look inside the Mercedes, and then the airplane's door opened, stairwell lowering to touch the runway. Now that he was closer, he was fairly certain the plane must have been a new model Bombardier Challenger, but he wouldn't have sworn to it.

A figure appeared, silhouetted at the top of the stairs.

"You don't look like you're in much of a hurry," Alena Boudreau said, her voice carrying even above the engines and the rain.

She treated him as if he were some errant teenager, admonishing him for his pace, never mind that he had just left his son behind on a day that had been promised to the kid. He ought to have been simmering with anger and frustration, but instead, his thoughts prickled with curiosity and admiration. Alena wore the whiteness of her hair like a crown, was nearly always the smartest person in the room, brutal with her adversaries, and always behaved as if she could see through to your secrets, whether you had any or not.

Good riddance to General Wagner, he thought.

"Reporting as instructed, Director," Walker said as he started up the stairs, hands on the railings, picking up his pace.

"I told you we're not going to stand on formality," she said, stepping back to allow him to board the plane.

"You did, yes. But frankly, I'll wait until I find out what we're up to here before I decide how cozy I want to get."

Alena scowled. "Don't worry, Dr. Walker. I've been known to get cozy, but never with my subordinates. It's a good rule."

He flushed. "That's not what I—"

"There, that's better," she said, smirking. "I like you off-balance. Have a seat. We need to talk, and I don't want to waste any more time."

Walker felt the engines cycling around him. Cool air blew from overhead. "You told me to bring my camping gear."

"You left it in the car. In a moment, you'll want to go get it." Alena reached inside her jacket and pulled out what appeared to be a phone but which unfolded into a full-size tablet, the sort with a liquid glass screen. "I'm going to show you something. Maybe you've already seen it. Thousands of people have, this morning, but I take it you had other things on your mind. By tonight, that number will be in the millions, thanks to the internet and the media's lust for horrifying video clips."

Walker frowned. "All right." It was far from the first time he'd been called in because of something horrifying in an online video. After sitting on the bench for months, Wagner's version of the naughty step, he was ready for any assignment, and since it had taken him away from his son, he figured it had better be damned important. The most horrifying things always were.

"First, the SRC," Alena said. "Here's the gist. You've worked for the Department of Defense under various cover organizations—"

"I work for DARPA, not the DoD."

"And everyone in DARPA works for the DoD. Don't waste my time, Walker."

"Ma'am." He nodded, not liking where this was going.

"We've had some questionable exposure in the last couple of years, first in Turkey and then with the Pandora Room. But you know all about those. Someday soon, you and I will have a talk about your actions, but not today. Right now, here's what you need to know. To have a fresh start, DARPA has created a new false front for our more esoteric research and investigations. It has a global face. We've brought in some like-minded scientists in cooperative foreign governments to share data . . . at least, a little bit of data. As far as the world knows, we're the Global Science Research Coalition, or the SRC. You report to me now. Otherwise, it's going to be business as usual for you. All the niceties can wait until this is over and we sit down in my office like ordinary people. That's all simple enough, I take it?"

Walker sank back into his chair. "You're not going to tell me what happened with General Wagner, are you? Why he was removed? What he's done to have what you called a 'no-good, very bad day'?"

"No. I am not. General Wagner is still overseeing various projects for DARPA. He's their responsibility, not ours."

The engine continued to cycle. The plane seemed to thrum with urgency. Outside, the rain fell harder. From his seat, Walker had just the right angle to see the headlights on Alena's Mercedes.

"Let's see the video," he said.

"This is Jericho Falls, New Hampshire, in the White Mountains," Alena explained. "The events on this video took place at about fifteen minutes past eleven o'clock this morning. Not even three hours ago."

She tapped the screen, opened a file, and turned it toward him as it began to play. It started with a Fourth of July parade, and he flinched at the discordant noise of the marching band going by. When the car plowed into view and the screaming started, she turned the volume down a bit, and he was grateful, but it was only when the man stepped out of the car that Walker began to understand why he was here.

"The woman who ran off," he said while Alena folded up her liquid tablet. "Who is she?"

"Just anyone. Her name is Maeve Sinclair. The people you saw die there, at the end, were her mother and brother—"

Walker felt sick. "Jesus Christ. What the hell is this?"

"Moments after that video ends, Blackcoats show up. There are helicopters. All from a place called Garland Mountain Laboratories. I'm working on finding out more, but all I know right now is what I've just told you, and that the driver of that car was a man named Oscar Hecht, an employee at Garland Mountain. Obviously, he was infected with something—"

"Nothing I've ever seen," Walker said. He felt a tightening in his chest, wondered how much she really knew. "There isn't a contagion on earth that can be passed that quickly, particularly by simple skin contact, and even if there were, there's never been a virus or bacterium that can infiltrate a body instantly, kill in seconds."

Alena exhaled a long breath. She sat up in her seat, back straight. "Are you finished?"

Walker had always liked this woman. Admired her. She had a reputation for being fearless, brilliant, dedicated, honest, and fair, but there were other facets to that reputation, and he was seeing one of them.

"Yes. I'm finished."

Alena stood. "To your insistence that there's nothing like this, all I can say is that clearly, there is now. I've brought comm units for you, as well as some equipment that may be helpful, but supplement that with your own gear as you please. Go to Jericho Falls. Find out what the hell is going on, but most importantly, find Maeve Sinclair and protect her at all costs."

A shiver went through him. He'd been so shocked by what he'd seen that he'd barely been thinking about the young woman who'd endured that horror, who must be terrified and grieving, maybe blaming herself. Who had run off into the mountains.

"The police will be searching for her—"

"Yes, and those Blackcoats from Garland Mountain as well," Alena agreed, moving to the exit. She paused at the top of the steps. "As Oscar Hecht was dying, *she* touched *him*. Moments later, she touched members of her family and they dropped dead, which means whatever contagion he was carrying, she's carrying it now. We have to assume everyone she touches is going to die. The police will be looking for her, and those Blackcoats, but they won't be the only ones. This video is online. It's already on the news channels. There will be others who want to know how Garland Mountain did this, who want to study Maeve Sinclair. Still others—and you know this, Walker, think about it—will want to be the one to personally take this woman's life, just on the chance that this power, this 'death touch,' will pass to them as it did to her from Oscar Hecht.

"Go and find her, Walker. Bring her back to me."

Walker's stomach twisted with nausea. "Because we're so different from whomever else is going to be hunting her? The SRC isn't going to be just as interested in studying her, figuring out how to use this for ourselves?"

Alena only shook her head. "The difference is, with me, she'll still be alive."

She went down the steps, climbed into her car, and was gone before Walker had even retrieved his gear from the Jeep. Ten minutes later, he was in the air, wondering what the hell he was getting himself into.

As always.

5

Rue helped Ted up the front steps of the home he'd shared with Ellen when the two of them had still been married. It had been Ted's childhood home, but he'd willingly moved out during the divorce, determined that his kids would grow up in this house. Ted had found himself a little two-bedroom cottage in the woods behind the old fire station, and it suited him just fine—the perfect place to drink or get high on Oxy or morphine or whatever he could get his hands on. Rue had tried so many times to convince him to get help, resisted all his efforts to push her away, until one day he'd told her he didn't want to die, but he didn't want to feel what it was like to be alive anymore.

That had done it. Something had broken inside him then, as if he'd heard himself speaking those words and cracked in half. Shaking, raging, he'd punched a hole in the wall of his cottage and then asked her to take him somewhere to get help. Rue had done it.

If Ted had managed to give up drinking at the same time, Rue thought Ellen might have taken him back after that. But a week after he'd gotten out of rehab, he'd reunited with his other oldest friend, whiskey. Said he needed the whiskey to help keep him buzzing so he'd stay away from the pills. The logic seemed absurd. His doctor said it would lead to further disaster, but so far it had been working.

After today, Rue figured all bets were off.

They'd gone to the hospital. X-rays showed three cracked ribs. He had a mild concussion. Lots of bruises and scrapes. He'd sprained his right knee, which remained swollen and blackened from smashing against the windshield. He would be in a lot of pain and discomfort for quite a while, but physically, he would recover.

She held Ted by one arm as if he were a hundred years old, escorted him up the front steps, used his key to get him through the front door. He gazed into some unseen space, some nothing world, and she wondered if his mind had gone completely numb or if his thoughts were about the son he had just lost, about how badly he'd spoiled his relationship with Ellen and how he'd never be able to make it up to her now. She wondered if coming home had been a good idea. There might be booze here. And even if he had kicked his pill addiction eight months ago, he'd still know how to get them if he really wanted them. That was the thing about broken people—there was always someone happy to help you shatter even further.

On the threshold, Ted seemed to wake abruptly from his somnambulism. His head snapped up and he glanced around, nearly knocking Rue into the shrubs to one side of the brick steps.

"Rose?" he said, his eyes red and rheumy, salty streaks on his face where his tears had dried. He still held his injured arm against his chest.

A massive oak tree spread a shady canopy across half the front yard. Rue remembered climbing that tree with Ted when she was a kid, sharing secrets and cigarettes. Now Rose sat in the shade of its leaves, twenty-one years old, grieving in silent agony in Priya's arms.

It was Priya who looked up at Ted now. "Go on inside, Mr. Sinclair. I've got her. Just give us a few minutes and we'll come in. I think she just needs . . ."

Priya tucked a lock of black hair behind her ear, as good as a shrug. Her expression crumbled, because the truth was she had no idea what Rose needed. Rue understood the look on her face because it mimicked the feeling in her own heart. What the hell was she supposed to do for Ted Sinclair?

"Thank you, sweetie," Ted said. "Thank you."

Priya wiped at her own tears and nodded. Ted shuffled into his house, Rue at his side, and he looked around the living room—at the two recliners in front of the TV and the magazines and coffee mugs and blankets thrown about the place, showing it was lived-in and loved and busy—and he brought a trembling hand up to cover his eyes.

Rue escorted him to the sofa and sat with him, one hand on his back as he took deep breaths. Slowly, he straightened up, reached out, and took her right hand in both of his.

"Thank you."

"You don't have to thank me, Ted. I'm just taking my best friend home."

Ted tried to smile.

"You should have stayed in the hospital," Rue said. "You know that."

He looked at her as if he hadn't heard. "My son is . . . Logan is gone."

Rue had no reply to that. They'd put a brace on his knee and wrapped his torso tightly enough that he could barely breathe, trying to get his ribs to heal. But there was no cure for having watched your child die, watching the woman you still loved die. And what about Maeve? He'd lost her, too, or so it seemed.

"You should sleep, Ted. I still can't believe the way you went over the top of that car. Jesus, that was . . ." Rue stopped herself. He'd been through more than enough already today.

Ted wetted his lips with his tongue and glanced over toward the ornate cabinet in the corner. He hadn't lived in this house for a long time, but he definitely remembered where his ex kept the liquor.

Rue's heart sank. The last thing she wanted to do was give him a drink, but she saw the shame and the plea in his eyes and reckoned that if anyone ever truly needed a drink, it was Ted Sinclair on this godforsaken day.

"I'll pour you one," she said, knowing how hard it would be for him to ask.

The gratitude in his eyes made her want to cry.

"What else can I get you?" she asked as she handed him a tumbler of Jameson Irish Whiskey.

"Information," Ted replied, sipping the whiskey. Some of the color returned to his face. "What's going on, Rue?"

"I don't know any better than you do. I'm sorry, but—"

"You know a hell of a lot about a hell of a lot," Ted said. "You saw what happened, what Maeve did, what that piece of shit in the car did in that crowd. I need to know what you think is going on here."

He took another sip of whiskey, then stared into the glass a moment before downing the rest in a single gulp. Exhaling through his teeth, wincing in pain, Ted stood up and limped over to the closet by the door. He dug around until he pulled out a pair of weathered brown hiking boots, then kicked off his shoes and slid to the floor, not bothering with a chair. He hissed with the pain of every movement, flushing red as his cracked ribs grated.

"I'm not going to ask what you think you're doing," Rue said, running a hand over the stubble on the shaved side of her head. "Get into bed, Ted. The police are up there looking for her now—"

"I'm her father," he said without looking up as he tried to lace his first boot with only one good hand.

"What about Rose?"

The question might have been unfair, given the circumstances. Rue knew that. But Rose sat out under the shade tree with her girlfriend, mourning and in shock but very much alive. Alive and safe. She needed her father as much as Maeve did.

"Can you stay with them?" Ted asked. "I know they're twenty-one and they're supposed to be adults now, but after this morning, I can't leave them without someone to watch over them. I'm sure Priya's parents will come, maybe stay with them both—Rose has gotten close with them, and she'll understand that I need to do this. She'll want me to do this."

Rue didn't share his certainty. "Of course," she said, watching as Ted began to lace up his second boot, wincing at the pain in his knee. "I think you're making a mistake, but I'm here for whatever you need. I'll talk to the police, and I'm going to figure out what the hell happened at that lab. Whatever happened at the parade today, it didn't start there. What's happened to Maeve didn't have to happen, and . . ."

She saw the way his face paled, and her words trailed off. Ted wiped at his eyes, hands trembling again. Rue knew he was in no condition to go up into the mountains alone. Hell, he shouldn't even leave the house. He had refused opioids at the hospital, so all they'd given him for his pain had been the equivalent of a fistful of Advil. What little it might be doing to blunt his pain would wear off soon. Rue couldn't let him go, but he would hate her for trying to stop him, just as she would hate him if the situation were reversed.

A rap came on the screen door. Rue and Ted both snapped around to see Chief Kaminski beyond the screen mesh, staring in at them. Len Kaminski had been chief for three years, and while the job would have aged most men, Rue thought Kaminski looked heartier and healthier than he had when he'd been a captain or a lieutenant. He'd lost beer weight, his face tan instead of ruddy, and while the graying of his hair had reached lightning speed, his eyes were clear and alert. The top job had given him renewed purpose, and Rue felt a wave of relief wash over her the moment he drew open the screen door, hinges squealing.

"Where you going, Mr. Sinclair?" Kaminski asked, like it was the most natural question in the world.

Ted blinked a few times, as if the words needed extra processing. "What kind of question is that?"

Kaminski ran a hand across his chin as if trying to decide if he needed a shave. "Let me start again. I need you to take a minute before you go running off and get yourself shot—"

"Shot?" Rue asked. "Did they shoot someone?"

"No, no, hang on," Kaminski said. "Just hear me out." He hooked his fingers into his belt. She had seen other cops do the same and wondered if they were trained not to stick their hands into their pockets, making it harder to draw a weapon or otherwise react in a crisis.

"I've called in the state police," he said. "A dozen of them are already here, with more on the way. Between my officers and those troopers, we've got seventeen people up on the mountain now, making a sweep that starts right where Maeve ran into the woods."

Ted shook his head. "She's not going to stick close to town, Chief.

My girls know these mountains. They camp and fish. If Maeve doesn't want to be found, she's going to head up the slope into deeper woods."

"Fair enough," Kaminski said, "but this is a methodical search. Let us do what we need to do."

Rue held up her hands. "Chief, I'm sorry, but seventeen people is nothing up on Champney. Those woods go on forever. I know you don't have a lot of personnel, and what happened at the parade . . . my God, it must be chaos over there still. But if Ted wants to go and look, and if he's too stubborn to follow the doctor's orders after the bashing he took, then he should go out looking for Maeve. And I'm sure we can round up plenty of people who will help."

"You think so?" Chief Kaminski said, a new edge to his voice. "You think lots of people who saw what happened today are gonna want to comb through the woods looking for Maeve?"

Ted took it like a punch in the gut. Rue saw him recoil. He rubbed the back of his good hand across his mouth, the way he always did when the craving dug its claws into him and he really needed a drink.

"Jesus, Len—" she said.

"Fuck you, Chief," Ted spat, face reddening, clearly not caring that the man carried a gun. "You didn't see it happen. That son of a bitch drove right through the crowd, killed people with his car and then with his bare goddamn hands. I'm lucky to be alive. Maeve did what she did to save lives, to stop that lunatic, and then he . . . he fucking gave her whatever the hell disease he was carrying."

"Yeah. Sure looked that way," Kaminski said. "You're living a nightmare day, Mr. Sinclair. Losing your ex and your boy like that. I can't begin to tell you how sorry I am. My point is that most people were either there or have seen video, and speculation is running wild. Whatever sickness Maeve's got in her now . . . well, that's the reason most people aren't gonna be rushing to join a search party."

Anger prickled the skin at the back of Rue's neck. She knew her face must have been flushing with it. "I've never seen anything like it, and this is my job. But I also know this town, and I've known Ted most of my life. People care for him and his family, and fear is not going to keep the people who really give a damn from helping him now."

"Maybe not," Kaminski said. "But it's not just that. One of the things I came to tell you—"

The house phone began to ring. Half a second later, Rue felt her cell phone start to buzz in her back pocket.

"No need to answer," Kaminski went on. "It's an automated call from the town, letting residents know that the feds have put us under quarantine. Even the state police and EMTs who've come in to help are stuck here until the quarantine is lifted."

Ted deflated, staring at his boots.

Rue doubted quarantine was necessary. The way Vargas and the other Garland Mountain Labs employees had behaved this morning, it was clear they were worried only about the driver of the car, the people he had touched, the people Maeve had touched, and Maeve herself. There didn't seem to be any implication the contagion could be airborne. Regardless of Garland Mountain's confidence, however, Rue approved of the quarantine. Whatever their lab had brewed up, Rue wanted to make absolutely certain nobody in Jericho Falls was unknowingly carrying that infection.

It relieved her to know that the government had stepped in, but she thought about Garland Mountain Labs and that Vargas woman, the Blackcoats and their helicopters, and she wondered just what the government's role might be. The Pentagon had employed private military contractors in the past, a euphemism for *mercenaries*, and utilized them in foreign lands. The soldiers working for Garland might not be American military, but they were certainly authorized by the federal government.

"Len . . . Chief . . . what the hell were they doing at that lab?" she asked.

Kaminski glanced at Rue and scratched the back of his neck. "Normally, we'd have heard from the CDC, but the quarantine order came from Homeland Security. Make of that what you will. I don't have a clue what the Garland Mountain folks were up to, but if it led to this . . ."

Ted took a step closer to him, sighing with discomfort at the pain in his ribs. "Maybe I'm not thinking straight. Inside it feels like a part of me is screaming all the time, even right now, while I'm talking to you."

Rue felt her heart break a little for this man who had always been so good to her.

"That's understandable. What you're going through—"

Ted put his good hand on Kaminski's arm. "Look me in the eye and tell me you don't think Maeve's in danger. Those helicopters and the soldiers they carried, they'd have killed the driver of that car if they'd reached him before he drove into the parade. I think they'd have killed Maeve if they'd gotten there in time and if there weren't so many people with cameras."

"You can't know that," Kaminski said.

"You're right. I can't. But you didn't do what I asked. So look me in the eye and tell me you don't think my daughter's in danger. Tell me you don't think they'll kill her. And if you really don't think that, then tell me you don't think they'll drag her back to Garland Mountain and put her in a cell and study her like she's one of their specimens, because whatever this sickness is, I've never heard of anything this good at killing people. It's in my daughter, Chief, and you know damn well they're going to want it more than they've ever wanted anything."

Chief Kaminski stared at him, breath coming in long sips of air, a terrible understanding darkening his eyes. He lowered his head. "Holy shit."

"He's right," Rue said. "It's one thing if your people or the state police find her first, Len, but if those other bastards get her—"

"We can't let that happen," Ted interrupted.

Kaminski paled. "You were about to go into the woods when I got here. Where were you headed?"

Rue wondered if Ted might hesitate, worried about trusting the chief, but maybe he had already realized what had only just occurred to her. They had nobody else to trust.

"My ex-father-in-law, Maeve's granddad, had an old cabin up there. She and Rose loved it when they were little, but their grandfather passed ten years back. If she's looking for a place to hide, that's the only one I can think of."

"Worth a look," Kaminski said. "Glad you got your boots on. Let's go."

Some of the color returned to Ted's face, along with a grim determination. He had a purpose. If he was out trying to help Maeve, maybe he wouldn't have to think about the fact that his son and his ex-wife had died in front of him. Died at the hands of his eldest daughter.

"Go," Rue said. "I already said I'd stay with Rose and Priya, and I'll get on my phone and start learning everything I can about Garland Mountain Labs."

Ted shot her a grateful look. She knew it masked his pain, hid away the internal screaming to which he'd just confessed. She also knew that he would need another slug of Jameson before he left, but there was strength in him, nevertheless.

He was going to need it.

Rose Sinclair lay on the grass in the shade of the tree that had watched over the family all her life, until today. As a girl, she'd held a strange fantasy in her heart, this idea that somehow the old oak tree with its sprawling branches wanted to shield and protect her, and not only her but Maeve and Logan, and Mom and Dad, too. It had a little magic in it, that tree, at least for her.

Today the magic had died.

She lay with her head on Priya's lap, a warm breeze rustling the leaves overhead, and tried to find solace in the way Priya's fingers stroked her face and pushed through her hair. There were raised voices in the house, and from somewhere not far away she could hear the heavy chop of a helicopter. Sirens wailed. A dog began to bark and then to whine, maybe a block away, and she wondered what had frightened it so. But not for long.

Her head hurt, a pressure that gripped her temples. Her eyes burned with dryness, now that she'd cried herself out. Down at the base of her brain, in that lizard part, she felt the urge to move, to get up and do something, to avenge what had happened to her mother and Logan, and to Maeve, wherever she had run. But she couldn't get her muscles to obey her commands when her mind's eye kept replaying the parade over and over, kept showing her the mental clip of the sick man staggering out of his car, those people dying, Maeve swinging the baseball bat . . . and what happened after.

Priya bent down and kissed her forehead, still stroking her hair. "I'm so sorry."

The husk of a thing that had been Rose felt a flicker of life inside. It seemed scary to think about, the idea that she would have to live in the world again. Like this, in the shade of the oak tree, the solidity of Priya there to hold her, she could push it away, build herself a little bubble in time where she didn't have to live in a world in which her mother and brother had died in front her, their bodies spirited away by some government agency.

In her mind, she could see her sister running between buildings, rushing into the woods, up to the mountain. Her face crumpled, and her chest ached.

"Maeve," she said, shuddering as if with a chill or a fever instead of an anguish she'd never known. God, she wished her sister were there.

Priya said nothing. Only kissed her temple again. Stroked her cheek. Turned her face upward and kissed her lightly on the lips. A hot tear landed on Rose's face, and her vision cleared enough for her to see that Priya had also resumed crying. Rose suspected they were both entirely sick of their tears, their grief, sick of themselves.

"I love you," Priya whispered.

Rose twined her fingers with Priya's. "Just seeing all of that . . . seeing those people die—"

Rose saw the hollowness in her eyes and knew they were both in shock. Priya might not have lost family, but she'd borne witness to something that would leave them both with trauma that would last forever. At twenty-one years old, forever might be a very long time.

The front door opened. Rose wiped at her tears and sat up. Side by side, backs against the huge oak, the two girls watched Rose's dad and Chief Kaminski come down the steps and cross the lawn toward them. Rose expected her father to look as broken and disoriented as he had earlier, but the man who came out of the house carried himself quite differently from the man who had entered it. He still limped and winced in pain. His eyes remained oddly dark and the circles beneath them had deepened, but the straightness of his spine and the set to his jaw showed the anger that had taken root in him, and she could see he had purpose now. That was good. He so often looked for something to blur his pain or his sadness. Anger might burn that right out of him.

Later, she thought. *Later on, when Maeve is safe . . . or when it's over and she's really gone, then he'll break. But not yet.*

The thought cut her deeply. She'd seen him drunk so many times, seen how lost he'd become when painkillers had become his life. Rose held Priya's hand a little tighter.

"Dad?"

He went down on one knee in front of her, grinning to hide the pain in his ribs. "Chief Kaminski and I are taking a run up to the cabin. If anyone's going to find her there, I want to make sure it's us."

Rose started to get up.

"No," her father said, one hand on her wrist. "Stay here. Auntie Rue is in the house. You and Priya just sit tight, talk to Rue if you need anything, and the chief and I will be back soon, hopefully with your sister."

Rose's heart fluttered in her chest. Her dad was the only family she had at the moment, and she knew he needed her even more than she needed him. She wanted to latch on to him and not let go, but she nodded. "Okay. We'll stay. But bring a jacket, Dad. Bring a pair of work gloves or something. Do not let her touch you, no matter what happens."

Pain flared in his eyes as he understood, but he rose to his feet. "You're right. I wasn't thinking." He told Chief Kaminski to hold on a minute and lumbered back inside, coming out with a light zippered sweatshirt and a pair of leather gloves.

"Take care of her for me," Ted said to Priya.

"I will," she said as the two girls rose.

Rose's dad hugged them both, gingerly. Priya's family still liked to pretend their daughter didn't love a girl, but all the Sinclairs had welcomed her into their lives as if they'd been waiting for her, holding space open for her since the day she was born. Rose doubted she and Priya would stay together forever, or even through college—so few high school couples managed it—but secretly, she could see herself married to this girl someday.

"I love you," Ted Sinclair said, to both of them.

Rose grabbed him by the shoulders, made sure he met her eyes. "Do not let her touch you. Don't do that to me."

"I won't," he promised.

Then he turned and climbed slowly into Chief Kaminski's car. The engine coughed to life, the tires kicked up gravel, and half a minute later all was quiet again in the shade of that oak tree. In that quiet, it occurred to Rose that she had been selfish. Priya had called her parents to tell them what had happened so they knew she hadn't been injured, but with all the sirens and helicopters, with the news, with people dead, they would be frantic about their daughter's safety. They would want her home. She might be twenty-one, but she was still their girl.

"Pri," Rose began.

The rumble of another engine interrupted them. For a moment, Rose thought her father and the chief had changed their minds, but then she spotted Bill McHugh's ugly old Chevy Corsica. Red and faded and dented without being repaired, the thing seemed both ancient and ageless, but it ran perfectly. He might not have taken care of the outside, but he looked after the engine.

He skidded into his driveway and jolted to a stop. McHugh popped open his door and climbed out of the car. The way he looked over at them, forehead crinkling, eyes so sad, it was as if Bill McHugh had lost family this morning. He strode across his yard and into the Sinclairs', looking like he wanted to scoop them up into his arms. Rose and Priya stood up and walked over to meet him halfway.

"Aw, Rosie, kid . . . I'm so sorry about your mom and Logan." Mr. McHugh shook his head, his hands weaving slowly in the air as if in search of his next words.

"Thanks. Thank you." She didn't know what else to say.

He'd been their neighbor all her life. His daughter Cara had babysat each of the Sinclair kids at some point in their lives, before drugs had nearly killed her and a Colorado rehab center had saved her. She'd never come home from the Rockies. Rose hoped the dark vein of addiction running through the country hadn't reached her there, but she knew it might, if Cara McHugh didn't have the strength to fight it off. Most people seemed to think beautiful little hamlets like Jericho Falls were too remote, too idyllic, for the epidemic to take root. But people like Cara McHugh and Rose's own father were living proof, and Chief Kaminski could have shown those doubters plenty of corpses if living proof wasn't evidence enough.

Rose stared at Bill McHugh, somehow even hollower than before.

"Can you believe this?" the man demanded. "After what happened this morning, you'd think they'd need all the help they could get, but I went and volunteered to help them troopers search for Maeve, and now they're telling me I can't go."

Priya stiffened. "What?"

"On top of that, state police say the town's quarantined and nobody's allowed to leave."

Rose frowned. Why hadn't her father told her that? "That's kind of you just the same, Mr. McHugh. Thank you."

Red-faced, McHugh glanced at the house. He grew a bit sheepish, as if realizing that raising his voice to a grieving, frightened young woman might not be the best way to show his support for the family.

"I'm sorry, Rosie. Please let me know if you need anything, all right? I'll be just next door."

She nodded to him. Priya took her hand, and they walked back to the shade tree as Mr. McHugh returned to his own property. They kept mum until they heard his front door bang shut.

Rose tugged her phone from her pocket. She had texted Maeve a dozen times with no response. She figured her sister had tossed her phone to avoid the SIM card being tracked. Their dad seemed to think Maeve would go to Granddad's old cabin, but Rose doubted that. Smart as Maeve was, she would know that would be the first place he would suggest the police look for her. She felt like screaming. She knew why Maeve had to run, why she felt she needed to hide, and she loved her sister, but at the same time she found herself hating her instead.

Rose stood, brushing at the seat of her cutoffs. "I've got to go, Pri. I've been all over the mountain with her. If anyone's going to find her, it'll be me."

Priya glanced up at the house. "I don't think that's the best idea."

Rue had not come out to check on them, but Rose knew she would. The woman had always been such a good friend to her father—to both of her parents—even now, on the family's most hideous day.

Rose took Priya's hand. "We have to go now. It'll take a little while to really lock down the town. Mr. McHugh leaves his car keys in the console between the seats. He never minded when Maeve had to borrow his car. I don't think he'll be angry with me, especially today. I'm gonna take his car and drive out to the end of Goodman Hill Road, hike in from there, and find Maeve."

"Babe," Priya said, a familiar caution in her voice. "People are dead."

Rose winced. "Yeah. My mother's dead. Logan's dead. I don't want Maeve to be dead, too. You honestly think anyone's going to have a better chance of finding her than I am?"

Priya gave a tiny shrug, shaking her head. "My parents . . . they're going to be furious if I go with you."

Rose lifted her hand, kissed her fingers, and nodded. "I know. But I've gotta go. I'll drop you off on the way."

"No, you won't. I'm not letting you go without me." Priya gestured toward the house. "But what about Rue?"

The sound of Mr. McHugh's rumbling Chevy engine hadn't brought Rue to the door. Rose reckoned she was on the phone or half-asleep, not responding to that loud growl. Taking Priya's hand, she walked over to the car and opened the door.

"Easier to ask for forgiveness than permission."

6

For the first half hour, Maeve had done nothing but climb. After the parade, and the BMW, and the man behind the wheel, she had run away to the mountain. The woods had swallowed her up, as she had known they would. There were many trails on Mount Champney that were well groomed, perfect for hikers most of the year and cross-country skiers in the winter, but there were also dozens of less traveled paths. She'd crashed through the trees at the edge of town, headed uphill, and intentionally gone into the deeper woods, avoiding paths entirely.

Nearly an hour after entering the woods, the silent screaming inside her skull had quieted enough for her to begin to string thoughts together. Mom and Logan were dead. People would be after her. She needed time to think, but she couldn't let anyone near her until she had gotten her thoughts in order. She would need a plan—a destination.

Now she had one, at least temporarily.

Maeve knew several ways to reach her granddad's old cabin, including a dirt road that wound up through the woods, but that would leave her too exposed. Very few people still used the dirt road, but hikers sometimes parked on the shoulder to access the mountain trails. After getting turned around several times, she located the Jericho snowshoe trail, where her granddad had brought her and Logan and Rose as kids. Rose had been little, then, and when she was old enough to really take advantage of the cabin, Granddad had been too old. And then he'd died.

Shafts of sunlight shone through the trees, illuminating patches of the narrow trail. Covered with snow, it made a decent path, but in summertime it was too narrow and overgrown, and rocks and thick roots jutted from the ground. Maeve stumbled several times as she jogged up the trail but managed to keep her feet moving under her. The rich pine and maple scents of the forest filled her lungs, as if the mountain had taken her into its embrace. Mostly in shadows, accompanied by the sounds of her own exertion, she allowed herself the luxury of feeling safe.

In the distance, she heard the thrum of a helicopter's rotors. It might have been a news chopper, but Maeve felt sure whoever might be up there, they were searching for her. She focused on the thump of her old blue Sperrys on the hardened ground, creating a pace and a rhythm, and that helped her not think about the parade and the car, the baseball bat and the blood, and the look of relief in the murderer's eyes.

She hadn't recognized it at first, but now the memory had crystallized. She could see those eyes, that last moment of his life, even after he'd lunged for her and she'd grabbed his wrist. He'd realized death had come for him and his rage had bled away, replaced by . . . gratitude? Maeve thought it might have been gratitude, yes. And she hated him for it.

Her mother's face swam into her thoughts, and Maeve pushed it away. Her side hurt from the effort of the climb, but she picked up her pace. Blood rushed to her head, heart pounding in her ears, and that helped her not think about the things she didn't want to think about. Helped her erase the gray-eyed image of her mom coughing, of the panic etched into her features as she fell. As she died at her daughter's hands.

No. Maeve slowed her jog to a stiff walk, still hurrying.

The snowshoe trail hit a switchback, and she turned left and followed. During the summer, most people would have had a difficult time locating the trail. In the early fall, downed trees would be cleared and overgrown brush would be trimmed back. The few markers were so faded they blended easily with the surrounding woods. But Maeve knew what she was looking for. In some places, the trail appeared to simply end, but she always found it again.

A cough built in her chest, burst like a dog's bark from her throat, and she blamed the pollen in the air even though allergy season had come and gone.

To her left, twenty feet from the trail, she saw the pile of rocks that her granddad told her had been a forest chapel in the nineteenth century. Now the rocks served as a rustic fireplace for winter hikers and snowshoers. People who knew where to find it would gather 'round with thermoses of coffee or flasks of whiskey, sing songs or roast marshmallows or snuggle up against the cold weather and remember a time when the dangers of the wild mountain woods could not be so easily left behind. Granddad had taken Maeve and her siblings there one late afternoon as the sun had set, cooked hot dogs on sticks, and talked to them about bears and wolves and other things that might be found in the forest when people were alone and foolish. Then he had escorted them home along the nighttime trail, and Maeve had marveled at the array of unsettling noises from among the trees. She had listened with wonder and terror, and she had never forgotten.

As she emerged from the trail into the grassy, rutted lot behind Granddad's old cabin, she tasted the salt of new tears on her lips. Her phone buzzed again in her pocket. It had been going off regularly, vibrating with both calls and text messages. She knew she couldn't hold on to it for long, but it remained a lifeline, a possibility, a way home if she had any hope of going home.

"Oh God," she whispered, putting her hands on her hips and taking a breath as she studied the back of the cabin.

One of the back windows had been broken. Moss had grown thick on the roof. An old birch tree had fallen, white and thin and skeletal, against the south side of the cabin, but the leaves had kept growing and one of the branches seemed to have merged with the wooden structure. The mountain seemed determined to take back this piece of land, and with Granddad gone from the world, Maeve's father hadn't done anything to prevent it.

She ached with a yearning stirred by memories. There had been a bed here once, a place for her to lay her head, to cuddle with Rose back when she had been little, to make blanket forts with Logan and play board games and read the books that Granddad pushed on her and which she nearly always liked a bit more than she let on.

If only, she thought. If only she could go in there now and find Granddad waiting, find little Rose with a blanket, find Logan with the Scrabble board. If only they could catch fish down by the falls and fry those fish in a skillet with garlic and lemon and a pinch of this and a dash of that. If only Mom and Logan weren't dead.

Maeve looked at her hands for the first time since she had run from the parade. She studied her palms, wondering why they weren't soaked with blood, why they hadn't turned red or black or purple as an ugly bruise, anything to show that they were no longer ordinary hands.

Her phone vibrated again.

With a deep breath, she slid it from her pocket. The last text had come from her dad. *I'm coming, Maeve. I promise I'll find you.*

"Please don't." She whispered the words to herself, and perhaps to her father wherever he might be. Certainly not to God. If she'd ever believed in any sort of god, this had cured her of that delusion forever. What god would have stood back and watched such horror unfold?

Shit. He would come here. She knew that as surely as she'd ever known anything. Her father would think of the cabin right away. Maeve stared at the broken window and wondered if her dad might already be inside waiting for her—she wondered if he hated her now, if he might be coming here to take her home or have her arrested.

Of course he hates you. So does Rose. Of course they do. After what you did.

"Get your shit together," she said out loud. Closing her eyes, she imagined ice flowing down through her, freezing her veins, cooling the heat of shame and grief, hardening her muscles and bones.

Maeve set off to the north side of the cabin. The pump had

rusted, but it took less than a minute to get water flowing again. It began as a brown trickle, then spat and sprayed, and finally ran clear enough that she felt safe taking a drink. Hurrying around to the front of the cabin, she found the old key stuck between the step and the frame of the front stairs, where it had always been. The front door lock barely turned. The key jammed. Maeve put her shoulder in it, and the lock tore through rotted wood with a dry crunch. The door swung inward.

From off in the woods came the sound of an engine. Maeve glanced over her shoulder, listening as the engine growled, coming nearer.

A hunger gnawed inside her, and she had to fight the urge to stand and wait. If the engine signaled her father's arrival—even if it was someone else on the hunt for her—at least she would not be alone. If they meant to punish her, hurt her, it would only be what she deserved.

The engine rumbled nearer. She wanted so badly for her father to hold her. Just throw his arms around her.

Maeve would touch him. Take his hands in hers. Rose would come, and Maeve would embrace her. They would cough, and black blood would drip from their eyes. They would jerk and seize and judder on the ground, in the dirt, and then they would die. She could see it happen in her mind's eye, as if she had already lived those moments.

Maeve couldn't breathe. It felt as if her insides were being clawed out. *No, no, no,* she thought, because she would not allow herself to hurt anyone else, especially not her dad or Rose. She would never touch another person if that was what it took to keep from killing. Never touch anyone, not in love or lust, not for simple joy or comfort. The reality of it began to suffocate her.

She coughed again, a new ache in her throat and chest. Her temples throbbed.

It's not fair, a greedy little voice said in her head. *Just wait for them. They want to comfort you. They want to hold you.*

It didn't sound like her own voice at all but like someone else, like a serpent whispering in a garden. Everyone had a selfish terror inside them, waiting for the worst moments of their lives to manifest. She told herself that she wouldn't fall prey to it. Wouldn't let fear make her small.

She ran inside and rifled through the dusty kitchen until she found an old plaid thermos Granddad had always used for his coffee. In her pocket, her phone buzzed again, and she pulled it out and tossed it onto the rickety little kitchen table. They could track it if they wanted to, but they would only track it to the place they'd already have decided to search for her. It buzzed again as she ran from the cabin.

In the yellow grass of the side yard, she filled the thermos from the rusted pump. The car roared louder, clear and carrying across the yard, the woods no longer damping the noise. Whoever it was had arrived at the cabin, but they hadn't found her yet.

Maeve darted across the grassy lot and into the woods, rejoining the snowshoe trail. Every footfall sounded too loud in her ears, but by the time she heard car doors slamming shut back at the cabin, she'd already split off onto what Granddad had called the Jackrabbit Trail, and she knew nobody would find her here. Not quickly, anyway.

Fifty yards along, she came to a tree that had been split by lightning before she was born, both sides continuing to grow. From the split in the trunk, she had a view down the slope and into the cabin's small clearing. A blue-and-silver police car sat silently on the dirt road in front of the cabin, windows dark. Maeve's heart thrummed like hummingbird wings, but she fought the urge to keep running.

The driver's door opened first. Chief Kaminski climbed out, gesturing to someone inside the car. He raised his voice, and some of the words carried on the breeze. "Stay put, Ted. I don't need any more bodies."

Ted.

The passenger door opened, and Maeve's father stepped out. Her heart leaped. She could still see it in her mind, the moment the BMW had struck him, the way he'd jumped to avoid being hit and smashed into the windshield, been thrown up and over, landed on the pavement. But he was alive, and he was here. In pain, from the careful way he moved . . . but here.

He slammed the door hard enough for the sound to echo up the mountain. Some of his words were lost, but Maeve heard *fuck you* and *my daughter* clearly enough. Her left hand shook as she lifted it to cover her mouth, to keep her from shouting for him the way her heart yearned to. How old had she been when she had stopped needing her father?

Stupid question. Such a dumb fucking question. The child she'd been had not vanished but had been absorbed into the adult woman she'd become. Once, she had been a little girl who had climbed into her father's lap every day when he came home from work. Those memories were fresh, and today they were sharp enough to cut her.

"Daddy," she whispered. Whatever he had become, whatever demons he'd faced, he was still the father she'd always known.

His love for her would put him in danger, and she had lost too much today.

Maeve began to turn away, but something prickled at the back of her neck, an icy pain that radiated up into her skull. Wincing, she staggered and braced herself against a tree, stifling the groan at her lips. A bird took flight from the branches overhead, and she breathed through her teeth until the spike of pain had subsided. Frozen, she listened for approaching footsteps, but when she managed to look down at the road again, she saw Kaminski and her father entering the old cabin. The front door hinges creaked so loudly Maeve could hear them from up on the hill.

Her gut rippled with a sudden twist of nausea. She coughed and wiped at her mouth only to see a black smear on the back of her hand. *It's in me. The sickness he touched them with . . .*

Maeve heard the static of a police radio back down the hill, but she couldn't make herself turn and look for her father this time. She knew what would happen if she touched him, but it felt as if there were two voices in her head, deeply at odds, like the angel and devil on the shoulders of a character in some old cartoon. Part of her wanted the comfort her father's embrace would bring, but another part—a hungry part—wanted to hug him for another reason.

An image flashed in her head of her father coughing and choking, of disease frothing from his mouth, of his throat turning purplish black as he fell to his knees, eyes rolling back in his head. Maeve cried out—she couldn't stop herself, not with this horror in her mind. Tears burned at her eyes, guilt and grief and rage clawing at her.

There's always Kaminski, said the voice in her head. *You could take him.*

Her hands itched with heat, fingers clenching with a need she refused to understand.

The echo of her own cry lingered in the air. She blinked, wondering if they'd heard it down at the cabin.

Maeve bolted, dashing up the Jackrabbit Trail, leaving her father behind for the second time that day, wondering if she would ever see him again, terrified of what might happen if she did. She hurled herself up the mountain, deeper into the wild wood. She coughed again, spat black sludge onto the underbrush, winced at the needles of pain in her skull, and wondered if what she was really looking for was a place to lie down and die.

Either way, she wasn't going to hurt anyone else. Not ever.

No matter what the voices in her head might say.

7

Walker basked in the glory of the Buick's air-conditioning, cranked as high as the vents would pump it out. His plane had landed at half past two at a small regional airport, where he'd been met by a typically nondescript DoD employee and handed the keys to a silver Buick Cascada convertible, seemingly fresh off the lot. Working for the SRC had accustomed him to rentals or beat-up loaners, dusty Jeeps and dented trucks. If the DoD guy wondered how Walker warranted this vehicle, he gave no indication, but Walker wondered enough for both of them.

The sky had been half-blue and half–ghostly white when the plane was in the air, but by the time it landed, that misty cover had spread farther and begun to darken. On the video from this morning, the day had begun with a beautiful blue sky, but as the clouds moved in, the day had turned gray and heavy with humidity. As he drove, Walker glanced out the window and said a little pagan prayer for rain.

A convertible. Jesus, these people.

He kept the top up.

The GPS took him winding along a valley, halfway 'round a lake, and through dense forest. Hawks wheeled across the darkening sky. Higher up, a helicopter sliced the air in unsettling silence. It should've made more noise, which identified it as either friend or enemy. Helicopters used for corporate or tourist purposes were never so quiet. They didn't need to be.

Garland Mountain Laboratories appeared on his left, half a mile earlier than the GPS indicated. Walker hit the brake and turned onto a narrow road that looked as if it might tunnel into the side of a wooded mountain slope. The road veered to the right, through a dense screen of trees, and he caught his first glimpse of the fence. A quarter mile later, he tapped the brake and brought the Buick to a purring halt at a high, barbed wire–topped gate replete with security cameras. Two guards stepped out of the shack by the gate, one of them wearing an assault rifle slung across his shoulder. It looked to Walker like a SIG 556R, a serious weapon, but it only spurred more questions in his mind.

Who are you people? he thought as the guard approached.

Walker rolled the window down. "I'm Dr. Ben Walker from—"

"Global SRC," the guard finished. "You're expected, Dr. Walker. Please proceed to the end of the road, park in Lot C. Someone will greet you there."

Walker studied the man's face, the lines at the corners of his eyes, the lean features, the way his stance created an illusion of ease until you looked at the tension in his jaw and the way his right hand never strayed far from the service weapon holstered at his hip. Military, no question about it. The training, at least.

"Don't you want my ID?" he asked.

The guard smiled as if the question were adorably quaint. "No, sir. We've got it covered."

He signaled for the one with the assault rifle to open the gate, and a moment later it began to roll back with a metallic squeal. Walker drove through, keeping an eye on the two guards in his rearview mirror. Of course they had known he was coming, and presumably the SRC had sent some identification through, but still the guards should have confirmed his ID. Walker glanced back at the cameras by the guard station and wondered how many there had been on the road into the facility and how good Garland Mountain's facial recognition software might be.

Lot C awaited him at the road's end, as promised, nearest to the main entrance, a small lot marked for visitors and VIPs, but with fewer than half a dozen spaces occupied. Walker pulled the conspicuous Buick into the spot nearest the door. As he climbed out of the car, he saw a woman exit the lab and stride toward him. She wore a vest top, black trousers, and black boots that gave her away as something other than what she seemed. When she approached him, she did not offer a hand to shake.

"Dr. Walker, I'm Cristina Vargas, one of the lab supervisors. I'll be your escort while you're here, and I'll be happy to answer any questions you have."

"I don't want to waste your time," Walker replied, studying her eyes. "But I do have questions. Honest answers will speed us along."

Vargas wrinkled her nose. "You think I'm going to lie to you?"

"My past experience has left me ill prepared for honesty from people in your position."

"What position is that?"

"People who are hesitant to let me through the door."

Vargas smiled at that. "All right, then. Come in, Dr. Walker. We'll make this as painless as we can and get you on your way. You have more important things to do than hang around our lab all day."

She brought him inside, through security and past multiple cameras. The guards he saw wore sidearms and eyed him with a steel that said they had used those weapons before in some earlier life. Walker nodded to let them know the message had been received and also to give them the same message in return.

The lab had been built into the face of the mountain. From the outside, it appeared to be only two levels, but when Vargas took him onto the elevator, the row of buttons confirmed his suspicion that the facility was larger than it seemed. Five levels in total, three of them underground. It must, he thought, have cost billions of dollars to build the place, and a lot of influence to do it quietly.

Vargas took him up to a small conference room on Level 2, where a bald and bearded white guy in a lab coat shifted uncomfortably in one chair, and a woman tapped away at a laptop. When Vargas brought

Walker in, Lab Coat looked at his watch—he actually wore one—and gave a put-upon sigh.

"Please make it quick, Dr. Vargas," the lab coat said.

"I'd appreciate that as well," Walker said, drilling Lab Coat with a smile he hoped would set the man's beard on fire. "Before anyone else dies from whatever the fuck you idiots let out of your lab."

The bald-and-bearded Lab Coat, who looked a bit like Rasputin now that Walker gave it some thought, flushed red with anger, likely more color than his pale basement-dwelling life normally allowed. His colleague didn't smile, exactly, but as she turned to look at Walker, the corner of her mouth lifted with a hint of amusement. A large woman with a tumble of natural curls and better fashion sense than Lab Coat, Walker recognized her immediately.

Dr. Katherine Isenberg had previously worked for DARPA. They'd crossed paths a few times, briefly, but he saw the flicker of recognition in her eyes and gave her a small shake of his head. She took the hint, swallowing any words of greeting. Walker preferred not to let the others know he and Kat Isenberg were acquainted, partly because of the other flicker he saw in her eyes, a glimpse of worry and urgency.

"That's how it's going to be?" Vargas asked, taking a seat at the table. She leaned back, studying Walker, steepling her fingers on her chest.

Nobody had offered him a seat, but Walker took one. "It doesn't have to be. Maybe I jumped the gun. So let's just get to it and see if I made the wrong assumption. Let's start with names and job titles. We've got Dr. Vargas . . . who does what, exactly?"

Vargas fumed. "I've told you. I'm a lab supervisor."

"For all of Garland Mountain Labs or for—"

Lab Coat rolled his eyes. "For one lab. Dr. Vargas is my supervisor."

Kat Isenberg gave a small wave. "Dr. Isenberg. Deputy lab supervisor. And this is Dr. Jones, project manager."

Walker wanted to ask about Dr. Jones's projects, but while he had Vargas here, he had a more important question.

"Who funds Garland Mountain Labs?"

Vargas smiled. "Next question."

"Okay. Now I know where we stand," Walker said, leaning back in his chair. "My guess is Homeland Security, but Defense has to be aware, and given what little I do know about your operation, it feels like DARPA."

Dr. Jones grunted. "You said you didn't want to waste time."

Walker hadn't liked any of this from the outset—the lab, the sickness, the idea that anyone could kill just by touching someone—but he particularly didn't like how close to home this felt. Whoever gave the researchers at Garland Mountain their marching orders, this was familiar territory, the sort of research DARPA did every day. But playing twenty questions with these people wasn't going to save a single life if the questions went unanswered.

"Just tell me what you're prepared to tell me about the guy in the BMW and what he could do," Walker said. "Then I'll do what I can to fix your fuckup."

Dr. Jones made a tsking sound with his tongue. "People who live in glass houses, Dr. Walker."

Walker bristled. "Meaning what, exactly?"

"We all have a job to do, that's all," Vargas said, kindlier than before. More concerned. "The man's name was Oscar Hecht. He worked here. The media will have that information fairly soon. Red Hands is a tactile bacterial infection—"

"Red Hands? That's what you—"

"Yes, that's what we call it," Jones interrupted. "Project: Red Hands. And yes, it's the result of intensive research and experimentation. Given whom you work for, you're in no position to lecture us. It wasn't supposed to ever leave the lab, but Hecht infected himself and then ran from his own idiocy. A fool and a coward, and now he's dead."

"And he took a lot of other people with him," Walker replied.

"Justin . . . ," Vargas cautioned.

Walker glanced at the man's name tag for the first time. *Dr. Justin W. Jones.* He didn't look like a Justin. Walker had preferred *Rasputin*.

Kat Isenberg tapped at the computer, nodding to herself. "Dr. Vargas, we're set."

Vargas exhaled. "Finally."

Walker cocked his head. "You want to share?"

"The quarantine perimeter is closed. Between our people, state police, and officers from police departments in surrounding communities, every road now has a checkpoint."

Something about the statement chilled Walker, but it took him a moment to sift his thoughts. He narrowed his eyes, studying Jones and Kat before fixing his gaze on Vargas.

"You have all the bodies here at the lab, don't you? The remains are quarantined here. Everyone from the Sinclair woman's family to Hecht himself."

Vargas gave a nod. "That's right."

"This is a tactile contagion, you said, and from the clips I've seen, I will take you at your word. The only way to get this sickness is to be touched by someone infected with it, and aside from Hecht and Maeve Sinclair—whose exceptions I assume you'll decline to explain—everyone touched with Red Hands dies less than a minute after contact."

"That's an exaggeration," Jones said. He ran a hand over his beard, unconsciously grooming himself. "Some lived nearly two minutes."

Walker wanted to punch him in the throat. He squeezed his eyes closed. When he opened them, he caught a strange expression on Kat's face. She had glanced at her lab partner with a look of disdain, even disgust. When she caught Walker looking at her, she gave a shake of her head and mouthed the words *I'm sorry*. Vargas and Rasputin hadn't seen—they were staring at Walker—but at least one person in this place had a soul.

"In other words," Walker said, "you know there isn't anyone else infected with this thing. I'd like you to walk me through exactly how you know that, how we got here, and what you're planning to do about it."

Vargas looked at him as if he'd lost his mind. The guy he thought of as Rasputin-in-a-lab-coat actually snickered, laughing at Walker rather than with him. As manager of Project: Red Hands, his work had cost lives, and he didn't seem all that broken up about it. Kat Isenberg met Walker's gaze, fidgety and frustrated, and he felt sure she would have talked to him if the other two weren't in the room.

"I think we're done here, Dr. Walker," Vargas said, gesturing toward the door. "We look forward to helping you bring Maeve Sinclair home safely, for her own protection as well as the protection of anyone she might encounter."

Jones stood. Kat Isenberg closed her laptop.

"This quarantine should comfort me," he told Vargas. "You spending so much effort on making sure Sinclair doesn't kill anyone else."

"But you're not comforted, are you?"

Walker shook his head. "I would be if I thought you cared more about the people who might die than you do about putting your genie back in the bottle."

The authorities had put the quarantine in place mostly for show—you couldn't have something contagious kill a bunch of people on a video the whole world had seen and do nothing. But the only person the masterminds at Garland Mountain actually wanted to confine to the area was Maeve Sinclair.

"Now, hang on," Jones said, face going red. "If you can get her here, we can help this woman."

Walker turned for the door. "You'd fucking better, Justin."

Vargas hurried to follow him out and escort him to the elevator. In the lobby, the security guards nodded to Walker, and then they were outside. The clouds had thickened and darkened, and a few drops of rain spattered the ground.

"We're doing all we can," Vargas said. "We all want to keep people safe."

"You're doing a bang-up job so far."

Walker headed for Lot C, where his convertible Buick loaner sat looking absurder than ever.

"What did you expect?" Vargas called. Hands stuffed into her pockets, she studied him with what seemed genuine curiosity.

"Excuse me?" Walker said.

"She's had a bad fucking day, yeah, her life is a goddamn tragedy," Vargas went on, "but what's in Maeve Sinclair is our research, and she belongs here at Garland. The decision may rest with someone higher up, but did you really think we'd be eager to help you be the one to lay hands on her?"

Walker felt his fists clench. He smiled, but if Vargas had known him better, the smile would have made her nervous. "You think she belongs to you."

"Of course. Who else? I told you, it's our research—"

"She's not research. She's a human being."

Vargas sighed heavily and rolled her eyes. "Grow up, Walker. This girl is death incarnate, and she's fucking AWOL." She waved him off. "Just go find her. We'll fight over her later. If she offers to shake hands, maybe just blow her a kiss instead."

She turned and walked back toward the facility entrance. Walker glanced around, surprised not to have an escort, but then he remembered all the cameras and the guards at the gate, and knew there were still eyes on him.

The cameras watched as he drove back to the gate, but it swung open without so much as a glance from the guard shack. They had known he was coming, and they knew he was leaving. Walker felt more conspicuous than ever in his silver convertible, and he sped up, the Buick surging along the narrow road beyond the gate, embarrassed and angry and filled with a new urgency.

When a dented red Hyundai pulled out from behind a tree to block the road, he barely had time to jam on the brake. The Buick skidded to a halt. The engine ticked and growled, and the wipers swished across the glass as Walker glared at the Hyundai, waiting for trouble. He'd lived moments like this before, and the next step nearly always included hard-eyed men with guns. Instead, the woman who stepped out of the Hyundai was tall and attractive, tattooed and grim-faced. She slammed her car door and walked directly toward him, and Walker knew then she had no intention of killing him. If she meant him harm, she would know better than to expose herself that way. If he'd had a gun, he could have put a dozen bullets in her.

Which reminded him that he shouldn't have left his gun packed in his bag, in the trunk. He hadn't expected to want it quite so soon.

As the woman approached the driver's window, Walker hit the button to lower it.

The first tattoo his gaze lit upon seemed to be a purple octopus encircling her forearm, the last thin tentacle like a bracelet on her wrist. He'd have liked her immediately if not for the way she'd just endangered both their lives.

"Can I ask your name?" she said, one hand on the roof, ducking to look through his window. Not an ounce of fear.

He had both hands on the steering wheel. "This is a strange ambush."

Her forehead wrinkled. "What?" Blinking, she stepped quickly back from the car, hands raised. "Look, I just want to know who you are. I spent fifteen minutes at the gate. Once the guard told me nobody would see me, he basically ignored me until I gave up. I saw you take the turn in my rearview mirror when I was leaving and I thought, no way are they letting this guy in. I'm pissed off, so I followed you back. Sure enough, I get to the gate and you're nowhere in sight, which meant you were inside. So I wanna know, who are you that they stonewalled me but let you through?"

Walker felt the seconds ticking past, but he could see the pain and determination in the woman's eyes.

"I don't work for the lab," he said. "They're assholes."

She didn't smile. "Implying you personally are not an asshole."

"I have my days." He extended his hand through the window. "Walker. Global Science Research Coalition."

"Rue Crooker," she said, shaking his hand. "Concerned fucking citizen."

Walker released her hand, glancing at the tentacles of her octopus tattoo. "Short version, my boss sent me to make sure this morning's tragedy doesn't get any worse. It's incredibly dangerous. You should really be at home until—"

Rue gave him a look of profound disappointment. "See, I liked you until right now."

"I'm sorry?"

"If you work for Global SRC, you know I'm not in any danger. The only people in danger are Maeve Sinclair and anyone who comes into contact with her."

Walker smiled. A breeze kicked up and blew the forest smells of pine and cedar through his window. "You may not like me anymore, but I now like you a hell of a lot, Ms. Crooker."

"*Dr.* Crooker."

"Of course you are." He tilted his head. "What sort of doctor might you be?"

"Biologist. I was there when it happened. Saw it all, and not on video. Also dealt with your friends from the lab—"

"They are definitely not my friends." Walker hesitated, knowing Alena wouldn't want to involve civilians, but this woman was already involved, and he had an assignment to complete. "You said only Maeve and anyone she runs into will be in danger, and you're right. For her sake, I need to be the one to find her. I assume you didn't drive over here and argue with the guards at the gate out of clinical interest."

Rue simmered. "They brought all the victims back here. People want to know what's being done with the remains of their loved ones and how long before they're released."

Walker put both hands on the wheel, felt the engine idling. "Yeah, but that's not why you're here. You came because you want answers. You're a biologist, and this isn't like anything you've ever seen. It's something that shouldn't even exist, and you wanna know what it is, how it does."

"And I want Maeve to be all right."

"You know her," Walker said.

Rue took another step back from the car. For a few seconds, she seemed to be evaluating him, and then she nodded to herself as if deciding. Reached up to scratch at the stubble on the shaved part of her scalp.

"Maeve's father is one of my closest friends. I've known the girl all her life. Her father, Ted, had a hunch about where she might go and headed up there with the chief of police, Len Kaminski. They'll be back at the house by now, with her or without her."

Walker swore under his breath, hands tightening on the wheel. "That could be very dangerous."

Rue tapped the roof of the car. "Follow me. I'll make an introduction."

"You trust me enough to do that?"

She scowled. "Someone has to help this family, and you're the only person I've encountered who seems willing. But don't flatter yourself, friend. After today, I don't trust anyone."

8

Three-quarters of an hour after Maeve had started on the Jackrabbit Trail, she noticed a narrower trail on her left. Unlike so many in these mountains, this path had no marker, no sign, no name to offer a hiker the comfort of familiarity or the assurance that if they wandered off and became lost, they were likely to find their way.

She took a breath, a prickle of fear at the back of her neck. The trail wended into a thick tangle of forest, much darker than the path she'd been on, but it appeared to continue up the mountain. More importantly, she knew she had never hiked this trail with her family, had never lugged her fishing rod through that gap. If her father tried to guess where she'd go next, he might well think to try the Jackrabbit Trail, but he'd never imagine she would go off by herself into the dark unknown.

Which made it her only choice.

Maeve wished she could stop, let them find her, but that just wasn't possible. She needed time to think. Right now, she couldn't see any way out of this, but she nurtured a small hope that if she could just stop and rest, something would occur to her.

Protecting her face from branches, she plunged along the narrow trail, so thick with trees and bushes that they scraped at her like brambles. If they had a good tracker, the person would doubtless be able to follow, but she wasn't going to make it easy for them.

Neither was the weather, apparently. Ten minutes after she'd started up the new path, stumbling on rocks and root braids that thrust from the dirt, it began to rain. The sun had been fading in and out all along, but it surprised her when she heard the pattering on the leaves over-head and then the thick rattling of heavier drops. Though it couldn't have been much past 2:00 p.m., it felt as if night had already fallen.

Maeve welcomed it. If the storm went on long enough, all traces of her passing this way would be erased.

Maybe nobody will ever find me. Maybe I'll die up here.

A racking cough bent her double and blurred her vision. Her chest had begun to ache, and she pressed both hands against her sternum. Her throat felt tender and swollen. Maeve coughed again, and she spat something thick and dark onto the rain-damp path. This couldn't be what she feared—not whatever had killed her mother and Logan. The people the driver had touched died instantly. She had killed him; he had touched her, passed whatever disease had cursed him onto her, but she wasn't supposed to be the one to get sick.

The trail widened a bit, turning northeast, up the face of the moun-tain, toward a ridge between Mount Champney and the neighboring Little Blackberry Mountain. Northeast felt like the safest direction. Off to the west were the real Jericho Falls, the waterfalls from which the town had gotten its name. The falls and the caves there brought out tourists and day hikers, and she knew whoever might be look-ing for her would assume she would strike out for the falls. A young woman on her own, up on the mountain, knowing there were caves where she could hide and people who might be willing to help her? The average middle-aged man wouldn't bet money on Maeve seeking out the hard terrain, the darkest woods. Her father would expect it, but she had to gamble on him not sharing those thoughts. Even if he blamed her for what had happened . . . even if he hated her now.

Her gut gave a sour twist, and she began to cough. Something in her felt *off*. She thought longingly of her grandfather's cabin, but she couldn't go back there. She continued along the narrow, overgrown trail. The rain fell so hard it began to pool and flow in little rivulets along the raised roots. Squirrels darted through underbrush. Twenty paces farther, the branches grew so close together that the trail virtually disappeared.

She plunged ahead. A thin branch scraped her cheek, and she hissed at the sting. Raindrops ran down her face as she pushed through, tripped on a root, and stumbled half a dozen steps to land sprawling on the path. The fall knocked the wind out of her. A rock jutting from the ground smashed into her left breast, and she groaned and rolled over, arms across her chest. She coughed a little. The ache in her throat throbbed, but as her breathing evened out, she managed to turn over and rise up onto her knees.

The trail had turned parallel to the mountain. The rain had lightened up. Ahead, the path sloped downward to a break in the trees. Silhouetted in the gray light, perhaps two hundred yards ahead, a broken, jagged stone chimney rose from a sloped roof. Maeve shot to her feet in panic, ready to bolt, fearful that she had unknowingly doubled back toward town.

Something skittered through the trees overhead, but she heard no voices, nothing to indicate there were people around. With cautious steps, she started down the path toward that broken chimney, trying to orient herself. As the path sloped, she ran through all her past fishing and camping trips with her family, and moments before she reached the aging, moss-covered stone structure off the trail, she realized she had found the Moonglow Inn.

It stood on a stony precipice overlooking the glacier-carved river gorge for which it had been named. Three hundred million years earlier, the Ice Age had caused glaciers a mile thick to move across the land, forging mountains, slashing valleys and deep gorges, shifting stone, leaving tunnels and caves and beautiful rock formations behind. Maeve's father tended to be a quiet man, but she believed he had a bit of poetry in him, because occasionally he would reveal a love for some beautiful place or story that had touched him.

Once upon a time, a trapper named Elwin Grey had been knee-deep in the river, looked up, and seen the full moon framed between the walls of the gorge, its light reflecting off glacial stone, and felt himself transported somewhere magical. Elwin Grey had named the place Moonglow River Gorge, and as more settlers moved in, the name had stuck. In high school, Maeve had written a paper about the native Abenaki people, who had surely had a name for the gorge before Elwin Grey's magical evening, but she didn't share that paper with her father. She didn't want to extinguish that little bit of poetry in him.

The Moonglow Inn had its own story. Maeve had never been there before. Like most who'd caught a glimpse of it, she had only seen the corner of its sagging roof from down in the gorge. But her father had told her the story of a Scottish laird who had fallen in love with the view from that precipice and believed others would as well. He'd sold his Highland estate and invested his money and influence building the inn. For a time, Maeve's father had told her, it had worked. Hunters and fishermen and bird-watchers came, people of wealth and breeding who wanted to explore the wild mountains. But the waterfalls to the west drew more visitors, more development, and no road could be built to reach the Moonglow Inn. By the time the Great War erupted in Europe, the Scotsman's dream had already faded, and before the war ended, the doors had been shuttered. Several times, investors had purchased the property in hope of reviving it, but over the course of a century, it had never actually reopened.

The Moonglow Inn had become a memory. A ruin. A stone heap covered in moss, broken windows looking out over the gorge. One wing of the inn had collapsed and slid over the precipice into the gorge about eighty years earlier. Hikers would sometimes make their way there, Maeve's father had told her, but it was far enough and spooky enough that the place did not draw vast numbers of partying teenagers the way it might have if it were closer to town.

The place was just empty. Crumbling. A dead shell of a thing, the hollow husk of a man's lost dream.

It was exactly what Maeve had been hoping for.

With the rain pattering the leaves overhead and the wind gusting over the rim of the gorge, she left the trail and explored the façade of the inn. Some of the windowpanes were intact, but most had been shattered. Maeve pressed against the swollen wood of the front door, and the rusted hinges squealed. She put her shoulder into it and yanked up on the handle as she pushed, and it scraped against the stone threshold just enough to give her room to squeeze through.

Her nausea had faded, but she grunted as she squeezed through the gap and inhaled the moldy stink of the rotting wood. Her stomach churned, bile at the back of her throat. Maeve forced it down, but the moment it passed she began to cough again. Each barking seal cough sent a spike of pain through her skull, and she felt something trickling from her nose. Reaching up, she wiped away something she first thought was blood, but which she saw, in the wan light coming through the broken roof, was putrid yellow and oily black.

She collapsed to the floor in what had once been the lobby. The thick pine beams of the floor had turned soft where the roof lay open to the elements, but here it retained its solidity and strength. Where the huge stone fireplace rose to the ceiling, the fallen portion of the chimney had crashed through the roof and lay in a pile on the floor. The rain fell through the opening. Across the lobby, a staircase rose into shadows and cobwebs.

The stairs seemed to call to her. They looked protected from the wind and rain, dry and warm. She could curl up at the top of the steps and figure out what to do next. Another cough rumbled in her chest, but she took small sips of breath, fighting it, staving off the pain that came along with it. Maeve stumbled toward the stairs, wheezing, barking, head throbbing, that disgusting crap in her throat.

Her eyes were wet. She went to wipe at them with her hands, but when she blinked, the gray interior of the crumbling lodge turned a filmy red.

Through the veil of red that covered her eyes, the room around her changed. A fire roared in the fireplace. The dying echo of laughter hung in the air. The stink of booze filled the lodge. The whole world turned crimsons and scarlets and bright candy-apple reds, but mostly bloodred, because all around her, strewn across the lobby, were bloated corpses dressed in the finery of another era. Their eyes were stained a reddish black, clotted with dried fluid. Their throats were swollen and black, their exposed skin covered in deep red blotches that had bled and scabbed and begun to rot as if acid had eaten down to the bone.

Maeve tried to scream, but her throat was so raw that pain silenced her. Another round of coughing racked her body, and she dropped to one knee. She drew a ragged breath, managed to stifle the next cough, and stared at her hands, which were trembling and pale in the storm light.

Pale, not veiled by that red film that had affected her vision.

The moment passed. The fireplace no longer roared with flame. The inn had returned to the moldering, broken, abandoned gray pile it had been upon her entrance into the place.

Maeve wanted to rise, to run, even to weep, but she didn't have the energy for any of those things. Instead, she lay on the floor, listened to the rain on the roof, and winced at the strange hunger that gnawed at her.

The itch returned to her hands and her fingers twitched while she lay there, yearning for something she refused to allow herself to imagine. Yearning for *contact*.

She closed her eyes for fear of what they might see.

Rose knew she ought to have come alone, but she was deeply grateful to have Priya with her. Without the comfort of her company, the warmth of her love, she'd have been alone with her grief. Images of her mother and Logan swam into her thoughts, and she shoved them out. Yeah, if she'd been alone, she knew she would have collapsed into helpless sobs by now. Full fetal position breakdown. Mom and Logan were dead, the two people who seemed to always look out for her the most. Now what, she was supposed to live with her father? Sometimes she loved him so much it hurt, but she couldn't trust him to do what he said or be where he promised, and that hurt even more.

"Gorilla Rock's just up here, isn't it?" Priya asked.

Rose smiled, surprised that Priya would remember. She wasn't much of a nature girl. They had overheard enough to know that Maeve had set out north and east from her granddad's cabin, so Rose had parked Mr. McHugh's old Corsica at the entrance to the Edison Campground and they'd hiked up the southern approach, hoping to intersect her path. Rose had halfway expected to be stopped by local or state police, but the quarantine didn't stop people from moving around Jericho Falls—only from leaving it. There had been a number of police cars parked along the trailheads, where cops and others out searching for Mae must have started up the mountain. There'd been a single state police car at Edison Campground, but it was empty. Whoever had driven it over, they'd been deployed up onto the mountain. Most of the cops who weren't part of the search must have been manning roadblocks on the main routes out of town or still helping with the cleanup downtown.

Maybe tomorrow there would be more searchers—National Guard or something—but for now, the numbers were limited. If they hadn't found Mae by then, Rose wondered how long it would be before they decided other people were or were not infected. The federal government would be monitoring the situation, but they had proven to be colossal fuckups when it came to the containment of contagion in the past. In the end, the only thing Rose cared about was that there was nobody there to stop them from going up the mountain after her sister.

"We follow the markers for the Eagle View Trail and we'll come to the fire pit," she said. "Gorilla Rock's not far after that."

She took Priya's hand and led the way. When the Sinclair siblings had been small, their father had taken them to Plug Pond to fish at least once a week during the summer. For him, fishing had always included drinking, but he'd had it under control in those days, or at least none of them ever seemed to notice how much he drank. It was just Ted Sinclair, catching fish, drinking beer, laughing with his kids.

She knew this part of the mountain well. Gorilla Rock had acquired its name over generations, first as a colloquialism, until someone had included it in a hiking brochure, and then the name became permanent. A piece of glacial stone, its broken edges formed what looked to be a protruding brow, shadowed eyes, a sloping forehead, so that it looked like the head of a brooding gorilla.

The first time Rose had climbed up to the rock, which stood twenty feet above the trail, she had found a depression in the back of the stone head. The way the ground sloped up to it, and the concavity in the rock, it was the perfect place for a girl to secrete herself away if she wanted to play hide-and-seek or just give her long-suffering father a heart attack.

She had been a mischievous girl.

Priya took Rose's hand again, her brow furrowed as she marched through the trees.

The trail had been marked with spots of blue paint to let hikers know they were on the right track, but this route was so well traveled that it would have been hard to miss. The thought caused a frown to crease Rose's forehead.

"Shit," she whispered. "Shit, shit, shit."

Priya squeezed her hand. "What is it?"

How could Rose explain the impact those blue paint spots had on her?

"This trail . . . it's too well known," she said, looking at Priya. "I'm so stupid. Maeve's probably a mess right now, but she's not stupid."

Rose cursed herself again, silently now. Maeve would be terrified and lonely and shattered by guilt. But if she wanted to hide on the mountain, she would be too smart to travel the most familiar trails.

"You're right," Priya said. "She's not stupid. She has to know she needs help. Do you really think she's going to hide somewhere your father wouldn't find her eventually?"

Rose looked at her, a rough heat rising in her cheeks. "You were *there*."

Priya squeezed her hand. "Finding her isn't enough, Rose. We've got to figure out what's been done to her, how to help her, and we can't do that if she's—"

"The last thing she wants is for my dad to find her," Rose said. "I'm sure she doesn't want us to find her, either."

Priya chewed her lip. "Then how are we supposed to find her?"

Rose looked up toward the mountain's peak. "Someone's going to. Which means it has to be us."

*   *   *

Priya kissed her tears. "Then let's focus. You said she wouldn't have come here. Where *would* she go? The peak? I know there are caves up there. Or maybe she just doubled back and headed for the falls. There are houses there, cabins, plenty of camps where she could try to hide."

"Maybe," Rose agreed, "but I don't think so. She'd have taken the Jackrabbit Trail from the cabin. If we start climbing from here, head straight up the mountain, we'll cross it. From there, we'll find some of the narrow trails that hunters and animals use. Not the kind of thing hikers would bother with. We find those and we search, and if we find any sign of her, there's no point in shouting her name. Chances are, she's not going to answer back. She doesn't want us anywhere near her if she thinks she might . . . that she could kill us."

Priya gave her a gentle kiss. "Lead the way."

Rose felt a hitch in her chest as she turned and left the path, hiking up the mountain through the woods. A flood of images flashed through her mind. Bouncing on Maeve's bed on Christmas morning, dragging her sleepy sister into their parents' room to wake them, the two girls teasing Logan, who would always be seated halfway down the steps waiting for them, more excited than any of them to see what Santa had brought.

Logan, gone.

Years had passed since Maeve had left for college. The bond between the sisters had evolved and matured. In some ways it had grown stronger, but Rose had often thought how much less fun growing up had made her relationship with Maeve. No more blanket forts.

As a little girl, Rose had often woken in the night, terrified of the darkness inside her closet. The door never quite shut all the way, and the age of the house had warped the frame so that it swung open slightly when the wind blew outside and the gusting made the house breathe in and out. On those nights, Rose would tiptoe into Maeve's room, climb into bed with her, warm and safe under the blankets with her big sister.

Maeve had never sent her out, never complained of being woken.

No matter how old they'd become, Maeve had always opened her arms, hugged Rose, stroked her hair, and kissed the top of her head. It had been Rose, eventually, who had decided she was too old for such displays.

Maeve could hide as deep in the woods as she liked. No matter how afraid Rose might be, no matter how much she grieved, she was going to find her sister. Maeve had never turned her back, and neither would Rose.

"Hey," Priya rasped, grabbing at the strap of her backpack.

Rose frowned, turning to look at her. They had hiked about twenty yards above Gorilla Rock.

"What's the—"

Priya held a finger over her lips, neck craned, listening to the woods. All Rose could hear was the patter of the rain on the leaves and the path. Thunder rumbled in the distance.

"I don't—" Rose started to say.

But then she did. A noise down in the clearing below Gorilla Rock, a padding of footfalls as if someone had dashed across the clearing, trying to make as little noise as possible. The noise went silent for a few seconds, and she was about to speak again when the sound of something in the brush carried up to them.

It might have been a lone hiker or someone searching for Maeve, but whoever it was, they were attempting to be quiet, and something about that made her skin crawl. She glanced up at Priya and saw what looked like a gleam of hope in her eyes, and only then did the other possibility occur to her.

Maeve.

Sliding and scrambling, slipping on the rain-slicked forest floor, she rushed down the slope, heedless of the noise she made as she crashed through branches.

She slipped. Cussing loudly, she flailed and tumbled the last few feet into the clearing. On her hands and knees, Rose looked up, glanced around, and ached with fresh loss as she saw the clearing remained empty.

"You heard it, right?" Rose asked, standing and brushing off dirt and pine needles. "Someone was here."

"I thought I did," Priya said, brows knitted. "Unless it was an animal. A deer. Maybe a bear, or a wolf—"

"Oh, that's a cheery thought," Rose replied. "Thanks for that."

Quiet descended on the clearing for a moment. Even the rain paused. No birds called, no squirrels foraged. The two of them stood and listened, but if anything had been there, it was gone now. They were alone.

Rose felt hollower, lonelier as she turned and started to climb up the mountain again. Priya being there, strong and calm and brave, should have comforted her, but suddenly the presence of this girl she loved only made her feel her loss more keenly.

How many hours until dark?

Rose began to lose hope.

9

Ted Sinclair liked movies about the apocalypse. Sometimes he would daydream about what it might be like—what kind of person he might prove to be—if the world ever really began to fall apart around him. Not that Ted was eager for nuclear war or a zombie uprising, but he loved those stories because they were about ordinary human beings having their mettle tested by the crumbling of civil society. He liked to tell himself that he would rise to the occasion, that instead of seeking the comfort of oblivion he would step up, fight for survival, for himself and the people he loved. Ted could picture himself a hero, living wild, running some guerrilla war campaign against an oppressor. But in that lizard brain at the base of his skull, he could feel a different instinct. A tremor, an urge.

He wanted pills. A little plastic bottle rattling with lovely tabs of Oxy. Better yet, a dose or two of fentanyl. The pills might kill him, but first they'd get him so high that dying wouldn't seem like such a terrible plan.

Which was exactly why he needed to stay far away from pills.

Alcohol, on the other hand, remained his very dear friend.

He stood in his living room, a generous tumbler of Jameson whiskey in his hand, and decided this wasn't the apocalypse quite yet, but it felt close. Death felt intimately near, tangible and possible. Ted had always loved apocalyptic movies, but now he decided he would hate those films for the rest of his life.

Rue Crooker had let his daughter Rose wander off with Priya, and instead of raising alarms, instead of screaming to the world that the last healthy, living member of Ted Sinclair's family had decided to go search an entire mountain range with her girlfriend, Rue had gone off to have a close-up look at Garland Mountain Labs. They'd been friends since childhood and he loved Rue, but he wanted to shake her. Had she really thought they would throw open their doors to her, let her see their research?

Ted sipped his third whiskey, letting its burn rush through him. He stared at Rue and at Chief Kaminski and at the stranger who sat on the arm of the sofa. Ted had told them all to make themselves comfortable, but death had come to this house and there was only so comfortable a stranger should make himself here. Today.

Whiskey blunted his apocalypse a little bit, but the end times had come to the Sinclair family. The rest of the world might be tuning in to CNN or Fox News or whatever, learning about the quarantine and Maeve Sinclair, the woman with the death touch. They might have watched the footage from the parade, entranced by tragedy, but they would all go on with their lives, and Ted had to stand in his living room with a stranger telling him what to do while his ex-wife and his son lay dead in some secret government lab and his eldest daughter ran away to the mountains to hide, while the youngest went in search of her.

And this Walker son of a bitch wanted Ted to sit here and just wait.

"I wish you could hear yourself, Mr. Walker," Ted said. He knew he was glaring, knew his upper lip had curled with disdain, but he couldn't help it.

"Dr. Walker," Rue corrected him.

"Just Walker is fine," the guy said.

"I don't give a fuck!" Ted snapped.

They all stared at him—Rue, Kaminski, Walker—and Ted felt his chest rising and falling, felt the warm flush in his cheeks. He knew he must look like a drunk about to get into a bar brawl, and maybe he felt that way. Shit, no *maybe* about it.

"You really think I'm going to stay here while my girls are up on that mountain?" Ted demanded, glancing incredulously from face to face. "I don't even know you."

Kaminski had perched on the edge of the big old green-and-gray striped chair that remained the oldest piece of furniture in the house. He leaned forward, his face full of so much sympathy that Ted wanted to kick him.

"Ted, you've got a concussion, broken ribs, and cartilage damage in one knee. You're not going to be much use crawling around those mountains. Between my officers, state troopers, and security officers from the lab—" Chief Kaminski started.

"Goddamned government thugs," Ted snarled.

"No argument," Kaminski said. "That's what they are. But they're up there with good police officers searching for Maeve. I'm going to radio up that Rose and Priya are on the mountain as well, but you know their priority has to be Maeve."

"Because she's dangerous," Ted sneered.

"You know she is," Rue said. She stood up from the sofa and approached him, put her hands over his as if she wanted to try to help him clasp his glass of whiskey, to take it away. Like he needed help. And maybe he did, the way his hands had started to shake.

"I guess I do," Ted said, looking Rue in the eye. "I watched them die. Watched Logan and . . ." He shook his head, blew out a breath, refused to cry in front of a stranger. Not again, anyway. He shot a look at the presumptuous bastard sitting on the arm of his sofa. "Walker, you really think you can get her off the mountain safely? I can't help feeling like no matter how good these cops are, the first one she comes near is going to shoot her to keep from dying the way my son and his mom did."

"If she comes off the mountain on her own, she'll probably come home, which means you'll see her first," Walker said. "If she stays up there, then I do think it's best for her safety and everyone else's if I find her first."

"How do you plan to do that?"

"It's not my first mountain or my first time tracking someone," Walker replied. "I've got some gear and some connections they don't have."

Ted exhaled. "What do you need from me?"

Walker gave a slow nod. It looked almost like a promise, but Ted couldn't allow himself to trust anyone.

"Any insight into her thought process would help," Walker said. "The police are focusing on the area around the waterfall, banking on Maeve heading for somewhere she might regard as safe."

"There's some logic in that," Ted admitted, glancing at Kaminski. "But she lit out from her granddad's cabin heading northeast, and I think she'll stay that way, either go straight up the mountain or to the west. Might not be as safe or as familiar, but she'll stay one step ahead as long as she can, and then she'll go to ground, find a place to hide. I've taken my kids fishing up there a hundred times, and we used to hike all over when they were little ones. We . . ."

A shudder went through him. Ted's breath hitched and he held up a hand, knowing if he uttered another word he would erupt into a torrent of sobbing.

Kaminski put a hand on his shoulder. "It's all right, Ted. I'm gonna take Dr. Walker up to the cabin, and he can start searching from there. The government goons want me to focus my people to the west, toward the falls, but that doesn't mean Walker has to follow those orders. Maybe we'll come across Rose and her girlfriend. If we do, I'll bring them home. You just need to stay here, answer the phone if it rings, and hope she comes home on her own."

Ted felt his legs weaken. The idea of staying here made him want to scream—these were his daughters, his last family, flesh and blood—but so did the idea of him not being here when one or both of them made it home to an empty house. It tore him apart. He wanted to collapse, but he'd been raised with more spine and dignity than that.

"You have anyone who can stay with you?" Kaminski asked. "Other family?"

Ted felt the thin smile on his lips. Other than Rue, he'd never been much for small talk with neighbors or friends, even the ones he liked. Shortly before Walker and Rue arrived, Ted had thought about calling his sister Dianna, but Di lived in Texas and they hadn't done more than exchange Christmas cards or share a cursory phone call in going on a decade.

His brittle smile grew thinner still. "I'll be all right."

Rue had hung back, standing in the archway that led into the living room. She matched his own brittle smile. "I'll stick around, if you'll have me, Ted. We're quarantined, anyway, and I know you're not going to eat a damn thing unless I force you to cook something for us both."

Ted stared. He wanted to be angry with her for letting Rose and Priya wander off, but he had known her so long and so well that her presence did ease his mind, at least a little. If not for Rue, he doubted he would ever have really understood what it felt like to have a real friend. It wasn't watching a ball game or bullshitting or fulfilling some kind of silent obligation. Real friendship was about deciding someone else's well-being was just as important to you as your own—or even more important. Someone who wasn't your spouse or your child.

"How do you feel about a quick egg fry?" he asked, draining the last of his whiskey.

It was what they'd always made in high school, when they'd come home much too late from a party, usually a little drunk or a little high. He'd crack some eggs and throw whatever he could find into the frying pan with them. Grated cheese, leftover taco meat, shreds of deli ham, chopped vegetables, Tabasco sauce.

"Sounds perfect," Rue said.

Whether Ted liked it or not, Kaminski was right. With his broken ribs and battered head, he wasn't likely to be able to hike all over the mountain without injuring himself further. He would be of no use to his daughters today, but Ted had gotten used to the feeling.

He looked at Walker and Kaminski. "Go. Bring them back. Both of them."

There were other things he wanted to say, words he didn't dare speak aloud. Words about making sure that whatever happened, Maeve did not lay a hand on Rose.

Ted would never have admitted it out loud, but part of him considered Maeve already lost.

God, forgive me, he thought, even though he had never been persuaded there was a God up there listening.

Now, more than ever, he figured prayers fell on deaf ears. Or no ears at all.

Which left Walker, a virtual stranger, who had confidence and determination but also a haunted look in his eyes, as if he had faced horror before and not emerged victorious.

But Walker was all they had.

Rue watched with condemnation in her eyes as Ted poured himself another drink.

10

Kaminski drove the route toward the cabin mostly in silence, for which Walker felt grateful. The rain came down hard, windshield wipers squealing out a rhythm as questions cluttered his mind. The federal government had to be involved or Garland Mountain Labs would not have been able to get the quarantine order. So who was pulling those strings? The Blackcoats were mercenary security forces, not U.S. military, but someone had to be signing their paychecks. There were too many unknowns.

His pack sat on the floor of Kaminski's car, nestled between Walker's boots. Alena Boudreau had not sent him to New Hampshire empty-handed. The SRC might not have the flair of Q from the James Bond films, but DARPA existed specifically to develop science. Not all of it was about finding new and clever ways to kill someone. So he did have a thing or two in that backpack that might help him track Maeve, if he was lucky.

Alena had also given him a small black box containing two comm units—a primary and a spare. They were tiny things, like AirPods, but they came in handy. Once he slipped one in his ear, he would be able to communicate with Alena directly. By now, the cell phone towers around Jericho Falls would be jammed, but the comm units didn't rely on those towers.

On the other hand, Alena was a long way from New Hampshire. It'd help if he had someone a little closer to handle some of the ground-work and keep him updated if he got into trouble. Walker glanced at Chief Kaminski and wondered if he could be trusted. More than that, he wondered if the chief would have time to help him, should the moment arrive when Walker needed that help.

His pack also held other, more standard gear. Flashlight. Night-vision goggles. And a gun.

Walker had a love-hate relationship with guns. He hated pulling the trigger, but he loved staying alive. Which brought him back to his frustration with the many unknowns he faced in his search for Maeve Sinclair. He didn't like it. The assignment was to get Maeve Sinclair off the mountain alive, but to do that, he needed to do the same for himself.

As Kaminski turned up a narrow road that snaked through the forest, Walker studied the houses they passed, wondering what the people inside were doing. The quarantine forced them to stay in Jericho Falls and established a curfew that confined them to their homes after dark, but it seemed most people were nervous enough to stay inside during the day as well. Walker reckoned they were going to get cabin fever pretty quickly.

The rainstorm that had moved in over the past hour or two had turned the afternoon gray and gloomy, but there were at least four or five hours of daylight left. It was July, after all. Midsummer.

"You can show me where to enter the trail her father talked about?" Walker asked.

"The Jackrabbit Trail," Chief Kaminski reminded him. "It's the only thing that makes sense. We know she was at the cabin. From what Ted said—"

"I don't love the idea of relying on him," Walker said. "The guy's an alcoholic and an addict. Never mind that he got his bell rung this morning. He's also drunk right now, while both his daughters are lost on a mountain."

He didn't specifically say he thought Ted Sinclair was a bad father, but the chief didn't have to be a genius to read between the lines. *Not that you're such a great dad yourself*, Walker thought, remembering the look in Charlie's eyes earlier in the day. And his words.

That was for later, though.

Walker felt a little sick at the thought. Charlie, it seemed, was always for later. He wondered if he had been too swift to judge Ted Sinclair or too slow to judge himself.

"You said you didn't want him with you because he'd slow you down," Chief Kaminski said.

"He would have," Walker replied. "But with all respect for the man's grief, I had to weigh how much help he might be against how much trouble. Better for everyone if he stays home. His ribs and his skull will thank me later."

Kaminski slammed on the brakes. "Son of a bitch."

They'd just come in sight of the late Granddad Sinclair's cabin. Several police cars and a K-9 unit van sat out front, but Walker only spotted two cops. The pair of beer-bellied officers on the cusp of retirement had apparently been left behind to establish the cabin as base camp.

But it wasn't the presence of the two cops that had startled Chief Kaminski. Two Blackcoats stood in front of the cabin near the aging police officers. Several other Blackcoats were walking the perimeter of the property, likely marking out trails and searching for signs of Maeve's presence.

"Do these guys really think she's coming back here?" Walker asked.

"She abandoned her phone at the cabin," Kaminski replied. "She's never coming back to this place. But you know the way swaggering dicks like them think. They look at Maeve as a scared young woman. Most of them probably figure she hasn't gone more than a hundred yards into the woods and any minute she's going to come back looking for some big, strong man to save her."

Kaminski put his vehicle in park, killed the engine, and climbed out. One of the two cops hurried toward him, glancing at the Blackcoats with bristling resentment.

"The good news," Kaminski went on, "is that the longer they think of her as soft and weak, the longer Maeve will be able to stay lost. Hopefully, that'll buy you the time you need to reach her first."

"Chief, I'm sorry," said the officer who trotted up to the vehicle. The man huffed with exertion after jogging a dozen paces, so it was no wonder he hadn't been assigned to a search party. "They showed up with federal ID. We had to let them look over the scene."

"Don't sweat it, Foley," Kaminski replied. "If they'd found anything useful, they wouldn't still be looking. Keep an eye on them, make a record of anything they try to remove from the site. Otherwise, let them alone. I don't want you getting into a pissing match with these guys, Foley. They'll end up killing you and burying you in a shallow grave."

Foley's eyes went wide, like he wasn't sure whether or not his police chief had been joking. Walker wasn't certain himself, but he said nothing until Foley had trotted away and Kaminski frowned thoughtfully.

"So where's this Jackrabbit Trail?" Walker asked.

Kaminski kept his back to the cabin so neither his own people nor the Blackcoats would be able to hear him or see the small gesture he made, pointing in the general direction of the northeast tree line.

"It's narrow, mostly overgrown. Might be marked, but most likely it's not. You can't miss the tree by the entrance—split by lightning some years back, but both sides are still growing."

Walker nodded. "I'll walk a little way before I head into the trees. Don't want to draw attention. But there's something you should know, Chief. You've got a lot on your hands, keeping the peace in town, keeping civilians off the mountain. You should be on the lookout for other people on the mountain, too—people who aren't civilians."

Kaminski shot a sidelong glance at the Blackcoats. "Tell me about it."

"I don't mean them. There could be others looking for Maeve," Walker said. "Dangerous people who want the ability to do what she can do. Warn your officers. It's not just one lost woman they need to be worried about up here. There's worse than that."

Kaminski massaged his left temple. "This gets better all the time. But thanks. I'll pass it along."

Walker opened the back door of the chief's car. Making sure the cops and Blackcoats couldn't see what he was up to, he dug into his pack and tugged out the black box containing the two comm earpieces. There were a dozen names for the little devices—earbuds, pods, comms, lobes, and others—but Walker had always thought of them as *earwigs*, the first name he'd ever heard for them. Once upon a time it had been necessary to hide such devices, but they were so readily available to consumers now that being seen talking to oneself no longer came off as crazy.

"Do something for me," he said, holding out an earwig to Kaminski. "Bring this back to Rue Crooker. Ask her to turn it on and monitor. I may need someone in Jericho Falls who understands the science."

Kaminski took the earwig, studied it in his open palm, and slipped it into his pocket. "Anything else?"

Walker put in his own earpiece, stuffed the box back into his pack, then took out his holstered weapon and clipped it to his belt. "Buy me whatever time you can."

He closed the car door. The sound made two Blackcoats look over at him, but he was with Chief Kaminski, so they kept searching the grounds of the cabin.

"You want me to keep the state troopers and my own people searching around the falls, keep them away from this side of the mountain?" Kaminski furrowed his brow.

"It'd help."

Kaminski glanced up toward the cabin. "I'll do my best."

With that, Walker started along the dirt road, back the way they'd come. He'd gone about thirty yards when he found himself around a curve and out of view. Darting into the woods, he started backtracking to the Jackrabbit Trail.

Maeve had a hell of a head start, but she was sick and scared and confused. Walker told himself he could find her. A quarter hour later, when he came to a place where footprints in half-dry mud had been obliterated with a stick, he actually believed it.

Staring at those footprints, he felt a little queasy and a shudder went through him, almost as if he could feel the sickness Maeve had left in her wake. Sickness, and something else, a skin-crawling sensation that made him glance yet again at his surroundings. A deep frown creased his forehead.

The trees on either side of the path seemed lower, denser, as if they might inch closer until they could strangle him. They were only trees, of course. But as he quickened his pace, the whole trail seemed tainted by that unsettling feeling. Walker thought perhaps it wouldn't be as difficult to find Maeve as he'd first imagined. He also thought finding her might turn out to be an absolutely terrible idea.

But he kept following the trail.

Whatever had infected Maeve Sinclair, it couldn't be allowed to roam free.

Viv Cheng and Leon Lewis had been assigned to Garland Mountain Labs within weeks of one another. Leon had been honorably discharged from a special ops group he was never allowed to mention, but he'd told Cheng as much as possible about his background. Cheng, on the other hand, had only been willing to say that she had done work for Homeland Security. Leon still wondered if that meant something covert or if she'd just been an ICE agent and been fired or quit. Of course, if she'd quit ICE as a conscientious objector or something, she wouldn't be employed by White Oak Security. The firm provided private armed security for at least a dozen sites on American soil that the government didn't want the public to know about. They couldn't use official U.S. military, so they used White Oak, one of several firms that provided what had come to be colloquially known as Blackcoats.

Most of the time, Leon liked his job. He'd been in blood-soaked deserts and climbed over corpses in ditches, so he didn't mind putting a bullet into someone for no reason other than that he'd been ordered to do so. But this felt different.

"You feel all right?" Cheng asked as they moved quietly along the narrow trail Ben Walker had chosen.

Leon snorted. "Do you? This feel all right to you?"

He regretted the words the moment they left his lips, but the old cliché about not being able to put the genie back in the bottle had never been truer. Cheng shot him a narrowed glance, and an uneasy quiet fell between them. Not silence. Up on the mountain, in the fucking woods, they would never find true silence.

Birds cried and wheeled far overhead, barely glimpsed through the branches that wove together to block all but shafts of daylight from hitting the trail. Gray, ugly light from a sky full of storm. Rain pattered the leaves and the trail. The wind kicked up and rustled a million leaves into a rough whisper that almost sounded like a voice. To Leon, it held a beauty he could not deny, the rustling of leaves telling him to breathe. To take it all in. Maybe telling him that this wasn't the kind of hunting people were supposed to be doing up here, in the quiet of the wild.

"What the fuck is wrong with you?" Cheng asked at last without glancing over her shoulder again. "I don't want to have to worry, Leon."

"Relax, Vivian. I'm here. I've got your back. Walker's one guy, and he may not like it, but we're on the same team."

Cheng halted, turned to scan his face. "Did you see the video clip? Sinclair touching those people, them falling down dead?"

"I saw it."

"Just making certain. 'Cuz it sure as hell isn't some D.C. scientist who's got me on my toes. The Sinclair woman might as well be the bogeyman or the Big Bad Wolf as far as I'm concerned," Cheng said. "I'll be honest, man, it's got me spooked. I'm looking behind every damn tree, worried she's gonna jump out at me. I'd rather run into a bear than this bitch."

Leon had seen the video, but he decided he and Cheng had viewed it very differently. Project: Red Hands wouldn't be the first science experiment to have gotten out of control and killed a bunch of people. This wasn't even the first time Leon had to work a containment job, keeping a fuckup quiet and limiting exposure. But the last time had been in Mosul, and the people they'd been hunting—the ones who'd invented the bioweapon—had been terrorists.

Who were the terrorists here?

Not Maeve Sinclair. He didn't like the idea of hunting an innocent woman and certainly not on American soil. Hell, there wasn't any terrain that felt much more American than this.

Cheng held up a fist. Leon stopped, listening hard. Sure enough, he could hear a voice drifting back to them, Walker talking on a phone or radio. The guy had paused, and Leon cursed himself for not paying enough attention. They couldn't afford for Walker to realize he was being followed—not yet. Dr. Vargas back at Garland Mountain thought Walker had an in with the family, that maybe he'd even been in touch with Maeve Sinclair. Cheng and Leon had been tasked with following him, just in case he really did know how to find the woman.

Cheng motioned for them to continue and started up the trail. Slowly. Quietly.

Leon started checking the trees on either side of the trail, unsettled by her description of Maeve Sinclair jumping out at them. The woman had done nothing wrong. Garland Mountain Labs had been responsible for everything that happened in Jericho Falls that day.

But if they did manage to find Maeve Sinclair, and she made the slightest movement toward him, Leon Lewis intended to shoot her in the damn face.

Twice.

Walker never loved the idea of working for DARPA. They spent a good deal of their budget developing projects that kept him up at night. What got him through to the sunrise was knowing how many lives their science also saved. DARPA had given him more than one opportunity to stave off global catastrophe, and that counted for something. Of late, he'd developed a recurring nightmare about the mass graves that would be necessary if nature ever unleashed a true pandemic, and he told himself those nightmares were reason enough to keep working for the SRC. As long as he could keep the scales tipped toward saving lives instead of taking them, the work was worthwhile.

And, of course, he liked the toys.

More than once, he had squirreled something out of the DARPA labs that hadn't been cleared for real-world deployment. Twice, Walker had been officially reprimanded for his sticky fingers, and once, the Department of Defense had threatened to imprison him if it should happen again. The threat had the desired effect, meaning Walker hadn't stolen anything from DARPA in about eighteen months, but that didn't mean he couldn't occasionally raid the lab like a girl rifling through her big sister's closet for the right outfit.

Today, however, the right outfit had been a loan from his new boss. Before sending him off on his flight north, Alena Boudreau had outfitted him with a set of TAGI goggles, newly developed by a DARPA scientist named Arun Lahiri. Walker hadn't bothered to tell Chief Kaminski about them—he hadn't wanted to get the chief's hopes up—but he had slipped them on fifty yards along the Jackrabbit Trail and he'd been entranced ever since.

TAGI stood for *thermal and gas imaging*, which seemed a very boring name for equipment that broke every rule. Walker had used infrared and thermal imagers before, but TAGI took the concept much further, able to identify not merely the presence of a heat signature but minute thermal changes in the landscape. Maeve Sinclair had passed this way too long ago to have left her own heat behind, particularly with the rain that had been falling, but in certain places her passing had disturbed the mud and leaves and pine needles, causing the release of small amounts of heat and gases related to the decomposition of the leaves. A broken branch released both moisture and accumulated ethylene gas, and TAGI logged each of these miniscule changes. Walker could not see Maeve's footprints, but it was evident that someone had come this way quite recently, and given what Ted Sinclair and Chief Kaminsky had said, Walker had to bank on it being Maeve. He would follow the trail as far as it would take him, and if he lost her, he would have to improvise.

He jogged along the path, careful not to catch his foot on a root or rock. As he moved, he tapped at his earwig. The comm unit came on line with a piercing electronic shriek. Walker swore, stumbled a bit, teeth bared. He reached up to dig the earpiece out, but the shriek quieted to a crackling noise and then nothing but the shush one might hear on the inside of a conch shell.

Frowning, he dug the earwig out anyway, studied it, then plugged it back into place as he picked up speed again.

"Call David," he said aloud.

The line buzzed only once before David Boudreau answered. One of the smartest people Walker had ever met, David looked younger than he was, some of that youthful appearance stemming from the chip that seemed forever on his shoulder. His mother had died when he was quite young, after which he had been raised by his grand-mother, Alena. At the time, she'd been a globe-trotting scientist and all-around troubleshooter, the kind of person who didn't have room in her life for a kid. Instead, David had been her sidekick, learned the tricks of the trade, surpassed his grandmother in intellect but not in wisdom. He'd been mauled badly in a gruesome field assignment in the Caribbean, a precursor to Walker suffering a similar but less se-vere attack in Guatemala several years later. They both had scars, they both took too many painkillers, but Walker could still make himself useful in the field. David hardly ever left the M Street apartment in D.C. where he lived. But he didn't have to leave to give Walker what he needed.

"I was wondering when I'd hear from you," David said.

"Someone's trying to block communications in the area."

"What, you can't say hello?"

"Hello, David."

"Hello, Walker. Of course they're blocking comms. Local phone service in Jericho Falls is out. Cell towers are being jammed. They don't want residents discussing the details of the quarantine with the rest of the world. More importantly, they don't want whoever's up there on the mountain with you—or on the way there—to have an easy time talking to each other, never mind tracking the woman with the death touch."

"Speaking of Maeve, could you skip ahead to where you tell me what you know? I've got signs of someone on this trail, but there's no guarantee it's her. What am I dealing with?"

"There's a lot of chatter," David said. "It's only been about five hours and the parade disaster clip has had millions of hits online. We're far from the only people who are going to be looking for her. I gather there are some already on location, but others will be on the way."

"Satellite surveillance?"

"Of course. At least one vehicle entered via a fire road to the southeast. Bolt cutters were used on the chain. They didn't bother being stealthy or trying to cover their tracks."

Walker slowed to a walk, adjusting his goggles as he peered at a heat signature off to his left. It darted away, skittering up a tree—just a red squirrel, terrified and irritated.

"The quarantine restricts residents to the settled parts of town," Walker said. "A single vehicle could just be libertarians flexing or a pack of teenagers acting out their rebellion fantasies. I would have been happy to tell the government to screw in a situation like this, when I was younger."

"You'd like to tell them to screw now," David reminded him.

Walker smiled. As he did, a sound came from behind him. He turned, goggles slipping a bit. As he adjusted them, a hawk took flight from the trees back along the way he'd come.

"Everything all right?" David asked.

"Just a bird. Our conversation is disturbing the local wildlife."

Walker broke into a light jog, following what he continued to hope was the same path Maeve Sinclair had taken. But he hadn't gone six paces when he faltered. To the right, a smaller path branched off. Calling it a trail would have been a generous use of the word, but the TAGI goggles showed plenty of disturbed leaf cover and small, snapped branches at the entrance to the path.

"You still there?" David prodded.

"I'm here. Tell me about my visitors," he said.

"The guys who cut the chain? No idea. A Jeep. We're working on backtracking it, trying to get IDs on the driver and any passengers. Meanwhile, you have other problems. At least two small aircraft have flown over in the past hour."

Walker ducked to avoid branches as he forged his way along this rougher path. "Any thoughts at all about who I'm going to run into out here?"

"Let me get back to you on that," David said. "Meanwhile—"

"Stay alive. I know."

The conversation ended. The earwig gave a little squeal of static, but nothing as deafening as earlier. Walker picked up the pace. Wearing the goggles made him feel as if he had slipped into some other world, but the smell of the woods and the mountain air and the solidity of the trail beneath him helped to ground him. He ought to have allies up here. The cops and the Blackcoats and Walker himself ought to have been seeking the same resolution, but he could not allow himself to trust in that assumption. Right now, he could trust only himself, and that knowledge made the shadows in the forest around him seem darker, and the skittering of wildlife in the underbrush took on a sinister quality.

A low burring noise made him look up, and despite the rain and the looming gray sky, he could make out the small airplane coming in from the north. As he watched, a small figure detached from the underbelly of the plane. Dread began to tighten around his heart. Seconds passed, and then the tiny figure unfurled into a bone-white parachute.

He bolted along the path, barely paying attention to the heat and gas signatures picked up by his goggles. Chief Kaminski didn't have enough people to sweep the whole mountain, so he sure as hell didn't have an airplane or someone willing to jump out of it. The Blackcoats would have come in with choppers, and for the moment, they were also focused mostly to the west, at least for now. Which meant that ghostly parachute belonged to someone else—someone determined to find Maeve, who didn't care that their arrival would be seen by some of those on the ground.

People like that were very, very dangerous.

He slowed his pace. Even if he left the trail, rushed through the trees, he would never be able to pinpoint exactly where the parachutist would land. On the off chance he guessed correctly, he would not reach the spot before the jumper could unbuckle their chute and set off into the woods. And then what? Walker began to think that leaving Ted Sinclair home had been a terrible idea. Injured alcoholic or not, at least Ted knew these paths and knew his daughter.

Focus, he told himself. *Stick to the hunt.* He could not allow himself to be distracted by the other hunters. Walker had known governments and spook agencies would send people after Maeve. David's report about the Jeep confirmed it. He needed to find Maeve before anyone else did.

Or maybe not. Whoever found her first might not live through the encounter. Maybe he just needed to be the first one to find her and survive.

11

Maeve woke to find that the roaring dragons that chased her through her dreams were the grinding, buzzing engines of dirt bikes coming toward the half-collapsed Moonglow Inn. The sound echoed off the walls as Maeve sat up, heart thumping inside her chest. Her head ached and her throat burned, but she propped herself up and listened as one engine seemed to move farther away and the other drew nearer.

She told herself it must be kids. A couple of teenagers from town, ripping through the woods on their dirt bikes. Her first boyfriend, Rick, had gotten his dirt bike thirdhand. It had been his dad's, then his older brother's, and by the time he'd gotten the beast it had been beaten to shit, rusted, and had bald tires. Rick had restored it the best he could, but mostly he only cared that it would run and that it had tires that could tear up the mud and rocket him along the mountain trails, even the ones where dirt bikes weren't allowed. Fifteen-year-old Maeve Sinclair had pretended to disapprove, but she'd loved that he liked to break the rules.

A bout of coughing broke her reverie. Dark spittle flew from her mouth, and a wave of nausea struck her. For a few seconds, she faded out as if falling into a trance. Or a fever. In those precious seconds, the dirt bike roared nearer, loud enough that it seemed to be breathing right outside the door.

"Idiot," she whispered, stumbling to her feet. Dizziness washed over her as she started for the broken wall, and she staggered to the right, arms raised as if trying to walk a tightrope.

The rain began to fall harder, a curtain of noise drawn over the whole mountain. It had a buzz of its own, so as she reached the edge of the broken wall, it took a moment to realize the dirt bike engine had gone silent. Her chest fluttered with the need to cough again, but she stifled the urge.

The part of the inn that had slid into the gorge had left a ruined, ragged edge, but the broken wall ended a dozen feet from the cliff, so she could slip out into the storm without falling hundreds of feet to the rocks below.

The wind pushed against her the moment she left shelter. A gust swept through the trees as if it meant to brush her over the edge, but Maeve held her footing. The storm hid the sound of her footfalls. As she reached the front of the old stone building, she glanced around the corner.

The dirt bike lay on its side as if the rider had ditched it, but she knew that couldn't be true. Somewhere off in the woods, the other dirt bike's engine still roared in a rise and fall. The rain had arrived early, but rough weather had been part of the forecast. These riders were not in this part of the woods in the middle of a rainstorm merely for recreation. They were searching for something. They had a purpose, a target.

She scanned the trees in front of the inn. In the gray gloom of the woods and the rain, the figure near the inn's façade had to move before Maeve noted his presence. She sucked in a breath as he took a step. The rider moved quietly, carefully, thinking to find her still inside the ruin of the Moonglow. Maeve watched as he reached into his coat and slid out a handgun. The gun glistened in the rain.

In the storm, all she could see was that he was white and needed a haircut and a shave. The rain had plastered his hair to his head, and he looked like he'd just been fished out of a pond, but the urge to go to him seized her.

He stepped inside the inn, the same way she had entered.

She scanned the woods, then stared at the toppled dirt bike. That other engine still roared out in the woods, and the last thing she wanted to do was to draw attention to herself, give her presence away, but she felt too sick to fight back or even hide very long if the rider was determined to find her.

Maybe he's only checking this place because he figures you'd need shelter. He's just guessing. He doesn't know you're here.

Maeve closed her eyes, felt the rain on her face and drizzling down the back of her neck, under her collar. She stepped out from hiding at the corner of the stone building, took another step, watching the darkness where the rider had vanished inside the inn, and then she bolted for the dirt bike. In her mind, she had already reached the bike, stood it up, straddled it, and kick-started the engine. Simple tasks. She counted them off in her head—lift, straddle, start up, give it some gas. Get the fuck out of here.

The driver darted his head out through the doorway. Silent, he watched her bolt through the rain. For the first time, she heard her own footfalls and knew they had given her away, that even with the rain and distant thunder, her boots on the trail had been too loud. If she'd gone quietly, she might have made it, but she'd wanted to rush, to get as far from here as possible, quick as she might.

He ran.

It took her only three more steps to realize he would intercept her, that she would never get on that bike before the rider could get his hands on her. In the back of her mind, a small voice tried to reason with her, tell her that maybe he wasn't after her at all, that he only thought she intended to steal his dirt bike and wanted to stop her.

But the man kept silent, and his silence told her that he had no questions about her identity or her intentions. Maeve knew only one choice remained to her, the same choice she'd made hours ago. She veered into the woods and kept running. Numbness spread through both of her feet. The pain in her throat returned. She coughed and wheezed.

The dirt bike roared to new life behind her.

Branches snagged her clothes and scratched her skin. One whipped across her cheek, stinging only an inch from her eye, and she felt blood trickle down her face like hot tears. The trees seemed to blur. Somehow, off the trail now, her feet managed to miss the roots. She scrambled over a fallen tree, jogged to the right. Through blurred vision, she saw more gray light and knew she had started shifting back toward the gorge.

The engine roared louder. Her chest burned. Her legs, so tired from her hike already, quivered with every step, ready to collapse beneath her. In the midst of the trees, she came upon a ridge of massive rocks carried here by glaciers millennia before, nearly piled one atop the other.

She heard the dirt bike engine whine and glanced over her shoulder. The bike shot from the trees fifteen yards away. Maeve reached into a place inside of her that existed only for survival. Rage lived there, along with sorrow. She ran along the stone ridge, searching for a place to climb, telling herself she could outpace the rider, that he'd have to leave his bike on this side and if she could get on the other side before he managed, she could still get away. But of course she'd forgotten about his gun, and now that she remembered, she knew she couldn't climb, couldn't give him such an exposed target. She would have to keep running, make it to the edge of the gorge and hope there was some other way.

Abruptly, she came to an opening between two of those ancient, glacial stones and ducked into it without hesitation. As she ran, coughing up thick black spittle, she knew.

This is useless. Where could she go, weaponless and on foot, where this man could not find her?

The path between the stones ended. Dark, rainswept forest stretched ahead. Behind her, she heard the dirt bike roar into the passage, engine echoing off the walls. Just to her right was a fallen sycamore tree. It had blown down in a storm, its whole root system exposed.

Branches had smashed against the stone ridge, several snapped off and others hanging by bark and fiber.

Maeve grabbed a broken branch, four feet long, thick as her wrist. The dirt bike engine roared over her left shoulder. She turned and swung the branch like she was aiming to knock the son of a bitch out of the ballpark. The thick, bare end of the branch caught him under the jaw. He came halfway out of the saddle, managed to keep one hand on the bike, which made him swerve straight at the fallen sycamore.

The front wheel hit a rut, twisted hard to one side, and the bike bucked the rider. He flailed as he flew through the rain. Maeve could only watch as a jutting, broken branch impaled him and he slumped over it, hanging like a scarecrow from the fallen tree.

She didn't even have the strength to scream.

The driver gasped, sucking air. His left arm began to shake as blood spilled from around the branch and down his leg, soaking through his trousers. Bloody froth spilled over his lips as he continued to try to breathe, and he turned his head to stare at her. His mouth moved as if he wanted to speak, and Maeve realized she needed to know whatever he could tell her.

"Who sent you?" she asked, approaching him, trying not to get too close. "What's happened at home? What are they saying . . . about me?"

As she took another step, his gaze shifted to her hands. Maeve had never seen such terror. He might have been dying, but what he feared more than anything was the idea of her touching him. In his fear, he began to snarl words at her in a language she thought might be Russian.

Tears welled in her eyes, slid down her cheeks, hot amid the cool trickles of rain on her face. Emotions warred within her. In their midst, one feeling burned the brightest, a gnawing she had felt earlier but which now seemed to inflate inside her. Her fingers flexed of their own accord, and she took another step closer, studying his scruffy beard and sodden clothes. Blood and rain dripped from his dangling feet.

Her aches and weariness seemed to diminish as she took another step toward him. The rider twitched and coughed, choking on his own blood. Somehow he mustered the strength to shake his head, to plead with her to stay away. Maeve lifted a hand, reaching toward him, basking in the breeze and the rain and relishing the thought of what it would feel like to take what she needed from him.

Like the driver at the parade had done.

Like she herself had done to her mother and Logan.

He would die, anyway. What difference would it make if she hastened him along? It might save him hours of anguish. In the back of her mind, a little voice pleaded with her to back away, but the *other* voice had grown louder. Like the drone of highway traffic or the whirl of a ceiling fan, it had become white noise, but she realized it had never left her. The presence shifted inside her skull, whispering, tempting her with promises. *Touch him. It's the only way. The sickness in you . . .*

Maeve knew the rest.

Her hands shook. She stared at the man, watched the blood and rain sluice off his boots, and noticed the gleam fading from his eyes. *No*, the voice inside her said. Shaking, yearning, she reached for him. One of her hands caught the back of his shirt, and images seared through her mind, flickers of the death she'd witnessed and the ones she'd caused. Her mother's throat had turned black. Her brother's eyes had gone blank and dull, vacant and unknowing.

"No!" Maeve screamed. She threw herself backward, staggered. Her gut twisted, and she breathed through her nostrils, forcing herself not to vomit. Instead, she turned her back on the dying man. She started back through the passage nature had cut into the stony ridge, but the roar of the other dirt bike rose abruptly, as if it had just found the path that would lead to her.

Maybe it had—maybe the driver had found the first dirt bike's trail.

She turned and rushed past the impaled man. As she darted into the trees, she spared a backward glance and saw that his eyes had glazed over. His body hung lifeless, all his muscles slack, and a part of her was relieved.

But the other part screamed inside the cage of her bones, enraged that she had let that life go to waste.

She staggered into the woods, numb with horror and guilt and fearful of the conflict between her head and heart. She ran as best she could, half listening to the dirt bike engine coming closer. Through the trees, she could see the edge of the forest and knew it had to be the gorge. She had to hide, had to be quiet. If the second rider couldn't hear her, no way would he find her in this rain with no trail around. She turned left, heading north, sixty or seventy feet from the edge, searching for a felled tree to shimmy under or a cluster of low bushes to crouch within.

The sound of the rain vanished.

Though she kept running, the noise of her footfalls went away.

Even the growling engine went quiet.

Maeve stopped, breathing hard, the only sound the thump of her heartbeat in her chest. Her back felt strangely cold, as if winter had peered across the seasons all the way to July and caught her in its gaze. But she knew it wasn't winter—it was something else. She turned to look and saw a figure wrapped in rough white cloth and draped in another layer that billowed around her, sheer and translucent. Red and black fluid dappled her shroud, stains peppered the cloth where it touched her body. Her hair had been shorn to mere inches and jutted at all angles, ragged and filthy. A leather mask had been tied across her face, cut and stretched to resemble a hawk or some other bird of prey, complete with jutting beak. The leather had been stained a deep crimson, the dark shade of blood that has begun to pool.

No rain touched her. The storm wind gusted the opposite direction from the unfelt breeze that billowed her funereal garments. Maeve stared at her, slowly shaking her head, backing away from the gnawing hunger she felt emanating from the thing in the woods, this thing that she knew had followed her. She would have screamed, but she knew that somewhere the other rider still hunted her.

At this thought, as if the vision could read her mind, the masked woman smiled. Her teeth were rotten and bleeding, her lips covered in sores.

The instant Maeve made the decision to flee, the noise rushed back into the world. The rain, the wind, her boots on the dirt, and that dirt bike growl, which now, thankfully, seemed farther away, as if the rider had lost her trail, if he'd ever had it to begin with.

She ran two hundred yards or more before she staggered and rested against a tree. Struck by a fresh bout of coughing, she spat blood and black bile. Little spots of blood welled from the pores on her arms, and the rain washed it away.

I'm dying, Maeve thought numbly, as if it were the most ordinary thing in the world.

And maybe it was. Dying seemed like precisely the right thing to do.

12

Rue stood by the window and watched the street outside the Sinclair house, pulse racing. She felt sure she had seen a figure out the side window, looming just beyond a tangle of shrubbery, but when she'd rushed to the window for a better look, there had been no sign of anyone. She darted around the first floor of the house, peering through window after window, but spotted nothing out of the ordinary. Rue had never been paranoid, but she could forgive herself today.

She made her way back to the living room and peered out the front window, wishing she had someone to share her fears with. The only other person in the house was Ted, but he was lying down upstairs after too much whiskey and too much pain, and giving him something else to fear was the last thing she would do to him.

Once in a while, a car passed by. Two doors down, on the other side of the road, a kid played basketball in his driveway in the rain. Tall and thin, tank top and shorts soaked through, he moved methodically back and forth across the pavement, taking shot after shot and sinking most of them. The kid focused so much on his shooting that it was as if he didn't notice the rain, and apparently he had the same attitude toward the quarantine. People in Jericho Falls weren't confined to their homes. The older folks would likely be at the supermarket, stockpiling in fear, not knowing how long the quarantine might last. She figured most of the younger residents were going out of their minds. No cell service, no texting, no Wi-Fi. It had all been cut off on purpose. The teenagers in town wouldn't have thought about landlines, but those had also been jammed.

"Quarantine," she muttered to herself.

This wasn't any quarantine Rue had ever heard of. She couldn't call her boss, couldn't call the governor's office to complain, couldn't see what people might be saying on social media. Anyone who wanted news would have to head to the town hall or the police station and find someone willing to talk. Rue had already made that trip once. The police station had been virtually abandoned aside from Len Kaminski's aunt Carole, who always worked the front desk, and a young cop named Burlingame. The moment she saw that, Rue knew she had wasted the trip. Aunt Carole and Officer Burlingame proved capable of only two responses—"I don't know" and "We'll ask the chief when he's back"—neither of which helped in any way.

The only place she could think of where she might actually get some answers was Garland Mountain Labs, and she wasn't quite ready to make the trip over there again. With communications in town virtually silenced, all her nascent little paranoias had grown to full size. The world had already seen the video clip, so what were they trying to hide? If they weren't trying to cover up the event itself, the moment Project: Red Hands got out of control, then why didn't they want the locals talking to each other or to anyone else? Could it really all be about Maeve? Were they that worried that someone would hear from her or try to help her?

Or did they expect worse things to happen in Jericho Falls? Things they didn't want the rest of the world to see?

The thought chilled her, settled deep into her bones. Rue watched the kid down the street shooting baskets and knew that whatever happened, she could not be like him, could not pretend the rain wasn't falling, that they weren't cut off, virtual prisoners of the devious pricks at Garland Mountain.

Something moved outside the window. Rue craned her neck to look sidelong across the front yard and saw a fat wild turkey ambling across the lawn. Another followed, and then a third. The little parade moved with an odd dignity as they crossed to the opposite side of the street and cut between houses before vanishing into the garden behind an old federal colonial. Growing up here, Rue had seen all sorts of animals in the wild, but turkeys had always been a particular fascination to her. They were contentious, inexplicably awkward birds. As a girl, it had occurred to her that she had never seen a turkey fly, and she wondered how they avoided predators if they couldn't get into the air. She wondered if perhaps they managed to fly high enough to get into the trees, and it thrilled her when she learned she had guessed it precisely. They were silly-looking creatures, but she admired their resilience and their sense of self-preservation. Life, it seemed, was all about self-preservation.

Rue went back to the sofa and picked up the notebook she'd been scrawling in for an hour. She had been at the parade, heard the crump of impact when Oscar Hecht had driven his BMW into the crowd. Spectators had fallen, broken and bleeding, some of them dead. And then Hecht had climbed out of the car, and the horror had only grown worse. Rue had been turning it over in her head, trying to see it from a new angle. Before someone had started jamming the internet, she had watched grainy footage of the crash and aftermath over and over, focused not on the car or the victims Hecht had struck but on the people he touched. The way they died.

Too fast.

Thirty or forty seconds from contact to death, that had been all it had taken. She visualized the contagion taking place, the virus or bacteria passed from one person to another. Bacteria seemed more likely to her, but she didn't want to assume anything yet. She had scrawled dozens of mathematical calculations in her notebook, jotting notes in the slanted script she had learned by copying her grandmother and which looked hopelessly old-fashioned on the page. One word stood out amid all the others—stood out because it had been circled a dozen times and underlined twice.

Accelerant.

Many scientists Rue knew were rigid in their belief that established science remained immutable, that the areas of existence still to be explained were open to discussion but that facts were simply facts. For instance, no contagion on earth could infect a host in mere seconds. The word for such a thing was *impossible*.

Rue had never liked that word. She tended not to think in terms of what might be possible or impossible but what was demonstrable. The world had seen video of a disease not only transferrable by contact but instantly fatal. Some of the comments online had suggested poison, and Rue had a whole list in her notebook, along with explanations for why she had crossed each one out. Poisons like arsenic and tetrodotoxin would take hours to kill someone who ingested them, longer if absorbed through the skin. Something like polonium would take days. Cyanide would do the job much more quickly, but still, the absorption rate would come into play. Consuming a liquid or inhaling a gas would be different, but nothing like that had happened at the parade.

Logic didn't support poison as the answer. If somehow Hecht had been immune but infused with some kind of poison developed at Garland Mountain Labs, how had he passed that same condition to Maeve Sinclair? Bacteria seemed only slightly more logical.

Naturally immune? Rue had scribbled in her notebook. *Carrier?*

Desperate for some explanation, this one seemed to come closest. Garland Mountain had bioengineered some kind of killer bacterium that could be transferred in seconds, by touch alone, and Oscar Hecht had been immune, a carrier. In Maeve Sinclair, he had found another like him. The fact that she'd touched him while he was dying was sheer coincidence; Maeve would have been infected either way.

Rue managed to make all of that sound almost rational in her mind, as long as she didn't let her thoughts stray to the tragic flaw in her logic. It was simple enough to believe Garland Mountain had made such breakthroughs, malicious mad scientist bastards that they were. But it was one thing to believe an infection could be transmitted so quickly, another thing entirely to swallow the idea that it would travel through the human body fast enough to kill in an instant. Absorbed through the pores, carried into the bloodstream, surfacing as suppurating sores, corrupting the lungs . . . she couldn't call it impossible because she had seen it. The effect was demonstrable, and Rue had no doubt that if Maeve touched her now, she would die the same way and with equal swiftness.

It just wasn't logical.

"It hurts my fucking head," she whispered.

"What's that?" a voice said behind her.

Rue jumped up from the sofa, turning around, one hand over her heart. "Jesus, Ted, you scared the life out of me."

He smiled weakly. "There's enough of that going around."

Rue's eyes widened at the poor joke, and Ted, realizing what he'd said, lifted a hand to cover his mouth. Grief clawed at the expression on his face, but he shook it off with a huff.

"Any word?" he asked, still muzzy from the whiskey.

There were dark circles under his eyes, and she couldn't help wondering if there were pills of any kind in the house. All he'd taken for the pain of his injuries had been whiskey and ibuprofen, and the allure of a stronger painkiller had to be powerful, especially for someone with an addict's memory of drug-induced bliss.

She pushed the thought away. Ted was stronger than that. He had to be.

"Nothing," Rue said, closing her notebook.

Ted shook his head sadly. "I should have gone." He shot her an accusatory glance. "I should be up there right now."

"You're not in any shape to do that, Ted. And there are dangerous people up there—"

"That's exactly why I should have gone. My daughter is—"

"Maeve is one of those dangerous people," Rue said. "She needs you alive. She needs you here when she comes home."

They had been friends a long time, but Rue had never seen him like this. Tormenting himself. Hating himself.

"You're a good man," she said. "You always were. You've suffered loss today that most people can't even imagine. Nobody expects you to—"

Ted threw up his hands. Tears came to his eyes. "Jesus, Rue, don't you get it? *I* expect me to. I need to be a better father than this. Ellen would have expected me to be stronger than . . ."

He trailed off, wincing and favoring the side where he'd cracked three ribs.

"Who am I kidding? Strong people don't become addicts. Strong people don't have to tell themselves they can give up drinking whenever they want."

Rue went to him, took his hands, forced him to look into her eyes. "You're a sensible man, a good man, a good father. Addiction is complex, but I know this much—it had its claws in you pretty damn deep, and you ripped those claws right out. I saw the way it hollowed you out, Ted. But you came back to life."

He smiled softly, still half-drunk, pale with pain and grief. "Nice try, Crooker. But I'm still a drunk."

"One monster at a time, buddy," she replied, tapping a finger on his chest. "One monster at a time."

"You don't think I'm letting them down? Letting Ellen down?"

"She's gone," Rue said. "She and Logan both. But her daughters are alive. Ellen would want you to do what was best for them, and you know it. I don't have kids, but I know it must make you want to scream, just sitting around and waiting. But we've covered this. You were hit by a car. You're a wreck. They could be anywhere by now. Just stay here. Be the sanctuary they will need when they come down off the mountain."

"A whiskey-soaked sanctuary."

"If that's the way it has to be," she replied.

Ted looked as if he wanted to argue, but instead he pulled her into a quick hug, rested his head on her shoulder a moment, and then turned away.

As he did, the doorbell rang.

Rue turned toward the sound, but Ted rushed by her, hurrying out to the foyer fueled by hope and desperation. She arrived in his wake, just as he opened the front door. Rue would have told him to be careful, all sorts of dark fears surfacing in the back of her mind, but the door already hung open and she looked over Ted's shoulder at Chief Kaminski.

Ted stared at him. "Please tell me something good—"

"No news either way, I'm afraid. Not yet," Kaminski said. He looked past Ted. "It's actually Rue I needed to see."

Ted visibly deflated. He turned and wandered back into the living room as if he'd forgotten Kaminski had arrived. Rue watched him go, tempted to get him another glass of whiskey, hating that temptation.

She looked at the chief. "What's going on?"

Kaminski reached into his pocket and withdrew a small nub of black plastic. "Communications earpiece. You ever use something like this?"

Rue took it, brows knitting as she lifted it to the light and turned it over. "Not exactly like it, but I have AirPods for my phone."

"Same basic idea. Walker asked me to give you this. Hoped you'd use it, monitor, wait for him to be in touch."

She held it in her palm. "He wanted you to give this to *me*?"

"Said he might need someone with your science brain down here, in town. Seemed like a compliment to me."

Rue closed her fist around the little plastic nub and shook it like a die. "I suppose. The kind of compliment that could get a woman killed. But I'll help however I can. I don't think this thing'll do much good, though. The cell towers are jammed."

Chief Kaminski smiled. "This one doesn't need cell towers. I'm headed back up the mountain. Someone's got to keep the damn Blackcoats from pushing my officers around. Meanwhile, give Walker a call. Maybe he can put a stop to this clusterfuck before it gets any worse."

Priya would never tell Rose, but she had begun to give up hope. The day had started hot, but once the wind and rain arrived the temperature had dropped precipitously, and up on the mountain with the breeze and the clouds, soaked to the skin, she felt a chill settling in. The humidity made it hard to breathe. Her feet squelched inside her shoes. She would have sold both kidneys for a cup of coffee.

Half an hour earlier, they'd heard what sounded like a bear lumbering through the trees, and she had spotted a deer a few minutes later, but the animal had bolted. Other than that, the nearest living thing seemed to be the pilot of the helicopter that made regular sweeps over the mountain. Priya didn't mention it to Rose, but the presence of the chopper reassured her. If they were still looking for Maeve, that meant she hadn't been captured yet and hopefully that she was still alive.

She exhaled, tugging on Rose's hand. "Sorry. Can we take a breather?"

Rose kissed her fingers. "Of course."

Grateful, Priya sat on a large rock and scanned the trees around them. Water dripped off the leaves. Little streams ran along the path, pooling beside thick roots, finding a path down the mountain. Pine needles and leaves were carried away.

She looked up to find Rose watching her. "What?" she asked.

"You're going to make me say it? That we're wasting our time?"

Priya exhaled. It was one thing to think it, another to hear the words spoken aloud. "I'm not going to say that. I'm with you, no matter how long we're up here. But I admit I'm worried about the rain. Even if we knew how to track someone, we're just guessing."

Rose turned to stare along the trail in the direction they'd been headed. "If she started on the Jackrabbit Trail, she'd have kept going east. That'd bring her to the gorge eventually, and she knows the gorge from fishing with my dad. She knows there are caves down there. She's going to need time to figure out her next step, somewhere to sleep tonight, out of the rain. If it were me, that's where I'd go."

Priya felt a flicker of hope. Or maybe it was just that she had faith in Rose. "The gorge it is," she said, rising from the rock. "You know how to get down there from here?"

Rose shrugged. "More or less."

Priya saw motion out of the corner of her eye, a ghostly figure that seemed to separate from the trees without a sound. The white woman couldn't have been more than five feet tall. The silver of her shoulder-length hair might have been natural or come out of a bottle, but either way, it added to her haunting pallor, as did the gleaming silver pistol in her hand.

"Hey, no," she muttered, holding her hands out to make sure the woman knew they didn't represent any kind of threat.

Rose stepped between Priya and the gun. "Who the hell are you?"

The little silver-haired killer ignored the question. "*You're* Rose Sinclair. Your sister is Maeve, the woman from the video. The one with the death touch."

They weren't questions.

The killer lowered her weapon, but it hung at her side, deceptively loose. Just from the way she stood and the dull, dead light in her eyes, Priya knew the gun was far from dormant. It might as well have been a snake, coiled to strike.

"You can call me Agatha," the woman said, with an accent Priya didn't recognize. "I'm bored to tears, honestly. Sick of trailing you two. I'm glad to hear you've got at least some idea of where to look for your sister; otherwise, I would have been very angry."

"What do you want with Maeve?" Rose asked.

Agatha lifted the big silver gun again, the barrel's mouth giving them a dark wink. "Lead the way, Rose. If I get the impression you're intentionally wasting my time, I'll put a bullet through your pretty girlfriend's head."

"You do that," Rose said, "and you'll never get what you want from us."

Priya grabbed a fistful of Rose's shirt and whispered to her. "Don't do anything stupid."

The woman grinned, left eye half-hidden behind the silver hair the rain had plastered across her face. "Let me tell you something now that may help you later on."

The gun barely twitched before she fired a bullet into the ground. It kicked up dirt and rainwater just inches from Rose's left foot.

"I kill for a living, and sometimes for pleasure. It took more effort just now for me to avoid killing you than it would to put a bullet in your heart," she said. "So let's go, shall we?"

Rose touched Priya's arm, encircled her wrist, and gave her a tug.

The echo of the gunshot still rang in her ears as she turned to follow Rose along the trail, with Agatha—whoever she really was—keeping pace ten feet behind. Whoever she was, Priya had no doubt this woman intended either to capture Maeve or simply murder her, and there was no way she could let that happen. Rose had lost enough.

Contrary to her own advice, Priya had a feeling she was going to have to do something very, very stupid.

13

Walker slid the TAGI goggles down to hang around his neck as he trekked through the rain. Any hope he'd had of following Maeve's trail had turned to mud, just like the ground underfoot. He had seen that parachutist floating toward the trees and he'd needed to make a split decision. Whoever had that chute would also be searching for Maeve, and he'd banked on them having more intel than he did, or at least a more efficient way to track her. It was a thin strand of hope to hang on to, but for the moment it was all he had.

Which troubled him.

Where are the satellites? he thought. American spy satellites could focus with such clarity that surveillance could count the whiskers in a man's beard. In the rain and through the trees, that might be more difficult, but Alena should be able to get some satellite surveillance of this damned mountain, give him some help.

Walker wondered if he'd been set up to fail. According to her reputation, Alena Boudreau didn't operate like that, but his doubts grew with every step. He had anticipated field support, more intel, more *everything* upon his arrival here. Instead, he had been dropped into town with zero guarantee of backup, and when he'd called in, the person on the line had been David Boudreau, Alena's grandson. The assignment felt very quiet, very insular, and it had his thoughts awhirl.

Whoever the parachutist was, they wouldn't have dropped onto the mountain without some sense of Maeve's location. Walker figured they had their own satellite surveillance working for them or some other way to find her. Which meant they either weren't American, or the Department of Defense didn't know Alena had sent Walker onto this mountain.

Or both.

He didn't like where this train of thought was heading, but he couldn't stop its progress. He had gotten himself into hot water with his bosses, and they had benched him until they felt they could trust him again, which he had known might be never. His employers had been furious at him for dropping the only sample of a potentially deadly bacterium into the ocean, but mostly because they wanted that contagion for themselves.

Of course they had sidelined him. The fact they hadn't court-martialed him or found some other way to lock him up could only be ascribed to their own self-preservation. He had saved a lot of lives, but even his friends had told him he would never be put into the field again, that nobody would trust him.

Yet here he was. In the field, alone, at the behest of a woman who claimed to have been put in charge of a new operation—the Global Science Research Coalition—just yesterday, and who needed his help.

How many times had Walker slipped something useful out of DARPA because nobody had been paying attention? Because, in that moment, it was an item nobody needed? That was him, Walker knew. Put into a box on a shelf or stored away in some climate-controlled warehouse like the Ark of the Covenant at the end of *Raiders*. And Alena Boudreau had sneaked in and snatched him off the shelf.

Soaked with rain, sick of trudging, covered with scratches, he knew the conclusion was inescapable. Alena had sent him up here because she didn't have anyone else to send and because he was expendable. She'd also sent him because he had a history of rash behavior, and if he fucked up, she could say it wasn't her fault, that was just Walker being Walker.

He trudged onward, growing more determined. One man, by

himself, without a trail to follow, had almost zero chance of locating Maeve now, if she didn't want to be found.

But that didn't mean he wouldn't try.

Walker slowed his pace, quieting his steps as he drew toward the area where the chutist had landed. From a distance, it was always difficult to gauge perfectly, but he felt he must be very close. Pausing, he closed his eyes and listened. Sure enough, he could hear the patter of the rain striking smooth nylon, and he started off to his left, slightly northward. Fifty feet through the trees and over a fallen oak, he saw the chute tangled in the trees. Whoever had arrived had dropped to the forest floor and run off into the woods.

He reached up to slide his goggles back into place and tapped the side to power them on again. Instantly, the new arrival's footfalls were revealed. A smile lifted one corner of his mouth as he followed the trail of broken branches and the heat of the chutist's passing. Given how quickly he'd closed the distance, he gauged he wasn't more than ten minutes behind.

Walker inhaled the scents of the forest and the rain, and his mind went back to the way this day had begun. He should have been in Virginia, camping in the mountains, swimming in the river with Charlie. If he closed his eyes, even for a moment, he could see the frustration and disappointment on his son's face. Charlie had grown up with broken promises and long absences that must have seemed like disinterest. Walker loved his son, but it wouldn't have felt like love to Charlie. Quite the opposite. In the nine months he had been benched, he had worked hard to repair their relationship.

Walker's own father had let him down so many times, in so many ways, that he always promised himself he'd never inflict that kind of hurt on Charlie. For years, he had told himself his situation was different. As a child, he had felt invisible in his own house. His father had been there in the flesh, but emotionally absent, usually halfway drunk and surrounded by a cloud of cigarette smoke. He'd been afraid of his own shadow, and his cowardice had filled him with such self-loathing that he'd gone off to Iraq to prove he could muster up some courage when his country needed him.

He'd died there.

Every time Walker lost himself in his work, every time an assignment took him away from home for weeks or months at a time, he told himself it wasn't abandonment. Lied to himself to make it okay. *Good thing I don't need you*, Charlie had said today.

Walker's father had been frightened of shadows, but Walker himself only feared one thing—that Charlie had been telling the truth.

He hadn't forgotten the exchange he'd had with Amanda this morning, either. It had been three years since their split, and he still remembered the smell of her hair and the way she had curled against him in the middle of the night, and the times he'd woken up with her nestled into the crook of his arm. There had been women since Amanda, one in particular. Seong didn't want anything to do with him now, and that was all right. He understood the choice she'd made. Amanda, though . . .

Walker wanted to get off this mountain.

His earwig buzzed. He tapped it.

"I'm here."

"Is this Dr. Walker?"

A woman's voice, but not Alena's. It took him a second to realize who it had to be. "Dr. Crooker?"

"Any luck in your search?"

Walker saw the bright flare above the path that indicated a branch had broken, and he frowned. The parachutist had gone this way, no doubt, but Walker did not want to catch up with him while talking to Rue. He slowed down, glanced both ways through the woods. If the chutist was close enough to hear his voice, he would hear the noise if the guy made a run for it.

"It's a big mountain," he replied. "I'm doing what I can, but if Maeve's father has any other suggestions about where she might have gone, I'd love to hear them."

Silence on the line. The wind kicked up and rain trickled down the back of his neck, drizzling along the small of his back. He shivered.

"Rue? You still there?"

"Yes. I'm just wondering if that's why you went to all the trouble of getting me this phone. The town is quarantined, someone—I'm guessing government—has blocked all phone communications, but you decided I ought to be an exception to that. But you don't even know me."

Walker smiled to himself. "That is why."

"Sorry? I don't—"

"I'm having significant trust issues right now, Dr. Crooker," Walker said. "I don't trust anyone I know, including my current and former employers."

"So you trust me because I'm a total stranger? How does that make sense?"

"I trust you because you're a bystander. You're in this because you live in Jericho Falls, and you were at that parade. You're in it because Ted Sinclair is your friend and he's suffered a tragedy that would crush any of us, and because you care about his daughters. I trust you because you stood up to the Garland Mountain people and didn't take any shit, and because you're a scientist, and if there's anything this world needs to learn, it's to trust our fucking scientists."

A soft chuffing noise came over the line. It took a second for him to recognize it as a laugh.

"That's funny?" he asked.

"You're just coming up with reasons to convince yourself."

Walker heard a rustling sound back the way he'd come. A squirrel or something, he was sure, but he had a sense this was larger than a squirrel. *Please don't be a bear*, he thought idly. He didn't have time to run from a goddamned bear.

"You're right," he said. "But those reasons are good enough for me."

"What do you want from me?"

"I want you to leave Ted there. I know it's awful to ask. Maybe you can get a neighbor to sit with him. But I need you to—"

"Abandon my best friend?"

"No. I need you to help him. I'm asking you to put yourself in danger for him."

"What kind of danger?"

"The kind that leads to people dead in the street at a parade."

"Jesus," Rue hissed in admonishment.

Walker hurried on before she could be angry with him. "I'd like you to go back to Garland Mountain and stick your nose in as much as possible, find out whatever you can about Project: Red Hands and what they did to Oscar Hecht. What it's done to Maeve. If I can find her, I intend to bring her in alive, but if there's any hope of helping her, we have to be able to hold her and understand what's happened to her. You have the skill set I need, Rue."

"Walker, I'm a civilian. They wouldn't even let me through the gate. I can't just—"

"You have the knowledge base, and you're really, really fucking pissed off. Am I wrong about either of those things?"

"No."

Another rustle in the trees. Walker looked that way. His goggles picked up a bit more light than they had before, streaks of heat where there hadn't been any before.

He started following the parachutist's trail again, listening for his pursuers. "I have the authority to hire outside consultants and to grant emergency interim security clearance—"

"Is that even a thing?"

"I'm offering you a temporary consulting position with the SRC so you can get into Garland Mountain and get some answers."

"You're basically deputizing me?"

"Yes."

"I don't have any ID," Rue said. "They won't take me seriously."

"When I was there, I spotted a familiar face. Kat Isenberg. I worked with her seven or eight years ago. She was with DARPA then, and I'm guessing Garland Mountain is under the DoD umbrella. Maybe she's not the person I thought she was, but if she is, then she can't possibly be comfortable with all of this. See what she can tell you, and see if she can get you into the lab."

"That's a tall order for a woman you worked with once, years ago."

Walker scanned the trees ahead for a place to hide. A place to wait for whoever trailed him to pass by. "She'll either want to do what's right, or she won't."

"How am I supposed to get in touch with her? The phones are jammed."

"The earpiece you're using now should only have two numbers programmed into it, with voice commands for Alpha and Beta. Alpha is me. Call Beta and you'll get the office of the director of the SRC. Whoever answers will be able to get a message to Kat. There's no way communications aren't working at Garland Mountain."

"So I just call her up?" Rue asked. "What's to stop her from just telling me to go to hell?"

"Humanity, I hope," Walker replied. "I need to sign off, Dr. Crooker. I hope you'll do this for me, but it's your call. If you get in touch with Kat Isenberg, tell her I have faith in her. Also, try not to get killed."

Rue swore. "I hope this wasn't your idea of a pep talk."

"I wouldn't ask if I had someone else with your expertise on the ground down there."

"Someone with my expertise who happens to be willing to do anything so her best friend doesn't lose more of his children today," she replied.

"I'm sorry it has to be you," Walker said.

He ended the call. Rue might be fuming, thinking him an asshole, but she would do as he'd asked. Walker didn't have time to be polite. He slipped the gun out of his waistband and held it down by his side as he stepped silently off the path and found a space between a pair of hundred-foot northern pine trees. The shadows in the woods had gotten longer and deeper, and in the gray light and the drizzle, it all felt like some strange otherworld. But this was no fairy tale.

None of the fairy tales he knew had guns in them.

Leon Lewis heard Walker's voice ahead on the path—not the words, just the distant mutter. From the shift in tone, he knew when Walker began to wrap up the call, and he held up a fist to signal Viv Cheng to freeze.

They had been quiet enough, but Leon had started to think maybe

Cheng had been right—maybe they ought to have hung back a little farther. In the rain, with the wind blowing, he doubted they'd made any noise that Walker had heard. They'd both been trained to move silently—*like a fuckin' ninja*, Leon would have said, except he didn't want to offend Cheng. She was of Chinese descent, not Japanese, but Leon liked to be what Aaron, his older brother, called "sensitive and shit."

Cheng touched his shoulder, and he nearly shot her in surprise. Shot her or shat himself. Leon hadn't realized how tense he had become over the past hour or so, shadowing Walker, but every muscle in his body seemed ready to snap.

With her usual scowl, Cheng motioned for him to continue forward. Leon hesitated until Cheng pointed to the ground and used two fingers to mime walking. Sometimes Leon could be slow on the uptake, but he got this right away, and he couldn't argue with her logic. They were not on a trail. They had pursued Walker into a part of the forest without any path at all, and that meant that with every second they delayed, they ran a greater risk of losing track of him. Leon had invested a lot of time and sly ninja shit into trailing Walker, and the last thing he intended to do was fuck it up. Never mind that he might well be demoted or even fired.

He steadied his nerves, took a breath, and started forward. Head cocked, he listened to the rain and to his own nearly silent footfalls. *Shit.* Not a peep from Walker. He tried not to think about the fallout if he and Cheng blew this assignment. Instead of searching the mountain for Maeve Sinclair, they had been told to follow one person, a single individual who had some serious training on his résumé but had never been in combat. Walker might have seen some crazy shit, but he wasn't special ops.

Leon quickened his pace. He heard Cheng make the little clucking noise with her tongue that always came out when she disapproved of something, but he kept on. Maybe he wasn't quiet as a ninja in that moment, but he told himself that the rain and wind would cover it.

Thunder cracked somewhere far across the sky. It boomed and rolled, and he picked up the pace even more, scanning the path ahead for any sign of Walker. It might not be nighttime, but with a storm as gray as this and in the dark shadows of the forest, the dark seemed deep enough.

His heart raced. *Shit, shit, shit.* Where had Walker gone? Unless he had started to run, there was no way he could have gotten so far ahead of them in such a short time. He had been on the phone only two minutes ago. The call finished and then he'd started moving. Leon and Cheng had paused, but not for this long. Anxiety flooded through him. Had Walker diverted through the trees, taking off at a new angle? Maybe he'd learned something in his call that had made him alter his course, but without a path, it would be impossible to know where. Leon cursed under his breath, wondering if his sister could still get him the job she'd once mentioned, as an investigator for the law firm that employed her.

A rustle came from behind him, along with a strangling noise that sounded a bit like Cheng's clucking tongue. Leon turned.

Walker stood behind Cheng, choking her with one arm across her throat. In his free hand he held a gun, the tip of its barrel nestled in the little concave space just behind her right ear, but his gaze locked on Leon.

"Who do you work for?" Walker asked.

Leon smiled. "We're all here doing the same job, Walker. Don't get crazy."

Walker jabbed the gun barrel into Cheng's skull, and she cried out.

"Specifically," Walker said. "Who do you work for?"

Leon lowered his weapon, let it drop onto the damp leaves, and slowly held his hands out in supplication. "We're on the same side. That's what I'm trying to tell you, man. We're White Oak Security."

"Mercenaries, yeah, I got that part," Walker sneered. "I want to know who your current client is. Who is paying the tab for you fuckers to sneak around up here? And what are they paying you to do that requires you to follow me?"

Leon's mouth had gone dry. He found himself wishing he hadn't dropped his gun. Not that he would have drawn on Walker while the guy had his weapon snug against Cheng's skull, but he didn't like losing the option bullets gave him. The knife clipped to his belt felt warm and familiar against his hip. It would be clean and shiny now, but it had been dipped in blood before. It would be a damn shame if he had to kill Walker, but better than having to go back and tell the boss he had lost the bastard in the woods.

"We don't have clients," Leon said. "We take orders. The boss doesn't tell us who the client is."

"Bullshit. You can figure it out."

Cheng bared her teeth. "Yeah, sometimes we can. Right now, we know it's government work, just like you."

"Not like me."

"Oh, Mr. Fucking Righteous," Cheng said. She tilted her head away from the gun, but Walker followed with its barrel, kept it nudged against her. "You're asking questions you already know the answers to. We're following you because we have orders to follow you. The boss told us you were here, told us to shadow you in case you found the target before we did."

Leon winced at the word. He saw Walker's eyes narrow the moment Cheng uttered those two syllables.

"Target," Walker echoed. "Maeve Sinclair is not a target. She's a victim."

"You gonna kill me or argue semantics?" Cheng asked.

Leon saw her legs tense, knew she would make a move. His fingers drifted toward his knife.

"I don't have time for either," Walker said. He drew back his hand, went to knock her on the skull with his gun.

Cheng twisted in his grasp, grabbed him by the throat, reached for his gun hand. As she moved, Leon unsheathed his knife, rushing toward them. Cheng wouldn't need him. She had Walker cold. He watched her thrust her left leg behind his right and drive him backward. Walker started to fall. As he did, he grabbed a fistful of Cheng's hair and dragged her after him. The momentum of his fall brought them both down. He yanked her over him, put a boot in her gut, kept her moving, hurled her at the trunk of a foot-thick birch with such force that the tree cracked and began to fall, branches catching on other trees on the way down.

"Son of a bitch," Leon muttered as he took aim at Walker's back, cocked back his knife hand, and snapped his wrist forward.

Walker wasn't there when the knife sliced the air. He'd dropped to the ground. The knife glanced harmlessly off a tree branch and skittered into the underbrush, and Leon found himself looking down the barrel of Walker's gun.

Cheng rushed at him from the left, had the drop on him for sure, but Walker jerked his gun hand up and fired. The bullet took Cheng in the shoulder, spun her around. Leon saw her blood spatter the leaves as she fell.

Walker slammed a boot down on the bullet wound.

"That placement was on purpose," he told Cheng. "I can shoot you somewhere else if you want."

"Christ's sake, we're on the same side," Leon snarled.

Walker stepped back, covering them both with his gun. "The possibility of that being true is the only reason I'm not leaving your corpses out here in the woods. You just outright told me you intended to murder Maeve Sinclair. Those aren't my orders, and I wouldn't follow them if they were. Give your boss a message for me. I'm going to get that woman somewhere safe, where she can be treated. I'm putting myself in between her and anyone who wants to stop that from happening."

Gun or no gun, Leon lunged for him, got hold of his wrist to keep the gun aimed up at the sky. Leon caught him with a punch to the gut, then the kidney, but Walker moved with the blows, and when Leon tried to hit him again, the bastard gave him a solid shot to the skull. Leon staggered, rattled, wondering if a man could be concussed by one fucking punch.

Other punches landed, all of them Walker's. Leon caught a glimpse of Cheng, unconscious now and bleeding in the dirt. Then Walker brought his gun down on Leon's head, and the lights went out.

14

Maeve huddled beneath the prickly branches of a pine tree, smears of sap on her arms and face. The earth moved, but this was no quake or tremor. She had felt this way before, drunk and lying in bed with the spins. Vertigo, or something like it.

Her vision blurred. Long minutes passed—she couldn't be certain how many—before drops of rainwater plinked into her left eye and forced her to focus. She felt the pine needles sticking to her soaking-wet clothes and knew she had to move. Maeve rolled onto her belly and crawled out from beneath the pine.

Maeve.

The world tilted again. Her stomach convulsed, and she vomited with such force that tears came to her eyes. The stink of it wafted up at her, and she recoiled even as her stomach twisted again and once more she went rigid as vomit poured out of her.

She breathed through her mouth to keep from smelling it. Forcing herself to crawl away, she found herself out in the open again, in the rain, and she let the cold water cleanse her.

It's rotting you from the inside, Maeve. Get up, you cowardly nothing. Can't you feel it? You're hungry.

And she was. God, she was. The inner voice might have been cruel, but she couldn't deny the truth of its words. What troubled her was the voice itself, the way it resonated in her bones as if the words were music played through the pipes of an organ. Was this madness? Sickness?

How could she be hungry after being so violently ill?

She tried to rise, stumbled, and then managed to walk. Her vision wavered, the path ahead unclear. Her thoughts were muddled as if the rain and the wind had penetrated her mind. In high school, she and Kristie Burns had gotten so drunk at a party in the woods that they'd tried to walk home and had gone two miles in the wrong direction before they'd realized. They'd made it to a street on the outskirts of town, headed toward North Conway, and Alec Bergen had pulled over to check on them. Alec and Kristie's older brother were best friends, and Kristie'd had a crush on him since she was in the sixth grade. That night, she had thrown up in the backseat of Alec's car, a stink that would never come out of the upholstery, and afterward Kristie could never stay in any room with Alec for more than thirty seconds. But at least they had made it home safely.

For a few seconds, Maeve found herself back inside that moment, living that night, riding in the back of Alec's shitbox Cadillac, an ancient rusted thing he'd gotten from his grandpa. *She blinks, breathes in, smells Kristie's puke—or her own—and then she isn't in the car or in the woods but standing at the edge of a field.*

Hungry.

There are soldiers in the field. Bulanovo, *says that dark voice inside her. She feels sun on her skin, hears the clang of crude swords and the grunts of men.* They're starving, *says the voice.* Killing each other so they might no longer be hungry. Can we do any less?

Maeve staggers forward with legs that are not her own. She feels tall, though her arms are thin and her clothing ragged. The smell on her now is something else, something worse, something like the awful, gut-churning stench of the rats who'd died and rotted in the wall of her family kitchen one spring.

She walks toward the soldiers as they clash. Her hands are outstretched. Their nostrils flare and foreheads wrinkle when her stench reaches them, as if she is only vaguely visible to them until that moment when they smell the stink of death. That moment when it becomes too late.

Her long, spindly fingers reach out to brush an arm, a cheek, the soft curve of a throat. One by one, they fall, those she touches, and they buck and writhe as the sickness turns them putrid. They wilt and die behind her like flowers in a field of war.

On her hands and knees in the mud and rain, Maeve coughed hard enough that bloody spittle flew from her mouth. Coughing racked her body again, her fingers sinking into the mud, but she forced herself to breathe evenly, slowly, shuddering.

Blinking, she stared at the muddy ground, at her fingers, nothing like the long, wicked claws she had just imagined.

"What the hell was that?"

Trembling, hands on her knees, she managed to rise to her feet. The wheezing remained in her chest, the pressure in her head. The voice lingered as well, the malignant presence that had been taking root in her thoughts, inside her skull. As she thought of it now, a soft sigh of amusement that slithered in her brain. *A tumor,* she thought. Could cancer grow that quickly, put pressure on some part of her brain that might make her have such hallucinations, might breed this fear and paranoia? Or could it just be fever, exhaustion, dehydration?

Snarling, she bashed her fists against her temples. Sick as she was, she knew she had to find something to eat and fresh water to drink.

Hungry?

Serpentine, the voice continued to snake through her thoughts. An image swam up into her mind of the guy on the dirt bike, impaled, bleeding, and on the edge of death. Again her hands clenched, itching. They yearned to return, to touch the dying man, but even if she would have done such a thing, it was too late. The rider had died.

Find another, Maeve.

Again she smashed her fists against her head. She didn't want to kill anyone else. Even if that meant the sickness gnawing at her would kill her.

A buzz filled the air, low but growing louder. The other dirt bike, she thought at first, before tracking the sound as coming from overhead and to the north. Hopeful, she looked up to find the sky almost completely hidden by the canopy of trees. Rain dripped from branches and leaves and pine needles. In the open places, gray light and still more rain slipped through, but she couldn't get a glimpse of the helicopter, even as the noise of its rotors droned nearer. Heart thumping, she hurried through the trees, searching for a clearing. She could turn herself in, get help. They might not be there to help her, she knew— after what she'd seen at the parade, after the infection had poisoned her, turned her into a carrier, a killer, a contagious thing—they might not want her alive. But that would be better than the urge inside her now, the desire to find someone to touch, some warm life to end.

"Please," she managed as she came to a place where slightly more of the gray sky showed itself above her. She screamed, "Please!" Maeve waved her hands back and forth, spotted the helicopter against the storm clouds. Too high. Too far. She waved harder, screamed louder.

She watched the chopper glide away until the trees blocked her view again. Adrenaline had masked her pain and discomfort for a minute, but now the ache in her throat and the throbbing in her skull returned. Her bones hurt as if they had been driven into her flesh. Maeve exhaled, coughed, and tried to clear her thoughts.

Instinct had made her head for the gorge earlier. She'd gotten side-tracked, but now she glanced around in search of the right direction. Whoever might be on this mountain looking for her, she could never trust their motives. Only her dad and Rose.

Descending into the gorge could be treacherous if you didn't know the right path to take, but there were caves in the gorge. It could take them days to find her, even if they knew where to look. Down there, she would either be trapping herself or saving herself.

She set off north through the trees.

Inside, the voice still lingered. She felt its awareness of her, like eyes watching her from the dark, only inside her thoughts instead of hiding in the trees. For the moment, however, the voice had gone quiet, and she had no visions of spindly fingers brushing death across the skin of the living, or of them falling to the ground, lesions bursting on their flesh.

The silence hung heavy in her thoughts, as if something held its breath, waiting.

15

Rose had never felt so exposed in her life. She and Priya walked hand in hand where the woods would allow it. The bitch with the gun followed right behind them, but they held hands as if this were an ordinary hike, the two of them exploring the wilderness. They had kayaked on the river but had never climbed any of the mountains together, never even gone fishing. Their dad had taken Rose and Maeve fishing many times, and she wondered why she had never taken Priya.

Agatha bumped her gun against the small of Rose's back, and she let out a kind of peep, a sound she'd never made in her life. Her face flushed with shame. Had she ever hated anyone as much as she did this tiny woman with her big goddamned gun? She didn't think so. Even the man who had driven his car through the crowd at the parade had been sick and fleeing something or someone. And she couldn't hate Maeve, even though her heart wanted to. Maeve would be suffering even more than Rose. After what she'd done, Maeve would be in agony.

But this fucking bitch? Rose burned with hatred for her.

"Talk to me, Rose," Agatha said. "Where are we headed?"

"Where you wanted to go. There are dozens of ways to get down into the gorge, but only a few of them are both quick and safe."

Agatha said nothing, just kept them moving with the specter of that gun.

"Can I ask you a question?" Priya said quietly.

Agatha's footfalls were quiet, but now they grew quieter, as if she had fallen back to make sure she could shoot them both. "Go on."

"How much do you get paid to kill someone?"

Rose stiffened. Her mouth went dry, but she kept walking. She squeezed Priya's hand in warning, but the question was already out.

Agatha laughed softly. "Well, Rose, looks like your girlfriend is more interesting than I thought. But what makes you think I kill people for money, honey? All sorts of people will want what Maeve has. Maybe I work for my government—"

"I don't think so," Priya interrupted. "You're a private contractor. That's why you're here alone. I don't know if someone paid you to be here or if you're looking at it as, like, an investment or something. But you work alone. And I was just wondering what it cost to hire you to kill someone."

Rose felt the chill of the rain that soaked her clothes, felt the way they clung to her, but now she felt the dampness of the air as well, and it seemed ready to suffocate her. This wasn't *Priya*, so what did Priya have in mind?

Agatha fell back another step or two. She laughed softly, muttered some profanity under her breath. "Let me get this straight—I have a gun pointed at you. In this moment, you have zero idea whether I intend to let you live through the day, and you're looking to hire me to murder someone else?"

Rose glanced over her shoulder. Agatha's amusement seemed genuine.

"Not necessarily to hire you," Priya replied, growing sheepish. "I'm just, y'know, looking for an estimate."

That did it. Agatha burst out laughing, stopped in her tracks. She kept her gun aimed at them, but the barrel wavered.

Priya plowed into Rose, letting go of her hand and practically sweeping her off to the left. Rose stumbled, but Priya kept her from falling, kept her moving. Panic alarms shrieked inside her, and she expected bullets to punch through the vulnerable softness of her back. Expected them, but didn't wait for them. Her body understood what it took her mind deadly seconds to process, that they were running, trying to escape, that they were about to die.

Gunshots popped and echoed through the forest. Rose felt the shots in her chest, each one slamming into her with sound alone, like standing too close when the fireworks went off. She heard shrapnel blown out of trees, heard bullets hit the dirt. It took only seconds.

As she lunged behind a huge oak, Rose realized Priya had let go of her hand.

She spun in time to see Priya cock her arm back like a pitcher on the mound and let fly with a jagged black rock the size of a baseball. Agatha leveled her pistol and fired. The bullet punched through Priya's right shoulder, spun her around, droplets of blood spraying the leaves around her.

Too late.

The rock Priya had thrown struck the left side of Agatha's face. Her head whipped to one side as she staggered backward, caught her boot on a root, tried to break her fall with her gun hand, and cried out in pain as something gave way in hand, or wrist, or fingers.

"Fucking run!" Priya said, clutching at her bloody shoulder as she crashed toward Rose, smashing branches out of her way.

Rose was already running.

Though she tried to fight it, she succumbed to the temptation to look back. She saw Agatha on her knees, cradling her right hand against her body. Blood smeared on the woman's cheek and stained the beautiful silver of her hair. The tiny killer looked fragile and pitiable, until the moment she turned her head and her gaze tracked them. Even from here, she looked disoriented, unfocused, but Rose felt seen.

Agatha might be down and bleeding, but still Rose felt hunted.

Maeve drifts in and out of the world. Outwardly, she struggles to draw breath, her throat so raw it seems lined with shards of glass, but another part of her feels exultant, ready to open her mouth and scream with pleasure. In that interior place, a shard of Maeve opens its eyes to find herself in a church of rough-hewn stone, torches blazing in sconces on the walls. She glides as if in the midst of a dance, inhaling the oily smoke from those torches and the sweat-stink of worshippers. Her hands dart out, caressing those who chant their prayers, and one by one she silences them.

Infects them.

Their lives are delicious.

Maeve follows a serpentine path among them, slithering contagion. She takes a withered old man by the hands and kisses him on the corner of his mouth, the adoring gesture of a favored granddaughter. She holds his wrinkled cheeks between her hands and watches the glint in his rheumy eyes go dark, watches the plague blossoms rise and burst on the sagging flesh of his throat and forehead, watches the bags beneath his eyes turn black and begin to blister with rot.

People scream in the church. Someone grabs a torch from the wall and brandishes it in her direction. She reaches out, and the haggard old woman thrusts the burning torch at her face. Maeve stops it with an open hand, grasps the oily flames, greasy smoke pluming up from her palm and fingers as they are engulfed in fire. The old woman shrieks at her, eyes wide with ferocity born of terror, yanks the torch from her grip, and thrusts it like a swordsman, right into Maeve's face.

Her hair ignites.

As flames engulf her head, she grabs hold of the fierce old hag's face, and the woman sags to her knees, topples to the stone floor, and cracks her skull open. . . .

In the real world, Maeve wept. Tears slid down her face.

Feverish, she staggered from tree to tree. The wind whipped against her, rain trickling down her back, mixed with sweat from her effort and her disease. Her left hand reached out again, searching for the next tree, but this time it found nothing to grasp. She lost her balance, stumbled forward.

Panic snapped her awake, reality burning almost as much as that dream-fire.

The gorge, she thought, and for an instant she imagined herself flying over the edge. Falling, falling, falling. She imagined *impact*.

But impact came too soon. Maeve sprawled on her side in the tall grass of a clearing. Rain pelted her, falling harder than ever. She had lost track of her direction, lost track of the gorge, yet it seemed of little importance now. Lying in the wet grass, she realized she must be closer to death than to salvation. Whatever she had hoped to do—hide, think, devise some escape or cure—the time for those hopes had passed.

I'm going to die.

The realization was not unpleasant. It settled into her, wrapped itself around her, and she embraced the idea. She'd killed the BMW driver, though she supposed she ought to be forgiven for that one. And her mother and Logan . . . the guilt clawed at her, but she knew no god would hold her responsible. But what about now? She felt the thing inside her, that hunger, the sickness, and the voice still whispered there. If she lived, she would surrender eventually, and someone would kill her.

This could only end one way.

Better to die now than to suffer or to kill again.

Maeve pushed herself up to a sitting position and drew her knees up toward her chest. She wrapped her arms behind her head, coughing, trying to get one unfettered breath of mountain air, the smell of rain. Maybe she should just wait there to die?

She smiled bitterly. It had been a foolish thought. Maybe? Where else could she go?

"Mama," she rasped and began to cough.

A finger of jagged lightning stabbed the gray sky, silent, and habit made her count the seconds until thunder boomed, echoing off the mountain, the sound rolling into the distance. Four seconds. The storm had grown worse.

She glanced up to search the sky for more lightning. As she did, she caught sight of a squat building across the clearing, caught in the shadows cast by trees and storm. Warm yellow light glowed in the two small windows in front. Barely more than a cabin with a wide front porch, it had several picnic tables arrayed in front, and paths worn down to the dirt led from several directions right to the front steps.

Ranger station, she thought, just before she spotted the sign. Even in the storm, the yellow painted words were visible.

Maeve struggled to her feet. She pushed her hands through her soaking hair and squeezed some of the rain out, pushed the whole mess behind her head, away from her face. Somehow, though she felt like never moving again, she straightened up to her full height. She would turn herself over to them. Whoever might be chasing her, they would either kill her or cage her or study what had happened to her, maybe all three in some particular order, but it didn't matter anymore. She just wanted this to end, and if the ending meant death, at least it would be faster than dying up here, sprawled on the ground in the rain.

She took one step toward the ranger station.

The front door opened.

The ranger didn't step out, but he held the door with one hand and craned his neck, peering through the rain at her.

"Hey," he called, "you okay? I spotted you from the window and I thought . . . You alone? Are you lost?"

Maeve gazed at the silhouetted figure in his pine-green uniform. She saw the other one behind him, a second ranger, an older man who grabbed him by the shoulder. The rain drowned out their conversation, but she watched the pantomime through the rain as the older man gestured toward her, face etched with concern, and the younger one, who had come to the door, looked hesitant.

The younger ranger took a step out onto the porch, the wind sweeping around him, plastering him with rain. "You the one they're looking for?"

Even from forty feet away, even in the storm, she could see the change in him. A young guy like him, maybe Maeve's age, did not take a job like this without thinking himself some kind of noble figure. When he had opened the door, he had looked the part, kind and caring. Now suspicion and fear clouded his features, and the fear reminded Maeve of this morning.

The look on her mother's face as she'd died.

"No," she whispered.

Maeve started to turn back the way she'd come, but her body seized as if she had been on a leash all along and now her owner had tugged it tight, calling her to heel. A cough erupted from her chest. Black spittle and bloody foam sprayed from her mouth, flecking the tall grass, and in the midst of wheezing, trying to catch her breath, a surge of black hostility flooded her mind. The anger burned her. Its venom tasted bitter in her mouth, and she sneered as she turned toward the ranger station.

The sneer vanished. Her face went slack, then pitiful and pleading, but none of those expressions belonged to her.

"Please," she called. "Help me."

No, she thought. But the voice that had come from her lips did not belong to Maeve, and for that moment—just those few seconds—she could not form her own words. The gift of speech had been stolen from her.

She wept, and the tears—at least—were her own.

The hunger came on her even more suddenly than the anger. It had been inside her all along, gnawing, yearning, but now it ripped into her with such power that she clutched at her gut and cried out.

"Son of a bitch," the young ranger said, striding across the porch and starting down the steps.

"Frankie, wait," the older one warned.

Frankie glanced over his shoulder. "Call it in, Abe. We can't just leave her."

In the doorway, his silhouette darker, taller, wider than Frankie's, Abe just stood there and watched, worry carved into his features. Frankie strode toward Maeve, and though she did not lick her lips, the temptation existed. The satisfaction and anticipation of watching him approach made her flex her fingers.

No. I don't want to, she thought.

The voice inside her disagreed. It wanted Frankie in a way that Maeve had never wanted anyone for anything, and that *want* radiated through her. *She can see it in that moment, striding up to the porch and taking Frankie into her arms, caressing his exposed skin while black boils erupt and the cough chokes him, and she tastes his life on her tongue and in the folds of her brain, the tingle of it from toes to fingertips.*

"You okay?" he asked again, approaching through the rain.

In her mind, she saw the sorrow and confusion in her mother's dying eyes, and that seared into her brain, a clarifying image. Maeve snarled as she ripped herself out of its control and turned away. She started to walk, forcing herself, and wondered if she could manage to run.

Distracted by pain and mesmerized by hunger, she barely heard the engine over the rain. Only when the rangers both turned to the right, no longer focused on her, did Maeve notice the droning buzz that grew louder with each tick of her life's clock.

The buzz belonged to the engine of a dirt bike.

She didn't have to wonder if this might be the one she'd heard earlier, the twin of the bike ridden by the man who had impaled himself on a fallen tree. The rider saw her and changed course, rear tire slewing through mud. He bent his head low over the handlebars, rain sheeting across him, and he drove straight for her.

Her hands reach toward the rider as he approaches. The buzz of his engine continues, as if originating within the confines of her skull, yet the vision before her shimmers like heat above a roadway and shifts, and she is elsewhere. The tall grass is gone, the mountain and the storm vanish. At her feet lies the twisted corpse of a man whose face is covered with a mask, whose exposed skin is dotted with pustules and bleeding from pores. Though it may only be a part of his costume, by his clothing she believes him some sort of nobility, perhaps even monarchy.

Screams fill the room. The shrieking sweeps over her like the weight of the air just before a storm thunders in. She looks up and sees them coming for her, terrifying phantasms, beaked monstrosities, cloaked shadows, and it's a moment or two before she recognizes these as merely costumes, like the one worn by the dead prince arrayed on the black marble floor. This is no tomb, as she'd thought a moment ago, but some kind of masquerade ball. It's a party.

The walls are black. The drapes tied back from the windows are the finest, most elegant black velvet. Only the windows vary in hue. Each glass pane is stained a bloody scarlet, lit from without by tripod candelabras whose flames cast a garish, flickering red light within.

The costumed celebrants rush toward her, their hands outstretched as if to punish her for some crime. She feels a smile stretch her lips, feels her face crack at the corners of her mouth as she reaches out her own hands to greet them. For the first time, she notices those hands, wrapped in rough, yellowed cloth, stained with blood and black effluent. She notices the fingers, bone-thin or perhaps merely bone. Skeletal.

The masquerade envelops her, tears at the fabric that shrouds her body.

As they claw her apart, they begin to cough. To choke. Purple bruises turn to erupting blisters on their skin. Black blood weeps from eyes and ears, and they begin to drop, one by one.

We all fall down, *she thinks* . . .

The buzz in her skull made her blink. She reeled and fell to her knees, the sickness overwhelming her at last. Maeve stared down at her hands. For a moment she saw the mummified skeletal fingers, but her vision cleared with another blink and they were only her hands after all. Maeve Sinclair, flesh and blood.

There were three spots on the back of her hand. Small blisters, sores that had appeared within the past hour. Maeve coughed, unable to rise from her knees, and she spat a wad of black phlegm from her throat.

She looked up and found herself in that clearing again. The tall grass, the muddy trails, the rain soaking her clothing. To her left stood the forest ranger station, to her right the dirt bike bore down on her. The rider squinted against the rain, teeth bared. His dark hair plastered his scalp, made him look almost like a corpse himself.

Maeve thought this must be real. She felt the rain, heard the dirt bike's growl.

She licked her lips, the hunger so bad she would have screamed if the pain in her throat would have let her. Maeve opened her arms as if to embrace the rider. The dirt bike roared toward her, and the rider reached inside his jacket, drawing out a handgun. One hand guiding the bike, he began to take aim, the engine snarling as it began to slow.

Something flashed in her peripheral vision. Brown against the gray light.

The young ranger hurtled through the rain, planted himself in the dirt bike's path. The rider swerved, one-handed. The front tire went sideways in the mud, the dirt bike slewed, and the rider flew into the air to hit the ground perhaps twenty feet from Maeve. He tucked his body in, protecting his head and his gun hand, skidded in the mud, and started to rise almost immediately. Mud smeared half his face, and his right eye seemed to open behind a wet, dark mask. He looked at her as he reached up to scrape that mud away. His gun dangled in his right hand, also smeared with mud.

Maeve shuddered with anticipation as she staggered toward him, arms outstretched. As he wiped the mud off, the young ranger slammed into him.

The two men went down together. The impact rolled them off the path and into the grass. The wind picked up, the rain slashed down at an angle. The thick humidity of the earlier storm had abated, and Maeve felt a chill now, as if the hot July summer had fled the mountain and surrendered entirely to this storm. She watched the rider and the ranger struggle, saw arms flail and punches land, and then the crack of a gunshot filled the air, momentarily blotting out the shush of the rain and wind.

The older ranger shouted as he came down out of the little cottage they used for their station. He clutched a radio in his right hand, barking into it, reporting on events as they unfolded. With his left hand, he wielded an aluminum baseball bat that certainly wasn't standard issue for the job.

Grunting with effort, the dirt bike rider tossed aside the young ranger's body. In that green uniform, the deep red flowing from his gunshot wound soaked in just a little darker than the rain, but Maeve could smell the copper tang of blood in the air.

The rider began to turn, gun still in his fist.

Maeve knelt beside him, gripped his arm before he could take aim. Her other hand cupped around the back of his neck, and she bent quickly to give him a soft peck on the forehead. She tasted the rain and his sweat. He struggled to turn the gun toward her, but a savage cough seized him. He wheezed, trying to catch his breath, and she slipped the gun from his hand and let it hang from her fingers as she rose and started along the path to the east.

A tremor swept through her, part pleasure and part pain. A sound escaped her throat, and she noticed immediately that the rawness, the ragged feeling of broken glass, had vanished. She felt as if she could scream now, as if she might sing. Warmth suffused her. The cold and pain, the sickness, had been leeched from inside her and into the man whose life she had just taken.

She dropped the gun into the tall grass and kept going, feeling strong. Alive.

"Stop!" the older ranger shouted from behind her. "Come back here, lady. You can't just walk away from . . . Jesus Christ, what did you do to Frankie?"

Maeve hesitated. Rotated her head to look at him. He reminded her of Jeff Bridges, the actor who always looked like he'd just woken from a bender. As strong and healthy as she felt, her fingers still twitched. A little knot of hunger growled in her chest. A longing that had quickly grown familiar to her, as much a part of her as the beat of her own heart.

"Run," she whispered, halfheartedly. Then she shouted it. "Run!"

She forced herself to turn away and take her own advice. Tall grass whipped at her. The soft, rain-soaked ground squelched underfoot as she ran for the trees.

The old ranger barked after her, screaming commands as if he thought she might actually obey them. A little voice deep in her brain told her she ought to do exactly that. She recognized it as the voice of the original Maeve, the one who had ceased to exist this morning. The other voice, the louder one, the darker one, demanded that she turn around, go back, and get the old ranger and eat his life. Consume him. Infect him.

But Maeve strode on. She forced herself to quicken her pace, running from the old ranger as much as she ran from the voices in her head.

Up ahead, the woods were dark. The trunks of trees looked almost like a shadow army, waiting in the rain.

Two of those dark forms shifted, and Maeve assumed she must be hallucinating again, until the first one stepped out of the trees and she saw the black, glistening armor, and knew that her troubles were not over. The soldiers had come for her.

Relief swept through her, despite the roar of that new voice. The one that yearned for life, lusted for death.

The two black-clad soldiers aimed their guns at her and began to shout her name, ordering her to raise her hands above her head. There was nowhere for Maeve to run.

A smile curved her lips, but it was not her own smile. That grin belonged to something else.

16

When Walker heard the whine of the dirt bike coming to him through the trees, he hesitated. The sound might mean anything, but in a summer rainstorm, with the town under quarantine, he figured it had to be someone hunting Maeve Sinclair. He crashed through the trees in the direction of the engine's growl. Thirty feet ahead, he saw gray light through the branches and realized he'd come to a clearing.

The engine noise changed to a high whine, became muffled, and then coughed out. Walker frowned as he realized there were voices coming from the clearing. He picked up his pace, ignoring the snapping branches and the clomp of his boots. Being overheard was a calculated risk. He drew his gun, fingers tightening on the grip as he scanned the woods.

The gunshot seemed so loud that the sound of rain vanished for several seconds. Walker didn't slow down, but his steps were more careful as he rushed to the edge of the clearing. He sought cover behind a massive oak. A gust of wind shook raindrops from seemingly every leaf overhead. He wiped at his eyes and stared at the scene playing out in the clearing.

The ranger station. An older, bearded man in uniform came out the door with a radio in one hand and a gleaming silver baseball bat in the other. In the clearing, two men seemed to grapple while a woman strode purposefully toward them.

No, Walker thought. *They're done grappling.*

One of the men was dead, the source of the gunshot, no doubt. The details resolved themselves in his head. The dead man wore a ranger's uniform, which made the other man the dirt bike rider. A killer, searching for Maeve.

As for the woman, he'd seen a photograph of Maeve, but soaked with rain and at a distance of fifty yards or more, she could have been anyone. Then he watched as she reached for the fallen rider's arm, turned away his gun hand, and kissed his forehead.

Seized by a coughing spasm, the rider began to die. Walker had witnessed the phenomenon on video, but it seemed different in person. Lonelier, both for the dying and the killer.

Maeve started to cut across the clearing. The old ranger came running after her.

Walker stepped out of the trees. He was off to her right, barely in her peripheral vision, and he thought he could catch up with her pretty damn fast with the noise of the rain covering his pursuit. The old ranger spotted him, turned toward him, pointed his baseball bat at Walker like Babe Ruth calling his home run. Then the old ranger tipped to one side, reeling as if drunk—or shot. He tried to stand up straight, but a second bullet blew half his skull across the tall grass.

Walker dove into the grass as something buzzed past his head. Might have been a horsefly, but he had a feeling this insect had been hotter and shinier. He pushed left through the grass and lifted his head enough to see Maeve. The two Blackcoats were right in her path, and instead of running or trying to hide in the grass, she had begun to jog toward them, hands in front of her as if one of the Blackcoats might be her long-lost lover.

For a heartbeat, Walker focused on those hands.

Bullets strafed the grass around him, and he understood only one move lay available to him. Taking a breath, he bent low and hustled through the grass. They would see him coming, or at least see the grass bending, so he darted back and forth, managing a jerking serpentine pattern. They didn't want to kill Maeve—he told himself that and hoped it was true—but they also weren't going to be thrilled with the idea of being touched by her.

Taser, he figured. They would tase her or shoot her with some kind of tranquilizer dart. Or they would just murder her out of terror.

Walker stood up, took aim, and put two bullets in the chest of a Blackcoat. The shots knocked the guy off his feet, but he wore body armor, so the odds were good he would be back in action momentarily.

Rushing through the grass, he put Maeve between himself and the other Blackcoat. This was the gamble, but it wasn't much of a risk. If this guy didn't have orders to take Maeve alive, Walker wouldn't reach her in time, anyway.

He ran. Full tilt. Grass whipped at him. He heard the standing Blackcoat shouting to the one he had shot, telling him to get up. Panicked.

Walker liked that panic. It bought him priceless seconds. Invaluable territory. Slightly bent to compensate for Maeve's height, he closed the distance. Fifty feet away from her. Forty. Thirty. At twenty feet behind her, Walker dodged to his left, every inch of his chest awaiting the bullet his body knew was inevitable. But he spotted the Taser in the Blackcoat's hand just as the fucker pulled the trigger on it. The prongs struck Maeve in the abdomen. In the rain, sparks and smoke spurted up from the contact points, but instead of stopping her, the shock seemed to speed her forward. Maeve threw her head back in pain or joy or some combination of the two, and she lunged for the Blackcoat with the Taser.

He'd expected the Taser to do its job. Now he started shouting for his partner. "Franco! Shoot her! Jesus, Franco, shoot—"

To his credit, Franco tried. Pressing one hand against his chest, where Walker's bullets would have hurt like a bastard, body armor or no, Franco got onto one knee and leveled his gun. This time, Walker shot him in the face.

He winced as the bullet whipped Franco back, lowered his gaze as the man crumpled to the ground. For all the training he'd had, all the danger he'd thrown himself into over the years, he had intentionally taken human life only a handful of times, and they still haunted him. He wished the other Blackcoat had not said Franco's name. He would rather not have known. Walker thought about Charlie, back at home, and wondered how it would make him feel to know his father had just killed a man.

"Maeve!" he called. "Maeve Sinclair, stop. Back away from him!"

She ignored him, if she'd heard him at all. She reached for the Blackcoat. He grabbed her wrists, tried to push her away, but she tore one hand free and grabbed at his face. Her fingers splayed across his forehead, palm covered his eyes and nose. The Blackcoat backpedaled, shoving her away at the same time to put as much distance as possible between them.

The guy stood there, hands out in front of him, staring at them. He'd discarded the useless Taser but still had his weapon. His eyes were wide as if he were waiting, like he might simply explode.

He shuddered. His free hand came up to cover his mouth, and he might have coughed behind that hand. When he lowered it, blood smeared his lips and blotches began to form on his face. Walker thought he might be crying.

The man seemed to remember his weapon then. He lifted it, took aim not at Maeve—who had just killed him—but past her, at Walker. In his last seconds, he meant to vent his rage and take someone with him.

Walker dove to the right, dropped into the tall grass, and landed ribs-first on a rock the size of a football. The rock smashed into his side and drove the air out of him. Pain slammed through him as he rolled over, clutching his side and wheezing. Gun in hand, he rose to one knee and forced himself up.

Mind fuzzed by the pain, trying to clear his head, he took aim at the place the Blackcoat had been, only to watch the man collapse and die before a bullet could be fired.

Maeve remained on her feet. She moved through the windswept grass and the pouring rain, hands still outstretched.

Only this time, those hands reached out for Walker.

* * *

Leon Lewis returned to consciousness with a sudden flutter of his eyelids and a painful throb in his skull. *Fucker hit me harder than I thought.* He sucked in a gasp so deep it made him wonder if he'd stopped breathing for a moment, but he was pretty sure Walker hadn't hit him hard enough for that.

"Asshole," he grumbled, pushing himself up.

He looked around to get his bearings. The day had turned darker, or maybe that was just the combination of the storm and the trees. Walker had knocked him out, but he must have rolled a bit when he'd fallen, because now he found himself backed up to a massive pine, like he was the ugliest present under the tree on Christmas morning. The rain dripped off the pine needles, but the tree shielded him from the worst of it.

Cheng hadn't been so lucky.

He swore again, rising as he stepped out into the rain. Leon searched himself for his phone, his comm unit, his gun, and couldn't find any of them. Walker had paused long enough to toss them into the woods, apparently. Of course he had.

"Asshole," he said again.

He tried to shake off the shroud that unconsciousness had left in his mind. Had the bastard given him a concussion? Leon thought maybe he had. But a concussion wasn't going to kill him. Cheng's bullet wound, on the other hand, might well be the end of her.

She lay on her side in the rain. Her gear was black, of course, so it was hard to tell how much blood she might have lost, but Leon could see the wound in her shoulder—practically the armpit. One of the vulnerable places in White Oak's body armor design. He knelt by her and checked the pulse in her neck. It was weak, but there, which meant the bullet hadn't struck the axillary artery, or she'd have bled out completely by now. Her chest rose and fell, so she was still breathing, but that didn't tell him how long she might stay that way.

"Viv," he said, giving her a shake.

Nothing.

Leon shook her again. "Vivian," he said. "Cheng, you still with me?"

Her eyelids twitched and opened blearily but then closed again, which made up Leon's mind. No way was Cheng walking off this mountain, and he couldn't carry her all the way. He started searching her body and wasn't at all surprised to find no phone and no gun. She didn't like to wear the earpiece comm, however, and Walker wouldn't have known that. Leon undid the Kevlar vest on her body armor and patted several inside pockets until he felt the small bump.

Relieved, he slipped it out and lodged it into his own ear, then tapped the button. "Oak Tree, this is unit thirteen. Anyone copy?" Static exploded in his ear, and then he heard a burst of cross talk. "Oak Tree, this is thirteen. Do you copy?"

"Go ahead, thirteen."

Leon exhaled. "Cheng's down. We need dust-off. Can you track and retrieve?"

Several seconds ticked by as the woman running logistics on this operation tried to track their location using the comm unit. Leon wondered if he'd lost the connection.

"Oak Tree?"

"Okay. I've got you, thirteen," she said. "How bad is the injury?"

"I'll do what I can, but tell them not to stop for red lights."

There were no red lights, of course. An evac team would be sent up, either on a chopper or some kind of ATV. In this weather, he guessed the latter.

"Half an hour or more," she warned.

Leon looked at Cheng, already figuring out how he could pad the wound, but the question of whether she had another half hour came down to how badly she was bleeding. There would be nowhere to tie a tourniquet, so it all came down to applying pressure to the wound.

"We'll hold on," he said, not at all sure Cheng would.

That was it. Evac was on its way. He ended the call, unzipped a pocket, and pulled out a small med kit. Cheng bared her teeth as he shifted her body, working the Kevlar body armor off, but he needed access to the injury. When she cussed him out by name, he felt a flicker of hope, though she didn't open her eyes to do it. With a small pair of surgical scissors, he cut away the blood-soaked fabric around her shoulder and pulled it back to look at the entry wound. Cheng continued to bleed, but while the flow seemed steady, it wasn't a gusher. No spurting blood, no massive pool beneath her. In either case, she'd have died before the evac team arrived.

"Okay," he said quietly. "We got this."

No exit wound, though, which presented a small problem. If there had been, he could have glued the bullet hole to stop the bleeding until a surgeon could get in there and do it right. But with the bullet still lodged in there, he didn't want to risk it. They had been taught to do some field dressing of wounds, but he had only halfway paid attention. He wanted to bash his skull against a tree for being so thoughtless. Instead, he racked his brain to remember what he could. Pressure was the key.

"Don't move around," he told Cheng. "The bullet's still in there. You don't want to make it worse, cause more bleeding."

Her eyes opened partway, and he could see the disdain in them. Leon managed a smile. Of course, Cheng knew as much about this as he did, probably much more. Viv Cheng would have paid way more attention when they were teaching field triage and all that shit. Right then, she was probably thinking he should have been the one to get shot—at least she would do a better job of patching him up.

"Sorry, partner. I'm all you've got," he told her. "We'll both be happier when—"

Leon heard an engine. He blinked in surprise and glanced around. The sound came from over his left shoulder, directly from the southern approach to the mountain. Relief flooded through him, but it only lasted a moment. No way could an evac team have gotten to them so quickly. It had been just a few minutes since he'd called for help. And now that he listened more closely to the rumbling engine, he knew it didn't belong on any ATV. This was something else, small enough to maneuver along some of the wider hiking trails but too big to come up through the trees to reach them.

"Who . . . the hell is that?" Cheng managed to ask.

Leon didn't hesitate. He knew he didn't have time for anything but movement. He used the knife to strip off the sleeve he'd already cut through on Cheng's shirt. Ripping open a packet of gauze, he pressed it to the wound. Blood soaked through instantly, and Cheng snarled in pain.

"I've gotta go, Viv. You know I do," he said. He folded up the sleeve he'd torn off and pressed it to the wound under her armpit. "Don't try using your free hand to hold this on. Just keep your arm clamped down. That should put enough pressure to stem the blood flow. You need to stay alive for maybe twenty minutes. Don't fuck it up."

He said the words with a gallows humor, but neither of them smiled.

"Someone else is after her," Cheng managed, her voice thin and reedy.

"We knew it would happen." Leon's job had just changed. There were plenty of Blackcoats up on the mountain searching for Maeve Sinclair. But the engine he'd just heard belonged to someone else. Russians, Saudis, maybe some cartel hit squad. Who the fuck knew? The important thing was that he had his orders. Whatever it cost, he absolutely could not let an outsider get to the target first.

He took Cheng's comm unit out of his ear. Tapped it to make sure the GPS locator was working. Tucked it into her hand. Whatever happened to him, the evac team would be able to find her.

"Cheng, listen—" he started to say.

Her eyelids fluttered and he thought she might have gone dark again, but she exhaled loudly, almost a sigh. "What the hell are you . . . waiting for?"

She held her bare arm close to her body, as tightly as she could. Leon stood. For a second or two, he watched the rain fall on her face and wondered how long before she passed out again and how much blood she had already lost.

Then he started running, following the Jeep's engine.

Rue drove through Jericho Falls as if there were nothing out of the ordinary going on. Several people walked their dogs on rainswept sidewalks. There were a few other cars on the road, all of them with headlights on to cut through the gloom of the stormy afternoon.

But this wasn't the Jericho Falls that Rue had known her whole life. An orange neon Open sign glowed in the front window of Al Forno Pizza, but only because someone had neglected to turn it off while abandoning the shop. Barrio Taqueria and the Red Hen Market had their lights on, and there were people inside—quite a few people, actually—but nearly everything else had closed down.

The icy knot in her chest seemed to get heavier, like a cannonball inside her, weighing her down. As dreamlike as the scene around them had become, she felt its reality, and that made it worse. A metallic taste in her mouth troubled her, and she thought she might be sick.

Is this shock?

It occurred to her that the things she felt might not be shock but instead the fading of shock. The morning had been the worst minutes of her life. The BMW, the screams, people dying in the street, Ted losing his son and ex-wife, Maeve running off after what had happened to her.

Poor Ted, she thought numbly. She had seen her best friend hit by a car that morning, and now it didn't even make the list of the top traumatizing things she had witnessed. The hits kept coming.

At least she might be able to do something to help. She could try, anyway. Better than hiding like everyone else. Better than staying home and hibernating or getting drunk like . . .

Rue shuddered. The thought that had bubbled up—*better than staying home and getting drunk like Ted*—made her feel horribly guilty, and yet she couldn't shake her disappointment in him. She loved him and she understood him, but she had spent her whole life hoping he would be *better*.

She took a left at the Speedway. It was hard to tell in the rain, but the gas station was open. The place had a run-down look that verged on postapocalyptic. Faded sign, old pumps, and a little market that looked more like a seedy liquor store. She was out on the southern edge of town. Another mile or so and she'd reach whatever roadblock had been set up.

Instead, she took a left on Pumpkin Patch Lane. A charming name for an old farm road. Up ahead, the lighted sign of the Candlelight

Inn gleamed. When Rue had called the SRC, she had spoken to a youngish-sounding man named David, who had sounded more than a little surprised that Walker had enlisted her help. The next thing he'd said still echoed in her thoughts.

"That's Walker, though," David had told her. "Always improvising."

Rue hadn't liked the way he'd said it, but her misgivings hadn't changed her mind about helping. If anything, it had made her more determined. It certainly seemed as if Walker had been sent to do a job and not given the backup and the tools to do anything more than improvise, even if his employers scoffed at his history of improvisation.

David had put in a call to Kat Isenberg and then called Rue back to say the woman had agreed to meet her.

"How can I be sure she's not setting me up?" Rue had asked. "Or that the people at Garland Mountain weren't listening in? I mean, I could be in real danger, right? Just showing up at this meeting?"

"Absolutely," David had agreed. "Nobody's forcing you, Dr. Crooker. Whatever you might learn, it won't help Walker find Maeve Sinclair."

"But it might help keep her alive if Walker does bring her down off the mountain."

"It might."

Rue pulled into the parking lot of the Candlelight Inn. Kat Isenberg had told David it would be open, and she was right. If not for the rain, Rue felt sure there would have been at least half a dozen motorcycles in the parking lot. The Candlelight did not draw tourist trade. Once upon a time it had been an actual inn with rooms for travelers, but those days were half a century gone. Instead, it was a combination bar and restaurant, a place with the greatest buffalo wings Rue had ever eaten and an array of artisan calzones that made her stomach rumble, even today. No pizza, just calzones.

The Candlelight needed a paint job and had two cracked windows in front. Even on a gorgeous sunny day, it would have been forbidding—hell, it looked halfway haunted—but today, in the late-afternoon rain, it looked like the last place anyone who didn't know it well would want to enter. Scientists from out of town, for instance.

Rue hurried through the rain between a pair of Ford pickups that looked like the before-and-after shots in a marketing campaign. She could smell the rust on the older one as she passed.

As she pushed through the door, the jukebox was blasting an old Black Crowes song. Bikers crowded the bar area, laughing and drinking in a way that made her think of long-dead Viking warriors in Valhalla, especially on a day when these guys had left their motorcycles at home. A popcorn maker crackled in the corner of the bar, the smell of oil and butter and stale beer filling the place as Rue walked into the restaurant portion of the inn. About half the booths and tables were taken, a fair accomplishment on an afternoon like this. People were having an early dinner, some of them families, others groups of friends with frightened eyes, everyone trying to figure out what would happen next.

At the back, near the restrooms, a heavyset fortyish woman sat in a shadowed booth. She wore a red raincoat still dappled with droplets, her hair pulled back in a ponytail. She looked skittish, glancing around nervously, her back to the wall like Michael Corleone, wanting to see anyone who approached her.

Rue slid into the booth across from her. "Ben Walker told me you might be a decent human being."

Isenberg rolled her eyes. "That sounds like Walker."

It seemed to break the ice, but only a little. The woman's gaze flickered over Rue's tattoos, the shaved part of her scalp, and then she met Rue's gaze with a new curiosity.

"Who are you, really? I don't have time for games."

"Dr. Isenberg, we need your help," Rue said. "You know this isn't a game."

The woman paled. She glanced around the room again, her expression desperate. For the first time, Rue realized that Kat Isenberg wasn't just being secretive.

She was terrified.

Maeve felt like a passenger in her own body. Distant thunder boomed, and her insides trembled with the noise. Her eyes could still see, she could smell the rain and the sodden earth, but to her it seemed as if she existed now in the back room of the house in her head. Like she had been locked in the kitchen while someone else took over the front room, filled up the foyer, waited with the front door flung wide. Waiting for someone to arrive.

Someone had.

"Maeve, listen to me," the man said, one hand out like some kind of referee. In his other hand, he held a gun by his side, like he'd forgotten it was there. But he hadn't forgotten; she could tell by the way he held himself, relaxed but also ready, like a bullwhip about to be snapped.

"My name is Ben Walker. I want to help you. The longer you stay out here in the open, the more danger you're—"

She lunged for him.

Not that she wanted to. Maeve Sinclair existed in the back of the house, locked in the kitchen at the back of her mind. The person whose presence filled the front of the house in her head . . . that was who lunged. *The hunger*, she thought. As if the hunger might be a person, a sentient, thinking being.

"Maeve!" he snapped.

The man. *Walker.*

The hunger turned toward him. Maeve stumbled after him through the rain and the tall grass. The sky hung so low and dark that it might as well have been winter instead of midsummer.

Her hands reached for him again. Maeve saw something in his eyes that made her blink and hesitate. She felt the hunger in her gut and heart and at the base of her skull, but the urgent kindness in his gaze made her want to fight it.

"I'm sick," she told him. A cough erupted from her throat. It staggered her, made her pause. Walker flinched, took half a step back.

He raised his gun, kept his gaze on her hands. "I want to help you," he said again, "but if you come after me again, I'm going to shoot you in the leg. If you keep coming, I'll shoot the other leg. I don't want to, but you've gotta keep your hands to yourself so I can get you out of here."

Maeve lowered her head, wavering on her feet. She took a choking breath and stepped forward. The hunger clawed at her insides, whispered in her head, but she fought against it. She had fed already, but the gnawing wouldn't abate for long.

Another step. She reached out.

The gunshot kicked up a muddy clod of dirt by her feet.

She braced herself, ready to jump at him. Her gaze locked on his. Those kind eyes had gone cold, and the part of her that was still just Maeve felt glad. It'd be easier to take him without that kindness she had seen in him.

The rain grew oddly loud, as if the rest of the world's noise had vanished. Maeve licked her lips, could practically feel the life that would flow into her when her fingers touched Walker. The gun worried her very little. Would a bullet kill her? She supposed it might, but the hunger understood nothing of fear.

Enveloped in the gentle shush of the rain, she smiled.

Walker wiped rain from his eyes.

Maeve took the moment, bent her knees—

Voices cried out in the rain. Shattered the gentle quiet.

She stumbled, hearing her name, hearing the anguish in those voices.

Walker scrambled backward a few steps, gun hand sweeping in an arc, just in case he needed to shoot someone else.

Maeve saw two shadows hurrying toward her through the rain. One clutched at her shoulder, moving slower than the other. The hunger flickered inside her, a little tremor of excitement.

Then she recognized them. Priya. Rose.

A smile touched Maeve's lips. Her little sister had come for her, despite what she had done. The beautiful pain of the moment made her want to cry.

But the hunger came first.

Maeve turned toward her sister and reached out her hands.

17

When Rose saw Maeve fighting in that clearing, alive and sopping wet, smeared with mud, her legs went weak with love and gratitude.

Her sister. Alive.

The current running through her all day had been loss and loneliness. Rose loved Priya, but she needed her big sister to love her and tell her everything would be all right. That they could grieve together and life would go on.

Relief overcame caution. Rose shouted her sister's name and ran toward her, but when Maeve glanced over, something about the look on her face made Rose falter. Her eyes had a glint of red, and her hands . . .

Her hands.

Rose slipped in the mud, stumbled several paces in reverse. The woman in front of her no longer had the face of the girl Rose had sometimes hated and always loved, sometimes looked up to and always envied. Logan and Mom were dead, her dad was a drunk, and now Maeve . . . she didn't even know the person looking back at her with her sister's eyes. The person who reached out for her now with killing hands . . .

Maeve's palms were open, fingers slightly crooked as she reached out. All the sadness spilled out of Rose in just a few words.

"Maeve, no. It's me. Please . . ."

A rock struck Maeve in the chest, big enough and with enough force to make her grunt and halt her approach. In the tall grass, in the rain, she shifted her gaze away from Rose—and a second stone caught her in the mouth.

Maeve shouted in pain, her eyes ablaze with it, and she shook her head. When she glanced up at Rose and Priya again, her focus seemed to clear. Her eyes saw them, *knew* them, as if Maeve had been gone from her own soul and now had come home.

"What the fuck?" Maeve groaned, blood on her lips and chin. Her hands went up to cover her mouth. "I think you broke my teeth!"

Priya looked pale, held her wounded arm against her body, but she had a third rock in her good hand, ready to attack again.

She advanced on Maeve, pointed a finger. "You look at me right now, bitch, and tell me you've got your head on straight. You were in some kinda fucking trance there, and I need to know you're out of it. You try to touch Rose again, and I swear to God I'll—"

Priya cut herself off mid-sentence, as if she'd been the one hit with a rock. Rose saw her head turn, and she followed her gaze. The stranger strode toward them in the rain, the grass shushing as he waded through it. The gun in his right hand seemed to have turned darker.

The stranger was tall and broad-shouldered. He looked rugged, like he'd done his share of work outside, and his dark hair needed cutting. He stopped a dozen feet away, watching as Maeve spit out a broken tooth and a mouthful of blood.

"You all right?" he asked her.

Maeve glanced at him in disgust. "Just fucking peachy."

"I meant are you going to try to kill anyone?"

Maeve winced, gingerly touching her lips. She looked at Rose with fear in her eyes. "Whatever it is . . . it's passed for now." She turned to the stranger. "But keep that gun handy."

"Hang on," Rose said, moving toward them.

The stranger slid the gun into the clip on his belt. "No time for hesitation. We've got to get some cover. It's a bad idea for us to be out in the open like this."

He started walking toward the trees. Rose, Priya, and Maeve all watched him go.

"Maeve," Priya began, cradling her wounded shoulder. "You have any idea who this guy is?"

Maeve shook her head.

The stranger paused. "My name's Walker. Happy to give you my CV when we're not so exposed, but let's start with, 'I'm the only person on this mountain I can guarantee is not trying to kill Maeve Sinclair.'"

Maeve narrowed her eyes. "What about locking up Maeve Sinclair? Cutting her open like a lab rat? I'm betting that's a popular motivation for folks today."

"No doubt," Walker replied. "And it could come to that. But if it's between your freedom and more people dying at your hands, which one are you gonna choose? Maybe you can be cured of this thing and maybe you can't, but we all know you can't run from it for very long."

Rose had never seen Walker before now, but she hated him already.

Mostly because he was right.

Ted sat on the recliner in front of his living room TV, a tumbler of Jameson in his hand, pondering the skill set he'd developed thanks to alcoholism. Even with his head muzzy from booze, he could still look at the level in the bottle and predict with stunning accuracy how much he could drink and still wake up the next day with his memories intact.

Ted studied the glass in his hand. "Shit."

He sat up and set the tumbler on the coffee table. He hated to see it there, glistening amber, but he could always drink it when he came home.

Not that he didn't want it. *The beautiful burn,* he called it. Jameson went down anything but smooth, but whiskey always gave him a weird sense of history, and the kind of connection to the earth he felt when he sat by the ocean at night and watched the waves roll in, or on a day when the rain and wind churned up the sky the way it had this afternoon.

He laughed at himself, relishing the just-the-right-amount-of-drunk he felt. "You're a fucking poet," he said to the empty house. "The bard of Irish whiskey."

The laughter almost choked him. His face contorted, and he knew the tears would come if he didn't do something to stop them, so he forced himself to stand up. Wavering on his feet, he cast a regretful glance at the lonely bottle and then turned his back. If he could go through this day and stay off pills, stay away from all the shit he'd once used to dull his emotions, he could turn his back on a half-empty bottle.

The irony wasn't lost on him. But whiskey had never dulled his emotions. It sharpened them. Exacerbated them. Sometimes clarified them.

If he stopped early enough.

Ted turned, grabbed the tumbler from in front of the TV, drained the last inch and a half from the glass. "Goddamn it!"

He'd flung the tumbler before he realized it had left his hand. The glass flew across the room and shattered against the fireplace mantel. Glittering shards exploded in all directions. Unsatisfied with that destruction, he reached for the bottle, gripped it by the neck, cocked his arm.

Pain spiked through him. His skull, his wrist, his ribs. All the strength went out of him, and he lowered the bottle, let it slip from his fingers to the carpet.

Jesus, that hurt.

Of course. He hung his head, cradling one arm with the other. His ribs were an orchestra of little pains that together made a symphony. He hadn't been honest with Rue about his injuries, about how much pain he was in. The whiskey had helped, but he knew what would really help.

Not a chance, Ted thought.

Disgust curdled inside him. Self-loathing had become his frequent friend, but never more than today. He was useless. His wife had died. His son, once upon a time his baby boy, whom he'd cradled against his chest. The boy he'd tossed into the air and spun on the grass, letting him know Dad would always be there to catch him, always be there to give him a safe, soft landing.

Dead.

And his girls . . .

Flushed with the warmth of the whiskey, he glanced around and spotted his phone on the coffee table. Unsteady on his feet, he took a moment to clear his head and then picked up the phone. It took him a full ten seconds of tapping at the screen before he remembered the assholes who had quarantined Jericho Falls—the people he was sure were responsible for all the horrors of the day—were jamming cell signals and internet.

Knowing it would do nothing, he opened Find My Friends. The phone kept searching for Maeve and Rose and Logan . . . and Rue. The four people he could track with the app. Kept searching . . . but found nothing.

He couldn't find Rue.

He couldn't find Maeve.

He couldn't find Rose.

Ted stood in his ex-wife's living room, though maybe his again now that she'd died, and hugged himself tightly. Nobody else around to do it. He shivered as the whiskey drove heat out of his body. He needed another glass to get him warm.

Blinking, gutted, lost, he looked down in surprise to find the bottle in his hand. The cap remained sealed, but that could be easily remedied.

For his pain. All varieties.

"Where the hell are you, Rue?" he whispered. He didn't add *when I need you*, because she had always been there when he'd needed her, even when he didn't deserve her friendship. Even now, she was out there trying to help him. Trying to help his daughters.

That guy had come, Walker. Then Chief Kaminski had shown up with the fancy earpiece, and Rue had gone off to try to get answers about Garland Mountain Labs.

Ted straightened up. Rolled his eyes. "Jesus, you idiot."

If he wanted to find Rue, there was only one place he could be sure she would turn up eventually.

He dug into his pocket, confirmed his car keys were there. A bottle of Aleve sat on the coffee table, and he knew he ought to bring it with him, but the bottle already in his hand contained all the painkiller he would need.

Jameson in hand, he went out without bothering to lock the door.

Started up his car, backed out of the driveway, and then drove off in search of some way to bring his daughters home safe and sound.

This is what a good father would do, he thought.

Steering wheel in one hand, bottle in the other.

18

Walker had been in worse situations—which, looking back over his life, told him it might be time to take stock of his choices—but he'd hardly ever been in those situations alone. Now he hustled through the woods following a trio of young women, one of whom could kill them all if the urge swept over her again.

So you're not alone, Walker thought, grimly amused. He would have been far better off by himself, or if he only had to worry about Maeve Sinclair.

He watched the three women, saw the way Priya held her left arm against her body, and wondered how much more exertion she could take, how much blood she had lost.

Maeve had taken point, with Priya and Rose following about ten feet behind her. They might love her, but neither of them were foolish enough to want Maeve in a blind spot. She seemed aware of her surroundings, able to carry on a conversation, but her gaze shifted constantly, twitchy as a junkie, and when Walker had tried to talk to her, she had kept glancing at shadowy spots among the trees as if she saw something there none of them noticed. She had dark bags beneath her eyes and splotches on her neck and arms, but her energy never flagged. The rest of them were tired, but Maeve forged ahead with a steady stride, blazing a trail for them.

Walker never let his right hand stray too far from his weapon. It wasn't at all safe for Rose and Priya to be so close to Maeve, but the younger Sinclair had made it clear she would not abandon her sister, and Priya refused to go anywhere without Rose.

He picked up his pace, catching up with them. The time had come for decisions to be made. Rose and Priya heard his heavy boots and turned, both wearing fearful expressions.

"What's wrong?" Priya asked. "Are they coming?"

"Not yet. But they will. We need to talk about that."

Walker passed them, carefully approaching Maeve. He called her name twice before she seemed to notice. When she turned toward him, he saw something strange in her eyes. Not sickness or malice, and not the hunger he'd seen in them in the clearing by the ranger station. This was something else—cunning and old—something sizing him up.

Then she blinked and sighed in relief, and she was simply Maeve.

"We need a plan," he told her.

"I agree."

While Rose and Priya caught up to them, Walker kept his focus on Maeve's hands and saw the others doing the same thing. She noticed.

"I'm okay," she said, standing in the rain. She looked at her sister. "I *won't* be. It hurts, and I've been hallucinating. The sicker I feel, the stronger the urge to . . . touch someone. I've done that a couple of times, both in self-defense. But I won't lie—I didn't care when I did it that it was self-defense. Afterward, I feel better for a little while, but the urge is still there."

They stood in the rain, watching each other for a reaction.

"Should we be afraid?" Rose asked gently.

Even in the rain, Walker could see that Maeve had tears in her eyes. And why not? That morning she had killed her mother and brother with just a touch, and now her sister wanted to know if Maeve might kill her, too.

"Of course you should," Maeve said, voice quavering.

Another few seconds passed wordlessly, and then Walker moved over to Priya and started working to expose her wound. Rose had been wearing an open, pink-and-black linen shirt over a black tank top, and she volunteered it now, for Walker to staunch and bind Priya's wound.

"Let's start with this," Walker said to Priya, tearing the shirt into strips. "Who shot you?"

Priya and Rose told him the tale of a diminutive silver-haired killer named Agatha. Priya thought she must be an assassin, while Rose thought she worked for a rival government who didn't want the United States to be able to use Maeve's affliction in combat or espionage.

Walker thought about the parachutist he'd seen and wondered if that might have been "Agatha." Both theories about this killer seemed reasonable, but in the end, it didn't matter who had sent her or if she had arrived in hopes of getting Red Hands for herself. All he knew was that she didn't work for whoever employed White Oak Security's Blackcoats and she didn't work for Garland Mountain Labs or the SRC. For a moment he considered backtracking and trying to stop this Agatha person himself, but he'd broken the TAGI goggles when he'd smashed to the ground back there in the clearing at the ranger station. Even if he'd still had them, they might not have been entirely useful in this rain.

No, he had to stay with Maeve. She'd been his assignment.

Walker examined the wound and bound Priya's shoulder. The bullet remained lodged in the wound, which had to be causing Priya a hell of a lot of pain. She needed a doctor—a hospital—but the wound had started to clot and scab, so she would survive as long as no infection developed.

There were a lot of other ways Priya might die before tomorrow, but that bullet wouldn't do it.

"Your turn," Priya said. "Tell us what you know."

Walker didn't hesitate. Alena Boudreau had needed to work fast and had been uncertain whom she could trust. Walker had been given a very long time-out, so he had been perfect for the job. He understood that much. What he had not expected was to be dropped off in Jericho Falls and essentially left to his own devices. Garland Mountain was working for someone with a hell of a lot of sway in the federal government, or they wouldn't have been able to get away with this quarantine.

He laid it out for Maeve and the rest as best he could. Garland Mountain. DARPA. White Oak. Agatha. But he left out his concern that Alena Boudreau and her new agency had sent him no backup, no satellite surveillance. It worried the hell out of him. What had the old woman gotten him into?

"Beyond this Agatha and the Blackcoats, there are some people in a small Jeep, according to my contact," Walker said. "We have to assume they're after Maeve as well. And apparently people on dirt bikes—"

"Two," Maeve said, dropping her gaze to watch the rain pelt her shoes. "There were two of them. Both are dead."

Nobody seemed in a hurry to ask for explanations, so Walker finished wrapping and padding Priya's wound as best he could.

"You three—you're family, or near enough," he said. "I'm nothing to you. I know that. You don't have to trust me, and you don't have to do what I say. That's all up to you. But I meant what I said before. Of all the people out here trying to find Maeve, I'm the only one I can guarantee isn't willing to let her die or get cut open for some scientist to study."

The wind picked up. They all seemed to shiver, but Walker thought it might not have been the wind or the rain that gave them a chill.

Rose cocked her head. "So this is like a *Terminator* moment? 'Come with me if you want to live'?"

"Basically," Walker replied.

"That's great and all," Priya said, "but how are you planning to get us out of here? If there's some kind of rescue team on the way, now would be the time to tell us."

Walker kept his eyes on Maeve. Her gaze kept shifting from open and anguished to cold and dispassionate, as if she couldn't decide how she felt about any of it. He told himself it was shock and confusion, but he made sure he could always see her hands, just in case.

"Nobody's coming. Not yet, anyway. I'm going to get in touch with my people and see what they can do. I believe Garland Mountain Labs is working for the Department of Defense, and honestly, ending up in DoD hands may be our best option, but with my employers oversee-ing your treatment."

Priya laughed derisively. "Please. You want us to just hand Maeve over to the people trying to kill her?"

Maeve shook her head. "The people in black are here to capture me. I think it may be a dead-or-alive situation. All Walker's saying is that he wants them to guarantee the 'alive' part." She looked at him. "That right?"

He nodded. "There's no way for you to sneak off the mountain. And even if you can hide, you won't be able to hide forever." Again he glanced around at their faces, saw the fear and pain and anger there. "What we need is time for me to try to work it out, to get a guaran-tee of your safety, and try to get you put into the custody of the SRC instead of letting White Oak hand you over to Garland Mountain."

They all looked at Maeve, but her gaze had drifted. Her fists opened and closed. Raindrops ran down her forehead. Walker and Priya turned instead to Rose.

"What the hell are you looking at me for?" Rose demanded.

Maeve laughed softly. She rubbed her hands together as if warming them, and everyone took half a step away, ready to fight or run.

"There you go," Maeve said, taking note of the reaction. "They're looking at you because nobody's in the mood to let me make decisions for myself. I can't be trusted." Maeve shot a hard look at Walker. "They're right not to trust me. So are you. But if the goal is to hide until you can get some guardian angel to make them promise not to kill me, then the only place we have any real chance is the gorge. I was trying to make it there before, but I got . . . turned around."

"All right," Walker said. "Let's go."

Rose pointed through the trees. "Maeve's already leading us in that direction."

They started off again, with Maeve in the lead and Walker bring-ing up the rear. He felt the gun clipped to his belt. As long as he had Maeve in view, he could end this at any moment. He only hoped she didn't make it necessary.

He heard the distant buzz of a helicopter, but after he'd listened for a couple of minutes, he felt sure the pilot was flying a search pattern, not headed directly for them. Carefully, keeping Maeve in sight, he dropped back farther and tapped at his earwig. It beeped quietly, waiting for someone to pick up the signal on the other end. Long seconds passed before the beeping ceased.

Static and then a voice. "Hello, Dr. Walker. Update?"

Not David Boudreau. Not Alena.

"Who is this?"

"I'm sorry," said the voice. "My name is Joel Sutherland. I'm Director Boudreau's assistant at the SRC. I'm the one fast-tracking your new salary and benefits package. I will not, however, get you coffee when you come to the office."

Dead serious. Dry.

Walker blinked, his boot skidding in a bit of rain-soaked mud. "Joel, are you being funny?"

"Apparently not," Joel replied, even more drily. "I understand if you're not in the mood. People with guns, strange diseases, bad weather, dead people."

This guy, Walker thought, unable to decide if he wanted to murder Joel or be his new best friend.

"Do you have an update, Dr. Walker?" Joel asked.

"For Alena, yes. Put her on," Walker replied.

"I'm afraid she's not available. Before you protest, she's in a high-level meeting at the moment that I believe relates to your current assignment."

"Okay, Joel. Then listen. I've contacted the Sinclair woman. Her mental state is in question, but she has not threatened me or the other civilians with us."

"Other civilians?"

From his tone, it seemed the apparently unflappable Joel was flappable after all.

"We're searching for cover. Time for Alena to show me what a good choice I made, taking this job. Whoever's backing Garland Mountain and their storm troopers, she needs to get them to back off so the SRC can take charge. Maeve will voluntarily place herself into the SRC's custody, but only SRC."

Joel whistled. "Nicely done. You must have an honest face."

"Do you maybe not understand the urgency here?" Walker said, the words clipped, angry.

"I do," Joel replied evenly. "There's a tug-of-war going on. Director Boudreau was briefly given the authority to do precisely what you're asking. Less than an hour after she was given that authority, it was revoked."

Something snagged on Walker's arm, but he plunged onward. A few scratches were the least of his concerns. Maeve might be the most dangerous person on the mountain, but there were other dangers. Bureaucracy could end up the one that got them killed.

"Elaborate," Walker said.

"Her authority was overridden by the undersecretary at the request of General Henry Wagner at DARPA. It seems General Wagner is presently on-site at Garland Mountain."

"Wagner." *Of course it is*, Walker thought.

Inside DARPA, the focus was always on science. The human race seemed to have developed a consensus that everything that could be learned about the world had already been learned, but science disproved that thought every day. Archaeologists dug up history that could be understood differently by modern minds. Biologists discovered new biospheres. Virologists encountered mutated bacteria. Astronomers learned more about the universe every time they opened their eyes.

Every waking moment, the world's governments and corporations were in a race to make the next breakthrough, and that competition heightened when the breakthrough in question might be used to kill people. DARPA wanted to make sure they were the first to get their hands on new dangers facing the world and the first to weaponize those discoveries. Of equal importance, their job was to anticipate the ways in which enemies might use such developments against the United States and create ways to counter those aggressions.

There were ethical, honorable ways to go about this work.

And then there was General Henry Wagner, who seemed like a benevolent enough creature until you dared to question his motivations or his definition of acceptable losses. Walker could remember sitting in a meeting with Wagner and several other DARPA officials, discussing the deaths of three researchers. They had been researching the use of the gene-editing tool CRISPR to create cheaper, more effective, and more precise biological weapons and had accidentally been exposed.

General Wagner had sighed and sipped his coffee. "You want to make an omelet, you have to break some eggs," he'd said as he reached for a cinnamon danish.

"Fucking Wagner," he said now. "Joel, can you get me on the phone with him?"

"Right now?" Joel asked.

Walker wiped rain from his face, pushed his hands through his soaking hair. "Yes, right now."

General Wagner felt at home in the sublevels of Garland Mountain Labs. He'd spent the lion's share of his career in secure facilities at the Department of Defense and within DARPA, dealing with the dichotomy between their public and private faces. The upper levels at Garland Mountain—the public face of the lab—weren't precisely a façade. Accounting, human resources, security, and conference rooms were all housed on those levels, along with dozens of corporate research projects that might involve sensitive or proprietary information but did not require government security clearance. Those levels looked like a thousand different office buildings General Wagner had been inside, a hundred pharmaceutical companies. Glass offices, low-walled cubicles, computer screens, freshly polished conference tables.

No matter how ordinary those upper levels seemed, however, the whole place felt like a mask. People milled about on their ordinary errands, and perhaps they were fully intent upon those tasks, but General Wagner believed they must think, even on their most mundane days, about the work going on beneath their feet.

The real work, he thought, glancing around sublevel 2.

Garland Mountain's lower levels were designed as a hexagon. Each level hosted six separate laboratories, inside each of which was a fully self-contained research operation. The main elevator bank thrust up from the hexagon's center. Circling this axis was a wide common space throughout which the designer had placed chairs and sofas, coffee tables, workstations, and other spots where the research teams from each of that level's six labs could socialize for either business or pleasure. They were encouraged to take breaks, to consult other teams whose members shared the same security clearance, to share excitement and frustration. The first CEO of Garland Mountain Laboratories, Arun Lahiri, had believed that such an environment would be good for both morale and progress, and the results had seemed to confirm that belief.

Hank Wagner didn't go for that happy bullshit.

Too many chances for people to share classified data.

In Garland SL2-Alpha, researchers were instructed not to socialize with staff from other labs. They worked, General Wagner was sure to make clear, for the Department of Defense. They had been vetted and achieved the top clearance level available to those civilians below the level of project director. As such, they were ordered to steer clear of other Garland Labs employees both on the premises and off. SL2-Alpha staff were to treat everyone else as if they were invisible. The researchers on other projects in the complex thought SL2-Alpha put "asshole" as the top requirement when hiring. General Wagner knew some of the staff working on Project: Red Hands had been bothered by this reputation, but he didn't give a damn. If they wanted to whine about it, they could be replaced, and they all knew it.

Now, more than ever, he needed them all to keep their mouths shut. There were well over one hundred hired guns from White Oak out there searching for a civilian, with orders to bring her in dead or alive, as if this were the Wild West. The parade video had racked up tens of millions of hits, and the media were on the story like a pack of rabid dogs. Homeland Security was doing its best to spin the whole thing, dropping hints about a possible terrorist release of a fatal bioweapon. That was enough to keep people away, but not to keep drones out of the sky.

And it wouldn't last.

The faster they found Maeve Sinclair and locked her into a sterile room at the back of SL2-Alpha, the sooner he could get to cleaning up the whole mess.

General Wagner sat at a desk in a glass-walled office on the upper levels of the complex, far above the secure lab where Project: Red Hands had been painstakingly researched and crafted, and where it had gotten out of control, all thanks to a biologist named Oscar Hecht, who'd started hearing voices and lost his marbles.

"Sir?"

Wagner narrowed his eyes to stare at Cristina Vargas, not willing to acknowledge that he had stopped paying attention.

"I'm listening, Dr. Vargas."

Vargas nodded. "I'm not sure what else to tell you at this point. We've got an autopsy room prepared, the surgery suite is ready if it becomes necessary, and the staff is confined to Alpha until further notice. If you can deliver Sinclair to us, we will learn whatever we can from her, no matter what condition she's in."

"And then?" General Wagner asked.

"That will be up to you, sir," Vargas replied. "Project: Red Hands has produced results—"

"Results you don't even understand," General Wagner sniffed. "All the brilliant minds on your team, and you can't explain why Hecht became infected."

"He infected himself, General," she said, brows knitting.

"I've traded bullshit with presidents, Dr. Vargas. Don't test me. You have a lot of data, a lot of research, and you have dozens of different plague cocktails in your fridge. What you don't have is a clue about what triggered the thing to work on Hecht. Yes, he purposely injected himself with something that killed every lab subject you've tried it on—"

"We'd never tried it on a human subject."

General Wagner held up a hand. "Until Hecht did it to himself. But until you can explain to me why it worked on Hecht and not on the animal subjects, and certainly not on Cheng—"

"You ordered that test, General."

Wagner shot to his feet, pounded his hand on the desk hard enough that the papers spread across it jumped. Vargas barely blinked, and it irritated him that he couldn't make her flinch.

"Enough!" he barked. "I'm not here to argue with you. That's not how this works, Dr. Vargas."

"Obviously," she muttered, sitting back in the chair.

Half an hour ago, White Oak Security had brought in one of their Blackcoats after the woman had been badly injured during the hunt for Maeve Sinclair. General Wagner had known nothing about her except her name—Vivian Cheng—and that to be employed by White Oak she had signed all the waivers necessary for them to run their test and claim they'd been trying to save her life.

Instead, the injection had killed her.

If they couldn't replicate what Hecht had done to himself, the whole project rested on getting Maeve Sinclair into this lab. Vargas insisted that they could learn much more if she were alive, but General Wagner knew that was a preference, not a requirement.

A knock on the glass door.

His aide, Sergeant Hannah Loring, shot him an apologetic look through the glass. She held a slender silver phone in her hand. General Wagner rolled his eyes but waved for her to enter. He had told her that he didn't want a call from anyone unless they were high enough up the chain to give him orders.

"What is it, Sergeant?"

Vargas vacated her seat to make room for Sergeant Loring in the small office. For her part, Loring ignored the empty seat and stood not quite at attention. She held the phone down by her hip and spoke quietly.

"It's Director Boudreau's office, General," Sergeant Loring said.

"Didn't I say—"

"You did, sir. But I'm told Director Boudreau is prepared to abandon any claims or protests, with a single condition that she will only share with you directly."

General Wagner rolled his eyes. He'd known Alena Boudreau for more than twenty years and knew this had to be part of one scheme or another. The woman had a moral compass that had made her a pain in his ass dozens of times, but she was a hell of a scientist and she got results. More than likely, she wanted to get some kind of guarantee from him about the Sinclair woman or score some promise from him about future cooperation.

"Oh, for fuck's sake. Give me the phone."

Sergeant Loring handed it over. General Wagner sighed as he put the phone to his ear.

"Alena, listen—" he began.

"Pardon me, General," said a male voice. "Please hold for Director Boudreau."

The office boy put him on hold. He wanted to throttle the prick. Alena making him wait like this was just like her. Wagner glared at Sergeant Loring, irritated that she hadn't made sure Alena was on the line already before putting him on.

He heard a click, the call being transferred, but it wasn't Alena Boudreau's voice that came on.

"Hello, Hank."

General Wagner stiffened. "Who the hell is this?"

"You did this, General. Your people got sloppy and let this malicious little bug slip out, and a lot of people died because of it. Because of you. They're still dying. Now you're gonna kill this woman or get her killed for something you did, for your mistake."

The general swore softly. He recognized the voice. "This isn't your business, Walker. You're on paid leave until I tell you differently. I don't know who the hell you think—"

"I don't work for you anymore. I work for the SRC now."

Fucking Alena, General Wagner thought. He wanted to spit.

"I'm on the mountain," Walker continued. "I'm going to get Maeve Sinclair, and I'm going to bring her down. I want your guarantee that no harm will come to her and that you will withdraw all searchers until this skirmish between you and Director Boudreau has reached a conclusion."

Wagner stared at Loring and Vargas. Neither of them could hear a word, and curiosity blazed in their eyes. He smiled thinly and turned his back to them. They would still be able to hear, but it felt more private this way, more personal.

"Maybe my team shares some blame," General Wagner said, "but so do you, Dr. Walker. You remember your assignment in Greenland. You and Hector Montez got all kinds of praise for your work there and for the germs you dug out of the permafrost. But you two assholes weren't as careful as you thought."

"What are you—"

"Heard from Montez lately, Walker?" Silence on the line. General Wagner sneered. "That's what I thought. Montez came back with a little infection. Nothing contagious, at least at first, but enough to panic us. Enough to start us down a line of research that's like nothing I've ever seen. I'll tell you this much, the idea of weaponizing sickness is a hell of a lot older than any of us imagined."

"Is Montez alive?"

"You must be a great friend to have," General Wagner said, twisting the knife. "Montez went off duty while you were in Iraq, almost a year ago. He's been dead seven months. And as far as your guarantees, you can fuck yourself. I've no interest in making her suffer any more than she already has, but if it comes down to her safety or the security of the nation, that's an easy choice to make. Bring her in, Walker. If she behaves, she'll be safe. If not, I make no promises. As for you, you're done. You and Alena Boudreau both."

He waited for a reply, but this time there was none. Walker had ended the call.

General Wagner dropped the phone onto the desk and smiled.

"Sergeant, pass the word along. We're not just looking for Maeve Sinclair up on that mountain. We're also looking for Dr. Benjamin Walker. The woman I'd like alive if possible. But if anyone feels like shooting Walker, I'll throw them a goddamn parade."

19

By the time they reached the gorge, Maeve had grown hungry again.

That was a lie.

She kept trying to tell herself *again* must be the correct word—after all, her symptoms had subsided along with the hallucinations. Seeing Rose had done that, as if Maeve had been slowly sinking into some interior darkness, losing herself, and Rose had reached down into the madness and hauled her out.

For a while, the whispers in her head, the illusions, the sickness seemed to have gone away. But the truth she could not hide from herself was that the hunger had never really left her. It lingered, hiding down inside her, a small twinge in her gut instead of the gnawing emptiness it had been.

Now, though, the gnawing had begun to return. And with it, the whispers. The presence that she felt in her mind, like a tumor putting pressure on the inside of her skull.

"Hey," Rose said, "you all right?"

They were at the edge of the gorge, at a place known as Walter's Descent. There were no stairs and no signs to identify the spot, nothing but a small cairn of rocks that hikers had built and a little spray of blue paint that a casual passerby would barely notice. The way down from here would not be easy, but it ought to be safe enough, even for the wounded Priya, whose love for Rose had earned a bullet wound. Maeve knew she ought to feel worse about it than she did. Not that she felt no guilt—just maybe not enough.

Regret, though—she had plenty of that for all of them.

"Maeve," her sister said.

"The rocks will be slippery from the rain," Maeve said, glancing around as if the treacherous descent had been the thought on her mind, instead of which one of them she might kill first.

No. She squeezed her eyes shut. Rose loved her, in spite of everything. Her too-serious sister with the rare, braying laugh and enormous, vivid blue eyes, always full of wonder . . . Maeve would throw herself into the gorge before she would hurt Rose.

She loves you? said the presence in her mind. The voice. The hunger. Maeve yearned for contact, for someone to love her and put their arms around her, to comfort her with an embrace, let her sink gratefully into someone's forgiveness.

She won't touch you. They fear you. Look at their eyes. You're a monster to them, when all you want is life. Warmth. All you want is the cure.

The rain pelted her face and the wind kicked up, making her shiver as she gazed at the people who had come for her. The presence filled her, not just her thoughts but her bones, her blood. Like the sickness that had begun to rise again, making her skin itch and bleed, lodging a cough in her chest, the presence wasn't just inside her now but around her, as if she radiated disease and hunger. And malice.

Priya stood next to Rose. Beautiful Priya, delicate on the outside, took no shit from anyone except her family. Spent so much time trying not to upset them that she had no energy left to appease the rest of the world. Tough inside.

Priya, Rose.

Walker.

Him. The hunger gnawed at Maeve, and she smiled to cover up the predator's growl that wanted to come out.

Rose approached her. Maeve flinched away, and her sister froze. They stared at one another for a second or two, wariness blooming anew in Rose's eyes. She'd seen that flinch and understood it, knew that Maeve didn't want her getting close and knew why.

She didn't come any closer.

"Eventually," Maeve said out loud. Only it wasn't Maeve who'd said it but the thing inside her.

For the first time, the presence had made it all the way to her voice.

Rose paled. Even in the rain, she visibly blanched. "You go first."

Maeve nodded. As she turned away, the tears came. A sob built in her chest, tearing at her throat, but unlike the dreadful hunger, she managed to keep it down. Crying, fighting the thing inside her, she started down Walter's Descent. She coughed, and it came out a cry that nobody could mistake for anything but anguish. Yet as the others followed, no one inquired. What could any of them say?

The trail wasn't much of one. Hands out for balance, she slipped a bit here and there, mostly because of the Sperrys she'd worn that morning. They were soaked, her feet squelching. Walter's Descent was a switchback trail, some of it rock-flecked dirt, some of it bare rock. There were jagged formations and places where hikers had lodged fallen trees to create steps. In a few places there were cairns and paint spots. In one spot, a third of the way down, someone had drilled into bare rock and implanted an iron handhold.

Priya had more trouble than the rest of them, but only in places where she needed to use her hands to keep from falling. She kept her left arm pressed against her chest most of the time, but the one time she had to use it, Maeve overheard her talking to Walker and it was clear the bleeding had started again.

They moved in relative quiet, and Maeve was glad of that. Had any of them attempted to speak with her, she feared what words would come out of her mouth. Her voice could not be trusted now, and neither could her vision. Ten minutes passed, then twenty, and with the exertion of the descent, she grew weaker. Sicker. Her tears dried, but the cough worsened and the pain she'd felt before deepened.

The edges of her vision turned red. Images tried to crowd into her mind and many times she shook her head to refuse them. More than once she paused and held on to the rocks, fearful that she would sink into a vision of the past—one of the moments of mental slippage that felt so much like memory. Horrific, impossible memories of hunger and sickness and murder.

Hollow.

Gnawing.

Hunger.

Resisting the lure of that slippage felt like trying to stay awake behind the wheel of a car. She coughed hard enough to make her sway on her feet. Leaned against the rocks to make sure she didn't unbalance in the wrong direction and fall out over the gorge. The hidden place might have been carved by ancient glaciers, but it was far from smooth. The rock slabs jutted out, and there were a hundred places she might strike on the way down if she fell. Edges that would break her, shatter bones, stave in her skull.

Maybe that's best, she thought, leaning against sheer stone.

"No," she whispered.

In that other voice.

Her eyes had closed. When she opened them, she saw a figure in the rain about twenty feet away, a tattered shroud, blistered skin taut over bones, tinted red, eyes bleeding black.

No, the hunger whispered to her. *No*, said Death.

Breathless, fear like ice along her spine, she lifted a hand to cover her mouth, and fresh tears slid down her face in the rain. Did the others see it? Had it come for them or only her?

Maeve stood up straight, away from the wall of the gorge. The urge to throw herself over, to break and bleed and be gone, tugged at her more powerfully even than the gnawing hunger. The presence tried to claw at her, as if to anchor her to the stone, to keep her alive, but her mind flashed forward to what came next—to the moment when she lost herself to the hunger and reached out to whomever was near.

It wouldn't matter who, in the end. The need would override any love, any hesitation. Walker wanted to save her, but no sense of self-preservation would save him from the yearning that made her begin to tremble, even now. That red hunger had a much stronger sense of self-preservation than Maeve herself had.

The red hunger.

The wraith . . . it was inside her. Its memories.

No, she thought. But now she had allowed the thought to blossom in her mind, and it took root. The hunger did not belong to her.

Back along the trail, Rose dropped down from one massive rock slab to another, canted the other direction. She glanced at Maeve, and her eyes narrowed with concern, but then she turned to reach up, offering Priya a helping hand.

Maeve fought it. Her hands shook, and then her whole body. The urge to wait, to reach for them, whichever one of them caught up to her first . . .

Red streaks like poison ran under the skin on her arms. Maeve stared at those streaks and at the sores where it almost looked as if she'd been burned, black divots in her flesh. She wondered how they could all even look at her, as sick as she seemed.

Maeve began to cough so hard that her throat bled again, and she sprayed red and black onto the rocks. The rain thinned it, began to erase it, but not before the others had seen it. They stared at her.

Walker passed Priya and Rose, moving quickly, dropping down from one stone slab to the next. He drew his gun. Rose shouted at him to put it away. Fifteen feet from Maeve, Walker paused to glance back at Rose.

"I just want to make sure I'm between you and her," he said.

Maeve laughed softly. Or something inside her did. "You and your gun," it said.

Walker narrowed his eyes, studying her. "That's right."

The gunshot came out of nowhere.

Chips of stone and dirt kicked up from the trail only inches from Walker's feet. Priya cried out as Rose grabbed her and slammed her against the wall of the gorge, shielding her. Walker pressed himself against the same slab of stone and turned to Maeve.

"Take cover!" he barked at her, eyes wide as he tried to figure out what to do next.

Maeve knew they were pinned here. Based on the angle of the shot, the shooter had fired from the same side of the gorge they'd come from, but farther to the south. That meant they hadn't found the entrance to Walter's Descent but were trying to make their way down into the gorge by a more precarious route.

Maeve stepped toward Walker. He stared at her.

"Take cover, goddamn it!"

Maeve coughed. She scratched at her left arm, tearing open one of the purple blisters there. It stung, but not too badly. The wind buffeted her as she leaned out away from the wall of the gorge to get a better look.

Three more gunshots in quick succession. One bullet took a chink out of the stone that jutted a few feet away from her, back the way they'd come. Rose shouted some profanity, still shielding Priya.

Maeve licked her lips. Tasted blood and something sour. Something awful.

Walker saw the look in her eyes. Took aim at her chest. "Don't do it. Fight it, Maeve."

She grinned her bloody grin, but there was very little of Maeve in it. She felt her lips part, felt her teeth bare. Maeve fought it—forced her eyes closed.

With her eyes closed, she sees that revelry again. The obsidian room, the bodies lying about her on the floor, covered with those plague sores, a pretty blond girl on her knees, vomiting something solid, a piece of her insides coming up. Her hands reach out in the glow of the red-glass windows—

Maeve opened her eyes. "Back up."

Her voice came out a rasp, but Walker must have seen something in her face. Maeve wondered if he saw her there or the presence. The hunger.

He backed up. Kept the gun trained on her as she shuffled past him.

"Rose. Priya. Get out of her way," Walker said.

Maeve hung her head. Shuffling past them, she paused a moment, hunger ripping into her. Her right hand strayed toward the back of Priya's neck, shaking with the effort to stop herself.

"Mae-Maeve," Rose said through trembling and tears, using the nickname only she, as the little sister, had ever had the privilege to use. And hadn't used for fifteen years, at least. "Please . . . don't."

Maeve pressed her eyes closed again. This time, instead of a glimpse of the hellish past, she saw this morning's nightmare. Mom. Logan. Dad broken in the street.

Her scream tore something loose inside her.

Maeve ran along the trail. When she hit the turn they'd all taken, she leaped upward. She hit the rocks ahead, jagged, slippery stone slabs, slicked with rain. Maeve did not fall. The shooter up on the wall of the gorge fired again, and the gunshots echoed all around.

The thing inside her was ascendant now, but for the first time, they worked in concert. Hunger weakened her and strengthened her at the same time. It overrode fear and hesitation. Even without sickness, Maeve could not do the things she did now, but the red hunger, the death she carried inside her—it could.

She crawled and climbed, leaped and scrabbled from rock slab to hard-packed soil. Her hands and feet found purchase, fingers thrust into cracks, and, spiderlike, she ascended.

A ferocious gust of wind tried to scrape her off the wall of the gorge. Maeve barely noticed. Instead, she zeroed in on a glimpse of silver, and then her gaze locked on the small, lithe woman with the gun. Her silver hair blew around her in the wind. The rain had lessened, the sky a bit less gray, and Maeve thought she saw the glint of the woman's eyes.

Or that might just have been the gun.

Agatha, she thought.

Agatha, the red hunger replied.

They both remembered the story Rose and Priya had told about the petite assassin. Maeve had listened to the story, and anything Maeve heard, so the death inside her also heard. Agatha had come to kill her, certainly, but would this assassin just shoot her through the head or wait until Maeve got close enough so Agatha could take the death touch from her the way Maeve had taken it from the BMW driver?

Maeve thought the latter.

So did the hunger.

Which meant Agatha would let her get close before she tried for a kill shot. The hunger shifted into the front of her mind, drove Maeve down into a dark little box at the base of her own brain where she could still see what her eyes could see, but her limbs were no longer hers to control. The hunger clawed and burned, but the burning was the fire of a furnace. An engine. She clambered up the rocks, fingertips finding cracks, knees scraping and banging, shoes scrabbling.

Agatha hid most of herself behind a stone slab, leaning out, arms steadied so that she could take aim. The little killer radiated confidence, so sure of her aim and her willingness to pull the trigger that even the uncanny speed and agility of Maeve's ascent hardly seemed to rattle her. Until it did. Agatha blinked and wiped rain from her eyes, furrowed her brow and resettled her aim, and Maeve could see the moment when she understood there was more than sickness here, more than just the germs bred in a lab. Impossibly, Maeve quickened her ascent and saw a ripple of fear in Agatha's eyes.

She pulled the trigger out of fear instead of precision. Defending herself instead of attacking. It threw her off, just slightly, and Maeve's speed did the rest. A bullet grazed her left hip, carved a bloody furrow, but then she lunged the final ten feet. Agatha squeezed off three more shots, but she did it while in motion. The killer tried to get out of the way of Maeve's scraped and bleeding hands, and none of her shots struck home.

The rest of the bullets never left her gun.

Maeve clapped her hands on either side of Agatha's face and rode her down onto the rocks, straddling her. The killer tried to bring her gun around, even knowing she had only seconds to live, and Maeve batted it from her hand, bent and kissed Agatha oh so gently on the mouth. As Agatha began to cough and her throat turned black and blisters boiled up on her skin, Maeve pushed the woman's silver hair away from her face and watched her die.

Inside, she cried.

Inside, she screamed.

But not really. She wanted to grieve and to feel disgust for the way the presence that had taken up residence inside her reveled in Agatha's death, but the infusion of life felt too good. She shuddered with the pleasure of it, suffused with a sense of well-being, a lightness and a strength she had not felt even a minute before.

As she sat astride the woman, there in a cleft in the side of the gorge, the red hunger subsided. Maeve felt its presence fade, and she regained control over her body. She still trembled with the aftereffects of the meal she'd just had, but now she trembled in horror as well.

A sob escaped her and she hung her head, eyes closed, not wanting to move but not wanting to look at the woman she'd just murdered.

Drowning in self-loathing, she heard voices shouting and she remembered the others. Rose and Priya. Whoever the fuck Walker might be.

Maeve climbed off the corpse of the killer and turned to look down into the gorge. The others had stopped three-quarters of the way down. Walker had his gun aimed up toward her, though Maeve couldn't imagine he could reliably target her from that distance. She glanced up at the rim of the gorge, only twenty feet above her head. Much closer to her than her sister and the rest. It would have been so easy for her to go up instead of down, to keep running, but where would she run?

No. Her only hope waited below. There were people who still loved her, though she didn't know how that was possible. If she kept running, someone else would find her soon enough. Walker had told her that many of them would be like Agatha, they would want her dead or not care if she lived. For whatever reason, he seemed to want to keep her alive. Treat her fairly. *Help* her.

"Maeve, please!" Rose shouted up to her.

"Hurry!" Walker called, his voice carrying. "They'll be coming."

Maeve stiffened. They should do something to hide the body, make it harder for the Blackcoats to track them, but Walker was right. All those gunshots, and now the shouting, would quickly bring other hunters to this place. It might be moments from now, or minutes, but it would be soon. They didn't have time to delay.

It would have been better if she could have left the others, gone off on her own again, but right now her best chance lay with them. Her only choice was down.

She moved swiftly, but not as swiftly as before. The red hunger still lurked within her, but in truth it had become her. In her bones. In her blood. In her guts and her heart and lungs. In her hands most of all.

Maeve felt the strength in herself, the ravenous need, the cunning and betrayal, and wondered if she might no longer be human.

But if not that, then what?

She clambered down the side of the gorge. The others waited at the bottom, warily watching. A moment before, Maeve had felt sated, trembling with satisfaction. Now, already, it had begun to fade. As she descended toward those upturned faces, she felt a twinge of hunger return.

20

Walker steadied his aim, moving the gun to track Maeve as she scrambled down the wall of the gorge. The others had frozen, and Walker didn't blame them. Over the years, he had seen many impossible things, he'd been trapped underground in a place so steeped in evil that he'd inhaled it with every breath, but the way Maeve moved now, swift and agile, limbs thrusting at unnatural angles . . . seeing that made him want to run. If it unsettled him so deeply, he could imagine what it did to those who loved her.

His aim didn't waver.

"Stop right there, Maeve," he called when she was about twenty feet above them.

One hand on an outthrust rock, she pirouetted, her left foot barely catching a foothold. Maeve looked down at him as if the others had vanished. Her eyes narrowed. They had a red tint that hadn't been there before. It might have been a thin caul of blood covering her eyes, or it might have been the eyes themselves.

She hung there, staring at his gun, and waited.

The last of Agatha's screams still lingered in his head. Rose and Priya seemed frozen, waiting to see what would happen next.

"Circle around us," Walker told Maeve, gesturing with the barrel of the gun. "Get to the floor of the gorge as fast as you can and then back away. Give us room to come down. If you get too close to anyone, I won't have a choice. You get me?"

"I get you," Maeve said. But it no longer sounded like Maeve. Her voice had a low, whispery quality, the way a snake might sound if it learned human language.

Maeve scuttled around to their left and kept descending.

Walker glanced at the others. "All that noise is going to bring people running. We've got minutes, but probably not too many. So move it, but don't let Maeve anywhere near you."

Priya and Rose went quickly. Unlike Maeve, they were still on Walter's Descent, and the trail became easier to traverse near the bottom. The rain had subsided to a drizzle, but they were still soaked and the rocks were slippery as they hustled.

Priya still held her left arm close to her body. Pale from blood loss and shock, exhausted, she struggled to stay upright. Rose steadied her as best she could. Walker lowered his weapon but kept glancing down at Maeve to make sure she had followed instructions.

"That's not her," Priya said. "You don't know her. That's not Maeve."

"She's sick. Infected," Walker said, pretending he didn't know what Priya meant. They had both seen Maeve's eyes and heard her voice. The changes in her were obvious even to someone who'd only met her today.

"Whatever she does, you can't kill her. Don't shoot her," Priya said.

Rose pushed the wet hair away from her eyes and looked at her. "I know you're trying to help, babe, but please . . ." She shot a hard look at Walker. "If she tries to kill one of us, you shoot her."

"Rose," Priya said, "you don't have to—"

Rose kept her gaze locked on Walker. "You saw her. She's something savage now. Rabid. This morning . . . she didn't know what she was doing. Now she does. If she comes for us, you stop her."

Walker gave her a single nod. As they started moving again, he watched the way Maeve waited for them at the bottom and he wondered. She moved jerkily, pacing back and forth like some kind of junkie in need of a fix. Priya said the woman down there wasn't

Maeve, and Walker couldn't escape the feeling that in some vital way, that might be true.

A dozen feet from the end of the trail, he lifted his weapon again, tracking Maeve.

"Start walking," he told her. "Lead the way. Find a cave or some kind of shelter. We need cover as fast as possible."

So many things buzzed in his head. General Wagner had people crawling all over the mountain. Agatha had been a solo operator. The two dirt bikers had been, what, Israeli or Russian? Then there were the people in the Jeep that David Boudreau had told him about. No sign of them yet. But all the noise from the gorge would draw Wagner's Blackcoats at the very least, and he had to assume his little group was running out of time to find a place to hide.

Alena would have gotten his message from Joel by now. She would be doing her best to get him evac from this disaster, get Maeve safely off the mountain. But Walker had been stranded before, and he knew he couldn't count on the cavalry arriving in time. He had to think of something.

The Moonglow River churned along the bottom of the gorge. They'd come down the west wall and emerged on the wide swath of inhospitable terrain that ran beside the river. The moment Walker reached bottom, he picked up his pace.

"Keep your eyes open," he said to everyone, including himself.

Maeve had turned south toward town and gotten a good thirty paces ahead of him, but he wasn't worried about her running. When she had murdered Agatha, she had been much nearer to the top of the gorge than the bottom. If she had wanted to run, she could have done it then.

He hurried after her, anyway, wanted to keep her in sight. Quick glances at the rim of the gorge, both ahead and behind, made him feel more like a target than ever. There were a thousand spots up there that a halfway decent rifle shot could have taken any one of them out. He listened for a helicopter or an engine. The Blackcoats had to have heard the gunshots, if not the screams. They would be coming soon.

He hoped Rose and Maeve were right about finding a place to hide down here. Massive stone slabs lay scattered along the bottom of the gorge like some ancient giant had been playing with blocks and forgotten to pick them up. In some places, hiking trails ran along the rough terrain of the riverbank, and in others they had to clamber over the slabs. Walker hesitated the first time he reached a place where he needed both hands, unwilling to be without his gun, but the urgency thrumming in his bones left him no choice. He holstered the weapon again and kept going.

The river rushed past, swift and deep, no more than forty feet across here. They could swim if they had to, but they'd be dragged downstream a ways before they reached the other side. Walker glanced over his shoulder. Priya's injury made it more difficult for her, forcing Rose to lag behind to help her over the obstacles in their path. Walker wished he could speed them along, but there was nothing to be done about it.

The gorge turned slightly leftward. Walker skidded down a slab at the water's edge. His left boot splashed into the river, but he caught himself just in time to prevent a full dunking. Both hands on the rock, he scrabbled up and over.

A deep shadow to his right drew his attention, and he saw the cave there, narrow but dark enough that he couldn't be sure how far it went back. Once he'd noticed that one, he realized there were others. The way the glacier had left these stones piled in its wake, thousands of years ago, it had created plenty of gaps.

Why hadn't Maeve stopped to investigate them? Why hadn't she shown Walker there were places to hide?

He slid down the opposite side of a slab and hit a narrow trail of tufted grass and weeds. His gaze ticked up to the rim of the gorge again, his heart pounding, skin prickling with the vulnerability of their exposure. The rain had all but stopped now, and for the first time he realized the sky had begun to clear. He hadn't noticed because the breaks in the clouds revealed not blue but the slate shade of dusk, sliding toward the indigo of sundown. The storm might be passing, but night was about to fall. Somehow the hour had grown late without him realizing. It must be nearly eight o'clock by now.

That could be good, in that they would be more difficult to track at night.

Or bad, in that they could easily fall and shatter bones on the stone slabs inside the gorge.

Shit. Shit, shit, shit.

Too many thoughts in his head.

He came to another huge slab. Walker glanced back at the others, saw them sliding down the last big stone he'd mounted, Rose still helping Priya, and he leaped upward, scaling the slab ahead. He scanned the trail ahead, the stones, the edge of the river.

No sign of Maeve.

"Down here, Walker."

He turned toward her voice, nearly lost balance again. His boots skidded and he dropped to his knees on the slab, just managing to keep from falling. On hands and knees, he stared into the shadowed crevice between the gorge wall and the slab beneath him.

Red eyes stared back at him. Bleeding red, rimmed with sickly black. If she hadn't been standing in the shadows, face etched with sorrow and regret, Maeve Sinclair would have looked like a murder victim instead of a killer.

Walker dared not move. She only had to reach up and touch his face and the countdown to his hideous death would begin. He wanted to reach for his gun. Felt its weight against his abdomen, handle jutting into his stomach.

She must have seen the fear in his eyes, because she took a step backward and spread her arms, hands out at her sides like Christ on the cross.

"Go ahead," she said. "Draw your gun. *Please.*"

The way she said that last word broke his heart. He had never heard such desperation and surrender in his life. She might have been nearly thirty years old, but the pain in her made him think of her father, Ted, and that made Walker think of his own son.

Charlie, he thought, wishing he had never taken this assignment. Wishing Alena had never called. With staggering clarity, it came to him that someday he would make a promise to his son, break it, and run off on an assignment from which he would never return. All Charlie's life, Walker had been disappointing him, but the idea that he might not be there to field the resulting resentment, that he might leave Charlie with no way to resolve his righteous anger, broke him.

Thinking of that ultimate abandonment, he felt a kind of fear he'd never known. His breath hitched in his chest. He raised his hands, sat back on his haunches, and stared into those bleeding red eyes as he drew his gun and took aim at Maeve Sinclair's heart.

This woman, who exuded death, smiled at him as if he'd just given her the sweetest gift.

"There's a cave down here," she said in her own voice, not that serpent's whisper that had come from her lips before. A cough erupted from her chest, but she calmed it and smiled again, black blood smeared on her mouth. "We can hide here."

Was she herself again, now that she'd taken Agatha's life? And if so . . . for how long?

Walker glanced to his right, heard Priya and Rose talking quietly as they began to scale the last slab, back the way Walker had come. Priya sounded desperate, worried she wouldn't be able to make it much farther.

"Before they join us," Maeve said, drawing his attention back to her red grimace of a smile, "I want you to listen to me."

Walker gave a tilt of his chin. "Go on."

"I'm still me, right now," Maeve said, her voice cracking. "But I'm . . . I'm not alone in here, Walker. There's something else. I thought it was the disease at first. It's so strong, I get so feverish and disoriented, so I thought it was just that. But it's more than that. I get so hungry, like it's tearing me apart inside. You have no idea, Walker. Oh, my God, it feels . . ."

She became lost in the memory of that feeling for a moment, and Walker felt like he might puke. What the hell had the bastards at Garland Mountain created? What had General Wagner set loose?

Walker exhaled. "Maeve?"

She wiped at her mouth. Swallowed hard, visibly. "If I can't control it, you'll know. I'll be . . . different. Like when I went after Agatha. If there's any chance I'm going to hurt my sister, you shoot me."

Walker frowned. Rose had said the same thing, but Priya had been the one to argue that Maeve didn't know what she was doing. "What about Priya?"

The smile twisted the corners of Maeve's mouth. She looked as if she might scream or laugh or both. She had said she was in control of herself, but Walker could see that had been a lie. This thing inside of her might not be holding the reins at the moment, but she must have been barely keeping it down.

"If you let me hurt my sister, I'll make sure to kill you next."

"Fair enough," Walker said.

To his right, Rose helped Priya across a bit of grassy trail beside the river, and they reached the massive slab atop which Walker knelt. Night had deepened. They'd be able to see Walker from that spot, but Maeve would still be hidden from them until they crested the slab.

"We can't stay out here in the open," Walker said. "Get inside the cave. I'll bring the others in."

"Okay," Maeve said, backing away, turning toward what he now saw was a gap between the next slab and the wall of the gorge. In the gloom, he could see that inside the cave, the floor sloped downward.

Maeve stopped and looked back at him. "Once we're hidden away, I need to ask you something."

Walker put his legs over the side of the slab and began to skid down after her. "Why don't you just ask me now?"

Maeve stood just inside the darkness. Only her hands and face were visible to him, her eyes narrowed. When she spoke again, he worried there might have been a hint of that snake's hiss in her voice.

"Have you ever read Poe's 'The Masque of the Red Death'?"

Walker said he had. Then Priya was right behind him, on the slab where Walker had perched only moments before.

Maeve's eyes gleamed red in the darkness. "Good," she whispered. "I hope that will make this easier."

She retreated into the shadows of the cave and was gone.

Walker had no choice but to follow.

* * *

Rue Crooker sat in the corner booth in the shadows at the back of the Candlelight Inn, wondering if anyone could hear their conversation. *Whisper*, she thought, studying Kat Isenberg. They spoke softly enough, she supposed, and the booth felt isolated, hidden away like the kind of table gangsters would choose in an old mob movie. Still, the conversation itself made her feel as if every ear in the place must be tilted toward them.

"You're talking about mythology," Rue said, brows knitted. "Folktales."

"I'm not saying this right," Isenberg replied. She let out a long breath. "History's a distillation, okay? Everything we know as 'facts' where history is concerned is just a distillation of information taken from a billion different sources. Artifacts and written records are a part of that, and we assume they're reliable, but think about evidence in a criminal case. Witness testimony is not always reliable. Even someone's journal recounting events is tainted by their personal perspective. Now add hundreds or thousands of years of distance between the writing of that journal and its discovery. How reliable is that journal now?"

Rue leaned over the table, picking nervously at the edges of the coaster beneath her beer glass, and spoke just loudly enough for Isenberg to hear her over the old Amy Winehouse song pumping out of the overhead speakers.

"You're saying history books are no different from a teenage girl's diary?"

Isenberg's nostrils flared with anger. "That is not what I said, Dr. Crooker."

Rue held up both hands. "I'm sorry. That came out as flippant, and it wasn't meant to. I understand what you're saying, and I don't disagree."

Mollified, Isenberg went on. "The point is that mythology is one of the things that intersects with history. Folklore, legend, and let's not forget religion. Actual events blur into myth on every level, including personal myth, the way so-called heroes and monarchs self-mythologize, even today. Maybe there was a guy named Jesus who walked on water or turned water into wine, or maybe not. Maybe Vlad Tepes really had visiting diplomats' hats nailed to their heads if they didn't remove them in his presence, or maybe not. Maybe JFK and Bobby Kennedy had regular three-ways with Marilyn Monroe, or maybe not. You following me?"

Rue smiled. "More or less. But none of those things comes close to what you're talking about. Unless you want to talk about Vlad Tepes being a vampire. That's more in line with—"

Isenberg pointed at her. "How do you know he wasn't? Truly. How do you know?"

Rue shrugged. "I guess I don't."

"I've seen things you wouldn't believe," she went on. "Including some files from an assignment your friend Walker was involved with in Ecuador or Guatemala or somewhere. I can't remember which. The point is, ask Walker about bloodsucking monsters who can't stand sunlight."

Rue rolled her eyes. "You've gotta be fucking kidding me."

The group at the nearest table grew hushed and shifted a bit, and Rue realized she'd been too loud. The two of them waited a few seconds for the susurrus of voices around them to return to its former dull roar, and then Rue leaned forward again, hands around her sweating beer glass.

"Can you just get to it, please? How did we get here? What is going on at the lab? How do we keep anyone else from dying?"

Isenberg exhaled. "I can't answer that last one. But maybe you're right. I need to back up." She took a long gulp of beer and steadied herself before continuing.

"The moment all of this turns on is the vanishing of an entire civilization in the Indus Valley, around 1500 B.C.E. In a couple of ancient cities in what would now be Pakistan, comparatively advanced civilization just stopped cold, as if one day everyone in the region decided to wander off into the wilderness and died."

Rue cocked her head. "You know they died?"

"We do," Isenberg said quietly, glancing around to make sure they weren't overheard. "Four years ago, we found them."

"Holy shit," Rue whispered.

"There are coded files on this at Garland Mountain," Isenberg said. "DARPA has them, too. I'm going to guess Walker's boss knows all of this by now. There are written records, clay and stone tablets discovered with the mass graves in the Indus Valley that tell the story. It started with a builder called Pandya Ko. He was digging clay for bricks and cut himself on something that gave him an infection."

Rue nodded. This, at least, sounded like science.

Isenberg exhaled. Hesitated. "I'm playing this through in my head," she said. "You aren't going to believe any of this until you see the files at the lab. If I can get you in."

"You'd risk that?"

Isenberg shrugged. "I'm not sure what other choice there is. If someone doesn't stop them, this is going to get bigger and so much worse." She closed her eyes as if she couldn't look at Rue while she continued her story. "The basics? Pandya Ko heard voices in his head. Or one voice, anyway. The infection in his blood spread and he grew sicker, and then he touched his sister, who had come to care for him, and she died."

"Sounds familiar."

Isenberg opened her eyes. "Yeah. But try this part. Pandya Ko said the voice in his head came from the god of death. That it had been born in the blood of 'the first war,' and thousands had worshipped it and killed in its name."

Rue stared at her. "You say that as if you believe it."

"You haven't seen the tablets. Read the translations. I'm not saying I believe it, but Pandya Ko did, and so did the village elder who executed him and who then acquired the same killing touch. That village elder, who went mad with disease and hunger and told all who would listen that he had to feed the death god. The name he gave it in his own language, on those tablets, translates to *Red Hands*."

"Project: Red Hands."

Isenberg nodded. "Exactly."

Rue slid lower in her chair, staring at her beer. She picked up the glass, took a small sip, and then followed that with a much larger one, downing half the glass.

"There's more?" she asked.

"A hell of a lot more," Isenberg confirmed. "The mystery of all those people vanishing, though of course they didn't vanish. Red Hands passed from person to person—there are six named in the story—over the course of weeks. It spread so much and so fast that whole populations fled into the mountains, and Red Hands followed. The hunger grew and the sickness spread. The story ends with conjecture. Whoever carved out this history in that ancient language believed the host basically imploded from the infection's hunger. From its need. Hundreds of people died, maybe thousands, as quickly as if an asteroid had impacted Earth, only it did no damage to the landscape. Everyone just dropped dead."

"Ashes, ashes, we all fall down," Rue rasped. "Jesus. This is what we're dealing with?"

"So it seems."

Rue shook her head. "It makes no sense. Something like this doesn't just vanish from the world and then resurrect itself centuries later. It's not like there was a vaccine for it, and then idiots decided not to vaccinate their kids. This thing was gone."

"Not gone," Isenberg said. "Just buried. Dormant. And we . . ." She paled, had to breathe through her nose for a few seconds as if she fought the urge to vomit. "We didn't just dig it up by accident. We found the tablets in 1997, and we've been looking for it ever since. Not just the remains of someone who'd died from being touched by a host but the active bacterial contagion that infected the first one. A research team in Greenland located that—among other killer bacteria—over a year ago, a place where we believe a similar but much older 'meltdown' occurred, buried under the ice. Oscar Hecht was a colleague of mine. The project was his. I noticed his behavior changing, we all did, but we thought it was just overwork. He put a lot of pressure on himself, and a lot came down from above as well."

The two of them fell quiet. Rue felt a chill settle deep into her bones. She thought the feeling would fade after a few seconds, but it lingered as she sat there, thinking about an ancient world where such a thing as a death god could exist. Not a god, perhaps, but some impossible hybrid of human and disease. Infectious bacteria were alive, after all, and the driving force of that life was to endure, to bloom into contagion.

Like all life, bacteria only wanted to propagate more of their species.

To infect.

And a deadly contagion existed only to kill.

"Sentient, malevolent disease," Rue said quietly. "That's not possible."

"You prefer 'death god'?" Dr. Isenberg lifted her beer to take a sip, but her hands were shaking so badly she had to use both of them to set the glass down again. "You can call it what you like. Believe whatever your science or religion allows. But it's real. And it's out there."

Rue put both hands flat on the table, steadying herself. "You know what this sounds like, right? Someone able to walk across a battlefield or through a village, just touching people and they drop dead?"

"Of course I do," Isenberg replied. "Poe became part of our research."

Hard as it was for Rue to wrap her mind around the history Isenberg had shared, this went a step too far. She had first read Edgar Allan Poe's fiction while in college. Her father had loved early American authors. Rue had tried reading Hawthorne and Melville in high school and been so bored that twice she had fallen asleep with her face holding her place in the book. Her drool had caused the pages of *Moby-Dick* to stick together, which was fine because she had never attempted to read it again.

She'd liked Poe, though, at least enough so that she could have an interesting conversation with her father about his writing. They'd always had so few interests in common that it made for a nice change, prompting her to delve further into the author's work. Her father had died two weeks before she'd graduated from college, and after that, she had never read anything by Poe again.

But she remembered his tale about wealthy nobility partying their asses off in seclusion, walled away from the rest of the world while the Great Plague ravaged Europe.

Isenberg kept glancing toward the door. She checked the clear plastic watch on her wrist, radiating urgency and unease.

"We have a lot of theories," she said. "We've discovered evidence to support some of them. For instance, we believe the implosion of the final host mentioned on those tablets led to some kind of sporophyte vegetation growing up inside the body's remains. We've found traces that support this theory. Spores might have blown anywhere or been carried by rodents."

"Rats," Rue said, seeing where the theory must be headed. "You think you can trace the plague back to this source with nothing but a single artifact as evidence?"

Isenberg slid her beer to the middle of the table, done with it and apparently ruffled by Rue's tone. "Who said we only had a single artifact?"

"And Poe? You have evidence to back that up?"

Isenberg faltered. She glanced away, then abruptly began to slide from the booth.

"Dr. Isenberg," Rue began, reaching out a hand to stop her. She needed this woman—not just her information but her insight into Garland Mountain Labs. If she was going to be able to do anything to help Ted and his surviving children, Rue couldn't let Isenberg just walk away.

But the woman fixed her with a hard look, flinching from her touch.

"The Poe connection is more than us fantasizing. We're not inventing things that aren't there," Isenberg said quietly. "It's fiction, obviously, a story. But like so many other stories, the author based it on something out of real life, a tale he'd heard or a piece of history he'd run across. A story of the era of the plague."

"How can you know that?" Rue asked.

"We didn't," Isenberg replied. There were shadows beneath her eyes, haunted by memories. "Oscar Hecht told us. He had . . . I guess you'd call them *visions*. And that voice in his head. Whispers about a time when death became a human thing that walked on two legs and hungered for the lives of others. You think I don't know how crazy this sounds? You think—"

"I was there," Rue said quietly, hoping her low voice would quiet Isenberg's rising tone. "I watched Hecht get out of the car. I saw him touch people and saw how ugly their deaths were. I don't think I can make myself believe Red Hands is some kind of prehistoric deity, but Poe's Red Death being some kind of parable about an infection that kills on contact and drives the host to madness? I saw it with my own eyes. The question isn't whether it exists; the question is: What the hell do we do about it?"

Dr. Isenberg stood beside the booth, there in the shadows at the back of the Candlelight Inn, and hung her head. "That's what we all want to know. It's all we've been working on. Bringing Maeve Sinclair off the mountain is one thing, but making sure it doesn't spread further is—"

"You're serious."

Isenberg stared at her. "What?"

Rue narrowed her eyes. "Your bosses were developing this for a reason. It's what DARPA does. Your research was about finding the best way to use Red Hands to kill U.S. enemies. However this ends, you know that will still be their plan."

The knowledge darkened the shadows on Isenberg's face. "Whatever research I've done, it's always been meant to keep innocent people safe, not get them killed."

Rue wanted to call her out, remind her that there were innocent people everywhere, not just in her home state or country, but now was not the time.

"Get me into Garland Mountain," Rue said. "Let's see what we can do to stop all of this and stop them from killing anyone else."

Isenberg nodded, but Rue knew neither of them really believed the killing had come to an end.

21

The assholes in the Jeep spoke German. Maybe it wasn't fair to call them *assholes*, but given the day Leon had been having, anyone who made it more difficult qualified as an asshole in his book. Exhausted, hungry, soaked to the gills, he forgot nearly everything he had ever been taught about stealth. Still, somehow, he managed to get within forty feet of the Jeep without tipping the Germans off to his presence.

It surprised him, hearing them speak German. He had expected Israeli Mossad or Russians. Any outsiders who were already in the mountains searching for Maeve Sinclair before the quarantine had taken full effect had to have responded immediately when the video of the parade massacre had first gone viral. That meant only individuals or agencies who would see the video and understand its implications and who could get someone there quickly enough to slip into the woods before the flyovers and patrols above and around the mountain. He wondered how anyone thought they would get the woman out, even if they could find her, but that wasn't his problem.

BND, he thought. The German spy agency was so well organized, so damned smooth, that they hardly left a trace. When things turned ugly and violent, or diplomats died mysteriously, the world thought CIA or Russian FSB or Mossad, even MI6, but BND mostly kept their heads down, their operations quiet and efficient, and their reputation intact.

They're our allies, Leon thought. It troubled him more than a little. Here was a cell of BND agents operating on U.S. soil. There were three of them in the Jeep—two men and a woman—and they were trying to determine their next move. The engine idled, quiet for a Jeep, and the female agent held a tablet in her hand, tapping the screen as the two men argued in low voices. Leon didn't speak German, but he heard Maeve Sinclair's name, and that was all he needed to know.

When the Jeep started moving again, he gripped his weapon. He couldn't let them get to Maeve before the Blackcoats, but he wouldn't be able to keep up with the vehicle for long. The question was whether he could kill all three of them before they put his lights out. He steadied himself, checked to see how many ammunition magazines he had, and started to slip through the trees, waiting for the sound of the engine revving.

Instead, the Jeep rumbled quietly as the driver pulled it into the trees. Branches snapped, the vehicle bumped over some rocks, and soon it was parked among the trees just off the trail, not hidden but not inviting investigation. The rain had slowed to a light sprinkle, not loud enough to cover the noise of an attack, so Leon crouched and watched from cover as the Germans abandoned the Jeep, checked their weapons, and started to hike through the woods. They had some intel about Maeve's location, Leon realized, and wherever she was, they couldn't bring the Jeep in after her.

That was good.

As long as they were on foot, he could keep up with them. He would wait for the moment with the best chance of taking all three of them out, and then he would kill them before they could reach her. His job wasn't worth dying for. Being a mercenary was far from the same thing as serving his country in uniform. But he understood just enough about the contagion inside Maeve Sinclair to know that he didn't trust anyone with it beyond the Department of Defense. And maybe not even them.

The Germans set off through the woods.

Leon followed.

The gun in his hand felt heavier than before.

Inside the cave, Walker felt much more vulnerable than when they'd been out in the open. Even at the bottom of the gorge, they were safer than they were down here in the dark with Maeve—or whatever malevolence lurked inside her.

You don't believe that story, he told himself. *The Red Death. Sentient murder god. Living infection. You cannot possibly believe that.*

The way Rose and Priya had looked at Maeve when she struggled to express the torment within her, the hunger tearing her apart, Walker knew they didn't believe her, either. Rose had suggested mental illness, a complete psychotic break to go along with the contagion and fever raging inside her. But the difference between Walker and the others hiding in that cave was that he had met evil before. He'd seen the anguish of those who'd done the worst thing imaginable without any control of their actions.

He'd seen sin and he'd faced monsters.

Walker did not want to believe the things Maeve had told them, but unlike the others, he had no reason to reject those claims. Sherlock Holmes had said that once one eliminated the impossible, whatever remained, no matter how improbable, must be the truth. In Walker's experience, the things Maeve claimed were a full and terrifying explanation of everything.

He didn't want to believe any of it, but he did.

Which was why he put Maeve at the back of the cave. After sharing her secrets and her theories, she had grown unsettlingly quiet. She had stayed quiet while Rose had very carefully bound her wrists with a zip tie from Walker's pack. Priya had spotlighted her with his penlight—the only illumination they had in here—and Walker had kept his gun aimed at her, but Maeve had not resisted.

Sometimes she seemed to be talking to herself, as if frustrated with their reaction to her story. But then even that noise faded, and now Walker could only hear the rasp of her breathing, and he wondered how much of what she had said was something more than fever and nightmare. He had seen two versions of Maeve with his own eyes, and it worried him that he couldn't tell which of them might be ascendant right now.

Rose was at the entrance to the cave, listening for voices or gunshots or any sign that they'd been discovered. Walker had set the penlight down on the rocks, aimed at Maeve, so he could watch her out of the corner of his eye while he tended Priya's wound.

It didn't look good.

The bleeding might have stopped by now, except Priya had continued to exert herself, climbing down Walter's Descent, then scrambling through the gorge. Walker used additional strips of the shirt they'd torn up earlier and kept fresh pressure on the wound, glancing at Maeve from time to time. She had remained silent as he worked on Priya. The penlight illuminated just enough for him to make out her body, propped against the wall of the cave. Her shoulders were slightly hunched and the glow of the light cast strange shadows across her face, but her eyes had a dark gleam that did not come from the flashlight.

Priya moaned as he released the pressure he'd been holding on the wound. Walker tossed aside the bloody wad of shirt fabric and reached for the penlight. He hesitated a moment, not wanting to leave Maeve in the dark for fear that when he shone the light on her again, she might have vanished. Or moved nearer to him. He shook it off and turned the light on the wound, leaning closer.

"Looks like the bleeding has stopped again. That's good. Let's try not to rip it open again."

Priya shivered as the nighttime chill of the cave settled in. Walker had a light sweatshirt he would offer, but not until the wound had more time to close up.

"You're wasting time," Priya said. "We can't stay here."

Walker took the penlight, barely hearing her, and turned it toward Maeve. Had her lips curled back into the merest suggestion of a sneer? Walker thought they had.

"You hearing me?" Priya wheezed. "We have to move."

Walker cocked his head, listening for movement from the front of the cave. Rose would shout if trouble came, but he didn't like the stillness. He hoped Rose was just allowing herself a few minutes to rest and recover.

"We need more time," Walker said.

Priya needed more than the rest of them, but Walker's main concern was what he would encounter when they finally reached Jericho Falls again. Alena might be trying to wrest control of the SRC from General Wagner, but that kind of internecine conflict never ended well. The best thing for Maeve, and for all of them, might be to wait it out and see how things stood when the conflict between Alena and the general concluded.

"We've got till morning, if that," Priya said. "You know by daybreak they'll be down here, sweeping the whole gorge with soldiers, helicopters. We're dead if we wait that long."

Walker nodded slowly, penlight in hand, turning it all over in his head. Priya's thoughts echoed his own, but he hadn't wanted to lay it out so bluntly. He had not counted on the light-headed young woman with the bullet wound and no military experience to decipher just how desperate their situation had become.

"I'm working on it," he told Priya. "You should rest while you can."

She had dark circles beneath her eyes, and even in the darkness of the cave, she looked pale and sickly. Not sick, not yet. But she was in rough shape.

Quiet laughter unfurled in the darkness, echoing off the walls like the hiss of serpents.

Walker turned the penlight on Maeve. When the light hit her, she didn't blink or flinch, didn't close her eyes against the glare. She tilted her head, birdlike, studying him. When she spoke, her voice sounded different. New.

Not new, he thought. *She sounds old.* Her voice held the rasp of crumbling parchment paper. A shudder went through him. Walker had experience in the presence of malevolence, but that only made the fear cut deeper.

"You should set her free," Maeve rasped. "All that noise you made, the gunfire, the shouting . . . they're out there hunting you now. Hunting me. Put me out for them to find. I'll touch them instead of you."

Walker felt his throat go dry. The voice hardly seemed to come from Maeve's lips. It was as if the darkness itself were speaking. He raised his gun hand, made sure she could see the barrel as he aimed again at her chest. If he'd had any doubt before that something else had taken up residence inside this woman, that doubt had vanished.

"We're not going anywhere."

Priya shifted, tried to sit up, and groaned with the effort. "Maeve, no. We won't let you put yourself—"

"That's not Maeve," Walker interrupted, penlight and gun both steady.

Priya swore. "You can't tell me you believe—"

"It's not her," Walker said. He glared at Maeve.

She only smiled and tilted her head the other direction as if he were life's greatest curiosity.

"Maeve?" Priya asked, her voice softer, weaker, less hopeful.

Keeping both gun and light on Maeve, Walker shuffled backward toward the front of the cave.

"Rose," he whispered hoarsely, hoping his voice would carry. "Come here a minute."

Until he heard the scuff of her shoes on the floor of the cave, he wasn't sure she had heard him. But then Rose appeared, hands sliding over the cave walls to either side, guiding herself through the darkness toward the glow from that penlight. The only light they had.

The light flickered. Walker shot a dark look at Maeve, wondering if the thing inside her could be responsible.

"I heard voices," Rose said. "I think someone passed by, but it's quiet out there now. They're moving fast, if that was them, and it almost had to be, don't you think?"

He did. The Blackcoats were making a sweep, but unless they brought in a ton of heavy equipment, huge lighting rigs, they wouldn't be able to even find, never mind search, every crevice and cave until morning. Even if they had brought thermal imaging equipment with them, it would take hours.

"I felt them," Maeve said. "There were five of them. All very strong."

Rose's eyes widened. In the glow of the penlight, Walker saw the way she looked at her sister, as if trying to figure out what Maeve had become and how she could destroy that monster without destroying her sister. Walker did not want to be the one to tell her such thoughts were impossible.

"Not sure if you can hear me in there, Maeve," he said now that they were all together. "We're going to wait one hour. It'll be darker and drier by then, and with any luck, the Blackcoats will have made camp. They'll be waiting for sunrise, when they can be more thorough."

He looked at Rose. "We can't still be here in the morning."

"Where do we go?" she asked, glancing around the cave in confusion. "In the dark, the rocks will be hard as hell to navigate. Someone's going to smash their skull open or break a leg, at least. Priya's in no condition to make the trek down the gorge to town, never mind that none of us wants to be out there in the dark with Maeve."

"That's not very nice," Maeve said, almost sounding like herself, just for a moment.

"Our choices are limited," Walker told her. "I'd rather take risks than wait for an ugly certainty."

Rose glared at him. "You called your boss. You said help would come."

"I still think it will. I just don't know if it will come in time."

Priya shifted. "So what's your plan? No offense, Walker. You look pretty strong, but you couldn't carry me that far even on a paved road."

"I'm not going to carry you," Walker said. "The river is. It's going to carry all of us."

Rose gaped at him. "You're out of your mind. Priya can't use her left arm. There are huge rocks in the middle of the river and places where it drops off, stretches of white water—"

"No, he's right," Priya said. "Whatever it takes, we can't just wait around."

"We could all die!"

"If we stay here too long, we *will* die. The Blackcoats will kill us." Priya glanced at Maeve. "Or she will."

Rose stared at her sister in despair. "So instead we float down the river with her? Walker can't keep a gun on her if he's halfway drowning."

Maeve began to shift in the glow of the penlight. She bent over, coughing, and moaned. When she glanced up again, a sheen of greasy sweat covered her face. Her eyes, however, had cleared.

"I won't hurt you, Rose," Maeve said, the words coming out as a growl, as if she had to fight to utter every syllable. "If you're afraid I won't be able to help myself, I understand. You should go without me. Go ahead, and I'll follow if I can."

Rose seemed to consider it. Priya said nothing, but it couldn't have been lost on her that Maeve had surfaced long enough to promise never to hurt Rose, but she'd made no such guarantees about the rest of them.

"I'm not going home without you," Rose said at last. "I can't."

"It's settled, then." Walker looked at Rose. "Keep watching the entrance. Listen for trouble. One hour, and we'll go."

She nodded, took one more look at her sister, and stumbled off into the dark. Walker turned the penlight to help light the way for Rose, careful to make sure none of its glow made it out to the cave opening.

Something shifted in the dark, the air inside the cave suddenly heavy, the way it felt just before the sky burst open with rain. His skull hurt and he winced, listened to Priya whisper something about her own pain.

Walker heard Maeve breathing right behind him. Her breath cold on his neck.

In his mind's eye, he could see those pale hands, hideous with plague spots, reaching for his throat. When he turned, the penlight followed, and he found himself inches from her, face-to-face. She exhaled at the same moment he inhaled, taking her sickness into his own lungs. It couldn't be passed that way, he knew that, but still he felt panic race through him, and he thought of Charlie. *I don't need you*, Charlie had said. But Walker needed his son, needed to live, to make it right.

The gun shook in his hand. He cursed himself for being too confident, for having survived horrors he'd thought were worse than this, not understanding that the worst horror would be the one he couldn't come home from.

The barrel of the gun hovered inches from Maeve's forehead, just above the bridge of her nose. He swallowed hard, forced himself to take another breath despite the terror and revulsion.

Her hands were still bound behind her back. Maeve made no effort to turn and touch him or to free herself. Against the wall, Priya called her name, pleaded with her not to kill them. But now Walker saw the anguish in Maeve's eyes and knew she continued to fight the infection inside her, continued to fight the monstrous hunger there.

"If you have to kill me, or if someone else does it," Maeve said, "make sure they burn the body. Leave nothing but ash."

Priya said her name, tried to get her attention, to plead with her to listen.

"I will," Walker said.

Maeve turned from them both and walked deeper into the cave, hands still bound behind her back. When Walker heard her begin to choke and cough and cry, he turned the light away to give her what little privacy he dared.

She cried softly for several minutes before she fell quiet again.

A little while later, the whispery laughter returned.

Walker waited and held tightly to the gun.

ZZ

Rue sat in the passenger seat of Kat Isenberg's old Prius, staring out the window in frustration. She plucked the little comm piece from her ear, tapped it, saw the little light turn green, and slipped it back into place. She'd been trying to reach Walker for the past forty minutes, called a dozen times, but all she could summon up with that phone was a harsh buzzing that sounded only vaguely like a cell phone ring. No answer. No sense at all that Walker knew she was trying to reach him or whether he might still be alive.

Tucked between her legs, in the space between her crotch and the car seat, her own phone vibrated, just once. With the quarantine, cell service had been blocked, but something had gotten through—maybe some kind of emergency notification? It felt like a jolt of reality, a shout-out from her ordinary life—the one that contained her work, her colleagues, her family, and a dating app that she'd been ignoring for weeks. A hole seemed to open beneath her, as if she could sink down through her seat and find herself back in that ordinary life, in a world of familiar things and the beauty of the mundane.

She tugged her cell out from under her thigh and saw a missed call from Ted Sinclair. Ted, whom she'd left at home to sleep and drink and grieve. Her friend, whom she'd abandoned, but only so she could do whatever possible to save him from further grief. The phone shouldn't have worked at all, but she knew half the population of Jericho Falls would still be making attempts to call or text, and folks from outside would be trying to call in. Ted had tried to reach her, and the connection had been made for the millisecond it took to get her phone to ring once before the jamming signal had interrupted.

Rue tried calling back and got nothing—not a buzz or a ring—just the Call Failed notification that had plagued phones all over Jericho Falls since the communication blackout had begun.

She set her cell on the dashboard, but she made no further attempt to call Walker. What would be the point? Either he couldn't answer right now or he wouldn't. Rue had started along her own path, and what happened next did not rely on Ben Walker. She had managed to get a guy named Joel on the phone at the SRC and told him she had a way inside Garland Mountain, that she hoped to help find a way to cure Maeve or at least control her contagion. Rue neglected to mention that it could take years.

"You ready to go?" Dr. Isenberg asked.

They had pulled onto the shoulder of the road, half a mile or so from the turnoff that led to Garland Mountain Labs.

Rue watched her in the dashboard light, this beautiful, brilliant, and deeply troubled woman.

"You sure you're up to this?"

Isenberg smirked. "Not at all. But I worked on Red Hands from the beginning, and a lot of people have died. People I'd see in shops and cafés in Jericho Falls, people who were kind to me and my coworkers and who had no idea what we were doing might kill them. I'm going to carry that for the rest of my life. So you can call this next part just more of me being selfish, I guess. If you and I can help Maeve—either cure her or at least keep her own government from killing her—then I'll do whatever I need to—"

A car whipped past them, so close it nearly scraped the paint off the Prius. Isenberg squeezed the steering wheel and swore to a messiah her faith didn't believe in.

"Fucking asshole!" she added, almost a punctuation.

Rue's heart raced, but before she could join in the righteous flinging of profanity, she spotted the back of the passing car in the glow of Isenberg's headlights. The offender drove a silver Chevy Malibu with *WR*7 as the first three digits of the license plate.

Ted. And there was only one place he could be headed.

"Drive," Rue said. "That was Ted Sinclair. We have to stop him."

Jaw set, hands tight on the wheel, Isenberg tore away from the roadside as fast as the old Prius could carry them. Every pothole made Rue think they were driving an enormous tin can, but the car moved faster than she would have reckoned. It helped that, as fast as Ted had been driving, he didn't realize anyone was following. Isenberg took a curve with reckless abandon, but she kept the car from skidding off the road. Far ahead, the Malibu's taillights flared bright red as Ted slowed to turn down the narrow path that led up to Garland Mountain Labs.

"Shit, go!" Rue snapped.

Isenberg floored it. They were on a straightaway, and it took only seconds for them to catch up to the place where Ted had hit the brakes. The Prius juddered and squeaked as if it might quit on them, but Isenberg managed the turn doing about thirty miles per hour. Rue saw Ted's taillights ahead, realized they'd closed half the distance, that they would be able to catch up to him, and for a heartbeat she felt relief. He'd be at least a little drunk and out of control, and there would be no telling what he might do when he reached the gate. But they could catch him, calm him down, explain the plan to him. *You should have gone to his house, explained it to him already,* she thought, but too late.

Too late in so many ways.

The Prius skidded to the right, the road muddy from the storm. Isenberg spun the steering wheel, but she overcompensated for the skid. The headlights found only trees ahead of them. Rue braced herself, had a moment to wonder if she had an airbag on the passenger side. Isenberg kept her cool, tapped the brakes, straightened out so that the car aimed directly for the trees as if that had been her intention all along. The tires gripped the road again. Isenberg steered back onto the road. The left side of the car thumped through ruts and took out some underbrush. They scraped an oak tree, shattering the driver's-side mirror.

But they were back on the road.

"Holy shit," Isenberg said, her breath ragged. "Holy shit."

Rue blinked, still braced for impact, stunned that they hadn't wrapped around a tree. She exhaled, shaking, and then saw the tail-lights far ahead of them. Isenberg accelerated again, but they had lost their momentum.

"We'll never catch him," Rue said.

She looked at the dashboard. Her cell phone had slid off at some point while they were fishtailing and hoping not to die, and she felt a pang at its absence. It would have done her no good, but she thought of that missed call from Ted. If he had been able to get through to her, this would all have gone so differently.

"Slow down," she said quietly.

Isenberg kept chasing, though she knew she couldn't catch him.

"Kat, stop the car!" Rue said.

The Prius bumped through potholes as Isenberg hit the brakes. The engine gave a little electric sigh as they came to a stop, and Isenberg shot her a confused look.

"What are we doing, Dr. Crooker?"

Rue didn't like the way the woman had said her name, but now wasn't the time to point out that her anger was misplaced.

"We can't catch him. Pull over and we'll sit here for five or ten minutes," she said. "It does us no favors to arrive right behind a guy who is obviously about to make a scene."

Isenberg pulled the car to the side of the road. Rue thought of a lot of ugly ways things could be going up ahead, from Ted ramming his Malibu through the front gates at Garland Mountain to the guards shooting him while he tried to jump the fence.

"How crazy is he right now?" Isenberg asked. "Scale of one to ten?"

As Rue spoke, she felt as if she were betraying her best friend, even though all she wanted was to help him.

"He's a recovering addict and a currently functioning alcoholic."

"Goddamn," Isenberg said.

Rue nodded. "Yeah. My sentiments, too. I'm sure Ted's been drinking. When Oscar Hecht drove into the parade crowd, Ted went up and over the hood. Hell, he went over the whole car. Cracked ribs and more. He's in no shape to fight anyone and no shape to climb fences."

"So you think he's just going to go up and politely ask them not to kill his daughter?" Isenberg said.

Rue didn't hold her tone against her. Isenberg had lost track of the fact that these people were like her family, that Ted might as well be her brother—hell, she loved him more than most people loved their brothers.

She turned in her seat. "Here's how it's going to go. Ted will go up and tilt at windmills. He'll shout and scream and make a scene. But he doesn't own a gun and he'd have no idea where to get one in the middle of all of this, so nobody is going to shoot him. They'll either turn him away or they'll let him into the public part of the complex and have some kind of PR hack sit with him and try to calm him down, reassure him, maybe even attempt to send him away. If they don't let him in, that's bad for us. We might not get in, either, because they'll be extra prickly. But if they let him in—"

"If they let him, he'll be their focus," Isenberg said. She turned to focus on Rue. "Ted flew by before you could tell me what the guy at the SRC said. Maybe now's the time to share?"

They had jumped right into a car chase, so Rue's mind had been elsewhere.

"Right," she said. "The short version is they don't know much, but they know Walker caught up with Maeve. He's also with her sister and others."

Isenberg nodded in relief. "That's good. That's something."

"Yeah. I just wish I could've told Ted that." Rue sighed. "Anyway, there's more. Apparently, there's a tug-of-war going on over how to handle this. The SRC's director is arguing the case in D.C. that it's best to quiet things down and cover them up. Make it disappear without just murdering a bunch of people, which it seems your boss is totally fine with. The good news is that this Joel guy hinted the whole thing may be shut down in an hour or two, but there's another wrinkle."

"The bad news?"

Rue felt queasy, remembering the chill she'd gotten when Joel had shared the last of his thoughts with her. "The general overseeing Project: Red Hands—"

"General Wagner."

Rue nodded. "That guy. There's apparently some doubt in D.C. as to whether he'll obey an order to stand down."

Isenberg shifted the car into gear. "I've been in plenty of meetings with the general, and that wouldn't surprise me at all."

"So where does that leave us?" Rue asked.

"The same place you are every morning when you wake up," Isenberg said, sadness in her eyes. "Hope for the best, and prepare for the worst."

Isenberg pulled back onto the road. She drove as if they were ordinary visitors on an ordinary day. Rue tensed as they approached the front gate but saw no sign of Ted or his Malibu. Isenberg pulled up to the guard booth and rolled her window down.

"Evening, Carlo," she said to the guard, brandishing her ID for him to scan. "I've got a guest tonight. Dr. Crooker from Boston University."

The guard scanned her ID and craned his neck to look inside the car. Rue leaned in so he could get a good view of her, flashing her B.U. identification to make his job a little easier, as if they had nothing to hide.

"Weird time for it, Dr. Isenberg," the guard said.

"On the contrary," Isenberg replied. "We've got a crisis on our hands. I can use all the help I can get."

Rue wanted to ask about Ted, but she knew that was a terrible idea. If he'd made trouble, the question would draw the wrong attention, and if he'd turned off into the woods somewhere along the road and hadn't come up to the gate at all, she'd be sending up a warning flare, so they'd be on the lookout for him.

The guard, Carlo, slid the door to the booth closed and made a call. He turned his back halfway toward them, glancing over his shoulder as he spoke, but in less than a minute he faced forward and slid the door open.

"Go on ahead, Dr. Isenberg. But as you've got a visitor, please park in the visitors' lot, and stay with Dr. Crooker at all times."

Isenberg clucked her tongue. "Even in the public areas?"

"Yes, ma'am."

"That's weird."

The guard tapped a button inside the booth. With a loud buzz, the gates clicked and began to swing open.

"It's a weird night," he said.

Rue held her breath as Isenberg tapped the accelerator. They drove through, and the gates swung closed behind them. Isenberg turned into the visitors' lot, which was vacant except for a familiar silver Chevy Malibu.

"That answers that," Isenberg said as she pulled into a spot and killed the engine.

"It can't be that easy," Rue said.

"Maybe they decided having Ted around could help them if and when they bring his daughter off the mountain."

Rue let that simmer for a moment. She hoped the explanation could be that simple. Was it possible her fear and paranoia about Garland Mountain's hunt for Maeve had been unfounded? Ted had been drinking earlier, but she supposed it was possible he had sobered up by now.

"I guess we'll find out," Rue said.

Isenberg looked at her. "We're not going to breathe a word about Ted Sinclair once we're inside. I know you're worried, but even if they rolled out the red carpet for him—and we both know that's unlikely—you can't let them connect you to him. Not if you want to see the research."

Rue sank back in her seat. "Maybe this was a bad idea. You do this research for a living. It's not likely I'll see anything in it that you haven't already."

"It's not just about that. I'm so immersed in the project that I can't see the forest for the trees right now. Walker wouldn't have asked you to get in touch with me if he didn't think you could be valuable."

Rue laughed softly. "It's not as if he picked me from a pool of biologists available inside the quarantine area."

"True," Isenberg said. She put a hand on Rue's shoulder, locking eyes with her. "He got lucky. People in Walker's job are trained to seize opportunity in the field and to improvise. You were opportunity, and he's improvising. Maybe you're right and you won't see anything that's going to help Maeve or help get this thing under control, but I've got a lot to show you, and if all you can do is pass along what you learn to Walker, that might still help him."

"And Maeve," Rue said, nodding to herself. "And Ted."

Isenberg popped open her door. "Exactly. So are you coming inside?"

Rue stared at Ted's Malibu for a few seconds, wondering. Walker would save Maeve or he wouldn't. Ted would be all right or he wouldn't. People were dying, others were crawling all over a mountain looking to commit murder, and she'd been told the most outrageous story today, been asked to believe something absurd and terrifying. If only she hadn't seen people choke and die with her own eyes, hadn't seen people sicken with plague at the touch of a hand . . . then she would've been able to tell herself it was all a hoax.

But the Sinclairs were like family to her. They had each been kind to her in a world far too short on kindness. Ted loved her. If it had been her being hunted up on that mountain, he would have done the same foolish thing he'd done tonight.

Rue opened her door and stepped out, leaning back in to peer at Dr. Isenberg. "Even if I'm out of my league, curiosity alone is enough to lure me in."

Isenberg climbed out, slammed her door. "Let's go."

Rue fell into step beside her, and they walked together toward the gleaming façade of Garland Mountain Labs.

"Not a word about what curiosity did to the cat?" Rue asked.

Dr. Isenberg kept walking. "I wouldn't dream of it."

The exchange was lighthearted. Meant to be funny.

Neither of them laughed.

23

The gun felt heavy in Walker's hand. He did not want to kill Maeve—had come up here to do the exact opposite—but if she went for Rose or for Priya, he would pull the trigger on her.

Maeve's wrists remained bound behind her, and her back was against the cave wall, but still Rose kept a safe distance between them.

"Look me in the eye and tell me you're still in control," Rose said.

Maeve closed her eyes. "I'm still here," she said. Sweat glistened on her face. The sores on her skin had deepened. The circles under her eyes were so dark they looked like bad mascara the morning after a party gone wrong.

Rose hugged herself as if she were trying to fight the urge to embrace her sister. "That's not the same thing."

"No," Maeve agreed. "It's not. But it's the best I can do without lying to you. All I can say is that if we're going, we should go as soon as we can, and once we're outside, you should all keep your distance."

Walker liked the sound of that. If the hunger inside Maeve wanted to take them, if the disease wanted to infect them, this was not the advice *it* would give.

"Good enough for me," he said.

Priya shuffled forward. Her face looked thinner and older. Pain and blood loss were wearing her down. "We can't expect her to swim with her hands tied."

Walker thought about the thing inside Maeve—the inhuman agility and strength she'd revealed. Maybe it would keep her alive, even with her hands tied, but Priya was right. He couldn't take that chance.

"She'll never get up the rocks out there, either," Rose pointed out.

Walker hadn't let his thoughts get that far, but she was correct.

"Fair enough," he said, studying Maeve, thinking about how to free her without touching her hands. "I've got a little knife in my pack. But you'll have to stay absolutely still. I can't risk—"

Her eyes were dark, her expression humorless. "I've got it," she said. "I just didn't want to give you a reason to shoot me."

With a grunt and a twist of her shoulders, she snapped the bonds from her wrists. They all stared for a few seconds, letting the knowledge sink in—she could have done that whenever she liked. Unnerving as it was, Walker took it as a good sign. If Maeve didn't have at least some control, she would never have stayed bound.

"You first," he said. "Now let's move it."

He motioned with the gun. When Maeve started forward, hunched to avoid bumping her head on the ceiling of the cave, he waited until they had ten feet of separation before following. Priya and Rose moved as if to go ahead of him, but Walker ushered them back. He had the gun, and he intended to put himself between the civilians and the malignant thing inside Maeve. She still had some control, but it seethed in her. He could almost feel it radiating from within her.

Gun in hand, he duckwalked through the cave. Up ahead, Maeve stepped out into the gorge and began to climb the massive rock that hid the cave entrance. His earwig squawked, a little burst of static. He winced and reached up to tap the earbud. It had been useless while they were in the cave, no signal at all. There seemed little point in using it now. Updates from Alena's office or from Rue Crooker wouldn't do much to protect them from the Blackcoats. In a minute or two, he'd be neck deep in the Moonglow River, and whatever information they might have for him would have to wait. If all went well, they would be in the clear by daybreak. If not, chatting again with Alena Boudreau's personal assistant wouldn't be the thing that kept them alive.

"It's gotten cold," Priya said quietly, not far behind him.

"The mountains at night," Rose replied as if that explained it all.

Walker hadn't noticed the chill, but now he felt it. His clothes had dried in the hours since they'd entered the cave, but they clung to him, damp and clammy, and as the night wind slithered down the tunnel, it felt far too cold to be July. New England could always bring the unexpected.

Stepping out of the cave, Walker felt grateful to stand upright. He aimed his weapon at the top of the rock that blocked the entrance just in case the thing inside Maeve lay in wait for them, but there was no sign of her, which troubled him nearly as much. The cool air washed around him, and for the first time he realized just how much it had gotten under his skin, being trapped in the cave with Maeve and her passenger. Her infection.

"Quickly now," he whispered over his shoulder as Priya emerged from the cave. "Watch your step, but don't slow down. We have no idea what's waiting for us."

He clambered up the rock, peering down at the edge of the river. The burble of its passing seemed louder in the dark. The sky had mostly cleared, but the crescent moon cast only a ghostly gleam on the terrain around him, not nearly the brightness it would have when full.

Still, it was enough.

"Maeve," he whispered, pulse quickening. Worried.

To his left, back the way they had come before nightfall, he heard her voice rasp, "Here." Relieved, he skidded down the massive stone and started up the next one, even as Rose helped Priya to climb up to the perch he had just abandoned. Priya grunted in pain, huffing with effort, but Rose would have to help her. Walker's responsibility was Maeve.

He dropped down from the next rock. Maeve watched him but made no move to approach. The two of them stood like gunfighters ready to duel. Only Walker had a gun, but Maeve had become her own weapon.

"All quiet?" Rose whispered as she dropped down from the rocks to stand beside Walker.

He nodded. Rose tracked the tension between him and Maeve but turned to help Priya slide down to the rocky terrain alongside the river.

"Go," Walker said, gesturing for Maeve to get into the river ahead of the rest of them. They'd discussed it in the cave. *Stay in the river unless you have no other choice*, he had told them. *Wait until you reach the bridge in Jericho Falls to get out. Don't drown. Whatever you do, don't let Maeve touch you.*

Rose pushed past Walker. He held his breath, not liking how close she was to her sister.

"Be safe," Rose told her. "I can't lose anyone else."

Maeve nodded.

"Wait. Please, hang on a second," Priya said, even paler in the glow of the moon. "I don't hear anything. I don't see anyone. This is crazy dangerous. Can't we just walk—"

Walker heard a single, distant pop, and the night broke open.

The brightest flare he'd ever seen soared up into the darkness over the gorge and burst into silent brilliance. The others squinted against the searing glare, but Walker knew what was coming next.

"Into the water!" he shouted, grabbing Rose and propelling her toward the river.

Gunfire erupted all around them. Bullets struck the rocks on the bank barely inches in front of Rose, and Walker realized his error. He lunged after her, grabbed the back of her shirt, and dragged her down, using his body to shield her. He couldn't save them all, but she had been closest to him.

Bullets smashed into stone. Shards flew. Some plinked into the water. Maeve kept walking toward the river as if she wanted to be hit.

"Go to Priya," Walker told Rose. "The two of you get back to the cave entrance."

"We'll be trapped," she said, eyes wild with terror.

Walker pulled Rose to her feet, ducked low, and got her moving back toward Priya. He didn't have to shout at them to go. They were already moving, scrambling over the first of the two massive stone slabs, exposed in the flickering, dying light of the flare.

Someone shot a second flare, erasing his hope that they might escape notice.

Walker took aim, scanned the ridge, tried to use the new brightness to his advantage. He saw one of the snipers and opened fire, but at this distance it was nearly hopeless, and he had no idea how many of them there were, or who they were.

Blackcoats. Had to be.

Mercenaries. Trained for this.

But none of them had been shot. Not one bullet had connected. *They're not aiming,* he thought. *Trying to take us alive.*

Alive was good. Alive got him home to Charlie. Alive meant the Sinclair sisters didn't have to die.

In the new brightness, he saw Blackcoats rappelling down the walls of the gorge. Up on the rim, others were hustling along, trying to reach a place to descend. He put it all together, realized this was the way he would have done it himself. The gunfire and screaming at dusk, when they'd come down Walter's Descent and Maeve had murdered Agatha, had told the Blackcoats where to search for them. The Blackcoats had come, searched the gorge, and then stationed themselves along the rough mile or so of the area where they thought the gunfire had originated, knowing that Walker couldn't risk waiting until morning. That he would have to make a break for it.

He'd had no choice. And General Wagner had known it.

But they wanted Maeve alive, maybe the rest of them, too. Maybe those were the general's orders.

All of this went through his mind in seconds.

Then a bullet struck Maeve in the chest, and all of Walker's calculus changed.

She started to scream, and the voice that tore from her throat sounded like nothing human.

When the flare went up, everything changed. Leon had followed the Germans eastward. They'd moved swiftly, with a grace and quiet he forced himself to match. Several times he had to pause, catching his breath as he listened for noises that would let him pick up their trail again. He feared he would lose them eventually, and then he would have abandoned his wounded partner for no reason and lost himself on the mountain for good measure.

Then the flare.

The Germans froze when they heard that first pop, craning their necks to look up at the forest canopy. Tired and focused on stealth and speed, Leon barely heard the pop, but the Germans stopped so abruptly that he took two more steps before he could halt himself. They seemed like the loudest steps he'd ever taken, but even if the Germans heard him, divine intervention arrived in the form of the flare, which burst across the sky like the fireworks that had been going off around the country all week.

Gunshots echoed across the mountain. Burst after burst. Pop after pop.

"Damn it!" the German woman shouted, in English, with no foreign accent. "They couldn't have waited another ten minutes?"

She barked orders in German, pointing through the trees. The two men with her unslung the rifles from their backs and bolted through the woods toward the place where the flare had originated. The woman raced after them, tugging a phone from her pocket.

"This is Virgo-One," she said, once more in English, breathing hard as she dodged between trees and leaped rocks and bushes. "We're out of time. The word is given."

Leon followed. She and the other Germans had given up any attempt at stealth now, but as loud as the gunfire might be, whipcracks echoing through the woods, he did not want to risk giving himself away. He moved as fast as he could, caught his foot on a fallen branch but recovered his momentum, and held tight to his gun while he ran.

The men were German. She had talked to them in German, given them their orders in that language, but the woman didn't sound German at all. *So who the hell is she?* He caught a glimpse of silver hair sticking out from beneath her black watch cap, and now that she was running all out, he noticed for the first time the effort she put into movement, as if it were a burden. How old was she, this woman who'd brought killers onto the mountain to hunt Maeve Sinclair?

Leon hurt all over. His whole body ached, his legs felt like dead-weight, and his heart raced along alarmingly fast. It had been the longest day of his life, and now it had gotten a hell of a lot longer and a hell of a lot more dangerous.

But maybe all of this—the flare, the gunfire—meant it was nearly over. Maybe there would be answers coming soon. The thought sent an anxious tremor through him. While he'd been tracking the supposed Germans, his focus had been simple. He'd thought he'd understood the situation and how he had interpreted the mandate of his mission. Now he wondered if he had understood anything at all.

He brushed past a massive pine tree, put one boot on a fallen oak and sprang over it, surprised to find himself on a rough trail. Not well traveled, by any means, but more of a path than he'd been on for the past half hour. Moving in the dark, with just wan moonlight, it had been slow going. Running after the Germans had been a gamble. Here, though, he could see the winding trail where other boots had trod in the past, enough to indicate the smoothest passage.

Gunshots continued, another flare burst in the sky ahead. The echoes were strange, though, an odd acoustic muffling that the trees could not explain.

He heard the crack of a rifle up ahead, much closer. Then another shot, and a third.

Leon slowed, chest burning with exertion. He got control of his breathing and slipped back into the trees, wishing he could stay on the trail but knowing it would be unwise. Those rifle cracks were so close they could only have been from the Germans. The mountain crawled with his own people from White Oak Security, and Leon figured some of those shots being fired came from his comrades' weapons. But White Oak personnel weren't the only people up here searching.

He caught his breath, slinking through the trees until he could see a vast, open space ahead where the forest came to an end. The meager moonlight showed the edges of a broad chasm, and he remembered the gorge that had been on the mission map. This had to be it. Now the strange echoes made sense. Someone had found Maeve Sinclair, and they were fighting over the right to claim her—or her corpse.

Leon slunk through the last line of trees. He spotted the two German snipers ahead of him, for that was surely what they were. They had taken a position on the ridge, side by side, and were aiming along the gorge. One of them pulled the trigger. The rifle shot made Leon flinch, but he peered to his right along the gorge, and now he saw what they were shooting at. Black-clad soldiers came from the woods to the south, joining others who were stationed there. They were shooting into the gorge; Leon figured they were keeping their targets pinned down there. He saw two dark figures go over the side on ropes, rappelling over the edge.

They had to be his Blackcoats. White Oak Security.

The Germans were shooting at them.

Somehow, through some miracle of luck and fumbling accident, Leon found himself in precisely the right place at precisely the right time. Maybe he wouldn't be the one who found Maeve Sinclair, but he could still save the lives of some of his buddies. Hell, it might be Luther Baskin down there or Angela Todd. Johnny Kennedy, the funniest asshole on White Oak's roster, the big Alabama bastard they called Prez.

As Leon raised his weapon and took aim, he let out a long breath and smiled to himself as he thought about saving Prez Kennedy's life and all the tequila those assholes would buy him when they learned what he'd done.

He felt a breath on his cheek, warm in the cool night air.

Then the cold kiss of the gun barrel against his temple.

Leon saw her then in his peripheral vision. Silver hair, black watch cap, wrinkles around her eyes. Much older than he'd realized. God, she had to be sixty at the very least.

"My name's Alena," she said. "What's yours?"

The Red Death's influence came in waves. The tiny bit of Maeve that could still pursue rational thought had developed theories about that, ideas involving proximity to the living and duration since the last time she'd passed the infection to another. None of that mattered now.

Her head throbbed, spiking with pain that she knew could be alleviated if only she would stop fighting, give the Red Death what it wanted. Yes. Not the hunger or Red Hands or whatever other label she might have given it—this wasn't just a presence, it was a consciousness. A living malignance, a disease that could override an infected host and spread the contagion within it, with purpose. Woven into the host body—into her body—so that the only cure for her own suffering was to communicate it to others. The pressure valve on her sickness was to share it. To spread the Red Death . . . in order for her to live.

The air in the gorge grew hot. The brightness of the flares turned the stone walls into red glass, or perhaps she existed now in two places—the solid world around her and the blur of memory and hunger that existed inside the Red Death. She saw through its ancient eyes just as it saw through her own. Gunfire echoed all through the gorge. Voices shouted to her to get down, to hide. The bullet wound in her left side pulsed, little dribbles of blood spilling out, the stain on her dirty tank top spreading.

Another bullet tagged her shoulder, and she jerked slightly.

She was no longer alone. The figure she had seen lurking nearby her, the one she had seen in her visions, the voice in her head, the insidious presence that made her skin crawl, made her feel as if she were coated with a thick film of gutter swill . . . it wasn't gone. Not vanished. The Red Death was just Maeve now, and Maeve had become it.

Bullets struck the rocks nearby. Some plinked into the water. Others smashed stone, sent chips flying.

Maeve turned to see that Walker had taken cover. She saw him reloading his gun. Behind a large stone slab, back toward the cave entrance, Rose poked her head out, screaming for Maeve to wake up.

"Snap out of it, for fuck's sake!" Rose screamed, her face contorted in fury. She looked like Mom when teenage Rose hadn't cleaned her room for a month. The thought made Maeve smile and then laugh, and she knew her mind had broken.

It felt nice.

Better.

Shouts from overhead made her twist around to stare at the Black-coats gliding down into the gorge on ropes. They shoved off the wall, dropped swiftly, and the first to reach the ground unclipped themselves from the ropes, reaching for their weapons. Idly, it occurred to her that they were going to kill her, and that would be all right.

But they would also kill Rose and Priya and Walker.

And they worked for the motherfuckers who had infected Oscar Hecht.

She ran toward the soldiers who had dropped into the gorge about fifty feet away. Others were still rappelling down the rock walls. Maeve smiled to herself as she leaped from stone to stone, closing the distance between them with inhuman speed. *Inhuman.* She embraced the word and the savagery that went with it.

Soldiers saw her coming when she'd crossed half the distance already.

Somewhere behind her, Rose and Priya and Walker would be watching, or maybe they would be in the midst of their own fight. A tremor of shame for what she had become passed through her, but she pushed it away—too late for that.

Bullets strafed her from above, chipping away at the rocks behind her. Too slow to catch her. The hunger of the Red Death ached in her bones, no longer a gnawing in her gut or a whisper in her skull but part of her now. Or simply . . . her.

The first two soldiers to unclip from the ropes let their guns hang from the straps around their necks, reaching for Tasers instead. They had time to take aim and fire, the Tasers stinging her. They were eager, ambitious, and they had thought to capture her alive.

In gratitude, she smashed their skulls against the stone wall of the gorge.

"Holy—" a Blackcoat shouted, a dozen feet to her right. The woman shouldered her weapon, pulled the trigger, interrupted herself so that she never finished that sentence.

Maeve wondered what the next word would have been. There were so many possibilities.

Instead, bullets sprayed the gorge. The woman's eyes were narrowed with purpose. Instead of fear, the Blackcoat had determination, and Maeve admired that. A bullet tore through her right side, cracked bones, skidded along her rib cage, and exited out her back. Another tore off her left ear.

Then Maeve landed on the Blackcoat, ripped off her face mask, and spit in her eyes.

She threw her head back, screaming in triumph and ecstasy as infection raced through the Blackcoat's body. Bloodstream. Lungs. Skin. Brain.

The Red Death sprang up from the shuddering, dying woman and turned to look up at the other soldiers as they descended.

They were coming for her.

She eagerly awaited them.

24

Walker could have made the river. He knew it. The water ran deep and fast; more importantly, it ran south and away from this shitshow. If he ran, dove, swam underwater for as long as he could hold his breath, and if they didn't have a sharpshooter with a scope talented enough to pick him off when his head bobbed above the water downriver . . . he could survive this.

Gun in hand, he tried and failed to catch his breath. He'd been under fire before. Nearly died multiple times. Inhaled the presence of evil. Climbed down a mountain with a demon trying to murder him. Been in an ordinary firefight, caught shrapnel from a terrorist's roadside bomb, watched a woman's bones crack and shift under her skin while she turned into something inhuman, and heard a nest of tiny, winged serpents whisper his name. But this was the first time his own government had tried to kill him, and it really pissed him off.

Go, he thought. *For Charlie's sake.*

"Walker!" Rose screamed.

He spun to see her glance around the side of the slab that blocked the cave entrance. Walker wanted to shout to her that she and Priya needed to get inside, but he would only be telling Rose something she already knew. She was a grown woman.

"Give me a goddamn gun!" she shouted.

He frowned. As if he had a gun to spare.

Rose shouted again, something different about her voice this time. He glanced back and saw her pointing, looked up, and saw two soldiers coming down into the gorge right above him. One of them had a weapon aimed straight down at Walker. The show-off thought he lived in a James Bond movie, that he could actually manage to track a steady aim while bouncing off the rock wall.

The Blackcoats overhead shouted something at Walker, ignoring Rose and Priya because they were unarmed. Walker put his hands up as if he meant to surrender. The show-off barked orders down at him. A third flare burst into the air above the gorge. The second had faded almost to nothing, and now Walker got a good look at these two guys who were coming for him and he scowled. The jackass showboating while he rappelled couldn't have been more than twenty-two.

Walker shot him in the ass.

He'd been aiming for the leg, but in the midst of his fear and desperation, he found room to laugh as the Blackcoat shouted in pain, arched his back, and tumbled off the wall. The rope had a safety line that snagged him ten feet from the ground. He jerked and bounced on the line, upside down, eyes rolling in pain. His hands dangled underneath him, gun drooping.

"Careful," Walker called up to him. "You're gonna drop that."

He jumped up and tore the gun from the Blackcoat's hands.

The second one kept shouting his partner's name—Puglisi—and trying to get a clear shot at Walker, who stayed under Puglisi like the guy was his umbrella. Puglisi bled on him, swore at him, called angrily to God to damn Walker for shooting him in the ass and how could being shot in the ass hurt this goddamn much.

Walker didn't have an answer for him, but he used the time wisely.

Holstering his sidearm, Walker opened fire with the HK the Blackcoat had so kindly brought to him. Bullets had been chipping away at the rocks around him for minutes now. More Blackcoats were coming down into the gorge. The moments when he could reasonably believe they had any way out of this disaster were ticking away, but he kept firing. In his mind, he pictured General Wagner burning in hell. He hoped it existed, hoped the general found his way there.

"Rose!" he shouted over his shoulder. "Priya! We're going into the water! It's the only way!"

"You're fucking crazy!" Rose called.

Up to his left, bullets chipped stone. Several of the Blackcoats had gotten into position where they might actually kill him. He had stuffed himself between a slab and the wall, with Rose and Priya sandwiched between the next slab and the cave opening.

He should have run the seven or eight steps and launched himself into the river. He knew that. His son waited at home, and he had spent enough years nearly making Charlie fatherless while trying to save some other kid's parents or some other parent's kids.

Maeve had been his assignment, and he had been determined to get her off the mountain alive, but he peered around the corner of the slab and saw her along the riverbank. She had a Blackcoat by the collar and smashed his face against the wall again and again, crushing his skull and pulping his face.

Is that even Maeve? Or is Maeve already gone?

More of them dropped toward her. Walker exhaled. They were so focused on her that he might have been able to get away, but if he left Rose and Priya to go home to his own son, he wouldn't ever be able to hold his head up. There was only one way to make it home to Charlie.

He took aim and pulled the trigger again, wondering how many Blackcoats he would have to kill.

His earwig buzzed. David Boudreau, he figured. Or Joel, or Rue Crooker.

"About goddamn time," he muttered as he tapped the plastic nub in his ear. "Whoever this is, you'd better have a way out of this."

"Hello, Benjamin," a soft voice rasped. "I'm sorry it's taken me so long to get back to you."

"Alena?" Walker snapped. He took aim and shot another of the Blackcoats descending toward Maeve. "That was the world's longest fucking meeting. Tell me you got the DoD to override General Wagner!"

"Oh, I did," Alena assured him. "But our friend the general has stopped answering his calls. He's ignoring the chain of command."

Walker sighed, ducking behind the slab again. He looked up, searching the dying flare light for any movement overhead. The Blackcoats were more interested in Maeve than they were in him or Rose and Priya, but that wouldn't last forever.

"Fantastic," Walker growled. "Now what the fuck are we supposed to do?"

"Keep your head down."

"What the hell is that supposed to—"

"Dear Benjamin," Alena said. "I'm afraid I haven't been entirely forthright with you."

As if that had been a cue, a fresh round of gunfire ripped through the gorge, but these bullets were coming from the north. Blackcoats rappelling down the wall took heavy fire. Some were shot and others tried to take cover behind ledges and outcroppings. Walker looked up at the western rim of the gorge, saw a Blackcoat jerk backward, clutching his chest, and tumble over the side.

"Alena," he said.

No reply. His earwig fuzzed with static.

The call had ended.

The fight continued.

Rose helped Priya back into the cave. The bullets could not chase them in, but the sounds followed, echoing and ricocheting loudly enough to hurt their ears. In the darkness, the mouth of the cave glowing with the flickering red light from the flares drifting down into the gorge, they held each other. Rose could feel Priya's heart beating against her chest, warm breath on her neck. She cupped the back of Priya's neck and clasped her even more tightly, as if the two women could merge if only they loved one another hard enough.

Rose sank into Priya's arms, wishing she could stay there, but instead she pulled away.

"No," Priya said, grabbing her wrist, eyes blazing. "We stay here.

It's not us they're trying to kill. They don't care about us. We stay here until they find us or until the sun comes up and it's all over. Do you understand me?"

Rose did understand. She averted her eyes. "Maeve . . ."

"You can't save her!" Priya snapped, wincing at the pain in her wounded shoulder. She released Rose's wrist and took hold of her face instead, forced Rose to meet her gaze. "She's been dead since the parade—since that asshole infected her. You know this. She's too sick to carry this for long. One way or another, she's as good as dead. But you . . ."

Priya's sternness collapsed into a sob. She pressed her lips together in a tight line. "You've lost so much. You and your dad, that's all you have left. And me, Rose . . . you have me. Just stay here with me, quiet. Just hold me till it's over."

Rose had never wanted anything more in her life. For a few seconds, she even thought she might do it. But as she inhaled the scent of the one she loved, images burst through. Memories of her mother and Logan. Of her dad and Maeve.

Maeve.

Grief opened under Rose like a gravity well, yet she knew her anguish must only be a pale shade of the pain Maeve felt. The horror and guilt and regret. And Maeve had that sickness rotting her from the inside, eating away at all the things that gave her identity. That gave her life.

"I'm sorry, love," Rose said quietly, the words almost obliterated by gunshot echoes. "You'll be safer here. I'll be back for you."

Priya sighed, breath hitching. Tears spilled from her eyes, shimmering in the red flare light.

Rose kissed her, lingering, and then pressed her forehead against Priya's for a few moments before she pulled away and stepped out of the cave without a backward glance.

Screams and bullets soared through the gorge. Rose slid along the side of the stone slab that blocked her view, lay flat against it, and crawled up far enough to get a glimpse northward. She spotted Walker immediately, sheltering behind the next slab to the north. He leaned out, assault rifle in his hands, and opened fire on two Blackcoats who were still descending.

Rose climbed up a bit farther. She heard screams and managed to peer over the top of the slab, where she had a view of the floor of the gorge and the broad swath of rocks and slabs that made up the riverbank. She saw Maeve there, fighting, half a dozen dead men strewn around her as if she were building herself a fort out of corpses.

One of them moved.

Not dead yet.

Gun out, taking aim.

Rose screamed as the Blackcoat fired. Bullets stitched across Maeve's back, punching her forward. She arched, let out a plaintive sound that carried through the gorge in spite of the barrage of gunfire, and then she sprawled onto the ground amid the scrub grass. In the guttering light of the bloody-red flare, Rose could see her sister's body jerking, legs twitching, as if she were trying to move, trying to rise, trying to keep fighting.

A fresh pair of flares soared into the air over the gorge, tiny red suns that cast their crimson glow over the grotesque panorama playing out below. Rose blinked, felt little breaths escaping her body, lay on that stone slab and stared at Maeve. She remembered what her sister had told her, the way Maeve had described the visions she'd had. "Like little glimpses into someone else's hell," Maeve had said.

The flares colored the night red, and Rose knew she was staring into her sister's hell.

Rose pushed up onto her feet, standing atop the slab. Gunfire echoed around the gorge, but it seemed far from her now, as if she were already a ghost and such crude violence existed in the land of the living.

"No!" Priya screamed, stumbling from the cave. "Rose, don't—"

But Rose had already dropped over the edge of the slab. By the time Priya scrabbled up to the perch she'd vacated, Rose had already clambered over the next one. Walker had been hiding behind it and must still be somewhere nearby, but the aperture through which she viewed the world had narrowed to include only Maeve.

Rose ran to her, hoping for the impossible.

The men who'd shot Maeve turned toward Rose with their guns, and she ignored them, calling her sister's name. When she reached Maeve's body, already thinking of it that way—her body—she halted, staring down at the blood pooling on the dirt and scrub grass. The Blackcoats barked at her to back away, to put up her hands or she would join her sister, and that sounded all right with Rose, but somehow she managed to raise her shaking hands. She tasted salt on her lips and only then felt the warm stripes of tears on her cheeks. There had been so many tears that she idly wondered if it was possible for a person's tears to run dry.

"Maeve?" She knelt beside her sister.

The gunmen screamed again. Shifting position, taking aim, growing shriller the way some men did when they weren't being obeyed.

Rose saw all of this in her peripheral vision, her conscious mind only vaguely taking note.

Maeve groaned. She struggled to roll onto her side, shuddering, blood burbling from her lips. As Rose reached toward her, Maeve managed to shake her head, eyes full of sorrow. In their lives, they had shared the joy and anger so many sisters felt, closeness that outsiders could never understand, mutual hostility that made for fragile reunions, laughter over jokes no one else would find amusing, the pain of watching their parents' marriage decay and collapse.

"Don't," Maeve said.

Dying.

The men with their Kevlar armor and their guns kept shouting. One of them took a knee, aimed straight at Rose's head, roared at her to back away from the body.

The body, and Maeve wasn't even dead yet. Rose had thought of her that way, but this felt different, offensive. Intrusive. Rose did not want Maeve to be *the body*, but this man, this hollowed-out, blackhearted bastard, had the gleam of excitement in his eyes. Thrilled to lay claim to *the body*.

Rose met his gaze. There were others around, more than she'd realized. Beyond these two were three more, two of them women. Others rappelled to the floor of the gorge just thirty feet to the north.

Maeve would not live.

Rose knew that.

But she'd be damned if the people who had created the infection that killed her would ever lay a hand on her.

Rose heard Priya crying out for her. She wished she could tell herself Priya would understand, but knew she never would.

Rose did it, anyway.

Slid forward and put her sister's head into her lap.

The Blackcoat's finger tightened on the trigger. Rose flinched as gunshots cracked the air close by, but it was the Blackcoat who jerked backward. His gun flew from his grip, and then a second bullet struck him in the left cheek and he fell dead to the ground. Two other Blackcoats died, bullets tearing into them, and the rest lunged for cover.

"Rose, what have you done?"

She didn't turn, but she knew the voice belonged to Walker. He had been there, behind the stone slab, fighting. He'd been shooting at the Blackcoats at the rim of the gorge and the ones coming down the walls, trying to keep their bullets away from the Sinclair sisters. But Rose didn't care about bullets anymore.

She caressed Maeve's face, wiped her tears and blood. Rose would have forgiven her, but there was nothing to forgive. Maeve had been wild with grief, needing someone to blame for the deaths of their mother and Logan, and Rose had wanted to hate her. Now she only wanted Maeve to feel loved, to know she was not alone in the end.

Rose watched the light dim in her sister's eyes and then go out. Maeve's head lolled to one side, her body going slack.

Then Rose's hands began to itch and grow warm. She felt a twinge in her gut.

Was that a whisper she heard, inside her skull?

Rose thought it might be.

No. You can't have her.

Maeve had never been pregnant. She didn't know what it might feel like to have life grow within her. She imagined the thing inside her as more like cancer—not a single tumor but tendrils of it, vines of black rot sending shoots through her bones, wrapping around her arteries, rooting in every muscle. Life, though. Sentient, the way a fetus might be. And like a fetus, it had been growing stronger and maturer, developing into something aware and full of purpose.

It scratched and gnawed inside her like a wild thing in a cage, desperate to be free to hunt and feed so it might grow stronger. So the ghost of death might walk the world again and spread its poison far and wide.

It had flourished inside her, lived and breathed in her. It had killed in her, but it wouldn't die with her.

Her wounds pulsed with the heat of blood leaving her body. Her vision dimmed as if light and color were fading from the world, but she stared up at Rose, lips moving as she tried to form words of regret and of warning, all such sentiments far too late to help any of them.

Too late, a voice echoed in her mind, and what remained of Maeve Sinclair could not tell if it was her own thought or that of the Red Death. *Farewell.*

"Rose," she tried to say aloud, and Rose looked at her.

Death felt like mercy, so Maeve did not mind it overmuch, but the hunger began to slip out of her. The malevolent disease slithered from her flesh and into Rose, and Maeve fought that as hard as she was able.

She blinked. Beyond her sister, she saw the withered crimson figure again, looming over Rose as if the two were allies now. Or as if it had claimed Rose as its own.

Maeve closed her eyes. The Red Death told her goodbye yet again, in more insistent tones, and she felt it struggle to break free from the anchor it had planted inside her. The hunger had tethered itself to her, and now Maeve refused to release it.

As she slid down into the dark and final comfort of death, Maeve still fought.

Not my sister, she thought. *Not Rose. You can't have her.*

Then all went quiet inside her, and Maeve Sinclair was no more.

Alena Boudreau didn't like to shout and she didn't like to fight, but she had found herself more than willing to do both when necessary. She cherished science and the thrill of discovery, but both had proven to be rife with dangers and secrets, and the world teemed with assholes willing to commit atrocities to acquire such things. That dilemma led to violent conflict and deceit. Because she was director of the Global Science Research Coalition, no one would expect her to be in a position to give orders that required human beings to be shot.

No one except those who understood the work they really did.

The work that DARPA did. The work the Department of Defense did. Every minute of every day, all over the world, there were a thousand ways to ignite catastrophe, epidemic, mass extinction, or global destruction. Humanity had built itself a delicately balanced house of cards. It would take very little to bring it all down.

If, from time to time, preventing such catastrophe meant resorting to violence, Alena Boudreau had learned to live with that.

"Just stand there and nobody will shoot you," she said, gesturing at Leon Lewis, unable to hide her irritation. He didn't look convinced, and maybe the gun in her hand had something to do with that, but tough shit. She hadn't come here to coddle mercenaries and worry about their feelings.

Static crackled in her ear. She shook her head, tapped the earpiece. "Walker, you still there?"

Most of what she heard over the connection had been gunfire, hard to distinguish from the sounds picked up by her other ear. Gunshots echoed up and down the gorge, from rim down to river. But they were quieting now.

"I'm here," Walker said. "I think Maeve Sinclair's dead."

"Shit!" Alena snarled. Leon Lewis flinched, watching her gun hand as if she were some kind of explosive device that might detonate if she became too unstable. She figured that wasn't far from the truth.

"There's more," Walker said.

He kept talking, but she snapped at him to hang on. "We're pulling the plug up here. Stay alive another minute or two, would you?"

Alena walked to the rim of the gorge. She had kept mostly to the tree line to avoid Blackcoat snipers. The two Germans she'd brought with her were former BND counterintelligence agents who had signed on to the SRC less than a week before. The moment she'd been named director, Alena had begun to reach out to colleagues and allies with whom she had worked over the years. If the SRC were to present to the world that they were a global coalition, they had to look the part. But not all her employees were going to be scientists.

None of those new hires had been officially logged or even vetted by the DoD as of yet. Alena had been engaged in a chess match with General Wagner, and she had been careful not to reveal her strategy. When DARPA had begun moving pieces around the board, shifting Wagner's responsibilities, creating Global SRC and naming Alena its director, she had suspected the general would try to hold on to his pet projects and wall them off, even from his superiors. There had been lies, obfuscation, his allies covering for him all through the shadowy corridors of government, but Alena had allies, too. And Walker . . . well, Ben Walker had been a stroke of luck. General Wagner had punished Walker not for breaking the rules but for taking away an opportunity to create yet another deadly bioweapon, when Garland Mountain had been developing one for him all along.

General Wagner had sidelined Ben Walker. With the secrecy necessary to her task, Alena hadn't been able to recruit many experienced field agents, but the general had left Walker on the bench, and she had been more than happy to put him back in the game.

A buzz in her ear. She tapped the comm unit. "Tell me."

"The order's been given, Director Boudreau. General Wagner will be informed shortly, but White Oak Security has been ordered to stand down."

"Thank you, Joel."

Alena did not smile as she signed off. There were too many dead for her to feel any sense of triumph. She went to Paul Dietrich, the senior of the two German agents she'd hired, and put a hand on his shoulder.

"Nearly done now, but don't lower your guard," she told him. "I don't trust anyone tonight."

Dietrich nodded. The other German, Oskar Lubitsch, spoke little English, but he didn't need a translation to understand. Alena raised the small pair of night-vision binoculars that hung from a strap around her neck. South along the ridge, she watched as the Blackcoats from White Oak Security lowered their weapons. They looked confused and a little bit lost, turning to their unit commanders.

When the Homeland Security agents emerged from the woods behind them, Alena held her breath. She'd made sure the order had come from White Oak's operations director before Homeland Security moved in because she thought that would avoid any further loss of life. The last thing she wanted was another hundred corpses on the mountain. Even so, she tensed as the DHS agents trained their weapons on the Blackcoats and forced them to disarm.

She braced for more gunshots, but none came.

Lowering the binoculars, she glanced over at Leon Lewis. "I haven't forgotten you, Leon. Come take a look at this."

He moved tentatively, eyeing the Germans, watching her carefully. Wordlessly, he took the binoculars and looked south, just as Alena had. She knew what he would see.

"Your operation's over," she told him. "Time to stand down."

Leon exhaled with obvious relief and passed the binoculars back to her. "Okay. So what now?"

"Now you get to go home," Alena replied. "Though if I were you, I'd think hard about my line of work. White Oak took on a client willing to send you to kill American citizens, including government employees. Maybe you're okay with that sort of thing—"

"I'm not," Leon said quickly, brow knitted in thought.

"You didn't seem the type, to be honest," she said. "The dust on this will settle, Leon. One way or another, it will be swept under the carpet, and some other atrocity will take its place. When things calm down, come and see me. I'm going to need people with at least a spark of conscience."

He looked at her a long moment, then nodded and turned away. Leon Lewis began walking along the rim of the gorge, off to join the rest of his unit, but Alena had a feeling he would not be with them for long.

Alena tapped her comm again. "Walker, you still there?" Static. She frowned. "Walker?"

"—hurry."

She swore, lifting the binoculars and rushing to the edge of the gorge so fast that Dietrich grabbed the back of her jacket to keep her from stumbling over. The night vision blurred as she turned, trying to get it to focus, searching for Walker.

"What is it?" she asked. "They should be surrendering."

"It's not the fucking Blackcoats," Walker said. "It's Rose Sinclair."

Walker felt like he'd be hearing the echoes of gunshots for the rest of his life. His eardrums throbbed in the aftermath. The Blackcoats moved in around Rose, barked at her to move away from her sister's body. They didn't seem to really understand what had happened, what it meant that Rose had been holding on to Maeve but hadn't gotten sick yet herself. Maeve had died, just as Oscar Hecht had died.

"Get away from her," Walker ordered, advancing toward the Blackcoats, sweeping his weapon in an arc, trying to warn them off.

There were over a dozen of them along the trail now, but most of those had come down the wall of the gorge some yards to the north. Of the ones still alive, there on the rocky bank of the Moonglow, only four were close enough to Rose that she might lunge for them, and Walker saw the murder in her eyes. They must have seen it, too, because although they had lowered their weapons moments ago, they raised them again.

"We told you, girl," one of the Blackcoats said, "get away from the body."

"Lower your weapons," Walker snapped at them. "Back away!"

The red glow of the flares had begun to fade and waver. Soon they would have only wan moonlight to see by. Walker took three careful steps on uneven ground, aimed his weapon at the Blackcoat who had spoken. The others turned their guns on him.

Rose slid closer to them, taking advantage of the distraction. Her eyes had their own red glow, and he knew that glimmer had nothing to do with the flares. It broke Walker's heart to see the predatory sneer that contorted her face. He thought of Ted Sinclair and all he'd lost, and in his heart, he cursed the man for not being up here on the mountain himself, injuries be damned.

"Don't do it, Rose," he said.

Guns shifted back toward her.

Walker took another step, stared hard at the Blackcoats. "Listen to me. You guys are done. This is over, and you need to withdraw right now. Nothing else needs to happen here. My team is going to lock this down. Nobody else needs to be hurt."

Rose spun around and marched toward him, screaming out her pain and fury. Instinct made Walker pivot and aim the gun at her, center mass. He flushed, hating himself in that moment, but he didn't turn his weapon away.

"Stay there, Rose. You don't need to hurt anyone else."

She spat on the rocks a few feet from him. Walker flinched, wondering if her body fluids were infectious.

"You tried to help, but Maeve is dead, anyway," she said, and he could almost hear her heart shattering as she spoke. "They murdered her. Truth is, they murdered her twice, and they took my mom and Logan."

She grinned. Something like tears dripped at the corners of her eyes, but these tears were dark streaks of red or black. Hard to tell in the flickering, hellish light of the dying flares.

"You think I'm going to let them just *surrender*?"

Rose lowered her head, then turned and stalked toward the nearest Blackcoat, the one with the big mouth. His eyes widened as she raised her hands, the reality finally hitting him. His gun twitched at his side. As he staggered backward, he brought the weapon up again.

Walker couldn't watch another member of the Sinclair family die.

He took aim and shot the Blackcoat in the chest. The guy stumbled and fell, and the others reacted. One of them fired at Walker, barely missing.

"Stop!" Walker shouted, tossing his gun to the ground. "He's wearing body armor! I was getting his attention. Just walk away. Fucking *run* away before she kills you!"

They must have seen the wisdom. As the other Blackcoats down in the gorge came toward them, those three began to retreat, shouting at their fallen comrade to follow. Bursts of static came from their comms, voices calling out names.

The fallen Blackcoat scrambled to his feet. Shaking, he backed away, gun pointed at Rose just in case she lunged at him.

Rose quickened her pace. Her muscles tensed. Walker saw the way she moved, the way she coiled, and knew he was too far away to stop her even if he dared to touch her.

Then Priya was there.

Eyes wide and pleading, cradling her left arm, she came around the side of the slab that had sheltered her from bullets and rushed at Rose and the Blackcoat, free hand up in front of her.

"Rose, no! Let it be over."

Rose took a step toward her, left hand reaching for Priya's throat. Priya recoiled in shock, and Rose faltered. Behind her, the last Blackcoat ran to join his comrades, boots pounding the path until he'd reached the safety of numbers. They all turned to watch, a Greek chorus of hired killers.

Rose stared at her hands. Black tears slid down her face. "I'm sorry."

"Let them help you," Priya told her. "Please." Priya started toward her, gently, warily. "I need you."

Rose jerked backward, stared at Priya. She shook her head and hugged herself tightly, determined to keep her hands to herself. She turned and walked to where her sister lay dead. Rose fell to her knees, huddling down as if against a cold winter, though it remained midsummer.

Then she looked up at Walker. "Whatever you think you can do, you'd better do it fast."

The last crimson flicker of the flare's light burned out, leaving only the moon.

But Rose's eyes still glinted red.

25

One New Year's Eve during his college days, Ted Sinclair spent the night in jail. He'd been drinking in a bar with friends, thanks to an amateurishly made fake ID and a doorman willing to look the other way in exchange for ten bucks and a promise not to cause any trouble. It wasn't the fake ID or the underage drinking that had landed Ted in jail, however—the blame for that rested squarely on the shoulders of a girl named Kristina Lawson. Ted and Kristina and four other friends had been seated at a round table in view of the bar. An absurdly handsome guy with creamy brown skin and the kind of fashion sense that would forever be beyond Ted had been seated at the bar and sent Kristina two drinks in a row. She smiled shyly at him, wagged her fingers in thanks, and played hard to get . . . until the moment *Chrystina Campbell* got up from the table and sashayed over to the guy at the bar to suggest he buy a drink for a girl who'd appreciate it.

What ensued would forever be called the Battle of the Christinas—it seeming fair not to use the correct spelling for either of them. They had been frenemies before the bar fight, but after fists had flown and fingernails had broken, the friend part could never be recovered. Ted had tried to intervene, been shoved into a pair of drunk bikers, and abruptly the scrap between the two young women turned into a full-on bar brawl.

Bruised and aching, nose broken, at least one rib cracked, Ted had curled up against the back wall of the jail's holding cell, grateful the blood clotting his nostrils prevented him from smelling the metal, lidless toilet that sat out in the open, never mind the dozen other men crowded into the cell. It came as no surprise that New Year's Eve was a busy night for cops breaking up drunken brawls, never mind arresting drunk drivers and petty thieves.

Tonight, he missed that piss-stained holding cell. At least back then he had known someone would come to get him, that he would be charged and released.

More than thirty years since then. *How the hell did all that time pass by so fast?*

Tonight, Ted found himself in a cell again, but this time nobody was coming to get him. He could always blame the booze, but the whiskey hadn't drunk itself.

Half-drunk, drowning in grief and worry, he'd climbed into his car and driven to Garland Mountain Labs with some barely formed idea that they owed him answers and that he could force those answers out of them with the sheer power of his alcohol-fueled righteousness. He'd parked in the lot, stormed to the front door, and been greeted by a guy named Justin Jones, who was the facility manager or something like that.

Ted wanted his daughters, and he'd been certain Garland Mountain not only knew where they were but could retrieve them. He also wanted the lab to admit responsibility for everything—for the horror at the parade, the deaths of his ex-wife and son, the hideous thing that had infected Maeve.

He'd sobered up just a little—enough to know what an idiot he'd been.

Security guards had grabbed him the moment Dr. Jones had allowed him to cross the threshold into the building. They'd halfway carried him to an elevator, descended a level or two, and muscled him into a chamber that looked as if it had been designed by Apple engineers. An iRoom. MacJail. The walls were off-white, softly illuminated by recessed bulbs. The furnishings were a pair of sleek white chairs and a dormitory-narrow bed with tightly fitted sheets and a square pillow.

A narrow pocket door in the corner opened into a tiny bathroom. In the main cell—because it could only be a cell—white plastic cups were racked beside a white plastic sink, providing a water supply. Each wall had a section where the surface formed a pattern that approximated something that might be considered art, though of course there were no windows. The space might have been sterile, but it would not have been entirely unpleasant if not for the locked door and the fact he didn't have the option to leave.

For the moment, Ted was a prisoner. He didn't know how long they would keep him here, but the presence of that bed didn't bode well. It suggested that the people who had designed the security holding cell for Garland Mountain Labs had anticipated a time when seizing an intruder would not necessarily lead to calling the appropriate authorities. If they had called the police to report him, nobody would be expecting him to sleep there.

He'd alternated between sitting in one chair or the other, then pacing to try to sober up, but he had yet to so much as perch on the bed, no matter how strong he felt the urge to lie down. Arms crossed, back aching, ribs and knee shrieking with pain that reminded him of the impact of Oscar Hecht's car. Had his body cracked the BMW's windshield? He couldn't remember now, but he thought it must have.

Images of Logan and Ellen paced around the edges of his mind like wolves just at the edge of the firelight, ready to attack once the fire burned down. He couldn't think of them now, though. His daughters needed him.

Maeve had needed him, and instead of being the father he should have been, he'd let shock and pain and grief take control. *And addiction*, he thought. *Don't forget that.*

His tongue pushed out, moistening his lips. A sheen of sweat covered him, though the climate in the MacJail had been set to the perfect temperature. Whiskey would help, but he and the whiskey both knew it wasn't sufficient. Like a husband always in the shadow of his wife's first love, the whiskey knew it would never be enough. He wanted painkillers. Morphine. Heroin. If he had been locked in here before he'd done rehab, Ted knew he would have been crawling out of his skin, would have hurt himself, would have done anything to get out of here.

He stood up from the chair, flushed with fresh anger.

Maeve *still* needed him. Rose had gone after her because Ted had been too weak or too selfish or too broken—the "too" didn't matter. Rose had put her life in jeopardy because Ted hadn't been the father his daughters needed.

For heroin, he'd have done anything to escape.

"What about for your daughters, Ted?" he said aloud.

Do they mean less to you than addiction?

He rushed at the door, planted his hands on the smooth surface, and started kicking. The door shook in its frame. He had tried to smash the lock, tried to pry the door open, to no avail, and even as he kicked and pounded against it, he knew he would only succeed in bruising his hands and scuffing his boots.

Helpless, furious, he kept pounding.

Ted opened his mouth to shout for someone to come talk to him, listen to him. Anything. Set him free, let him keep looking. Keep him locked up if they had to, but don't leave him alone.

"Just tell me!" he screamed. "Tell me they're still alive!"

Every impact of his boot or his fist sent shock waves of pain through him. He felt cracked ribs shifting, felt something behind his knee tug and tear. Ted didn't care. There were two kinds of pain, and when you'd experienced both it was easy to see that only one of them mattered.

He hauled his boot back again, took a breath to shout, and in that slim, quiet instant, he heard something outside the door. Ted pressed his ear against the door. Out in the corridor, boots thundered past. Urgent voices barked sharp commands. The door vibrated against his cheek.

Something had happened. No alarms blared, but those sounds were an alarm all their own. Ted couldn't tell if it boded well for Maeve and

Rose, but one thing seemed certain—inside Garland Mountain Labs, the shit had hit the fan.

Justin W. Jones had lived his share of bad days. He'd held his mother's hand while she closed her eyes for the last time. At the age of eleven, he had stood on his front lawn and watched his father drive away, knowing in his gut the son of a bitch would never return and hating himself for wishing it weren't true. While pursuing his Ph.D., he had kissed the woman in charge of the lab where he'd spent three years and intended to spend at least two more. His first inkling that he'd misread their intimate rapport was her fist smashing his nose.

Today, though. The worst day of his life. No contest.

Justin strode along the corridor with six Garland security guards in their crisp tan uniforms. All of them wore sidearms and grim expressions. Several managed to keep a cold glint in their eyes, and he wondered if they were simply good at hiding their emotions or if they truly were unruffled by the path events had taken. People were dead, more were dying. The security team might not know the nature of the contagion that had escaped the lab, but they surely knew those with upper-level clearance considered it catastrophic. How those few stayed so calm, he would never know. And Justin couldn't ask them. He only knew their names from the ID badges they wore. Before today, they might as well have been masked storm troopers, for all he had given a crap about them.

Now he needed them to care about their jobs. Needed them to care very much. Maybe even care about him.

At the end of the corridor, he bent to press his eye to a retina scanner. The light above the door pinged green, and the door unlocked. He shoved it open and marched through with the security team in his wake.

On the other side of the door was another corridor, the mirror image of the first except that its walls were glass. To the left, the glass looked down into the central axis of the private lab space. To the right, the glass made up the windows of smaller labs, offices, and small conference areas.

"Dr. Jones, should we expect resistance?" one of the guards asked.

Justin glanced back at her, a flutter in his chest. "Be ready for anything."

They reached the end of the glass corridor. The last door on the right stood open. He could hear a voice shouting from inside the large office. Seven steps from the doorway, he wanted to turn and run, but there would be no running from any of the colossal fuckups of the past couple of days. Justin hoped he could live through it, and fortunately the best chance of that had just been handed to him by his contract manager at DARPA.

He knocked on the open door, and the three men inside looked up. Justin didn't wait to be invited in, just stepped through the door with the security team following. They spread out to either side of him, taking up half the office.

General Henry Wagner sat behind the desk in his on-site office, what he'd often called his home away from home in the many months that he'd been working in tandem with Garland Mountain Labs on Project: Red Hands. The two men from White Oak Security who stood behind him at attention were the only Blackcoats who hadn't been detailed to search for Maeve Sinclair, which was fortunate.

"Justin," the general said, even the name a scowl of dismissal. He scanned the faces of the security team, and though he must have known the answer, he asked the question, anyway. "What the fuck is this?"

At six foot four and on the high side of 250 pounds, General Wagner was an intimidating presence. He scared Justin far more than the two stone-faced Blackcoats. If the general had leaped up from his desk and started bellowing, as he'd done more than once in Justin's presence, things might have gone even worse. But Project: Red Hands had turned into the worst thing that had ever happened to Justin W. Jones, a storm of black clouds, crashing thunder, and death-strike lightning. The path to blue skies ran right through General Wagner—ran right over him, if Justin were being honest—and so fear would have to be forgotten.

"I'm sorry, General," Justin said in a quiet voice that cracked as he spoke. He cleared his throat, lifted his chin, put more authority into the words. "I've received direct instructions from DARPA director Steven Delacruz that you have been relieved of your authority in this matter and at this facility."

Wagner's upper lip curled in disgust. "Oh, have you? And to whom has that coward handed the reins?" The general smashed his hands down onto the desk. Through a sneer, he rose from the chair, towering over the rest of the people in the room. "Never mind. I know the answer to that."

"I'm sorry, General," Justin said.

"You have no gift for lying, Jones," the general said. He glanced back at the two Blackcoats, perhaps considering making a fight of it, but then he looked at the security team again. "This is your mess. I'll make certain that's not forgotten. When the cleanup begins, I promise you will be swept away with the rest of us."

Justin stiffened. He stared at the Blackcoats, realizing they planned to do nothing to aid the general. Wagner himself simmered with anger but did not appear ready to die in a useless gunfight over an order from his own superiors.

"I guess we'll see, General," Justin said. "But either way, we won't be the ones doing the cleanup. Whatever happens next, at least there's that small mercy."

General Wagner came out from behind the desk. The Blackcoats stayed where they were as the security guards surrounded the general and escorted him out of the office.

"I never asked for mercy," Wagner said as they led him away.

"Probably for the best, then, that no one's offering it."

Justin hung his head as he walked behind the security team. The procession made him think of his youth as an altar boy, and that rang painfully true. Penitent then, and penitent now. But in those days, he had been far more likely to be forgiven.

All he wanted now was for it all to be over. Whatever his penance, whatever the cost to bring this to an end, he would gladly pay it.

All of her adult life, Rue had looked different from most people. The hairstyle and color, the tattoos, were her way of letting the way she felt on the inside make its way to the surface. As a girl, she had considered herself quite ordinary-looking. Not ugly, not pretty, just unremarkable. So often, she had felt invisible, ignored by a world to which she had much to offer. Peacocks could spread their feathers, show the full kaleidoscope of their colors, strut with pride. More than anything, Rue wanted to be seen. She wanted to be a peacock, to be fully herself, to show all the colors inside her. She didn't need to be admired for them, but she refused to stay invisible.

Tonight, she had regretted that choice for the first time in her life.

"Stop panicking," Kat Isenberg said, reaching over to take her hand. "Take a breath, be still, and focus on the work."

Rue tried to take her advice, took a deep breath and let it out. They were inside Garland SL2-Alpha, the one lab inside Garland Mountain that was not under the auspices of the lab's director but those of the federal government. General Henry Wagner held the top spot, overseeing SL2-Alpha. Dr. Cristina Vargas was the lab supervisor, with Dr. Isenberg as her deputy, and a guy named Justin Jones was the project manager specifically overseeing Red Hands. None of them were in SL2-Alpha tonight. The shit had hit the fan, and they all had more important things to worry about. Red Hands had been born in this unit, and the research had blown up into absolute catastrophe for them.

Any other night, Rue would never have made it into SL2-Alpha, never mind into the restricted access sublevels of Garland Mountain Labs. But this wasn't any night, and she had Kat Isenberg with her. With Dr. Vargas absent, Kat was in charge.

"You're going to be fired," Rue said to her now, quietly, as Kat bent to peer over her shoulder. Kat had typed in her password to give Rue access to all the Red Hands research. It was not only a breach of security but would likely be considered a federal crime.

"Possibly executed," Kat replied, and Rue couldn't tell if she was joking. "Just do the work. Let me worry about the fallout."

It hadn't surprised her that Kat had gotten her into Garland Mountain. Without Vargas there to recognize her, and with the pressure and chaos unfolding, Kat's authority had been enough. But when they had gotten onto the elevator at the center of the facility's hexagon and Kat had used her ID to select a classified sublevel, Rue had been certain that a voice would come over an intercom or an alarm would go off, and the two of them would end up in plastic handcuffs or something similar.

Instead, several other people had gotten onto the elevator, looking harried and anxious, even a little afraid.

"What's going on?" Kat had asked.

A skinny thirtysomething guy with his beard and hair shorn down to about an inch—the sort of thing someone did when they didn't want to ever have to fuss with their appearance—looked at Kat with an angry spark in his eyes.

"You oughta know," Skinny replied. "It's your project that's causing all this bullshit."

"Jason," one of the others cautioned.

Skinny Jason rolled his eyes. "Please. It's just the truth. Dr. Isenberg is a grown-up. She can handle a little truth." He cut a sidelong glance at Rue, his expression full of disapproval of her as well, though it seemed more for her association with Kat than for her appearance.

"I can, actually," Kat said. "So share it with me?"

Skinny Jason tsked and fixed her with a glare. "We're all in the dark here. Aside from your people and maybe a handful of supervisors, we don't even know what you're all doing to fix this. All we've been told is that Dr. Hecht was infected and he took off and infected a bunch of other people, and now they're all fucking dead. Great job, government scientists."

Rue saw the way the words hurt Kat, the way her eyes crinkled as the sting set in.

"Hey," Rue said. "There's no need for—"

"Who the fuck are you?" Skinny Jason asked.

Kat didn't give her a chance to answer. "She's a consultant we've brought in to try to resolve this quickly."

Skinny Jason reappraised Rue. "Well, I hope you're smarter than this batch."

The elevator door had opened and they'd all gotten off at sublevel 2. Others were moving through the common area that surrounded the elevator bank. Some carried boxes or metallic containers in their arms and were waiting for the elevator to go back up. Several of the labs around the hexagon on sublevel 2 were dark inside, the doors closed and presumably locked. Rue had wondered but said nothing.

Inside Garland SL2-Alpha, two research assistants were still working when Kat used her ID to unlock the door, ushering Rue inside. It had been from those assistants that they'd learned General Wagner had arranged for the COO of Garland Mountain to order the rest of the labs shut down and the research teams sent home if they lived inside the quarantine zone. Others were to evacuate if they could find somewhere else to stay.

"It's like last call at the bar," one of the assistants said. "They don't have to go home, but they can't stay here."

Wagner had also sent Dr. Vargas and several others from SL2-Alpha over to join the Blackcoats. Maeve Sinclair had apparently been located. It would only be a matter of time before she would be brought in, dead or alive, and Vargas had been tasked with overseeing the process of getting her back to Garland Mountain without allowing anyone else to be exposed to Red Hands.

"General Wagner asked that we let him know as soon as you returned," the other assistant said, reaching for a phone.

"Don't do that," Kat had said.

The two assistants shot her twin looks of concern. General Wagner had given them an order. They were scientists, but they worked for DARPA, and Wagner was the top of their hierarchy. Could Dr. Isenberg countermand his order?

"The general—"

"Is only going to get in the way of the work we have to do, right here and right now," Kat said.

The assistants both hesitated.

"Hi," Rue said, getting their attention. "I'm a new face and a new name, but all four of us have the same goal here—trying to make sure nobody else dies. If not a cure, we need a counteragent, something that will save Maeve Sinclair's life if we can manage it. If not, then something that will inhibit infection in others. You wouldn't be a part of this project if you weren't all brilliant. I don't know about you, but I don't trust your General Wagner to use that brilliance to save lives instead of using it to help cover his ass. You want to call him, get him down here to give Dr. Isenberg her marching orders? Be my guest."

"Actually," Kat said, "you two should go with the rest. The way things are going, you'll be safer outside than inside."

The two assistants had stared at her. The standoff lasted all of three seconds before they gathered their things and departed.

Rue had spent the past couple of hours poring through the work Dr. Hecht had done on Project: Red Hands before he had purposely infected himself. The bacterium presented as unlike anything Rue had encountered before, and yet there were elements that were familiar, strands that mirrored the structure of other germs. Like linguists managing to translate a few specific phrases in an ancient, unknown language, she thought she and Kat could use those few strands to unravel the rest of Red Hands and find a cure. Or if not a cure, at least a treatment.

If they had the time.

"That was a big sigh," Kat said. "I don't like the sound of that."

"I think we can do it," Rue replied. "If General Wagner will let us. If we can work it out before they drag us out of here."

A buzzer sounded inside the lab. Rue glanced up to see that Kat had stepped back and was looking out toward the door.

"Um, I think you need to see this," Kat said.

Rue swore, thinking she had jinxed them with her own words. She rose and followed Kat through the lab, out to the glass wall at the entrance, beyond which they could see the common area and the elevator bank. Men and women in white shirts and dark jackets hustled through the common area.

"Who the hell is this now?" Rue asked.

Kat shook her head. "Not a clue."

A woman arrived at the entrance to SL2-Alpha. She gave them a little wave, then knocked at the door to the unit. Only then did Rue spot the three bold yellow letters inscribed over the left breast on her navy-blue jacket.

DHS. Department of Homeland Security.

"Holy shit," Kat said. "General Wagner must be furious."

Rue smiled. "For better or worse, something tells me General Wagner isn't your boss anymore."

The DHS agent knocked again, looking less pleasant and less patient than a moment before.

"For better or worse," Kat echoed.

She buzzed the agent in.

26

Maeve drifted in a red limbo, a space that might have felt like sleep if not for the taste of blood and sorrow on her lips. She thought her eyes were open, but could see only a kind of crimson fog. Or perhaps it might have been a cloud, and she was flying through it. A sound reached her, someone shouting. Metal clanged against metal, perhaps swords clashing or armor turning away a dagger strike. There came a roar that might have been a black bear or . . .

Or an engine. It had to be an engine.

Sleep now, darling.

Only when she heard the words did Maeve realize she did not float there alone. She tried to move, sit up, tilt her head to seek out the shape that lurked just at the edge of her vision, but she found herself paralyzed. Now that her companion had spoken, she felt it there in the fog beside her, crawling toward her. It crept below her, behind her, slipped up and whispered in her ear.

You've been so very ill. Rest now. The time of pain and hunger has passed.

Something sharp touched her scalp, a finger, joined by others. As it caressed her, ran its fingers through her hair, Maeve tried to scream. Her lips would not move. The terror trapped itself inside her, a tumor no surgery could remove, and it grew with every heartbeat, building pressure that had no release.

Her eyes widened. God, she wanted to cry, but like her scream, the tears would not come. The red fog began to darken, to blacken.

"—*touch her. Those wounds are weeping. Put your hands up, and don't go near her.*"

A voice. Not the one that whispered to her, not the one that enveloped her in sorrow. A different voice, this one angry.

"*None of us are that stupid,*" yet another voice replied. "*Look at her. Jesus, her throat is so bloated. You ever see anything like this?*"

"*You'll all be quarantined,*" the first voice said. And then, as if to a third someone, beyond her hearing, he said, "*Get him out of here. Get them all out. Nobody without a hazmat suit comes within fifty yards of her. Tell Vargas not to approach. She can supervise from up on the ridge.*"

Maeve had been cold until now. She hadn't realized just how cold until her bones began to grow warm, heating her from within. Floating in that fog, she began to feel the weight of her body for the first time. Pain cramped her chest and clawed at her throat, and she wanted to talk, to cry out to the whisperer that he had promised she would feel no more pain.

Go away, he told her. *You're a fool to fight this. You can't trap me here. I'm hungry, my darling, and I will grow with that hunger. Infection has taken you. There's no room left in this flesh for you.*

The fingers caressing her face pushed through her skin, began to tug at her face as if the whisperer meant to strip her down to muscle and gristle and hide beneath the mask of her life. But the tugging ceased and the intrusion worsened. She felt the whisperer sliding into her, lifting her face, pushing in beside her as if he had raised the edge of her comforter and slipped beside her in bed in the middle of the night.

Then she knew him. Saw him, and saw herself. One of them dead and the other hideously alive. This was no withering, gnawing hunger. What inhabited her now breathed malice, flexed predatory sinew. Sickness fled her. The pain, the heat, the desire . . . once upon a time, human beings had carried in their souls an intimate knowledge of evil. Most of the world had breathed it in so often, seen it in the eyes of others enough times, that they could no longer recognize it for what it was. How it felt.

Only a flicker of self remained inside her, a thing that recognized itself as Maeve Sinclair. Recoiling from the filth that polluted her, she regretted not surrendering to death. The whisperer had warned her, tried to send her away, and she had fought him.

Rose.

Out there somewhere, her sister had been infected. As the hunger, the Red Death, had clawed its way into Rose, Maeve had twisted her thoughts around the presence within her and held on with everything she had, all the things that made her Maeve. Dying, the infection had passed from her to Rose, but Maeve had grasped hold and refused to relinquish it.

Now they were here—Maeve and the hunger. The whisperer. Lost in red limbo. And she understood what a terrible mistake it had been.

As the last spark of herself, the last shard of Maeve Sinclair, winked out, she felt the comfort of a sheet being drawn over her corpse.

They would come back for her body, the hunger knew.

The hunger, after all, was all that remained inside the corpse of Maeve Sinclair. It stirred, and deepened . . . and it waited.

Walker bumped around in the back of a Jeep, head muzzy with exhaustion. His eyes burned. He ought to have felt relieved it was over. He sure as hell ought to have felt safer in the back of the Jeep than he had with a bunch of Blackcoats shooting at him, but this didn't feel like safety, and he could not allow himself to think it was over.

So much for mission accomplished, he thought.

Maeve Sinclair lay dead back in the gorge, a bunch of researchers and DHS agents overseeing the quarantining and transfer of her corpse.

Alena Boudreau sat next to Walker, the two of them knocking shoulders as the Jeep rattled along a trail that would lead them off the mountain. They were about six miles from Garland Mountain Labs. In the Jeep, on the trails, then the road, it might take them fifteen minutes to reach the facility. Walker wondered if he could manage to avoid smashing Alena in the skull for that long. Sure, she was a seventysomething-year-old woman, but she'd also sent him on this assignment with only a fraction of the information she ought to have given him. If he had known what she was up to behind the scenes, that the cavalry would be coming, Walker would have done things differently. Maeve might still be alive.

In the front passenger seat, Priya nursed her wounded shoulder, which had already received some first aid from a medic. Walker didn't think it was physical pain that made Priya turn her face from the driver and swipe at her eyes. The driver pretended not to notice her tears. In the backseat, Walker and Alena said nothing. No words that might embarrass Priya, nor any words of comfort.

What could they say?

Priya loved Rose. Walker had seen the love between them, the desperation, the fear for one another. Either one of those young women would do anything, sacrifice any part of themselves—even all of themselves—for the other. But Priya sat silently crying in the front seat of the Jeep, and Rose rode in the vehicle ahead of them—a boxy yellow hazmat ambulance that hadn't been made for this terrain. It bumped along, just ahead of the Jeep, a lonely, terrified, grieving young woman in the back.

Walker could not have stopped Rose from touching Maeve. If he'd spotted her moving toward her sister earlier than he had, what could he have done? Shoot her to save her?

Even so, it haunted him.

"You're awfully quiet," Alena said.

Walker turned to stare at her, the seat crinkling beneath him. In his mind, the picture of Maeve Sinclair falling, the bullets punching through her, would not be erased.

"You used me," he said quietly, glancing at Priya, hoping the rumble of the Jeep would blot out much of what he said. "Wagner put me on the sidelines. You made your move, brought in your people. You needed someone capable of finding the woman, someone who could lock her down, keep the situation from getting worse without letting her fall into Wagner's hands. His project blew up in his face, and you saw your chance."

"General Wagner has been running black box operations even his superiors didn't know about," Alena said. "When subordinates expressed safety concerns, they suffered retribution. Wagner ordered Red Hands tested on CIA prisoners in an off-book facility in Romania. Oscar Hecht was the perfect partner for him. There isn't a line Wagner won't cross, and Hecht felt the same way. These are men who don't play by anyone's rules. Hecht is dead, and thanks to him and Wagner, so are a lot of other people. So tell me, Benjamin, what have I done that has so upset you? I offered you a job, and you accepted."

He could see the vein in her temple pulse while she spoke. Her passion and dedication in her work were the stuff of legend, but he'd never heard she was ruthless.

Walker shook his head. "Alena—"

"Director Boudreau, if you still work for me."

He locked eyes with her. "Alena," he repeated. "The people we work for do a lot of unpleasant things. Ugly things. Most of the time, there's a reason for that ugliness, a higher purpose, and I believe in that higher purpose. But you left me in the dark and used me—"

"I didn't know who I could trust."

"—and as a result, people are dead who might otherwise be alive."

He stopped himself from mentioning Rose Sinclair. Priya had to be listening to all of this now, even in her shock and sadness. Rose might not have become the carrier of Red Hands if Alena had been open with Walker about what was really going on, and he didn't want to hurt her further with an *if*. That word could be the most painful in the English language. Life and death were full of ifs, and they never saved anyone an ounce of anguish.

"We'll talk more when this is over," Walker said, nodding toward the back of Priya's head so Alena would understand his reticence.

She raised an eyebrow. "It's already over, Walker. It's under control."

Walker went silent. The Jeep bumped through several potholes and ruts, and then pulled out onto the road. Just a few minutes and they would be at Garland Mountain. He looked through the windshield at the yellow hazmat ambulance ahead of them, and he thought of Rose.

It's under control, Alena had said.

Walker wished he could believe that.

Driving up to the rear gate of the Garland Mountain Labs complex, they passed two Humvees heading in the opposite direction—Blackcoats withdrawing. Dismissed. Walker glanced at the driver of the second Humvee as they went by, saw the angry line of his lips pressed together, and felt as if this whole thing might really be over.

The guards at the rear gate took one look at Alena's ID and waved them through. The Homeland Security agent behind the wheel of the Jeep didn't bother with a parking space; he drove right up to the paved walkway by the heavily fortified rear doors and killed the engine. Alena thanked him and climbed out. Walker went around to help Priya. She gave him a dark look, as if she blamed him for her injuries, maybe for all the day's horrors, but she accepted his aid in climbing from the Jeep and leaned on him for support as she started up the walkway.

"It's an exodus," she said, nodding toward the many people and cars in the parking lot.

Lab coats, T-shirts, suit jackets—something like twenty people were loading plastic containers and metallic cases into their cars, presumably files and research, and were leaving Garland Mountain like rats leaving a sinking ship.

Walker helped Priya shuffle a bit faster along the walkway, trying to catch up with Alena. "You're letting all these people leave? You don't know what research they're taking with them."

Alena reached the door, showed her ID, and the guard inside buzzed them through. She yanked the door open and held it for them. Her blue eyes sharpened.

"They're not our concern. Better they be out of the way, somewhere safe."

Priya hesitated to enter the building. She held back, taking long breaths, and Walker worried that blood loss had finally caught up with her and she might collapse. The aboveground levels of the Garland

Mountain complex were sprawling, and he knew they must have some kind of medical facility inside.

"You okay?" he asked. "Do you need me to—"

Priya turned to glare at Alena, who still held the door open for them. "I want to see Rose."

"She's already here," Alena replied. "They're getting her settled in a containment room. You'll be able to see her very soon."

"I don't trust you," Priya said.

Alena smiled thinly. "Fair enough. Trust is currency. We shouldn't give it to people who haven't earned it. Give me a chance to try."

After another moment's hesitation, Priya nodded, and Walker escorted her through the door and past the guards, who buzzed them through an inner door and into an industrial-looking lobby area, much more utilitarian than the gleaming reception area at the main entrance. Across the lobby, a pair of techs in hazmat suits were spraying some kind of orange-tinged foam onto the walls and floor of an open elevator, making it clear which direction they had taken Rose. Nobody else wore hazmat suits, and nobody stepped forward to try to disinfect Walker, Priya, or Alena, so the Garland Mountain team still felt the sickness couldn't be transmitted except by Rose's touch. But Rose had touched the walls, railings, or doors inside the elevator, so they weren't taking any chances.

"This way," one of the guards said, gesturing to the left, where a set of steel doors buzzed to let them in. The guard pulled the door open and held it as they went through.

Perhaps in a kind of protective gesture, Walker went ahead of them, so whatever waited on the other side, he would encounter it first. Priya had taken a bullet many hours before and still managed to shuffle along behind him. She needed further care before she collapsed completely, but he knew Rose would be her first priority. Alena came last, but Walker knew she wasn't going anywhere.

Three figures approached them along the corridor, one of them a ginger-haired Homeland Security agent with her hand resting on the butt of her gun. She stalked slightly behind the other two, walking as if she had found herself in a combat zone. But the two men who preceded her were the ones who caught Walker's full attention. One of them was the arrogant lab coat he'd thought of as Rasputin when they'd met almost twelve hours before. The man's name tag floated in Walker's memory—Justin W. Jones.

The other guy shouted Priya's name and rushed along the corridor toward her.

Ted Sinclair.

Walker stepped aside to let Ted get to Priya. Bleary-eyed, disheveled, Ted paused with his hands outstretched. He'd been about to pull Priya into a hug, but now he saw the bloody field dressing on her shoulder and the blood soaking through her T-shirt, and his face crumbled.

"Oh, Pri," Ted said.

"It's okay," she said, sliding her right arm around him and leaning her head against his chest. "Just be gentle."

Alena, Walker, Dr. Jones, and the ginger DHS agent stood awkwardly in the corridor as the two of them wept together. Priya had been tough, holding her grief and fear inside, but now she let her tears flow. Walker had been nurturing a lot of ugly thoughts about Ted Sinclair over the course of the day, but as he watched the tenderness and love with which Ted comforted Priya, he softened. Ted might be a drunk and an addict—hell, Walker could smell the whiskey sweating out of his pores—but he was a good enough father that his daughter's girlfriend put her faith in him, leaned on him like this.

Walker decided he wasn't in any position to judge another father.

"They're taking care of Rose," Ted said, holding Priya at arm's length. She might have been a grown woman, almost done with college, but he wiped her tears away as if she were his child. "I know she's infected. Dr. Jones explained what's happening. They're searching for a cure, and in the meantime, they think they might be able to make the infection . . . stop, or . . ."

Ted looked at Justin W. Jones, searching for the right words.

"Dr. Isenberg might be able to force the infection into dormancy. Suspend the symptoms," Jones said, glancing at Walker and Alena. "It's a long shot, but if it works . . . well, it won't keep Rose from being contagious. She'd have to remain quarantined. But it would prevent her from getting any sicker in the meantime, giving us more time."

Alena pushed past Walker, staring at Jones. "This is something you were developing after Oscar Hecht was infected?"

Jones thought the question over. "Not exactly. But they were able to use Hecht's notes to build on."

"Let me guess. You had Hecht researching how to control the infection," Walker said, glaring. "Turn it on and turn it off, so it would be a more effective murder weapon."

Priya shot him an admonishing glance. "It doesn't matter. The only thing we care about is whether or not it will help Rose."

"And Maeve," Ted added. He glanced at Walker. "They brought Rose in, but Dr. Jones said they had to be more careful with Maeve. That she's on the way."

Walker flinched, his stomach twisting into a knot. He glanced at Priya, saw the sorrow and pity contort her features, watched Ted Sinclair as he read the look that passed between them.

"What?" Ted said, shaking his head. "No. Dr. Jones said—"

Alena stared at the lab director with a sneer of disgust. "Dr. Jones is a fucking coward."

Walker put a hand on Ted's arm. "I'm sorry, Ted. I said I'd get her off the mountain—"

Ted pulled away from Walker, lips pressed tightly, trembling. He started to speak and then only shook his head again. In less than twenty-four hours, he'd lost a son and a daughter and their mother, the woman with whom he'd shared a life and three children. The only one left was Rose.

This time, Priya was the one to comfort him.

A long minute passed in the silence of grief. Finally, Alena went over and put a hand on Ted's arm. "Mr. Sinclair, why don't Dr. Jones and I take you to see Rose now? We can't be in the room with her at the moment, but we can speak to her through glass."

Ted stood a bit straighter and nodded. Alena gestured to Dr. Jones, and the four of them started down the corridor, back the way Jones and Ted had come, apparently to find an elevator that wasn't in the midst of being sterilized. Walker watched Priya, thinking she might turn and give a wave of farewell, but she had more important things on her mind.

"Dr. Walker, yes?" the ginger DHS agent said.

"That's right."

"I'm supposed to take you down to sublevel two. Apparently, they're waiting for you."

Walker cast a final glance at Ted Sinclair. Whiskey or no whiskey, it said something about the man that he hadn't drunk or drugged himself into a coma after the day he'd had. Walker silently wished him well, then turned to the DHS agent.

"Lead on."

A knock on the glass door. Rue jerked upright in her chair, knocking over Dr. Isenberg's nearly empty coffee cup. A little brown dribble spilled onto an array of paperwork before she'd snatched up the cup. She muttered a quiet profanity as she glanced over at the door to see Ben Walker on the other side of the glass. Rue burst into a smile of relief and victory, but Walker didn't reciprocate.

"Oh no." Rue stood and hurried to the door. "Please, God . . ."

As she opened the door, Kat Isenberg came up from the back of the lab, summoned from her work by Walker's knocking.

"Dr. Crooker," Walker said, clasping her hand and then reaching out to shake with Isenberg. "Kat, I won't ask how you are. I can only thank you."

"I'm glad to see you, Walker," Isenberg said.

Rue searched his eyes. "I tried you so many times on the stupid earbud."

Walker blinked as if he'd forgotten about it. He dug the plastic nub from his ear and tossed it into the trash can by Isenberg's desk. "I was in the gorge, then in a cave since sunset, until a little while ago. Once I found Maeve—"

"You *did* find her? Oh, God, from the look on your face, I thought the worst. Kat and I have made some progress," she said, all in a rush.

"They were already working on ways to modulate the symptoms, manipulating the bacterium. It's pretty harrowing, honestly, when I think about what they were trying to accomplish, but once Kat and I started looking at that research specifically with an eye toward diminishing the severity of the symptoms instead of—"

"Rue," Walker said.

"The point is, we think we can slow it down. Right now, it wouldn't help the newly infected much. It might buy them a couple of hours of pretty agonizing life, but it wouldn't save them. But we're looking at Dr. Hecht's samples from after he infected himself, testing on them, trying to see what we can do for Maeve—"

"Rue, stop," Walker said, holding up a hand, eyes squeezed shut. He opened them, glanced at Dr. Isenberg, then turned again to Rue. "You're not working to help Maeve anymore. You're working to help Rose. Maeve is—"

"No," Rue said, shaking her head.

"She's gone. But Rose is still here, and you can help her."

Rue heard a quiet little cry of anguish, like the air leaving a balloon. It took a moment before she realized the sound had come from her.

"Poor Ted," she said. "Oh, Maeve. She was the sweetest little girl, so smart. When she went through her teen years, the hostility broke Ted's heart. Then when she went to college and it was like she saw him with new eyes and she was so kind to him, it was like the greatest gift. He was so . . ."

Rue hung her head. Kat Isenberg reached out and held her hand, squeezed her fingers. Rue couldn't wrap her mind around it—Maeve and Logan and Ellen, all gone, and now Rose sick with the same thing, infected by Red Hands. Tainted by something Dr. Isenberg thought might actually be evil. Real, malevolent evil.

"Is Ted . . . ?"

"He's with Rose and Priya," Walker said. "Priya's been shot, but she's going to be all right. The bullet didn't hit anything vital, and she's tough as nails."

"Always has been," Rue said. "Rose fell for her senior year in high school. Priya lets her parents turn a blind eye to the two of them, but she holds her head up, never apologizes for who she is. She's tough. But I guess she'll need to be."

Rue gave Kat's hand a grateful squeeze, then pulled away and went to sit back down at her desk. "Come on. Let's get back to work. The Sinclairs are like my family. This right here is the only way I know how to help Ted and Rose, so that's what I'm going to do."

"Okay. I'll be back in a while, see if I can help at all," Walker said. He reached for the door, but paused to look at Isenberg. "There's a hunger in them, y'know. The one who carries the contagion—Hecht, then Maeve, and now Rose. The longer they go without infecting someone, without killing someone, the worse the sickness hits them. But there's a hunger, too, driving them to want to pass that infection along. If you can treat Rose's symptoms, keep her from succumbing to the sickness, will that limit the hunger?"

"I wish we could tell you," Isenberg replied. "Theoretically, the answer's yes, but . . ."

"But?" Walker asked.

Rue stared at the computer screen, not looking up at them. "But it depends how much of the malignance in Rose is rooted in the bacteria, and how much is just . . . evil."

The only thing Rose wanted was a blanket. As cool as the mountain air had been out there in the dark, even in July, it felt even colder in the little room where they had her locked up. A clean room, they called it. Not in the sense of being neat and tidy, though it was both of those things, but in the sense of being sterile. Of course, sterile also meant mind-numbingly boring.

"Try not to think of it as a jail cell," said the Homeland Security agent who had opened the door for her when they'd put her in the room.

As jail cells went, Rose had to admit it leaned toward fancy. The whole room was off-white and looked to be made of plastic. The bathroom seemed to be one piece, as if it had been carved out of that white plastic and then slotted into place. The toilet and sink had biohazard symbols on them, as did the bathroom door, which made Rose feel a bit like a superhero. Or a weapon.

They'd given her a soft, cozy sweatshirt with *Garland Mountain Labs* on it, like it came from a souvenir store, or like these scientists and security guards had their own softball team. The pants, though, were thin cotton hospital scrubs, hence her desire for a blanket.

She had a bed. Between that and the bathroom, she thought she might be in this quarantine room for a while, but she wondered how they were going to handle feeding her. Certainly they wouldn't have gone to all this trouble if they were going to let her starve to death.

Stop, she thought. *Don't think about food.*

Rose sat on the edge of a chair, looking at her reflection in the blank screen of the TV attached to the wall. *Don't think about it.*

She was hungry. Not thinking about being hungry didn't make the hunger go away. What she wondered, though, was whether she felt hungry for food . . . or for something else. Her throat had begun to hurt. A tickle of a cough irritated the back of her throat. In her dark reflection, she could see dark splotches on her neck and heavy circles under her eyes like she'd let some goth punk girlfriend do her makeup.

So . . . hungry, she thought.

And froze, staring at her own eyes in that reflection, because the voice in her head just now hadn't sounded like her, had it?

Rose hugged herself, bent over, perched on the edge of the chair. This was quarantine. She was supposed to be alone here, but Rose knew she would never truly be alone again. She opened her mouth to scream, but a little bell rang in her room, and she whipped around to see a green light blinking on the wall.

There were four doors in her clean room—one a closet, one the bathroom, one the door through which the men in hazmat suits had brought her, and a fourth, which had been locked when she'd tried the latch. Now that green light blinked just inches from the latch on the fourth door. Rose stood, went to the door, turned the latch . . . and it opened.

"Oh, Rosie," her father said.

Rose stared at him, then at Priya, who'd been given a sweatshirt that matched Rose's own. A spot of blood showed through the fabric, where she'd been shot, but Priya did not look quite as pale as before.

A hard plastic chair was the only piece of furniture on Rose's side of the glass, and she sat quickly, mostly to avoid falling down. She hugged herself, staring at the two of them. First at Priya, then at her dad.

She thought of Maeve.

"Daddy," she said, suddenly a little girl again. "I'm so sorry."

Her father's eyes were a bit glassy, like he'd been drinking, but he stood straight enough that she knew his thoughts were clear. Their side of the visiting room was no bigger than Rose's—except there were two chairs over there—but neither Ted nor Priya bothered to sit down. Ted put both hands on the glass that separated them. He moved slowly, and she could tell his cracked ribs still pained him, but he barely seemed to notice as he looked in at her.

"You were brave," he told her. "You found your sister. I should've been there. I should've . . ."

He glanced away, as if he couldn't meet her gaze.

Rose knew nothing she could say would make him feel better. His injuries would have held him back. He'd never have found Maeve. Rose and Priya had gone off on their own without consulting him because none of them had been thinking clearly, logic fogged by trauma and grief. Now here they were.

"Babe," Priya said.

Her left arm had been put in a sling, but Priya reached to touch the glass with her right hand, fingers splayed. Rose covered it with her own hand, an inch of glass between them, protecting Priya from the disease eating away at Rose.

Rose put her forehead against the glass, and Priya did the same.

"They think they can help you," Priya said quietly. "They're working on it."

Rose lifted her head, now eye to eye with Priya, but she said nothing about the prospect of these scientists helping her. Priya hadn't been infected, but after being with Maeve and seeing what had happened to her, what was inside her, they knew that the scientists at Garland

Mountain Labs hadn't developed this malignant contagion . . . they had *unleashed* it.

There's no putting the genie back in the bottle, she thought.

Or, at least, Rose hoped the thought was her own.

"Fight it," Priya said as if she could see the doubt and worry in Rose's face. "I love you, Rose. I love you, and I need you."

Rose could only give her a quiet nod. She would fight the influence of the thing whispering, even now, deep inside her. For Priya's sake, yes, and for her dad's sake. She was all he had left. But mostly, she would fight for Logan and Mom and for Maeve, all of whom the hunger had taken from her. *Rose and the Red Death*, she thought. *Only one of us will live.*

This time, she knew the thought was her own.

But the whispers were still there, slithering in her skull.

Rose looked at Priya and her dad. The way they stood, even the way they looked at her, she could see they thought this was over.

But it wasn't over. Not at all.

27

If someone had asked her even two hours earlier, Cristina Vargas would have predicted an unmitigated disaster for Project: Red Hands. Already, Oscar Hecht's decision to experiment on himself had led to a pile of corpses, including his own. Hecht had killed eight people with his BMW at the parade and another nine with his bare hands before Maeve Sinclair had bashed his skull in with a baseball bat. In addition to Hecht, Maeve had gone on to kill her mother and brother. The chaos in video clips made it difficult to say with certainty whether the other two people who'd died the morning of July 4 had been touched by Hecht or by Maeve, but either way, they were dead.

Then the slow-motion massacre had moved up onto Mount Champney. They didn't have a head count yet, but between those shot to death and those infected with Red Hands, the dead numbered in the dozens. General Wagner had been much less concerned with how to spin the news than he'd been with capturing Maeve Sinclair, but everything had changed now. The general had been removed, and it would be up to Homeland Security to devise a story to explain the video that the whole world had seen of Oscar Hecht, as well as the quarantine, and the deaths in the mountains above Jericho Falls.

Vargas mustered a morbid grin. At least it wasn't *her* job.

She stood on the rim of Moonglow River Gorge. The whole

area had turned into a hive of postcrisis activity. Muddy Jeeps and three-wheelers lined the rim, some parked between trees. Homeland Security had accounted for nearly all the White Oak Security employees—living or dead—who had been working for General Wagner. Bodies were being loaded onto wagons and into the backs of Jeeps. Some asshole with a drone had been taken into custody, his drone destroyed. The state and local police had been informed that Maeve Sinclair had been found and they'd been asked to stand down.

One thing Vargas had to say for SRC Director Alena Boudreau— the old bitch worked fast. And she knew how to utilize her assets. Vargas had initially worried that her involvement with Red Hands would end her career, but so far it appeared that the general would suffer the consequences and that Vargas would be retained to continue her research. The bad news was that Maeve Sinclair had died.

But Rose Sinclair had been infected. That might not have been good news for Rose, but for Vargas, it was Christmas morning. They would have a living subject and two dead ones—Maeve and Oscar Hecht, not to mention the bodies of all those Maeve and Oscar had killed.

A gust of wind swirled across the rim of the gorge. Vargas shivered and looked up at the sky, breathing in the mountain air. It must have been going on 3:00 a.m. by now, she thought, and the last of the clouds had begun to clear off, exposing the stars and a crescent moon. It had been a long time since she had slept, but she felt energized. Exhilarated. Sleep could wait.

The distant buzz of an approaching helicopter arrived on the next gust of wind, just as a Garland Mountain lab monkey named Hurwitz trotted up to her.

"Dr. Vargas, they're prepping to move the body. The chopper's almost here," Hurwitz said.

So earnest and dutiful. Alena Boudreau would be cleaning house now that she had taken over, but Hurwitz couldn't be sure if Vargas would still have any power, so he was kissing her ass just in case. She nearly snapped at him—did he think she couldn't hear the helicopter approaching? Instead, she thanked him with a beatific smile and turned to look down into the gorge. Even when Hurwitz took up position beside her, almost elbow to elbow, as if they were equals, Vargas did not slap him down. Like Hurwitz, Vargas couldn't be sure what the new boss might do. She had to be careful, just in case this obsequious, snot-nosed lab monkey landed higher up the ladder than Vargas herself.

Fucking politics, she thought.

Down in the gorge, retrieval teams were still zipping corpses into body bags. They wore hazmat suits, despite Vargas's certainty that they couldn't be infected by contact with Maeve Sinclair's victims. Vargas and her deputy, Kat Isenberg, had examined Oscar Hecht's body themselves and were fairly sure that even contact with Maeve's corpse wouldn't release contagion. Whatever activated the passage of the infection from host to victim, it went dormant when the host died. At least, it had gone dormant in Oscar.

But better safe than sorry.

The helicopter buzzed over the tops of the trees. Vargas and Hurwitz both squinted and covered their eyes as the spotlights beneath the chopper swept the rim of the gorge. Arrays of emergency lights had been set up down at the bottom of the gorge to help with the investigation and body retrieval. The helicopter's spotlights added to those lights, and now the area around Maeve's corpse lit up like high noon in the desert. Several techs in hazmat suits backed away from Maeve's corpse, waving to the chopper. Two of them knelt by the body, and Vargas saw they had not finished preparing it for airlift. The techs had shifted the corpse onto a backboard to preserve its condition, and now they lifted it, then lowered it into the thick, yellow, plastic body bag specifically crafted for potentially infected human remains. Black biohazard symbols were printed all over the yellow plastic.

"It's finally over," Hurwitz said as if he'd been running the show all along.

Vargas glanced at him. "It's just starting, actually. Unless you need a vacation."

Hurwitz smiled thinly. "Are you . . ."

He narrowed his eyes and leaned forward, as if he meant to pitch himself over the edge. Vargas looked into the gorge, following Hurwitz's gaze, and felt a chill envelop her. She took a step back from the rim.

The corpse of Maeve Sinclair stood up, yellow biohazard body bag pooled around its ankles. Hazmat-suited techs scrambled away from her, but the dead thing reached out and caught the back of one tech's hood. Maeve yanked the tech toward her, ripped open the plastic hood, then shoved the tech away from her. Grasping at the rip in his hood, the tech staggered a dozen feet, fell to his knees, and sprawled face-first onto the rocks at the edge of the Moonglow River, twitched once, and went still.

Dead.

Maeve hadn't touched him.

"Oh, fuck this," Hurwitz said, backing quickly away from the rim. He turned and started running toward the nearest mud-spattered Jeep.

Vargas couldn't run. She could barely think. None of this made sense. The whole point of Red Hands was that it passed through skin-on-skin contact. She moved closer to the rim, resisting the urge to flee. The thing that had been Maeve Sinclair turned south and began to stagger in that direction, first slowly and then with unsettling speed. Its jerky, flailing movements suggested that whatever had happened to Maeve, even if she were somehow still alive—or alive again—her brain had stopped worked properly.

"Shoot her," Vargas said quietly. Then she unclipped the radio at her belt, thumbed the button. "This is Cristina Vargas. We have Subject Two secured at the lab. We do not need Subject One. Eliminate her."

"Dr. Vargas," a voice came back, fuzzed with static. "Director Boudreau specifically—"

"Fuck her! She's not here!" Vargas barked, voice cracking in panic. Her stomach churned and her heart pounded, and it occurred to her that there had been emotions she had never understood before now. Terror. Real terror. Her hands clenched and her palms turned slick with sweat as she shook her head and leaned farther over the edge, watching as hazmat-suited techs climbed rocks to get out of Maeve's path and others retreated north. One of them jumped in the river, swept south in the current.

They had seen what Vargas had seen. Maeve had never touched the tech she'd just killed.

Not just terror, Vargas thought. *Revulsion*. For all Oscar Hecht's talk about whispers in his head, about the Red Death, she'd thought it all absurd. But she watched Maeve spider-crawl over massive stone slabs and reach the wall of the gorge, and she understood that the thing down there in the gorge must be evil. Vargas would have said, even two minutes ago, that evil existed only in myth.

A whimper escaped from her lips.

She thumbed the radio again. "Did you hear me? Kill her, god-damn it!"

Still, they held off. The helicopter hovered, the pilot uncertain what to do next, rotors blasting a wicked downdraft into the gorge.

Then Maeve started climbing the wall, scrabbling on rock and dirt and clawing straight upward. The Blackcoats were gone and these Department of Homeland Security agents had a different set of or-ders, but at least one of them must have felt the terror that Vargas felt. A single gun opened fire, and then others followed. A bullet struck Maeve Sinclair in the head, blew out the side of her face, and she swung away from the wall, clinging by the fingers of one hand.

Her feet found purchase. Her free hand dug into a crevice. She leaned her head back and in the chopper's spotlights. The single eye remaining in the intact left side of her face glared up at the DHS agents. Maeve shook as if in a seizure, managed to cling to the rock face, and then she screamed in a voice that sounded more like a wounded beast than anything human.

The helicopter veered off. The rotors whined as it cut southeast, sliced diagonally into the gorge, and struck the opposite wall. The whole gorge shook with the impact. The crump and scream of tearing metal filled the air, blotted out by the whine of the chopper's engine, and then the fuel tank exploded. The wreckage scraped along the rock wall and landed, burning, on the opposite bank of the river.

A DHS agent opened fire on Maeve. Bullets struck the rocks around her. A second agent fired, and then a third, a chorus of gunfire.

Vargas had been an atheist since the age of eleven. Without realizing it, she began to pray silently.

The gunfire halted. One of the DHS agents went to his knees, coughing. A second agent clutched at his neck, trying to breathe, and then tumbled over the edge and fell into the gorge, bones cracking as he struck outcroppings all the way down.

Vargas could only watch as, one by one, every person up on the rim coughed and staggered and collapsed. Two more slipped off into the gorge. In the back of her mind, Cristina Vargas screamed at herself to run, but her heart simply wasn't in it. In her heart, she knew it would make no difference.

In the driver's seat of a Jeep tucked between two pine trees, Hurwitz managed to start the engine before he choked and vomited a stream of black and yellow bile. He collapsed onto the steering wheel. The horn beeped once. The engine kept running.

Bleeding, broken fingers grabbed the rocky ledge at the top of the gorge, and Maeve Sinclair crawled up onto the rim. Jerking limbs shifting as if she popped bones back into place, she stood and turned to scan the trees and the landscape to the north.

Forty yards away, Cristina Vargas covered her mouth to silence the mewling noise that escaped her. The air between them rippled with some invisible pulse, and she felt an oily film on her skin. Death enveloped her with a shift in air pressure. She tried to clear her throat. Her ears popped. Vargas tried to reach up to grab hold of her head, staggered by the pain that clamped around her skull, but she felt too weak even for that. When she coughed, it racked her body so fiercely that she went down on one knee. Black spittle sprayed from her lips, and she fell onto her side.

Lying there, floating on a wave of death, she saw the corpse of Maeve Sinclair turn southward and begin to run along the rim of the gorge, headed downhill. Off the mountain.

Vargas gave a final, rattling cough and saw no more.

* * *

"Walker, could you please take a seat? You're irritating the hell out of me."

He stood near the door, hands stuffed in his pockets, head bobbing and tapping one foot as if in time with music none of the others could hear.

"Nervous energy," Walker said, staring at Alena. "Sorry."

"Sit down," she replied, not attempting to disguise it as anything but a command.

"No, ma'am. Director Boudreau. I don't think so."

Alena rolled her eyes. They weren't off to a great start, the two of them. He knew he must be getting on her already frayed nerves, but the woman had used him as a pawn in her own power games, and Walker was in no mood to worry about pissing her off. General Wagner had an infinite black void where his ethics ought to have been, whereas Alena seemed like a human being, a woman with a moral compass. Even so, it would take time to decide whether or not he trusted her or even wanted to work for her. His time on the bench had its benefits, and the idea of making amends with his son had a lot more appeal than continuing to work for people who would employ men like General Henry Wagner.

"Suit yourself." Alena sighed and turned her attention back to the others at the conference table.

Walker remained standing. Kept tapping his foot to that unheard rhythm. Most importantly, he stayed in that spot, just a few inches from the door. The sooner he could get out of there, the better. The farther from New Hampshire he could get when this was over, the happier he would be.

"What's to become of General Wagner?" Justin W. Jones asked.

Alena cocked her head. "You miss him already, Dr. Jones?"

Idiot, Walker thought.

"No, no," Jones replied, backpedaling fast. "He's the DoD's problem now. I just have a lot of questions, as you might imagine. Are you going to stay on-site, work out of Garland Mountain, now that the SRC has taken over our government contracts? Or will you put someone else here to oversee those? I just—"

Ted Sinclair slammed a hand onto the table. "Are you fucking kidding me?" He glared at Jones, fuming.

"You have something to say, Mr. Sinclair?" Alena asked.

Ted shot her a withering glance. "This is the conversation you want to have right now? Human resources? Rose is downstairs in a fish tank, and the rest of my family is . . . is gone. I know you're all worried about the cover-up, how you're going to clean up this mess, and who's going to get fired and who's going to *prison*—"

On the last word, he shifted his gaze toward Justin W. Jones.

"But all I want is some reassurance that everything that can be done for my daughter will be done and that nobody is going to try to separate me from her."

Alena softened. Walker thought he might be seeing her real self for the very first time.

"We're all living in the dark, Ted. I don't know what's going to happen now, but here are the things I can promise," she said. "As long as I've got anything to say about it, the team here will do everything possible to help both of you. That includes letting you decide how you want to handle your comings and goings at this facility. If you want to be here 24-7, you'll have anything you need for as long as you need it."

Ted seemed to want to shout again, but he must have seen something in Alena's eyes, perhaps the same thing Walker had just seen, because he gave a nod and exhaled as if he had found some comfort in this for the first time. His eyes dampened, and he reached up to wipe at them, turning away from the table for a moment.

"One small order of business," Walker said. "Mr. Sinclair's best friend is Dr. Rue Crooker, a biologist from Boston University. Right now, she's downstairs helping Kat Isenberg try to figure out how to help Rose, and they're apparently making some progress."

Alena gave him a quizzical glance. "Dr. Crooker works here?"

"Not technically," Walker said. He gave a small shrug. "I deputized her."

"How the hell did she get through security?" Dr. Jones asked.

"Dr. Isenberg brought her in as a visitor, then sneaked her down to the lab."

Jones swore, but Walker ignored him. He had no power here.

"You don't have the authority to do anything like that," Alena said.

"My role is . . . ill defined so far," Walker reminded her. "I'm not sure I even work for you, to be honest. But what I would recommend is that you hire Dr. Crooker immediately, whatever the cost, to work with Dr. Isenberg on this. In fact, it wouldn't be a terrible idea to give her the job of overseeing all the government-sponsored research that comes into Garland Mountain. Rue Crooker actually has ethics, maybe even a soul. This place could use her. And let's be honest, Alena, the SRC could use her, too."

"I'll take it under advisement," Alena said. "Now let's—"

"Walker's right," Ted Sinclair said, his voice cold, words clipped. "You said you'd give me what I need to feel like Rose is being taken care of. What I need here is Rue."

Alena tried to hide her pique. She managed a thin smile, then gave Walker a reproachful glance. "We'll make it happen. Anything else?"

"I'm sure there will be," Ted said. "But now's not the time. I need to sober up. I need to get some rest. I need to go back and make sure Rose is okay, and I need to talk to Priya. Her parents will have to be called. I'm sure they're crazy worried about her."

Justin W. Jones sat up a bit straighter. Unsure of his place now, he kept his gaze on Alena. "There's the matter of secrecy. We're still working out a story for the media."

Alena held up a hand to silence him. "Not now, Dr. Jones."

Ted stood up, his chair scraping the floor. "Don't worry, you heartless pricks. I know anything you're going to do to help us now is contingent on us cooperating. I'll make sure Priya understands, too. I'll make the government pay for what we've lost eventually, but right now, I'm too tired and too sad to think straight, so I'll put off my mercenary demands until I can take a breath without wanting to scream."

His eyes brimmed with tears as he looked at Dr. Jones. "If you have people you love, I hope they die horribly, gasping for breath. I hope you're there to see it. I hope they know you're watching and they look at you like they don't understand why you're not helping them, and you never sleep again without being haunted by the memory of their eyes in that moment."

Walker cringed, all the breath knocked out of him by those words.

Justin W. Jones looked as if he might throw up. "Jesus Christ. That's—"

"Cruel?" Ted gave a hollow laugh. "I meant every word. I'd regret not saying it. I blame you and everyone else who could have stopped this from happening in the beginning. My dead children blame you. Rose, downstairs, is fucking death personified. She'll never hug her father or her girlfriend again. She blames you, Jones. I hope you live a very long life without a moment's peace."

Alena and Jones had both lowered their heads.

Ted strode from the room, fists clenched at his sides.

A moment later, Walker followed.

Priya sat cross-legged on the floor, her muddy sneakers against the glass that separated her from Rose. "It's hard to know what to say, except 'I love you.'"

Rose faced her, also on the floor, the soles of her Sperrys pressed to the glass. She lowered her head, staring at her hands, which hung between her legs, fingers splayed, like creatures in hibernation. Waiting to be woken.

Seconds ticked past. Priya's heart clenched.

"Rose?"

Rose looked up.

"I said I love you." Priya reached forward and pressed a hand against the glass.

"I heard you, babe. I love you, too. You know I do," Rose said. She didn't reach out to touch the glass, but she did lift her gaze to meet Priya's. "You should go home."

"What? No way."

Rose leaned toward the glass but still did not reach out to touch it. "You should be with your family—"

"You're my family."

This time, Rose did reach for the glass, but not for tenderness. She slapped her palm against it, making Priya flinch. "You've been shot. You need real doctors. A hospital. You need to be with your parents, and you need sleep before you work out what to do next."

Priya's bullet wound throbbed with heat and pain. She leaned away from the glass, just slightly, lowering her hand. "You think I'm going to abandon you?"

"That's not—"

Priya stood. "I know what you mean. I don't entirely disagree. And yes, I'm going to see my parents and calm them down, but I'm twenty-one, Rose. We're not little high school giggle-girls. What I feel for you isn't some crush. It's not something I can just turn off or burn black candles and write in my journal about. I fucking love you. Okay, we're still young in comparison to old people, but we're old enough to have lived a little, met some shitty human beings, and I know what I want in this life, and that's you."

Rose did not stand. She placed the palms of both hands on the glass and looked up at Priya. "You can't have me, Pri. Not unless they have a cure, and do you honestly think that's going to happen anytime soon? Until then, this glass will always keep us apart. This glass, or some hazmat suit, or something else. You really think you'll be okay with a girlfriend you can never touch, who can never touch you?"

"It won't be never! They'll find—"

"What if they don't?"

Silence filled the space between them, more of a barrier than the glass could ever have been. Exhaustion gripped Priya, as if strength had been bleeding out of her. Depleted, only sorrow left, she told herself Rose needed rest, same as she did.

"You've lost so much," Priya told her. "I can't imagine what you're feeling. But I promise you haven't lost everything. I'm not going anywhere."

On the other side of the glass, Rose sat in silence, tears running down her face.

Priya lowered herself to the floor again. She sat facing her love and reached out to press both hands to the glass. It wasn't much, but it was all they had.

"Rosie," she began.

"I love you, too," Rose said without looking up. "So much."

Priya smiled, even as the sadness tore her apart.

Long seconds passed.

Then alarms began to wail, red lights flashing overhead. Heavy footfalls thundered by, right outside the door, people shouting.

"What the hell?" Priya asked, turning toward the door. "What now?"

"Maeve," Rose said. "She's here."

Priya stared at her. "That's not . . . Babe, Maeve is dead."

Rose stiffened, spine rigid. Her head turned, chin lifted, as if she heard something Priya's ears could not.

"You may be right," Rose said. "But dead or not, she's coming for me."

28

The alarms shrieked, red lights flashing. Walker imagined the inner corridors of NORAD when nuclear apocalypse was imminent. He turned to look at Dr. Jones. Alena might be in charge now, but Jones knew the facility and its protocols.

"Talk to me, Jones!"

Justin W. Jones had gone pale pink in the flashing red lights. He looked like he might vomit. Whatever had happened, this was not a drill.

"Alena, get up!" Walker barked.

He didn't have to tell Ted Sinclair. The man reached for Alena, but she shook him off, and then all of them were standing, moving toward the door. Walker reached for the knob, convinced that the alarms would put them into lockdown, meaning locked in, but when he turned the knob, the door swung open.

The two Homeland Security agents out in the corridor were barking questions on their comm units, but they looked as disoriented as Walker felt. He turned and grabbed Jones, hauled him close.

"What is this?"

"Alpha Red," Jones snapped, whipping his head around, desperate to be free. "Terrorist attack or bioagent release. It's never happened before. It can't be—"

Ted grabbed Walker's arm. "Rose. I've got to get to her."

"It could *be* her," Alena told him. "It must be."

"What about Priya?" Ted said. "I can't just—"

Walker nodded, turning to Jones again. "There a safe room on this floor? Quarantine space, in case of contamination?"

Dr. Jones started to point south along the corridor, toward an array of glass-walled offices. Walker spotted a darkened hallway, lost in shadow between the flares of the red emergency lights. He spoke, but his words were lost in the blare of the klaxons.

Walker looked at the DHS agents. "Take Director Boudreau and Dr. Jones. Get them into a safe room, and stay there till the all-clear."

Alena's eyes narrowed. He could see cold calculations running in her head. If she felt a fraction of Walker's own terror, she didn't show it.

"Move!" Alena snapped at Jones.

Jones started nodding and kept nodding as he hurtled down the corridor ahead of them. Alena and the DHS agents followed. Walker glanced at Ted, saw that the other man understood his intentions without him needing to voice them, and together they ran the opposite direction, toward the elevators.

The red lights turned the halls into a strobing crimson hell. Walker raced ahead of Ted Sinclair, who limped as fast as he could manage on his injured knee. Ted called out questions as he tried to keep up, but Walker ignored them. He had no answers.

As he turned a corner, he heard the first gunshots.

His breath caught in his throat, and he froze in the hall, listening. In the quiet between the cries of the alarm, more gunfire erupted. Ted caught up, grabbed Walker's sleeve. Walker shook him off, precious seconds ticking by as he racked his brain. Terrorists, maybe. Someone had sent the assassin, Agatha, unless she'd been a solo operator. Then there'd been the killers on dirt bikes, trying to get to Maeve, to kill her and take the death touch from her.

"What is this?" Ted asked, staring at him, wide-eyed.

Walker held up a hand to silence him, thinking. Could it be General Wagner? Would he have gone this far? A traitor to his nation?

Would White Oak Security have allowed their Blackcoats to kill DHS agents and armed security at a top-secret research facility under government supervision?

"Fuck it," Ted snarled. "And fuck you."

He hurried onward, heedless of the gunfire. Walker knew he was right. The only way to answer his questions was to live through this, but right now, all Ted Sinclair cared about was protecting Rose and Priya, and Walker understood that. If Charlie were here, he would have made the same choice.

Charlie. Walker thought Charlie might have told him to go back and take shelter in a safe room with Alena and Dr. Jones. But Walker had never made his choices based on safety. His grandfather had been a malicious bastard, his father had been a coward, but both men had given him the same gift, one thing they both had in common and had passed to Walker. A single quote from a century before, which Walker had used in his high school yearbook. "A ship in harbor is safe, but that is not what ships are built for."

Walker hadn't been built for safe harbor.

He followed Ted Sinclair, running through strobing red lights, running toward gunfire.

They reached the elevator hub. Gunfire echoed down the corridor to the left. Double doors down that end smashed open. Two guards and a quartet of DHS agents backed through the doors, firing at invaders Walker couldn't see.

Ted punched the call button, which glowed orange. Lockdown or not, the elevator still worked.

Walker took his arm and pressed him into the narrow well of the elevator door, seconds ticking by, waiting for the doors to slide open. Gunshots echoed down the corridor, punctuating the clamor of the alarm. Walker reached for his gun, and his fingers grasped nothing but air—the guards had taken it from him when they'd arrived.

He worried the elevator wasn't coming, that the button had lit up but lockdown meant the lift wouldn't really be working.

He stared at the backs of the DHS agents and security guards as they kept backpedaling.

A DHS agent stumbled, tripped over his own feet. For a heartbeat, Walker thought him an idiot, but then he saw the man turn onto his hands and knees, gasping and grabbing for his throat. Purple blotches blistered his neck. Dark spittle flew from his mouth.

A security guard and another DHS agent grabbed for one another as they fell, sprawling on the floor. By then, the first had died, black blood pooling around him, and the other three had begun to cough and gasp and stumble.

Over their heads, Walker saw a single figure striding along the corridor toward him, cast in shadows and flashes of crimson light. Beyond her, scattered in the hall back the way she'd come, were more corpses.

"Ted," Walker said, grabbing the back of his neck. "Run."

Ted stared at her. "Rose. Oh, God . . . my Rosie."

"That's not Rose."

"But you . . . you said Maeve was dead."

Walker shoved him hard, got him moving back the way they'd come, had to catch Ted to keep him from falling when his bad knee went out.

"She was," Walker said. "I swear to God, she was."

There'd been a bright red Exit sign twenty feet back. The door showed a pictograph of a person walking up some stairs, along with the words AUTHORIZED USE ONLY—ALARM WILL SOUND. He almost laughed as he kicked the release bar and the door swung inward.

Walker pulled and shoved and half-carried Ted, who cried out in pain as they ran and stumbled down the stairs. The man had cracked ribs and had torn something in his knee. Whatever numbing his drinking had provided had worn off now, scoured away by pain, but Walker couldn't let him stop or even slow down. With every flight of stairs, every landing, he waited for the coughing to start. If Maeve saw the stairwell door open, she would start down after them. Would the concrete and steel protect them, slow the spread of the contagion that had begun to blossom out from her? He prayed it would. Prayed, unsure who or what might be out there to listen.

They reached sublevel two. Walker blinked in surprise when he saw the sign, then barreled through the door, hauling Ted behind him. Somehow the alarm sounded even louder here. The red lights flashed. He spun in a circle, trying to figure out which direction the quarantine chamber might be. They weren't in the hexagon at the core of the building but in a side corridor. Down the hall, he saw the open space of the common area around the hexagon, the main elevator bank, and he hauled Ted in that direction.

"We have to find Rose and Priya," Ted said.

"That's what we're doing. But we need a safe room or we'll be dead. Priya, too. One of the labs, if we can get through."

"Not without them!"

Walker turned to snap at him. "I know!"

They reached the hexagon. He skidded to a halt and spun around, the klaxons blaring into his brain. Two guards stood by the elevator, guns drawn. He was about to run to them, warn them that Maeve would be coming, and then the red lights flashed brightly and he saw the lab beyond them. A pair of women stood beyond the glass, looking out.

Rue Crooker and Kat Isenberg.

"Come on!" Walker ordered.

Ted ripped himself from Walker's grasp. "Not without Rose."

Walker reeled on him. "Where do you think Maeve is going? Rose is infected now. That happened because Maeve died, Ted. She died. I saw her corpse. Shot to death, bled out. Red Hands didn't kill Rose because it needed her as a host. Something's happened that we can't possibly understand, but Maeve didn't come here by accident. She's looking for something, and the only thing that makes any sense is that she's looking for Rose. For them to be together."

Ted took a step away from him. Stumbled, nearly fell.

A figure appeared down the hall, beyond the lab where Rue and Kat waited. A shadow between red flashes. Walker felt his heart sink, waited for the sickness to carve him up, but then the red light strobed again and he saw it wasn't Maeve at all.

Priya ran toward them. "Ted! Oh, thank God. Please, you've gotta come. Rose is fighting it, but she needs you. Please!"

Ted raced to her, barely a trace of his limp now, and the two of them vanished around the corner.

The elevator doors opened, and the two guards stepped on. They'd watched the whole thing unfold, guns at the ready, but hadn't opened fire. One of them looked deathly pale, but not sick. Not yet. Neither of them wore a hazmat suit.

Walker ran toward the lab, where Rue and Kat were gesturing madly for him to hurry.

He thought of Ted and Rose. Of Ted and Maeve. Of Ted and Logan. He ran faster.

Stop fighting, Rose thought. *They're right there. All you have to do is reach for them. If you need them, you know they will not deny you. That's what love is, Rose. That is what love is.*

"No," she rasped, lips flecked with bitter black spittle. She licked it away, swallowed it down, fought the urge to throw it back up. "You're not . . . me. That's not . . ."

"Rosie. Love?" her father said, so gently. He uttered a little sob and wrapped his arms around himself, and she knew he did it because the glass kept him from reaching for her, holding her and comforting her the way a parent should. The way a true parent would want to.

"That's not love!" Rose cried.

She began to cough, turned away from her dad and Priya. Huddled her face in the corner of her isolation room.

"Fight it, Rose," Priya said quietly.

She understood, more than Rose's father did. Priya had been on the other side of the glass when the hunger had really begun to claw into Rose. She'd cried as Rose had described to her the voice in her head, the insidious things it said to her, the suggestions it made. The way she wanted to touch Priya, how she wanted to rationalize it.

The hunger had stabbed her in the chest seconds after the alarms began to sound. It had been nestled inside her, somewhat under control, and Rose had believed she had time, that she could hold it off.

Then the alarms blared and the red lights flashed and the hunger pounced, as if it had been waiting for the moment she would be off-balance.

And it whispered to her.

He loves you. He'll do anything for you.

Rose had told Priya to find her dad. Much as she loved Priya, and as broken as her father so often seemed, she needed him now the way she had when she'd been a young girl, waking in the dark after a bad dream, afraid of every shadow. Afraid of getting out of her bed and afraid of staying in. Her mother was dead. Rose needed her father to tell her everything would be all right in the end, that they could help her. That they could rip this hunger and its whispers from inside her. She needed her dad to lie to her.

To hold her.

No. Not hold her. Anything but that.

Rose turned to him. Her throat felt ablaze with pain, torn up on the inside. Trickles of fluid ran down her face, but they weren't tears. Plague lesions had formed and were leaking.

"You have to go," she told them, looking from her dad to Priya. "You shouldn't have come in here with me."

"We can't," her father said, face etched with sorrow, his heart breaking over and over and over again. "I told you. We're safer in here than out there. As long as you can control it, we're safer. Maeve is out there."

Rose shook her head. Every muscle felt the urge to reach for him, to embrace him, to kiss Priya, to infect them and take their lives to feed the hunger and the disease in her. But she leaned against the wall and wrapped her arms around her knees.

Fuck you, she thought, and this inner voice belonged to her. *You can't have them.*

The Red Death whispered to her in return, the voice slithering inside her skull. *The sickness will rot you down to snot and marrow.*

Rose didn't care.

She looked at Priya and then at her father.

"That thing out there," she said. "It's not Maeve."

* * *

Walker stared at Kat Isenberg, heart pounding, glad to be on the inside of the secure door of the lab. Each of the sublevel labs at Garland Mountain had been built with contamination protocols. The moment the alarms had gone off, each lab had sealed itself to keep any contagion from escaping and also to prevent any outside contaminant from getting in. They were safe in here, or so Walker told himself. Images of the guards and Homeland Security agents dropping dead in the upstairs corridor swam into his head, and he pushed them away. Nobody really knew what they were dealing with here. All they could do was press on.

"You're sure about this?" Walker asked.

Kat threw up her hands. "Of course I'm not sure. Rue's only been here half a day. Her instincts are fantastic, and we worked on this together, but I have no idea if it's—"

"Just tell him!" Rue said, plugging her ears with her fingers. The alarms were drilling into all their brains by now.

Kat nodded. "Vargas and Hecht and I were working on a bacteriophage engineered to shock the infection into dormancy. It's not a cure. The introduction of the phage won't kill the bacteria, but it should slow it down. Might even put it into hibernation inside the cells."

Walker could have kissed them both. "Inject me."

Rue unplugged her ears. "We don't know what it'll—"

"It might keep me from being infected," he said. "If it doesn't, it'll diminish the effects enough that it should buy you time to keep working."

Walker didn't need to see the glance the two scientists exchanged to know they agreed with his assessment. They were all scientists.

"Inject me," he said again. "Then give me the biggest syringe you have. I'm going to find Maeve. Nothing else has stopped her, but if anything can—"

Something slammed against the glass door. Kat Isenberg gave a jump and cried out. Walker spun around, but he saw Rue's expression even before he turned and he knew what he would see.

Maeve Sinclair's corpse dragged a bloody palm across the glass, made a fist, and began to pound on the door. So many bullet wounds had torn up her body that the fabric of her clothes had become almost indistinguishable from her flesh. All ripped, all bloody. One half of her face had been obliterated. Shards of her skull jutted from brain matter like shark's teeth.

The grin on what remained of her lips and the red gleam in her single eye were enough to tell him that it wasn't Maeve looking through the glass at them.

Walker wished he had time to mourn her.

"Kat, tell me you have that injection ready."

Rue told her to stop, to wait, but Kat grabbed Walker's arm. They'd been working down here for hours and had studied a hundred possible solutions. He winced as she injected him with the only one any of them believed might make a difference.

Walker held out his hand.

The thing inside Maeve Sinclair watched as Kat put a second syringe in Walker's palm.

It stopped slapping its bloody hands against the glass and its half smile widened as if it knew what came next. As if it dared Walker to try.

"Rue," Walker said. "Open the goddamn door."

"No," she said. "Don't do this."

Kat Isenberg whispered some small kindness to Rue and then gently moved her out of the way, reaching for the controls that would override the contamination protocol and allow her to open the door. To let Walker out . . . or to let the monster in.

Another wet slap hit the glass.

Walker glanced over and saw it wasn't Maeve's hand but her ruined face. She slumped into the door and slid down, collapsing, leaving a smear of blood and mucus and black rot on the glass. For a second or two, she leaned against the door, and then the dead thing toppled backward and slid onto the floor.

The malevolent grin on that half face remained, but the red light winked out in that one dead eye, and the corpse lay still.

* * *

Rose felt a different sort of ache. Not the hunger that gnawed her insides but a kind of lure, hooked into her chest, drawing her with such power that it could not be refused. The alarm continued to blare, but the noise had receded somehow, as if muffled by this new yearning. The red lights flashed on the faces of her father and her girlfriend, but she barely saw them now.

"What are you doing, Rose?" Priya asked, her voice little more than a whisper in the dark, the scratching of a mouse trapped in the wall.

Rose exhaled, weakness deflating her. She leaned against the glass wall, looked through it, and wondered where Priya had gone. Earlier, they had been able to gaze at one another through the glass.

"Hey! Rose! Snap out of it!" Priya shouted.

She clapped her hands loudly. Rose blinked and swiveled her head to look at Priya.

"Where are you going?" Priya asked.

Ted stood behind her, hands on Priya's shoulders. "Rosie, just stay here. Please. You can't go out there."

In the strobing red glare, Rose saw her own hand wrapped around the doorknob. The same door her dad and Priya had used to join her in the isolation room. They'd come in here because they thought they would be safer with her than out there in the corridors with Maeve on the hunt.

Rose could feel Maeve out there now, and she understood what Priya and her father did not—sharing this room with her couldn't keep them safe. Rose might be able to control the hunger, the Red Death that whispered into her brain, but Maeve had already lost that fight. The infection had gotten deep into Maeve, eaten into her marrow, and all that remained of her now was the Red Death. Rose could feel it out there in the halls of Garland Mountain—coming for her. The Red Death might feed on others along the way, might spread its contagion, infect everyone it came near, but the whispers inside Rose's head knew the truth.

The rotting, living death had been torn in half, split between the Sinclair sisters, and it wanted to be reunited.

"I can't stay here," Rose managed to say before a ragged cough burst from her lips. She gasped to catch her breath. Bitter black fluid leaked from her eyes and nose. She looked over at her dad and Priya. Sounds had retreated again, their voices were muffled, but it was better that she could not hear their pleas.

"You'll be safe without me," she said, looking sadly at her father. "I'm going out to give her what she wants."

Priya started to reach for her, anguished, heart breaking. Ted wrapped his arms around Priya and pulled her away, held her back. He stared at Rose, crying, but he would not let Priya be infected.

"Thank you, Daddy," Rose said.

She opened the door they had unlocked when they'd come looking for her. Rose wasn't a prisoner any longer, and neither was the death inside her.

The door slammed behind her, and Rose went out to meet her sister.

Walker crouched by the glass door of Garland SL2-Alpha and stared at Maeve Sinclair's ravaged corpse. He had watched her die twice tonight and wanted to be sure. The closer he looked, the more he focused, he understood how impossible it was for her to have gotten this far. Bullets had torn apart her chest. Broken bone jutted from her side. Her right knee looked shattered. But of course it was her face, her skull, the visible wreckage of her brain, that told the tale. Even in the pulsing red light, he could see the black lesions on her brain. Blisters leaked a thick fluid that looked more like paste than blood.

"Stay back from the door," Rue said over Walker's shoulder.

"She's dead."

"Walker," Kat Isenberg replied, "she's right. We don't know that. Until someone shows up to confirm and start the cleanup, let's not take any chances."

He kept staring at Maeve. Her one good eye had filmed over, and now a viscous, milky caul had begun to form on the retina.

"It doesn't make sense," he said. "The Blackcoats killed her in the gorge, but here she is. You both saw her. She had enough strength to get all the way down here, but then her body just gives out?"

"For Christ's sake," Rue said, "*look* at her."

"That's what I'm doing."

Rue came and stood beside him. She didn't crouch down, though her view of the corpse would be obscured by the smear of blood and fluid that Maeve had left on the glass.

"She's not moving," Rue said. "She's not going to move. Whatever drove her to get her here, the bacteria inside her, the Red Death, her body finally took enough damage that she couldn't go any farther."

Walker stared. "Maybe."

As he stood and turned toward them, a wave of disorientation swept over him. He wavered on his feet, and Rue grabbed his arm to steady him.

Isenberg hurried over to them. "What is it? Do you feel sick?"

The question made Rue back away from him as if touching him had burned her. She looked at her hands, eyes flaring with worry. Isenberg watched him through heavily lidded eyes, but he could practically see the anxiety bristling inside her. Her body language gave away her fear.

"Just a little light-headed," he promised them. "Yes, probably from the bacteriophage you shot me up with, but I don't feel sick. Not even a cough."

"It wouldn't infect you like that, anyway," Isenberg said.

"I know that," Walker replied, then pointed at Rue. "Tell her."

Rue flushed. "I don't need to be told. I'm just jumpy after every-thing. Jumpy and tired."

Walker saw the tension leave them, and he exhaled. "All right. So we just wait for a cleanup crew to handle this. I hope you have a deck of cards or something."

Isenberg started talking about what she thought would happen now, wondering who might be left alive in the building and how long it might take for someone to come investigate.

Rue glanced back along the corridor that led deeper into the lab, where there were two isolation rooms, conference rooms, offices, and additional laboratory spaces. "You're telling me there aren't hazmat suits in all these labs, just as basic equipment provided?"

"There are at least four," Isenberg replied. "But do you really want to be the first one out there, checking out Maeve's remains, with no backup at all? Not me. Either way, we're all going to get to know each other much better in the next couple of days. The quarantine on this whole facility is going to be thorough and—"

Rue pointed through the glass. "Here we go. Faster than I'd have thought."

Walker turned, pressed his face to the glass, and saw four people in shapeless yellow hazmat suits working their way along the wide common area around the elevator hub in the middle of the hexagon. All four had guns, and they moved like soldiers instead of scientists—though Walker himself was both and knew others who fit the same description.

The alarm stopped blaring.

"Thank God," Isenberg sighed.

Walker's eardrums pulsed with the same rhythm, as if the alarm had not gone silent. A tinny buzz in his ears reminded him of a dozen crowded music clubs from his misspent college years. The red emergency lights kept flashing, but as irritating as they were, he would endure them forever as long as he didn't have to hear the klaxons anymore.

"Hey!" Rue called, slapping the glass door of SL2-Alpha. "Over here!"

One of the hazmat-suited guards spotted them, started in their direction, and then halted as he spotted the wreckage of Maeve's corpse. He pointed, said something to his comrades, and slowly they began to approach.

Walker leaned against the glass, waiting for them.

Out the corner of his eye, he saw something twitch, and looked down at Maeve's remains.

The dead thing's right hand shot upward, stretching as if it had just woken from a long sleep. As it did, skin and rotting flesh tore and split. Long, spindly, skeletal fingers pushed out from within. The skin of her arm hung down in strips. The skeletal fingers reached up, sank sharpened tips into cheek and skull and brain, and ripped. The other hand propped the dead thing up and it began to rise.

The Red Death tore Maeve Sinclair's ruined body off as if it were nothing but a costume, a skin suit. It had grown like a tumor inside her, infected her, taken her over. It broke skull away, cracked off ribs, removing the Maeve husk like a lobster shell.

Behind Walker, Rue Crooker had begun to pray.

"I think it's . . . Is it the devil?" Kat Isenberg asked, her voice hitching, both hands up behind her head. She trembled, shook her head, stepped back from the glass. Her eyes hinted at encroaching madness. "We woke it up, Walker! Oh, God, we woke it up!"

Draped in ribbons and scraps and dripping fluids of Maeve, the withered, red cadaverous thing heard the shouts of the guards in their hazmat suits. They opened fire. Bullets ripped into the dead thing, ricocheted off the glass, and the Red Death turned to glare at the yellow hazmat suits awash in the flashing crimson lights.

It seemed to expect them to fall.

When they did not, safe inside their hazmat suits, it moved with unnerving speed. Those spindly fingers were sharp enough to tear through the yellow suits. Men and women screamed, kept firing their guns, and then were coughing. Falling. Dying.

"We have to do something," Walker said quietly, almost to himself.

Rue laughed in a way that told him something inside her had broken. "Do what? What the fuck can we do?"

"Not you," Walker said, looking at her. "I had the injection."

He turned and stared at her, then Isenberg. "Both of you get into an isolation room. Right now. Ten seconds and I'm opening this door! Go!"

They hesitated.

Walker was about to shout at them again when Rue pointed out through the glass.

"Look."

He turned . . . and saw Rose.

Had Rose been looking only with her eyes, she would never have stopped screaming. She saw the broken, shredded human remains sprawled on the floor surrounded by little puddles of blood and viscera, and she knew it had once been her sister. But from thirty feet away, in front of the doorway to SL2-Epsilon, she felt Maeve's presence. The yearning that drew her to this place, at this moment, came not only from the contagion inside her—the infection she and Maeve had shared—but from a deeper, even more primal connection.

She stared at the withered husk before her, at the red gleam in its black eyes and the way its dried skin pulled back from yellow teeth into a corpse's grin, and she saw both death and beauty there. The Red Death had been an infection, now torn free of its host, but some part of Maeve had infected it in return.

"Sister," Rose said.

The husk staggered toward her, dragged its feet, smearing Maeve's blood in its wake. It gained strength, spine straightening, thin arms rising as the red emergency lights continued to flash, so that its movements seemed a zoetrope nightmare. One step in each moment of darkness, one step bathed in red light. Bones cracked as it stretched its hands out for her, fingers bent into claws.

In the silence, Rose heard Walker and Rue pounding on the glass door of SL2-Alpha. In the next flash of red light, she saw them there, banging, gesturing to her, calling out. They understood nothing. How could they know what it felt like to have the Red Death seething inside her? To feel the urge, the yearning so strong that the word *hunger* could never describe the ravenous need? How could they understand what it felt like to know you were one part of a whole, to feel the pull of your other half, to scream inside your own skull and fight with your soul to run the other direction, but to watch your body move toward death regardless?

At least I won't be alone, Rose thought, staring into that cadaverous grin, those hellish, eternal eyes, and searching for her sister there.

Rose opened her arms, and the Red Death stepped into that embrace.

Walker smashed his fist against the glass. He started to scream Rose's name again, but when the husk slid its arms around her and lay its head so gently on her shoulder, he saw a sorrowful peace on Rose's face.

He held his breath and could only watch as new blemishes emerged on Rose's neck and cheek, blistering, cratering, bleeding black.

Beside him, Rue cried out, pounding on the glass.

Walker grabbed her arm, turned her toward Isenberg. "Get in the isolation room. Right now."

As he grabbed the larger syringe, Rue started to argue, but Isenberg reached for her hand and tugged her away from him. The two of them rushed deeper into the lab. Walker called out to them to tell him when they were about to seal the isolation room door. Eight or nine seconds was all it took before he heard Isenberg shout and then the slam of the door.

He slapped the fat black button on the wall, an emergency disengage for the lab's entry door. Air hissed as the containment seal breached, and he closed his eyes for a moment, filled with a regret he could not express. The last thought he'd had before hitting that button should have been of his son. The injection Isenberg had given him made him feel nauseated and unsteady, his vision blurred slightly, which meant it had done *something* to him. Maybe killed him, maybe inoculated him. All these years, he had made one decision after another to put himself at risk with hardly a thought for the scars he would leave behind.

I'm sorry, he thought to a son who would never hear him.

Syringe clutched like a dagger, he ran toward the husk, unsure what it would do, knowing only that he had crossed the threshold. He breathed in the air that had killed so many others. His head throbbed with pain, and that swirl of nausea worsened. He waited for a cough, waited for a tickle in his throat, waited for the pain of fissures rotting on his skin.

He raised the syringe.

Red lights flashed, turning the embrace between Rose and the Red Death into a flickering grotesquerie. In the quiet, he could hear Rose weeping over the sound of his own footfalls and the beating of his heart. He crept toward the husk, thumb on the syringe, aiming for the back of its neck.

Walker's breath caught in his throat.

He froze in place and watched as the husk began to wither even more. The dried skin pulled taut over its bones. It shriveled in Rose's arms. The leathery skin crumbled, cascading to the floor in a fine red dust. Rose opened her eyes, releasing a moan that echoed with loss. She fell to her knees and tried to grasp the Red Death's bones in her hands, but they gave way at her touch and spilled to the floor into the growing pile of red dust, as if that was all they had ever been.

Rose drew a heavier breath, there on her knees, trembling. To Walker's eyes, she looked thinner, as if she, too, had begun to wither.

He spoke her name, and she looked up at him, scarlet eyes gleaming brightly.

"Help me," she whispered in a voice he'd never heard before.

Walker plunged the syringe into her neck, then stood back to wait.

Seconds passed before he allowed himself to hope. Then Rose coughed once, reached up to touch the blisters on her neck, and climbed unsteadily to her feet. The red tint in her eyes remained, but it had diminished.

She spoke in a raspy whisper, as if the words came from a long way off.

"Get me back into isolation," Rose said. "I'll . . . hold on as long as I can."

Behind her eyes, he thought he saw something else looking out.

"Whatever they're going to do," she said, "tell them to work fast."

29

The remaining hours of darkness passed quickly. Rue managed to fall asleep shortly after sunrise, though she had only the clock to let her know morning had come. On a plastic mattress worthy of a college dormitory, sweaty under a synthetic blanket, she managed four hours of fitful sleep in which she dreamed she woke in a snowbound winter cabin. Logs crackled in the fireplace while the beams of the cabin groaned with gusts of wind. In her dream, Rue nestled herself into the arms of a lover, sprawled on the floor in front of the fire. At peace.

She woke to the slamming of a door, saw where she was, and lay rigid on the bed, listening, waiting to hear a scream or an alarm. A full minute passed before she could slow her heartbeat to something resembling its normal rhythm.

A knock came at the door.

Rue sat up, looked blearily around at the cell she'd slept in. Dr. Isenberg had told her that almost everyone who worked in the sublevel labs ended up crashing in the isolation rooms at least once. As exhausted as she had been this morning, the space hadn't bothered her, but now an urgency filled her. A claustrophobic frisson that made her drag the sweaty blanket around her and hurry to the door.

When she opened it, Walker waited on the other side.

She blinked. "You don't look dead."

"The jury's still out."

"Seriously," Rue said. "They've cleared you? After Isenberg injected you with that bacteriophage?"

"I'm not contagious," Walker replied. "Doesn't mean they're letting me out of here anytime soon. They let me sleep for two hours, but mostly they've been taking my blood and other fun samples."

Rue could see how exhausted he must be. The bags beneath his eyes were dark crescents, and his skin had a sallow hue. But there were no plague blossoms, no black bruising on his throat, and at least thus far, he didn't seem to be coughing.

"You're actually okay? After being so close to that . . . to Maeve?"

"I wasn't kidding. The jury is definitely still out. There's no trace of the Red Hands bacterium in my blood culture or cells. Just the phage."

"That injection shouldn't have been so effective," Rue said. "Not if you were exposed to Red Hands. Maeve was radiating that contagion like some kind of cloud around her. Based on what Alena said last night, up at the gorge, it killed people who were almost a hundred yards away."

Walker shrugged. "By the time she got to us, I think she'd almost burned out. It had used her up. Director Boudreau and I think what you call a 'cloud' had limits. When her body gave in, the aura effect dissipated. I wouldn't have wanted the thing that ripped its way out of her to touch me—or Rose, for that matter—but I think I got lucky."

Rue leaned against the doorframe, wrapped in her blanket. "I'm glad. Enough good people died yesterday."

"I'm still stuck here for a while, though," Walker said. "I'm guessing four or five days of poking, prodding, tests, and observation to see if I start unraveling. I'd like to get home, but I'm also glad to stick around and see how things go for Rose."

Rue lifted her eyebrows.

Walker nodded. "She's alive. And sick, but not any sicker than she was when you fell asleep. Isenberg is working with the SRC team that Alena brought in."

A darkness seemed to pass over his face. Walker exhaled, eyes downcast. "The only voice coming out of her is her own, so far, but you can see it in her eyes sometimes, when she looks at you. The infection is still there, and so is the other thing. The *old* thing. Sometimes you can feel it watching."

"Last night, Isenberg said she thought if we could kill the infection in Rose, we could get rid of it."

Rue and Walker studied each other for a moment. She'd noticed neither of them wanted to name the ancient presence rooted inside Rose Sinclair. Neither of them wanted to call it the Red Death, as if someone using the term Poe had coined would lend the thing even more malignant power.

"Speaking of Alena," Walker said, "I hear she offered you a job."

"Last night," Rue confirmed. "Though I get the impression it's more about locking me into the penalties for revealing government secrets. If I'm an employee—"

Walker scowled. "Don't kid yourself. She needs you way more than the university does. You've already proven your usefulness."

"I strip-mined Oscar Hecht's research and took a shot in the dark when we were desperate."

"Okay," Walker said. "Have it your way. But I hope you take the job."

"I've been searching for biological secrets to unlock my whole life. After the things I've seen, there's no way I can go back to my old job. Besides, Kat Isenberg told me she wants someone to boss around." Rue shrugged. "I've got a few days to think it over. None of us are going to be released from quarantine till then, at least, so I might as well make myself useful in the meantime."

Walker held on to the door. "I'm glad to hear it. And I'm grateful, Rue. I don't want that to get lost in all of this. Alena sent me up here on an assignment. This was my job. But you got into it just because you cared about Ted and his family. Not many people would have stuck with it when they realized how dangerous things were becoming."

Rue flushed. "He's my best friend. They're my family, too."

"I know," Walker said. "And he's asking for you. Why don't you go and see him before you get to work."

"I'll do that. Thank you," Rue replied. "How is he?"

"Edgy. Probably itchy for a drink, but he's focused on his daughter. Determined. Standing tall."

Rue surprised herself by smiling. That was something, at least.

Rose couldn't bear to tell her father she wanted to be alone. Flush with fever, racked with chills, plagued by whispers and hunger pangs, she had barely slept at all. The isolation room she found herself in now had a bit more personality than the one she'd been in the night before. The researchers in this lab had painted the walls a soothing blue, and phosphorescent paint had been used to dapple the ceiling with glow-in-the-dark stars, but that didn't make it any easier to look at her father and Priya through the glass.

When Rue came to the door, knocking softly, and called Ted out into the corridor to speak with her, Rose felt weak with gratitude.

Priya slept on the other side of the glass. The Homeland Security agents had carried a bed in from another part of the lab so that they could all be together, despite being separated by the glass. Rose watched Priya sleep, and it soothed her to know she would be okay. Her bullet wound had been seen to. Her parents had been called. Someone on the outside had apparently met with them in the early hours of the morning, shortly after it had all come to an end, and explained that she would be quarantined here at Garland Mountain for several days along with Rose and Ted. Priya had spoken to her father, and then Ted had gotten on the phone.

Now Priya slept. Rose exhaled softly, spreading her fingers across the glass, heart aching as she watched Priya's chest rise and fall. Her face looked peaceful, as if none of the horrors of the prior day had ever happened.

She's going to leave you, a voice whispered in her head.

It wasn't her own voice, but it didn't belong to the Red Death, either.

"I know," Rose said quietly, pressing on the glass. The hunger had diminished but not disappeared. Sadness clawed at her now more than hunger. The voice understood.

Priya would have to leave. Rose would have to stay. Priya's family would want her out of here, out of danger. She would argue at first, but Rose would insist. She would break Priya's heart if she had to, to make sure she would be safe.

It wouldn't be safe in here, Rose knew. Not until the SRC found a way to help her.

Maybe not ever.

Alena Boudreau had promised they would never stop trying. They had already found a way to suspend the spread of the bacteria, to reduce the infection, which Alena said gave her faith they might be able to kill it. *Burn it out*, she'd said.

For now, the fever remained.

And the voices.

Dad won't leave you here alone, one of those voices said.

Rose smiled and wiped at her eyes. She'd been stubborn, trying not to cry. The hunger might still be in her, the malignant old god, the dead thing that spoke to her. But the other presence inside her felt even stronger, and it soothed her fever and gave her courage.

I won't ever leave you, either, it said, inside her head. *I love you.*

"I love you, too, Maeve," Rose whispered, leaning against the glass of her cage. "I love you, too."

Walker had showered and shaved. They'd come for more blood tests and given him orange juice and coffee and had scrounged up a box of Pop-Tarts from somewhere. He'd met with Alena three separate times, talked to Kat and Rue. He'd seen Ted Sinclair only briefly, and that was enough. With General Wagner gone, the man's grief and pain needed a target, and Walker didn't feel like volunteering for that assignment. The longer Ted went without a drink, the worse it would be.

Ted planned to use quarantine to dry out. Walker didn't bother to

PHANTOM

Tor Books by Terry Goodkind

TERRY GOODKIND

PHANTOM

TOR ®

A TOM DOHERTY ASSOCIATES BOOK
NEW YORK

PHANTOM

Edited by Patrick Nielsen Hayden

Map by Terry Goodkind

A Tor Book
Published by Tom Doherty Associates, LLC
175 Fifth Avenue
New York, NY 10010

www.tor.com

Tor® is a registered trademark of Tom Doherty Associates, LLC.

Library of Congress Cataloging-in-Publication Data

Goodkind, Terry.
    Phantom / Terry Goodkind.—1st ed.
      p. cm.
    "A Tom Doherty Associates Book."
    ISBN-13: 978-0-765-30524-4 (regular edition) (acid-free paper)
    ISBN-10: 0-765-30524-0 (regular edition) (acid-free paper)
    ISBN-13: 978-0-765-31554-0 (limited edition)
    ISBN-10: 0-765-31554-8 (limited edition)
    1. Married people—Fiction.   2. Missing persons—Fiction. I. Title.

PS3557.O5826P44   2006
813'.54—dc22

2006014138

First Edition: July 2006

Printed in the United States of America

0 9 8 7 6 5 4 3 2 1

To Phil and Debra Pizzolato,
and their kids, Joey, Nicolette, Philip, and Adriana,
who constantly remind me of the value of life
by bringing their love and laughter to mine

The following individuals have been invaluable
in helping to bring *Phantom* to life.

Brian Anderson
Jeff Bolton
R. Dean Bryan
Dr. Joanne Leovy
Mark Masters
Desirée and Dr. Roland Miyada
Keith Parkinson
Phil and Debra Pizzolato
Tom and Karen Whelan
Ron Wilson

Each of these people has been there for me when I needed them most.
Each is a person of unique ability who played a key role in making
this book happen. Each of them brings joy to my life by just
being themselves.

In loving memory of Keith Parkinson.

Those who have come here to hate should leave now, for in their hatred they only betray themselves.

—translated from *The Book of Life*

PHANTOM

Kahlan stood quietly in the shadows, watching, as evil knocked softly on the door. Huddled under the small overhang, off to the side, she hoped that no one would answer that knock. As much as she would like to spend the night in out of the rain, she didn't want trouble to visit innocent people. She knew, though, that she had no say in the matter.

The light of a single lantern flickered weakly through the slender windows to either side of the door, reflecting a pale, shimmering glow off the wet floor of the portico. The sign overhead, hung by two iron rings, grated and squealed each time it swung back and forth in the wind-borne rain. Kahlan was able to make out the spectral white shape of a horse painted on the dark, wet sign. The light from the windows wasn't enough to enable her to read the name, but because the other three women with her had talked of little else for days, Kahlan knew that the name would be the White Horse Inn.

By the smell of manure and wet hay, she judged that one of the dark buildings nearby had to be a stable. In the sporadic displays of distant lightning, she could just make out the hulking shoulders of dark structures standing like ghosts beyond the billowing sheets of rain. Despite the steady roar of the deluge and the rumble of thunder, it appeared that the village was sound asleep. Kahlan could think of no better place to be on such a dark and wretched night than bundled up under bed covers, safe and warm.

A horse in the nearby stable whinnied when Sister Ulicia knocked a second time, louder, more insistently, evidently intending herself to be heard over the riot of rain, yet not so loud as to sound hostile. Sister Ulicia, a woman given to reckless impulse, seemed to be taking a deliberately restrained approach. Kahlan didn't know why, but imagined that it had to do with the reason they were there. It also might have been nothing more than the random nature of her moods. Like lightning, the woman's smoldering bad temper was not only dangerous but unpredictable. Kahlan couldn't

always tell exactly when Sister Ulicia would lash out, and just because she
so far hadn't didn't mean that she wouldn't. Neither of the other two Sisters was in any better mood or any less inclined toward losing their temper. Kahlan supposed that soon enough the three of them would be happy
and quietly celebrating the reunion.

Lightning flashed close enough that the blinding but halting incandescence briefly revealed a whole street of buildings crowded close around
the muddy, rutted road. Thunder boomed through the mountainous countryside and shook the ground beneath their feet.

Kahlan wished that there was something—like the way lightning revealed things otherwise hidden in the obscurity of night—that could help
illuminate the hidden memories of her past and bring to light what was
concealed by the murky mystery of who she was. She had a fierce longing
to be free of the Sisters, a burning desire to live her own life—to know
what her life really was. That much she knew about herself. She knew,
too, that her convictions had to be founded in experience. It was obvious
to her that there had to be something there—people and events—that had
helped make her the woman she was, but try as she might to recall them,
they were lost to her.

That terrible day she stole the boxes for the Sisters, she had promised
herself that someday she would find the truth of who she was, and she
would be free.

When Sister Ulicia knocked a third time, a muffled voice came from
inside.

"I heard you!" It was a man's voice. His bare feet thumped down
wooden stairs. "I'll be right there! A moment, please!"

His annoyance at having been awakened in the middle of the night was
layered over with forced deference to potential customers.

Sister Ulicia turned a sullen look on Kahlan. "You know that we have
business here." She lifted a cautionary finger before Kahlan's face. "Don't
you even think of giving us any trouble, or you'll get what you got the last
time."

Kahlan swallowed at the reminder. "Yes, Sister Ulicia."

"Tovi had better have gotten us a room," Sister Cecilia complained.
"I'm in no mood to be told the place is full."

"There will be room," Sister Armina said with soothing assurance, cutting off Sister Cecilia's habit of always assuming the worst.

Sister Armina wasn't older, like Sister Cecilia, but nearly as young and attractive as Sister Ulicia. To Kahlan, though, their looks were insignificant in light of their inner nature. To Kahlan, they were vipers.

"One way or another," Sister Ulicia added under her breath as she glared at the door, "there will be room."

Lightning arced through the greenish, roiling clouds, releasing an earsplitting boom of thunder.

The door opened a crack. The shadowed face of a man peered out at them as he worked to button up his trousers under his nightshirt. He moved his head a little to each side so that he could take in the strangers. Judging them to be less than dangerous, he pulled open the door and with a sweeping gesture ushered them inside.

"Come on in, then," he said. "All of you."

"Who is it?" A woman called out as she descended the stairs to the rear. She carried a lantern in one hand and held the hem of her nightdress up with the other so that she wouldn't trip on it as she hurried down the steps.

"Four women traveling in the middle of a rainy night," the man told her, his gruff tone alluding to what he thought of such a practice.

Kahlan froze in midstride. He'd said "four women."

He had seen all four of them and had remembered as much long enough to say so. As far as she could recall, such a thing had never happened before. No one but her masters, the four Sisters—the three with her and the one they had come to meet—ever remembered seeing her.

Sister Cecilia shoved Kahlan in ahead of her, apparently not catching the significance of the remark.

"Well for goodness' sake," the woman said as she hurried between the two plank tables. She tsked at the foul weather as the wind drove a rattle of rain against the windows. "Do get them in out of that awful weather, Orlan."

Streamers of fat raindrops chased them in the door, wetting a patch of pine floor. The man's mouth twisted with displeasure as he pushed the door closed against a wet gust and then dropped the heavy iron bar back in the brackets to bolt the door.

The woman, her hair gathered up in a loose bun, lifted her lantern a little as she peered at the late-night guests. Puzzled, she squinted as her gaze swept over the drenched visitors and then back again. Her mouth opened but then she seemed to forget what she had been about to say.

Kahlan had seen that blank look a thousand times and knew that the woman only remembered seeing three callers. No one could ever remember seeing Kahlan long enough to say so. She was as good as invisible. Kahlan thought that maybe because of the darkness and rain the man, Orlan, had merely made a mistake when he'd said to his wife that there were four visitors.

"Come in and get yourselves dry," the woman said as she smiled in earnest warmth. She hooked a hand under Sister Ulicia's arm, drawing her into the small gathering room. "Welcome to the White Horse Inn."

The other two Sisters, openly scrutinizing the room, took off their cloaks and gave them a quick shake before tossing them over a bench at one of the two tables. Kahlan noticed a single dark doorway at the back, beside the stairs. A fireplace made of stacked, flat stones took up most of the wall to the right. The air in the dimly lit room was warm and carried the distractingly enticing aroma of a stew in the iron pot hung from a crane pushed to the side of the hearth. Hot coals glowed out from under a thick layer of feathery ashes.

"You three ladies look like drowned cats. You must be miserable." The woman turned to the man and gestured. "Orlan, get the fire going."

Kahlan saw a young girl of maybe eleven or twelve years slip down the stairs just far enough so she could see into the room from under the low ceiling. Her long white nightdress with ruffled cuffs had a pony stitched in coarse brown thread on the front, with a row of loose strands of dark yarn making up the mane and tail. The girl sat on the steps to watch, tenting her nightdress over her bony knees. Her grin revealed big teeth that she had yet to grow into. Strangers arriving in the middle of the night apparently was an adventure at the White Horse Inn. Kahlan dearly hoped that that was all there would be to the adventure.

Orlan, a big bear of a man, knelt at the hearth, stacking on a few sticks of wood. His thick, stubby fingers made the wedges of oak look to be little more than kindling.

"What would possess you ladies to travel in the rain—at night?" he asked as he cast them a look over his shoulder.

"We're in a hurry to catch up with a friend of ours," Sister Ulicia said, offering a meaningless smile. She kept her tone businesslike. "She was to meet us here. Her name is Tovi. She will be expecting us."

The man put a hand on his knee to help himself up. "Those guests who stay with us—especially in such troubled times—are pretty discreet. Most don't give their names." He lifted an eyebrow at Sister Ulicia. "Much like you ladies—not giving your names, that is."

"Orlan, they're guests," the woman scolded. "Wet, and no doubt tired and hungry, guests." She flashed a smile. "Folks call me Emmy. My husband, Orlan, and I have run the White Horse since his parents passed away, years back." Emmy gathered up three wooden bowls from a shelf. "You ladies must be famished. Let me get you some stew. Orlan, get some mugs and fetch these ladies some hot tea."

Orlan lifted a meaty hand on his way past, indicating the bowls his wife cradled in an arm. "You're one short."

She twitched a frown at him. "No I'm not; I have three bowls."

Orlan pulled four mugs down from the top shelf of the hutch. "Right. Like I said, you're one short."

Kahlan could hardly breathe. Something was very wrong. Sisters Cecilia and Armina had frozen dead still, their wide eyes fixed on the man. The significance of the couple's chitchat had not escaped them.

Kahlan glanced to the stairwell and saw the girl on the steps leaning toward them, gripping the rails, peering out, trying to fathom what her parents were talking about.

Sister Armina snatched Sister Ulicia's sleeve. "Ulicia," she said in an urgent whisper through gritted teeth, "he sees—"

Sister Ulicia shushed her. Her brow drew down in a dark glare as she turned her attention back to the man.

"You are mistaken," she said. "There are only three of us."

At the same time she was talking she prodded Kahlan with the stout oak rod she carried, shoving her farther back into the shadows behind, as if shadows alone would make Kahlan invisible to the man.

Kahlan didn't want to be in the shadows. She wanted to stand in the light and be seen—really seen. Such a thing had always seemed an impossible dream, but it had suddenly become a real possibility. That possibility had shaken the three Sisters.

Orlan frowned at Sister Ulicia. Holding all four mugs in the grip of one meaty hand, he used his other to point out each visitor standing in his gathering room. "One, two, three"—he leaned to the side, looking around Sister Ulicia, to point at Kahlan—"four. Do you all want tea?"

Kahlan blinked in astonishment. Her heart felt as if it had come up in her throat. He saw her . . . and remembered what he saw.

It can't be," Sister Cecilia whispered as she wrung her hands. She leaned toward Sister Ulicia, her eyes darting about. "It's impossible." Her familiar, incessant but meaningless smile was nowhere in evidence.

"Something's gone wrong. . . ." Sister Armina's voice trailed off when her sky blue eyes glanced Sister Ulicia's way.

"It's nothing more than an anomaly," Sister Ulicia growled under her breath as she leveled a dangerous look at the two of them. Never ones to be servile, the two nonetheless showed no evidence of wanting to argue with their stormy leader.

In three strong strides Sister Ulicia closed the distance to Orlan. She seized the collar of his nightshirt in her fist. With her other hand she swished her oak rod in the direction of Kahlan, standing in the shadows back near the door.

"What does she look like?"

"Like a drowned cat," Orlan said in ill humor, obviously not liking her hand on his collar.

Kahlan knew without doubt that using such a tone of voice with Sister Ulicia was the wrong thing to do, but the Sister, instead of exploding in a rage, seemed to be just as astonished as Kahlan.

"I know that, but what does she look like? Tell me what you see."

Orlan straightened, pulling his collar away from her grip. His features drew tight as he appraised the stranger only he and the Sisters saw standing in the weak light of the lanterns.

"Thick hair. Green eyes. A very attractive woman. She'd look a lot better if she were dried out, although those wet things on her do tend to show off what she's made of." He began to smile in a way that Kahlan didn't like one bit, even if she was overjoyed that he really saw her. "Mighty fine figure on her," he added, more to himself than the Sister.

His slow and deliberate evaluation made Kahlan feel naked. As his gaze roamed over her, he wiped the corner of his mouth with a thumb. She could hear it rasp against his stubble. One of the sticks of wood in the hearth caught flame, brightening the room in its flickering glow, letting him see even more. His gaze wandered upward, and then caught on something.

"Her hair is as long as . . ."

Orlan's bawdy smile evaporated.

He blinked in surprise. His eyes widened. "Dear spirits," he whispered as his face went ashen. He dropped to a knee. "Forgive me," he said, addressing Kahlan. "I didn't recognize—"

The room rang with a crack as Sister Ulicia whacked him across the top of the head with her oak rod, dropping him to both knees.

"Silence!"

"What's the matter with you!" the man's wife cried out as she rushed to her husband's side. She squatted, putting an arm around his shoulders to steady him as he groaned and put a big hand over the bloody wound on the top of his bowed head. His sandy-colored hair turned dark and wet under his fingers.

"Are all of you crazy!" She cradled her husband's head to her breast, where a red stain grew against her nightdress. He appeared stunned senseless. "Unless you travel in the company of a spirit, there are only three of you! How dare you—"

"Silence," Sister Ulicia growled in a way that gave Kahlan an icy shiver and made the woman's mouth snap closed.

Rain pattered against the window while in the distance a slow rumble of thunder rolled through the forested hills. Kahlan could hear the sign squeaking as it swung to and fro each time the wind gusted. Inside the house it had gone dead silent. Sister Ulicia looked over at the girl, now at the bottom of the steps, where she stood gripping the simple, square, wooden newel post.

Sister Ulicia fixed the girl in a glare that only a sorceress in a vile mood could marshal. "How many visitors do you see?"

The girl stood wide-eyed, too frightened to speak.

"How many?" Sister Ulicia asked again, this time through gritted teeth in a voice so threatening that it made the girl's grip on the newel post tighten until her fingers stood out white and bloodless against the dark wood.

The girl finally answered in a meek voice. "Three."

Sister Armina, looking like bottled thunder, leaned close. "Ulicia, what's going on? This isn't supposed to be possible. Not possible at all. We cast the verification webs."

"Exterior," Sister Cecilia corrected.

Sister Armina blinked at the older woman. "What?"

"We only cast exterior verification webs. We didn't do an interior review."

"Are you out of your mind?" Sister Armina snapped. "In the first place it isn't necessary and in the second place who would be fool enough to be the one to do an aspect analysis of a verification web from an interior perspective! No one ever does such a thing! It isn't necessary!"

"I'm only saying—"

With a withering look, Sister Ulicia silenced them both. Sister Cecilia, her wet curls plastered to her scalp, looked like she was about to finish her complaint, but then decided instead to remain mute.

Orlan seemed to recover his senses as he pulled away from his wife's embrace and began to stagger to his feet. Blood ran down his forehead and to either side of his broad nose.

"Were I you, innkeeper," Sister Ulicia said, turning her attention back to him, "I'd remain on my knees."

The menace in her voice gave him pause for only a moment. He was clearly angry as he rose up to his full height, letting his bloody hand drop away from his head. His back straightened, his chest expanded, and his fists tightened. Kahlan could clearly tell that his temper was outpacing his sense of caution.

Sister Ulicia indicated with her rod that she wanted Kahlan to back away. Kahlan, ignoring the direction, instead stepped closer to Sister Ulicia, hoping to change the rush of events before it ended up being too late.

"Please, Sister Ulicia, he will answer your questions—I know he will. Let him be."

The three Sisters turned unpleasantly surprised looks on Kahlan. She had not been spoken to, or asked to speak. Such insolence would cost her dearly, she knew, but she also knew what was liable to happen to the man if something didn't change, and right then it seemed to her that she was the only one who could effect a change.

Besides, Kahlan knew that this was her only chance to find out something about herself—to perhaps find out who she really was and maybe even why she could remember only the most recent parts of her life. This man had clearly recognized her. He very well might be the key that could unlock her lost past. She dared not let the chance slip away—even if she had to risk the Sisters' wrath.

Before the Sisters had a chance to say anything, Kahlan addressed the man. "Please, Master Orlan, listen for a moment. We're looking for an older woman named Tovi. She was to meet these women here. We were delayed, so she should already be here, waiting for us. Please, answer their questions about their friend. This could all be quickly resolved if you would hurry upstairs and get Tovi for them. Then, like this passing storm, we will all soon be out of your lives."

The man reverently dipped his head, as if a queen had asked his help. Kahlan was not only surprised, but completely bewildered by such an act of deference.

"But we have no guest named Tovi here, Mot—"

The room lit with a blinding flash—lightning that was the match of anything out in the raging storm. The twisting rope of liquid heat and light that ignited from between Sister Ulicia's hands blasted across Orlan's chest before he could finish the appellation he had been about to use. The jarring concussion from being so close to the explosive detonation of such thunderous power hammered deep into the core of Kahlan's chest. The impact threw Orlan back, sending him crashing through a table and both benches, slamming him against the wall. The deadly contact with such power had nearly cut the man in half. Smoke curled up from what was left of his shirt. A glistening red splatter of gore marked the wall where he'd hit before slumping to the ground.

In the aftermath of the deafening blast, Kahlan's ears rang in what seemed the sudden silence.

Emmy, her eyes wide with the shock of an event that had in an instant forever altered the course of her life, wailed the single word "No!"

Kahlan pressed a hand over her mouth and nose, not just in revulsion, but to mask the smell of blood and the stench of burned flesh. The lantern that had been on the table had been thrown to the floor and extinguished, leaving the room mostly to the wavering shadows cast by the fire in the hearth and the sporadic flashes of lightning coming in the slender windows.

Had it not been a night already filled with thunder and lightning, such a blast would surely have awakened the entire town.

The wooden bowls Emmy had been holding clattered down onto the floor and rolled drunkenly away. She screamed in horror and ran toward her husband.

Sister Ulicia came unhinged. In a fury she intercepted Emmy before she could reach her dead husband.

Sister Ulicia slammed the woman against the wall. "Where's Tovi! I want answers and I want them right now!"

Kahlan saw that the Sister had brought her dacra to hand. The simple weapon looked like nothing more than a knife handle with a sharpened metal rod in place of a blade. All three Sisters carried a dacra. Kahlan had seen them use the weapons when they had encountered Imperial Order scouts. She knew that once the dacra had pierced a victim, no matter how minor the penetration, it took only a thought on the Sister's part to kill. With the dacra it was not the wound itself that killed, but rather the Sister who, through the dacra, extinguished the spark of life. If the Sister didn't withdraw the weapon, along with her intent to kill, there was no defense, and no chance of salvation.

A confusing, faltering flash of lightning lit the room through the narrow windows beside the door, throwing long spikes of shadows across the floor and against the walls as two Sisters together snatched the panicked woman, struggling to control her. As the fit of lighting ended and a dark pall again descended over the room, the third Sister raced up the stairwell.

Kahlan went for the girl.

As she ran toward her mother, Kahlan intercepted the girl, hooking her around her middle, holding her back. Her eyes went wide in panic, her mind unable to maintain the memory of seeing Kahlan even long enough for her to be aware of who or what had grabbed her—seemingly out of thin air. Far worse, though, she had just seen her father killed. Kahlan knew that the girl would never be able to forget such a terrible sight.

Over the steady drumbeat of rain and wind, Kahlan heard the footfalls of the Sister upstairs as she rushed down the hallway. She paused intermittently, stopping at each room to throw open a door. Any guests who had been awakened by the commotion and shouting, and dared to come out of their room into the dark hall, were about to face a Sister of the Dark on a rampage. Those still asleep behind their doors would face no less.

Emmy cried out in pain. Kahlan knew why.

"Where is she!" Sister Ulicia yelled at the woman. "Where's Tovi!"

Emmy screamed, begging that her daughter not be harmed.

Kahlan knew that it was a grave tactical mistake to betray to an enemy what you feared most.

In this case, however, she supposed that such information was irrelevant; not only was it pretty obvious what a mother would fear, but the Sisters needed no such leverage. Seeing her mother in a state of unbridled terror was only serving to frighten the child all that much more. She struggled mightily. Despite her frantic effort, such a slender girl was no match for Kahlan.

Holding the girl tightly, Kahlan pulled her back through the doorway beside the stairs and into the darkened room beyond. In the flashes of lightning coming through a window at the rear, Kahlan saw that it was a kitchen and storage area for supplies.

The girl cried in wild panic that was the match of her mother's.

"It's all right," Kahlan whispered in the girl's ear as she held her tight, trying to calm her. "I'll protect you. It's all right."

Kahlan knew that it was a lie, but her heart would not allow the truth.

The slender slip of a girl pawed at Kahlan's arms. It must have seemed to her as if she were being held by a spirit clutching at her from the underworld. If she even saw Kahlan, Kahlan knew that the girl would forget her before her mind could transform perception into cognition. Likewise, Kahlan's words of comfort would evaporate from the girl's mind before they had a chance to even begin to be comprehended. Within an instant after seeing her, no one ever remembered that Kahlan existed.

Except Orlan. And now he was dead.

Kahlan hugged the terrified girl tight. She didn't know if it wasn't really more for her own sake than the girl's. At that moment, keeping the girl away from the terror of what was befalling her parents was all Kahlan could do. The girl, for her part, writhed madly in Kahlan's arms, trying to twist away, as if she were being held by a monster intent on bloody murder. Kahlan hated adding to her terror, but letting her go out into the other room would be worse.

Lightning flashed again, making Kahlan glance to the window. The window was large enough for her to get through. It was dark outside, and the dense forest lay tight up to the buildings. She had long legs. She was strong and quick. She knew that if she chose, she could, in a few heartbeats, be through the window and into the thick of the woods.

But she had tried to escape the Sisters before. She knew that neither night nor woods would conceal her from women with such dark talents. Kneeling there in the dark, her arms holding the girl in a tight embrace, Kahlan began to tremble. The mere contemplation of an attempt at escape was enough to make her brow bead in sweat for fear that such a notion would unleash within her the embedded constraints. Her head swam dizzily with the memory of past attempts, memories of the agony. She couldn't take such suffering again—not when it was to no purpose. Escaping the Sisters was impossible.

When she glanced up, Kahlan saw the dark shadow of a Sister descending the stairs.

"Ulicia," the woman called out. It was Sister Cecilia's voice. "The rooms upstairs are all empty. There are no guests."

In the front room Sister Ulicia growled a dark curse.

The shadow of Sister Cecilia turned from the stairs to fill the doorway, like death itself turning its withering gaze on the living. Beyond, Emmy wailed and wept. In her confusion, grief, pain, and terror she was unable to answer Sister Ulicia's shouted questions.

"Do you want your mother to die?" Sister Cecilia asked from the doorway in that deadly calm voice of hers.

She was no less cruel or dangerous than Sister Armina, or Sister Ulicia, but she had a quiet, composed way of speaking that was somehow more terrifying than Sister Ulicia's screaming. Sister Armina's straightforward threats were simple and sincere but delivered with a bit more bile. Sister Tovi had a kind of sick glee in her approach to discipline and even torture. When any of them wanted something, though, Kahlan had long ago learned that to deny them would only bring nearly unimaginable suffering, and in the end what they had wanted in the first place.

"Do you?" Sister Cecilia repeated with calm directness.

"Answer her," Kahlan whispered in the girl's ear. "Please, answer her questions. Please."

"No," the girl managed.

"Then tell us where Tovi is."

In the room behind Sister Cecilia, the girl's mother gasped in a terrible rattle and then went silent. Kahlan heard bony thumps as the woman hit the wood floor. The house fell quiet.

From the dim, flickering light beyond the doorway, two more shadows glided up behind Sister Cecilia. Kahlan knew that Emmy would answer no more questions.

Sister Cecilia slipped into the room, closer to the girl Kahlan held tightly in her arms.

"The rooms are all empty. Why are there no guests in your inn?"

"None have come," the girl managed as she shook. "Word of the invaders from the Old World has scared people away."

Kahlan knew that that made sense. After leaving the People's Palace in D'Hara and swiftly traveling south through mostly remote country on a small riverboat, they still had encountered detachments of Emperor Jagang's troops more than once, or been through river settlements where those brutes had been. Word of such atrocities would have spread like an ill wind.

"Where is Tovi?" Sister Cecilia asked.

Holding the girl protectively away from the Sisters, Kahlan glared up at them. "She's just a child! Leave her be!"

A shock of pain slammed into her. It felt to Kahlan as if every fiber of every muscle had violently ripped. For an instant, she didn't know where she was or what was happening. The room spun. Her back hit the cupboards with bone-breaking force. Doors flew open. Pots, pans, and utensils cascaded out, bouncing and clattering across the wooden floor. Dishes and glasses shattered as they came crashing down.

Kahlan slammed facedown onto the floor. Jagged, broken shards of pottery slashed her palms as she tried unsuccessfully to break her fall. When she felt the end of something razor-sharp pressed against the side of her tongue in back she realized that a long sliver of glass had pierced her cheek. She clenched her jaw, snapping off the glass between her teeth so that it wouldn't slash open her tongue. With effort she managed to spit out the bloody, daggerlike piece of glass.

She lay sprawled on the floor, stunned, disoriented, unable to fully gather her senses. Grunts escaped her throat as she tried without success to move. She found that as those sounds slipped out, she couldn't draw a new breath back in. Each bit of air that escaped her lungs was a bit of air lost to her. Her muscles strained to pull the wind back into her lungs. The pain lancing through her middle was paralyzing, acting to counter her effort to get a breath.

In desperation she gasped, at last managing to pull in an urgent breath. She spat out more blood and sharp splinters of glass. She was just beginning to feel the twinge of pain from the fragment still stuck through her cheek. Kahlan couldn't seem to make her arms work, couldn't lift herself up from the floor, much less reach up to pull out the piece of glass.

She turned her eyes upward. She could make out the dark forms of the Sisters closing in around the girl. They lifted her and shoved her back against a heavy butcher block standing in the center of the room. A Sister held each arm as Sister Ulicia squatted down before the girl to meet her panicked gaze.

"Do you know who Tovi is?"

"The old woman!" the girl cried out. "The old woman!"

"Yes, the old woman. What else do you know about her?"

The girl gulped air, almost unable to get the words out. "Big. She was big. Old and big. She was too big to walk real good."

Sister Ulicia leaned close, gripping the girl's slender throat. "Where is she? Why isn't she here? She was supposed to meet us here. Why is she gone?"

"Gone," the girl cried. "She's gone."

"Why! When was she here? When did she leave? Why did she leave?"

"A few days back. She was here. She stayed with us for a while. But she left a few days back."

Sister Ulicia, with a cry of rage, lifted the girl and heaved her against the wall. With all her effort, Kahlan struggled to her hands and knees. The girl crashed down to the floor. Ignoring how wobbly she felt, Kahlan crawled across the floor, across broken glass and pottery, and threw herself protectively across the girl's body. The girl, not knowing what was happening, cried out all the more.

Footsteps came toward her. Kahlan saw a cleaver lying on the floor nearby. The girl cried and struggled to get away, but Kahlan held her protectively against the floor.

As the shadows of the woman came closer, Kahlan's fingers closed around the wooden handle of the heavy cleaver. She wasn't thinking, she was simply acting: threat, weapon. It was almost like watching someone else doing it.

But there was a kind of deep inner satisfaction at having a weapon in her hand. Her fist tightened around the blood-slicked handle. A weapon was life. Flashes of lightning glinted off the steel.

When the women were close enough, Kahlan suddenly raised her arm to strike. Before she could begin to accomplish her task, she felt a gut-wrenching blow, as if she had been rammed by the butt end of a log. The power of that blow hurled her across the room.

A hard impact against the wall stunned her. The room seemed like it was far away, off at the far end of a long, dark tunnel. Pain swamped her. She tried to lift her head but couldn't. Darkness pulled her in.

The next time she opened her eyes, Kahlan saw the girl cringing before the Sisters as they towered over her.

"I don't know," the girl was saying. "I don't know why she left. She said she had to be on her way to Caska."

The room rang with silence.

"Caska?" Sister Armina finally asked.

"Yes, that's what she said. She had to get to Caska."

"Did she have anything with her?"

"With her?" the girl whined, still sobbing and shivering. "I don't understand. What do you mean, with her?"

"With her!" Sister Ulicia screamed. "What did she have with her! She had to be carrying things—a pack, a waterskin. But she had other things. Did you see anything else of what she had with her?"

When the girl hesitated, Sister Ulicia smacked her across the face hard enough to have loosened her teeth.

"Did you see anything she had with her?"

A long string of blood from the girl's nose lay horizontally across her cheek. "When she was at supper one day, I went to take her clean towels and I saw something in her room. Something strange."

Sister Cecilia leaned down. "Strange? Like what?"

"It was, it was like a . . . a box. She had it wrapped in a white dress, but the dress was silky smooth and it had partly slipped off the box. It was like a box—only it was all black. But not black like paint. It was black like night itself. Black like it would take the light right out of the day."

The three Sisters straightened and stood in silence.

Kahlan knew exactly what the girl was talking about. Kahlan had gone in and taken all three of those boxes from the Garden of Life in the People's Palace—from Lord Rahl's palace.

When she had brought the first one out, Sister Ulicia had been furious at Kahlan for not bringing all three of them out at once, but they were larger than expected and there had been no room to hide them all in her pack, so Kahlan had at first brought out only one. Sister Ulicia had wrapped that vile thing in Kahlan's white dress and had given it to Tovi, telling her to hurry and be on her way, that they would all meet up later. Sister Ulicia hadn't wanted to risk getting caught in the palace with one of the three boxes and so she hadn't wanted Sister Tovi to wait while Kahlan went back up into the Garden of Life after the other two boxes.

"Why did Tovi go to Caska?" Sister Ulicia asked.

"I don't know," the girl wept. "I don't know, I swear I don't. I only know that I heard her say to my parents that she had to be on her way to Caska. She left a few days back."

In the quiet, lying against the floor, Kahlan struggled to breathe. Each breath sent agonizing stitches of pain through her ribs. She knew that it was only going to be the beginning of the pain. When the Sisters finished with the girl they would turn their attention to Kahlan.

"Maybe we had better get some sleep in out of the rain," Sister Armina finally suggested. "We can start out early."

Sister Ulicia, her fist with the dacra on her hip, paced between the girl and the butcher block, thinking. Shards of pottery crunched under her boots.

"No," she said as she turned back to the others. "Something is wrong."

"You mean with the spell-form? You mean because of the man?"

Sister Ulicia waved a hand dismissively. "An anomaly. Nothing more. No, something is wrong about the rest of it. Why would Tovi leave? She had explicit instructions to meet us here. And she was here—but then she leaves. There were no other guests, no Imperial Order troops in the area, she knew we were on our way, and yet she leaves. It makes no sense."

"And why Caska?" Sister Cecilia asked. "Why would she head for Caska?"

Sister Ulicia turned back to the girl. "Who visited Tovi while she was here? Who came to see her?"

"I already told you, no one. No one at all came here while the old woman was staying with us. We had no other callers or guests. She was the only one here. This place is out of the way. People don't come here for stretches."

Sister Ulicia went back to her pacing. "I don't like it. Something is wrong about this, but I can't put my finger on it."

"I agree," Sister Cecilia said. "Tovi wouldn't just leave."

"And yet she did. Why?" Sister Ulicia came to a stop before the girl. "Did she say anything else, or leave a message—perhaps a letter?"

The girl, sniffling back a sob, shook her head.

"We have no choice," Sister Ulicia muttered. "We're going to have to follow Tovi to Caska."

Sister Armina gestured toward the front door. "Tonight? In the rain? Don't you think we ought to wait until morning?"

Sister Ulicia, deep in thought, looked up at the woman. "What if someone shows up? We don't need any more complications if we're to accomplish our task. We certainly don't need Jagang or his troops getting a whiff of us being about. We need to get to Tovi and we need to get that box—we all know what's at stake." She took the measure of both women's grave expressions before going on. "What we don't need are any witnesses who can report that we were here and what we're looking for."

Kahlan knew very well what Sister Ulicia was getting at.

"Please," she managed as she pushed herself up on shaky arms, "please, leave her be. She's just a little girl. She doesn't know anything of any value to anyone."

"She knows Tovi was here. She knows what Tovi has with her." Sister Ulicia's brow drew tight with displeasure. "She knows we were here looking for her."

Kahlan struggled to put force into her voice. "She is nothing to you. You're sorceresses; she is but a child. She can do you no harm."

Sister Ulicia glanced briefly over her shoulder at the girl. "She also knows where we're going."

Sister Ulicia looked deliberately into Kahlan's eyes. Without turning to the girl behind her, and with sudden force, she slammed her dacra back into the girl's midsection.

The girl gasped in shock.

Still staring down at Kahlan, Sister Ulicia smiled at such a deed as only evil could smile. Kahlan thought that this must be what it would be like looking into the eyes of the Keeper of the Dead in his lair in the darkest depths of the eternity of the underworld.

Sister Ulicia arched an eyebrow. "I don't intend to leave any loose ends."

Light seemed to flash from within the girl's wide eyes. She went slack and fell heavily to the floor. Her arms sprawled out at crazy angles. Her lifeless gaze stared fixedly right at Kahlan as if to denounce her for not keeping her word.

Her promise to the girl—*I'll protect you*—rang through Kahlan's mind.

She cried out in helpless fury as she pounded her fists against the floor.

And then she cried out in sudden pain as she was flung back against the wall. Rather than crash to the floor, she stuck there as if held by a great strength. The strength, she knew, was magic.

She couldn't breathe. One of the Sisters was using her power to constrict Kahlan's throat. She strained, trying to get air, as she clawed at the iron collar around her neck.

Sister Ulicia approached and put her face close to Kahlan's.

"You are lucky this day," she said in a venomous voice. "We don't have time to make you regret your disobedience—not right now, anyway. But don't think that you are going to get away with it without suffering the consequences."

"No, Sister," Kahlan managed to say with great effort. She knew that not to answer would only make it worse yet.

"I guess that you're simply too stupid to comprehend how insignificant and powerless you are in the face of your betters. Perhaps this time, when you are given another lesson, even one as lowly and ignorant as you will understand it."

"Yes, Sister."

Even though she knew quite well what they would make her endure to teach her that lesson, Kahlan would have done the same thing again. She regretted only failing to protect the girl, as she had promised. The day she had taken those three boxes out of Lord Rahl's palace, she had left in their place her most prized possession: a small statue of a proud woman, her fists at her side, her back arched, and her head thrown back as if facing forces that would subdue her but could not.

Kahlan had gathered strength that day in Richard Rahl's palace. Standing in his garden, looking back at the proud statue she'd had to leave there, Kahlan had sworn that she would have her life back. Having her life back meant fighting for life, even if it was the life of a little girl she didn't know.

"Let's go," Sister Ulicia growled as she marched toward the door, expecting everyone to follow.

Kahlan's boots thumped down on the floor when the force pressing her to the wall abruptly released her.

She collapsed to her knees, her bloody hands comforting her throat as she gasped for air. Her fingers encountered the hated collar by which the Sisters controlled her.

"Move," Sister Cecilia ordered in a tone that had Kahlan scrambling to her feet.

She glanced over her shoulder and saw the poor girl's dead eyes staring at her, watching her go.

Richard stood suddenly. The legs of the heavy wooden chair he'd been sitting in chattered as they slid back across the rough stone floor. His fingertips still rested on the edge of the table where the book he'd been reading lay open, waiting, before the silver lantern.

There was something wrong with the air.

Not with the way it smelled, or with the temperature, or with the humidity, although it was a warm and sticky night. It was the air itself. Something felt wrong about the air.

Richard couldn't imagine why he would suddenly be struck with such a thought. He couldn't even begin to imagine what it was that could be the cause of such an odd notion. There were no windows in the small reading room, so he didn't know what it was like outside—if it was clear, or windy, or stormy. He knew only that it was deep in the night.

Cara, not far away behind him, stood up from the thickly padded brown leather chair where she, too, had been reading. She waited, but said nothing.

Richard had asked her to read several historical volumes he'd found. Whatever she could find out about the ancient times when the Chainfire book had been written might prove helpful. She hadn't complained about the task. Cara rarely complained about anything as long as it didn't in any way prevent her from protecting him. Since she was able to stay right there in the room with him, she'd had no objections to reading the books he'd given her. One of the other Mord-Sith, Berdine, could read High D'Haran and had in the past been very helpful with things written in the ancient language often found in rare books, but Berdine was far away at the People's Palace. That still left uncountable volumes written in their own language for Cara to review.

Cara watched him as he peered around at the paneled walls, his gaze passing methodically over the ornamental oddities on the shelves: the lacquered boxes with inlaid silver designs, the small figures of dancers carved from bone, the smooth stones lying in velvet-lined boxes, and the decorative glass vases.

"Lord Rahl," she finally asked, "is something wrong?"

Richard glanced back over his shoulder. "Yes. There's something wrong with the air."

He realized only after seeing the tense concern in her expression that it must have sounded absurd saying that there was something wrong with the air.

To Cara, though, no matter how absurd it might have sounded, all that really mattered was that he thought there was some kind of trouble, and trouble meant a potential threat. Her leather outfit creaked as she spun her Agiel up into her fist. Weapon at the ready, she peered around the little room, searching the shadows as if a ghost might pop out of the woodwork.

Her brow drew tighter. "The beast, do you think?"

Richard hadn't considered that possibility. The beast that Jagang had ordered his captured Sisters of the Dark to conjure and send after Richard was always a potential threat. There had been several times in the past when it had seemed to appear out of the very air itself.

Try as he might, Richard couldn't tell precisely what it was that felt wrong to him. Although he couldn't put his finger on the source of the sensation, it seemed like maybe it was something he should remember, something he should know, something he should recognize. He couldn't decide if such a feeling was real or merely his imagination.

He shook his head. "No . . . I don't think it's the beast. Not wrong in that way."

"Lord Rahl, on top of everything else, you've been up most of the night reading. Perhaps it's just that you're exhausted."

There were times when he did wake with a start just as he began to doze off, foggy and disoriented from the gathering descent into the dark grasp of nightmares that he never remembered when he woke. But this impression was different; it was not something borne out of the dullness of dozing off to sleep. Besides, despite his fatigue, he hadn't been about to fall asleep; he was too anxious to sleep.

It had been only the day before that he had finally convinced the others that Kahlan was real, that she existed, and that she wasn't a figment of his imagination or a delusion caused by an injury. At long last they now knew that Kahlan was not some crazy dream he was having. Now that he at last had some help, his sense of urgency to find her drove him on and kept him wide awake. He couldn't bear to take the time to stop and rest—not now that he had some pieces of the puzzle.

Back near the People's Palace, questioning Tovi just before she died, Nicci had learned the terrible details of how those four women—Sisters Ulicia, Cecilia, Armina, and Tovi—had invoked a Chainfire event. When they unleashed powers that had for thousands of years been secreted away in an ancient book, everyone's memory of Kahlan—except Richard's—had in an instant been wiped away. Somehow, his sword had protected his mind. While he had his memory of Kahlan, his sword had later been forfeited in the effort to find her.

The theory of a Chainfire event had originated with wizards in ancient times. They had been searching for a method that would allow them to slip unseen, ignored, and forgotten among an enemy. They postulated that there was a method to alter people's memory with Subtractive power in a way that all the resulting disconnected parts of a person's recollection would spontaneously reconstruct and connect themselves to one another, with the direct consequence being the creation of erroneous memory to fill the voids that had been created when the subject of the conjuring was wiped from people's minds.

The wizards who had come up with the theoretical process had, in the end, come to believe that unleashing such an event might very well engender a cascade of events that couldn't be predicted or controlled. They speculated that, much like a wildfire, it would continue to burn through links with other people whose memory had not initially been altered. In the end, they had realized that, with such incalculable, sweeping, and calamitous consequences, a Chainfire event had the very real potential to unravel the world of life itself, so they had never dared even to test it.

Those four Sisters of the Dark had—on Kahlan. They didn't care if they unraveled the world of life. In fact, that was their ultimate goal.

Richard had no time to sleep. Now that he had finally convinced Nicci, Zedd, Cara, Nathan, and Ann that he wasn't crazy and that Kahlan existed in reality if no longer in their memories, they were committed to helping him.

He desperately needed that help. He had to find Kahlan. She was his life. She completed him. She was everything to him. Her unique intelligence had captivated him from the first moment he met her. The memory

of her beautiful green eyes, her smile, her touch, haunted him. Every waking moment was a living nightmare that there was something more he
should be doing.

While no one else could remember Kahlan, it seemed that Richard
could think of nothing else. It often felt to him as if he were her only connection to the world and if he were to stop remembering her, stop thinking
about her, she would finally, once and for all . . . truly cease to exist.

But he realized that if he was to accomplish anything, if he was to ever
find Kahlan, he sometimes had to force his thoughts of her aside in order
to concentrate on the matters at hand.

He turned to Cara. "You don't feel anything odd?"

She arched an eyebrow. "We're in the Wizard's Keep, Lord Rahl—who
wouldn't feel odd? This place makes my skin crawl."

"Any worse than usual?"

She heaved a sigh as she ran her hand down the long, single blond braid
lying over the front of her shoulder.

"No."

Richard snatched up a lantern. "Come on."

He swept out of the small room and into a long hall layered with thick
carpets, as if there were too many carpets on hand and the corridor had
been the only place that could be found to put them. They were mostly
classic designs woven in subdued colors, but a few peeking out from underneath were composed of bright yellows and oranges.

The carpets muted his boots as he marched past double doors to each
side opened into dark rooms. Cara, with her long legs, had no difficulty
keeping up with him. Richard knew that a number of the rooms were libraries, while others were elaborately decorated rooms seeming to serve
no purpose other than to lead to other rooms, which led to other rooms,
some simple and some ornate, all a part of the inscrutable and complex
maze that was the Keep.

At an intersection Richard took a right, down a hall with walls thickly
plastered in spiral designs that had mellowed over the centuries to a warm
golden brown. When they reached a stairway Richard hooked his hand on
the polished white marble newel post and took to the stairs heading down.
Glancing up the stairwell, he could see it climb around the square shaft
high up into darkness, into the distant upper reaches of the Keep.

"Where are we going?" Cara asked.

Richard was a bit startled by the question. "I don't know."

Cara shot him a dark look. "You just thought we would go search through a place with thousands upon thousands of rooms, a place as big as a mountain, a place built partly into a mountain, until you happen across something?"

"There's something wrong with the air. I'm just following that perception of it."

"You're following air," Cara said in a flat, mocking tone. Her suspicion flared again. "You aren't trying to use magic, are you?"

"Cara, you know as well as anyone that I don't know how to use my gift. I couldn't call upon magic if I wanted to."

And he most certainly didn't want to.

If he were to call upon his gift the beast would be better able to find him. Cara, ever protective, was worried that he would carelessly do something to call the beast that had been conjured at the orders of Emperor Jagang.

Richard turned his attention back to the problem at hand and tried to discern what it was about the air that seemed so strange to him. He put his mind to analyzing precisely what it was that he sensed. He thought that it felt something like the air during a thunderstorm. It had that edgy, spooky quality.

At the bottom, several flights down the white marble stairs, they emerged in a simple corridor made of stone blocks. They followed the corridor straight through several intersections and came to a halt as Richard stared down a dark spiral of stone steps with an iron railing. Cara followed as he finally started down. At the bottom they passed through a short passage with a barrel ceiling of oak planks before coming out into a room that was the center of a hub of halls. The round room had speckled, gray granite pillars all around the outside holding gilded lintels above each passage that went off into darkness.

Richard held out the lantern, squinting as he tried to see into the dark passages. He didn't recognize the round room, but he did recognize that they were in a part of the Keep that was somehow different—different in a way that made him understand what Cara meant when she said the place made her skin crawl. One of the corridors, unlike the others, led at a rather steep angle down a long ramp, apparently toward some of the deeper areas of the Keep. He wondered why there would be a ramp, rather than yet more of the endless variety of stairs.

"This way," he told Cara as he led her down the ramp and into the darkness.

The ramp seemed endless in its descent. Finally, though, it emptied into a grand hall that, while not more than a dozen feet wide, had to be seventy feet high. Richard felt like an ant at the bottom of a long, narrow slit deep in the ground. To the left side rose a natural rock wall that had been chiseled right out of the mountain itself while tightly fit, enormous stone blocks formed the wall on the right. They passed a series of rooms in the block wall as they made their way onward in what seemed an endless split through the mountain. As they moved steadily ahead, the lanternlight was not strong enough to reveal any end in sight.

Richard suddenly realized what it was that he sensed. The air felt the way it occasionally felt in the immediate area around certain people he knew who were powerful with the gift. He remembered the way the air itself seemed to crackle around his former teachers, Sisters Cecilia, Armina, Merissa, and especially Nicci. He remembered times when it seemed as if the air around Nicci might ignite, so great was the singular power radiating from her. But that sensation had always been in close proximity to the individual; it had never been a pervasive phenomenon.

Even before he saw the light coming from one of the rooms in the distance, he felt the air coming from the place. He half expected to see the air in the entire hallway beginning to sparkle.

Immense, brass-clad doors stood open, leading into what appeared to be a dimly lit library. He knew that this was the place he was looking for.

Walking through those doors with elaborate, engraved symbols covering them, Richard froze in midstride and stared in astonishment.

A flickering flash of lightning came in through a dozen, round-topped windows and illuminated row upon row of shelves all around the cavernous room. The windows, rising two stories, ran the entire length of the far wall. Two-story polished mahogany columns rose up between them, hung with heavy dark green velvet draperies. Gold fringe lined the edges of the drapes, and swagged tassels held them back from the windows. The small squares of glass that made up the soaring windows were not clear, but thick and composed of numerous rings, as if the glass had been overly thick when poured. When the lightning flashed it made the glass seem to light as well. Lanterns with reflectors all around the room lent the place a

soft warm glow and reflected off the polished tabletops here and there between the confused disarray of books lying open everywhere.

The shelves were not what Richard had at first expected. There were indeed books on a number of them, but other shelves held clutters of
objects—everything from neatly folded sparkling cloth, to iron spirals, to
green glass flasks, to complex objects made of wooden rods, to stacks of
vellum scrolls, to ancient bones and long, curved fangs that Richard
didn't recognize and couldn't begin to guess at.

When the lightning flashed again, the shadows of the window mullions
running over everything in the room, running across tables, chairs,
columns, bookcases, and desks, made it appear as if the whole place were
cracking apart.

"Zedd—what in the world are you doing?"

"Lord Rahl," Cara said in a low voice from right over his shoulder, "I
think your grandfather must be crazy."

Zedd turned to peer briefly at Richard and Cara standing back in the
doorway. The old man's wavy white hair, standing out in every direction,
looked a pale shade of orange in the lamplight, but white as snow whenever the lightning flashed.

"We're a bit busy right now, my boy."

In the center of the room, Nicci floated just above one of the massive
tables. Richard blinked, trying to be sure that he really saw what he
thought he saw. Nicci's feet were clear of the table by a hand's width. She
stood poised dead-still in midair.

As impossible and startling as such a sight was, that wasn't the worst of
it. On the top of the table was drawn a magical design known as a Grace.

It appeared to have been drawn with blood.

Like a curtain encircling Nicci, unmoving lines also hung suspended in
the air above the Grace. Richard had seen a number of gifted people draw
spell-forms before, so he was pretty sure that that was what he was seeing,
but he had never seen anything approaching this midair maze.

Consummately complex, composed of lines of glowing green light, it
hung in the air like a three-dimensional spell-form.

In the center of that intricate geometric framework Nicci floated as still
as a statue. Her exquisite features seemed frozen to stone. One hand was
lifted out a ways. The fingers of her other hand, at her side, were spread.

Her feet weren't level, as if standing, but dangled as if she were in mid-jump. Her fall of blond hair was lifted out a little, as if in the midst of that jump up into the air her hair had risen away from her head, just before she was about to come back down . . . and at that precise instant she had been turned to stone.

She didn't look alive.

Richard stood transfixed, staring at Nicci poised in midair just above a heavy library table, a net of glowing green geometric lines tangled all around her. Nothing on her moved. She didn't appear to be breathing at all. Her blue eyes stared unblinking into the distance, as if gazing on a world only she could see. Her familiar, exquisite features looked perfectly preserved in the greenish cast given off by the glowing lines.

Richard thought that she looked more dead than alive, the way a corpse in a casket looked just before being laid to rest.

It was an impossibly beautiful and at the same time profoundly alarming sight. She appeared to be nothing so much as a lifeless statue made of flesh and light. Skeins of her blond hair in twisting, gentle arcs and curves, even individual strands of hair, stood out unmoving in midair. Richard kept expecting her to finally and suddenly finish her fall back to the table.

When he realized that he was holding his breath he at last let it out.

Seemingly in sympathy with the tempestuous intensity of the lightning out beyond the wall of windows, the air in the room fairly crackled with the power that had been focused into what was obviously, even to Richard's untrained eye, an extraordinary conjuring. It had been that rare quality to the air that had first caught his attention back in the small reading room.

For the life of him, Richard could not imagine what was going on, what could be the purpose of such a use of magic. He was at once fascinated by it and disconcerted that he knew so little about such things. More than anything, though, he found the sight darkly frightening.

Having grown up in Westland, where there had been no magic, he sometimes wondered what he had missed—especially at times like this, when he felt hopelessly ignorant. But at other times, like when Kahlan had been taken, he hated magic and wished never again to have anything to do with it.

Those devoted to the teachings of the Imperial Order would find cynical satisfaction at such cold thoughts about magic coming from the Lord Rahl.

Despite having grown up unaware of magic, Richard had since come to learn a few things about it. For one, he knew that the Grace drawn under Nicci was a powerful device used by those with the gift. He also knew that drawing it in blood was something that was rarely done and even then in only the gravest of circumstances.

As he glanced at the glistening lines of blood that made up the form of the Grace, Richard noticed something that made the hair at the back of his neck stand on end. One of Nicci's feet was poised over the center of the Grace—the part representing the Creator's light, from where emanated not only life but the rays that represented the gift that passed through life, the veil, and then on into the eternity of the underworld.

Nicci's other foot, however, was frozen mere inches above the table beyond the outer ring of the drawing—over the part representing the underworld.

Nicci hung suspended between the world of life and the world of the dead. Richard knew that such a thing was hardly trivial happenstance.

He focused beyond the startling sight of Nicci floating in midair and in the shadows beyond saw Nathan and Ann occasionally illuminated by flashes of lightning, like ghosts flickering in and out of existence. They, too, solemnly watched Nicci in the center of the glowing spell-form.

Zedd, one hand on a bony hip, his other running a slender finger down his smooth jaw, slowly moved around the table, observing the ever-growing, ever more intricate pattern of glowing green lines.

Outside, through the tall windows, lightning continued to flash in harsh fits, but the rumble of thunder was muted by the thick stone of the Keep.

Richard gazed up at Nicci's face. "Is she . . . is she all right?"

Zedd looked over as if he had forgotten that Richard had entered the room. "What?"

"Is she all right?"

Zedd's bushy brows drew together. "How would I know?"

Richard threw his arms up and let them flop down in dumbfounded alarm. "Well, for crying out loud, Zedd, aren't you the one who put her there?"

"Not exactly," Zedd muttered, rubbing his palms together as he moved on.

Richard stepped closer to the table below Nicci. "What's going on? Is Nicci all right? Is she in danger?"

Zedd finally looked back and sighed. "We don't exactly know for sure, my boy."

Nathan came out of the shadows and toward the table, into the greenish light. The tall prophet's dark azure eyes were clearly troubled. He opened his hands in a gesture of reassurance, his long white hair brushing his shoulders as he shrugged slightly. "We think she is all right, Richard."

"She should be just fine," Ann assured him as she joined Nathan.

The broad-shouldered prophet towered over her. In her plain woolen dress, with her graying hair gathered back into a loose bun, she looked all the more plain beside Nathan. Richard thought that just about anyone would probably look plain beside Nathan.

Richard gestured, indicating the net of geometric lines that encased Nicci. "What is this thing?"

"A verification web," his grandfather said.

Richard frowned. "Verification? Verification of what?"

"Chainfire," Zedd told him in a somber voice. "We're trying to figure out precisely how a Chainfire event functions so that we can see if there is a way to reverse it."

Richard scratched his temple. "Oh."

He was liking the whole thing less and less. He desperately wanted to find Kahlan, yet he was deeply worried for what could happen to Nicci in such an attempt to unravel mysterious powers created by ancient wizards. As First Wizard, Zedd had abilities and talents that Richard could not begin to fathom, and yet those wizards in ancient times far surpassed Zedd's gift. With as much as Zedd, Nathan, Ann, and Nicci knew, as powerful as they all were, they were still dabbling with things outside their experience, things beyond their ability, things that even those ancient wizards feared. Still, what choice did they have?

Besides caring deeply for Nicci, Richard needed her to help him find Kahlan. While the others might in some areas be more powerful or more knowledgeable than Nicci, the sum of everything about her put her on a different plane. She was probably the most powerful sorceress ever to have drawn a breath. What others could do with a great effort, Nicci could do with a glance. As remarkable as that was, to Richard that was probably one of the least remarkable things about Nicci. Other than Kahlan, he didn't know anyone who could focus on a goal as tenaciously as Nicci. Cara could be just as unflinching about defending him, but Nicci was able to center that kind of tenacity on anything she set her mind to. Back when she had fought against him, her reckless determination made her not just brutally effective but profoundly dangerous.

Richard was glad all that had changed. Since the search for Kahlan had begun, Nicci had become his closest and most steadfast friend. Nicci knew, though, that his heart belonged to Kahlan and that could never change.

He raked his fingers back through his hair. "Well, why is she up there in the middle of the thing?"

"She's the only one of us who knows how to use Subtractive Magic," Ann said in simple summary. "A Chainfire event needs Subtractive elements to ignite it and then to make it function. We're trying to understand the whole spell—both the Additive and Subtractive components."

Richard supposed that made sense, but it still didn't make him feel any better about it. "And Nicci agreed to this?"

Nathan cleared his throat. "It was her idea."

Of course it was. Richard sometimes thought the woman had a death wish.

It was times like this that he wished he knew more about such things. He was feeling ignorant again. He gestured up at the totality of everything floating above the table. "I never realized that verification webs used people. I mean, I never knew that such webs were cast around someone like that."

"Neither did we, exactly," Nathan said in that deep, commanding voice of his.

Richard felt uncomfortable under the prophet's gaze, so he turned to Zedd. "What do you mean?"

Zedd shrugged. "This is the first time any of us has ever done an aspect analysis of a verification web from an interior perspective. To do so requires Subtractive Magic, so casting a verification web in this manner probably hasn't been done in perhaps thousands of years."

"Then how did you know how to do it?"

"Just because none of us has ever done such a thing," Ann said, "doesn't mean we haven't studied various accounts of it."

Zedd gestured to one of the other tables. "We've been reading the book you found—*Chainfire*. It's more complex than anything any of us has ever seen before, so we wanted to try to understand everything about it. While we've never done an interior perspective before, it's really just an extension of what we already know. As long as you know how to run a standard verification web, and you have the required elements of the gift, you can perform the aspect analysis from an interior perspective. That's what Nicci is doing—that's why she had to be the one to do it."

"If there's a standard process, then why would this method be needed?"

Zedd lifted a hand toward the lines around Nicci. "An interior perspective is said to show the spell-form in more revealing detail—down to a more elemental level—than you see in the standard verification process. Since it is said to show more than can be learned in the standard process, and Nicci was able to initiate it, we all decided that it would be an advantage to do it this way."

Richard was starting to breathe a little easier. "So then using Nicci in this way is just an abstract analysis. It means nothing more."

Zedd looked away from Richard's eyes as he lightly rubbed the furrows on his brow. "This is only a verification process, Richard, not an ignition of the actual event, so, in a sense, it's not real. What the real spell does in an instant, this inert form stretches out into a lengthy verification process so as to enable a comprehensive analysis. Although not without its risks, that's not the viable spell itself you see around Nicci."

Zedd cleared his throat. "When the actual spell would have been cast, though, instead of Nicci, that would have been Kahlan, and it would have been all too real."

Goose bumps ran up Richard's arms. His mouth felt so dry that he could hardly talk. He could feel his heart pounding through the veins in his neck. He wanted that not to be true.

"But you said that you needed Nicci in order to cast this web. You said that you could only do it because she can work Subtractive Magic. Kahlan wouldn't have been able to do that for the Sisters—and in any event she wouldn't have cooperated."

Zedd shook his head. "The Sisters were casting the real spell around Kahlan. They had command of Subtractive power and would have had no need for Kahlan's cooperation. We needed Nicci to work it from inside, using both Additive and Subtractive aspects, so that we can try to determine how it functions. The two aren't analogous."

"Well, how—"

"Richard," his grandfather said, gently cutting him off, "as I said, we're rather busy. Right now is not the time to discuss this. We need to observe the process so we can try to figure out the equational behavior of the spell. Let us do our job, will you?"

Richard slipped his hands into his back pockets. "Sure."

He glanced back at Cara. She wore what people might see as a blank expression, but to Richard, as well as he knew her, it revealed a great deal and seemed to reflect his own suspicions. He turned back to his grandfather. "Are you having some kind of . . . trouble?"

Zedd cast the others a sidelong glance and only grunted before turning back to studying the geometric forms surrounding the woman floating before him.

Richard knew his grandfather well enough to know by his drawn features that he was either unhappy or very worried. Richard didn't think that either prospect augured well. He began to worry himself—for Nicci.

As the others stood back to take it all in, frowning in concentration as they pondered the way the glowing verification web continued to trace new lines through space, Richard stepped closer. He slowly walked around the table, finally studying—for the first time, really—the lines crisscrossing through the air all around Nicci.

As he moved in closer and stepped around the table, he realized that the lines actually formed a cylinder in space, like something flat that had been rolled up, with Nicci inside that cylinder. That meant that all the lines were simply a two-dimensional drawing, even if they did wrap around until they met. Richard mentally flattened out that cylindrical form, much like unrolling a scroll, in order to see it in his mind as a more customary line drawing. When he did so, he began to realize that there was something oddly familiar about the network of lines.

The more Richard studied it, the more he couldn't stop staring at it, as if it were pulling him in . . . drawing him into the pattern of lines, angles, and arcs. There seemed to be something he should recognize about it all, but he couldn't figure out what.

He thought that perhaps he should regard a spell-form that had been cast around Kahlan, as this terrible thing had been, to be evil, but he didn't feel that way. The spell-form existed; it did not possess the quality of being good or evil.

The ones who cast the web around Kahlan were the real evil. Those four Sisters were the ones who had used the spell for their own evil ends. They had used it as part of their plan to have the boxes of Orden and to free the Keeper from the underworld—to loose death on the living. All in return for beguiling promises of immortality.

Gazing at the lines, Richard began to scrutinize the rhythm in those lines, their patterns, their flow. As he did so, he began to get an inkling of their significance.

He was beginning to see purpose in the design.

Richard pointed to a place near Nicci's extended right arm, just below her elbow.

"This place, here, is wrong," he said as he frowned into the fabric woven of light.

Zedd came to a halt. "Wrong?"

Richard hadn't realized that he'd said it out loud, at least not loud enough for others to hear. "Yes, that's right. It's wrong."

Richard went back to studying the lines, tilting his head to better follow them along as they went through a complex intersection of routes coming around from all directions to end up before Nicci's middle. He was beginning to grasp the meaning of those routes and the larger intent of the design.

"I think there's a supporting structure missing." He aimed a finger off to his left. "It seems like it should have started back there, don't you think? It looks like this place, here, should have a line going up this way and then back to that spot near her elbow."

His attention riveted on the rhythm of lines, Richard was largely lost to the rest of the room.

"It's impossible for you to know such a thing," Ann said flatly.

He wasn't discouraged by her skepticism. "When someone shows you a circle and it has a flat spot in it, you know it's wrong, don't you? You can see the intended design and know that the flat spot doesn't belong there."

"Richard, this is not some simple circle. You don't even know what you're looking at." She caught herself before her voice rose any more, clasped her hands before herself, and took a deep breath before going on. "I'm simply trying to point out that there are a great deal of complexities involved here that you are not aware of. The three of us haven't even begun to be able to unravel the mechanism behind the spell-form, and we have extensive training in such things. Despite our training and knowledge, it's still far from complete enough for us to grasp the manner in which it functions. You don't understand the first thing about such complex motifs."

Without turning to her, Richard flicked a hand to dismiss her concern. "Doesn't matter. The form is emblematic."

Nathan cocked his head. "It's what?"

"Emblematic," Richard murmured as he studied an intersection of lines, trying to identify the primary strand through the architecture of the lineation.

"So?" his grandfather sputtered after Richard again fell to silent preoccupation.

"I understand the jargon of emblems," he said, absently, as he found the primary thread and traced it along a rise and fall and swirl of the pattern, all the time coming more in tune with its intent. "I told you that before."

"When?"

"Back when we were with the Mud People." Richard immersed himself in the flow of the design, trying to perceive the ascendant course among the lesser branches. "Kahlan was there. So was Ann."

"I'm afraid that we don't remember," Zedd admitted after seeing Ann shake her head in frustration. He sighed unhappily. "Yet one more memory surrounding Kahlan lost to us because of what those Sisters did."

Richard didn't really hear him. Growing ever more agitated, he waggled a finger back and forth at a breach in the lines just below Nicci's elbow. "I'm telling you, there's a line missing, here. I'm sure of it."

Richard turned to his grandfather. He saw then that everyone was staring at him. "Right here," he told them as he pointed again, "from the end of this upward rising arc, to this intersection of triangles, there should be a line."

Zedd frowned. "A line?"

"Yes." He didn't know why they hadn't spotted it before. It was stone cold obvious to Richard, like a song sung with a note of the melody left out. "A line is missing. An important line."

"Important," Ann repeated in weary exasperation.

Richard, becoming more unsettled by the moment, wiped a hand across his mouth. "Very important."

Zedd sighed. "Richard, what are you talking about?"

"There is no way you could know such a thing," Ann scoffed, her patience wearing thinner by the moment.

"Look," Richard said turning back to them, "it's an emblem, a design."

Zedd scratched the back of his head, glancing briefly to the window as a particularly violent fit of lightning flared so close that it released a crack of thunder that felt like it might loosen the stone walls of the Keep.

He turned back to Richard. "And the design . . . tells you something, Richard?"

"Yes. Such a design is like a translation from another language. In a way, it's what you're trying to understand by doing this verification web.

This form characterizes a concept in much the same way that a math equation expresses physical attributes, such as an equation expressing the ratio of the circumference of a circle to the diameter. Emblematic forms can be a kind of language, too, the way mathematics is a form of language. They both are able to reveal something about the nature of things."

Zedd patiently smoothed back his hair. "You see emblems as a form of language?"

"In a way. Take the Grace underneath Nicci, for example. That's an emblem. The outer circle represents the beginning of the underworld while the inner circle represents the limits of the world of life. The square separating them represents the veil between those worlds. In the center is an eight-pointed star, representing the Creator's Light. The eight lines radiating out from the points of that star all the way out through the outer circle represent the gift carried from Creation all the way through life, across the veil, and beyond, into death. The whole thing is an emblem; when you see that emblem, you see it as a whole concept. You might say that you understand the language of it.

"If, during the casting of a spell, someone with the gift doesn't draw the grace correctly—hasn't spoken the language correctly—it won't work as intended and might even cause trouble. Say you saw a Grace with a nine-pointed star, or with one of the circles missing, wouldn't you know it was wrong? If the square representing the veil was drawn incorrectly, then under the right circumstances it could even theoretically breach the veil and allow the worlds to bleed together.

"It's an emblem. You understand the concept it represents. You know what it should look like. If it's drawn wrong, then you recognize it as wrong."

When the flashes of lightning flickered to a stop, the room felt forsaken in the weak light of lamps. Distant thunder rumbled ominously up from the valley below.

Zedd, standing stock-still, studied Richard with more focus than he had been studying the verification web. "I've never looked at it in quite that way before, Richard, but I grant that you might have a point."

Nathan arched a brow. "He certainly does."

Ann sighed. "Perhaps."

Richard turned from their dour expressions back to the glowing lines. "This, right here," he said, gesturing, "is wrong."

Zedd stretched his neck to peer at the lines. "Let's just say for the sake of argument that you're right. What do you think it means?"

Richard's heart hammered as he made his way around the table, swiftly tracing lines through the spell. He used a finger, keeping it just clear of the lines of light, to track the primary pathways, the sweeps of the pattern, the fabric of the form.

He found what he was expecting. "Here. Look here, at this newly formed structure that has built up around these older, original lines. Look at the disordered nature of this new cluster; they're a variable, but in this emblem of lines it should all be a constant."

"Variable . . . ?" Zedd sputtered, as if having thought he was following Richard's reasoning, had instead suddenly found that he was completely lost.

"Yes," Richard said. "It's not emblematic. It's a biological form. The two are clearly different."

Nathan wiped both hands back over his white hair as he sighed but remained silent.

Ann's face had gone crimson. "It's a spell-form! It's inert! It can't be biological!"

"That's the problem," Richard said, answering her point rather than her anger. "You can't have these kind of variables tainting what's supposed to be a constant. It would be like a math equation in which any of the numbers could spontaneously change their value. Such a thing would render math invalid and unworkable. Algebraic symbols can vary—but even then they are specific relational variables. The numbers, though, are constants. Same with this structure; emblems have to be constructed of inert constants—you might say like simple addition or subtraction. An internal variable corrupts the constant of an emblematic form."

"I don't follow," Zedd admitted.

Richard gestured to the table. "You drew the Grace in blood. The Grace is a constant. The blood is biological. Why did you do it that way?"

"To make it work," Ann snapped. "We had to do it that way in order to initiate an interior perspective of the verification web. That's the way it's done. That's the method."

Richard held up a finger. "Exactly. You deliberately introduced a controlled biological variable—blood—into what is a constant—a Grace. Keep in mind though, that it remains outside the spell-form itself; it's merely an empowering agent, a catalyst. I think it must be that such a variable in the Grace allows the spell you initiated to run its course without being influenced by a constant—the Grace. Do you see? It gives the verification web not only the power invoked by the Grace, but the freedom gained through the biological variable to allow it to grow as it needs to in order to reveal its true nature and intent."

When Zedd glanced her way, Cara said, "Don't look at me. Whenever he starts in like this I just nod and smile and wait until the trouble starts."

Zedd made a sour face. One hand on a hip, he took a few paces away before turning back. "I've never in all my years heard such an explanation of a verification web. It's quite a unique way of looking at it. The most troubling thing is that, in a perverse way, it actually makes sense. I'm not saying that I think you're right, Richard, but it certainly is a disturbing notion."

"If you're right," Nathan said, "it would mean that we've been children playing with fire all these years."

"That's if he's right," Ann added under her breath. "Sounds a tick too clever to me."

Richard stared up at the woman frozen in space, the woman who could not at the moment speak for herself. "Whose blood did you use to draw the Grace?" he asked the others behind him.

"Nicci's," Nathan said. "She suggested it herself. She said it was the proper method and the only way to make it work."

Richard turned to them. "Nicci's. You used Nicci's blood?"

Zedd nodded. "That's right."

"You created a variable . . . with her blood . . . and you put her inside of it?"

"Besides being what Nicci told us had to be done," Ann said, "we have a lot of research and reason to have confidence that this is the proper method of initiating an interior perspective."

"I'm sure you're right—under normal circumstances. Since you all know the proper method for doing such things, then that can only mean that the corruption is far different than any ordinary problem that could be anticipated to arise in the verification process." Richard raked his fingers back through his hair. "It would have to be something . . . I don't know. Something unimaginable."

Zedd shrugged. "You really believe that having Nicci in there when she was the source of the blood to power the web could mean something troublesome, Richard?"

Richard pinched his lower lip as he paced. "Maybe not if the originating spell-form you were verifying were pure. But this one isn't. It's contaminated by another biological variable. I think that providing the source of the control variable—Nicci—might allow the contamination all the latitude it needs."

"Meaning?" Nathan asked.

Richard gestured as he paced. "Meaning that it's like throwing oil on a fire."

"I think the storm is letting our imaginations get carried away," Ann said.

"What biological variable could possibly contaminate a verification web?" Nathan asked.

Richard turned back and stared at the lines, following them around to that terrible arc that ended when it should be supported. He glanced across the empty space to the waiting intersection.

"I don't know," he finally admitted.

Zedd stepped closer. "Richard, your ideas are original, and they are certainly thought-provoking, I'll grant you that. And it could be that they may provide us useful insights to help us understand more than we otherwise might have. But not everything you say is correct. Some of it is simply wrong."

Richard glanced back over his shoulder. "Really? Like what?"

Zedd shrugged. "Well, for one thing, biological forms can be emblematic as well. Is not an oak leaf biological? Don't you recognize that emblematic form? Isn't a snake something that can be expressed with an emblem? Isn't a whole entity, say a tree or a man, able to be represented emblematically?"

Richard blinked. "You're right. I never thought of it that way, but you're right."

He turned back to the spell-form, viewing the area of biological contamination with new eyes. He scanned the confusing mass, trying to make sense of it, trying to discern a pattern. Try as he might, though, it seemed useless. There was no pattern.

But why not? If its delineation was biological in origin, as he knew it was, then, according to Zedd, there should be some kind of source pattern expressed within that depiction. But there was none. It was nothing more than a confusing mass all tangled up in a nest of meaningless lines.

And then he realized that he thought he recognized a small portion within that mass. It looked . . . somehow liquid. But that made no sense, because he saw another part that looked almost the opposite. That other fragment looked more like an emblematic representation of fire.

Unless there was more than one element to it. A tree could have an oak leaf emblem, an acorn, or the form that represented the whole tree. And what was to say that it couldn't be three different things all contaminating the spell-form together.

Three things.

He saw them, then—each of those three elements.

Water. Fire. Air.

They were all there, all tangled together.

"Dear spirits," Richard whispered, his eyes going wide.

He straightened. Goose bumps tingled up his arms. "Get her out of there."

"Richard," Nathan said, "she's perfectly—"

"Get her out of there! Get her out now!"

"Richard—" Ann started.

"I told you—the spell-form has a flaw!"

"Well that's what we're trying to find out, now, isn't it?" Ann said with exaggerated patience.

"You don't understand." Richard gestured toward the wall of softly glowing lines. "This isn't the kind of flaw that anyone would be looking for. This one will kill her. The spell is no longer inert—it's mutating. It's becoming viable."

"Viable?" Zedd's expression twisted with incredulity. "How could you possibly—"

"You have to get her out of there! Get her out now!"

Although she couldn't move, couldn't speak, Nicci was aware of everything that was being said, even if the voices sounded hollow, distant, temporal, as if coming from some faraway world beyond the greenish shroud.

She wanted to scream *Listen to him!* But, held tightly as she was within the bosom of the casting, she could not.

More than anything, she wanted out of the terrible tangle of crushing power that encased her.

She hadn't understood the true meaning of an interior perspective before—none of them had. None of them could have guessed at the reality. Only after initiating the process had she discovered that such a perspective was not simply a way to view a verification web in more detail from the inside, as they had thought, but rather a means for the person doing the analysis to experience it within themselves. By then it was too late and she could not tell the others that what it meant was that she would be perceiving the spell-form by having it ignited within her. The part surrounding her was the mere aura of the conjured power that had dawned within her. It had at first been a revelation bordering on the divine.

Not long after they had initiated it, though, something had begun to go wrong. What had been a profoundly beautiful form of vision had deteriorated into horrific agony. Every new line that sliced through space around her had a corresponding interior aspect that felt as if it were slashing through her soul.

In the beginning she had discovered that pleasure was part of the mechanism by which one perceived the spell as it unfolded. In much the same way in which pleasure could confirm wholesome, fitting aspects of life, it likewise revealed the intricate nature of the spell-form in all its glory. It felt like watching a particularly beautiful sunrise, or tasting a delightful confection, or gazing into the eyes of someone you loved and having them gaze back in the same way. Or, at least, it was like what she imagined it would feel like to have them gaze back in that way.

She had also discovered that, as in life, pain pointed out grievous disorders.

Nicci would never have guessed that such a method had once been commonly used to analyze the inner functioning of a constructed magic—of gauging its inner health. She would never have guessed the complexity or extent of what the method could reveal. She would never have guessed how much it could hurt when something within the spell went awry.

She wondered if she would still have insisted on doing such a thing had she known. She guessed that she would have, if it had a chance of helping Richard.

At that moment, though, there was little else that mattered to her but the pain. It was beyond anything she had ever experienced. Not even the dream walker himself had been able to give her this much pain. It was almost impossible for her to think of anything but her want of being free from the agony. So great was the magnitude of the taint within the spell that there was no doubt in her mind that experiencing it would, for her, be fatal.

Richard had shown them the place it had begun to go wrong. He had pointed out the fundamental defect. That contamination concealed within the spell was pulling her apart. She could feel her life bleeding away beyond that terrible outer circle of the Grace. That Grace, drawn with her blood, had become her life, and it would be her death.

For the moment, Nicci straddled two worlds, neither of them wholly real to her. While still in the world of life, she could feel herself inexorably slipping into that dark void beyond.

All the while, the world of life around her was losing its vibrance.

She was at that moment willing to let it all go, to let herself slip forever into the eternity of nonexistence, if only it would mean that the pain would end.

Even though she could not move, Nicci could see everything in the room—not with her eyes, but with her gift. Even beyond the suffering, she recognized such an exotic form of sight as an extraordinary experience. Vision through her gift alone had a singular quality that approached omniscience. She could see more than her eyes had ever allowed her to see. Despite her agony, there was a quiet majesty to it all.

Beyond the net of greenish lines, Richard looked from one startled face to another.

"What's the matter with all of you? You have to get her out of there!"

Before Ann could launch into a lecture, Zedd gestured for her to keep quiet. Once sure her lips would stay pressed tightly together, he turned his attention back to his grandson.

Another line departed an intersection and traced a path through space. It felt to Nicci like a dull knitting needle taking a stitch in her soul, pulling the agony of that thread of light through her as it bound her ever more tightly to a dark death. It was all she could do to remain conscious. Surrender was seeming sweeter by the moment.

Zedd gestured up toward her. "We can't, Richard. These things have to run a course. The verification web runs itself through a series of connections and in that way reveals information about its nature. Once the verification process has begun, it's impossible to halt it. It has to run its course to completion and then it extinguishes."

Nicci knew the grim truth of it.

Richard seized his grandfather's arm. "How long?" He shook the old man like a rag doll. "How long does the process take?"

Zedd pried Richard's fingers off his arm. "We've never seen a spell like this. It's hard to say. But as complex as it's proving to be I can't imagine it taking less than three or four hours. She's been in there an hour already so it will be hours yet before it runs its course and extinguishes."

Nicci knew that she didn't have hours. She had mere moments before the pull of the contamination drew her forever beyond the veil and into the world of the dead.

She thought it a strange way for her life to end. So unexpected. So uneventful. So pointless. She would at least have wanted it to be an end that in some way would have helped Richard, or to have been after they knew that they had accomplished something. She wished her death could have at least bought him something of value.

Richard turned back to gaze up at her. "She won't last that long. We have to get out of there now."

Inwardly, through her agony, she smiled. To the end. Richard would fight to the end against death.

"Richard," Zedd said, "I can't imagine how you could possibly know such a thing, and I'm not saying that I don't believe you, but we can't shut down a verification web."

"Why not?"

"Well," Zedd said as he sighed, "the truth is, I don't even know if such a thing is possible, but even if it were, none of us knows how to do it. The standard verification process builds safeguards to shield itself from tampering. This thing is an order of magnitude more complex and involved."

"Rather like trying to dismount in midgallop while racing along a ridgeline," the tall prophet said. "You need to wait until the horse is finished running before you jump off, or you will only be leaping to your death."

Richard returned to the table, frantically studying the structure constructed of light. Nicci wondered if he realized that, while it was to a degree tangible, what he was seeing existed mainly as a mere aura representing the real power raging through her.

As another line advanced from an intersection at an angle that was dreadfully wrong, Nicci gasped inwardly. She felt something vital within her being slowly ripped open. The pain of it sang through the marrow of her bones. She saw darkness layered over the room, and knew she was seeing into another world, the dark world where there would be no more pain.

She began to allow herself to drift toward that world.

And then she saw something in the otherworldly shadows. She caught herself, held herself back from the dark brink of death.

Something with glowing eyes, like twin coals, gazed out from the dark shadows. The malevolent intent of that furnace gaze was fixed on Richard.

Nicci struggled desperately to call out a warning. It cleaved her heart that she could not.

"Look," Richard whispered as he gazed up at her, "there's a tear running down her cheek."

Ann sadly shook her head. "Probably because she isn't blinking, that's all."

Richard's hands fisted in frustration as he moved around the table, trying to decipher the meaning of the lines. "We have to find a way to shut the thing down. There has to be a way."

Richard's grandfather laid a hand gently on the back of Richard's shoulder. "I swear, Richard, I would do as you want if I could, but I know of no method to halt a verification web. And what is it that has you so fired up, anyway? Why the sudden urgency? What is it that you think is con-taminating the spell-form?"

Nicci's attention was locked on the thing watching out from the shadowy world of the dead. Whenever the lightning flared, illuminating the room, the thing with the glowing eyes wasn't there. Only when darkness again fell over the room could she see it.

Richard's eyes turned from studying the lines to gaze up at Nicci's face. She wanted nothing so much as for him to reach out and pull her free of the agony of the spell that had impaled her on lethal shards of magic, but she knew that he could not. Right then, she would have willingly given up her life for one moment in his arms.

Richard's answer finally came in a soft resignation. "The chimes."

Ann rolled her eyes. Nathan let out a sigh of relief, as if he now knew that Richard was merely imagining things.

Zedd's brow lifted. "The chimes? Richard, I'm afraid that this time you've gotten it wrong. That simply isn't possible. The chimes are underworld elements. While they certainly lust to enter our world, they can't. They're forever trapped in the underworld."

"I know very well what the chimes are," Richard said in a near whisper. "Kahlan freed them. She freed them to save my life."

"She couldn't possibly know how to do such a thing."

"Nathan told her how, told her their names: Reechani, Sentrosi, Vasi. Water, fire, air. Calling them was the only way for her to save my life. It was an act of desperation."

Nathan's mouth fell open in surprise but he offered no argument. Ann cast a suspicious glare up at the prophet.

Zedd spread his hands. "Richard, she may have thought she was calling them, but I assure you, such a thing is monumentally complex. Besides, we would know if the chimes were free in our world. Be at ease about this much of it. The chimes are not loose."

"Not anymore," Richard said with grim finality. "I banished them back to the underworld. But Kahlan always believed that because she unknowingly brought them into our world it had engendered the beginning of the destruction of magic itself—the cascade effect, as you once described it to us."

Zedd was taken aback. "The cascade effect . . . you could only have heard that from me."

Richard nodded as he stared off into memories. "She tried to convince me that magic had been tainted by the presence of the chimes, and that banishing them back to the underworld would not halt that taint. I never knew whether or not she was right. Now I do."

He pointed up at that awful place before Nicci, that core of her pain, her agony, her end.

"There is the proof. Not the chimes, but the corruption their presence caused: the contamination of magic. That contamination has infected this world. It was drawn to the strength of this magic. It has infected the Chainfire spell and it will kill Nicci if we don't get her out of there."

The room had grown darker yet. Nicci could hardly see through the veil of pain. But she could still see those sinister eyes behind Richard, in the shadows, watching, waiting. No one but Nicci knew that it was there, in that spectral place between worlds.

Richard would never know what hit him.

Nicci had no way to warn him.

She felt another tear roll down her face.

Richard, seeing that tear drip from her jaw, leaned close. With quiet determination, he used a finger to trace the primary pathways, the supporting junctures, and the main framework of the emblem, as he called it.

"It should be feasible," he insisted.

Ann looked beside herself but she remained silent. Nathan watched with stony resignation.

Zedd pushed his simple robes farther up his bony arms. "Richard, it's impossible to shut down a regular verification web, much less one such as this."

"No, it's not," Richard said, irritably. "Here. See here? You have to interrupt this route, here, first."

"Bags, Richard, how am I supposed to do such a thing! The spell shields itself. This web is powered by Subtractive as well as Additive Magic. It has integral shields constructed of both."

Richard stared at his grandfather's crimson face a moment before turning back to the maze of lines. He gazed up at Nicci again and then carefully inserted a hand in through the net of lines to touch Nicci's black dress.

"I won't let it have you," he whispered to her.

No words had ever sounded sweeter, even if she knew he could not understand the impossibility of his promise.

When his finger touched her dress, the patterns shifted from two-dimensional to three-dimensional forms that looked more like a thornbush than a spell-form.

It felt to Nicci as if he had just twisted a knife through her insides. She struggled to remain conscious. She focused on the glowing eyes in the shadows. She had to find a way to warn Richard.

His hand paused. He carefully pulled it back out. The pattern flattened to two-dimensional.

Nicci would have sighed in relief could she breathe.

"Did you see that?" he asked.

Zedd nodded. "I certainly did."

Richard glanced back over his shoulder at his grandfather. "Is it supposed to do that?"

"No."

"I didn't think so. It's supposed to be inert, but the biological variable contaminating it has changed the nature of the host spell-form."

Zedd's expression tightened as he considered. "It seems pretty obvious that whatever is going on, it's changing the way the spell works."

Richard nodded. "Worse, it's a random variable. The contamination caused by the chimes' presence in this world is biological—it evolves. Probably so that it can attack different kinds of magic. This spell will undoubtedly continue to mutate. There's probably no way to predict how it will change, but from the evidence here, it appears that it's only going to become more virulent. As if Chainfire isn't trouble enough, this could make it worse. It could even be that everyone affected by it will develop problems beyond their memory loss revolving around Kahlan."

"What makes you say that?" Zedd asked.

"Just look at how many memories of events only tangent to Kahlan you've all lost. The lost memories could even be the means by which the contamination infects those people touched by the effects of the Chainfire event."

As if the Chainfire event being loosed on the world weren't potentially deadly enough, it now seemed catastrophic beyond imagining.

Ann was bottled fury. She gritted her teeth. "Where did you learn such gibberish?"

Zedd flashed her a scowl. "Be quiet."

"I told you, I understand emblematic designs. This one is a mess."

Nathan glanced to the windows as they lit with flashes of lightning. When the room again fell to darkness, Nicci could again see the thing watching from a dark world.

"And you sincerely believe that it's somehow harming Nicci?" Zedd asked.

"I know it is. Look at this divergence, right here. Such a thing is lethal even without this added breach over here. I know a lot about representational designs involving lethality."

Zedd gave Richard a forbidding look. "I need to know what you're talking about, what you mean by 'representational designs involving lethality.' "

"Later. We have to get her out of there, first, and we have to get her out now."

Zedd shook his head in resignation. "I wish I knew a way, Richard, I truly do, but as I've said, I don't. If you try to pull her out of there before the verification has run its course, that alone will kill her for sure. That much I do know."

"Why?"

"Because her life is in a way suspended. Don't you see that she isn't breathing? The spell-form surrounding her supports her life while she cannot, while the web runs through the verification. She is, in a way, now a part of the spell itself. Pull her out, and you will be pulling her out of the mechanism that is keeping her alive."

Nicci's heart sank. For a moment, she had begun to believe Richard, to believe that he could do it. It was not to be.

All the while the glowing eyes watched. She could see the shape of it, now, standing there in the dark shadows beside a tall shelf. It looked something like a man twisted into a fearsome beast of sinew and knotted muscle. Its eyes gleamed out from the darkness of death itself.

It was the beast that hunted Richard. The beast sent by Jagang, the dream walker.

She would have done anything to stop it, to keep it from Richard, but she could not move a muscle. With every new line of light, she was being stitched tighter and tighter to her fate, pulled inexorably into the darkness of eternity beyond life.

"Even if it's mutating," Richard said as if thinking aloud, "it still has elements that support it while it grows."

"Richard, a verification web is self-generating. Even if it was mutating like you say, there is no way to halt such an event."

"If it can be shut down," Richard murmured, "it will release her—then we won't be pulling her out of it while her life is still being supported by the spell."

Sighing, Zedd shook his head as if he thought Richard hadn't understood a thing he'd said.

Richard studied the lines one last time, then abruptly reached out and placed his finger at an intersection that had been created back before the area of contamination.

The line extinguished at his finger.

"Dear spirits," Nathan said as he leaned in.

The shadow took a step forward. Nicci could now see its fangs.

The line that had extinguished felt as if it pulled her insides out with it. Nicci fought to cling to life. If he really could do it, if he really could extinguish the spell, she had a chance to warn him.

If she could hold on that long.

Richard withdrew his finger. The line ignited again. It lanced through her like a razor-sharp spear. The world flickered.

"See?"

Zedd reached out to duplicate what Richard had done, but with a yelp of pain pulled his hand back as if he'd been burned.

"It's shielded with Subtractive Magic," Ann said.

Zedd shot her a murderous scowl.

"And remember the shields back at the Palace of the Prophets?" Richard asked her. "Remember how I was able to pass through them?"

Ann nodded. "I still have nightmares about it."

Richard reached out again, quickly this time, and again blocked the line of light. Again it extinguished.

Richard then put a finger from his other hand at an intersection preceding the darkened line. In a blink, more lines went dark. He moved his first finger to insert it at another key point, working his way back through the pattern, causing the spell to turn in on itself.

The darkened line raced around Nicci, hitting intersections, making turns, sweeping through and darkening arcs. The line Richard had extinguished ceased to exist in the pattern, its absence causing an interruption in the vitality of the rhythm.

Nicci marveled at the reaction of the spell-form within her. She could sense in detail the process of it dismantling, like a flower closing its petals.

The room again seemed to shimmer in Nicci's gifted vision, as if lightning were flaring, but she knew that this was not lightning.

The glowing eyes peered about, as if it, too, sensed the fluctuation in the flux of power Richard had interrupted.

Didn't anyone but Nicci realize that Richard was using his gift to penetrate such shields? Were they blind? The use of his gift drew the beast out of the underworld.

Outside, real lightning flashed and thunder boomed. The room flickered not only with the lightning but with the disruption of power within the spell-form. The wall of windows flashed between blinding brightness and inky obscurity.

It felt to Nicci as if both of those powerful discharges thundered right through her. She could not understand how she was still alive. It could only be that Richard was shutting down the spell without destroying it. He was methodically extinguishing it, like snuffing out the flames on a row of wicks.

Focused in concentration, Richard put his other hand down lower and blocked another line. The line went dark, racing back through the complex matrix.

The shadow of the beast began to step out of the underworld, partially into the world of life, pulling and flexing its arms with the difficulty of the task, testing its newborn muscle. Fangs glistened in the lamplight as the jaws stretched wide.

Their attention riveted on the lines around Nicci, no one noticed.

Holding a block in one network of lines, Richard carefully inserted a finger to occlude a preceding framework.

The entire web, having lost not just its most important supporting structure, but its very integrity, began to come apart. Angles opened. Intersections disjointed, letting connecting lines sag away. Other lines collided, sparking flashes of white light upon contact that made yet more lines go dark.

All of a sudden, the web of remaining lines collapsed downward, like a curtain falling. Nicci could feel the network of power laced all through her slough away. As the falling lines of light hit the Grace they went dark. In an instant, they were gone.

Free from the tangle, Nicci abruptly dropped to the table as she gasped a breath, like a scream drawn inward. Her legs had no strength to hold her and she crumpled, toppling over the edge of the table.

Richard caught her in his arms as she fell. Her dead weight took him to one knee. He maintained his balance, cradling her in his arms, saving her from hitting the stone floor.

Outside, lightning went wild, casting the room in fits of flickering light.

It was then that the beast, a soulless creature created for a single purpose, materialized fully out of the world of the dead and into the world of life.

And sprang straight for Richard.

Hanging limp and helpless in Richard's arms, despite how much she tried, Nicci simply could not bring forth enough strength to warn him of the beast about to crash down on him. She would have given her last breath to deliver that warning but, right then, she had no breath.

It was Cara, throwing all her weight at the charging creature, who deflected the full force of the attack and saved Richard from a killing strike. The beast's fangs caught only air as it crashed past Richard, but its claws ripped through the flesh at the back of his shoulder. Knocked off balance from Cara's tackle, the beast stumbled past Richard and smashed headlong into one of the heavy shelves. Bones, books, and boxes tumbled down.

The thing scrambled to its feet, snarling, fangs bared, muscles taut. Stretching for a moment to its full height, it was a good foot taller than Richard and its shoulders were nearly twice as wide. Bony projections marked its hunched spine. Dark, leathery flesh, like that of a desiccated corpse, covered powerful muscles.

It was a creature that wasn't really alive, and yet it moved and reacted as if it were. Nicci knew that it had no soul, and for that reason it was all the more dangerous. It had been conjured in part from the lives and Han—the gift—of living men. It acted with the single-minded purpose that had been instilled in it by its creators: Jagang's Sisters of the Dark.

As it immediately recovered and again went for Richard, Cara lashed out with her Agiel. The beast didn't appear to be harmed in the least by the weapon, but it abruptly halted and twisted toward the Mord-Sith with shocking speed and strength, backhanding her hard enough to send her flying. She crashed into a bookcase, toppling it back. Cara didn't rise from the jumble of books and splintered wood.

As lightning flashed outside the tall windows, Zedd used the opening to thrust out a hand, unleashing a shimmering bolt of power that lit the room. Shards of white-hot light exploded against the dark hide of the beast's chest, leaving lines of soot radiating outward as evidence of the contact that didn't appear to have caused any real harm.

Nicci, after Richard had laid her on the floor, was just starting to be able to pull desperately needed air into her lungs. She put an elbow out to prop herself up as she gasped for breath. She saw blood running from Richard's shoulder and down his arm. As he rose to meet his attacker he reached for his sword, but his sword was no longer there, at his hip.

Slowed for only an instant, he instead drew a knife from a sheath at his belt. As he met the threat racing toward him he slashed with the blade, making solid contact that sent the creature reeling. Staggered by the blow and knocked from its feet, it tumbled across the stone floor, stopping only when it collided with one of the massive shelves. A ragged flap of leathery flesh hung like a flag from the injured shoulder. Without slowing, without pause, the beast sprang into a somersault and landed on its feet, ready to renew its attack.

Ann and Nathan both threw fiery bolts at it. Rather than incinerating it, the conjured flames splashed off the beast. Unharmed, it roared with fury. Flashes of lightning glinted off the razor-sharp blade poised motionless in Richard's fist. The creature seemed all fangs and claws as it again lunged for him.

Richard stepped aside, gracefully turning with the beast's onrushing charge, and with a backhanded swing slammed his knife hilt-deep into the center of its chest. It was a perfectly executed strike. Unfortunately, it seemed to have had no more effect than anything else that had been tried.

The creature wheeled with impossible speed and seized Richard's wrist. Before it could catch him up in its powerful arms, Richard twisted under the grip and came up behind his attacker. He gritted his teeth with the mighty effort of twisting the creature's powerful arm up behind its knobby back. Nicci heard joints pop and bone snap. Rather than the injury slowing the beast, it whirled around, swinging the broken arm like a flail. Richard ducked and rolled away as deadly claws scythed past.

Zedd used the opening to ignite a sphere of seething liquid fire. Even the lightning seemed to pause in the presence of such profound power brought to life. The room vibrated with the howl of the deadly, concentrated inferno Zedd unleashed. The knot of churning flames shrieked through the dark room, illuminating the tables and chairs, the shelves and columns, and the faces of everyone watching as it swept past.

The beast glanced back over its shoulder at the tumbling, hissing yellow conflagration wailing across the room and defiantly bared its fangs at the approaching fire.

It struck Nicci as an odd thing for the creature to do, almost as if it didn't fear fire conjured by a wizard. Nicci had trouble imagining anything that could withstand such an onslaught—or not fear it. This was no mere fire, after all, but a menace that burned with phenomenal ferocity.

An instant before the writhing sphere of wizard's fire reached its target, the creature simply winked out of existence.

Absent an objective, the fire splashed down on the stone floor, exploding across the carpets and breaking over tables like a rogue wave crashing ashore. Although conjured for a specific enemy, Nicci knew that runaway wizard's fire could easily annihilate them all.

Before it could destroy the room or anyone in it, Zedd, Nathan, and Ann immediately cast yet more webs—Zedd doing his best to recall his power while the other two suppressed and smothered the flames before they had a chance to get out of control. Clouds of steam billowed up as they all worked to contain any errant droplets of the tenacious fire. It was a tense moment before they knew that they had succeeded.

Beyond the fog of vapor, Nicci saw the beast materialize out of the darkness.

It appeared behind Zedd, back in the shadows where she'd first seen it step into the world of life. Nicci was the only one who realized that it had returned in a different place. She had never before seen the creature slip in and out of the world of the dead at will, but she knew that was the method by which it was able to track and follow Richard across vast distances. She knew, too, that no matter the form it took, it would never rest until it had him.

Richard spotted the beast coming for him before any of the others and called out a warning to Zedd, standing directly in the path of the wild charge. Zedd blocked that charge by massing the air itself into a densely compressed, angled shield. The trick deflected the beast's course by just enough. Richard used the diversion to slash at his attacker. Before his knife could make contact, the beast again winked out of existence, only to return an instant later once past Richard's blade.

It almost seemed to be toying with them, but Nicci knew that that wasn't the case. It was merely employing varying tactics in its soulless quest to have Richard. Even its seemingly angry roars were merely a tactic meant to weaken its victim with fear, thereby giving it a chance to strike. Instilling the capacity for emotion in it would have produced limitations; therefore Jagang's Sisters had left such qualities out. The beast was incapable of actually feeling anger. It was simply unremitting in its purpose.

Ann and Nathan released a torrent of power concentrated into thousands of small, rock-hard, deadly points that could have shredded the hide right off an ox, but before the hurtling fragments could rip into the creature, it again effortlessly evaded the attacks by stepping into a shadow and coming out once again in another place.

Nicci realized that none of them had the ability to stop the thing.

Struggling to recover her strength, she scrambled across the floor to check on Cara. Still lying against a wall, Cara was dazed and having difficulty regaining her senses. Nicci pressed her fingers to the Mord-Sith's temples, trickling in a thread of magic to wake her and revive her strength. She seized the woman by her leather outfit when she suddenly tried to scramble to her feet.

"Listen to me," Nicci said. "If you want to save Richard, you have to listen to me. You can't stop that thing."

Not one to take instruction well, especially when it came to protecting Richard, Cara saw the immediate threat and sprang into action. As the beast spun around, focused on Richard, Cara threw herself at it, down low, rolling under it, knocking it from its feet. Before it could recover, she leaped on the beast's back, as if mounting a wild stallion, and jammed her Agiel into the base of its skull. It was a move that would have killed any man. When the beast reared up on its knees, she hooked the weapon across the front of its throat.

With its good arm, the creature snatched Cara's Agiel and effortlessly ripped it from her grip. Cara vaulted for the weapon and snatched it back, but it cost her a blow that again sent her tumbling across the floor.

As everyone clambered back from the creature, trying to stay out of the reach of its deadly claws, it threw its head back and roared. The sound was so deafening that everyone winced. Flashes of lightning lit beyond the windows, throwing blindingly bright light and a jumble of confusing shadows through the nearly dark room, making it difficult to see.

Zedd, Nathan, and Ann conjured shields of air and used them to try to force the threat back, but the beast was able to crash through the shields and charge for their creators, forcing them to dodge out of harm's way.

Nicci knew that the three of them could not stop such a menace with the power they had. She didn't see how Richard could, either.

As the others continued to fight with every bit of ability and cunning they could muster, Nicci again seized a fistful of Cara's leather outfit at her shoulder and hauled her close.

"Are you ready to do it my way? Or do you want Richard to die?"

Cara, panting from the exertion, looked ready to spit fire, but she heeded Nicci's words. "What do you want me to do?"

"Be ready to help me. Be ready to do exactly as I ask."

After receiving a nod of agreement, Nicci scrambled back up onto the table. She placed one foot in the center of the Grace drawn in her own blood, and the other out beyond the outer circle.

Zedd, Nathan, and Ann threw everything they could conjure at the rampaging beast: webs of arcing power that could have cut stone, intensely focused force that could have bent iron, a hail of air concentrated into nodules hard enough to pulverize bone. None of it had any effect on the creature. In some cases it wasn't affected by their power, while at other times it swiped at the assaults, brushing them aside, or avoided them altogether by winking out of existence only to reappear once the threat had passed.

It again turned its attention to its purpose and lunged for Richard. He dodged to the side and once more used his knife to rip through the creature's tough hide, trying to sever an arm. That, too, Nicci knew, would do no good.

As the others shouted instructions, trying to find a way to destroy the threat, Cara, torn between helping Richard and following instructions, turned and peered up at Nicci. "What are you doing?"

Nicci, not having the time to answer questions, pointed. "Can you lift that candelabra?"

Cara glanced back over her shoulder. It was made of heavy wrought iron and held two dozen candles, none of them lit.

"Probably."

"Use it like a lance. Drive the beast back toward the windows—"

"What good is that going to do?"

The beast lunged at Richard, trying to get its arms around him.

Richard twisted away and in the process landed a powerful kick to its head that did no more than momentarily stagger it.

"Just do as I say. Use it like a lance to drive the creature back. And make sure that the others stand back and stay clear."

"You think that if I can club it with the candelabra that will stop it?"

"No. It learns. This will be something new. Just drive it back. It should be momentarily confused, or at least cautious. As soon as you force it back, throw the candelabra at it and then get yourself clear."

Cara, her lips pressed tightly together in frustrated fury, considered for only an instant. She was a woman who knew that hesitation could bring harm. She grabbed the heavy main post of the candle stand in both hands and with a mighty effort lifted it. The candles fell from their cups, bouncing and rolling across the stone floor. It was clear to Nicci how heavy the iron stand was. She thought, though, that Cara had enough muscle to handle it. There was no doubt that she had the mettle.

But Nicci could no longer worry about Cara. She put the woman from her mind and straightened both arms, extending her hands down toward the bloody depiction of the Grace beneath her. She disregarded her doubts, her fears, and, as she had done countless times before, drew her mind back into the core of Han within herself. This time, above the Grace, it felt like falling back into an icy pool of power.

Ignoring the fate she was condemning herself to, she turned her palms upward and lifted her hands, using that icy pool of power within herself to begin to bring the verification web back to its induction point. From within the dominion of the Grace, Nicci concentrated on a mental image of removing the countervailing blocks within the spell-form that kept it contained and inert. With deliberate intent, once she had exposed the inner field that only she could see, she used both sides of her power to connect opposing junctions.

In an instant the green lines again started twisting their way up, like some ravenous vine made of light. In a heartbeat, the network of lines was as high as her thighs.

Cara thrusted and stabbed at the beast. Several times she made solid contact with her unwieldy iron weapon, knocking the creature back a step. Each time it took a step back, she immediately jabbed again, forcing it back another step, then another. Nicci had been right—the creature reacted cautiously to the unexpected nature of the attack.

She hoped that Cara could get the beast back not only far enough but in time.

Bolts of lightning arced through the night sky, illuminating the wall of thick glass windows. Compared with the forces of the storm, the oil lamps were so weak as to be nearly useless. The flashes back and forth between blinding light and darkness made it difficult to see.

As the glowing, greenish lines that were the mere reflection of the inner aspect of a spell that had been created thousands of years before by men long ago lost to history wove their way up around her, that inner spell-form once again ignited, lancing through her far faster than it had the first time. Nicci hadn't been entirely ready. She went blind before she expected to. She struggled to breathe while she still could, while she still had a remnant of control.

Her gifted vision began to flicker back and forth between both worlds, between the light of life and eternal blackness. The dark void beyond came and went in flashes, much like the lightning outside the window, but with blinding darkness rather than blinding light. Straddling both worlds, Nicci felt as if her soul would be ripped apart.

She ignored the pain and focused on the task at hand.

She knew that she could not destroy such a beast with her power alone. Sisters of the Dark had, after all, created it with the help of ancient powers that she could not begin to fathom. The conjured creature was the match of anything Nicci knew how to call forth. It would take something more than mere sorcery.

Back near the windows, the beast finally dug in and halted its brief retreat. Cara jabbed at it, but the snarling beast would retreat no more. Cara was having difficulty handling the heavy iron candle stand. When Richard started to come to her aid, she yelled at everyone to get back. When he didn't obey, she swung the candle stand around, making him jump back and letting him know that she meant business.

Putting all her strength into the effort, Nicci brought her palms up, preparing to do the impossible.

She had to find the cusp between nothing and the ignition of power.

She needed not power, but its precursor.

The green lines advanced farther up around her in their determined work of encasing her in the totality of the spell. Nicci tried to draw a breath, but her muscles would not respond. She needed the breath—just one breath.

When the world of life flashed back into her gifted vision, she pulled with all her might and at last drew that breath.

"Now, Cara!"

Without hesitation, Cara heaved the heavy candelabra. The beast easily caught the massive iron candle stand in one clawed hand, lifting it high. Behind it, through the windows, lightning cracked and boomed.

Nicci paused, waiting for a lull in the flashes.

When it came, when the room plunged back into darkness, she cast out—not power, but its antecedent.

That casting bathed the beast in the agonizingly almost: the inductive ignition of power . . . absent the consequence.

She could see that the creature felt the strange sensation of the promise of the profound . . . not quite conjured, not yet delivered. It blinked in confusion, unsure if it really felt something, wanting to act, yet not knowing what it was that it felt or what to act against.

Without the successful launch of any direct attack of Nicci's power, the beast appeared to decide that she had failed and again defiantly lifted the candelabra high over its head, like a trophy won in battle.

"Now," Zedd called to Ann and Nathan as he rushed forward, "while it's distracted."

They were about to ruin everything. Nicci could do nothing to halt their interference. Cara, never one to be gentle in her duty, did do something. She drove the three of them back like a sheepdog herding strays. They protested as they retreated, demanding she get out of the way.

Nicci watched it all happening from a distant place on the cusp between worlds. She could no longer help Cara. The woman would have to handle it herself. Somewhere in the faraway world of life, Zedd fumed at the Mord-Sith and tried to launch an attack, but Cara used the threat of ramming him with a shoulder to drive him back, throwing him not only off balance, but distracting him from his intentions.

In that other world, the dark world beyond life, what Nicci had deliberately created was a void of effect, cause without consequence, a constructed expectation of a material release of her darker power, which she also deliberately failed to provide.

Time itself seemed to stand still, waiting for what must be but would not come.

The tension in the air around Nicci was palpable. The green lines around her raced ever faster through the air in an effort to completely reestablish the verification web, to have her life held suspended.

The flaw, like a spider in its web, waited for her.

She knew she had only a fleeting moment before she would be unable to do anything.

This time, her end would at least gain something of value.

Nicci fed the field around the beast yet more of the open gateway to a profound release of power which she purposely withheld.

The stress between what existed and what did not yet exist, and would not happen, was insufferable.

In an instant, that terrible, intolerable void, that vacuum of power that Nicci had created in both worlds, was filled with the deafening release of a bolt of lightning that came crashing in through the window, while its twin, from the world beyond the world of life, ripped through the veil, drawn to the need unfulfilled around the beast—compelled to complete what Nicci had begun but would not finish. This time, there was no safety in escape to another world; both worlds had together unleashed their fury.

Shattered glass rained through the room. The thunderous boom shook the stone walls of the Keep. It seemed as if the sun itself were exploding in through the window.

The lines racing around Nicci came up like a shroud.

Through her gifted vision she saw the completion of the link she had established, saw the lightning find the void around the beast and fulfill the terrible empty obligation she had created.

The explosion of that lightning was beyond anything that she had ever seen before. Creating the precursor in both worlds lent the lightning the power of both worlds, Additive and Subtractive, creative and destructive, intertwined in a single calamitous discharge.

Nicci was frozen by the spell, and could not close her eyes against the blinding flash of light and dark that tangled together, striking both ends of candelabra and blasting down through the beast.

In the violent corona of crackling white light, the beast came apart, driven to dust and vapor by the intensity of the heat and power focused in the void Nicci had created.

Gales of rain and wind roared in through the shattered window. Outside, yet more lightning flickered through the roiling greenish clouds. When the lightning outside lit the room, they could all see that the beast was gone.

For now, anyway, it was gone.

Through the net of green lines, Nicci saw Richard racing across the room toward her.

That room seemed so distant.

She saw the dark world close in around her.

When her horse whinnied and stamped its hooves, Kahlan slipped her hand farther up the reins, closer to the bit, to hold the nervous animal in place. The horse didn't like what it smelled any more than Kahlan did. She reached up and gently stroked the underside of the horse's chin as she waited behind Sisters Ulicia and Cecilia.

Light gusts ruffled the cottonwood leaves overhead, making the glossy leaves shimmer in the midday light. In the shade of those huge cotton-woods, dappled sunlight danced over the grassy hilltop, while overhead a few cottony white clouds dotted the blindingly bright blue sky. When the breeze shifted around and came in from their backs, it brought relief not only from the sweltering heat. Kahlan allowed herself a deeper breath.

She used a finger to wipe sweat and grime from under the metal collar locked around her neck. She wished she could have a bath, or at least jump in a stream or a lake. The summer heat and dusty traveling had conspired to turn her long hair into an itchy, tangled mess. She knew, though, that the Sisters didn't care how uncomfortable she was and that they wouldn't be pleased if she were to ask if she could have a chance to wash up, the way they often did. The Sisters didn't care in the least about Kahlan's wants, much less her comfort. She was their slave, no more; it mattered not if the collar she wore around her neck chafed and rubbed her skin raw.

As Kahlan waited, her mind wandered to the statue she had given up, the statue she'd had to leave in Lord Richard Rahl's palace. While she had no memory of her past, she had memorized every line of that figure of a woman with flowing hair and robes. There was something quietly noble about her spirit, about the way the figure stood with her back arched, her hands fisted, and her head thrown back as if in defiance of invisible forces that would subdue her.

Kahlan knew all too well what it felt like to have invisible forces sub-duing her.

From the quiet hilltop they watched as Sister Armina made her way across the open landscape below. There was no one else in sight. The long grasses looked almost liquid as they waved and bowed in the breeze. Sister Armina finally trotted her bay mare up the hill. She circled her horse around and came to a halt beside the rest of them.

"They're not there," she announced.

"How far ahead are they?" Sister Ulicia asked.

Sister Armina lifted an arm to point. "I didn't go much beyond those hills there. I didn't want to take a chance on being spotted by any of Jagang's gifted. As near as I can tell, though, the stragglers and camp followers have only moved on a day or two ago."

When the breeze at their backs slackened, it allowed the smell to drift up the hill again. Kahlan wrinkled her nose. Sister Ulicia noticed but didn't comment. The Sisters didn't seem to be at all bothered by the stench.

Sister Ulicia abruptly turned and stuffed a boot in a stirrup. "Let's go have a look over the hills beyond," she said as she swung up into her saddle.

Kahlan mounted up and followed after the other three women as they trotted their horses down the hill. She thought it odd how the Sisters seemed unusually jumpy. They tended to be arrogantly bold in whatever they did, but now they were being cautious.

To the left towered the rugged, blue-gray shapes of lofty mountains. The rock slopes and cliffs were so imposing that there were few places where trees could gain a foothold. Some of the peaks were so high that they had snow atop them despite it being summer. Kahlan and the Sisters had followed those mountains south since finding a place to cross over them after leaving the People's Palace. In those travels, the Sisters had avoided going near people whenever they could.

Kahlan gave her horse's reins a little more slack. The hills they rode across were rutted with gullies that made it difficult traveling at times. Kahlan knew that there would probably be roads down out of the hills, but the Sisters didn't generally like to travel on roads and kept off them whenever possible. As they moved through the tall grass among the scattered trees, they stayed in the concealing shelter of the folds of land between hills.

Before Kahlan could see any of what lay ahead, the unmistakable, gagging stench of death grew so terrible that she could hardly breathe. Cresting a hill, she finally saw the city spread out below. They all paused, gazing down at the empty roads, the burned buildings, and the carcasses of what looked to be horses.

"Let's be quick," Sister Ulicia said. "We'll take the main road on the other side for a ways and get close enough to be sure of where they are and exactly the direction they're headed."

They spurred their horses into canters as they rode in silence down out of the hills and into the fringes of the city. The place looked to have been built up around a meandering bend in a river and the crossings of several roads that were probably trade routes. The larger of two timber bridges had been burned. As they crossed a narrow second bridge in single file, Kahlan glanced down at the water. Bloated bodies floating facedown had collected in the reeds. Even before she had seen them, the stench of death had been so heavy in the air that she had lost her interest in going for a swim. She just wanted to be away from the place.

As they rode in among the buildings, Kahlan held a scarf over her nose and mouth. It didn't help much. She thought she might vomit from the fetid smell of rotting flesh. It seemed peculiar that it was so strong.

She soon discovered why.

They rode past side streets where corpses were piled in the hundreds. A few dogs and mules lay dead among them, the legs of the mules standing out straight and stiff. From the way the bodies were jammed into the narrow side streets, Kahlan thought that the people must have been herded into confined spaces from which escape was impossible and then slaughtered. Most of the dead, animal and human, were ripped open with ghastly wounds. Some of the dead had broken lances jutting from them, while others had been killed by arrows. Most, though, appeared to have been hacked to death. Kahlan noticed one other thing about them: they were all older people.

Many of the buildings in one section of the city were burned down. Only in a few places did wisps of smoke still curl up from some of the thicker piles of rubble. The charred wooden beams looked like the scorched skeletons of monsters. It appeared to be a day or two since the fires had burned themselves out.

Stepping their horses along the narrow cobbled street between two-story buildings looming up to either side of the road, they peered about in silent appraisal of the destruction. The buildings still standing had all been looted. Doors were broken in, or lay in the street nearby. Kahlan didn't see a single window that hadn't been broken. Curtains lay draped over a few of the tiny balconies overlooking the street. A few of those balconies held a body. Besides the fragments of wood from doorframes and the broken glass, the streets were littered with trivial items: random articles of clothing; a bloody boot; pieces of broken furniture; broken weapons; broken pieces of wagons. Kahlan saw a doll with yellow yarn for hair lying facedown, its back flattened by a hoofprint. All of the items had the look of having been picked over by a number of hands and, after being judged to be worthless, discarded.

Daring to look into the dark buildings they passed, Kahlan saw the real horrors. They were not merely the bodies of murdered townspeople. There were the bodies of people who looked to have been murdered for sport, or out of a sheer brutality. Unlike the bodies heaped in the side streets, these people were not older. They looked like they might have been people trying to protect their shops or homes. Through one broken shopwindow she saw that a man, wearing the kind of apron used by cobblers, had been nailed to a wall by his wrists. From the center of his chest protruded dozens of arrows, making him look like a grotesque pincushion. His mouth and each eye had been penetrated by an arrow. The man had not only been used for target practice, but as an object of monstrous humor.

In other dark buildings, Kahlan saw women who had all too obviously been raped. A shirtsleeve still on one arm was all that covered one woman on a floor. Her breasts had been mutilated. In another place, a girl, looking not to yet have grown into womanhood, lay sprawled on a table, her dress pushed up past her waist. Her throat had been cut through to her spine. Her legs lay splayed out, a broomstick left shoved in her as a final act of disdain. Kahlan felt numb as she saw one horrifying sight after another, each of such lurid cruelty that she could not imagine the kind of men who could have committed such acts.

By the manner of dress of many of the dead, the men appeared to be simple working people. They were not soldiers. For the crime of trying to protect their homes and businesses they had been butchered.

As Kahlan passed one small building she saw, in a back corner against a brick wall, a pile of small children—mostly babies. It was reminiscent of the way autumn leaves collected in a corner, except these all had once been living people with a life ahead of them. The gore on the brick wall betrayed where their heads had been bashed in. It was apparent that the killers had wanted to dispatch them as efficiently as possible. On the silent ride through the city, Kahlan saw several more places where the very young had been cast into piles after being murdered in a fashion that could only be described as entertainment for the most monstrous of men.

Although there were not very many women among the dead, Kahlan didn't see one who was fully clothed. The ones she did see were either older or pretty young. Their treatment had been bestial beyond imagining and their deaths slow.

Kahlan swallowed back the lump in her throat as she wiped her eyes. She wanted to scream. The three Sisters didn't seem to be particularly moved by the carnage in the city. They watched down the side streets and gazed at the surrounding hills, apparently concerned about any sign of a threat.

Kahlan had never been so happy to leave a place as she was when they finally made their way out of the city and took a road leading southeast. The road turned out not to be the escape from the outrages of the city that she thought it would be. Along the way the ditches were here and there filled with the bodies of unarmed young men and older boys, probably executed for trying to escape, resisting the idea of slavery, as lessons to the others, or simply for the sport of murder.

Kahlan felt dizzy and hot. She feared she might be sick. The way she swayed in her saddle only made her nausea worse. The stench of death and charred flesh followed them in the bright sunshine as they rode among the hills on the far side of the city. The smell was so pervasive that it felt as if it had saturated her clothes and was even coming out in her sweat.

She doubted that she would ever again sleep without nightmares.

Kahlan didn't know what the name of the city had been, but it was no more. There hadn't been a single person left alive. Anything of any value had either been destroyed or looted. From the number of corpses, as vast as they had been, she knew that many of the city's inhabitants, mostly the women, the ones of the right age, anyway, had been taken as slaves. After seeing what had happened to the women left dead in the city, Kahlan could vividly imagine what would happen to the women taken away.

The broadening plane and the hills to either side for as far as Kahlan could see had been trampled by what had to be well beyond mere hundreds of thousands of men. The grasses had not simply been flattened by countless boots, hooves, and wagon wheels, but had been ground to dust under the weight of unthinkable numbers. The sight put into perspective the magnitude of the masses that had passed through the city, and in a way was more horrifying than the ghastly scenes of death. A force of men this huge bordered on a force of nature itself, like some terrible storm that cut a swath across the face of the land, mercilessly destroying everything in its path.

Later in the day, as they approached the crest of a hill, the Sisters carefully maneuvered into a position that put the sun low at their backs so that anyone ahead would have to stare into the sun to see them. Sister Ulicia slowed and stood in her stirrups, stretching for a careful look, then signaled the rest of them to dismount. They all tied their horses to the carcass of a scraggly old pine split in two by lightning. Sister Ulicia told Kahlan to stay close behind them.

At the edge of the hill, as they crouched silently in the weedy grass, they finally caught their first glimpse of what had come through the fallen city. In the dim distance, spread across the hazy horizon, was what at first appeared to be a muddy, brown sea, but was actually the dark taint of an army of such numbers that it was beyond counting. Carried on the wind, in the quiet, late-day air, Kahlan could just make out the distant, bloodcurdling sounds of howls, women's screams, and men's raucous laughter coming from the massive mob.

The sheer weight of such multitudes would have crushed the defenses of any city. Any armed opposition would hardly have been noticed by an army as vast as this one. Men gathered in such numbers could not be halted by anything.

But as much as this army seemed to be a mass, a mob, a thing, she knew that it was wrong to think of it in those terms; this was a group of individuals. These men had not been born monsters. Each had once been a helpless babe cradled in a mother's arms. Each had once been a child with fears, hopes, and dreams. While an occasional aberrant individual could, because of a sick mind, grow up to be a remorseless killer, this many individuals had not. Each was a killer by conviction to a cause, a killer by choice, all united under a banner of perverse beliefs that gave sanction to their savagery.

These were all individuals who when confronted with the choice had willfully cast away the inherent nobility of life, and chose instead to be servants of death.

Kahlan had been horrified at the butchery she'd seen back in the city, nauseated by the things she had seen. For a time she'd hardly been able to breathe, not just from the stench of death, but from her tearful despair at such mindless brutality, at such monumental and intentional depravity. She felt a sense of sickening dread for those helpless souls yet to face the horde and a crushing loss of any hope that life could ever be worth living, that it could ever be reasoned and secure, much less joyous.

But now, at the sight of the source of the slaughter, the great force of men who had all willingly perpetrated such atrocities, all those desolate feelings melted away. In their place smoldering anger ignited, the kind of inner rage she didn't think a person very often felt in their life. Remembering the old people who had been hacked apart, the infants dispatched by bashing in their brains, and the savage treatment of the women, Kahlan could think of little else but her burning desire for vengeance for the silent dead.

That sense of rage seethed through her, a rage so terrible that it seemed to forever change something within her. In that moment, she felt a profound affinity with the small statue she'd had to leave in Richard Rahl's peaceful garden, an understanding of its spirit that she hadn't had before.

"It's Jagang, all right," Sister Cecilia finally said in a bitter voice.

Sister Armina nodded. "And we have to get past him if we're to get to Caska."

Sister Ulicia gestured to the wall of mountains to the left. "Their army, with all their horses, wagons, and supplies, can't cross the narrow passes between those peaks, but we can. As slow as Jagang moves, we can easily get over the passes and then to Caska long before they can travel south to get past the mountains and then move up into D'Hara."

Sister Cecilia stared off to the horizon. "The D'Haran army doesn't stand a chance against that."

"That's not our problem," Sister Ulicia said.

"But what about our bond to Richard Rahl?" Sister Armina asked.

"We're not the ones attacking Richard Rahl," Sister Ulicia said. "Jagang is the one going after him, seeking to destroy him, not us. We are the ones who will wield the power of Orden and then we will grant Richard Rahl what only we will have the power to grant. That is enough to preserve our bond and protect us from the dream walker. Jagang and his army are not our problem and what they aim to do is not our responsibility."

Kahlan remembered being at the People's Palace and wondering what the man was like. Even though she didn't know him, she feared for him and his people having to face what was coming for them.

"It will be our problem if they get to Caska before us," Sister Cecilia said. "Besides catching up with Tovi, Caska is the only other central site we can get into for now."

Sister Ulicia dismissed the notion with a flick of her hand. "They're a long way from Caska. We can easily cut the distance and outpace them by going over the mountains rather than down, around, and then back up as they will have to do."

"You don't think they might quicken their pace?" Sister Armina asked. "After all, Jagang might be eager to finally finish off Lord Rahl and the D'Haran forces."

Sister Ulicia huffed at the very idea. "Jagang knows the D'Haran army has nowhere else to go—Richard Rahl has no choice now but to stand and fight. The matter is as good as decided. It's only a matter of time.

"The dream walker is in no hurry, nor could he be—not with an army that huge and unwieldy. And even if they could quicken their pace they have to travel a much greater distance so that still wouldn't get him to Caska before we can get there. Besides, Jagang's army is the same now as it has been since they first took over the Old World, decades ago, and as it has been throughout this entire war. They never hurry their pace. They are like the seasons—they move with great force, but very slowly."

She cast a meaningful look at the other two Sisters. "Besides, they've just stripped the city of women. Jagang's men will be eager to enjoy their new spoils."

The blood drained from Sister Armina's face. "Don't we know the truth of that."

"Jagang and his men never tire of the use of captive women," Sister Cecilia said, half to herself.

Sister Armina's color came back in a red rush. "I'd love to string Jagang up and have my way with him."

"We'd all enjoy a bit of dealing out lessons to those men," Sister Ulicia said as she stared off into the distance, "but we have better things to do." She smirked. "Someday, though . . ."

The three Sisters were silent for a time as they gazed off at the vast horde spread across the horizon.

"Someday," Sister Cecilia said in a low, rancorous voice, "we will open the boxes of Orden and we will have the power to make that man twist in the wind."

Sister Ulicia turned and headed back toward the horses. "If we are ever going to open one of the three boxes, then we will first have to get to Tovi and the last box—and to what else is in Caska. Forget about Jagang and his army. This is the last we'll have to see them—until the day comes when we've unleashed the power of Orden and we can have a bit of fun dealing out our own, personal retribution to the dream walker."

Nicci opened her eyes. She saw only vague shapes.

"Zedd is angry with you."

Even though it sounded as if it had come from some hazy, faraway place, she knew that it was Richard's voice. She was surprised to hear it. She was surprised to hear anything. She thought that by all rights she should be dead.

As her vision started coming into focus, Nicci rolled her head to the right and saw him sitting huddled close on a chair that had been pulled right up beside the bed. Leaning forward, elbows on his knees, his fingers folded neatly together, he was watching her.

"Why?" she asked.

Looking relieved to see her awake, he leaned back in the simple wooden chair and smiled that crooked smile of his that she so loved seeing.

"Because you broke the window back in that room where you were all doing the verification web."

In the light of a lamp glowing softly beneath a milky white shade, she saw that she was covered up to her armpits in a luxuriously embroidered gold bedcover with lustrous sage green fringe. She had on a satiny nightdress that she didn't recognize. The sleeves went all the way down to her wrists. It was pale pink. Not her color.

She wondered where the nightdress had come from and, more to the point, who had undressed her and put it on her. Back at the Palace of the Prophets, so long ago, Richard had been the first person she'd ever met who didn't expect that he had a right to her body or some other aspect of her life. That forthright attitude had helped start the process of reasoning that eventually led to her casting off a lifetime of teachings of the Order. Through Richard, she had come to truly see that her life belonged to her alone. Along with that comprehension, she had since then discovered the dignity and self-worth in propriety.

Right then, though, she had concerns other than finding herself in a pink nightdress. Her throbbing head felt impossibly heavy against the cozy pillow.

"Technically," she said, "the lightning broke the window. Not me."

"Somehow," Cara said from another chair tipped back against the wall beside the door, "I don't think the distinction will much impress him."

"I suppose not," Nicci said with a sigh. "That room is in the hardened section of the Keep."

Richard twitched a frown. "It's where?"

She squinted slightly in an effort to bring his face more into focus. "That section of the Keep is a special place. It's hardened against intentional interference as well as aberrational and errant events."

Cara folded her arms. "Mind giving us the translation?"

The woman was in her red leather. Nicci wondered if that meant there was more trouble about or if she was just surly from the beast paying them a visit.

"It's a containment field," Nicci said. "We know very little about the ancient, bewilderingly intricate makeup of the Chainfire spell. It's hazardous to even study such unstable components all tangled together the way that one is. That's why we were using that particular place to run the verification web. That room is in the original core of the Keep—an important sanctuary used for tasks involving anomalous material. Various kinds of both constructed and free-formed conjuring are apt to contain innate tangential outflows that can convey domain breaches, so when working with them it's best to confine such potentially hazardous components to a containment field."

"Oh, well, thanks for the translation," Cara said in a cutting tone. "It's all so clear, now. It's a field thing."

Nicci nodded as best she could. "Yes—a containment field." When Cara's frown only darkened, Nicci added, "Doing magic in there is like keeping a wasp in a bottle."

"Oh." Cara let out a sigh, finally grasping the simplified concept. "I guess that explains why Zedd was so grumpy about it."

"Maybe he can fix it back to the way it was," Richard offered. "Surprisingly enough, the room isn't too badly torn up. It's mostly the broken windows that he's riled about."

Nicci lifted a hand in a weak gesture. "I don't doubt it. The glass in there is unique. It has embedded properties designed to contain conjured magic from escaping—and to prevent gifted assaults. Its function is much the same as shields, except that it deters power rather than people."

Richard considered a moment. "Well," he finally said, "it didn't prevent an attack from the beast."

Nicci stared off at the bookshelves built into the wall opposite the bed. "Nothing can," she said. "In this case the beast didn't come through the windows or walls—it came through the veil, emerging out of the underworld right into the room; it didn't need to come through any shields or containment field or refractory glass."

Cara's chair thumped down. "And it nearly tore your arm off." She shook a finger at Richard. "You were using your gift. You drew it to you. If Zedd hadn't been there to heal you, you would likely have bled to death."

"Oh, Cara, every time you tell the story I seem to bleed more. No doubt the next time I hear it told I'll have been torn in two and stitched back together with magic thread."

She folded her arms as she tipped her chair back against the wall. "You could have been torn in two."

"I wasn't as badly hurt as you make it out. I'm fine." Richard leaned in a little and squeezed Nicci's hand. "At least you stopped it."

She met his gaze.

"For now," she said. "That's all."

"For now is enough for now." He smiled in quiet satisfaction. "You did good, Nicci."

His gray eyes mirrored his inner sincerity. Somehow the world always seemed better when Richard was pleased that someone had accomplished something difficult. He always seemed to value what people achieved—always seemed to delight in their triumphs. It invariably lifted her heart when he was pleased with something she had done.

Her gaze strayed from his face. She noticed the small statue standing on the table just behind him. The lamplight highlighted the flowing hair and robes that Richard had once so carefully carved into the figure of his impression of Kahlan's spirit. The lustrous statue, sculpted from walnut, stood as if in silent defiance of some invisible force attempting to suppress that spirit.

"I'm in your room," Nicci said, half to herself.

A curious frown twitched across his brow. "How did you know?"

Nicci looked away from the statue to gaze out the small, round-topped window through the thick stone wall to the left. A delicate, pale blush of color was just visible in the lower reaches of a black, star-filled sky as dawn gradually approached.

"Lucky guess," she lied.

"It was closer," Richard explained. "Zedd and Nathan wanted to get you in a bed, get you comfortable, so they could evaluate what they needed to do to help you."

Nicci knew by the lingering, icy feeling coursing through her veins that they had done something more than mere evaluation.

"Rikka and I undressed you and put you in a nightdress Zedd found for us," Cara explained to the unspoken question she must have seen in Nicci's eyes.

"Thanks." Nicci lifted a hand in a vague gesture. "How long have I been unconscious? What happened?"

"Well," Richard said, "after you jumped back up into that spell-form the night before last and called the lightning to stop the beast, the verification web nearly took you for good. After I got you out, Zedd thought you needed to rest more than anything so he did a little something so that you would sleep. You were a bit delirious from the pain you were in. He said that he helped you drift off so you wouldn't have to suffer it. He told us that you would sleep all of yesterday and last night, and then awake around dawn today. I guess he had it right."

Cara rose to stand behind Richard and peer down at Nicci. "No one thought that Lord Rahl would be able to get you out the second time. They thought your spirit was too far gone into the underworld to ever get you back—but he did it. He got you back."

Nicci looked from Cara's smug smile to Richard's gray eyes. They didn't reflect anything of the difficulty of the task. She had trouble imagining how he could have accomplished such a thing.

"You did good, Richard," she said, making him smile.

He and Cara turned toward a soft knock at the door. Zedd quietly eased the door open to peek in. When he saw that Nicci was awake, he shed his care and strolled in.

"Ah," he observed, "back from the dead, it would appear."

Nicci smiled. "Wretched excursion. I don't advise a visit to the place. Sorry about the windows, but it was either—"

"Better the windows than what might have happened to Richard."

Nicci was cheered to hear him say as much. "That was my thought."

"Sometime you will have to explain to me exactly what you did and how you did it. I wasn't aware that any form of conjured power could breach those windows."

"It can't. I simply . . . invited a confluence of natural power to come in through the windows."

Zedd regarded her with an unreadable look. "About the windows," he finally said in a measured tone, "we might be able to use your ability with both sides of the gift to restore them."

"I'd be glad to help."

Cara took a step forward. "When Tom and Friedrich eventually get back from patrolling the surrounding countryside I'm sure that they'd be able to help with the window's woodwork. Friedrich, especially, knows about working with wood."

Zedd nodded as he smiled briefly at the suggestion before turning to his grandson. "Where have you been? I went looking for you this morning and couldn't find you. I've been looking for you all day."

Nicci realized that the windows were hardly his primary concern.

Richard glanced briefly at the statue. "I read a lot last night. When it got light I went for a walk to think about what to do next."

Zedd sighed at the answer. "Well, as I told you after you broke the first spell-form holding Nicci, we need to talk about some of the things you said."

It was clear that it was not a matter of casual curiosity but a pointed demand.

Richard stood to help stuff pillows behind Nicci when he saw her start to sit up. The pain was becoming no more than a fading memory. Zedd had obviously done something more than help her sleep. Her head was starting to clear. She realized that she was hungry.

"So talk," Richard said as he sat back down.

"I need you to explain precisely how you were able to know how to shut down a verification web—especially one as complex as the Chainfire event matrix."

Richard looked more than a little weary. "I told you before, I understand the jargon of emblems."

Zedd clasped his hands behind his back as he started to pace. Concern was clearly etched in the lines of his face. "Yes, about that, you mentioned that you know a lot about 'representational designs involving lethality.' I need to know what you meant by that."

Richard took a deep breath, letting it out slowly as he leaned back in his chair. Having grown up around Zedd, he obviously knew quite well that when Zedd wanted to know something it was easiest to just answer the questions.

Richard turned his wrists over across his knees. Strange symbols girded the leather-padded silver wristbands he wore. On the center of each band, at the insides of his wrists, there was a small Grace. That alone was alarming enough, since Nicci had seen Richard use them to call the sliph so that they could travel. She couldn't begin to imagine what the other symbols meant.

"These things all around the bands—the emblems, designs, and devices—are pictures representing things. Like I said before, they're a jargon, a language of sorts."

Zedd waggled a finger at the designs on the wristbands. "And you can make out meaning in them? Like you did with the spell-form?"

"Yes. Most are ways of fighting with the sword—that's how I was first able to recognize them and how I began to learn to understand them."

Richard's fingers idly sought reassurance in the touch of the weapon's hilt, but it was no longer there at his hip. He caught himself and went on.

"Many of these are the same as the designs outside the First Wizard's enclave. You know—on those brass plaques on the entablature above the variegated, red stone columns, on the round metal disks all along the frieze, and also carved into the stone of the cornice."

He glanced over his shoulder at his grandfather. "Most of these emblems overtly involve combat with a sword."

Nicci blinked in surprise as she listened. Richard had never told her about the symbols on the wristbands. As First Wizard, Zedd had been the keeper of the Sword of Truth, and it was his duty to name a new Seeker when needed, but given his reaction, she didn't think that even he had known about this. She supposed that was understandable. The sword, after all, had been made thousands of years before by wizards with prodigious power.

"That one." Zedd thrust a bony finger at an emblem on one of Richard's wristbands. "That one is on the door to the First Wizard's enclave."

Richard turned his other wrist and tapped a starburst pattern on the top of the silver band. "As is this one here."

Zedd pulled Richard's arms closer, inspecting the wristbands in the lamplight. "Yes . . . those are both on the door." He squinted a frown at Richard. "And you honestly believe that they mean something, and that you've learned to read them?"

"Yes, of course."

Zedd, his wiry brows drawing low, was still clearly dubious. "What do you think they mean?"

Richard touched a symbol on the wristbands and one like it on his boot pins. He pointed out the same design within the gold band around his black tunic. Until he pointed it out, Nicci hadn't realized that it was hidden there, among the rest of what seemed to be nothing more than an elaborate decorative strip. The pattern looked like two rough triangles with a sinuous, undulating double line running around and through them.

"This one is a kind of rhythm used for fighting when outnumbered. It conveys a sense of the cadence of the dance, movements without iron form."

Zedd cocked an eyebrow. "Movement without iron form?"

"Yes, you know, movement that's not rigid, not prescribed and inflexible, yet is still deliberate, with specific intent as well as precise objectives. This emblem describes an integral part of the dance."

"The dance?"

Richard nodded. "The dance with death."

Zedd's jaw worked a moment before his voice returned. "Dance. With death." He stammered a moment more with the halting beginnings of a flurry of questions before finally pausing and then retreating to something simpler. "And how does this connect with the symbols at the First Wizard's enclave?"

Richard burnished a thumb across the forms on the left wristband. "The symbols would have meaning to a war wizard—that, in part, is how I figured it out. Symbols have significance in many professions. Tailors paint shears on their window, a weapons maker might paint the outline of knives over his door, a tavern might have a sign with a mug on it, a blacksmith an anvil, and a farrier might nail up horseshoes. Some signs, a skull with crossed bones beneath it for instance, warn of something deadly. War wizards likewise put signs up on the First Wizard's enclave.

"Even more importantly, each profession has its own jargon, a specialized vocabulary specific to that craft. It's no different with a war wizard. The jargon of his profession has to do with lethality. These symbols here and outside the First Wizard's enclave are in part the sign of his craft: bringing death."

Zedd cleared his throat, then looked down and pointed at another symbol on Richard's wristband. "This one, here. This one is on the door to my enclave. Do you know its meaning? Can you paraphrase its intent?"

Richard turned his wrist slightly as he glanced down at the starburst symbol. "It's an admonition not to allow your vision to lock on any one thing. The starburst is a warning to look everywhere at once, to see nothing to the exclusion of everything else. It's a reminder that you mustn't allow the enemy to draw your attention in a way that directs your vision and makes it settle on one thing. If you do, you will see what he wishes you to see. Doing so will allow him to blind you, in a manner of speaking, and he will then come at you without you seeing him and you will most likely lose your life.

"Instead, like this starburst, your vision must open to all there is, never settling, even when cutting. To dance with death means to understand and become as one with your enemy, meaning with the way he thinks within the range of his knowledge, so that you know his sword as well as your own—its exact location, its speed, and its next move before it comes without having to wait to see it first. By opening your vision in this way, opening all your senses, you come to know your enemy's mind and moves as if by instinct."

Zedd scratched his temple. "You're trying to tell me that these symbols, signs specific to war wizards, are all instructions for using a sword?"

Richard shook his head. "The word 'sword' is meant to represent all forms of struggle, not just combat or fighting with a weapon. It applies just as much to strategy and leadership, among other things in life.

"Dancing with death means being committed to the value of life, committed with your mind, heart, and soul, so that you are truly prepared to do what is necessary to preserve life. Dancing with death means that you are the incarnation of death, come to reap the living, in order to preserve life."

Zedd looked thunderstruck.

Richard seemed somewhat surprised by Zedd's reaction. "All of this is much in keeping with everything you've ever taught me, Zedd."

The lamplight cast sharp shadows across Zedd's angular face. "I suppose that in a way it is, Richard. But at the same time it's so much more."

Richard nodded as he rubbed a thumb across the softly glowing silver surface of a wristband. He seemed to search for words. "Zedd, I know that you would have wanted to be the one to teach me about all the things having to do with your enclave—like you wanted to be the one to teach me about the Grace. As First Wizard it was your place to do so. Perhaps I should have waited."

He brought up a fist in conviction. "But there were lives at stake and things I had to do. I had to learn it without you."

"Bags, Richard, how would I teach you about such things?" he said in resignation. "The meaning of those symbols has been lost for thousands of years. No wizard since, since . . . well, no wizard I know of has ever been able to decipher them. I have trouble imagining how you did."

Richard shrugged one shoulder self-consciously. "Once I began to catch on, it all became pretty obvious."

Zedd cast a troubled look at his grandson. "Richard, I grew up in this place. I've spent a great deal of my life here. I was First Wizard when there were actually wizards here to direct." He shook his head. "All that time those designs were on the First Wizard's enclave, and I never knew what they meant. It may seem simple and obvious to you, but it is not. For all I know, you're just imagining that you understand the emblems—just making up meaning you want to be there."

"I'm not imagining their meaning. They've saved my life countless times. I learned a great deal about how to fight with a sword by understanding the language of these symbols."

Zedd didn't argue but instead gestured at the amulet Richard wore around his neck. In the center, surrounded by a complex of gold and silver lines, was a teardrop-shaped ruby as big as Nicci's thumbnail. "You found that in my enclave. Do you also have an idea of what it means?"

"It was part of this outfit, part of the outfit worn by a war wizard, but unlike the rest of it, like you said, this was left in the protection of the First Wizard's enclave."

"And its meaning?"

Richard's fingers reverently brushed the amulet. "The ruby is meant to represent a drop of blood. The emblems engraved in this talisman are the symbolic representation of the way of the primary edict."

Zedd pressed his fingers to his forehead, as if confounded by yet another confusing conundrum. "The primary edict?"

Richard's gaze seemed lost in the amulet. "It means only one thing, and everything: cut. Once committed to fight, cut. Everything else is secondary. Cut. That is your duty, your purpose, your hunger. There is no rule more important, no commitment that overrides that one: cut."

Richard's words came softly, with a kind of knowing, deadly seriousness that chilled Nicci to the bone.

He lifted the amulet out away from his chest, his gaze fixed on its ornate engravings.

"The engraved lines are a portrayal of the dance and as such they have a specific meaning." He traced a finger along the swirling designs as he spoke, as if following a line of text in an ancient language. "Cut from the void, not from bewilderment. Cut the enemy as quickly and directly as possible. Cut with certainty. Cut decisively, resolutely. Cut into his strength. Flow through the gaps in his guard. Cut him. Cut him down utterly. Don't allow him a breath. Crush him. Cut him without mercy to the depths of his spirit."

Richard glanced up at his grandfather. "It is the balance to life: death. It is the dance with death or, more precisely, the mechanism of the dance with death—its essence reduced to form, its form prescribed by concepts.

"It is the law a war wizard lives by, or he dies."

Zedd's hazel eyes were unreadable. "So these marks, these emblems, ultimately regard a war wizard as a mere swordsman?"

"The same overriding principle I told you about before applies to this just as it does the other symbols. The primary edict is not meant to merely convey how a war wizard fights with a weapon, but, more importantly, with his mind. It's a fundamental understanding of the nature of reality that must encompass everything he does. By being true to the primary edict, any weapon is an extension of his mind, an agent of his intent. In a way it's what you once told me about being the Seeker. It's not the weapon that matters so much as the man who wields the weapon.

"The man who last wore this amulet was once First Wizard. His name was Baraccus. He also happened to have been born a war wizard, as am I. He, too, went to the Temple of the Winds, but when he returned, he went into the First Wizard's enclave, left this there, came out, and committed suicide by leaping off the side of the Keep."

Richard's gaze drifted into distant visions and memories. "For a time, I understood and ached to join him." Nicci was relieved when the haunted look in his gray eyes was banished by the return of his easy smile. "But I came to my senses."

The room rang with the silence, as if death itself had just silently glided through the room, paused for a moment, and then moved on.

Zedd at last smiled himself as he gripped Richard's shoulder, giving his grandson an affectionate joggle. "I'm glad to know I made the right choice in naming you Seeker, my boy."

Nicci wished that Richard still had the sword that belonged with the Seeker, but he had sacrificed it for information in an attempt to find Kahlan.

"So," Zedd said at last, getting back to the matter at hand, "because you know about these symbols, you believe you understood symbols within the Chainfire spell-form."

"I was able to shut it down, wasn't I?"

Zedd clasped his hands behind his back again. "You have a point there. But that doesn't necessarily mean that you could read forms within the spell as emblems, much less know that the spell-form was corrupted by the chimes."

"Not the chimes themselves," Richard patiently explained, "but the contamination left behind as a result of the chimes having been in this world. That corruption is what infected the Chainfire spell. That's the issue."

Zedd turned away, his face hidden in shadows. "But still, Richard, even if you actually do understand something of the emblems having to do with war wizards, how can you be sure that you accurately understand this, this"—he gestured in the vague direction of the room where it had all happened—"this other business with the Chainfire spell and the chimes?"

"I know," Richard insisted in a quiet voice. "I saw the mark of the nature of the corruption. It was caused by the chimes."

He sounded tired. Nicci wondered how long he'd been up. Because of the arid timbre to his voice and the slightest unsteadiness in his movements, she suspected that it had probably been days since he'd slept. Despite how weary he might have been, he sounded resolute in his conviction. She knew that it was his worry for Kahlan driving him on.

Nicci, having been pulled out of the spell-form by him twice, wasn't one to want to so easily discount his theory. More than that, though, she had come to understand that Richard had an insight into magic that was very different from the conventional wisdom. At first she had thought that his perception of how magic functioned in part through artistic concepts was a product of his having been raised without having been taught about magic, without having any exposure to it, but she had since come to see that that unique insight, along with his singular intellect, had enabled him to grasp an essential nature of magic that was fundamentally different from the orthodox teachings.

Nicci had come to believe that Richard might actually understand magic in a way not envisioned by anyone since ancient times.

Zedd turned back, his face illuminated by the warm glow of lamplight on one side and, on the other, the faint, cold light of dawn. "Richard, let's say you're right about the meaning of the symbols on those wristbands and the ones like them on the First Wizard's enclave. Understanding those things does not mean that you can understand the lines within a verification web. It's a completely different, and unique, context. I'm not doubting your ability, my boy, I'm really not, but dealing with spell-forms is a vastly complex matter. You can't leap to the conclusion—"

"Have you seen a dragon in the last couple of years?"

Everyone in the room fell to stunned silence at Richard's sudden change of topic—and not just to any subject, but one that could only be described as strange at best.

"A dragon?" Zedd ventured, at last, like a man inching out onto a newly frozen lake.

"Yes, a dragon. Do you recall seeing a dragon since we left our home in Westland and came to the Midlands?"

Zedd smoothed back some of the wavy tufts of his white hair. He glanced briefly to both Cara and Nicci before answering. "Well, no, I can't really say that I recall having seen any dragons, but what does that have to do—"

"Where are they? Why haven't you seen any? Why are they gone?"

Zedd looked at his wits' end. He spread his hands. "Richard, dragons are very rare creatures."

Richard leaned back in his chair, crossing one leg over his other knee. "Red dragons are. But Kahlan told me that other types are relatively common, with some of the smaller ones kept for hunting and such."

Zedd's expression turned suspicious. "What are you getting at?"

Richard gestured with a sweep of a hand. "Where are the dragons? Why haven't we seen any? That's what I'm getting at."

Zedd folded his arms across his chest. "I give up. What are you talking about?"

"Well, for one thing, you don't remember—that's what I'm talking about. The Chainfire spell has affected more than just your memory of Kahlan."

"Don't remember what?" Zedd sputtered. "What do you mean?"

Instead of answering his grandfather, Richard looked back over his shoulder. "Have you seen a dragon?" he asked Cara.

"I don't recall any." Her gaze remained fixed on him. "Are you suggesting that I should?"

"Darken Rahl kept a dragon. Since he was the Lord Rahl at the time, you would have been at hand so you would probably have seen it."

Zedd and Cara shared a troubled look.

Richard turned his raptor gaze on Nicci. "You?"

Nicci cleared her throat. "I always thought they were mythical creatures. There aren't any in the Old World. If there ever were, they haven't existed for ages. No records since the great war have any mention of them."

"What about since you came to the New World."

Nicci hesitated at recounting the memory. She realized, though, by the way he patiently and silently waited for her answer, that he wasn't going to let the subject go. She knew that whatever obscure equation he was working to solve wouldn't involve anything trivial. Under his silent scrutiny, Nicci felt not only a compulsion to answer, but a rising sense of foreboding.

She threw the bedcovers back and swung her feet down off the side of the bed. She didn't want to be lying there any longer—especially when speaking about that time. Gripping the side rail, she met Richard's gaze.

"When I was taking you away to the Old World, before we left the New World, we came across colossal bones. I never got down off my horse to look at them, but I remember watching you walk through those rib bones—rib bones that were well beyond twice your height. I had never seen anything like them. You said that you believed that it was the remains of a dragon.

"I thought that they must have been ancient bones. You said they were not, that they still had scraps of flesh on them. You pointed out all the flies buzzing around it as proof that it was what was left of a rotted carcass, not ancient remains."

Richard nodded at the memory.

Zedd cleared his throat. "And have you ever seen a dragon, Richard? One that was alive, I mean."

"Scarlet."

"What?"

"That was her name: Scarlet."

Zedd blinked with incredulity. "You have seen a dragon . . . and it has a name?"

Richard stood and went to the window. He rested his hands on the stone opening, leaning his weight on it as he gazed out.

"Yes," he said at last. "Her name was Scarlet. She helped me, before. She was a noble beast."

He turned back from the window. "But that's not the point. The point is that you knew her, too."

Zedd's eyebrows lifted. "I knew this dragon?"

"Not as well as Kahlan or I, but you knew her. The Chainfire event has obviously corrupted your memory of it. Chainfire was meant to make everyone forget Kahlan, but everyone is forgetting other things as well, things that were connected with her.

"For all I know, you might once have known the meanings of the emblems outside the First Wizard's enclave better than I do. If you did, that memory is lost to you. How many other things have been lost? I don't know much about the various ways to use magic, but when we were fighting the beast the other night it seemed to me that in the past all of you used more inventive spells and powers than the simple things you tried against the threat—except maybe what Nicci did at the end.

"This is what the men who came up with the Chainfire spell feared most. This is why they didn't ever want it ignited. This is why they never even dared test it. They feared that once such an event was initiated it might spread, destroying connections removed from the primary target of the spell—in this case Kahlan. Your memory of Kahlan is lost. Your memory of Scarlet is lost. Your memory of even having seen dragons is apparently lost as well."

Nicci stood. "Richard, no one is arguing that the Chainfire spell isn't terribly dangerous. We all know that. We all know that our memories have been damaged by the ignition of a Chainfire event. Do you have any idea how disturbing it is to be intellectually aware that we all did things, knew things, and knew people that we now can't remember? Don't you realize how haunting is to be in constant dread of what memories are lost, and what others might be lost? That your very mind is eroding? What are you getting at, anyway?"

"Just that—what else is being lost. I think that the destruction is expanding through everyone's memory—that their minds are eroding, as you put it. I don't think that Chainfire was a single event of merely forgetting Kahlan. I think that the spell, once activated, is an ongoing, dynamic process. I think that everyone's memory loss is continuing to spread."

Zedd, Cara, and Nicci all looked away from Richard's unwavering gaze. Nicci wondered how they could expect to help him if none of them were consciously capable of using their own minds, much less keeping what they still had from day to day.

How could Richard trust any of them?

"I'm afraid that as bad as that much of it is, it gets more involved and far worse," Richard said, the heat having left his voice. "Dragons, like many creatures in the Midlands, need and use magic to live. What if the corruption caused by the chimes extinguished the magic that they need in order to live? What if no one has seen any dragons for the last couple of years because they no longer exist and with Chainfire are now forgotten? What other creatures with magic might have also vanished from existence?"

Richard tapped a thumb against his own chest. "We are creatures of magic. We have the gift. How long until that taint left by the chimes begins to destroy us?"

"But perhaps . . ." Zedd's voice trailed off when he could think of no argument.

"The Chainfire spell itself is contaminated. You all saw what it was doing to Nicci. She was in the spell and she knows the terrible truth of it." Richard began pacing as he spoke. "There is no telling how the contamination within the spell might change the way it works. It might even be that the contamination is the reason that everyone's memory loss is spreading beyond what would have otherwise happened.

"But worse yet, it appears that the corruption has worked in conjunction with the Chainfire event in a symbiotic fashion."

Zedd looked up. "What are you talking about?"

"What is the mindless purpose of the chimes? Why were they created in the first place? For one single function," Richard said in answer to his own question, "to destroy magic."

Richard paused his pacing to face the rest of them as he went on. "The contamination left by the chimes is destroying magic. The creatures that need magic to live—dragons, for example—would likely be the first to be affected. That cascade of events will continue. But no one is aware of it because the Chainfire event is simultaneously destroying everyone's memory. I think this may be happening because the Chainfire spell is contaminated, causing everyone to forget the very things being lost.

"In much the way a leech numbs its victim so that they won't feel their blood being drained away, the Chainfire spell is making everyone forget what is being lost because of the corruption of the chimes.

"The world is changing dramatically and no one is even aware of it. It's as if everyone is forgetting that this is a world that is influenced by, and in many ways functions through, the existence of magic. That magic is dying out . . . and so is everyone's memory of it."

Richard again leaned on the sill and stared out the window. "A new day is dawning, a day in which magic continues to die out, and no one is even aware that it is fading away. When it passes entirely, I doubt that anyone will even remember it, remember what once was.

"It's as if all that was this world is passing into a realm of mere legend."

Zedd pressed his fingers to the table as he stared into the distance. The light of the lamp accentuated the deep creases of his drawn features. His face had gone ashen. At that moment, Nicci thought that he looked very old.

"Dear spirits," Zedd said without looking up. "What if you're right?"

They all turned to the sound of a polite knock. Cara pulled the door open. Nathan and Ann stood beyond the doorway, peering in.

"We ran the standard verification web," Nathan said as he entered behind Ann, glancing around at the somber expressions.

Zedd looked up expectantly. "And?"

"And it reveals no flaws," Ann said. "It's perfectly intact in every way."

"How can that be?" Cara asked. "We all saw the trouble with the other one. It nearly killed Nicci—and would have if Lord Rahl hadn't gotten her out."

"Our point, exactly," Nathan said.

Zedd's gaze fell away. "An interior perspective is said to be able to reveal more than the standard verification process," he explained to Cara. "This is not a good sign. Not a good sign at all. The contamination apparently buried itself as deeply as possible in order to conceal its presence. That's why it wasn't seen in the standard verification web."

"Or else," Ann offered as she slipped her hands into opposite sleeves of her simple gray dress, "there is nothing really wrong with the spell. After all, none of us has ever run an interior perspective before. Such a thing hasn't been done in thousands of years. It's possible we did something wrong."

Zedd shook his head. "I wish it were so, but I now believe it to be otherwise."

Nathan's brow drew down with a suspicious look, but Ann spoke before he had a chance.

"Even if the Sisters who unleashed the spell ran a verification web," she said, "they likely would not have run an interior perspective, so they wouldn't have suspected that it was contaminated."

Richard rubbed his fingertips back and forth across his brow. "Even if they knew that it was contaminated, I don't think they cared. They wouldn't be concerned about what damage such contamination might cause the world. Their goal, after all, was to get the boxes and unleash the power of Orden."

Nathan looked from one grim face to another. "What's going on? What's happened?"

"I'm afraid that we've just learned that memory may only be the beginning of our loss." Nicci felt rather odd standing before them in a pink nightdress as she pronounced the end of the world as they knew it. "We are losing who we are, what we are. We are losing not just our world, but ourselves."

Richard no longer seemed to be paying attention to the conversation. He was standing stock-still, staring out the window.

"Someone is coming up the road to the Keep."

"Maybe it's Tom and Friedrich," Nathan said.

Zedd shook his head as he made for the window. "They wouldn't be back from a patrol of the surrounding countryside this soon."

"Well, it could be that they—"

"It's not Tom and Friedrich," Richard said as he started for the door. "It's two women."

What is it?" Rikka called out as Richard, Nicci, and Cara ran toward her. Nathan and Ann had already fallen far behind. Zedd was somewhere in the middle.

"Come on," Richard shouted to her as he ran past.

"Someone is coming up the Keep road," Cara called back over her shoulder as Rikka joined in the charge through the halls.

Richard veered around a long stone table set against the wall beneath a huge painting of a lake. Sheltered trails could be seen burrowed through the deeply shadowed pine groves. In the distance, through a bluish haze, majestic mountains rose up to catch brushstrokes of golden sunlight. It was a scene that made Richard long to be back in his Hartland woods on the trails he knew so well. More than anything, though, the painting always reminded him of the magical summer he'd spent with Kahlan in the home he had built for her far back in the mountains.

The summer of Kahlan's recovery from her terrible injuries, as he showed her the natural beauty of his forested world and she once again blossomed back to health, had been one of the happiest times of his life. It had ended all too suddenly when Nicci had arrived without warning and taken him away. He knew, though, that if Nicci had not interrupted it, something else would have. It had been a dream time that had to end; until the looming threat from the Imperial Order was halted, no one could live their dreams. They would all, instead, be swept up in the same nightmare.

They turned a corner around a green marble pillar with a gold capital and base and all plunged down a spiral run of granite steps, Richard and Nicci in the lead with the two Mord-Sith following close on their heels. The stairwell was small for the Keep, but would have dwarfed anything Richard had ever seen growing up back in Westland.

At the bottom, he slid to a halt, momentarily pausing to decide which would be the quickest route; in the Keep it wasn't always the way it would seem. Besides that, it was as easy to get lost in the Keep as it was to lose one's direction in a birch forest.

Cara pushed through between Richard and Nicci, not only to be sure that there would be a red-leather-clad guard to each side of him, but so that she would be the one out ahead of him. As far as Richard knew, Mord-Sith didn't have rank, but Rikka, like the other Mord-Sith, always wordlessly conceded Cara's unspoken authority.

Richard recognized the unique pattern of the thin black and gilded bands lining both sides of the mahogany wainscoting in one of the paneled corridors to the side. From almost since the time he had learned to walk, Richard had used the details of his surroundings to know his way. Like trees in the woods that he recognized because of some peculiarity like a twisted limb, a growth, or a scar, he had learned to navigate through the Keep and places like it by the details of architecture.

He gestured. "This way." Cara charged off ahead of him.

As they ran, their boot strikes echoed off the stone floor of the hall. Nicci was barefoot. He was somewhat surprised that without shoes she could keep up running across the rough stone. Nicci was not the kind of woman Richard ever envisioned running in bare feet. Even running in bare feet, though, she still looked somehow . . . regal.

It wasn't all that long ago that Richard would not have imagined Nicci ever running again. He was still surprised that he had managed to get her out of the spell-form after the lightning had exploded through the window. For a time, he was sure that they had lost her. If Zedd had not been there to help after Richard had shut down the verification web, they very well might have.

They turned down another hall; long carpets quieted their run and finally led them between two highly polished red marble columns and into the oval-shaped anteroom. A balcony, supported by pillars and arches, ran around the perimeter of the room. The doorways at the back of the balcony were all corridors, arranged like the spokes of a wheel, that led to different levels and areas of the Keep.

Richard bounded down the five steps ringing the room inside the columns and ran past the great clover-leaf-shaped fountain centered in the tiled floor. The fountain's waters cascaded down successive tiers of ever wider, scalloped bowls to end up in a pool contained by a knee-high white marble wall that also served as a bench. A hundred feet overhead a glassed roof flooded the room with warmth and light.

When he reached the far side of the room, Richard pushed ahead of Cara and threw open one of the heavy double doors. He paused on the top of the dozen wide granite steps outside. Nicci halted beside him, to his left, with Rikka on the far side of her. Cara took a defensive place close by on his right. All of them were still catching their breath from the brief but swift run through the Keep.

The grass in the paddock across the way was lush and green in the early-morning light. Beyond the paddock the wall of the Keep rose straight up, making the inner courtyard seem like a cozy canyon. The passing of millennia had left the soaring wall of tightly fitted, dark stone stained with pale tan sediment. Creamy drips of calcium deposits gave the impression that the rock was slowly melting.

Two horses clopped through the dark, arched opening to the left, which tunneled under part of the Keep to gain access to the inner courtyard. Richard couldn't tell who it was, hidden as they were back in the deep shadows of the broad, low archway, but whoever it was must have known where they were going and they apparently weren't afraid to enter an interior area of the Keep, an area used not by visitors but by wizards and those who had worked with them at the complex. But that was long ago. Still, Richard recalled his own trepidation the first time he cautiously ventured this far into the grounds of the Keep. His hackles rose at who might be bold enough to ride right into such a place.

When the two riders emerged into the light, Richard saw that one of them was Shota.

The witch woman locked eyes with him and smiled that quiet, knowing, private smile she wore so naturally. Like most other things about Shota, Richard didn't entirely trust the smile as significant, much less sincere, and so he couldn't be sure that it augured well.

He didn't recognize the woman, maybe ten or fifteen years older, who rode deferentially half a length behind Shota. Short, sandy hair framed the woman's pleasant face. Her eyes were as intensely blue as the sky on a sparkling clear autumn day. Unlike Shota, she wore no casual smile. As they rode, her head swiveled and those blue eyes searched, as if she feared an imminent attack of demons who might materialize out of the dark stone of the surrounding walls.

Shota, by contrast, looked calm and self-confident.

Cara leaned past Richard toward Nicci. "Shota, the witch woman," she whispered confidentially.

"I know," Nicci answered without taking her eyes off the beautiful woman riding toward them.

Shota brought her horse to a halt close to the steps. As she straightened her shoulders she casually rested her wrists across the saddle's pommel.

"I need to see you," she said to Richard as if he were the only one standing there. The smile, sincere or not, had vanished. "We have much to talk about."

"Where is your murderous little companion, Samuel?"

Shota, riding sidesaddle, slipped down off her horse in a way that Richard imagined must be how a spirit would slip to ground, if spirits rode horses.

A hint of indignation narrowed Shota's almond-shaped eyes. "That is one of the things we need to talk about."

The other woman dismounted as well and took the reins to Shota's horse when the witch woman lifted them to the side, much the way a queen would, not knowing or caring who would take them, but expecting without any doubt whatsoever that someone would. Her gaze remained fixed on Richard as she glided closer to the broad granite steps. Her thick, wavy auburn hair tumbled down over the front of her shoulders and glistened in the early light. Her revealing dress, made of an airy, rust-colored fabric that complemented perfectly the color of her hair, seemed to float with her effortless strides, clinging to her every curve, at least the ones it covered.

Shota's gaze finally left Richard to take in Nicci with an "I dare you" look. It was the kind of look that would have withered just about anyone. It failed to wither Nicci in the least. It struck Richard that he was probably in the presence of the two most dangerous women alive. He half expected dark thunderclouds to roll in and lightning to flicker, but the sky remained defiantly clear.

Shota's gaze finally slid back to Richard. "Your friend Chase has been gravely hurt."

Richard didn't know what he had been expecting Shota to say, but that wasn't even close. "Chase . . .?"

Zedd suddenly arrived and pushed his way through between Richard and Cara. "Shota!" he declared in a huff. His face had gone red and it wasn't from his run through the halls. "How dare you come into the Keep! First you swindle Richard out of the sword, and then—"

Richard lifted an arm out across his grandfather's chest to stop him from charging down the steps. "Zedd, calm down. Shota says that Chase has been badly hurt."

"How does she think—"

Zedd's voice abruptly clipped off when Richard's words finally sank in. His wide eyes turned back toward Shota. "Chase, hurt? Dear spirits . . . how?"

Zedd suddenly caught sight of the other woman standing a little farther back, holding the reins to the horses. He squinted against the bright light. "Jebra? Jebra Bevinvier?"

The woman smiled warmly. "It has been quite a while. I wasn't sure that you would remember me, Wizard Zorander."

This time Richard didn't try to stop Zedd when he rushed to descend the steps. He embraced the woman in a warm and protective hug.

"Wizard Zorander—"

"Zedd, remember?"

She drew back to peer up at his face. A smile broke through the sadness that weighed so heavily in her eyes. Her smile ghosted away. "Zedd, my vision has gone dark."

"Gone dark?" Concern tightening his features, he straightened and gripped her by the shoulders. "How long ago?"

A terrible anguish flooded back into her blue eyes. "Nearly two years."

"Two years . . ." Zedd said, his voice trailing off in dismay.

"I remember you, now." Richard said as he moved down the steps. "Kahlan told me about you."

Jebra cast Richard a puzzled frown. "Who?"

"The phantom he chases," Shota said, her unwavering gaze fixed on him as if daring him to argue.

"The woman he seeks is no phantom," Nicci said, drawing Shota's attention. "Thanks in part to the pricey and rather equivocal suggestions you offered, we have discovered the truth of what Richard has been telling us all along. Apparently you are still in the dark about it."

Nicci's icy look reminded Richard that she had once been known as Death's Mistress. The cold authority in her voice matched the look. There were few women in the world as widely feared as Nicci had once been—except perhaps for Shota. Nicci's demeanor indicated that she was clearly a woman still to be feared.

Shota, unfazed, deliberately took in the length of Nicci's pink night-dress. Richard expected a smirk. Instead, a hot look flashed in Shota's eyes.

"You have been sleeping in his bed." She sounded almost surprised by her own words, as if the information had come to mind unexpectedly.

Nicci shrugged with satisfaction at Shota's ire. "So I have."

The slightest smile in turn curled the corners of Shota's mouth. "But you have not succeeded in bedding him yet." Her smile widened. "Have you tried, my dear? Or do you fear the sting of rejection?"

"I don't know, why don't you tell me how it felt, then I'll decide."

Richard gently pulled Nicci back from the edge of the step before the two woman did something stupid—like try to scratch out each other's eyes. Or reduce each other to ashes.

"You said you were here for a reason, Shota—this had better not be it."

Shota heaved a soft sigh. "I found your friend Chase. He was gravely injured."

"So you said. How was he injured?"

Shota's gaze didn't shrink from his. "He was hurt by a sword you would be quite familiar with."

Richard blinked in astonishment. "Chase was hurt by the Sword of Truth? Samuel attacked Chase?"

"I'm afraid so."

Zedd shook a bony finger at Shota. "This is your doing!"

"Nonsense." Shota, too, lifted a finger as Zedd stepped closer, but in warning rather than accusation. The gesture, and her words, kept Zedd from taking another step. "I need no sword to accomplish harm." She arched an eyebrow. "Like to see, wizard?"

"Stop it!" Richard descended the steps two at a time and put himself between Shota and his grandfather. He turned a glare of his own on Shota. "What's going on?"

She sighed unhappily. "I'm afraid that I don't entirely know."

"You gave Samuel my sword." Richard tried to keep the heat out of his voice, to keep from letting his anger show, but he feared that it wasn't working very well. "I warned you about his nature. Despite my warning, you insisted that he have it. I want to know what he is up to. Where is Chase? How badly is he hurt? And where is Rachel?"

Shota's brow twitched. "Rachel?"

"The girl with him—the girl he adopted. The two of them were on their way back to Westland. Chase was going to bring his family back to the Keep. You mean to say that the girl wasn't there, with him?"

"I found him gravely injured." For the first time, Shota looked disconcerted. "There was no girl with him."

As he watched Rikka take the reins to the two horses and pull them toward the paddock, Richard tried to imagine what was going on, why Rachel hadn't stayed with Chase. He worried about the possible reasons, worried for what might have happened to Rachel. Knowing how resourceful and devoted she was, Richard wondered if she had gone for help and was now wandering around all by herself.

Another thought struck him. "And how was it that you just happened to come across Chase?"

Shota wet her lips. She looked reluctant to say something obviously distasteful to her, but finally she did. "I was hunting Samuel."

Surprised, Richard glanced at Nicci. Her expression showed no reaction and her features appeared so absolutely devoid of emotion that for an instant it reminded Richard of a similar look he had from time to time seen on Kahlan. A Confessor's face, she had called it. Confessors would occasionally shed all emotion in order to do the terrible things that were at times necessary.

"How is Chase?" Richard asked, considerably quieter. He wanted to know why Shota was hunting Samuel, but at the moment there were more important worries weighing on his mind. "Is he going to be all right?"

"I believe so," Shota said. "He'd been run through with a sword—"

"With my sword."

Shota didn't argue the distinction. "I'm not a healer, but I do have certain abilities and I was able to at least reverse his journey toward death. I found some people who could care for him and help him recover. I believe he is safe for the time being. It will be a while before he is on his feet again."

"And why didn't Samuel kill him?" Cara asked from the top step.

"He stabbed Tovi the same way," Nicci said. "He didn't kill her, either."

"Samuel is certainly capable of murder," Richard pointed out.

Shota clasped her hands before herself. "Samuel apparently couldn't muster the courage to kill with the sword. He has done so in the past— when the sword was his before—and so he knows the pain it causes when it is used to kill." She arched an eyebrow at Richard. "I'm sure you know well what I'm talking about."

"It's a weapon that does not belong in the wrong hands," Richard said.

Shota ignored Richard's gibe and went on. "His is the way of a coward. A coward will often leave the person to die on their own, away from his sight."

"They suffer all the more that way," Zedd pointed out. "It's more cruel. Perhaps that was his reason."

The witch woman shook her head. "Samuel is a coward and an opportunist; his goal is not cruelty but rather is entirely self-centered. Cowards don't necessarily think things out. They act on whim. They want what they want when they want it.

"Samuel will rarely bother to consider the consequences of his actions; he simply snatches something when he sees an opportunity, when he sees something he desires. He shrinks from the pain it would cause him to kill with the sword and so he fails to complete the killing he initiated on impulse. If the person he injures suffers an agonizing and prolonged end, it doesn't matter to Samuel because he isn't around to witness it. Out of sight, out of mind. That was what he did to Chase."

"And you gave him the sword," Richard said, unable to disguise his anger. "You knew what he was like and you still made it possible for him to do this."

Shota regarded him a moment before answering. "That's not the way it was, Richard. I gave him the sword because I thought it would make him content. I believed that he would be satisfied to have it back in his possession. I thought it would mellow his lingering resentment at having the sword so abruptly taken from him."

Shota cast a brief but murderous look at Zedd.

"So, you didn't consider the consequences of your actions," Richard said. "You simply wanted what you wanted when you wanted it."

Shota's gaze slid back to Richard. "After all this time, and everything that has happened, you are still as flippant as ever?"

Richard wasn't in a mood to apologize.

"I'm afraid that there is more to this," Shota said, somewhat less heatedly, "more than I realized at the time."

Zedd rubbed his chin as he considered the situation. "Samuel must have stabbed Chase and then kidnapped Rachel."

Richard was surprised by Zedd's suggestion; he hadn't thought of that. He had assumed that Rachel had gone to find help.

He turned a frown on Shota. "Why would Samuel do such a thing?"

"I'm afraid that I don't have any idea." Shota looked up at Nicci, still standing at the top of the granite steps. "Who is this woman you say he stabbed? This Tovi?"

"She was a Sister of the Dark. And it is no idle accusation. Tovi didn't know the person who stabbed her, didn't know who Samuel was, but she certainly knew the Sword of Truth; she was once one of Richard's teachers back at the Palace of the Prophets. Just before she died she told me how she and three other Sisters of the Dark had ignited a Chainfire spell around Kahlan to make everyone forget her. They then used Kahlan to steal the boxes of Orden from the People's Palace."

Shota's brow creased. She looked truly perplexed.

"The boxes of Orden are in play," Richard added.

Shota flicked a hand dismissively as she stared off in thought. "That much I have come to know. But I did not know how it came to be."

Richard wondered how much more of the story she knew, but he told it anyway. "Tovi was taking one of the boxes of Orden away from the People's Palace, in D'Hara, when Samuel jumped her, ran her through with the sword, and then stole the box she was carrying."

Shota again looked surprised, but the look was quickly banished by quiet fury as she silently considered what she'd been told.

"I've known Chase my whole life," Richard said. "While anyone can make a mistake, I've never known him to be caught off guard by someone lying in wait. I can't imagine that Sisters of the Dark are much easier to ambush. Gifted people of their level of talent and ability have a sense of people being around them."

Shota looked up at him. "Your point?"

"Samuel was somehow able to surprise a Sister of the Dark, and a boundary warden." Richard folded his arms across his chest. "What's more, every time Samuel tries to accomplish something evil you always act all surprised and disavow any knowledge of what he was up to. What's your part in all this, Shota?"

"None. I had no idea of what he was up to."

"Unlike you to be so ignorant."

Her cheeks mantled. "You don't know the half of it." She finally turned away from him and headed for the steps. "I told you, we have much to talk about."

Richard caught her arm, turning her back. "Did you have anything to do with Samuel being able to sneak up on Chase or surprise Tovi and steal that box? Other than providing him with the weapon to accomplish the deed and no doubt telling him all about the power the boxes of Orden contain, I mean."

She searched his eyes for a time. "Do you wish to kill me, Richard?"

"Kill you? Shota, I've been the best friend you've ever had."

"Then you will put your anger aside and listen to what we have come to tell you." She pulled away from the grip on her arm and again started for the steps. "Let's get inside and out of this foul weather."

Richard glanced to the blue sky. "The weather is beautiful," he said as he watched her ascend the steps.

At the top she halted to share a brief glare with Nicci before turning to look down at Richard. It was the kind of haunting, timeless, troubling look that he imagined only a witch woman could conjure.

"Not in my world," she said in a near whisper. "In my world it's raining."

Shota glided down the steps to stand before the fountain. The diaphanous fabric of the dress that covered her statuesque form moved ever so slightly, as if in a gentle breeze. The gushing, cascading, effervescent waters danced and sparkled in the light from the skylights far above, putting on an exhilarating performance for the gathered audience. Shota stared absently at it for a moment, as if preoccupied with her own private thoughts, and then turned to the small crowd waiting just inside the huge double doors. They all stood silently, watching her, as if awaiting a queen's pronouncement.

Behind Shota, the water in the fountain sprayed high into the air. The exuberant surge of spray abruptly stopped. The last of the water, still rising just before the flow had cut off, reached its zenith, a dying liquid arc, and fell back as if slain. The dozens of uniform streams of water overflowing the down-turned points in the tiers of bowls, as if embarrassed by their frothy frolic, slowed to a stop and finally fell silent.

Zedd stepped to the brink of the steps, a forbidding look settling into the lines of his face. As he halted, the swirl of his simple robes gathered around his legs. At that moment it struck Richard that his grandfather looked very much like who he was: the First Wizard. If Richard had thought that Nicci and Shota had looked dangerous, he realized that Zedd was no less so. At that moment he was a thundercloud harboring hidden lightning.

"I'll not have you tampering with anything in this place. I indulge you because you have come here for reasons that *may* somehow be important to us all, but my leniency will not tolerate your meddling with anything here."

Shota flicked a hand, dismissing his warning. "I assumed that you would not acquiesce to me going any farther than this room. The fountain is noisy. I don't want Richard to fail to hear anything I or Jebra has to say."

She lifted an arm toward Ann, standing beside Nathan, watching, almost unseen in the deep shadows of the balcony and soaring red pillars. "It is a matter that has been close to your heart for half of your life, Prelate."

"I am no longer Prelate," Ann said in a quietly commanding voice that sounded very much as if she still were.

"Why were you hunting Samuel?" Cara asked, drawing the witch woman's attention.

"Because he was not supposed to have left my valley in Agaden Reach. Moreover, he should not have been able to do so without my expressed permission."

"And yet he did," Richard said.

Shota nodded. "So I went looking for him."

Richard clasped his hands behind his back. "How is it, Shota, that you weren't aware that Samuel was going to leave you? I mean, considering your power, vast knowledge, and all that business you've explained to me about how a witch woman can see the way that events flow forward in time. For that matter, how was he able to do so without your consent?"

Shota did not shrink from the question. "There is only one way."

Richard bit back the sarcastic remark that came to mind and instead asked, "And what would that be?"

"Samuel has been bewitched."

Richard wasn't sure that he'd heard her correctly. "Bewitched. But you're the witch woman. You're the one who does the bewitching."

Shota clasped her hands, looking down at the floor a moment as she folded her fingers together. "He was bewitched by another."

Richard descended the five steps. "Another witch woman?"

"Yes."

Richard took a deep breath as he glanced around to see the others sharing troubled looks. No one appeared inclined to ask, so he did. "You mean to say that there is another witch woman around, and she bewitched Samuel away from you?"

"I thought that I had made that perfectly clear."

"Well . . . where is she?"

"I have no idea. Certain issues in the flow of time are my business—I have seen to it. For me to be this blind to events that eddy so tightly through my purview can only mean that another witch woman has deliberately occulted those flows from me."

Richard stuffed his hands in his back pockets as he tried to reason it out. He paced briefly before turning back to her.

"Maybe it wasn't a witch woman. Maybe it was a Sister of the Dark or someone like that. A gifted person. Maybe even a wizard. Jagang has those, too."

"To manipulate a witch woman in an insignificant way is far from an easy task." She shot a brief glare up at Zedd. "Ask your grandfather."

Shota gestured around at some of the people in the room before her gaze returned to Richard. "A gifted person, even such as these, no matter how talented, could not begin to achieve a deception as comprehensive as this one has been. Only another witch woman could slip herself unseen into my domain. Only another witch woman could draw a shroud over my vision and then bewitch Samuel into doing what he has done."

"If your vision is shrouded," Cara asked, "how can you be so certain that Samuel has been bewitched? Maybe he was acting on his own. From what I've seen of him, he needs no mysterious enchantress to coax him into impulsive behavior. He seemed plenty treacherous all on his own."

Shota slowly shook her head. "You have only to look at what you've told me to see that this involves not simply cunning but knowledge beyond Samuel's ability. A Sister of the Dark was attacked; a box of Orden was stolen from her. In the first place, how would Samuel be aware that this woman had anything valuable? I didn't know of her myself because that is part of what has been hidden from me, so I couldn't have told him—not even absently, carelessly, or inadvertently, which is what you're thinking. So, Samuel didn't learn of it from me. If he happened across a treasure of some sort there is no doubt that Samuel is fully capable of doing whatever he could to snatch it, that much I concede."

"You mean the way he acquired the Sword of Truth in the first place?" Zedd asked.

Shota met his gaze briefly but chose to return to the matter at hand rather than confront the challenge. "Secondly, how would Samuel know where he could find a Sister carrying a box of Orden? You can't seriously mean to suggest that you think he simply was wandering around—way off in D'Hara—and by chance happened across this very Sister of the Dark, stabbed her, and robbed her of what she was carrying only to have it turn out to be one of the boxes of Orden?"

"I have to admit," Richard said, "I never have much believed in coincidence. It certainly doesn't seem plausible in this case, either."

"My thoughts, exactly," Shota said. "And then there's Chase. Due to his grave condition I wasn't able to learn much from him, but I was able to discover that he had been ambushed. Another coincidence—Samuel happening across and randomly attacking someone and it just happens to be someone else you know? I hardly think so. That leaves the question of why Samuel would be lying in wait for a man you know. Why would he attack him? What thing of value did Chase have?"

"Rachel," Zedd answered as he stared off, rubbing his chin in thought.

"But what would he want with a girl?" Cara asked. When several people glanced her way with troubled looks, she added, "I mean, that girl in particular?"

"I don't know," Shota said. "And that's the problem. As I've said, the events surrounding all of this are blocked to me, but blocked in a way that I didn't recognize, so I was unaware that anything was being hidden. It's obvious that there is a hand directing Samuel. That hand could only be another witch woman's."

"Do you know her?" Richard asked. "Do you know who it is, or who she might be?"

Shota regarded him with as forbidding a look as he had ever seen grace such feminine features. "She is a complete mystery to me."

"Where did she come from? Do you have any idea about that much of it?"

Shota's scowl only darkened. "Oh, I think I do. I believe she came up from the Old World. When you destroyed the great barrier several years back she no doubt saw an opportunity and moved into my territory—in much the same way that the Imperial Order saw an opportunity to invade and conquer the New World. By bewitching Samuel she is sending a message that she is taking my place, taking what is mine—including my territory—as her own."

Richard turned toward Ann, off at the side of the anteroom. "Do you know of a witch woman in the Old World?"

"I ran the Palace of the Prophets, guiding young wizards and a whole palace full of Sisters toward the way of the Light. I paid great heed to prophecy in that task but, other than prophecy, I didn't really involve myself in the goings-on in the rest the Old World. From time to time I heard vague rumors of witch women, but nothing more than rumors. If she was real, she never stuck her head up for me to know of her."

"I never knew anything of a witch woman, either," Nathan added with a sigh. "I never even heard the rumors of such a woman."

Shota folded her arms. "We're a rather secretive lot."

Richard wished he knew more about such things—although knowing one witch woman had proven on more than one occasion to be trouble enough. It seemed that there might now be twice the trouble.

"Her name is Six," Nicci said into the quiet anteroom.

Everyone turned to stare at her.

Shota's brow drew down. "What did you say?"

"The witch woman down in the Old World. Her name is Six, like the number." Nicci's expression had that cool absence of emotion again, her features as still as a woodland pond at dawn after the first hard freeze of the season. "I never met her, but the Sisters of the Dark spoke of her in hushed tones."

"It would be those Sisters," Ann grumbled.

Shota's arms slowly dropped to her sides as she took a step away from the fountain, toward where Nicci stood on the expanse of marble floor at the top of the steps. "What do you know of her?"

"Nothing much. I've only heard her name, Six. I only remember it because it was unusual. Some of my superiors at the time—my Sisters of the Dark superiors—apparently did know her. I heard her name mentioned several times."

Shota's countenance had turned as dark and dangerous as that of a viper with its fangs bared. "What were Sisters of the Dark doing with a witch woman?"

"I don't really know," Nicci said. "They may have had dealings with her, but if they did I never knew about it. I wasn't always included in their schemes. It may be that they only knew of her. It's possible they never even met her."

"Or it's possible that they knew her well."

Nicci shrugged. "Maybe. You'd have to ask them. I suggest you hurry—Samuel has already killed one of them."

Shota ignored the taunt and turned away to stare into the still waters of the fountain. "You must have heard them say something about her."

"Nothing very specific," Nicci said.

"Well," Shota said with exaggerated patience as she turned back around, "what was the general nature of what they were saying about her?"

"I only got a sense of two things. I heard that the witch, Six, lived far to the south. The Sisters mentioned that she lived much deeper down in the Old World, in some of the trackless forests and swampland." Nicci gazed resolutely into Shota's eyes. "And they were afraid of her."

Shota folded her arms across her breasts again. "Afraid of her," she repeated in a flat tone.

"Terrified."

Shota appraised Nicci's eyes for a time before finally yet again turning to stare into the fountain, as if hoping to see some secret revealed in the placid waters.

"There's nothing to say that it's the same woman," Richard said. "There's no evidence to say that it's this witch woman, Six, from the Old World."

Shota glanced back over her shoulder. "You, of all people, suggest that it's mere coincidence?" Her gaze again sought solace in the waters. "It doesn't really matter if it is or not. It matters only that it is a witch woman and she is bent on causing me trouble."

Richard stepped closer to Shota. "I find it pretty hard to believe that this other witch woman would have bewitched Samuel away from you just to show you up and have what's yours. There has to be more to it."

"Maybe it's a challenge," Cara said. "Maybe she is daring you to come out and fight."

"That would require her to make herself known," Shota said. "She has done just the opposite. She is deliberate and calculating about remaining concealed so that I can't fight her."

As he considered, Richard rested a boot on the marble bench surrounding the fountain. "I still say there has to be something more to this. Having Samuel steal one of the boxes of Orden has darker implications."

"The more likely answer points to none other than your own hand, Shota." Zedd's words drew everyone's attention. "This sounds more like one of your grand deceptions."

"I can understand why you would think so, but if that were true then why would I come here to tell you of it?"

Zedd's glare didn't falter. "To make yourself look innocent when you are really the one in the shadows directing events."

Shota rolled her eyes. "I don't have time for such childish games, wizard. I have not been directing Samuel's hand. My time has been spent on other, more important matters."

"Such as?"

"I have been to Galea."

"Galea!" Zedd snorted his disbelief. "What business would you have in Galea?"

Jebra laid a hand on Zedd's shoulder. "She came to rescue me. I was in Ebinissia, caught up in the invasion and then enslaved. Shota pulled me out of the middle of it."

Zedd turned a suspicious look on Shota. "You went to the crown city of Galea to rescue Jebra?"

Shota glanced briefly at Richard, a clouded look laden with meaning. "It was necessary."

"Why?" Zedd pressed. "I'm relieved to have Jebra at last rescued from that horror, of course, but what exactly do you mean when you say that it was necessary?"

Shota caught a diaphanous point of the material making up her dress as it lifted ever so gently upward, like a cat arching its back, craving a gentle stroke from its mistress's hand. "Events march onward toward a grim conclusion. If the course of those events does not change then we will be doomed to the rule of the invaders, bound to the mandate of people whose conviction, among other things, is that magic is an evil corruption that must be eradicated from the world. They believe that mankind is a sinful and corrupt being who should properly be unremarkable and helpless in the face of the almighty spectacle of nature. Those of us who possess magic, precisely because we are not unremarkable and helpless, will all be hunted down and destroyed."

Shota's gaze passed among those watching her. "But that is merely our personal tragedy, not the true scourge of the Order.

"If the course of events does not change, then the monstrous beliefs that the Order imposes will settle like a burial shroud over the entire world. There will be no safe place, no refuge. An iron mandate of conformity will be locked around the necks of all those left alive. For the delusion of the common welfare, in the form of lofty slogans and vacuous notions that incite the feckless rabble into nothing more than a mindless lust for the unearned, everything good and noble will be sacrificed, deadening civilized man into little more than an organized mob of looters.

"But once everything of value is plundered, what will be left of their lives? By their contempt for the magnificent and disdain of all that is good, they embrace the petty and the crude. By their rabid hatred for any man who excels, the beliefs of the Order will doom all men to grubbing in the muck to survive.

"The unwavering view of mankind's inherent wickedness will be the collective faith. That belief, enforced through ruthless brutality and unspeakable hardship, will be their enduring high-water mark. Their legacy will be mankind's descent into a dark age of suffering and misery from which it may never again emerge. That is the terror of the Order—not death, but life under their beliefs." Shota's words cast a pall over the room. "The dead, after all, can't feel, can't suffer. Only the living can."

Shota turned to the shadows, where Nathan stood. "And what say you, prophet? Does prophecy say it otherwise, or do I speak the truth?"

Nathan, tall and grim, answered quietly. "As far as the Imperial Order goes, I'm afraid that prophecy can offer no testimony to the contrary. You have aptly and succinctly described several thousand years of forewarning."

"Such ancient works are not easily understood," Ann cut in. "The written word can be quite ambiguous. Prophecy is not a subject for the inexperienced. To the untrained it can seem—"

"I sincerely hope that is a judgment based on a shallow opinion of my looks, Prelate, and not my talent."

"I was only . . ." Ann began.

Shota dismissively flicked a hand as she turned away. Her gaze settled on Richard, as if he were the only one in the room. She spoke as if addressing him alone.

"Our lives may be the last lives lived free. This may very well be the end for all time of the best of what can be, of striving for values, of the potential for each of us to rise up and achieve something better. If the course of events does not change, then we are now witnessing the dawn of the worst of what can be, of an age where, lest anyone dare live better through their own effort and for their own ends, mankind will be reduced to living the Order's idealized lives of ignorant savages."

"We all know that," Richard said, hands fisted at his sides. "Don't you understand how hard we've been fighting to prevent that very thing? Don't you have any idea of the struggle we've all endured? Just what do you think I've been fighting for?"

"I don't know, Richard. You claim to be committed, and yet you have failed to change the course of events, failed to stem the tide of the Imperial Order. You say that you understand, yet still the invaders come, subjugating more and more people with every passing day.

"But even that is not what this is about. It is about the future. And in the future, you are failing us."

Richard could hardly believe what he was hearing. He wasn't just angry but appalled that Shota would say such a thing. It was as if everything he had done, every sacrifice he had made, every effort, was meaningless to her—not only now, but in the future.

"You have come to tell me your prophecy that I will fail?"

"No. I have come to tell you that the way it now stands, unless you change things, we will all fail in this fight."

Shota turned from Richard and lifted an arm up toward Nicci. "You have shown him the dull, numb death that is all that can result from the beliefs held by the Order. You have shown him the bleak existence that is all there is under their dogma, that life's only value is in how much of it you sacrifice, that your life's only purpose is a means to an otherworldly end: a lifeless eternity in the next world.

"In that, you have done us all a great service and you have our gratitude. You have truly fulfilled your role as Richard's teacher, even if it was not in the way you had expected. But that, too, is only a part of it."

Richard didn't see how his captivity—being made to live a harsh life down in the Old World—could be regarded as a service. He hadn't needed to live through it to understand the hopeless futility of life under the rule of the Imperial Order. He didn't dispute one word Shota had said about what would befall them if they didn't prevail, but he was angered that she seemed to think that he needed to hear it again, as if he did not grasp what they were fighting for and as a result was failing to be fully committed to their cause.

Richard didn't know how it happened, because he had not seen her move, but Shota was suddenly right before him, her face mere inches from his.

"And yet, you are still not cognizant of the totality of it, still not resolved in a way that is essential."

Richard glared at her. "Not resolved? What are you talking about?"

"I needed to find a way to make you understand, Seeker, to make you see the reality of it. I needed to find a way to make you see what is in store for the people of not just the New World, but the Old World as well—what is in store for all of mankind."

"How could you possibly think that I—"

"You are the one, Richard Rahl. You are the one who leads the last of the forces that resist the ideas that fuel the conflagration that is the Imperial Order. For whatever reasons, you are the one who leads us in this struggle. You may believe in what you fight for, but you are not doing what is necessary to change the course of the war or else what I see in the flow of events forward in time would not be as it is.

"As it now stands, we are doomed.

"You need to hear what is going to be the fate of your people, the fate of all people. So I went to Galea to find Jebra so that she could tell you what she has seen. So that a Seer can help you to see."

Richard thought that maybe he should have been angry at the lecture, but he could no longer summon anger; it was slipping away. "I already know what will happen if we fail, Shota. I already know what the Imperial Order is like. I already know what awaits us if we lose in this struggle."

Shota shook her head. "You know what it is like after. You know what it is like to see the dead. But the dead can no longer feel. The dead can't scream. The dead can't cry in terror. The dead can't beg for mercy.

"You know what it is like to see the wreckage the morning after the storm. You need to hear from one who was there when the storm broke. You need to hear what it was like when the legions came. You need to hear the reality of what it will be like for everyone. You need to know what will happen to those alive if you fail to do what only you can do."

Richard glanced up at Jebra. Zedd's comforting arm encircled her shoulders. Tears ran down her ashen face. She trembled from head to toe.

"Dear spirits," Richard whispered, "how can you be so cruel as to think for an instant that I don't already know the truth of our fate should we lose?"

"I see the flow of the future in this," Shota said in a quiet voice meant for him alone. "And what I see is that you have not done enough to change what will be, or else it would not be as I see it. It is as simple as that. There is no cruelty involved, simply truth."

"Just what is it you expect me to do, Shota?"

"I don't know, Richard. But whatever it is, you are not doing it, now, are you? As we all slide into unimaginable horror, you are doing nothing to stop it. You are instead chasing phantoms."

Richard wanted to tell Shota a thousand things. He wanted to tell her that the Imperial Order was hardly the only threat bearing down on them. He wanted to tell her that with the boxes of Orden in play, if not stopped, the Sisters of the Dark would unleash power that would destroy the world of life and give everyone over to the Keeper of the Dead. He wanted to tell her that if they didn't find a way to reverse the Chainfire spell it could very well reap the destruction of everyone's memories and minds, robbing them of their means of survival. He wanted to tell her that if they didn't find a way to purge the world of the contamination left by the chimes, then all magic would be extinguished, and that contamination could very well have already engendered a cascade effect that, if not halted, had the potential, all by itself, to destroy all life.

He wanted to tell her that she didn't know the first thing about the woman he loved, the woman so dear to him. He wanted to tell her how much Kahlan meant to him, how afraid he was for her, how much he missed her, how his dread of what was being done to her kept him from being able to sleep.

He wanted to tell her that right then the Imperial Order was only one of their dire problems. But, seeing Jebra standing there trembling under the comforting shelter of Zedd's arm, he thought that there would be a better time to bring up all of those other matters.

Richard held out a hand, beckoning Jebra to come forward. Her sky blue eyes brimmed with tears. She finally, hesitantly, descended the steps toward him. He didn't know the specifics of the frightening things she had been through, but the strain of them was written all too clearly on her gaunt face. The lines there bore silent testimony to the hardships she had endured.

When she took his hand he gently covered it with his other in a small gesture of reassurance. "You've traveled a great distance and we value your help in our efforts. Please tell us what you know."

Her short sandy hair fell forward around her tear-stained face as she nodded. "I will do my best, Lord Rahl."

Under Shota's watchful eye, Richard led Jebra across the floor toward the fountain. He had her sit on the short marble wall containing the stilled water.

"You went with Queen Cyrilla back to her home," he prompted. "You were taking care of her because she was sick—driven insane by her time in the pit with all those terrible men. You were to help her to recover if she could and advise her if she did."

Jebra nodded.

"So . . . when she returned to her home did she begin to get better?" Richard asked, even though he knew that much of it from Kahlan.

"Yes. She was in a stupor for so long that we thought she would never get better, but after she was home for a while she finally did start to come round. At first she was only aware of those around her for brief periods. The more she recognized familiar surroundings, though, the longer those periods of clarity grew. Slowly, to everyone's joy, she seemed to come back to life. She eventually emerged from her long lethargy—like an animal coming out of hibernation. She seemed to shake off her long sleep and return to normal. She was full of energy, full of excitement to be home again."

"Queen Cyrilla was the queen of Galea," Shota said to Richard. "She inherited the crown, rather than—"

"Prince Harold," Richard finished as he looked up at the witch woman. "Cyrilla's brother was Harold. Harold declined the crown, preferring to lead the Galean army."

Shota arched an eyebrow. "You seem to know a lot about the monarchy of Galea."

"Their father was King Wyborn," Richard said. "King Wyborn was also Kahlan's father. Kahlan is half sister to Cyrilla. That is the reason I know so much about the monarchy of Galea."

If Shota was surprised to hear it, or if she didn't believe him because Kahlan was involved, she didn't betray either. She finally broke eye contact with him and went back to her pacing, allowing Jebra to continue her story.

"Cyrilla resumed her place on the thrown as if she had never left. The city seemed exhilarated to have her back. Galea had been struggling in its recovery from the horrifying time that the advance army of the Imperial Order had sacked the crown city. That attack had been a massive tragedy with tremendous loss of life.

"But with those invaders long gone the repairs of the destruction had been under way for quite some time. Even the burned buildings were being rebuilt. Businesses had started up again. Commerce had returned. People once again came to the city from all over Galea to make a better life for themselves. Families had begun to grow and knit together again. With hard work, prosperity had begun to return. With the queen back, it seemed to invigorate the spirit of the city all the more, and make the world seem right again.

"People said that lessons had been learned and such a tragedy would never happen again. To that end, new defenses were built, along with a much larger army. Cyrilla, like many of the people of Galea, put that appalling time behind her and was eager to be about the business of her land. She accepted audiences and kept her hand in many of the matters of state. She kept herself immersed in every sort of activity, from mediating trade disputes to attending formal balls where she danced with dignitaries.

"Prince Harold, being the head of the Galean army, kept her informed of the latest news about the invasion of the New World, so she was fully aware that the horde was pouring into the southern reaches of the Midlands. I always knew when she had received the latest reports; I would find her twisting her handkerchief, mumbling to herself, as she paced in a dark room without windows. It almost seemed to me that she was seeking the dark hiding place in her mind—the stupor she had been in before—but she couldn't find it, couldn't get back into it."

Jebra gestured briefly up the steps to the old man watching her speak. "Zedd told me to watch over her, to give her what advice I could. Even though she may have outwardly appeared to be her old self, and she didn't lapse back into the wooden daze, I could tell that she remained on the edge of insanity. My visions were unclear, probably because of that, because while she may have seemed normal again, she was still inwardly haunted by terrible fears. It was much like the land of Galea; things appeared normal but, with the Imperial Order in the New World, things were hardly normal. There was always a dark, underlying tension.

"When we heard from the scouts that the Order was moving up the

Callisidrin Valley, coming up the center of the Midlands intent on dividing the New World, I advised the queen that she must support the D'Haran army, that she must send the Galean army to fight with the rest of the forces of all the lands that had been joined together with the D'Haran Empire. I tried to tell her, as did Prince Harold, that our only chance at a real defense was in unity with the forces resisting the Order.

"She would not hear of it. She said that it was her duty as the queen of Galea to protect Galea alone, not other peoples or other lands. I tried to make her see that if Galea stood alone then it stood no chance. Cyrilla, though, had heard stories of other places that had been invaded, stories of the Order's ruthless brutality. She was terrified of the men of the Order. I told her that she would be safe only if we helped stop the invaders before they ever reached Galea.

"We received desperate requests for troops. Ignoring those requests, Cyrilla instead commanded Prince Harold to gather all the men he could into arms and that he use the army to protect Galea. She said that his duty, that the duty of the Galean army, was to Galea alone. She commanded that the invaders not be allowed to cross the borders, not be allowed to set foot on Galean soil.

"Prince Harold, who at first had tried to advise her of the wisest course of action, abandoned his own advice and in an act of pointless loyalty acceded to her wishes. She commanded that the defenses be set up to protect Galea at all costs. Prince Harold went to see to her instructions. She didn't care if the rest of the Midlands, or the entire New World for that matter, fell to the Order, as long as the Galean army—"

"Yes, yes." Shota impatiently rolled a hand as she paced before the woman. "We all know that Queen Cyrilla was loony. I didn't bring you all this way to describe life under a batty queen."

"Sorry." Ill at ease, Jebra cleared her throat and went on. "Well, Cyrilla grew impatient with me, with my insistent advice. She told me that her decision was final.

"With her determined commitment to a course of action, it finally fixed events, fixed our future and our fate. I think that for this reason I was at last beset with a powerful vision. It started not with the actual vision itself, but with a bloodcurdling sound that filled my mind. That terrible sound set me to trembling. With the frightening sound the visions came flooding forth, visions of the defenders being crushed and overrun, visions of the city falling, visions of Queen Cyrilla being given to the howling gangs of men to be . . . to be used as a whore and an object of amusement."

One hand held across her abdomen, her elbows tight against her sides, Jebra wiped tears back off one cheek. She briefly smiled up at Richard, a self-conscious smile that could not hold back the horror he could so clearly see in her eyes. "Of course," she said, "I'm not telling you all of the terrible things I saw in that vision. But I told her."

"I don't expect that it did any good," Richard said.

"No, it didn't." Jebra fidgeted with a strand of her hair. "Cyrilla was enraged. She summoned her royal guard. When they all rushed in through those double, tall blue and gilt doors she thrust a finger at me and proclaimed me a traitor. She ordered me thrown into a dungeon. The queen screamed orders to the guards as they were seizing me that if I spoke even one word of my visions—my blasphemy, as she called it—then they were to cut out my tongue."

A little laugh rattled out, a laugh incongruous with her trembling chin and wrinkled brow. Her words came out in a thin whine of apology. "I didn't want my tongue cut out."

Zedd, having made his way down the steps, laid a reassuring hand on the back of her shoulder. "Of course not, my dear, of course not. At that point it would have done you no good to have pressed the issue. No one would expect you to go beyond what you did; it would have served no purpose. You did your best; you showed her the truth. She made the conscious choice to be blind to it."

Fussing with her fingers, Jebra nodded. "I guess that her insanity never really left her."

"Those who are far from insane often act in an irrational manner. Don't excuse such conscious and deliberate actions with so convenient an explanation as insanity." When she gave him a puzzled look, Zedd opened his hands in a gesture of pained frustration at an old dilemma he had seen all too often. "All sorts of people who strongly want to believe in something are frequently unwilling to see the truth no matter how obvious it is. They make that choice."

"I guess so," Jebra said.

"Seems like, rather than heed the truth, she instead believed a lie that she wanted to believe," Richard said, remembering part of the Wizard's First Rule, the rule he had learned from his grandfather.

"That's right." Zedd swept an arm out in a grim parody of a wizard granting a wish. "She decided what she wished to happen and then assumed that reality would bend to her wishes." His arm dropped. "Reality doesn't indulge wishes."

"So Queen Cyrilla was angry with Jebra for speaking the truth aloud, for bringing it out where it could not be so easily overlooked and ignored," Cara said. "And then punished her for doing so."

Zedd nodded as his fingertips gently rubbed Jebra's shoulder. Her tired eyes had closed under his touch. "People who for whatever reason don't want to see the truth can be acutely hostile to it and shrill in their denunciation of it. They frequently turn their venomous antagonism on whoever dares point out that truth."

"That hardly makes the truth vanish," Richard said.

Zedd shrugged with the straightforward simplicity he saw in it. "To those seeking the truth, it's a matter of simple, rational self-interest to always keep reality in view. Truth is rooted in reality, after all, not the imagination."

Richard rested the heel of his hand on the hickory handle of the knife at his belt. He missed the sword being at hand, but he had traded it for information that eventually led him to the Chainfire book and the truth of what had happened to Kahlan, so it had been worth it. Still, he sorely missed the sword and worried over what Samuel might be using it for.

Thinking of the Sword of Truth, wondering where it was, Richard stared off at nothing in particular. "Seems hard to fathom how people can turn away from seeing what is in their own best interest."

"Doesn't it, though." Zedd's voice had changed from a tone of casual conversation to that thin, reedy tone that told Richard there was something more on his mind. "Therein lies the heart of it."

When Richard looked his way, Zedd's gaze focused intently on him. "Willfully turning aside from the truth is treason to one's self."

Shota, arms folded, paused in her pacing to lean toward Zedd. "A wizard's rule, wizard?"

Zedd arched an eyebrow. "The tenth, actually."

Shota turned a meaningful look on Richard. "Wise advice." After holding him in the grip of that iron gaze for an uncomfortably long time, she went back to her pacing.

Richard imagined that she thought he was ignoring the truth—the truth of the invading army of the Imperial Order. He wasn't in the least bit ignoring the truth, he just didn't know what more she expected he could do to stop them. If wishes worked he would already long ago have banished them back to the Old World. If he only knew what to do to stop them, he would do it, but he didn't. It was bad enough to know the horror that approached and feel helpless to stop it, but it infuriated him that Shota seemed to think he was simply being obstinate in not doing something about it—as if the solution was within his grasp.

He glanced up the steps at the statuesque woman watching him. Even in a pink nightdress she looked noble and wise. While Richard had been raised by people who encouraged him to deal with things the way they really were, she had been indoctrinated by people who were driven by the beliefs taught by the Order. It took a remarkable individual, after a lifetime of authoritarian teachings, to be willing to see the truth.

He gazed into her blue eyes for a long moment, wondering if he would have had her courage . . . the courage to grasp the nature and magnitude of the terrible mistakes she had made, the courage to then embrace the truth and change. Very few people had that kind of courage.

Richard wondered if she, too, thought that he was neglecting the invasion of the Imperial Order for irrational and selfish reasons. He wondered if she, too, thought that he was not doing something vital that would save innocent people from horrific suffering. He dearly hoped not. There were times when Nicci's support seemed like the only thing that gave him the strength to go on.

He wondered if she expected him to give up trying to find Kahlan in order to turn his full attention to trying to save a great many more lives than just that one, no matter how precious. Richard swallowed back the anguish; he knew that Kahlan herself would have made that demand. As much as she had loved him—back when she remembered who she was—Kahlan would not have wanted him to come after her if it meant that he would have to do so at the expense of trying to save so many more people who were in mortal danger.

The thought he had just had suddenly struck home: back when she knew who she was . . . who he was. Kahlan couldn't love him anymore if she didn't know who she was, if she didn't know who he was. His knees went weak.

"That's the way I saw it," Jebra said, opening her eyes and seeming to come awake as Zedd withdrew his comforting touch, "that I had done my best to show her the truth. But I didn't like being in that dungeon. Didn't like it one bit."

"So what happened then?" Zedd scratched the hollow of his cheek. "How long were you down in the dungeon?"

"I lost track of the days. There were no windows, so after a time I didn't even know if it was day or night. I didn't know when the seasons changed, but I knew that I had been there long enough for them to come and go. I began to lose hope.

"They fed me—never enough to be satisfied, but well enough to keep me alive. Every once in a great while they left a candle burning in the dingy central room beyond the iron door. The guards weren't deliberately cruel to me, but it was terrifying being locked away in the darkness of that tiny stone room. I knew better than to complain. When the other prisoners cursed or complained or raised a ruckus they were warned to be silent and, on occasion, when a prisoner didn't follow those orders, I could hear the guards carry out their threats. Sometimes the prisoners were there only a short time before being taken to their execution. From time to time new men were brought in. From what I could see as I peeked out the tiny window, the men they brought in were a violent and dangerous lot. Their vile oaths in the pitch black sometimes woke me and gave me nightmares when I fell back to sleep.

"The whole time I waited in dread of having a vision that would reveal to me my final fate, but such a vision never came. I hardly needed a vision, though, to know what the future held. I knew that as the invaders drew close, Cyrilla would likely come to think of it as my fault. I've had visions my whole life. People who don't like the things that happen to them often blame me for having told them what I saw. Rather than use that information to do something about it, it's easier for them to take out their displeasure on me. They often believed that I had caused their troubles by telling them what I had seen, as if what I saw was by my choice and brought to be through malice on my part.

"Being locked away in that dark cell was almost beyond endurance, but I could do nothing other than endure it. As I sat there endlessly, I could understand how being thrown in the pit had driven Cyrilla mad. At least I didn't have the brutes to contend with—those kind of men were locked in the other cells. As it was, I thought that I would surely die there, forsaken and forgotten. I lost track of how long I had been locked away from the world, from the light, from living.

"All the while I never had any more visions. I didn't know at the time that I would never have another.

"Once, the queen sent an emissary to ask if I would recant my vision. I told the man who came to see me that I would happily tell the queen any lie she wished to hear if she would only let me out. It must not have been what the queen wanted to hear because I never saw the emissary again and no one came to release me."

Richard glanced over to see Shota watching him. He could read in her eyes her silent accusation that he was doing that very thing—wanting her to tell him something other than what she saw was in store for the world. He felt a stab of guilt.

Jebra gazed up at the skylights high overhead, as if soaking up the simple wonder of light. "One night—I only later learned that up in the world it was night as well—a guard came to the tiny window in the iron door to my cramped little room. He whispered that Imperial Order troops approached the city. He told me that the battle was at last about to begin.

"He sounded almost cheered that the agony of waiting was finally over, that the reality of it relieved them all of having to pretend otherwise for their queen. It was as if knowing the truth of what was coming somehow made them faithless traitors, but that treason against the queen's wishes would now be transferred to reality. Still, that was only part of the queen's delusions, the part that was too obvious to avoid.

"I whispered back that I feared for the inhabitants of the city. He scoffed, said that I was daft, that I had not seen Galean soldiers fight. He professed confidence that the Galean army, a force of well in excess of one hundred thousand good men, would trounce the invaders and send them packing, just as the queen had said.

"I kept silent. I dared not contradict the queen's wishful illusions of their invincibility, dared not say that I knew that the massive numbers of Imperial Order troops I had seen in my vision would easily crush the defending army and that the city would fall. Locked in my cell as I was, I could not even run.

"And then I heard that strange, sinister sound from my vision. It ran shivers up my spine. My skin went cold with goose bumps. At last I knew what it was: it was the wail of thousands of enemy battle horns. It sounded like the howl of demons come up from the underworld to devour the living. Not even the thick stone walls could keep out that terrible, piercing sound. It was a sound announcing the approach of death, a sound that would have made the Keeper himself grin."

Jebra rubbed her shoulders, as if the mere memory of the shrill call of the battle horns had again given her goose bumps. She took a deep breath to regain her composure before she looked up at Richard and went on with her story.

"The guards all ran to the city's defenses, leaving the dungeon unguarded. Of course, the iron doors they locked behind themselves were more than enough to prevent anyone from escaping. After they were gone some of the prisoners let out cheers for the approaching Imperial Order, for the imminent fall of Galea, for what they believed would be their impending liberation. But soon they, too, went quiet as cries and screams swelled in the distance above us. Silence settled into the dark dungeons of the palace.

"Soon I began to hear the clash of arms, the collective cries of men in mortal combat, coming closer all the time. Along with the yells there were the awful shrieks of the injured. The shouts of soldiers grew louder as the defenders were driven back. And then, the enemy was in the palace. I'd lived in the palace for a time and I'd come to know so many of those people up there who were about to face . . ."

Jebra paused to wipe tears from her cheeks. "Sorry," she mumbled as she pulled a handkerchief from her sleeve and dabbed at her nose before clearing her throat and going on.

"I don't know how long the battle raged, but there came a time when I heard the booming sound of a battering ram bashing against the iron doors above. Each blow rang through the stone walls. When one door fell, the sounds came closer as the next door then came under assault until it, too, was breached.

"And then dozens of soldiers, all shouting battle cries, suddenly spilled down the stairs and into the dungeon. They brought torches with them, filling the room outside my cell with harsh light. They were probably looking for a treasure room, for plunder. Instead they found a filthy place of empty seclusion. They all rushed back up the stairs and left us to the dark, to quiet, heart-pounding fear.

"I thought that that was the last I would see of them, but it wasn't long before the soldiers returned. This time they brought screaming women back with them—some of the palace staff. Apparently the soldiers wanted to be alone with their fresh prizes, wanted to be away from all the other men who might steal them away or fight them for such valuable living plunder.

"The things I heard drove me to push myself back into the farthest corner of my cell, but that was no real withdrawal; I could still hear all of the ghastly business. I could not imagine the kind of men who would laugh and cheer at such terrible deeds as they were doing. Those poor women—they had no one at all to help them, and no hope of rescue.

"One of the younger women apparently broke from the man holding her and in a wild panic ran for the stairs. I heard voices yelling out for the others to grab her. She was quick and strong but the men easily caught her and threw her to the floor. When I heard her begging for her life, crying 'please no, please no,' I recognized her voice. While one man held her down, another put a boot on her knee and lifted her foot until I heard her knee pop. As she screamed in pain and terror, he did the same to the other leg. The men laughed, telling her that now that she wouldn't be running away again she could put her mind to her new duties. And then they started in on her. I have never in my life heard such frightful screams.

"I don't know how many men came down into the dungeon, but more and more arrived in turn. It went on for hour after hour. Some of the women wept and wailed the whole time they were being assaulted. Such carrying-on brought great gales of laughter from the men. But these were not men, they were monsters without conscience or restraint.

"One of the soldiers found a stash of keys and went around unlocking the cell doors. He laughed and hooted as he threw open the doors, declaring the liberation of the oppressed, and invited the prisoners to get in line to have their revenge on the wicked people who had persecuted and oppressed them. The girl whose knees they'd broken—Elizabeth was her name—had never oppressed anyone in her young life. She'd always smiled as she went about her work because she was so happy to have employment at the palace, and because she was infatuated with a young carpenter's apprentice who worked there as well. The prisoners poured out of their cells, only too eager to join in."

"Why didn't they pull you out?" Richard asked.

Jebra paused for a gulp of air before continuing. "When my cell door was thrown open I pressed myself up into the darkest corner in the back. There was no question as to what would happen to me if I went out, or if I was discovered. What with the screams of the women, the hollering, the laughter of the soldiers, and the scuffling over places in line, the men somehow didn't realize that I was hiding in the darkness at the back of my cell. There wasn't much light down in the dungeon. They must have thought the little room was empty, as some of the others were, for no one bothered to stick a torch in and have a look—after all, the rest of the prisoners were all men, all criminals, and all only too eager to come out. I'd never spoken to them, so they wouldn't have known that there was a woman down in the dungeon with them or they obviously would have come in after me. Besides, they were all . . . quite preoccupied."

Jebra's face, twisted in anguish, sank into her hands. "I could not begin to tell you what terrible things were being done to the women only a short distance from me. I will have nightmares about it for the rest of my life. Rape was only part of the purpose of those men. Their real lust was violence, a savage desire to degrade and hurt the helpless, to have the power of life and death over them.

"When the women stopped struggling, stopped screaming, stopped breathing, the men decided to go find themselves some food and drink to celebrate their victory, and then snatch some more women. Like best friends on a holiday, the men all took vows that they would not rest until there was not a woman left in the New World that they had not taken."

With both hands Jebra raked her hair back from her face. "After they all rushed off it fell still and quiet in the dungeon. I remained pressed to the back of my cell, the hem of my dress stuffed in my mouth, trying to keep from making a sound that would betray me as I shook and wept uncontrollably. My nostrils were filled with the terrible smell of blood and other things. Funny how after a time your nose has a way of becoming dulled to smells that at first made you sick.

"Still, I couldn't stop trembling—not after I hearing all the ghastly things that had been done to those women. I was terrified that I would be discovered and receive the same treatment. As I hid in the cell, afraid to come out, afraid to make a sound, I could understand how Cyrilla had gone mad under such mistreatment.

"All the time I could hear the sounds from above, the sounds of battle still raging, the sounds of pain and horror, the screams of the dying. I could smell oily smoke. It seemed like the battle, the killing, would go on forever. The women lying out beyond my open cell door, though, did not make any sound at all. I knew why. I knew that they were beyond any concerns of this world. I prayed that they were now in the tender comforting arms of the good spirits.

"I was exhausted from my constant state of fright, but I could not sleep—dared not sleep. The night wore on and eventually I saw light coming down the stairwell; the iron doors to the dungeon were no longer there to shut out the world above. Still, I dared not go out. I dared not move. I stayed where I was all day, until the room fell pitch black again with night. The rampage and looting above continued without abatement. What had begun as a battle had turned into a drunken celebration of victory. Dawn did not bring any quiet from above.

"I knew that I couldn't remain where I was; the stench of the dead women was becoming unbearable, as was the thought of being down there in the dark hole among the rotting corpses of people I knew. Yet such was my fear of what waited above that I stayed where I was that day and then again the entire night.

"I was so thirsty, so hungry, that I began to see goblets of water on the floor beside loaves of bread. I could smell the warm bread only a few feet away. But when I reached for them they were not there.

"I don't remember exactly when it was, but there came a time when I so ached for an end to the constant paralyzing dread that I came to accept and almost welcome my end. I knew all too well what was in store for me, but I reasoned that the agony of my terror would at last be over. I so wanted it to be over. I knew that I would have to endure suffering, humiliation, and pain, but I also knew that, just like the women who lay dead not far from me, it would eventually end and I would no longer have to suffer.

"So, I finally dared to step out of the darkness of my cell. The first thing I saw was Elizabeth's dead eyes staring right at me, as if she were looking over, waiting for me to emerge, so that I could see what had been done to her. Her expression seemed a silent plea for me to testify on behalf of justice. But there was no one to testify to, no justice to be had, just my silent witness of her forlorn end.

"The sight of her, along with the other women, drove me back in.

Seeing the nature of the tortures they had been subjected to, I was finally able to connect those atrocities with my memories of their screams. It set me to weeping uncontrollably. I cowered in terror, imagining myself subjected to such things.

"And then, overwhelmed by a fit of blind panic, I covered my nose with the hem of my dress against the terrible smell and ran through the tangle of twisted, naked limbs and bodies. I bolted up the stairs, not knowing what I was running toward, only knowing what I was running from. All the way as I ran I prayed for the mercy of a quick death.

"It was a shock to see the palace again. It had been a beautiful place, the painstaking renovations after the previous attack a few years back having only recently been completed. Now it was beyond being a wreck. It was impossible for me to understand why men would take the effort to break things the way they had, that they could find joy in such tedious acts of destruction. Grand doors were ripped off their hinges and broken to bits. Marble pillars had been toppled. Parts of shattered furniture lay scattered about. The floors were fairly covered with the litter of pieces of other once grand things: shards of beautifully glazed pottery; fragments of little ears and noses and tiny fingers from porcelain figurines; splintered wooden scraps showing a bit of a once carefully carved and gilded surface; flattened tables; art that had been torn to shreds or the faces in paintings ground threadbare under heavy boots. The windows were all broken out, drapes pulled down and trampled, statues defaced or broken, walls bashed in in places, covered with blood in others, elaborate rooms defecated in, the feces used to write vile words on the walls along with oaths of death to the Order's northern oppressors.

"Soldiers were everywhere, pawing through the residue left behind by yet other soldiers, picking over the dead, looting anything they could carry off, smashing elegant decorations out of sheer contempt, joking as they stood in lines outside rooms waiting their turn at the women captives. As I stumbled in a daze through the wreckage of the palace, I kept expecting to be grabbed and dragged off to one of those rooms. I knew that there was no avoiding my fate.

"I had never seen the likes of these men. These were men who inspired unbridled terror. Great, hulking, unwashed men in scarred and bloodstained leather armor. Most of them were covered in chains and belts and studded straps. Many had their heads shaved, making them look all the more muscled and menacing. Others glared out from beneath mats of long, tangled strands of greasy hair. They all looked savage and hardly human. Their faces were blackened with the grimy soot of fires and streaked through with sweat. Their language was loud, coarse, and boldly vile.

"Seeing such men stalking through the grand pastel pink or blue rooms seemed almost comical, but there was nothing amusing about the bloody axes at their belts, their swords greasy with gore, or the flails, knives, and iron-spiked cudgels hanging at hand around their waists.

"But it was their eyes that stopped you in your tracks. All had the kind of eyes that had not just become comfortable with the messy craft of butchery . . . but had taken a lustful liking to it. All looked upon every living thing they saw with a single evaluation: is this something to be killed? But their eyes had an even crueler cast when they took in any of the women captives being passed from hand to hand. That look was enough to stop a woman's breath, if not her heart.

"These were men who had abandoned any pretense at civilized manner. They did not bargain or barter the way normal men did. They took whatever they wanted, and even fought each other over the most insignificant plunder. They crushed and destroyed and killed on whim without consequence or conscience. These were men beyond the realm of civilized morality. These were savage brutes turned loose among the innocent."

Ⅰf there were soldiers everywhere, then why didn't they snatch you and drag you off?" Cara asked with the kind of casual yet pointed directness that only a Mord-Sith could so effortlessly muster, as if the very concept of propriety was beyond her.

The same question had occurred to Richard, but at that moment he had not been able to summon his voice.

"They thought she had been designated as a servant," Nicci said in a quiet, knowing voice. "Since she was walking around unmolested that long after the onset of the assault, the men would have assumed that there was a good reason, that those in command had reserved her for other duties."

Jebra nodded. "That's right. An officer who spotted me right off pulled me into a room with other men who were gathered around maps spread out over tables. The room hadn't been ruined as had most of the others. They demanded to know where their food was, as if I should know.

"They were just as ferocious-looking as the rest of the men and I would not have known at first that they were the officers except by the deference paid them by the other soldiers who came and went with reports. Some of these officers were a bit older and had an even harder edge to them, a more calculating look in their eyes, than the regular soldiers who always gave them a wide berth. When they looked at me I knew they were men who expected immediate answers.

"I grasped at that glimmer of hope—that I might live if I played along. I bowed with an apology and told them I would see to the food at once. They said that I had better, apparently more interested in eating than dealing out punishment. I rushed off to the kitchens, trying to act with a sense of purpose while being careful not to run for fear that the men would see a woman running and react like wolves to a fawn bolting from cover.

"There were several hundred others in the kitchens, mostly older men and women. Many of them I recognized, as they had long cooked for the palace. There were younger, stronger men there as well who were needed

to manage some of the work that was too heavy for the scullions or the el-
derly, work such as handling the carcasses for butchering or turning the
heavy spits. They were all working frantically among the roaring fires and
steaming pots as if their lives depended on it, which of course they did.

"When I entered the kitchens people hardly noticed me, as they were all
rushing about, preoccupied in various tasks. Seeing everyone was already
working at a fever pitch, I grabbed up a large platter of meats and offered
to take it back up to the men. The people in the kitchens were only too
happy to have someone else who was willing to go out among the soldiers.

"When I returned with the food the officers who had sent me abandoned what they had been doing. They appeared to be ravenously hungry.
They sprang up from the couches and chairs and used their bare, filthy
hands to snatch the meat off the tray. As I set the heavy tray on one of the
large tables, one of the men peered up at me as he chewed a mouthful. He
asked why I didn't have a ring in my lip. I didn't know what he was talking about."

"They put rings through the lower lips of slaves," Nicci said. "It marks
them as the property of men of rank and keeps the soldiers from taking
them as plunder. It gives those in command servants at their disposal for
menial work."

Jebra nodded. "The officer yelled orders. A man grabbed me and held
me while another came forward. He pulled my lower lip out and shoved an
iron ring through."

Nicci stared off into the distance. "They use iron as a reference to iron
kettles and such. An iron ring signifies kitchen workers and such."

Richard saw the glaze of suppressed rage in Nicci's blue eyes. She, too,
had once worn a ring through her lower lip, although hers had been gold to
denote that she was the personal property of Emperor Jagang. It was no
honor. Nicci had been used for things far worse than menial tasks.

"You're right about that," Jebra said. "After they put the ring in my lip I
was sent back to the kitchens to get them more food and wine. I realized
then that the other people in the kitchen wore iron rings as well. I was in a
numb daze as I ran back and forth to get the officers what they demanded.
I snuck a gulp of water or a mouthful of food whenever I could. It was
enough to save me from collapse.

"I found myself thrown in with other frightened people who worked at
the palace who were now taking orders from the officers. I hardly had

time to consider how I had by chance managed to escape a worse fate. As much as it throbbed and bled, I was glad to have that iron ring through my lip because when any soldier saw it he changed his mind about his intentions and let me be.

"Before long I was sent out with heavy satchels of food and drink for officers in other areas of the city. Out in the countryside surrounding the city I began to discover the true extent of the horror that had befallen Ebinissia."

When Jebra sank into a distant daze, Richard asked, "What did you see?"

She looked up at him, as if she had almost forgotten that she was telling her story, but then she swallowed back her anguish and went on. "Outside the city walls there were tens of thousands of dead from the battles. The ground for as far as the eye could see was covered with mangled corpses, many bunched in groups where they had died making their last stand. The sight seemed unreal, but I had already seen it before . . . in my vision.

"The worst of it, though, was that there were a number of Galean soldiers still alive, though grievously wounded. They lay here and there on the field of battle beside their dead brethren, wounded and unable to move. Some moaned softly as they lay near death. Others were more alert, but unable to move for one reason or another. One man was trapped, his legs crushed under the weight of a broken wagon. Another had been pinned to the ground by a spear through his gut. Even though in great pain, he wanted so desperately to live that he dared not pull himself off the shaft and release what it held in place. Others had legs or arms so badly broken that they were unable to crawl over the chaos of dead soldiers, horses, and rubble. With soldiers constantly patrolling, I knew that if I stopped to offer any comfort or aid to these wounded men I would be spotted and killed.

"As I made my way back and forth from the outposts I had to pass through this awful battlefield. The hills where this final engagement had taken place were dotted with hundreds of people slowly making their way among the dead, methodically picking through their belongings. I later learned that they were a small army of people who trailed behind the Imperial Order troops—camp followers—living off the scraps that the Order soldiers left in their wake. These human vultures pawed through the dead soldiers' pockets and such, making their living on death and destruction.

"I recall one older woman in a dingy white shawl coming upon a

Galean soldier who was still alive. Among other wounds, his leg had been gashed open to the bone. His hands trembled with the endless, solitary effort of holding the massive wound closed. It seemed a miracle that he was even still alive.

"As the old woman in the shawl pulled at his clothes, looking for anything valuable, he begged her for a sip of water. She ignored him as she tore open his shirt to see if he had a neck chain with a purse, as some soldiers did. In a weak, hoarse voice he again pleaded for a sip of water. She instead pulled a long knitting needle from her belt and, as he lay helpless, shoved it in the man's ear. Her tongue poked out of the corner of her mouth with the effort of twisting the long metal needle around inside his brains. His arms flinched and then went still. She drew the length of her knitting needle back out and wiped it off on his pant leg as she muttered a complaint that that would keep him quiet. She replaced her knitting needle in her belt and went back to rifling through his clothes. It struck me how well practiced she had seemed at the grisly task.

"I saw other camp followers use a rock to bash in the head of any man they found alive just to be certain he wouldn't surprise them by striking out when they were busy hunting for any loot. Some of these scavengers didn't bother to do anything to the wounded man unless he could still use his hands and tried to fend them off; if he was alive, but unable to resist, they merely helped themselves to what they could find and then moved on. But there were people who lifted a fist in the air and shouted in triumph whenever they found a fallen soldier still alive, one they could dispatch, as if doing so made them a hero. Occasionally there were those who came upon the helpless wounded and enjoyed torturing them in the most ghastly manner, amused by the fact that the men could neither run nor fight them off. It was only a matter of a few more days, though, before all the wounded survivors were dead, either from succumbing to their wounds, or finally being dispatched by the camp followers.

"Over the next few weeks the Imperial Order soldiers celebrated their great victory with an orgy of violence, rape, and plundering. Every building was broken into and thoroughly searched. Anything of value was looted. Other than the small numbers of the people like me who had been designated as servants, no male escaped capture and no woman escaped the clutches of those vile men."

Jebra wept over her words. "No young woman should ever have to

endure what was done to those poor creatures. The captured Galean soldiers as well as the men and boys of the city were well aware of what was
happening to their mothers, wives, sisters, and daughters—the Order
troops saw to that. Several times, small groups of the captives who could
no longer bear it rose up to try to stop the abuse. They were slaughtered.

"Before long the captives were sent in great gangs to dig seemingly
endless pits for the dead. When they had finished digging the pits they
were forced to recover all the rotting bodies for mass burial. Those who
resisted ended up in the pits as well.

"Once all the dead had been collected and thrown into the pits, the men
then had to to dig long trenches. After that, the executions began. Nearly
every male over the age of fifteen was to be put to death. There were tens
of thousands of people who had been caught up in the Order's net. I knew
that it would take weeks to butcher them all.

"The women and the children were forced at swordpoint to watch their
menfolk being put to death and thrown in the great open pits. While they
watched, they were informed that this was an example of what happened
to those who resisted the just and moral law of the Imperial Order. They
were lectured throughout the endless executions, lectured on how it was
blasphemy against the Creator to live as they had been living, solely for
their own selfish ends. They were told that mankind had to be purged of
such corruption and would be better for it.

"Some of the men were beheaded. Some were made to kneel before the
pits and then brawny men with iron-capped cudgels walked down the line
and with a powerful swing bashed in the heads of each man in turn while
a couple of captives in chains followed behind, throwing each freshly
killed man in the trench. Some of the prisoners were used for target
practice with arrows, or spears. Fellow soldiers laughed and mocked the
drunken executioner if his sloppy aim failed to achieve a clean kill. It was
a game to them.

"I think, though, that the sheer magnitude of the grisly business brought
a somber mood over some of the Imperial Order soldiers and they turned
to drinking as a way of masking their revulsion so that they could join in,
as was expected of them. It's one thing to kill in the heat of combat, after
all, but quite another to kill in cold blood. But kill in cold blood they did.
As the victims fell into the trenches they were covered over with dirt by
those who would soon join them.

"I recall one rainy day when I had to bring food to officers standing under the shelter of what once had been a canvas awning over a shop, now held up with lances. They were there to watch an execution that was being put on as an elaborate spectacle. The terrified women who were to witness the death sentences being carried out were brought straight from the rape rooms by their captors. Many of the women were still only half dressed.

"By the many sudden cries of recognition and names shouted out, it soon became obvious to me that the Order interrogations had identified the husbands of the women and had singled them out. The couples were being brought together in a macabre reunion, separated but in full view of one another.

"The women, huddled together and helpless, were made to watch as the wrists of their men were tightly bound behind their backs with leather thongs. The men were forced to kneel near the fresh pits, facing the women. Soldiers came down the line and in turn held each man's head up by his hair, then sliced open his throat. I remember the executioners' powerful muscles glistening in the rain. Holding their victims by the hair, after cutting his throat, they heaved each body back into the pits before going on to the next man in line.

"The men waiting to be slain wept and trembled as they cried out the names of their beloved, cried out their undying love. The women did likewise as they watched their men murdered and then thrown in on piles of other men still thrashing and gasping in the throes of death. It was as horrific, as wrenchingly sorrowful, as anything I have ever seen.

"As they saw their loved ones killed, many of the women fainted, collapsing to the muddy ground covered in vomit. As the steady rain fell, others, in wild terror, screamed the names of the man they saw about to be put to death. They struggled against the iron grip of guards who laughed as they dragged the women away in turn, shouting out the details of their intentions to her husband who was about to die. It was a twisted kind of cruelty that inflicted suffering on a scale that I could not begin to adequately convey.

"Families were not only being torn apart forever, but being wiped out. Did you ever hear that old question: How do you think the world will end? This was how. This was the world ending for thousands upon thousands of people . . . only it was ending one person at a time. It was one long drawn out withering of lives, the final ending of each individual's world."

Richard gripped his temples between the thumb and fingers of one hand so hard that he thought he might crush his own skull. With great difficulty he managed to control his breathing and his voice. "Didn't anyone manage to escape?" he asked into the ringing silence. "During all of these various rapes and executions and all, didn't anyone escape?"

Jebra nodded. "Yes. I believe that a few made it out but, of course, I had no real way to know for sure."

"There were enough who escaped," Nicci said in a quiet voice.

"Enough?" Richard shouted as he turned his fury on her. He caught the flash of rage that had slipped through his control and brought his voice back down. "Enough for what?"

"Enough for their purpose," Nicci said, gazing into his eyes, solemnly enduring what she saw there. "The Order knows that there are people who escape. During the height of the brutality, the worst of the horrors, they deliberately relax security so as to be sure that a few, at least, will escape."

Richard's mind felt as if it were hopelessly adrift in a thousand scattered, disheartened thoughts. "Why?"

Nicci shared a long look with him before she finally answered. "To spread such a fear that it will grip the next city in terror. That terror will insure that people in the path of the advancing army will surrender rather than face the same brutal treatment. In this way victory comes without the Order having to fight every inch of the way. The terror that is spread by escaping people who tell others what they saw is a powerful weapon that crumbles the courage of those yet to be attacked."

With the way his heart was pounding, Richard could understand the terror of waiting for the Order to attack. He raked his fingers back through his hair as he redirected his attention to Jebra. "Did they murder all the captives?"

"A few of the men—ones who were deemed not a threat for one reason or another—were sent with other people from the city out into the countryside in gangs to work the farms. I never knew what happened to these people, but I presume that they are still there, toiling as slaves to raise food for the Order."

Jebra's gaze sank as she pulled some strands of hair back from her face. "Most of the women who survived became the property of the troops. Some of the younger and more attractive women had a copper ring put through their lower lips and were reserved for the men of rank.

Carts frequently prowled the camp, collecting the bodies of women who had died during their abuse. No officer ever raised any objection to the brutal treatment these women received out in the tents among the troops. The dead were taken to the pits and thrown in. No one, not even Imperial Order soldiers who died, were ever buried with their name on a marker. They were all thrown in the mass graves. The Order does not believe in the significance of any individual and does not mark their passing."

"What of the children?" Richard asked. "You said that they didn't kill the younger boys."

Jebra took a deep breath before she began again. "Well, from the very first, the boys had been gathered together and organized by age into groups of what I can only describe as boy recruits. They were regarded, not as captured Galeans, not as the conquered, but as young members of the Imperial Order liberated from people who would only have oppressed them and corrupted their minds. The blame for the wickedness that necessitated the invasion was placed on the older generations, not these young people who were said to be innocent of their elders' sins. Thus they were separated, physically and spiritually, from the adults, and thus was begun their training.

"The boys were drilled in a manner that was like playing games, grim as it must have been to many. They were treated relatively well and kept occupied every moment in contests of strength and skill. They were not allowed to pine for their families—that was described as showing weakness. The Order became their families, whether they liked it or not.

"At night, while I could hear the cries of women, I could also hear the boys as they sang together, under the leadership of special training officers." She gestured as an aside. "I had to bring these officers food and such, so I had a chance to see what was happening to these boys as the weeks and then the months passed.

"After training for a time the boys began to earn rank and standing within their group for a variety of things—whether it be in games of skill and strength, or in memorizing their lessons in the righteous ways of the Order. As I would rush about in my duties for the officers I would see the boys standing at attention before their groups, reciting back the things they had been taught, speaking of the glory of being part of the Order, of their honorable duty to be part of a new world dedicated to the advancement of mankind, and of their willingness to sacrifice for that greater good.

"Even though I never really had the chance to learn the specifics of what these boys were being taught, I remember a line shouted incessantly as they stood at attention: 'I can be nothing alone. My life has meaning only through dedication to others. Together we all are one, of one mind, for one purpose.'

"After emotionally charged rallies the boys were brought in their groups to watch executions of 'traitors to mankind.' They were encouraged to cheer when each 'traitor' died. Their Order leaders stood proud and tall before the boys, backs to the bloodbath, saying, 'Be strong young heroes. This is what happens to the selfish betrayers of mankind. You are mankind's future saviors. You are the future heroes of the Order, so be strong.'

"Whatever trepidation the boys may have had at first, under the long and ceaseless indoctrination, guidance, and constant encouragement of the officers, those boys cheered. Even if it was not sincere at first, it seemed to become so in the end. I saw how the boys began to believe—with real fervor—the things they were being taught by adults.

"The boys were encouraged to use knives issued them to stab the freshly killed 'traitors.' This was only one of the ways they were systematically desensitized to death. In the end, the boys were earning rank by participating in the executions. They stood before empty-eyed captives and lectured them on their selfish ways, their treason to their fellow man and the Creator. The boy then condemned that individual captive to death and on occasion even carried out the deed. Their fellows applauded their zeal for helping to purge mankind of those who had resisted the holy teachings of the Order, those who had turned away from their Creator and their divine duty of service to their fellow man.

"Before it was over, almost every one of those boys had a hand in the butchering of the captives. They were praised as 'heroes' of the Order. At night, in their barracks, the few boys who would not go along with participating in the executions became outcasts and were eventually stigmatized as cowards or even sympathizers of the old ways, for being selfish and unwilling to support their fellow man—or, in this case, boy. They were most often beaten to death by their group.

"These few boys, in my eyes, were the heroes. They died alone at the hands of their fellow boys, boys who had once played and laughed with them but had now become the enemy. I would have given nearly anything to have been able to give these few noble souls at least a hug and a whisper of my thanks that they had not joined in, but I could not, so they died alone as outcasts among former friends.

"It was madness. It seemed to me that the whole world had gone insane, that nothing made sense anymore, that life itself made no sense anymore. Pain and suffering became the definition of life; there was nothing else. Memories of any kind of joy seemed like dim dreams and no longer real. Life dragged on, day after day, season after season, but it was life that revolved around death in one way or another.

"In the end, the only people of Galea left alive were the boys and the women who didn't die during the brutal rapes and then as whores for the soldiers. In the end, the older boys were participating in the rapes as part of their initiation and as rewards for their enthusiasm during their assignments, including the executions.

"Many of the women, of course, managed to kill themselves. Every morning, on the cobblestone streets at the foot of the taller buildings, were found the broken bodies of women who, seeing no future but degrading abuse, had managed to throw themselves out of windows or off roofs. I don't know how many times I would happen on a woman off in some dark corner, her wrists slashed by her own hand, her lifeblood having drained away along with any hope. I couldn't say that I blamed them for their choice."

Richard stood with his hands clasped behind his back, staring into the still waters of the fountain, as Jebra went on in endless detail of the events following the great victory by the brave men of the Imperial Order. The senselessness of it was almost too monumental to comprehend, much less endure.

The slashes of sunlight coming in through the skylights above slowly crept across the marble bench around the pool, across the expanse of floor, up and across the granite steps. The bloodred stone of the columns glowed as the sunlight ceaselessly, incrementally, advanced up their length while Jebra chronicled everything she knew of what had happened while she had been a captive of the Order.

Shota stood unmoving nearly the entire time, usually with her arms folded, her fair features fixed in a vaguely grim cast, watching Jebra tell her story, or watching Richard listen to it, as if making sure that his attention didn't wander.

"Galea had reserves of food aplenty for their citizens," Jebra said, "but not for anything like the numbers of invaders now occupying the city, who themselves did not have plentiful supplies with them. The troops stripped every storehouse of food. They emptied every larder, every warehouse. Every animal for miles around, including the great many sheep that were raised for wool and the milk cows, were butchered for food. Rather than keep the chickens for a steady supply of eggs, they, too, were killed and eaten.

"As the food ran low the officers sent off messengers with ever more urgent requests for resupply. For months the supplies did not come—no doubt in good part because winter had set in and slowed them."

Jebra hesitated, and then swallowed, before going on. "I remember the day—it was during a heavy snowstorm—when we were ordered to cook some fresh meat the Imperial Order soldiers delivered to the kitchens. It was freshly killed, headless, gutted human carcasses."

Richard abruptly turned to stare at Jebra. She gazed up at him as if from a place of insanity, as if in fear that she would be condemned for what she knew was beyond the pale. Her blue eyes brimmed with tears of supplication for forgiveness, as if she feared he would strike her dead for what she was about to confess.

"Have you ever had to butcher a human body for cooking? We had to. We roasted the meat, or stripped it from the bones to make stews. We dried rack upon rack upon rack of the meat for the regular soldiers. If the soldiers were hungry and there was nothing to feed them, bodies would be delivered to the kitchens. We went to extraordinary lengths to stretch what supplies of food we had. We made soups and stews with weeds, if we could find them beneath the snow. But there was just not enough food to feed all the men.

"I witnessed many things that will give me nightmares the rest of my life. Seeing those remorseless soldiers standing in the open doorway, the snow blowing in behind them, as they dumped those bodies on the floor of the kitchen will be one of the things that forever haunts me."

Richard nodded and whispered, "I understand."

"And then, early this past spring, the supply wagons finally began arriving. They brought great quantities of foodstuffs for the soldiers. I knew, despite the seemingly endless wagons full of supplies, that it would not last a long time.

"Beside the supplies, there were also reinforcements to replace the men who had been killed in the battle to crush Galea. The numbers of Order troops occupying Ebinissia were already overwhelming; the extra soldiers seemed to add to my numb sense of hopelessness.

"I overheard newly arrived officers reporting that more supplies would be coming, along with yet more men. As they streamed in from the south, many were sent on missions to secure other areas of the Midlands. There were other cities to be taken, other places to be captured, other pockets of resistance to be crushed, other people to be enslaved.

"Along with the supplies and the fresh troops came letters from the people back home in the Old World. They were not letters to any specific soldiers, of course, since the Imperial Order had no way of knowing how to find any individual soldier within their vast armies, nor would they have cared to, since individuals, as such, were unimportant in their eyes. Rather, they were letters sent to the general delivery of the 'brave men' fighting for the people back home, fighting on behalf of their Creator, fighting to defeat the heathens to the north, fighting to bring backward-thinking people the salvation of the Order's ways.

"At night, every night for weeks, the letters that had come with the supply wagons would be read to assembled groups of men—most of whom couldn't read themselves. They were letters of every kind, from people telling of the great sacrifices they had made in order to send food and goods north to their fighting men, to letters extolling the great sacrifices the soldiers were making to advance the divine teaching of the Order, to letters from young women promising their bodies in service to brave soldiers when they returned from vanquishing the uncivilized and backward enemy to the north. As you can imagine, this last kind of letter was quite popular and they were read over and over to hoots and wild cheering.

"The people of the Old World even sent mementos: talismans to bring victory; drawings to decorate the tents of their fighters; cookies and cakes that had long ago rotted; socks, mittens, shirts, and caps; herbs for everything from tea to bandages; scented handkerchiefs from enraptured women eager to offer themselves in duty to the soldiers; weapons belts and such made by the corps of young boys who trained with groups of other boys their own age until the day they could also go north to smite the people who resisted the Creator's wisdom and the Imperial Order's justice.

"The long trains of supply wagons, before they went back to the Old World to get more of the supplies necessary to support the enormous army up in the New World, were loaded down with loot to be taken back to the cities of the Old World that were supplying the food and goods needed by the army. It was like a loop of trade—booty for supplies, supplies for booty. I suppose that seeing endless wagonloads of plundered riches streaming south was also intended to be a great incentive for the people back home to continue to support what has to be the enormous cost of the war effort.

"The army that had invaded was far too large to fit in the city, of course, and with the reinforcements arriving with each train of supply wagons the endless sea of tents spread even farther out into the countryside, blanketing the hills and valleys all around. The trees for a goodly distance had all been stripped and used for firewood throughout the previous winter, leaving the landscape around the crown city looking lifeless and dead. The new grasses never grew beneath the teeming masses of men, the countless horses, and variety of wagons, so that it seemed that Galea had been turned to a sea of mud.

"From new units just arrived, men coming up from the Old World were formed into strike forces that were sent to attack other places, to spread the rule of the Imperial Order, to establish dominion. It seemed that there was an endless supply of men to enslave the New World.

"I was working to exhaustion feeding all the officers, so I was frequently around the command personnel and often overheard invasion plans and reports of cities that had fallen, tallies of prisoners taken, accounts of the numbers of slaves sent back to the Old World. On occasion some of the more attractive women were brought back for the use of the men of rank. The eyes of these women were wild with fear of what was to become of them. I knew that their eyes would soon enough become dull with longing for the release of death. It all seemed to me one endless attack, one long endless savagery that showed no signs of ever ending.

"The city by then, of course, had been all but emptied of the people who once had called it home. Almost every male over fifteen had long ago been put to death and the handful who hadn't had been sent off as slave labor. Many of the women—the ones too old or too young to be of use to the Order—had been put to death if they were in the way, but many had simply been left to starve to death. They lived like rats in the dark crevices of the city. Last winter I saw droves of old women and little girls who looked like skeletons covered in a pale veneer of flesh begging for scraps of food. It broke my heart, but to feed them would only end in execution for them and for me. Still, if I could get away with it, I sometimes slipped them food—if there was any to be had.

"In the end it was as if the population of Galea's crown city, hundreds of thousands of people, had for the most part been wiped from existence. What was once the heart of Galea is no more. It is now occupied by soldiers in the hundreds of thousands. The camp followers began setting up homes in the places long since plundered, simply taking over what was someone else's. More people from the Old World began to drift up to take places and live in them as their own.

"The only Galean women left alive were for the most part slaves used by the soldiers as whores. After time many became pregnant and gave birth to children fathered by the soldiers of the Imperial Order. These offspring are being raised to be future zealots for the Order. Virtually the only Galean children left alive after the first year of occupation were the boys.

"Drilled endlessly in the ways of the Order, those boys became the Order. They had long since forgotten the ways of their parents or their homeland, or even common decency. They were now Imperial Order recruits—newly minted monsters.

"After months and months of training, groups of the older boys were sent to be the first wave of attackers against other cities. They were to be the flesh that dulled the swords of the heathens. They went eagerly.

"I had once thought that the brutes who are the Imperial Order were a distinctly different, savage breed of people, unlike the civilized people of the New World. After seeing how those boys changed and what they became, I realized that the people who are the Order are really no different than the rest of us, except in their beliefs and the ideas that motivate them. A crazy thought, perhaps, but it seems that through some mysterious mechanism anyone is susceptible to being beguiled into falling for the Order's ways."

Jebra shook her head in dismay. "I never really understood how such a thing could come about, how the officers could teach boys such dry lessons, how they could lecture them that they must be selfless, that they must live a life of sacrifice for the good of others, and then, as if by magic, those boys would march off merrily singing songs, hoping to die in battle."

"The premise is pretty simple, really," Nicci said, offhandedly.

"Simple?" Jebra's brow lifted with incredulity. "You can't be serious."

Oh yes, simple." Nicci descended the steps one at a time in a slow, measured manner as she spoke. "Both boys and girls in the Old World are taught the same things by the Fellowship of Order, and in the same basic manner."

She came to a halt not far from Richard and loosely folded her arms as she sighed—not out of weariness, but rather with a weary cynicism. "Except that with them it's started not all that long after they're born. It begins with simple lessons, of course, but those lessons are expanded and reinforced over their entire lifetime. It's not unusual to see pious old people sitting through the lectures given by brothers of the Fellowship of Order.

"Most all people are drawn toward ordered social structure and they yearn to know how they fit into the larger scheme of the universe. The Fellowship of Order provides them with a comprehensive and authoritative sense of structure—in other words, tells them the right way to think as well as a proper way to live their lives. But it's most effective when started with the young. If a young mind is molded to the Order's dogma then it usually becomes inflexible and fixed for life. As a result, any other way of thinking—the very ability to reason—generally withers and dies at a young age and is lost for life. When such a person is aged, they will still sit through the same basic lessons, still hang on every word."

"Simple?" Jebra asked. "You said the premise is pretty simple?"

Nicci nodded. "The Order teaches that this world, the world of life, is finite. Life is fleeting. We are born, we live for a time, and we die. The afterlife, by contrast, is eternal. After all, we all know that people die but no one ever comes back from the dead; dead is forever. Therefore, it is the afterlife which is important.

"Around this core tenet, the Fellowship of Order ceaselessly drums into people the belief that one must earn their eternity in the glory of the

Creator's light. This life is the means to earn that eternity—a test, in a way."

Jebra blinked in disbelief. "But still, life is . . . I don't know, it's life. How can anything be more important than your own life?" She softened her skepticism with a smile. "Surely that isn't going to convince people to the Order's brutal ways, convince them to turn away from life."

"Life?" With sudden menace in her glare, Nicci leaned down a little to-ward Jebra. "Don't you care about your soul? Don't you think that what happens to your very own soul for all eternity might be of serious and earnest concern to you?"

"Well, of course I, I . . ." Jebra fell mute.

As she straightened, Nicci shrugged with a mocking, dismissive ges-ture. "This life is finite, transitory, so, in the scheme of things, in contrast to an eternal afterlife, how important can a fleeting life in this miserable world be? What true purpose could this brief existence possibly have, other than to serve as a trial of the soul?"

Jebra looked uncomfortably dubious yet unwilling to challenge Nicci when she framed it in such a way.

"For that reason," Nicci said, "sacrifice to any suffering, any want, any need of your fellow man is a humble recognition that this life is meaning-less, a demonstration that you acknowledge eternity with the Creator in the next world to be the consequential concern. Yes? By sacrificing you are avowing that you do not value man's realm over eternity, the Creator's realm. Therefore, sacrifice is the price, the small price, the pittance, that you pay for your soul's eternal glory. It's your proof to the Creator that you are worthy of that eternity with Him."

Richard was amazed to see how easily such a rationale—delivered by Nicci with confidence, command, and authority—intimidated Jebra into silence. While listening as Nicci towered over her, Jebra had occasionally glanced to the others, to Zedd, to Cara, to Shota, even to Ann and Nathan, but seeing none of them offering any objection or counterarguments, her shoulders began to hunch as if she wished she could disappear into a crack in the marble floor.

"If you confine your concerns to being happy in this life"—Nicci casu-ally swept an arm out, indicating the world around her as she glided re-gally back and forth before them—"if you dare to revel in the senseless trivialities of this wretched world, this meaningless, brief existence, that is a rejection of your all-important eternal next life, and thus a rejection of the Creator's perfect plan for your soul.

"Who are you to question the Creator of all the universe? How dare you put your petty wishes for your insignificant, pathetic little life ahead of His grand purpose of preparing you for all of eternity?"

Nicci paused, folding her arms with a kind of deliberate care that implied a challenge. A lifetime of indoctrination gave her the ability to express the Order's carefully crafted tenets with devastating precision. Seeing her standing there in her pink nightdress somehow only seemed to underscore her derision of the triviality of life. Richard remembered all too well Nicci delivering that very same message to him, only at the time she had been deadly serious. Jebra avoided Nicci's piercing gaze, instead fixing her stare on her hands nested in her lap.

"To bring the ways of the Order to other people, Galea for example," Nicci said as she resumed her pacing lecture, "many of the Order's soldiers had to die." She shrugged. "But that is the ultimate sacrifice—one's life—in an effort to bring enlightenment to those who do not yet know how to follow the only right and true path to glory in the next world. If a person sacrifices their life in the struggle on behalf of the Order to bring salvation to backward, ignorant, and unimportant people, then they earn eternity with Him in the next world."

Nicci lifted an arm, sheathed in the satiny, pink material of the nightdress, as if to reveal something magnificent but invisible standing right there before them. "Death is merely the doorway to that glorious eternity."

She let the arm drop. "Because an individual life is unimportant in the scheme of things that really matter, it's obvious that by torturing and killing individuals who resist, you are only helping to sway the masses of the unenlightened over to enlightenment—so you are bringing those masses salvation, serving a moral cause, bringing the Creator's children home to His kingdom."

Nicci's expression turned as grim as her pretense had been. "People who are taught this from birth come to believe it with such blind zeal that they see anyone living in any manner other than according to the Order's teachings—in other words failing to pay the rightful price of sacrifice in return for eternal salvation—as deserving of an eternity of unimaginable agony in the dark cold depths of the Keeper's realm of the underworld, which is exactly what awaits them unless they change their ways.

"Very few people who grow up under this indoctrination have enough of their reasoning ability still intact to be able to think their way out of this bewitching circular trap—nor do they want to. To them, to rejoice in life, to live for themselves, is trading eternity for a brief and sinful frolic before a looming doom-without-end.

"Since they must forgo the enjoyment of this life, they are going to be only too quick to notice anyone who fails to sacrifice as they should, fails to live by the canons of the Fellowship of Order. Besides, recognition of sinfulness in others is deemed a virtue because it helps to direct those who neglect their moral duty to turn back to the path of salvation."

Nicci leaned down toward Jebra and lowered her voice to a sinister hiss. "Much the same as killing nonbelievers is a virtue. Yes?"

Nicci straightened. "Followers of the Order develop an intense hatred for those who do not believe as they do. After all, the Order teaches that wicked sinners who refuse to repent are no less than Keeper's disciples. Death is no more than such enemies of the righteous deserve."

Nicci spread her arms in a forbidding gesture. "There can be no doubt about any of this since the Order's teachings are, after all, merely the wishes of the Creator Himself, and thus divinely elicited truth."

Jebra was now clearly too cowed to offer an argument.

Cara, on the other had, was clearly not cowed. "Oh, really?" she said in an even, but contrary, tone. "I'm afraid that there's one fly in the ointment. How do they know all this? I mean, how do they know that the afterlife is really anything at all like they portray it?"

She clasped her hands behind her back as she shrugged. "As far as I know, they haven't visited the world of the dead and then returned. How would they know what it's like beyond the veil?

"Our world is the world of life, so life is what's important in this world. How dare they demean it by making our only life the price for something unknowable? How can they begin to claim that they know anything at all about the nature of other worlds? I mean, for all anyone really knows, the spirit world could be a mere transitory state as we slip into the nonexistence of death.

"For that matter, how would the Fellowship of Order know that these are the Creator's wishes—or that He has any wishes at all?" Cara's brow drew down. "How do they even know that Creation was brought about by a conscious mind in the form of some divine breed of king?"

Jebra looked relieved that someone else had finally objected.

Nicci smiled in a curious manner and raised an eyebrow. "There's the trick of it."

Without looking over, she lifted her arm back toward Ann, standing across the room in the shadows. "It's the same method by which the Prelate and her Sisters of the Light know their version of the same gruel to be true. Prophecy, or the high priests, or some humble but deeply devout person has heard the intimate whispers of the divine, or has seen into a sacred vision He has sent them, or has been visited in dreams. There are even ancient texts that profess to have infallible knowledge of what is beyond the veil. Such lore is mostly a collection of the same kind of whispers and visions and dreams that in the distant past were set down as fact and have become 'irrefutable' simply because it is old.

"And how are we to verify the veracity of this testimony?" Nicci swept her arm out in a grand gesture. "Why, to question such things is the greatest sin of all: lack of faith!

"The very fact that the unknowable *is* unknowable is what they claim gives faith its virtue and makes it sacrosanct. After all, what would be the virtue in faith if that in which we have faith could be known? A person who can maintain absolute faith without any proof whatsoever must possess profound virtue. As a consequence, only those who take the leap of faith off the bedrock of the tangible into the emptiness of the imperceptible are righteous and worthy of an eternal reward.

"It's as if you are told to leap from a cliff and have faith that you can fly, but you must not flap your arms because that would only betray a fundamental lack of faith and any lack of faith would infallibly insure that you would plummet to the ground, thus proving that a failure of faith is a personal flaw, and fatal."

Nicci ran her fingers back into her blond hair, lifting it off her shoulders, and then, with a sigh, she let her arms drop. "The more difficult the teachings are to believe, the greater the required level of faith. Along with the commitment to a higher level of unquestioning faith comes a tighter bond to those who share that same faith, a greater sense of inclusion in the special group of the enlightened. Believers, because their beliefs are so manifestly mystic, become ever more estranged from the 'unenlightened,' from those who are suspect because they will not embrace faith. The term 'nonbeliever' becomes a commonly accepted form of condemnation, demonizing anyone who chooses"—Nicci tapped a finger to her temple—"to stick to the use of reason.

"Faith itself, you see, is the key—the magic wand that they wave over the bubbling brew they have concocted to render it 'self-evident.'"

Ann, despite the glare of contempt for a Sister of the Light-turned-traitor-to-the-cause, offered no argument. Richard thought it a rare choice on her part, and one that at that moment was particularly wise.

"There," Nicci said, shaking a finger as she paced, barefoot, "there is the crack in the Order's imposing tower of teachings. There is the fatal flaw at the center of all convictions contrived in the imagination of men. Such things in the end, even though they may be sincere, are nothing more solid than the elaborate product of whimsy and self-deception. In the end, without the rock of reality, an insane person who hears voices in their head is equally sincere and equally credible.

"That is why the Order vaunts the sanctity of faith and teaches that you must dismiss the wicked impulse to use your head, that you must instead abandon yourself to your feelings. Once you surrender your life to blind faith in their account of the afterlife, they claim that then, and only then, the doorway to eternity will magically open for you and you will know all.

"In other words, knowledge is to be gained only through rejection of everything that actually comprises knowledge.

"This is why the Order equates faith with holiness, and why its absence is deemed to be sinful. This is why even questioning faith is heretical.

"Without faith, you see, everything they teach unravels.

"And since faith is the indispensable glue that binds together their tee-tering tower of beliefs, faith eventually gives birth to brutality. Without brutality to enforce it, faith ends up being nothing more than a fanciful daydream, or a queen's empty belief that no one will attack her throne, that no enemy will breach the borders, that no force can overthrow her de-fenders, if she merely forbids it.

"After all, I don't need to threaten you to get you to see that the water in that fountain is wet or that the walls of this room are constructed from stone, but the Order must threaten people to make them believe that an eternity of being dead will be an eternal delight, but only if they do as they're told in this life."

As she glared into the still waters of the fountain, Richard thought that

Nicci's blue eyes might turn that water to ice. The cold rage in those eyes was born of things she had seen in her life that he could not begin to imagine. On the dark and quiet evenings alone with her, the things she had been willing to confide in him were terrible enough.

"It's a lot easier to convince people to die for your cause if you first make them eager to die," Nicci said in a bitter voice. "It's a lot easier to get boys to bare their breasts to arrows and swords if they have faith that doing so is a selfless act that will make the Creator smile and welcome them into the eternal glory in the afterworld.

"Once the Order teaches people to be true believers, what they have really done is to forge monsters who will not only die for the cause, but kill for it as well. True believers are consumed by an implacable hatred for those who don't believe. There is no more dangerous, no more vicious, no more brutal an individual than one who has been blinded by the Order's beliefs. Such a believer is not shaped by reason so he is not bound by it. As a consequence, there is no mechanism of restraint on his hatred. These are killers who will only too happily kill for the cause, absolutely secure in the knowledge they are doing the right and the moral thing."

Nicci's knuckles stood out white and bloodless as her fists tightened. Though the room seemed to ring with the sudden, terrible silence, the power of her words still echoed through Richard's mind. He thought that the strength of the aura crackling around her might provoke a sudden lightning storm within the anteroom.

"As I said, the premise is pretty simple." Nicci shook her head in bitter resignation, the emotion draining from her bleak pronouncement. "For most of the people of the Old World, and now the people of the New World, there is no choice but to follow the Order's teachings. If their faith wavers they are sternly reminded of the eternity of unimaginable suffering that awaits the faithless. If that fails to work, then faith will be driven into them by the point of a sword."

"But there must be some way to redeem these people," Jebra said at last. "Isn't there a way to bring them to their senses and get them to cast off the teachings of the Order?"

Nicci looked away from Jebra to stare off into the distance. "I was brought up from birth under the Order's teachings and I came to my senses."

Still staring off into a dark storm of memories, she fell silent for a moment, as if she were reliving her seemingly endless struggle to grasp at life, to escape the haunting clutches of the Order.

"But you cannot imagine how profoundly difficult it was for me to emerge from that realm of dark beliefs. I doubt that anyone who has not been lost in the suffocating world of the Order's teachings can begin to grasp what it's like to believe that your life is worthless and of no value, or grasp the shadow of terror that falls over you every time you try to turn away from what you have been taught is your only means of salvation."

Her watery gaze hesitantly drifted to Richard. He knew. He had been there. He knew what it was like.

"I was redeemed," she whispered in a broken voice, "but it was far from easy."

Jebra looked encouraged by what Richard knew was no real encouragement. "But it worked for you," she said, "so maybe it will work for others."

"She is different from most of those under the spell of the Order," Richard said as he gazed into Nicci's blue eyes, eyes that betrayed the naked emotion of how much he meant to her. "She was driven by a need to understand, to know, if what she had been taught to believe was true or if there was more to life, if there was something worth living for.

"Most of those taught by the Order have no such doubts. They block out those kinds of questions and instead tenaciously cling to their beliefs."

"But what makes you think that they won't change?" Jebra didn't look ready to abandon the thread of hope. "If Nicci changed, then why can't others?"

Still gazing into Nicci's eyes, Richard said, "I think they're able to block out any doubt in what they believe because they've internalized their indoctrination, no longer viewing it as specific ideas that have been drilled into them. They begin to experience the ideas they've been taught as feelings, which evolve into powerful emotional conviction. I think that's the trick to the process. They are convinced within their own minds that they are experiencing original thought rather than those discrete ideas that have been taught to them as they grew up."

Nicci cleared her throat as she looked away from Richard's gaze and turned her attention once more to Jebra.

"I think Richard is right. I was aware of that very thing within my own thinking, aware of that inner conviction that was actually born of a carefully crafted manner of instruction.

"Some people who secretly value their lives will join in a revolt if they can see that there is a realistic chance to win—that's what happened in Altur'Rang—but if there isn't that chance then they know that they must repeat the words that the followers of the Order want to hear or risk losing their most valuable possession: life. Under the Order's rule, you believe as they teach you, or you die. It's as simple as that.

"There are people in the Old World working to join together those who will revolt, working to set the fires of freedom for those who want to seize an opportunity to control their own destiny. So there are those who truly want a chance at freedom and will act to gain it. Jagang, too, knows of such efforts and has sent troops to crush those revolts. But I also know only too well that most of the people of the Old World would never willingly cast off their beliefs; they see doing so as sinful. They will work to ruthlessly crush any uprising. If need be, they will cling to their faith right into their graves. The ones—"

Shota irritably lifted a hand, cutting Nicci off. "Yes, yes, some will, some won't. Many wiffle-waffle. It doesn't matter. Hoping for a revolt is pointless. It's just idle wishing for salvation to arrive out of the blue.

"The legions of soldiers from the Old World are here, now, in the New World, so it's the New World that we must worry about, not the Old World and what the mood for revolt might or might not be. The Old World, for the most part, believes in the Order, supports the Order, and encourages the Order to conquer the rest of the world."

Shota glided forward, directing a meaningful look at Richard. "The only way for civilization to survive is to send the invading soldiers of the Order through that doorway to their longed-for eternity in the world of the dead. There is no redeeming those whose minds are lost to beliefs they are eager to die for. The only way to stop the Order and their teachings is to kill enough of them that they can't continue."

"Pain does have a way of changing people's minds," Cara said.

Shota gave the Mord-Sith a nod of approval. "If they come to truly understand without any doubt that they will not win, that their efforts will lead to certain death, then perhaps some will abandon their belief and cause. It very well could be that despite their faith in the teachings of the Order, few of them actually, deep down inside, really want to die to test it.

"But what of it? Does that really matter to us? What we do know is that a great many really are so fanatical that they welcome death. Hundreds of thousands have already died, proving that they really are willing to make that sacrifice. The rest of these men must be killed or they will kill us all and doom the rest of the world to a long, grinding descent into savagery.

"That is what we face. That is the reality of it."

Shota turned a hot look on Richard. "Jebra has shown you what will happen at the hands of these soldiers if you don't stop them. Do you think those men entertain any rational notions of the meaning of their lives? Or that they might join in a revolt against the Order if given a chance? Hardly.

"I'm here to show you what has already happened to many so that you will understand what is is going to happen to everyone else if you don't do something to stop it.

"A precise understanding of how the soldiers of the Order came to be, the choices they have made in their lives that brought them rampaging into the lives of innocent people, and the reasons behind those choices, are beyond being our concern. They are what they are. They are destroyers, killers. They are here. That is all that matters, now. They must be stopped. If they are dead, they will cease to be a threat. It's as simple as that."

Richard wondered how in the world she expected him to accomplish such a "simple" thing. She might as well be asking him to pull the moon down out of the sky and use it to crush the Imperial Order army.

As if reading his mind, Nicci spoke up again. "We may all agree with you, with everything you have come here to say—and in fact we didn't need you to tell us what we already know, as if you think us children and only you are wise. But you don't understand what you're asking. The army that Jebra saw, the army that marched up into Galea and so easily crushed their defenses and killed so many people, is a minor and rather insignificant unit of the Imperial Order."

"You can't be serious," Jebra said.

Nicci finally withdrew her glare from Shota and looked at Jebra. "Did you see any gifted?"

"Gifted? Why, no, I guess not," she said after a moment's thought.

"That's because they didn't warrant having their own gifted to command," Nicci said. "If they had gifted, Shota would not have been able to so easily get in there and then take you right out of the place. But they had no gifted. They're a relatively minor force and as such they're considered expendable.

"That's why the supplies took so long to reach them. All supplies first went north to Jagang's main force. Once they had what they needed they then allowed supplies to go to other units, like the one up in Galea. They are only one of Jagang's expeditionary forces."

"But you don't understand." Jebra stood. "They were a huge army. I was there. I saw them with my own eyes." She dry-washed her hands as she glanced around at everyone in the room. "I was there, working for them month after month. I saw how massive their numbers were. How could I not grasp the extent of their forces? I've told you about all they accomplished."

Unimpressed, Nicci shook her head. "They were nothing."

Jebra licked her lips, distress settling into her expression. "Perhaps I have not done an adequate job of describing it, of making clear just how many soldiers of the Order invaded Galea. I'm sorry that I've failed in making you understand how easily they crushed all those determined defenders."

"You did a very good job of reporting accurately what you saw," Nicci said in a gentler tone as she squeezed the woman's shoulder in sympathetic reassurance. "But you only saw a part of the whole picture. The part you saw, frightening as it surely was, was insignificant compared to the rest of it. What you saw could not begin to prepare you for seeing the main force led by Emperor Jagang. I've spent a great deal of time in Jagang's main encampments; I know what I'm talking about. Compared to their main force, the one you saw does not qualify as imposing."

"She's right," Zedd said in a grim voice. "I hate to admit it, but she's right. Jagang's main army is vastly more powerful than the one that invaded Galea. I fought to slow their advance up through the Midlands as they steadily drove us back toward Aydindril, so I ought to know. Seeing them come is like watching the approach of uncountable minions of the underworld come to swallow the living."

He looked stoic in his simple robes, standing at the top of the five steps, watching, listening to what others had to say. Richard knew, though, that his grandfather was anything but indifferent. Zedd's way was often to listen to what others had to say before he had his say. In this instance there was no need for him to correct anything that he'd heard.

"If the Order troops in Galea have no gifted," Jebra said, "then perhaps if some of those with the gift were to go there you could eliminate them. Perhaps you could save those poor people who are still alive, who have endured so much. It is not too late to at least save some of them."

Richard thought that what she was really asking, but feared to speak aloud, was if this was only a minor force with no gifted among them, then why hadn't some of those present done something to stop the slaughter she'd witnessed. Before Richard had ever left his woods of Hartland, he might very well have harbored the same vague sense of resentment and anger toward those who had not done anything to save them. Now he felt the torment of knowing how much more there was to it.

Nicci shook her head, dismissing the idea. "It's not so feasible as it might seem. The gifted might be able to take out a large number of the enemy and for a time create havoc, but even this expeditionary force has sufficient numbers to withstand any attack by the gifted. Zedd, for example, could use wizard's fire to mow down ranks of soldiers, but as he paused to conjure more the enemy would be sending wave upon wave of men at him. They might lose a lot of men, but they are not deterred by staggering casualties. They would keep coming. They would throw rank after rank of men into the conflagration. Despite how many would die, they would soon enough overwhelm even one as talented as the First Wizard. And then where would we be?

"Even something as simple as a band of archers could take down a gifted person." She glanced at Richard. "All it takes is one arrow finding its mark, and a gifted person will die the same as any other."

Zedd spread his hands in a gesture of frustration. "I'm afraid that Nicci is right. In the end, the Order would be in the same place with the same result, even if with fewer men. We, on the other hand, would be without those with the gift that we sent against them. They can replenish their troops with nearly endless reinforcements, but there will be no legions of gifted coming to our aid. As callous as it may seem, our only chance lies not with throwing our lives away in a futile battle that we know has no chance of success, but with being able to come up with something that has a real chance to work."

Richard wished that he believed that there was some solution, some plan, that had a real chance to work. He didn't think, though, that there was any chance that they could do anything other than prolong the end.

Jebra nodded, her glimmer of hope sparking out. The deep creases that lent a sagging look to her face along with the lasting web of wrinkles at the corners of her blue eyes made her look older than Richard suspected she really was. Her shoulders were slightly rounded, and her hands rough and callused from hard labor. Even though the men of the Order had not killed her, they had sapped the life out of her, leaving her forever scarred by what she had been through and what she'd been forced to witness. How many others were there, like her, alive but forever withered under the brutality of the occupying forces, hollow shells of their former selves, alive on the outside but lifeless inside?

Richard felt dizzy. He could hardly believe that Shota would bring Jebra all this way to convince him of how terrible the Order really was. He already knew the truth of their brutality, of the nature of their threat. He'd lived for nearly a year in the Old World under the repression of the Order. He had been there at the start of the revolt in Altur'Rang.

Jebra's firsthand testimony, if anything, was only helping to convince him of what he already knew—that they didn't stand a chance against Jagang and the Imperial Order forces. The entire D'Haran Empire would probably have been able to stop the unit that had descended upon Galea, but that was nothing compared with the main army of the Imperial Order.

Back when he'd first met Kahlan he'd fought hard to stop the threat to everyone brought by Darken Rahl. As difficult as it had been, Richard had been able to end that threat by eliminating Darken Rahl. He knew, though, that this threat was different. As much as he hated Jagang, Richard knew that he could not think of this in the same terms as the last battle. Even if he could somehow kill Jagang, that would not stop the menace of the Imperial Order. Their cause was monolithic, ideological, not driven by the ambitions of one individual. That was what made it all seem so hopeless.

Shota's vision—what she foresaw in the flow of time as the world's hopeless future if they failed to do something to stop the Imperial Order— certainly didn't seem to Richard to have required any great talent or special sight. He didn't need to be a prophet to see how dire a threat the Order was. If not stopped, they would rule the world. Jebra, in that sense, had told him nothing new, nothing that he didn't already know.

Richard recognized all too well that, the way things stood, when the forces of the D'Haran Empire finally met Jagang's army in the final battle, those brave men, who were all that stood in the Order's way, were all going to die. After that, there would be no opposition to the Imperial Order. They would rampage unchecked and in the end they would rule the world.

Shota was far from stupid, so she obviously knew all that, and had to know that he would know it as well.

So, he wondered, why was she really there?

Despite his dark mood over Jebra's frightening account of what she had seen, Richard had to think that Shota very likely had some other reason for her visit.

Still, Jebra's story had been difficult to listen to without it stirring not only his anguish, but his anger. Richard turned away and stared into the stilled water of the fountain. He felt the weight of gloom settling around his shoulders. What could he do about any of it? It felt as if this and all the other troubles pressing in around them were pushing Kahlan away from his thoughts, away from him.

At times she hardly even seemed real to him. He hated it whenever he had such a thought. Sometimes, when he remembered her wit, or the way she smiled so easily when she rested her wrists on his shoulders and locked her fingers together behind his neck and gazed at him, or her beautiful green eyes, or her soft laugh, or her touch, or the tight smile she gave no one but him, she seemed more like a phantom who existed solely in his imagination.

The very thought of Kahlan not being real sent a spike of tingling dread surging up through his insides. He had lived with that numbing fear for a long, dark period. It had been terrifying to be alone in his belief that she existed, terrifying to doubt his own sanity, until he had at last found the truth of the Chainfire spell and convinced the others that she was indeed real. Now, at least, he had their help.

Richard mentally shook himself. Kahlan was no phantom. He had to find a way to get her out of the clutches of Sister Ulicia and the other two Sisters of the Dark. It didn't help, though, that the thought of Kahlan being a captive of such ruthless women caused him such anguish that he sometimes couldn't bear to think about it, to think of what terrible things they might do to the woman who was his world, the woman he loved more than life itself, and yet he could not make his mind focus on anything else.

Despite what Shota believed he should do, Richard had to remember that, besides Kahlan being lost in the vortex of the Chainfire spell, there were other ominous dangers, like the boxes of Orden being in play, and the damage left behind by the chimes. He couldn't ignore everything else just because the witch woman came marching in to tell him what she thought he should do. It could even be that Shota's true goal was some complex scheme, some hidden agenda, involving this other witch woman, Six. There was no telling what Shota was really up to.

Still, Richard had come to have great respect for her, as had Kahlan, even if he didn't entirely trust her. While Shota often seemed to be an instigator of trouble it was not necessarily because she was deliberately trying to cause him grief; sometimes her intent was to help him and at other times she was simply the messenger of truth. And while she was always right in the things she revealed to him, those things almost always turned out to be true in ways Shota hadn't predicted—or at least in ways she hadn't revealed. As Zedd often said, a witch woman never told you something you wanted to know without also telling you something you didn't want to know.

The first time he met her, Shota had said that Kahlan would touch him with her power and so he should kill her to prevent that from happening. As it turned out, Kahlan did use her Confessor's touch on him, but that was how he had been able to trick Darken Rahl and defeat him. Shota had been right, but it had happened in a manner that turned out to be vastly different from the way she'd presented it. Even though she had been right, strictly speaking, if he had followed her advice Darken Rahl would have survived to unleash the power of Orden and rule them all, or the ones left alive.

In the back of his mind lurked the prediction Shota had made that if Richard married Kahlan she would bear a child that would be a monster. He and Kahlan had been wed. Surely that prediction would not turn out the way Shota had presented it either. Surely Kahlan would not give birth to a monster.

It was Zedd who finally spoke, bringing Richard out of his private thoughts. "What ever happened to Queen Cyrilla?"

The room was dead still for a time before Jebra answered. "It was as it had been in my vision. She was handed over to the lowest of the soldiers to use as they wished. They were eager to get at their prize. It went very badly for her. Her worst fears came to pass."

Zedd cocked his head, apparently believing that there was more to the story. "So that was the last you saw of her?"

Jebra folded her hands before herself. "Not exactly. One day, as I was rushing to deliver a platter of freshly roasted beef, I came upon a raucous group of men playing a game that the Imperial Order troops were very fond of watching. There were two teams with the gathered men shouting and yelling them on. The men were all betting on which team would win. I don't know what the game was—"

"Ja'La," Nicci said. When Jebra turned to look at her, Nicci said "The game is called Ja'La. In theory it's a game of athletic ability, skill, and strategy; in practice, under the rules the Order plays it by, Ja'La is all of that and in addition it's quite brutal. Ja'La is Jagang's favorite sport. He has a team of his own. I remember once when they lost a game. The whole team was put to death. The emperor soon had a new team of the most skilled, toughest, most physically imposing players to be found. They did not lose. The full name of the game is Ja'La dh Jin. In Emperor Jagang's native tongue it means 'the game of life.' "

Jebra frowned in recollection. "Yes, I guess I do recall hearing it called Ja'La. I always saw it played with a heavy ball. A ball heavy enough to on occasion break the bones of the players."

"The ball is called a broc," Richard said without turning.

Nicci glanced over at him. "That's right."

"Well," Jebra said, resuming her story, "on this particular day, as I was taking the platter to the commanders, I had to go to the place where the game was being played. There were thousands of troops gathered to watch. I was directed to a small stand for the commanders and had to make my way through the cheering throngs. It was a terrifying journey. The men saw the iron ring of a slave in my lip so none dared to pull me away to their tents, but that didn't stop their hands on me." Jebra's gaze sought the floor. "It was something that I had to endure often enough."

She finally looked up. "When I reached the commanders, down close to the playing field, I saw that the men starting up a new game weren't using the ball that they usually used." She cleared her throat. "They were using Queen Cyrilla's head for the ball."

Jebra sought to fill the uncomfortable silence. "Anyway, life in Galea had been changed forever. What was once a center of commerce is now little more than a vast army camp from where continuing campaigns against some of the free areas of the New World are launched. The farms out in the country, run by forced labor, don't produce as they once did. Crops fail or are poor. The needs of the vast armed forces in Galea are huge. Food is always scarce but the supplies that regularly come up from the Old World keep the soldiers fed well enough to carry on.

"I worked day and night as a slave to the needs of the Imperial Order commanders. I never again had any visions after the one about Queen Cyrilla. It seemed odd to me to be without my visions. I'd had them my whole life, but after that terrible vision about Queen Cyrilla a couple of years back, no more came. My gift as a Seer seems to have vanished. My vision has gone dark."

By the glance from Nicci, Richard knew that she suspected what he was thinking.

"Eventually," Jebra said, "I was one day snatched away from the middle of all those troops. It was Shota who somehow got me out. I'm not entirely sure how it happened. I just recall that she was there with me. I started to ask something but she told me to keep my mouth shut and to start walking. I remember turning back once to look and there was the army spread out across the valley and up into the hills, but they were a great distance behind us. I don't know how it had happened, really, that we were so far away." She frowned into her dim memories. "We were just walking. And here I am. I'm afraid, though, that because my visions have gone dark I can no longer be of any help to you."

Richard thought she should know the truth, so he told her. "Your vision probably went dark because several years back the chimes were in this world for a time. They were banished back to the underworld, but the damage was done. I think that the presence of the chimes in the world of life began the disintegration of magic. It must be that it disrupted your ability. Your gifted vision is probably lost, or, even if it returns in part or for a time, it will eventually be completely extinguished."

Jebra looked dazed by the news. "My whole life I have frequently wished that I had never been born with the vision of a Seer. In many ways it made me an outcast. I often wept at night, wishing to be free of my visions, wishing they would leave me be.

"But now that you tell me that my wish has been granted, I don't think that I ever really meant it."

"That's the problem with wishes," Zedd said as he sighed. "They tend to be things that—"

"The chimes?" Shota interrupted. By her tone of voice as well as her frown, Richard knew that she wasn't interested in hearing about wishes. "If such a thing were true, then why has there been no other evidence of it?"

"There has been," Richard said with a shrug. "Creatures of magic, such as the dragons, have not been seen in the last couple of years."

"Dragons?" Shota coiled a long wavy lock of hair around a finger as she appraised him silently for a moment. "Richard, people can go for a lifetime and never catch a glimpse of a dragon."

"And what of Jebra's visions going dark? After the chimes were in this world her visions ceased. Like other things of magic, her unique ability is flickering out. I'm sure that we aren't even aware of most of them."

"I would be aware of them."

"Not necessarily." Richard raked his hair back off his forehead. "The problem is, Chainfire—which I first heard about from you—is a spell that was ignited by four Sisters of the Dark to make everyone forget Kahlan. That spell is contaminated by the chimes, so besides Kahlan, people are forgetting other things as well, such as dragons."

Shota looked anything but convinced. "I would still be aware of such things because of the way they flow forward in time."

"And what about this other witch woman, Six? I thought that you said that she was masking your ability to see the flow of time."

Shota ignored his question and pulled the finger free of the skein of auburn hair. As she folded her arms. Her almond-shaped eyes remained fixed on him.

"If the shadow of the Order darkens mankind, none of it will matter, now, will it? They will put an end to all magic, as well as all hope."

Richard didn't answer. Instead he turned to the still waters, to his brooding thoughts.

Shota tilted her head, gesturing toward the steps as she spoke quietly to Jebra. "Go up there and see Zedd. I need to talk to Richard."

As Shota glided closer to Richard she cast Nicci a threatening glare. He wondered why Shota hadn't also told Nicci to go back up the steps with Jebra to talk to Zedd. He surmised, though, that the witch woman probably knew that Nicci wouldn't follow any such orders. He certainly didn't want to see them in a test of wills. He had enough to worry about without those on the same side battling among themselves.

When Richard glanced over and saw Jebra ascending the steps he also saw that Ann and Nathan had already made their way around the room to stand near him as well. When she reached him, Zedd circled a comforting arm around Jebra's shoulders as he murmured words of reassurance, but his gaze was on Richard. Richard appreciated his grandfather watching out for him and keeping an eye on the witch woman just in case she had any ideas about pulling one of her tricks. Zedd probably knew far better than any of them just what Shota was capable of. He also harbored a deep mistrust of the woman, not sharing at all Richard's view that Shota, at her core, was driven by the same convictions as they were.

As much as he might appreciate her central purpose, Richard was well aware that Shota sometimes pursued that purpose in ways that had in the past caused him no end of grief. What she viewed as help sometimes ended up being nothing but trouble for him.

He was all too aware that Shota also on occasion had her own agenda—such as when she had given the sword to Samuel. Richard suspected that she was up to something now as well, he just didn't know what or what was behind it. He wondered if it might have something to do with eliminating the other witch woman.

"Richard," Shota said in a soft, sympathetic tone, "you have heard the nature of the terror that is descending upon us. You are the only one who can stop it. I don't know why it is so, but I do know that it is."

Richard did not spare her for her gentle tone or her concern about their common enemy. "You dare to express your deep distress over the suffering and death brought by the Order and your conviction that only I can do something to stop the threat, and yet you conspired to withhold information just so that you could wrest the Sword of Truth from me?"

She didn't rise to the challenge. "There was no conspiring, as you put it. It was a fair trade—value for value." Her voice remained serene. "Besides, the sword would not be of any help to you in this, Richard."

"A poor excuse for you giving it to that murderous Samuel."

Shota arched an eyebrow. "And, as it turns out, had I not, then those Sisters of the Dark who stole the boxes of Orden would probably have united by now. With all three boxes together, they very well might have already opened one, very well might have already unleashed the power of Orden, very well might have already turned us all over to the Keeper of the dead. What good would the sword do you if the world of life were ended? It seems that Samuel, for whatever reason, has prevented a cataclysm."

"Samuel also used the sword to kidnap Rachel. In the process he nearly killed Chase—and apparently intended to."

"Use your head, Richard. The sword served us all by buying us time, even if it was at a cost that none of us likes. What are you going to do with the time you now have that you otherwise would not? More to the point, what good would the sword do you, now, against the threat of the Order?

"Besides, with the sword anyone can be a Seeker—a pretend Seeker, anyway. A true Seeker does not need the sword to be the Seeker."

He knew that she was right. What would he do with the sword? Try to cut down the Imperial Order single-handedly? Just as Nicci had explained to Jebra how those with the gift could not overcome vast numbers just because they could wield magic, the same applied to the sword. Still, Shota had given the sword to Samuel, and now Samuel seemed to be acting on the orders of a different witch woman, one who apparently had no one's interest at heart but her own.

Worse, what sense did it make to fret over a single weapon when so many were dying at the hands of the Order, when that single weapon would not preserve their lives or freedom? Richard knew that the sword was not the real weapon; the mind that directed it was what really mattered.

He was the true Seeker. He was the true weapon. Samuel couldn't take that.

And yet, he had no idea what to do to stop the threat, to halt any of the dangers closing in around them.

Nicci stood not far away—distant enough to give Shota her chance to talk to him, but close enough to step between them in an instant if the talk turned to threats, or to something Nicci didn't like.

Richard stared into Nicci's blue eyes a moment before turning again to meet Shota's gaze. "And just what is it that you expect me to do?"

Without being aware of her coming closer, he suddenly realized that he could feel Shota's breath against his cheek. It carried the faint scent of lavender. The fragrance felt as if it drew the tension right out of him.

"What I expect," Shota said in an intimate whisper as her arm slipped around his waist, "is for you to understand.

"To truly understand."

Distantly alarmed by what might be her veiled intent, Richard thought that he should back out of her firm embrace. Before he could move a muscle, Shota lifted his chin with a finger.

In an instant, he was kneeling in the mud.

The sound of the steady downpour roared around him, drumming on the roofs and awnings, pattering in the puddles, spattering mud on the walls of buildings, on broken carts and on the legs of the milling mob. Soldiers in the distance shouted orders. Bony horses, their heads hanging, their legs caked with mud, looked miserable as they stood impassively in the rain. A group of soldiers off to the side laughed among themselves while some others not far away chatted in trivial, bored conversation. Nearby wagons rumbled and bounced as they rolled slowly down a road, while in the distance a few dogs barked ceaselessly in a manner born of habit.

In the gloomy light of the leaden overcast everything looked a murky shade of grayish brown. When he glanced to his right, Richard saw that there were other men lined up, kneeling in the mud beside him. Their drab, sodden clothes hung limp from slumped shoulders. Their faces were ashen, their eyes wild with fright. Behind them lurked the maw of a deep pit, looking like nothing so much as a dark opening into the underworld itself.

With a growing sense of urgency, Richard tried to move, to shift his balance, so that he could scramble to his feet and defend himself. It was then that he realized his wrists were bound behind his back with what felt like leather thongs. When he tried to twist out of the tightly wound bindings, the leather cut deeper into his flesh. He ignored the searing pain and strained with all his might, but he could not break free. An old dread of being helpless with his hands tied welled up in him.

All around him towered hulking soldiers, some in armor made of leather, or out of rusty metal discs, or chain mail, while still others wore nothing more protective than crude hide vests. Their weapons hung from wide belts and studded straps. None of the weapons were ornate. They were simple tools of their trade: knives with homemade wooden handles riveted onto the heels of the blades; swords with leather wound around wooden grips to hold them to the tangs; maces made of crudely cast iron atop a stout hickory handle or wrought-iron bar. Their coarse construction made them no less effective for their task. If anything, the lack of adornment served to emphasize their only purpose and in so doing only made them look all the more sinister.

The greasy hair of those who didn't shave their heads was matted by the steady rain. Some soldiers had multiple rings or sharpened metal posts in their ears and nose. The grime layering their faces appeared impervious to the rain. Many a man had a swath of a dark tattoo across his face. Some of the tattoos were almost like masks, while others swept over cheek and nose and brow in wild, snaking, dramatic designs. The bold tattoos made the men look all the less human, all the more savage. The eyes of the soldiers flicked back and forth, seldom pausing on any one thing, giving the men the look of restless animals.

Richard had to blink the rainwater out of his eyes to see. He tossed his head, flicking strands of his wet hair back off his face. It was then that he saw men to his left as well, some weeping helplessly as soldiers held up those who would not, or could not, kneel upright in the sloppy mud. The sense of panic was palpable. The floodwaters of that panic spread to Richard, rising up through him, threatening to drown him.

This wasn't real, he knew . . . but, somehow, it was. The rain was cold. His clothes were soaked. An occasional shiver rattled through him. The place stank worse than anything he could ever remember, a combination of acrid smoke, stale sweat, excrement, and putrefying flesh. The cries of those around him were all too real. He didn't think he would have been able to imagine moans so devoid of hope and at the same time so desperately frightened. Many of the men trembled uncontrollably, and it wasn't from the cold rain. Richard realized, as he stared at them, that he was one of them, much the same as them, just one of the many on their knees in the mud, one of many with their hands bound behind their backs.

It was so impossible that it was disorienting; somehow he was there. Somehow Shota had sent him to this place. He could not conceive of how such a thing could be possible; he had to be imagining it.

A rock hidden beneath the mud dug painfully into his left knee. Such an unforeseeable, trivial detail seemed like it had to be real. How could he possibly imagine something so unexpected? He tried to shift his weight, but it was difficult to balance. He managed to push his knee to the side a little, off the sharp rock. He couldn't be imagining such a thing.

He began to wonder if it was everything else that he had actually been imagining. He wondered if it all had just been a dream, a diversion, a trick of his mind. He began to wonder if it could be possible that the Chainfire spell had somehow made him forget what was really happening, or if reality was just so terrifying that he had somehow blocked it out of his mind, withdrawing to an imaginary world, and now, suddenly, under the stress of the situation, he had snapped back to what was real. He began to realize that, even if he didn't know exactly what was going on or how he could be so confused, what really mattered was that this actually was real and somehow he was only now awakening to it. In fact, that's just what it felt like to him, like he had just awakened, disoriented and confused.

If he had been confused before, now he was desperately trying to remember, to understand how he had come to be where he found himself, how he had ended up on his knees in the mud among Imperial Order soldiers. It seemed like he could almost remember how he had gotten there, almost recall it all, but it remained just out of reach, like a forgotten word that was lost somewhere in the dark well of the mind.

Richard looked down the line to his left and saw a soldier grab a fistful of man's hair and yank his head upright. The man screamed—short, terror-choked sounds driven by a heaving chest. Richard could easily see that despite the man's frantic effort, he had no chance of escape. The sounds of his tearful pleas raised goose bumps on Richard's arms. The soldier behind the kneeling man brought a long, thin knife around in front of the man's exposed throat.

Again, Richard tried to tell himself that he had been right before, that it wasn't real, that he was somehow just imagining it. But he could see the chip in the blade of the crudely honed knife, see the man swallowing over and over in panting panic, see the grim grin on the soldier's smug face.

When the knife sliced deep across the man's throat, Richard flinched in shock at the sight, as the man flinched with the shock of pain.

The man thrashed, but the soldier holding him by the hair had no trouble restraining his victim. The rain-slicked muscles of his powerful arm bulged as he exerted more effort to cut down through the man's throat a second time, far deeper, and nearly all the way around. Blood, shockingly crimson in the gray light, gushed out with each beat of the man's still throbbing heart. Richard winced as the fresh smell of it made his nostrils flare.

He tried to tell himself that it wasn't real, yet, somehow, as he watched the man weakly twisting, watched as a bib of blood grew down the front of his shirt, soaked down the crotch of his pants, it was all too real. With one final effort, his neck gaping open, the man kicked his right leg out to the side. The soldier, still holding the man by the hair, heaved him back into the pit. Richard heard the dead weight splash down heavily in the bottom.

Richard's heart pounded against his chest wall so hard that he thought it might burst. He felt sick. He thought he might vomit. He strained frantically to wrench his hands free, but the leather only cut deeper into his flesh. The rain was washing sweat into his eyes. The leather thongs had been in place for so long that just moving against them burned painfully enough into the raw wounds to bring fresh tears to his eyes. That didn't stop him, though. He grunted with effort, putting all his muscle into the struggle to break his bonds. He could feel the leather rasping against the exposed tendons in his wrists.

And then Richard heard his name called out. He instantly recognized the voice.

It was Kahlan.

His whole life hammered to a halt when he looked up, across the way and into her dazzling green eyes. Every emotion he had ever had washed through him in an instant, leaving behind a kind of weak and terrible agony that ached all the way down to the marrow of his bones.

He had been separated from her for so long. . . .

Seeing her, seeing every detail of her face, seeing the little arch in the wrinkle in her brow that he had forgotten about, seeing the exact way her back curved as she stood turned slightly, seeing the way her hair parted naturally under the weight of the rain, seeing her eyes, her beautiful green eyes, told him that he could not possibly be imagining it.

Kahlan stretched out an arm. "Richard!"

The sound of her voice paralyzed him. It had been so long since he had heard her singular voice, a voice that from the first time he'd met her had riveted him with its intelligence, its clarity, its grace, its bewitching charm. But now there was none of that in her voice. All those qualities had been stripped away until all that was left was anguish beyond bearing.

Matching the distress in her voice, Kahlan's exquisite features twisted in horror at seeing him kneeling in the mud. Her eyes were rimmed with red. Tears streamed down her cheeks along with the rain.

Richard knelt frozen in terror, frozen at the sight of her, right there, so close yet so far. Frozen to discover that she was there, in the middle of thousands upon thousands of enemy troops.

"Richard!"

Her arm desperately stretching for him again. She was trying to get to him, but she couldn't.

She was being held back by a burly soldier with a shaved head.

Richard noticed for the first time that the buttons on Kahlan's shirt were gone, ripped off, so the shirt hung open, exposing her to the leers of the soldiers.

But she didn't care. She only wanted Richard to see her, as if that was all that mattered in life, as if that single sight of him was her whole life. As if she needed only that to live.

A painful knot swelled in his throat. Tears welled up. Richard whispered her name, too shocked by the sight of her to bring forth more.

Frantic, Kahlan again reached out for him, straining against the restraint of the soldier's meaty hand. His tight grip left white prints of his fingers in the flesh of her arm.

"Richard! Richard, I love you! Dear spirits, I love you!"

As she tried to tear away, to lunge toward him, the soldier circled a powerful arm around her middle, inside her open shirt, holding her back. The man reached around and, with a finger and thumb, seized Kahlan's nipple, twisting it as he glanced up, grinning with meaning, making sure that Richard saw what he was doing.

A small cry of surprised pain escaped Kahlan's throat, but otherwise she ignored the soldier, instead screaming Richard's name in abject terror.

Fired by rage, Richard furiously tried to get to his feet. He had to get to her. The soldier laughed as he watched Richard struggle. There was no way another chance would come along. This was it; this would be his only chance.

As he began to force his way to his feet, a guard rammed a boot into Richard's gut so hard that it doubled him over. Another soldier kicked him in the side of the head for good measure, stunning him nearly senseless. The world dimmed. Sound melted together into a dull drone. Richard struggled to remain conscious. He didn't want to lose sight of Kahlan. There was no sight in the whole world that meant more to him than the sight of her.

He had to find a way to get her out of the middle of this nightmare.

As he fought to regain his breath, the big hand of a soldier seized his hair and yanked him upright. Richard gasped, trying to draw a breath against the stupefying pain of the blows. He felt warm blood running down the side of his face, washing cold mud down his neck.

As his head was pulled upright, Richard's gaze fell on Kahlan again, on her long hair now tangled and matted by the rain. Her green eyes were so beautiful that he thought his heart might burst with the pain of seeing her again but not being able to hold her in his arms.

He wanted so badly to hold her in his arms, to comfort her, to protect her.

Instead, another man was holding her in his arms. She tried to squirm away. He cupped her breast, squeezing until Richard could see that it was hurting her. She beat at him with her fists, but he held her fast. He laughed at her futile efforts as his gaze again slid to Richard.

Kahlan fought him, but at the same time ignored what he was doing, ignored the distraction. What he was doing was not what mattered most to her. Richard was what mattered most. Her arms frantically stretched out toward him.

"Richard, I love you! I've missed you so much!" She was overcome with sobs of sheer misery. "Dear spirits, help him! Please! Somebody help him!"

To his left, the next man in line tried with all his might to back away as his throat was sliced deep. Richard could hear the man's frantic gasps gurgling through the gash that opened up his windpipe.

Richard felt faint with panic. He didn't know what to do.

Magic. He should call his gift. But how was he to do that? He didn't know how to call forth magic. And yet, in the past he had been able to do it.

Rage.

In the past his gift had always worked through his anger.

Seeing the soldier holding Kahlan, hurting her, provided him with more than enough anger. Seeing another of those monsters come in close to her, leering down at her, touching her intimately, only fanned the wild flames of his anger.

His world went red with rage.

With every fiber of his being Richard tried to ignite his gift with the essence of that fury. He clenched his jaw, gritting his teeth with the monumental concentration of his wrath. He shook with rage, expecting an explosion of power to match that rage. He saw what he needed to do. It seemed so close. He imagined it cutting down the soldiers. He held his breath against the storm that was about to be unleashed.

It felt like falling unexpectedly, without any ground below him to catch his fall.

The rain continued to plunge from the gray sky as if to drown his effort. No magic arced through the empty space between Richard and the man who held Kahlan. No conjured lightning erupted. No justice was at hand.

In all his life, if there was anything there, this was the moment it would have come—that much he knew beyond any doubt. There could be no more urgent need, no more desire, no more wrath for the woman he loved. But no power was there, no redemption at hand.

He might as well have been born without the gift.

He had no gift. It was gone.

It felt to Richard as if the world was caving in around him. He wanted everything to slow down, to give him time to find a solution, but everything swirled in a terrible rush. It was all happening too fast. It was so unfair to have to die like this. He hadn't had a chance to live, to have a life with Kahlan. He loved her so much and he hadn't really been able to be with her, just the two of them, living in peace. He wanted to smile and laugh with her, to hold her, to go through life with her. Just to sit in front of a fire with her on a cold, snowy night, holding her close to him, safe and warm, as they talked about the things that mattered to them, about their future. They should have a future.

It was so unfair. He wanted to live his life. Instead, it was to end in this miserable place for no good reason. For nothing. He wasn't even able to make his death mean something, to die fighting for life. Instead, he was going to die here in the rain and mud, surrounded by men who hated all that was good in life, while Kahlan was forced to watch it happen.

He didn't want her to see this. He knew that she would never be able to get the sight of it out of her mind. He didn't want to leave her with that last, horrific memory of him struggling in the bloody throes of death.

He made another attempt to get up, as did most of the other men. The soldier behind him stepped on his calves, bearing down with all his weight. The pain felt distant. Richard was in a daze.

He wanted nothing in the world so much as to get Kahlan away from the men who were holding her, groping her. Kahlan screamed in rage at them, clawed at them, swung her fists at them, and at the same time cried in helpless terror for Richard.

He twisted with all his might against the leather thongs binding his wrists but, rather than part, they only cut deeper. He felt like an animal caught in a trap. His hands had gone numb. He could no longer feel the warm blood dripping off his fingertips.

He didn't want to die. What was he to do? He had to stop this. Somehow, he had to. But he didn't know how. In the past, anger was the means to reach his gift, to call forth its power. Now, there was nothing but a helpless confusion.

"Kahlan!"

He couldn't seem to help himself from being swept up in the terror of it, in the blind panic of it. He couldn't stop the headlong rush of it. Couldn't regain his sense of control over himself. He was being swept away in a river of events he could not control or stop. It was all so senseless. It was all so overwhelmingly pointless, so monumentally brutal.

"Kahlan!"

"Richard!" she cried as she again reached out for him. "Richard, I love you more than life! I love you so much. You're everything to me. You always have been."

Sobs caught her breath, turning them to gasps.

"Richard . . . I need you so badly."

His heart was breaking. He felt that he was failing her.

A soldier seized Richard by the hair.

"No!" Kahlan screamed, holding out a hand. "No! Please no! Somebody please help him! Dear spirits, somebody, please!"

The soldier leaned down, a cruel smile twisting his grime-streaked face.

"Don't worry, I'll see to her . . . personally." He laughed in Richard's ear.

"Please," Richard heard himself say, "please . . . no."

"Dear spirit, please, somebody help him!" Kahlan cried to those around her.

She could do nothing and she knew it. There was no chance for him and she knew it. She was reduced to begging for a miracle. That, in itself, fed the flames of hot dread burning out of control within him. This was the end of everything.

"She's a real looker," the soldier said as he leered across the way at Kahlan, proving what Richard knew—that no miracle was at hand.

"Please . . . leave her be."

The soldier behind him laughed. That was what he had wanted to hear.

Richard was choking on the sob welling up in his throat. He couldn't breathe past it. Tears ran down his face along with the rain. She was the only woman he had ever loved, the one person who meant everything to him, meant more than life itself to him.

Without Kahlan there was no life, there was only existence. She was his world.

Without Kahlan life was empty.

Without him, he knew, Kahlan's life would be just as empty.

He saw other women not far from Kahlan, all being held by soldiers, all screaming for their men. He saw them saying things much like the things Kahlan was saying, offering the same words of love, the same calls for someone to save them. The soldiers taunted the men kneeling in the mud with vile oaths.

Seeing the women in the hands of the soldiers, one of the kneeling men to Richard's right struggled hard enough to earn himself a lightning-quick stab to the gut. It didn't kill him, but it was enough to keep him from fighting while he was made to wait his turn. As he knelt stiff and still, his wide eyes stared down at his own pink, glistening insides slowly bulging out of the gash. The screams of the man's wife seemed like they could have split the clouds above.

The man immediately to Richard's left gasped his last breath, thrashing in uncoordinated movements as the soldier holding up the man's head sawed the large knife back and forth across the victim's exposed throat. When finished, the soldier growled with the effort of heaving the dead weight back into the open pit. Richard heard the body thud down in the bottom of the open grave atop other bodies. He could hear gurgling gasps coming from the dark hole.

"Your turn," the soldier holding Richard said as he stepped around behind him to assume the role of executioner. The man leaned close. His breath stank of ale and sausage. "I need to finish this. I've a meeting with your lovely wife as soon as I'm done with you. Kahlan, isn't it? Yes, that's right—one of the other women confessed that your wife's name was Kahlan. Don't you worry, lad, I won't give Kahlan much of a chance to grieve, reminiscing about you. I'll have her full attention—I can promise you that. After I've had my satisfaction from her, others will have their turn on her."

Richard wanted to break the man's neck.

"Think about that as your wicked soul slides into the dark, eternal agony of the underworld, as you fall into the cold, merciless grasp of the Keeper. That's where all your kind goes—to the justice of eternal suffering—and that's as it should be, seeing as how we've all sacrificed everything to come up here to this forsaken land so we can bring divine Light and the law of the Order to all you selfish heathens. Your sinful way of life, your mere existence, offends the Creator—and it offends those of us who bow to Him."

The man was working himself up into a righteous rage.

"Do you have any idea what I've sacrificed for the salvation of the souls of your people? My family went hungry, went without—sacrificed—so that they could send everything to our courageous troops. My brother and I gave ourselves over to the fight for our cause and everything we believe in. We both came north to do our duty to our emperor and our Creator. We both devoted our lives to the cause of bringing goodness to you people. We fought in countless bloody battles against those who resist our efforts on behalf of what is right and just. We saw countless of our brethren die in those battles.

"I saw the glory of our army of the Order continue on in the fight for salvation while your people sent the wicked gifted against us. Those gifted conjured evil made of magic. My brother was blinded by some of that magic. He screamed in agony as that magic bloodied his eyes and burned his lungs. The infections that swiftly befell him made his whole head swell, his sightless eyes bulge. He could only moan in agony. We left him to die alone, so that we could move on in our noble struggle, as was only right.

"Your wife and those like her will now sacrifice themselves to give us a small diversion in this miserable life as we labor in that noble struggle. It's her small payment on a debt of gratitude for what we have given over for our fellow man in order to bring the word of the Order to those who would otherwise turn away from their duty to faith.

"Someday your sinful wife will join you there in the darkness of the underworld, but not until after we're finished with her. Just don't expect her to be joining you any time soon, as I expect she'll be whoring for the brave soldiers of the Order for some time to come, what with how the men like to get their hands on a good-looking woman like her in order to take their minds off the drudgery of their honorable work. I expect she'll be kept good and busy, since there is so much honorable work to do"—he waggled his knife before Richard's eyes—"like this business here. With the relief us men get from her, we'll have the strength to redouble our determination to eliminate all those who will not submit to the ways of the Order."

It was insanity. Richard could hardly believe that there were men this irrational, this devoted to such mindless beliefs, but there were. They seemed to emerge everywhere, multiplying like maggots, devoted to destroying anything joyful and beneficial to life.

He choked back his words, his rage. Nothing angered men like this as much as reason or truth or life or goodness. Such qualities only incited such men to destroy. Because Richard knew that anything he said would only provoke the man and make it worse for Kahlan, he kept quiet. That was all he could do for her, now.

Seeing that he had not goaded Richard into an appeal, the soldier laughed again and threw a kiss toward Kahlan. "Be with you shortly, love—soon as I'm done divorcing you from your worthless husband, here."

He was a monster, shortly to be headed for the woman Richard loved, toward a defenseless, terrified woman who was only beginning to suffer at the hands of these brutes.

Monster.

Could this be what Shota had meant?

The witch woman had once said that if Richard and Kahlan ever married and lay together, she would conceive a monster. They had always assumed that Shota had meant that if they conceived a child, then their child would be a monster because that child would have Richard's gift and Kahlan's Confessor power.

But maybe that was not at all the real meaning behind Shota's foretelling.

After all, nothing Shota warned them about ever turned out the way she had made it seem, even the way she herself believed. Shota's warnings and predictions always seemed to come about in a completely unforeseen manner, in a way that they had never even imagined, but at the same time Shota's predictions had always turned out to be true.

Was this what Shota's prediction had really meant? Was this the complex set of events finally reaching the climax of her prophecy? Shota had warned them emphatically not to marry or Kahlan would bear a monster child. They had married. Could this be how Shota's prophecy unfolded? Could this have all along been the real meaning behind her warning? Were these monsters to sire a monster?

Richard was choking on his tears. His death would not be the worst of it. Kahlan would suffer the worst of it, suffer a living death at the hands of those brutes, mother their monster.

"Richard, you know I love you! That's all that matters, Richard—that I love you!"

"Kahlan, I love you, too!"

He couldn't think of anything more to say—anything more meaningful. He guessed that there was nothing more meaningful, nothing more important to him. Those simple words spoke a whole life's worth of meaning, a whole universe of meaning.

"I know, my love," she said with a brief spark of a smile that flashed for an instant in her beautiful eyes. "I know."

Richard saw a blade sweep around before his face. He instinctively backed away. The man straddling his legs was ready and jammed a knee between Richard's shoulder blades, stopping him from falling back, then pulled his head up by his hair.

Kahlan, seeing what was happening, screamed again, flailing at the men holding her. "Don't pay any attention to them, Richard! Just look at me! Richard! Look at me! Think about me! Think of how much I love you!"

Richard knew what she was doing.

"Remember the day we were married? I remember it now, Richard. I remember it always."

She was trying to give him the last gift of a pleasant, loving thought.

"I remember the day you asked me to be your wife. I love you, Richard. Remember our wedding? Remember the spirit house?"

She was also trying to distract him, to keep him from thinking about what was happening. Instead, it only reminded him of Shota's warning that if he married her she would conceive a monster.

"Touching," the soldier behind him said. "It's the passionate ones like her who are good in the sack, don't you think?"

Richard wanted to rip the man's head off, but he said nothing. The man wanted him to say something, to beg, to protest, to wail in agony. As a last act of defiance against such men, Richard denied him the satisfaction.

Kahlan cried out her love, and that she wanted him to remember the first time she had kissed him.

Despite everything, that made him smile.

At the moment, she didn't care what was going to happen to her, she just wanted to distract him, to ease the pain and terror of his last moments of life.

His last moments.

It was all ending. It was all over. There was no more.

Life was over. His time with the woman he loved was over. There would be no more.

The world was ending.

"Richard! Richard! I love you so much! Look at me, Richard! I love you! Look at me! That's right, look at me! You're the only one I ever loved! Only you, Richard! Only you! That's all that matters—that I love you. Do you love me? Tell me, please, Richard. Tell me. Tell me now."

He felt the blade catch on the thin veneer of flesh covering his throat.

"I love you, Kahlan. You alone. Always."

"Touching," the soldier growled in his ear as he held the blade against Richard's throat. "While you're down in the pit, bleeding out, I'll have my hands all over her. I'm going to rape your pretty little wife. You'll be dead by then, but before you die, I want you to know exactly what I'm going to do to her, and that there's nothing you can do to stop it, because it's the Creator's will being done.

"You should have long ago bowed to the ways of the Order, but instead you've fought to keep to your sinful ways, your selfish ways, and turned away from everything right and just. For your crimes against your fellow man you will not only die, but you will suffer for all eternity at the hands of the Keeper of the underworld. Suffer greatly.

"As you go to the dark afterlife, I want you to go there knowing that if your precious Kahlan lives, it will only be as a whore for us. If she lives long enough, and she has a boy child, he will grow up to be a great soldier of the Order, and to hate your kind. We'll see to it that he comes here someday to spit on your grave, to spit on you and those like you who would have raised him in your wicked ways, raised him to turn away from serving his fellow man and the Creator.

"You think on that as your spirit is being sucked down into darkness. As your body grows cold, I'll be with the nice warm body of your love, giving it to her good. I want to make sure you know that before you die."

Richard was already dead inside. It was over, life and the world were ended. So much lost. Everything lost. For nothing but a mindless hatred of every value, of life itself, by those who chose instead to embrace the emptiness of death.

"I love you now and always, with all my heart," he said in a hoarse voice. "You've made my life a joy."

He saw Kahlan nodding that she'd heard him, and her lips mouthing her love for him.

She was so beautiful.

More than anything, he hated to see her inconsolable grief.

They stared into one another's eyes, frozen in that instant that would be the last instant that the world existed.

Richard gasped in a cry of terror, anguish, and sudden sharp pain as he felt the blade bite flesh, felt it slice mortally deep into his throat.

It was the end of everything.

S top it," Nicci growled.

Richard blinked. His mind reeled in confusion. Nicci had Shota's wrist in an iron grip, holding her hand away from him. But Shota still had an arm around his waist.

"I don't know what you're doing," Nicci said in a tone so dangerous he thought that surely Shota would shrink back in fear, "but you will stop it."

Shota did not shrink back, nor did she look the least bit fearful. "I am doing what needs to be done."

Nicci was having none of it. "Back away from him, or I will kill you where you stand."

Cara, Agiel in hand and looking even more displeased than Nicci, stood close on the other side of the witch woman, blocking her in. Before Shota could return the threat in kind, Richard collapsed heavily to the marble bench surrounding the fountain.

He was panting, gasping, and in a state of ragged terror. In his mind's eye he could still see Kahlan in the hands of those thugs, still feel the sharp blade slicing deep into him. His fingers lightly brushed across his throat, but there was no gaping wound, no blood. He desperately didn't want to let go of the sight of Kahlan, but at the same time it was so horrifying a glimpse of her hopeless dread that he wanted nothing so much as to forever wipe it from his mind.

He wasn't completely sure where he was. He wasn't sure exactly what was happening. It wasn't at all clear to him what was real and what wasn't.

He wondered if he was on the cusp of death and this was some confusing death-dream before all his lifeblood drained out of him, some final delusion to torture his mind as he passed from existence. He groped, trying to feel for other bodies there with him in the pit.

While Cara stood protectively before him, shielding him from the witch woman, Nicci immediately abandoned her altercation with Shota to sit beside him. She circled an arm around his shoulders.

"Richard, are you all right?" she leaned down, looking into his eyes. "You look like you've seen the walking dead."

Ignoring Cara, Shota folded her arms as she stood over them, watching Richard.

In his mind, the sound of Kahlan's screams still echoed, the sight of her as she cried out his name still tore at his heart. It had been so long since he had seen her. To see her again so suddenly, and like that, was devastating.

"Richard, it's all right," Nicci said. "You're right here, with me, with all of us."

Richard pressed a hand to his forehead. "How long was I gone?"

Nicci's brow twitched. "Gone?"

"I think Shota did something. How long was she . . . doing whatever she did?"

"I didn't let her do anything—I stopped her before she could begin. The instant she touched you under your chin I stopped her. She didn't have enough time to do anything."

Richard could still see Kahlan in his mind's eye, still see her screaming for him as the grimy hands of Imperial Order soldiers held her back.

He ran his trembling fingers back through his hair. "She had enough time."

"I'm so sorry," Nicci whispered. "I thought I stopped her soon enough."

He didn't think he could go on. He didn't think he could summon the strength to draw another breath. He didn't think that he would ever again be able to do anything but abandon himself to despair.

He could not hold back his anguish, his pain, his tears.

Nicci drew his face against her shoulder, wordlessly sheltering him in the refuge of her embrace.

It all seemed so futile. It was all ending. It was all over. He'd always said that they didn't have a chance to defeat Jagang's army. The Order was too powerful. They were going to win the war. There was nothing Richard could do about it, nothing left to live for but waiting for the horror of death to catch them all.

Shota stepped up on the side of him, beside where he sat on the short marble wall, opposite Nicci, and started to lay a hand on his shoulder. Cara snatched the witch woman's wrist, stopping her.

"I'm sorry to have to do that, Richard," Shota said, ignoring the Mord-Sith, "but you need to see, to understand, to—"

"Shut up," Nicci said, "and keep your hands off him. Don't you think you've brought him enough pain? Does everything you do have to be injurious? Can't you ever help him without trying to hurt him or cause him trouble at the same time?"

As Shota withdrew her hand, Nicci cupped hers to his face and with a thumb wiped a tear from his cheek. "Richard . . ."

He nodded at her tender concern, unable to summon his voice. He could still see Kahlan crying out for him as she tried to fight off the hands of those men. As long as he lived he would be haunted by that sight. At that moment he wanted more than anything to spare her the pain of seeing him executed and of her being in the cruel clutches of the Order. He wanted to go back, to do something, to save her from such inhuman abuse. He couldn't bear her world ending as she saw him murdered like that.

But it wasn't real. He couldn't have been there like that. Such a thing was impossible. He could only have imagined it.

Relief began to seep into him.

It wasn't real. It wasn't. Kahlan wasn't in the hands of the Order. She wasn't seeing him being executed. It was just a cruel trick by the witch woman. Just another of her illusions.

Except it had been real for all those people in Galea as well as untold other places where the Order had been. Even if it hadn't been real for Richard, it had been all too real for them. That was what it had been like. Their worlds had ended in just that manner. He knew exactly what they had suffered. He knew exactly what it felt like.

How many countless, unknown, unnamed, good people had lost their chance at life in just that way, all for the otherworldly ambitions of those from the Old World?

A new dread suddenly overwhelmed him. He had the gift. He was a war wizard. For most of those with the gift, it manifested itself in one specific area. But being a war wizard meant that he had elements of all the various aspects of the gift, and one aspect of magic was prophecy. What if what he had seen was really a prophecy? What if that was what was to happen? What if what he had seen was really a vision of the future?

But he didn't believe that the future was fixed. While some things, such as death, were inevitable, that didn't mean that everything was fixed or that one couldn't work toward worthy goals in life, couldn't avert disasters, couldn't alter the course of events. If it was a prophecy, it only meant that he had seen what was possible. It didn't mean that he couldn't try to stop it from happening.

After all, Shota's prophecies never seemed to come out the way she presented them. And anyway, what he had seen, what he had just experienced, was most likely Shota's doing.

Richard squeezed Nicci's hand in silent appreciation. Her other hand on his shoulder returned the squeeze. Her concern melted a little under the warmth of a small smile of relief at seeing him recovering his wits.

Richard rose up before Shota in a way that by all rights should have made her take a step back. She stood her ground.

"How dare you do that to me? How dare you send me to that place?"

"I did not send you anywhere, Richard. Your own mind took you where it would. I did nothing but release the thoughts you had suppressed. I spared you what would have otherwise come out in nightmares."

"I don't remember my dreams."

Shota nodded as she studied his eyes. "This one you would have remembered. It would have been far worse than what you have just suffered. It is better to face such visions when you can confront them for what they are, and grasp what truth they contain."

Richard could feel the blood heating his face. "Is that what you meant, before, when you said that if I married Kahlan she would bear a monster? Is that the real meaning hidden in your convoluted prophecy?"

Shota showed no emotion. "It means what it means."

Richard could still hear the words of the Imperial Order soldier telling him what he was going to do to Kahlan, telling him how she was going to be treated, telling him how she would give birth to children who would grow up to spit on the graves of those who had wanted to live their own lives for themselves, those who believed in everything he held dear.

Richard abruptly lunged for Shota and in an instant had her by the throat. The collision and his fierce determination to take her down carried them both over the short wall and into the fountain. With Richard on top, grappling her, their momentum drove them both under the water.

Richard hauled her up by her throat. "Is that what you meant!"

Water streamed from her face. She coughed it out.

He shook her. "Is that what you meant!"

Richard blinked. He was standing. He was dry. Shota stood before him. She was dry. His hands were still at his sides.

"Get ahold of yourself, Richard." Shota arched an eyebrow. "You are still partly in your dreams."

Richard looked around. It was true. He wasn't wet and neither was Shota. Not one wavy auburn hair on her head was out of place. Nicci's brow twitched when he glanced over at her. She looked puzzled by what could be the cause of his confusion. It must be true; he was still dreaming. It really was just a dream, just like his execution, just like seeing Kahlan. He'd only imagined that he had Shota by the throat.

But he wanted to.

"Was that what you meant when you said that Kahlan would bear a monster child?" Richard asked, a little more quietly, but with no less menace.

"I don't know who this Kahlan is."

Richard's jaw flexed as he gritted his teeth, thinking of having her by the throat for real. "Answer the question! Is it?"

Shota lifted a cautionary finger. "Believe me, Richard, you really don't want a witch angry with you."

"And you don't want me angry with you, so answer me. Is that what you meant?"

She smoothed the sleeves of her dress as she chose her words carefully. "In the first place, I have revealed to you at different times, in the various things that I've told you, what I see of the flow of events in time. I don't remember this woman, Kahlan, nor do I remember anything having to do with her. So, I don't know what event or prediction you are talking about, as I don't remember it either."

Shota's face took on the kind of darkly dangerous look that reminded him that he was talking to a witch woman whose very name inspired terrified trembling among most of the people of the Midlands. "But you are venturing into serious matters of grave peril in that flow of events forward in time." Her brow drew down in displeasure. "What, precisely, do you mean about a . . . monster child?"

Richard turned to gaze into the still waters of the fountain as he thought about the terrible things he'd seen. He couldn't bear to say it aloud. Couldn't bear to say it in front of others, to even suggest aloud that Shota had once made a prediction that he feared might actually mean that Kahlan would conceive a child fathered by the monsters of the Imperial

Order. It felt to him as if saying it out loud might somehow make it true. It was so painful an idea that he pushed the whole notion aside, and decided instead to ask another question.

He turned back to her. "What does it mean that I couldn't call my gift through anger?"

Shota sighed heavily. "Richard, you must understand something. I did not give you a vision. I did nothing more than help you to release hidden thoughts that were your own. I did not give you a dream of my making, nor did I plant any ideas in your mind. I merely made you aware of your own intellection. I can't tell you anything about what you saw because I don't know what you saw."

"Then why would you—"

"I only know that you are the one who must stop the Order. I helped you bring your own suppressed thoughts to the surface in order to help you to better understand."

"Understand what?"

"What you must understand. I no more know what that is than I know what you saw within your own mind that so upset you. You might say that I am merely the messenger. I have not read the message."

"But you made me see things that—"

"No, I did not. I opened the curtain for you, Richard. I did not make the rain you saw out of that window. You are trying to blame me for the rain, instead of appreciating the fact that I did nothing but open the curtain so that you could see it with your own eyes."

Richard glanced over at Nicci. She said nothing. He looked up the steps at his grandfather standing with his hands loosely clasped, silently watching. Zedd had always taught him to deal with the reality of the way the world was, taught him not to rail at what some believed was the invisible hand of fate controlling and conjuring events. Was he doing that to Shota? Was he trying to blame her for revealing things that he hadn't seen, or hadn't been willing to see?

"I'm sorry, Shota," he said in a quieter voice. "You're right. You did indeed show me the rain. I don't have a clue as to what to do about it, but I saw it. I shouldn't blame you for what others are doing. I'm sorry."

Shota smiled in a small way. "That is part of the reason why you are the one, Richard—the only one who can stop the madness. You are willing to see the truth. That is why I brought Jebra with such terrible accounts of what is happening at the hands of the Order. You need to know the truth of it."

Richard nodded, only feeling worse, feeling even more despairing over not having any idea of how to do what she thought he could.

He met Shota's unflinching gaze. "You've made a great effort to bring Jebra here. You've come a very long way. Your future, your very life, depends on this no less than does my life or the lives of all free people, all those with the gift. If the Order wins we all die, including you.

"Isn't there anything you can tell me that will help me to do something to stop this madness? I could use any help you can give me. Isn't there anything you can tell me?"

She stared at him a moment before speaking, stared as if her mind were in other places. "Whenever I bring you information," she said at last, "it angers you—as if I were the one creating what is, rather than merely reporting it."

"We're all facing slavery, torture, and death, and you're suddenly miffed about getting your feelings hurt?"

In spite of herself, Shota smiled at his characterization. "You think that I simply pluck revelations out of the air, as if I were picking a pear."

The smile faded as her gaze focused off into the distance. "You could not begin to understand the personal cost of bringing forth such shrouded knowledge. I do not wish to undertake such a formidable task if that dearly gained knowledge is going to do nothing but feed a grudge."

Richard shoved his hands in his back pockets. "All right, I get your point. If you're going to make such an effort, you expect me to consider it earnestly. We all have everything at stake, Shota. I'd value whatever you can tell me."

While Richard did honestly believe that Shota was telling him what she saw of the flow of events in time, he didn't believe that the meaning of such tellings was necessarily straightforward or what Shota believed they meant. Still, she had always offered him information that in some way had been central to the issues at hand—Chainfire being only the latest. While her revelation of the word *Chainfire* had been without an explanation that would help him, that clue alone had sustained his effort to find the answer to what had happened to Kahlan. Without that single word he would never have recognized that particular book as the one holding the key to discovering the truth.

Shota took a deep breath, finally letting it out in resignation. She leaned toward him the slightest bit, as if to emphasize how serious she was.

"It is for your ears alone."

Richard glanced at Cara and Nicci. By their expressions there was no doubt in his mind as to what they thought of the very idea of leaving him without their protection. While he knew they were convinced of the necessity of their being close at hand, he didn't really believe that he would be any safer for their watchful guard a step away rather than a few dozen— after all, Shota had just demonstrated as much. It was obvious, though, that they didn't share such a view.

Richard thought that maybe he could find a solution that would satisfy everyone. "They're on the same side. What difference—"

"The difference is that it is my wish." Shota turned to the fountain, turning her back on him, and folded her arms. "If you want to hear what I have to say, then you will honor my wishes."

Richard didn't know if she was merely being obstinate or not, but he did know that this was not the time to test the point. If he was going to get any help from Shota he needed to show her his trust. Likewise, Nicci and Cara were just going to have to trust him.

He gestured toward the steps. "Please, both of you, go up there with Zedd and wait."

Nicci clearly didn't like the idea any more than did Cara, but she recognized by the look he gave her that he needed her to do as he asked. She shot the back of Shota's head a hot glare. "If for any reason I believe you are about to harm him, I will reduce you to a charred cinder before you have a chance to act."

"Why would I harm him?" Shota looked back over her shoulder. "Richard is the only one who has a chance to stop the Order."

"Exactly."

Richard watched as Nicci and Cara wordlessly turned and ascended the steps. He had expected more of an argument from Cara, but was glad not to have it.

He shared a long look with his grandfather. Zedd seemed to be uncharacteristically quiet. For that matter, so did Nathan and Ann. All three watched him as if studying a curiosity found under a rock. Zedd gave Richard a slight nod, urging him to go on, to do what needed doing.

Richard heard the fountain behind him abruptly start to flow again. When he turned back he saw the waters shooting up into the air at the pinnacle, falling back, and streaming from the points of the bowls to dance at last in the lower pool.

Shota sat on the short marble wall surrounding the pool, her back to him as she leisurely trailed the fingers of one hand through the water. Something about her body language made the hair at the back of Richard's neck stand on end.

When she turned to look back over her shoulder, Richard found himself looking into the face of his mother.

His muscles locked stiff.

"Richard." Her sad smile showed how much she loved and missed him. She didn't look to have aged a day from his last boyhood memory of her.

As Richard stood frozen in place she rose fluidly before him.

"Oh, Richard," she said in voice as clear and liquid as the waters of the fountain, "how I've missed you." She slipped one arm around his waist as she ran the fingers of her other hand tenderly through his hair. She gazed longingly into his eyes. "How I've missed you so very much."

Richard immediately choked off his emotions. He knew better than to be lulled into believing it was really his mother.

The first time he'd met Shota she had appeared to him as his mother, who had died in a fire when Richard had been but a boy. At the time, Richard had wanted to take Shota's head off with his sword for what he interpreted as a cruel ruse. Shota had read the thought and reproached him for it, saying that appearing as she had was an innocent gift of a living memory of his love for his mother and her undying love for him. Shota had said that the kindness had been at a cost to herself that he would never be able to understand or appreciate.

Richard didn't think that this time she was giving him a gift. He didn't know what she was doing, or why, but he decided to confront it calmly and without jumping to conclusions.

"Shota, I thank you for the beautiful memory, but why is it necessary to appear as my mother?"

Shota's brow, in the likeness of his mother's, wrinkled in thought. "Do you know the name . . . Baraccus?"

The hairs at the back of Richard's neck, that had only just begun to settle, again stiffened. He gently placed his hands on her waist and with great care backed her away.

"There was a man named Baraccus who was First Wizard back in the time of the great war." With one finger, Richard lifted the amulet hanging at his chest. "This was his."

His mother nodded. "He is the one. He was a great war wizard."

"That's right."

"Like you."

Richard felt himself blush at the idea of his mother calling him "great," even if it was Shota in her guise.

"He knew how to use his ability; I don't."

His mother nodded again, a slight smile curling the corners of her mouth just as he remembered. His mother had smiled that way when she'd been proud that he had grasped the point of a particularly difficult lesson. He wondered if Shota meant that memory to have meaning.

"Do you know what happened to him, to Baraccus?"

Richard took a settling breath. "Yes, as a matter of fact, I do. There was trouble with the Temple of the Winds. The Temple and its invaluable contents had been sent to the safety of another world."

"The underworld," she amended.

"Yes. Baraccus went there to try to fix the trouble."

His mother smiled as she again ran her fingers through his hair. "Just as you did."

"I suppose."

When she finally finished fussing with his hair, her beautiful eyes turned down, her gaze settling again on his. "He went there for you."

"For me?" Richard looked at her askance. "What are you talking about?"

"Subtractive Magic had been locked away in the Temple, in the underworld, withdrawn from the world of life so that no wizard would again be born with it."

Richard didn't know if she was merely repeating what he had learned or if she was giving him what she believed to be the facts. "From the accounts of the time that I've studied, that's what I've come to suspect. As a consequence, people were no longer born with the Subtractive side of the gift."

She watched him with a kind of calm seriousness that he found disturbing in the extreme. "But you were," she finally said in a way that carried great meaning concealed in simplicity.

Richard blinked. "Are you saying that he did something while he was at the Temple of the Winds so that someone would again be born with Subtractive Magic?"

"By 'someone,' I presume that you mean . . . you?" She arched an eyebrow as if to underscore the sobriety of the question.

"What are you suggesting?"

"None has been born with Subtractive Magic and more, born a war wizard, since then, since the Temple was sent from this world."

"Look, I don't know for sure if that's true but even if it is that doesn't mean—"

"Do you know what war wizard Baraccus did upon his return from the Temple of the Winds?"

Richard was taken aback by the question, wondering what relevance it could have. "Well, yes. When he returned from the Temple of the Winds . . . he committed suicide." Richard gestured weakly to the vast complex above them. "He threw himself off the side of the Wizard's Keep, off the outer wall overlooking the valley and the city of Aydindril below."

His mother nodded sorrowfully. "Overlooking the place where the Confessors' Palace would eventually be built."

"I suppose so."

"But first, before he threw himself off that wall, he left something for you."

Richard stared down at her, not completely sure that he'd heard her correctly. "For me? Are you sure?"

His mother nodded. "The account you read was not privy to everything. You see, when he returned from the Temple of the Winds, before he threw himself from the side of the Keep, he gave his wife a book and sent her with it to his library."

"His library?"

"Baraccus had a secret library."

Richard felt like was was tiptoeing across fresh ice. "I didn't even know he had a wife."

"But Richard, you know her." His mother smiled in a way that made the already stiff hair at the back of his neck stand out even more.

Richard could hardly breathe. "I know her? How is that possible?"

"Well," his mother said with a one-shouldered shrug, "you know of her. Do you know the wizard who created the first Confessor?"

"Yes," Richard said, confused by her change of subject. "His name was Merritt. The first Confessor was a woman named Magda Searus. There is a painting of them across the ceiling down in the Confessors' Palace."

His mother nodded in a way that made his stomach knot. "That's the woman."

"What woman?"

"Baraccus's wife." -

"No . . ." Richard said as he touched his fingers to his forehead, trying to think it through. "No, she was the wife of Merritt, the wizard who had made her into a Confessor, not Baraccus."

"That was later," his mother said with a dismissive gesture. "Her first husband was Baraccus."

"Are you sure?"

She nodded firmly. "When Baraccus returned from the Temple of the Winds, Magda Searus was waiting for him, where he had asked her to wait, in the First Wizard's enclave. For days she had waited, fearful that he would never return to her. To her great relief he finally did. He kissed her, told her of his undying love, and then, in confidence, and after securing her oath of eternal silence, he sent her with a book to his hidden, private, secret library.

"After she had gone he left his outfit—the one you now wear, including those leather-padded silver wristbands, the cape that looks as if it has been spun from gold, and that amulet—in the First Wizard's enclave, left them for the wizard he had just insured would be born into the world of life . . . left them for you, Richard."

"For me? Are you sure that they were really meant for me, specifically?"

"Why do you think that there as so many prophecies that speak of you, that wait for you, that name you—'the one born true,' 'the pebble in the pond,' 'the bringer of death,' 'the *Caharin*'? Why do you think those prophecies that revolve around you came about? Why do you think that you have been able to understand some of them when no one else for centuries, for millennia, has been able to decipher them? Why do you think that you have fulfilled others?"

"But that doesn't mean that it was explicitly meant to be me."

With an indifferent gesture, his mother declined to either support or deny his assertion. "Who is to say what came first, the Subtractive side finally finding a child to be born in, or it finally finding the specific child it was meant to be born in. Prophecy needs a kernel to spark its growth. Something must be there to engender what will be, even if it is merely the color of your eyes that has been passed down to you. Something must make it come about. In this case, is it chance or intent?"

"I would like to think a chance series of events."

"If it pleases you. But at this point, Richard, does it really matter? You are the one born with the ability that Baraccus released from its confinement in another world. You are the one he intended to be born, either by chance or specific intent. In the end, the only thing that matters is what is: you are the one born with that ability."

Richard supposed that she was right; exactly how it came to be didn't change what was.

His mother sighed as she went on with the story. "Anyway, it was only then, after he had made his preparations for what he had insured would come about, that Baraccus emerged from his enclave and leaped to his death. Those who wrote the accounts did not know that he had already been back long enough to send his wife on an urgent covert mission. She returned to discover that he was dead."

Richard's head spun. He couldn't believe what he was hearing. He felt dizzy from the unexpected account of ancient events. He knew, though, from having been to the Temple of the Winds, that such things were possible. He had given up the knowledge that he had gained there as the price of returning to the world of life. Even though he'd lost that knowledge, he was left with a sense of how profound it had been. The one who had demanded the price of leaving behind what he had learned in exchange for his return to Kahlan had been the spirit of Darken Rahl, his real father.

"In her grief, Magda Searus volunteered herself to be the subject of a dangerous experiment that Merritt had come up with, volunteered to become a Confessor. She knew there was a good chance that she would not live through the unknown hazards of that conjuring, but in her grief, with her beloved husband, the First Wizard, dead, her world had ended. She didn't think that there was anything for her to live for, other than finding out who was responsible for the fateful events that had resulted in her husband's death, so she volunteered for what everyone expected might very well be a fatal experiment.

"Yet she survived. It was only much later that she began to fall in love with Merritt, and he with her. Her world came back to life with him. The accounts of that time are in spots blurred, with pieces missing or misplaced in the chronology of events, but the truth is that Merritt was her second husband."

Richard had to sit down on the marble bench. It was almost too much to take in. The implications were staggering. He had trouble reconciling the coincidences: that he had been the first in thousands of years to be born with Subtractive Magic, that Baraccus had been the last one to go to the Temple of the Winds until Richard himself, that Baraccus had been married to a woman who became the first Confessor, that Richard had fallen in love with and married a Confessor—the Mother Confessor herself, Kahlan.

"When Magda Searus used her newborn Confessor power on Lothain, they discovered what he had done at the Temple of the Winds, what only Baraccus had known."

Richard looked up. "What did he do?"

His mother gazed into his eyes as if she were looking into his soul. "Lothain betrayed them when he was at the Temple by seeing to it that a very specific magic that had been locked away there would at some future point be released into the world of life. Emperor Jagang was born with the power that Lothain allowed to seep out of the safety of its confinement in another world. That magic was the power of a dream walker."

"But why would Lothain, the head prosecutor, do such a thing? After all, he had seen to it that the Temple team was executed for the damage they had done."

"Lothain had probably come to believe, as did the enemy in the Old World, that magic should be eliminated from the race of man. I guess his zealotry found a new fixation: he imagined himself as savior of mankind. To that end he insured the return of a dream walker to the world of life, to purge the world of magic.

"For some reason, Baraccus was unable to seal the breach created by Lothain, unable to undo the treason. He did the next best thing. He saw to it that there would be a balance, a counter, to the damage done, someone to fight against those forces bent on destroying those with the gift, someone with the required ability.

"That would be you, Richard. Baraccus saw to it that you would be born to counter what had been done by Lothain. That is why you, Richard Rahl, are the only one who can stop the Order."

Richard thought he might be sick. It all made him feel as if he were but a cosmic pawn being used for a hidden purposes, a dupe doing nothing more than playing out the plan for his life contrived by others, performing his predetermined part in a battle across the sweep of millennia.

As if reading his mind, Shota, still looking and sounding for all the world like his mother, laid a compassionate hand on his shoulder. "Baraccus saw to it that there was a balance to counter this damage. He did not preordain how that balance would function or how it would act. He did not take your free will out of the equation, Richard."

"You think not? It seems to me that I'm merely the final piece of this game being put into play at long last. I don't see my free will, my own life, my choice, in any of it. It would seem others have determined my path."

"I don't think that is true, Richard. You might say that what they have done is not unlike training a soldier to fight. That training creates the possibility of accomplishing the goal of winning the battle should a battle come to pass. It doesn't mean that when the battle does comes the soldier won't run away, that he will instead stand and fight, or even that if he does fight to the best of his ability and training that he will win. Baraccus saw to it that you have the potential, Richard, the armor, the weapons, the ability, to fight for your own life and your own world should the need arise, nothing more. He was just giving you a helping hand."

A helping hand sent across the gulf of time. Richard felt drained and confused. He almost felt as if he no longer knew himself, knew who he really was, or how much of his own life was of his own making.

It felt to him as if Baraccus had suddenly materialized out of the dust of ancient bones, a phantom come to haunt Richard's life.

There was one thing that still nagged at him, one other bit that still didn't make sense. How could the head prosecutor, Lothain, turn on his beliefs, turn on everyone in the New World? It struck Richard as too convenient an explanation that he fell under the power, the allure, of the beliefs of the Old World.

And then it came to him—realization welling up through him in a rush with the power of floodwaters. The substance of it nearly took his breath. Something about the ancient accounts had always bothered him. Shota had stirred his memory of the things that had happened and in so doing all the existing pieces suddenly fell into place. Now he understood what was wrong with the story, what had always bothered him about it. Once he understood, he didn't know why he hadn't realized it long before.

"Lothain was a zealous prosecutor," Richard said, half to himself. It all came out in a rush as he spoke, his eyes wide and unblinking. "He didn't find a new fixation for his zealotry. He didn't turn on them.

"He wasn't a traitor. He was a spy.

"He had always been a spy. He was like a mole, tunneling ever closer to his objective. Over a long period of time he worked himself into a position of power. He also had accomplices covertly working under him.

"Lothain was a wizard who had become not just widely respected but powerful. With his political power he had access to the highest places. When the opportunity finally presented itself, an opportunity that he had helped engineer, he acted. He saw to it that his co-conspirators were assigned to the Temple team. Just like the Order today, Lothain and his men had a strong faith in their cause. They were the ones who corrupted the mission. It wasn't a change of heart, a misguided act of conscience. It had been planned all along. It was deliberate.

"They were all willing to sacrifice themselves, to die for what they believed was a higher cause. I don't know how many of the team were actually spies, or if all of them were, but the fact is that enough were that they accomplished their goal. It could even be that they convinced the others to go along with them out of a confused sense of moral obligation.

"It was inevitable, of course, that the other wizards at the Keep would soon enough realize that the Temple of the Winds project had been compromised. When they did, Lothain was only too ready to prosecute the entire Temple team, and saw to it that they were all executed. He didn't want anyone left alive who could betray the extent of what they had actually done.

"Lothain had intended all along for their precise actions to be kept secret so that successful countermeasures could not be undertaken. Those spies whom Lothain had assigned to the Temple team went to their graves willingly, taking their secrets with them. By prosecuting and sentencing the entire Temple team, Lothain was able to bury the entire conspiracy that he had devised. He eliminated everyone who had any knowledge of the true damage that had been done. He was confident in the knowledge that one day his cause would sweep aside all opposition and they would rule the world. When that happened, he would be the greatest hero of the war.

"There was only one minor problem remaining. After the trial, those in charge insisted that someone must go to the Temple of the Winds to repair the damage. Lothain couldn't allow anyone else to go, of course, because they would find out the true extent of the sabotage and might possibly be able to undo it, so he volunteered to go himself. That had been his plan all along—to follow up on the team himself, if need be, and cover up the truth.

"Because he was the head prosecutor, everyone believed that he had the absolute conviction to set matters right. When Lothain finally reached the Temple of the Winds, he not only saw to it that the damage could not be repaired, he used the knowledge he gained there to make it worse, to make sure that no one would find and fix the breach. He then covered up what he had done, intending to make it appear as if all had been set right.

"There was only one problem: the alterations he made, using the knowledge of the Temple itself, turned out to be enough to set off the Temple's protective alarms. From the Temple, in that other world, Lothain was unaware of the red moons the Temple had awakened in this world, and when he returned he was caught. Even so, he didn't care; he looked forward to dying, to gaining eternal glory in the afterlife for all that he had accomplished, just as Nicci explained about the way the people of the Old World think.

"The wizards at the Keep needed to know the extent of the damage Lothain had caused. Even though he was tortured, Lothain did not reveal the extent of the plan. To discover the truth of what had happened, Magda Searus became a Confessor. But she was inexperienced at the task and still learning as she went. Even though she used her Confessor power, she didn't realize, at the time, the importance of asking the right questions."

Richard looked up at the face of his mother. "Kahlan told me once that just getting a confession was easy. The hard part was understanding how to ask the right questions to get the truth. Merritt had only just devised the powers of a Confessor. No one yet understood the way those powers functioned.

"Kahlan was trained her whole life to be able to do it properly, but back then, thousands of years ago, Magda Searus didn't yet grasp how to ask all the right questions, in the right order. Even though she believed she had gotten Lothain to confess to what he had done, she failed to uncover the true extent of his treachery. He was a spy, and despite the use of the first Confessor, they failed to discover it. As a result, they never knew the full extent of the subversion carried out by Lothain's men on the Temple team."

His mother studied him from under a brow set in concentration. "Are you sure of this, Richard?"

He nodded. "It finally all makes sense to me. With what you've added to the story, all the pieces that I could never before fit in place now fit. Lothain was a spy and he went to his death never revealing who he really was, or that he had placed his own men on the Temple team. They all died without ever revealing the true extent of the damage they had done. No one, not even Baraccus, realized the full extent of it."

His mother sighed as she stared off. "That certainly explains some of the missing gaps in what came to me." She looked back at him as if in a new light. "Very good, Richard. Very good indeed."

Richard wiped a hand across his weary eyes. He didn't feel any great sense of pride in reaching down into the dark muck of history and pulling up such despicable deeds, deeds that were still slipping across time to haunt him.

"You said that Baraccus left a book for me?"

She nodded. "He sent it away with his wife for safekeeping. It was meant for you."

Richard sighed. "Are you sure?"

"Yes." His mother carefully folded her fingers together. "While still at the Temple of the Winds, Baraccus wrote the book with the aid of knowledge that he gathered there. No eyes but his have ever read it. No living person has so much as opened the cover since Baraccus finished writing it and closed the cover himself. It has, since that time, been lying untouched in his secret library."

The idea of such a thing gave Richard a chill. He had no idea where such a library could be, but even if he found the right library that would not tell him what he needed to know. He didn't suppose that there was a chance, but he asked anyway.

"Do you have any idea what this book is called? Or maybe what it's about?"

His mother nodded solemnly. "It is titled *Secrets of a War Wizard's Power*."

"Dear spirits," Richard whispered as he looked up at her.

Elbows on his knees, his face sank into his hands. He was so overwhelmed that he couldn't seem to take it all in. The last man who had visited the Temple of the Winds, three thousand years before Richard had, had somehow, while there, seen to it that the Temple would release Subtractive Magic, which Richard had been born with, in part, so that he could get into the Temple of the Winds to stop a plague started by a dream walker who had been born because a wizard, Lothain, had been there first and seen to it that a dream walker would be born in order to rule the world and destroy magic. And further, that same man who had seen to it that Richard would be born with Subtractive Magic had left Richard a book of instruction on the very magic it seemed he had bestowed on Richard in order to defeat the dream walker.

After Baraccus returned and committed suicide, the wizards had abandoned any further attempts to get into the Temple of the Winds to answer the call of the red moons, or for any other reason, as impossible. They were never able to get in to undo the damage the Temple team and then Lothain had done. Only Baraccus had been able to take action to counter the threat.

Very possibly, Baraccus himself had insured that no one else could get into the Temple of the Winds, probably so that there would be no chance that any other spy could ruin what Baraccus had done to insure that there would be a balance to the threat, namely, Richard's birth.

Richard looked up. His mother was no longer there. In her place stood Shota, the loose points of her dress floating gently as if in a breeze. Richard was sad to see his mother gone but at the same time it was a relief since it was so disorienting to try to speak to Shota through the specter of his mother.

"This library where Baraccus sent his wife with the book *Secrets of a War Wizard's Power*, where is it?"

Shota shook her head sadly. "I'm afraid that I don't know. I don't think that anyone but Baraccus and his wife, Magda Searus, knew."

Richard wore the war wizard outfit last worn by Baraccus, wore the amulet worn by Baraccus, carried the gift for Subtractive Magic very likely because of Baraccus. And Baraccus had left him what sounded like an instruction book on how to use the power he had seen to it that Richard had been born with.

"There are so many libraries. Baraccus's private library could be among any of them. Do you have idea at all which one it could be?"

"I know only that it is not among any other library, as you suggest. The library Baraccus created was his alone. Every book there is his alone. He hid them well. They remain undiscovered to this day."

"And for some reason he saw fit not to leave those books in the safety of the First Wizard's enclave?"

"Safety? Not long ago, Sisters of the Dark, sent by Jagang, violated this place. They took books, among other things, to the emperor. Jagang hunts books because they contain knowledge that helps him in his struggle to rule the world for the Order. Had the book Baraccus wrote for you been left here at the Keep, it very well might now be in Jagang's hands. Baraccus was wise not to leave such power here, where anyone could find it, where every First Wizard to come after him might have discovered it and tampered with it, or even destroyed it lest it fall into the wrong hands."

That was what had happened to *The Book of Counted Shadows*. Ann and Nathan, because of prophecy, had helped George Cypher bring it back to Westland with the intent that when he was old enough, Richard would memorize that book and then destroy it lest it fall into the wrong hands. It turned out that Darken Rahl would eventually need to get his hands on that book in order to open the boxes of Orden—the same boxes that were now in play because of Ann's former Sisters, who now had Kahlan, the last Confessor, who, because of what was written in that book, had helped him defeat Darken Rahl.

Richard lifted out the amulet he wore, which had once belonged to Baraccus. He stared at the symbols making up the dance with death. There was just too much for it all to be coincidence.

He peered up at Shota. "Are you saying that Baraccus foresaw what would happen and put the book in a place of greater safety?"

Shota shrugged. "I'm sorry, Richard, I don't know. It may be that he was simply being cautious. Considering his reasons, and what is at stake, such caution certainly seems not only to have been warranted, but wise.

"I've told you everything I can. You know all the pieces of the puzzle, of the history, that I'm unaware of. That doesn't mean that this is all there is to it, but from other sources you also know additional parts of the history, so you now know more of the story than I do. For that matter, you probably now know more of it than any person alive since war wizard Baraccus was the First Wizard."

Out of all she had told him, nothing would do him any good unless he could find the book Baraccus had meant for him to have. Without that book, Richard's war wizard powers were a mystery to him and next to useless. Without that book, it seemed that there was no hope of defeating the army that had come up from the Old World. The Order would rule the world and magic would be eradicated from the world of life, just as Lothain had planned. Without the book, Baraccus's plan was a failure, and Jagang was going to win.

Richard gazed up at the glassed roof a hundred feet overhead, which let in some of the somber, late-day light to balance the glow of the lamps down in the heart of the room. He wondered when the lamps had been lit. He didn't recall it happening.

"Shota, there could be no greater need for such knowledge. How am I supposed to succeed in stopping the Order if I can't use my ability as a war wizard? Can't you give me anything, any idea at all, of how to find this book? If I don't find some answers, and soon, I'm dead. We all are."

She cupped his chin as she looked down into his eyes. "I hope you know, Richard, that if I knew how to get that book for you, I would do it. You know how much I want to stop the Imperial Order."

"Well, why do you get specific information. Where does it come from? Why is it that it comes to you at specific times, like now? Why not the first time I met you? Or when I was trying to get into the Temple of the Winds to stop the plague?"

"I suppose that it comes from the same place you get answers or inspiration when you mull over a problem. Why do you come up with answers to problems when you do? I think about a situation and sometimes the answers come to me. Fundamentally, it's no different, I suppose, than how anyone comes up with ideas. It's just that my ideas are unique to a witch woman's mind and they involve events in the flow of time. I suppose that it's much the same as how you suddenly came to know the truth about what Lothain had done. How did that come to you? I suppose that it works much the same for me.

"If I knew where the book *Secrets of a War Wizard's Power* was, or had any idea of how to find it, I wouldn't hesitate to tell you."

Richard heaved a sigh and stood. "I know, Shota. Thank you for all you've done. I'll try to find a way for what you've told me to be of help."

Shota squeezed his shoulder. "I must go. I have a witch woman to find. At least, thanks to Nicci, I now know her name."

A thought struck him. "I wonder why she's named Six?"

Shota's countenance darkened. "It's a derogatory name. A witch woman sees many things in the flow of time, especially those things having to do with any daughters she might bear. For a witch woman, the seventh child is special. To name a child Six is to say that she falls short, that she is less than perfect. It's an open insult, from birth, for what a witch woman foresees of her daughter's character. It's a pronouncement that her daughter is flawed.

"Naming her Six probably earned the mother her own murder at the hands of that daughter."

"Then why would the mother so openly declare such a thing? Why not name the daughter something else and avoid the probability of her own murder."

Shota regarded him with a sad smile. "Because there are witch women who are believers in the truth, because truth will help others avoid danger.

To such women, a lie would be the bud of much larger trouble that would grow from it. To us, truth is the only hope for the future. To us, the future is life."

"Well, it sounds like the name fits the trouble this one is causing."

Shota's smile, sad though it had been, vanished. Her brow tightened with a dark look. She lifted a finger in warning. "Such a woman could easily conceal her name. This one, instead, reveals it the way a snake bares its fangs. You worry about everything else, and leave her to me. A witch woman is profoundly dangerous."

Richard smiled a little. "Like you?"

Shota didn't return the smile. "Like me."

Richard stood alone by the fountain as he watched Shota ascend the steps. Nicci, Cara, Zedd, Nathan, Ann, and Jebra were huddled off to the side, engaged in whispered conversation among themselves. They didn't pay any heed to Shota as she passed, like an unseen apparition.

Richard followed her up the steps. In the doorway, silhouetted by the light, Shota turned back, almost as if she had seen an apparition herself. She reached out and for a time rested a hand on the doorframe.

"One other thing, Richard." Shota studied his eyes for a moment. "When you were young, your mother died in a fire."

Richard nodded. "That's right. A man got in a fight with George Cypher, the man who raised me, the man I thought at the time was my father. This man who started the fight with my father knocked a lamp off the table, setting the house on fire. My brother and I were asleep in the back bedroom at the time. While the man dragged my father outside and was beating him, my mother raced in and pulled my brother and me from the burning house."

Richard cleared his throat with the pain that still haunted him. He remembered the quick smile of her relief that they were safe, and the last quick kiss she had given him on his forehead.

"After my mother was sure that we were safe, she ran back inside to save something—we never knew what. Her screams brought the man to his senses and he and my father tried to save her, but they couldn't . . . it was too late. They were driven back by the heat of the flames and could do nothing for her. Filled with guilt and revulsion at what he had caused, the man ran off sobbing that he was sorry.

"It was a terrible tragedy, especially because there was no one else in the house and nothing worth saving, nothing worth her life. My mother died for nothing."

Shota, standing silhouetted in the doorway, one hand resting against the doorframe, stared at him for what seemed an eternity. Richard waited silently. There was some kind of terrible significance evident in her posture, in her almond eyes. She finally spoke in a soft voice.

"Your mother was not the only one to die in that fire."

Richard felt goose bumps race up his legs and arms. Everything he had known for nearly his whole life seemed to be vaporized in an instant by the lightning strike of those words.

"What are you talking about? What do you mean?"

Shota shook her head sadly. "I swear on my life, Richard, I don't know anything else."

He stepped closer and grasped her arm, being careful not to grip it as hard as he easily could have under the sudden power of his burning need to understand why she would say such a thing.

"What do you mean, you don't know anything else? How can you say something so inconceivable and then just say that you don't know anything else? How can you say something like that about the death of my mother—and then just not know any more. That doesn't make sense. You must know something more."

Shota cupped a hand to the side of his face. "You did something for me the last time you came to Agaden Reach. You turned down my offer and said that I was worth more than to have someone against their will. You said that I deserved to have someone who would value me for who I am.

"As angry as I was with you at that moment, it made me think. No one has ever turned me down before, and you did it for the right reasons— because you cared about me, cared that I have what will make my life worthwhile. You cared enough to risk my wrath.

"When I assumed the likeness of your mother, that gift in some way influenced the flow of information coming to me. Because of that, just now as I was about to leave, that single thought came into my awareness: Your mother was not the only one to die in that fire.

"Like all things that I glean from the flow of events in time, it came to me as a kind of intuitive vision. I don't know what it means, and I don't know any more about it. I swear, Richard, I don't.

"Under ordinary circumstances I would not have revealed that small bit of information because it is so charged with possibilities and questions, but these are hardly ordinary circumstances. I thought you should know what came to me. I thought you should know every scrap of everything I know. Not all of what I learn from the flow of time is useful—that's why I don't always reveal to people isolated things like this. In this instance, however, I thought you should know it in case it comes to mean something to you, in case it might come to help you somehow."

Richard felt numb and confused. He wasn't sure that he believed it really meant what it sounded like it meant.

"Could it mean that she wasn't the only one to die because a part of us died with her that day? That our hearts would never be the same? Could it mean that she was not the only one to die in that fire in that sense?"

"I don't know, Richard, I really don't, but it could be. It may in that way be insignificant as far as being something that would actually help you now. I don't always know everything about what the flow of time reveals or if it is meaningful. It could be as you say and nothing more.

"I can only be a help if I relay information accurately, and so that is what I did. That is the exact way it came to me and in that precise concept: Your mother was not the only one to die in that fire."

Richard felt a tear run down his cheek. "Shota, I feel so alone. You brought Jebra to tell me things that gave me nightmares. I don't know what to do next. I don't. So many people believe in me, depend on me. Isn't there something you can tell me that will at least point me in the right direction before we're all lost?"

With a finger, Shota lifted the tear from his cheek. That simple act somehow lifted his heart in a small way.

"I am sorry, Richard. I don't know the answers that would save you. If I did, please believe that I would give them eagerly. But I know the good in you. I believe in you. I do know that you have within you what you must to succeed. There will be times when you doubt yourself. Do not give up. Remember then that I believe in you, that I know you can accomplish what you must. You are a rare person, Richard. Believe in yourself.

"Know that I believe you are the one who can do it."

Outside, before starting down the granite steps, she turned back, a black shape against the fading light.

"If Kahlan was ever real or not no longer matters. The entire world of life, everyone's life, is now at stake. You must forget this one life, Richard, and think of all the rest."

"Prophecy, Shota?" Richard felt too heavyhearted to raise his voice. "Something from the flow of time?"

Shota shook her head. "Simply the advice of a witch woman." She started for the paddock to collect her horse. "Too much is at stake, Richard. You must stop chasing this phantom."

When Richard went back inside everyone was crowded around Jebra, engaged in hushed conversation filled with sympathy for her ordeal.

Zedd paused in the middle of what he was saying as Richard joined them. "Rather odd, don't you think, my boy?"

Richard glanced around at the perplexed expressions. "What's odd?"

Zedd spread his hands. "That somewhere in the middle of Jebra telling her story Shota simply up and vanished."

"Vanished," Richard repeated, cautiously.

Nicci nodded. "We thought she would stick around and have something to say after Jebra finished."

"Maybe she had to go find someone to intimidate," Cara said.

Ann sighed. "Maybe she wanted to be on her way after that other witch woman."

"Maybe, being a witch woman, she isn't much for good-byes," Nathan suggested.

Richard didn't say anything. He had seen Shota do this before, like when she had shown up at his and Kahlan's wedding and given Kahlan the necklace. No one had heard her then, either, when she had spoken to Richard and Kahlan. No one had seen her leave.

Everyone went back to their conversation, except for his grandfather. Zedd looked distant and distracted.

"What is it?" Richard asked.

Zedd shook his head as he laid his arm around Richard's shoulders, leaning closer as he spoke intimately. "For some reason, I find my mind wandering to thoughts of your mother."

"My mother."

Zedd nodded. "I really miss her."

"Me too," Richard said. "Now that you mention it, I guess I've had her on my mind as well."

Zedd stared off into the distance. "Part of me died with her that day."

It took Richard a moment to find his voice. "Do you have any idea why she went back into the burning house? Do you think there was anything important in there? Maybe someone we didn't know about?"

Zedd shook his head insistently. "I felt sure that there had to have been some good reason, but I went through the ashes myself." His eyes welled up with tears. "There was nothing in there but her bones."

Richard glanced out the door and saw the spectral shadow of Shota atop her horse start down the road without looking back.

Rachel hesitated deep within the dark entrance. It was becoming difficult to see. She wished she couldn't make out what was drawn on the walls, but the fact was she could. All the way into the cave she had tried not to look too closely at the strange scenes covering the stone walls all around her. Some of the images made goose bumps rise on her arms. She could not imagine why anyone would want to draw such horrible, cruel things, but she certainly could understand why they would put them down in the cave, why they would want to hide such dark thoughts from the light of day.

The man unexpectedly shoved her. Rachel stumbled forward and fell flat on her face. She gasped a breath to regain the wind that had been so abruptly knocked out of her. She spit out dirt as she pushed herself up on her arms. She was too angry to cry.

When she peeked back over her shoulder she saw that, instead of watching her, he was gazing ahead into the darkness with those unsettling golden eyes of his, as if his mind had wandered and he'd forgotten all about her. Rachel glanced back toward the light, wondering if she could make it past his long legs. She reasoned that she could feign going one way and then dodge the other. That might work. But he was a lot bigger than she was and could no doubt run faster even if her legs hadn't been all wobbly from having been tied for so long. If only he hadn't taken her knives away from her. Still, if she was quick, she thought she might possibly be able to get enough of a start to make it.

Before she had a chance to try, the man noticed her again. He seized her by the collar and hoisted her to her feet, then shoved her on ahead, deeper into the black maw of the cave. Rachel struggled to find her footing over rock outcroppings and to jump fissures. Seeing some kind of movement ahead, she paused.

"Well, well . . ." came a razor-thin voice from back in the darkness. "Visitors."

The last word had been drawn out so that it almost sounded like the hiss of a snake.

Rachel's skin went icy cold as she stared, wide-eyed, into the darkness, fearing who could be the owner of such a voice.

Out of that darkness, as if from out of the underworld itself, a shadow materialized, gliding forward into the dim light.

Shadows didn't smile, though, Rachel realized. This was a woman, a tall woman in long black robes. Her long, wiry hair, too, was black. In contrast, her skin was so pale that it made her face almost appear to be floating all by itself in the darkness. It reminded Rachel of the skin of an albino salamander that hid under leaves on the forest floor during the day, never touched by the sunlight. All of her, from the coarse black cloth of her dress to her parched flesh stretched tightly over her knuckles to her stiff hair, seemed as dry as a sunbaked carcass.

She wore the kind of smile that Rachel imagined a wolf wore when dinner dropped in unexpectedly.

Although her eyes were blue, it was a blue that was as blanched as her skin, so that it almost seemed that she might be blind. But the way those eyes deliberately took Rachel in left no doubt that this was a woman who could not only see just fine in the light, but probably in pitch darkness as well.

"This had better be worth it," the man behind Rachel said. "The little brat stabbed me in my leg."

Rachel glared back over her shoulder. She didn't know the man's name. He had never bothered to tell her. Ever since capturing her he'd spoken very little, in fact, as if she were not someone but something—an inanimate object—that he had merely collected. The way he'd treated her made her feel like she was nothing more than a sack of grain thrown over the back of his saddle. But, at that moment, the grief, fear, thirst, and hunger during the long journey were only dim annoyances in the back of her mind.

"You killed Chase," she said. "You deserve more than I did."

The woman frowned. "Who?"

"The man with her."

"Ah, him," the woman in black said. "And you killed him?" She sounded only mildly curious. "Are you certain? Did you bury him?"

He shrugged. "I guess he's dead—men don't recover from such wounds. The spell concealed me well enough, just as you promised it would, so he never even noticed I was there. I didn't take the time to stop and bury him, though, since I knew you wanted me back as soon as possible."

Her thin smile widened. Coming ever closer, she finally reached out and ran her long, bony fingers back through his thick hair. Her ghostly blue eyes studied him intently.

"Very good, Samuel," she cooed. "Very good."

Samuel looked like a hound that was getting scratched behind the ears. "Thank you, Mistress."

"And you brought the rest of it?"

He nodded eagerly. A smile warmed his face. Rachel had thought him a cold-looking man, maybe because of his strange, golden eyes, but when he smiled it seemed to mask his nature. With that smile he was a better-looking man than most, although to Rachel he was, and always would be, a monster. A warm smile wasn't going to change what he had done.

Samuel seemed suddenly in a good mood. Rachel hadn't ever seen him this happy. Although much of the time she'd been in a sack, tied over the back of his horse, so she supposed that she didn't really know if he'd been in a good mood or not. She didn't really care.

She just wanted him dead. He had killed Chase, the best thing that had ever happened in Rachel's entire life. Chase was the best man who had ever lived. Chase had taken her in after she'd escaped from Queen Milena, the castle at Tamarang, and that terrible Princess Violet. Chase had loved her and had taken care of her. He taught her things about taking care of herself. He had a family he loved and who loved and needed him.

But now they had all lost him.

Chase was so big and so good with his weapons that Rachel hadn't thought that anyone could ever defeat him, especially not a man by himself. But Samuel had appeared like a ghost and run Chase through while he slept, run him through with that beautiful sword that Rachel just knew couldn't belong to him. She hated to think of how he had gotten that sword and who else he'd hurt with it.

Samuel stood looking like an idiot, his arms hanging, his shoulders slumped, as the woman ran her fingers back through his hair, whispering comforting, fawning words. It seemed completely unlike him. Up until then Samuel had always seemed confident and sure of himself. He always made it clear to Rachel that he was in charge. He always knew exactly what he wanted. In the presence of this woman, though, he was different. Rachel half expected his tongue to hang out and for him to start drooling.

"You said you brought the rest of it, Samuel," she said in her hissy voice.

"Yes." He lifted an arm back toward the light. "It's on the horse."

"Well, don't leave it out there," the woman said, her voice taking on an impatient edge. "Go and get it."

"Yes . . . yes, right away." He seemed only too eager to do her bidding and scurried off.

Rachel watched him rushing back through the cave, making his way over rocks that lay in his path, sometimes using his hands on the ground for balance, hurrying past the creepy gallery of drawings and toward the cave entrance. She noticed then light flickering on the dark walls. When she heard the sputtering sizzle she realized that it was light from a torch. She turned back around to see someone else, carrying a torch, appearing out of the darkness.

Rachel's jaw dropped.

It was Princess Violet.

"Well, well, if it isn't the orphan Rachel come back to us," Violet said as she stuck the torch in a bracket on the rock wall before taking up a place beside the woman in black.

Rachel's eyes felt like they might pop out of her head. She couldn't seem to make her mouth close. Her voice had fled down into the pit of her stomach.

"Why, Violet, dear, I do believe you've scared the little thing witless. Lose your tongue, little one?"

Princess Violet was the one who had lost her tongue. But now it was back. Somehow, as impossible as it seemed, it was back.

"Princess Violet . . ."

Violet's back stiffened as she straightened her broad shoulders. She seemed to be half again as big as the last time Rachel had seen her. She was meatier-looking. Older-looking.

"Queen Violet, now."

Rachel blinked in astonishment. "Queen . . . ?"

Violet smiled in a way that could have frozen a bonfire.

"Yes, that's right. Queen. My mother, you see, was murdered when that man, Richard, escaped. It was his doing. He is responsible for my mother's death, for the death of our beloved former queen. He brought us all nothing but grief and terrible times." She heaved a sigh. "Things have changed. I am queen now."

Rachel couldn't make it work in her head. Queen. It all seemed impossible. Mostly, though, it was dumbfounding that Violet could again speak after having lost her tongue.

A humorless smile spread on Violet's lips as her brow drew down. "Kneel before your queen."

Rachel couldn't seem to make sense of the words.

Violet's hand came out of nowhere, striking Rachel so hard that it knocked her sprawling.

"Kneel before your queen!"

Violet's shriek echoed back and forth in blackness.

Gasping in pain and shock, Rachel held one hand to the side of her face as she struggled to her knees. She felt warm blood running down her chin. Violet was a lot stronger than before.

The painful slap was like her past slamming right back down on her, as if everything had been a dream and she was waking again to the nightmare of her former life. She was all alone again, with no Giller, no Richard, no Chase to help her. She was again helpless before Violet without a friend in the world.

Violet's smile had vanished. As she stared down at Rachel kneeling before her, her eyes narrowed in a way that made Rachel have to swallow.

"He attacked me, you know. Back when he was Seeker, Richard attacked me, hurt me, for no reason." She planted her fists on her hips. "He hurt me bad. Attacked and hurt a child! My jaw was broken. My teeth were shattered. My tongue was severed, just as he had once promised to do. I was left mute."

Her voice lowered into a growl that chilled Rachel to the bone. "But that was the least of my suffering."

Violet took a breath to calm herself. With the palms of her hands she smoothed down her pink satin dress at the hips.

"None of my mother's advisors were any help. They were bumbling fools when it came down to doing anything worthwhile. They offered endless potions and poultices and aromas and incantations. They said prayers and made offerings to the good spirits. They applied leeches and hot jars.

None of it worked. My mother was buried without me there. I was unconscious at the time.

"Not even the stars had anything to say about my condition or chances. The advisors mostly stood around wringing their hands—and probably plotting who would steal the crown when I finally died. I suspect that if it wasn't soon then one of them would have helped me along into the afterlife with my mother. I heard their worried whispers about me becoming queen."

Violet took another calming breath. "In the middle of my nightmare of pain and suffering, of anguish and grief, of my growing concern about being murdered, Six arrived and helped me." She gestured up at the woman standing beside her. "Just when I needed it most, Six came along and helped save me, helped save the crown and Tamarang itself, when no one else could or would."

"But, but," Rachel stammered, "you're not old enough to be a queen."

She knew it was a mistake the instant the words had left her tongue, before her better judgment had time to stop them. Violet's other hand whipped around, slapping Rachel across the other cheek. Violet seized her by the hair and roughly pulled her back up onto her knees. Rachel cupped a hand to the new throbbing ache and with the other hand wiped blood from her mouth.

Violet shrugged, indifferent to the pain and blood she had caused. "Anyway, I grew up in the last few years. I'm no longer the child I was back then, the child you still think of me being, back when you lived here, enjoying our kindness and generosity."

Rachel didn't think that Violet had grown up enough to be a queen, but she knew better than to say so again. She also knew better than to think of enslavement as "kindness."

"Six helped me as I recovered. She saved me."

Rachel stared up at the pale, smiling face. "I offered my services. Violet welcomed me into the castle. Her mother's advisors certainly weren't doing her any good.

"Six used her power to heal my broken and grossly infected jaw. I had grown weak from only being able to sip a thin broth. With Six's help I was at last able to begin to eat again and recover my strength. New teeth even came in. I don't suppose that anyone ever grew a third set of teeth before, yet I did.

"But still I could not speak, so when I was well enough, strong enough, Six used her remarkable powers to grow me a new tongue." Her fists tightened at her sides. "The tongue that I lost because of the Seeker."

"The former Seeker," Six corrected, under her breath.

"The former Seeker," Violet acknowledged, considerably calmer.

A smug smile returned to Violet's plump face. It was a smile that Rachel knew all too well. "And now you have been brought back." Her tone expressed a threat that her words hadn't named.

"What about all the others?" Rachel asked, trying to buy time to think. "All the queen's advisors?"

"I am the queen!" It seemed that, along with the rest of her, Violet's temper had gotten bigger as well.

A gentle touch on the back from Six brought a brief glance up and a smile to Violet's face. She again took a calming breath, almost as if she had been reminded to watch her manners.

She finally answered Rachel's question. "I have no need for my mother's advisors. They were, after all, worthless. Six fills that role now, and does so much better than any of those fools.

"After all, none of them could grow me a new tongue, now could they?"

Rachel glanced up at Six. The wolf's grin was back. The ghostly blue eyes seemed to be staring right into Rachel's naked soul.

"Such a thing was far beyond their abilities," the woman said in a quiet voice, but one that carried the undertone of profound power. "However, it was well within mine."

Rachel wondered if Violet had ordered all the advisors put to death. The last time Rachel had been at the castle, Violet, at her mother's side, was just beginning to order executions. Now that she was queen, with Six to back her, there would be nothing to restrain Violet's whims.

"Six gave me my tongue back. Gave me my voice back. The Seeker thought he had taken all of that from me, but now I have it back. Tamarang is safely in my hands."

Had it not been so frightening a thought, so horrifying a concept, Rachel might have laughed at the very idea of Violet being queen. Rachel had been Violet's playmate, her companion—really nothing more than her personal slave. Violet's mother, Queen Milena, had gotten Rachel from an orphanage, intending her to be someone upon whom Violet could practice leadership, someone younger whom Violet could easily handle, and abuse.

Rachel had not only escaped, she taken Queen Milena's precious box of Orden with her, eventually giving it over to Richard and Zedd and Chase.

That had been a long time back. Violet looked to be about in her middle teens by now, although Rachel wasn't good at guessing older people's ages. She was a lot bigger than the last time Rachel had seen her, that much was for sure. Her dull hair was even longer. Her bones had gotten heavier, thicker. Like the rest of her, her face was still plump, but with those small, dark, calculating eyes, it had lost its childlike quality. Her chest was no longer flat, either, but had grown womanly. She looked like an adult just about to emerge from her cocoon. She had always been much older than Rachel, but now she seemed to have spurted up and widened the gap.

Even so, she didn't seem anywhere near old enough to be a queen.

But queen she was.

Rachel's knees, naked against the rock, were hurting something fierce. She didn't dare to ask to get up, though. Instead, she asked a question.

"Violet—"

Smack.

Before she had time to think, Violet had struck, seemingly out of nowhere, as if she had been waiting for an excuse. Rachel's vision swam sickeningly. It felt like the blow might have knocked teeth loose. Rachel gingerly felt with her tongue before she was sure they were all still in place.

"Queen Violet," Violet growled. "Don't make that mistake again or you will be put to torture as an instigator of treason."

Rachel swallowed back the lump of terror. "Yes, Queen Violet."

Violet smiled at the triumph. She was indeed the queen.

Rachel knew that Violet had a taste for only the most exquisite things, the most elaborate decoration, whether it be draperies or dishes, the most beautiful dresses, and the the most precious jewels. She insisted on surrounding herself with the best of everything—and that had been back when she'd only been a princess. That made it seem all the stranger that she would be in a cave.

"Queen Violet, what are you doing in this awful place?"

Violet stared down at her a moment, then waggled what looked like a piece of chalk before Rachel's face. "My heritage, my inheritance."

Rachel didn't understand. "Your what?"

"My gift." She shrugged offhandedly. "Well, not exactly the gift, but something akin to it. You see, I come from a long line of artists. You remember James? The court artist?"

Rachel nodded. "He had only one hand."

"Yes," Violet drawled. "A man a little too forward for his own good. Just because he was a relative of the queen he thought that he could get away with certain indiscretions. He was wrong."

Rachel blinked. "Relative?"

"Distant cousin, or something like that. He shared some little trace of the royal bloodline. That exceptional bloodline carries a unique gift for . . . artistry. The family of the rulers of Tamarang still carry the thread of that ancient talent. My mother didn't have the ability, but through that bloodline, it turns out that she did pass it along to me. At the time, though, the only one we knew of who still had that rare talent was James. Thus it came to be that he served as the court artist, served the crown, my mother, Queen Milena.

"The Seeker, the previous Seeker, Richard, before he caused the trouble that resulted in the murder of my mother, also murdered James. Our land was for the first time in history without the services of an artist to protect the crown.

"At the time we weren't aware that I, in fact, carry the ancient talent." She gestured to the tall woman beside her. "Six saw it in me, though. She told me of my remarkable ability. She has been helping me learn to use it, guiding me in my . . . art lessons.

"A lot of people were opposed to me becoming queen—some, even, among the crown's highest advisors. Fortunately, Six told me of the covert plots." She lifted the chalk before Rachel's face. "The traitors found drawings of themselves down here on these walls. I made sure that everyone knows what happens to traitors. With that, and with Six's help and counsel, I became queen. People no longer dare oppose me."

When she had lived at the castle before, Rachel had thought that Violet was dangerous in the extreme. She'd had no idea at the time just how much more dangerous she would become. Rachel felt a sense of crushing hopelessness.

Violet and Six glanced up when they heard Samuel rushing back in. Fearing that Violet was liable to whack her again, Rachel decided not to turn and look. She could hear Samuel panting, though, as he got close.

Violet swished her hand, commanding Rachel aside and out of the way. Rachel immediately scrambled to comply, only too happy to be out of the reach of Violet's arm, if not her authority.

Samuel had a leather bag held closed with a drawstring. He set the bag down carefully and opened it. He looked up at Six. She rolled her hand, urging him to get on with it.

It appeared to be a box of some kind. When it came out of the bag, Rachel saw that it was as black as doom itself. She thought that they all very well might be sucked into that black void and vanish into the underworld.

With one hand, Samuel held the sinister thing up to Six. Smiling, she lifted it out of his hand.

"As promised," she said to Violet, "I present you with Queen Violet's box of Orden."

Rachel remembered Queen Milena lifting that same box with the same kind of awed reverence. Except that now it wasn't all covered in the silver, gold, and jewels. Zedd had told Rachel that the real box of Orden had been under those jewels. This had to be that box that had all along been inside when Rachel had spirited it away from the castle just as Wizard Giller had asked her to do.

Now Giller was dead, Richard no longer had his sword, and Rachel was back in the clutches of Violet. And now Violet had herself a precious box of Orden, just as her mother had.

Violet smirked. "You see, Rachel? What need have I of those old, useless advisors? Could they have accomplished any of what I have accomplished? You see, unlike those weak people you threw in with, I always persevere until I succeed. That's what it takes to be a queen.

"I have the box of Orden back. I have you back." She waggled the chalk again. "And I will have Richard back to face his punishment."

Six sighed. "Enough of this happy reunion. You have what you asked for. Samuel and I need to go have a talk about his next assignment, and you need to get back to your 'art' lesson."

Violet smiled conspiratorially. "Yes, my lesson." She glared down at Rachel. "There is an iron box waiting for you back at the castle. And then there is the matter of your punishment."

Six bowed her head. "I will be off, then, my queen."

Violet flicked her hand in a gesture of dismissal. Six grasped Samuel's upper arm and started away with him. He had to watch his balance to keep his footing as he stepped over and around rocks. Six seemed to glide through the dim light without any trouble at all.

"Come along," Violet said in the kind of pretend cheerful tone that made Rachel's blood run cold. "You can watch me draw."

As Violet grabbed the torch Rachel stood on wobbly legs, then followed her queen, the light of the flagging flame illuminating walls covered with endless drawings of terrible things being done to people. There was not a spot on the walls that didn't have some sort of horrific scene. Rachel missed Chase something fierce, missed his reassurance, his smile when she had done a lesson well, his comforting hand on her shoulder. She loved him so much. And Samuel had killed him, killed all her hopes and dreams. She felt numb despair as she followed Violet deeper into the darkness, deeper into the madness.

Nicci spotted Richard far off down the long rampart, standing at the crenellated outer wall not far from the base of a soaring tower, gazing out over the deserted city far below. Twilight had muted the colors of the dying day, turning the distant rolling summer-green fields to gray. Cara stood not far from his side, silent but watchful.

Nicci knew Richard well enough that she could easily read the heightened tension in his body. She knew Cara well enough to see the reflection of that stress lurking in her intently calm appearance. Nicci pressed a fist over the knot of anxiety tightening in her middle.

Overhead the slate gray clouds roiled, spitting an occasional fat drop of rain. Distant thunder rumbled through the mountain passes, promising a tempestuous night to come. Despite the dark, seething clouds, the air was strangely still. The heat of the day had abruptly vanished, as if fleeing before the storm that was about to break.

As she came to a stop, Nicci rested a hand on the crenellated wall and took a deep breath of the humid air.

"Rikka said that you needed to see me. She said it was urgent."

Richard looked the match for the brewing storm. "I have to leave. At once."

Nicci had somehow expected just that. She glanced past Richard, to Cara, but the Mord-Sith showed no reaction. Richard had been brooding for days. He'd been quietly distant as he considered everything he had learned from Jebra and Shota. Zedd had advised Nicci to leave him to his deliberation. Nicci had not needed such advise; she probably knew his darker moods better than anyone.

"I'm going with you," she said, making it clear that she was leaving no room for discussion.

He nodded absently. "It will be good to have you with me. Especially for this."

Nicci was relieved not to have him argue, but the knot of anxiety tightened over the last part of what he'd said. There was a palpable sense of danger in the air. At that moment her concern was to insure that—whatever he was about to do—he was as well protected as she could manage.

"And Cara is going too."

Still, he gazed off into the distance. "Of course."

She realized that he was looking south. "Now that Tom and Friedrich are back, Tom will insist on coming along as well. His talents will be valuable."

Tom was a member of an elite corps of protectors to the Lord Rahl. Despite his amiable appearance, Tom was more than formidable in his duty. Men like him were not advanced to such trusted positions of protection to the Lord Rahl because they had nice smiles. Like other D'Haran protectors to the Lord Rahl, Tom had come to feel passionately about his duty to protect Richard.

"He can't come with us," Richard said. "We're going in the sliph. Only Cara, you, and me are able to travel in the sliph."

Nicci swallowed at the thought of such a journey. "And where are we going, Richard?"

At long last, his gray eyes turned to her. He gazed into her eyes with that way he had about him, as if he was looking into her soul.

"I've figured it out," he said.

"You've figured what out?"

"What I must do."

Nicci could feel her fingers tingling with a shapeless dread. The look of terrible resolve in his gray eyes made her knees weak.

"And what is that you must do, Richard?"

He puzzled a moment. "Did I ever tell you thanks for stopping Shota when you did, when she was touching me?"

Nicci was not disconcerted by Richard's abrupt change of topic. She had learned that it was Richard's way. It was especially characteristic when he was greatly troubled. The more agitated he was, it seemed that there were all the more things going on in his head at the same time, as if his thoughts were in a whirlwind of inner activity that pulled everything up into that tumultuous rush of deliberation.

"You told me, Richard."

About a hundred times.

He nodded slightly. "Well, thanks."

His voice had turned absent, distant, as he descended back into the dark depths of some inner equation upon which the future hinged.

"She was doing something painful to you, wasn't she."

It was not a question, but a statement that Nicci had come to believe more and more in the days following Shota's visit. Nicci didn't know what Shota had done, but she wished she had not allowed even that brief touch. There was no telling how much the witch woman could have conveyed in that touch, even as abbreviated as it had been. Lightning, after all, was brief as well. Richard had never said what Shota had shown him, but it was ground that Nicci, for some reason, feared to tread upon.

Richard heaved a sigh. "Yes, she was. She was showing me the truth. That truth is in part how I've come to understand at last what it is I must do. As much as I dread it . . ."

When he drifted into silence, Nicci patiently prodded him. "So, what have you figured out you must do?"

Richard's fingers tightened on the stone as he looked out again over the darkening countryside far below, and then to the somber jumble of mountains rising up beyond.

"I was right in the beginning." His gaze turned to Cara. "Right when I took you and Kahlan away to the mountains far back in Westland."

Cara frowned. "I remember you saying that we were going back into those deserted mountains because you had come to understand that we could not win the war by fighting the army of the Imperial Order. You said that you could not lead them in such a battle that they were sure to lose."

Richard nodded. "And I was right. I know that now. We can't win against their army. Shota helped me to see that. She may have been trying to convince me that I must fight that battle, but in part because of all that she and Jebra showed me, I know now that we can't win it.

"Now, I know what I must do."

"And what would that be?" Nicci pressed.

Richard finally pushed away from the stone merlon. "We have to go. I don't have time to lay it all out right now."

Nicci started after him. "I threw some things together. They're ready. Richard, why can't you tell me what you've decided?"

"I will," he said, "later."

"You're wasting your time," Cara said under her breath to Nicci as she fell in with her behind Richard. "I've already paddled up that creek until I got too tired to paddle anymore."

Richard, hearing Cara's remark, took Nicci by the arm and pulled her forward. "I'm not finished thinking it all through. I need to finish putting it all together. I'll explain it when we get there, explain it to everyone— but right now we don't have the time. All right?"

"Get where?" Nicci asked.

"To the D'Haran army. Jagang's main force will soon be heading up into D'Hara. I have to tell our army that we have no chance to win the battle that is coming for them."

"That ought to cheer their day," Cara said. "Nothing makes a soldier feel better on the eve of battle than their leader telling them that they are about to lose the battle and die."

"You want me to tell them a lie, instead?" he asked.

Cara's only answer was a scowl.

At the end of the rampart Richard pulled open the heavy oak door at the base of the tower. Inside was a room where some of the lamps were already lit. Nicci could hear people rushing up the stone steps to the side.

"Richard!" It was Zedd following behind the big, blond-headed D'Haran, Tom.

Richard halted, waiting for his grandfather to reach the top of the steps and make it into the simple stone room. Zedd rushed closer, gulping air.

"Richard! What's going on? Rikka came by in a rush saying that you were leaving."

Richard nodded. "I wanted you to know that I've got to go, but I won't be gone for long. I'll be back in a few days. Hopefully, in the meantime you and Nathan and Ann can find out something in the books that will be helpful with the Chainfire spell. Maybe you can even work on coming up with some solution to the contamination from the chimes."

Zedd waved irritably at the suggestion. "While we're at it, would you like me to cure the sky of that thunderstorm?"

"Zedd, don't be angry with me, please. I have to go."

"All right, but where are you going—and why?"

"I'm ready, Lord Rahl," Tom said as he hurried into the room.

"I'm sorry," Richard told him, "but you can't go. We're going to need to go in the sliph."

Zedd threw his arms up in the air. "The sliph! You do your best to convince me that magic is failing, and now you intend to put your life in the hands of a creature of magic? Are you losing your mind, Richard? What's going on?"

"I'm aware of the danger, but I must take the risk." Richard gestured. "You know that starburst symbol on the door of the First Wizard's enclave, up there?" When Zedd nodded, Richard tapped the top of his silver wristband. "It's the same as this one here."

"What about it?" Zedd asked.

"Remember, I told you that it has meaning? It's an admonition not to allow your vision to lock on any one thing. It's a warning to look everywhere at once, to see nothing to the exclusion of everything else. It means you mustn't allow the enemy to draw your attention and make you focus on what he wishes you to see. If you do, you will be blind to everything else.

"That's what I've been doing. Jagang has been forcing me—forcing everyone—to focus on one thing. Like a fool, I've been doing just that."

"His army," Nicci guessed. "That's what you mean? That we've all been focusing on his invasion force?"

"That's right. This starburst means that you must open to all there is, never settling on just one thing, even when cutting your enemy. It means that instead of focusing on one thing, you must open your mind to everything, even when it is necessary to keep that one central threat at the center of your attention."

Zedd cocked his head. "Richard, you've got to focus on the threat that's about to kill you. His army is millions of men strong. They're coming to crush all opposition and enslave us all."

"I know. That's why we can't fight them; we will lose."

Zedd's face went crimson. "So you propose to allow their army to roll into the New World unopposed? Your plan is to let Jagang's army freely overrun cities and allow to happen all the things Jebra told us had happened in Ebinissia? You want to so easily allow all those people to be slaughtered or enslaved?"

"Think of the solution," Richard reminded his grandfather, "not the problem."

"Not very comforting advice to those having their throats cut."

Richard froze and stared at his grandfather, seemingly struck silent by Zedd's words.

"Look," Richard finally said, running his fingers back through his hair, "I don't have time for this right now. I'll talk to you about it when I get back. Time is of the essence. I've already wasted far too much of it. I only hope that we still have enough time left."

"Enough time for what!" Zedd roared.

Nicci heard footsteps rushing up the stairwell. Jebra dashed into the room.

"What's going on?" she asked Zedd.

Zedd waved a hand in Richard's direction. "My grandson has decided that we must lose the war, that we must not fight Jagang's army."

"Lord Rahl, you can't be serious," she said. "You can't seriously consider allowing those brutes . . ." Jebra's voice trailed off as she stepped forward, peering up at Richard. She stilled in midstride. She staggered back a step.

The blood drained from her face.

Her jaw dropped open. Her jaw trembled as she tried without success to bring forth words. Her features slackened with dread.

Her blue eyes rolled back in her head as she fainted.

As she toppled back, Tom caught her in his arms and laid her gently on the granite floor. Everyone closed in around the unconscious woman.

"What happened?" Tom asked.

"I don't know," Zedd said as he knelt down beside the woman, pressing his fingers to her forehead. "She's fainted, but I'm not sure why."

Richard headed for the door that opened to the iron stairs running down the inside of the tower. "I'll leave you to take care of her, Zedd—you're the expert at healing. She's in good hands. I can't afford to waste any more time right now."

He turned back from the doorway. "I'll be back as soon as I can—promise. We shouldn't be more than a few days."

"But Richard—"

He had already started down the iron steps. "I'll be back," he called up at them, his voice echoing from the gloom.

Without hesitation, Cara followed after him down into the dark tower.

Nicci didn't want to let him get too far without her, but she knew that he would have to call the sliph, so she had a few moments. As Zedd checked different spots on Jebra's head, Nicci squatted down beside the unconscious Jebra, across from him.

Nicci felt the woman's brow. "She's burning up."

Zedd looked up in a way that nearly stopped Nicci's heart. "It's a vision."

"How do you know?"

"I know about seers in general and this one in particular. She's had a powerful vision. Jebra is more sensitive than most seers. Her emotions, with a certain kind of vision, sometimes overcome her. This vision had to have been something that was so powerful it rendered her unconscious."

"Do you think it was about Richard?"

"There's no way to tell," the old wizard said. "She will have to be the one to tell us."

Zedd may not have been willing to venture a guess, but Jebra had looked up into Richard's eyes just before she fainted. Nicci didn't have time to be discreet. She couldn't allow Richard to leave without her—and she knew that he would if she wasn't there when he was ready to go—but at the same time she couldn't leave without knowing if Jebra had had a vision about him that could reveal something important.

Nicci slipped her hand under the woman's neck, pressing her fingers to the base of Jebra's skull.

"What are you doing?" Zedd asked, suspiciously. "If you're doing what I think you are, that's not just reckless but dangerous."

"So is ignorance," Nicci said as she released a flow of power.

Jebra's eyes popped open. She gasped.

"No . . ."

"There, there," Zedd comforted, "it's all right, my dear. We're right here with you."

"What did you see?" Nicci asked, getting right to the point.

Jebra's panicked eyes turned to Nicci. She reached up and snatched the collar of Nicci's dress.

"Don't leave him alone!"

There was no need for Nicci to ask who Jebra was talking about. "Why? What did you see?"

"Don't leave him alone! Don't let him out of your sight—not for an instant!"

"Why?" Nicci asked again. "What will happen if he is left alone?"

"If you leave him alone, he will be lost to us."

"How? What did you see?"

Jebra reached up and with both fists pulled Nicci's face closer. "Go. Don't let him be alone. What I saw does not matter. If he's not alone, then it can't happen. Do you understand? If you let him get separated from you and Cara it will not matter what I saw—it won't matter for any of us. I can't tell you the means of separation, only that no matter what you must not let it happen. That's all that's important. Go! Stay with him!"

Nicci swallowed as she nodded.

"You'd better do as she says," Zedd told Nicci. "There's nothing I can do in this. It's up to you."

He reached out and grasped her hand, not as First Wizard, but as Richard's grandfather. "Stay with him, Nicci. Protect him. In so many ways he's the Seeker, the Lord Rahl, the leader of the D'Haran Empire, but in other ways he's still a woods guide at heart. He's our Richard. Protect him, please. We're all depending on you."

Nicci stared at him, at an appeal that seemed unexpectedly personal, an appeal that seemed to rise above all the wider needs of protecting the freedom of the New World and reduced it all to a simple love for Richard the man. She understood in that instant that without the sincere and simple concern for Richard as an individual, none of the rest of it mattered.

As she started to rise, Jebra pulled Nicci back down. "This is not a 'maybe' kind of vision, a possibility. This is certain. Don't let him be alone or he will be at their mercy."

"Whose mercy?"

Jebra bit her lower lip as her blue eyes welled up with tears. "The dark witch."

Nicci felt a shudder of icy dread ripple up her shoulders.

"Go," Jebra whispered. "Please, go. Hurry. Don't let him leave without you."

Nicci sprang up and rushed across the room. At the doorway she paused and turned back. Her heart was pounding so hard that it made her sway on her feet.

"I swear, Zedd. He will have my protection as long as I draw breath."

She watched as Zedd nodded, a tear running down his weathered cheek. "Hurry."

Nicci turned and ran down the iron steps, taking them two at a time, her footfalls echoing around the enormous tower. She wondered what else

Jebra saw in her vision that awaited Richard if he became separated from them, if he was left alone, but in the end Nicci decided that it didn't really matter what that visionary fate was, it only mattered that, no matter what, Nicci not allow it to happen.

Bats fluttered in undulating clouds up through the tower, funneling out through the open windows at the top, intent on their nightly hunt, as Nicci raced down the steps. The rushing sound of thousands of webbed wings made it seem the tower was exhaling in a long, low moan. She passed iron doors on landings without pause. She sometimes had to snatch the rail to keep her footing. At the bottom she raced around the walkway that surrounded the fetid water standing at the bottom of the tower. The black water rippled as small creatures slipped into the inky sanctuary.

Nicci ran in through the doorway that had been blasted open when Richard had destroyed the great barrier that had once separated the Old World from the new. The towers that powered that barrier had stood since the great war, three thousand years before. In more recent times, Jagang and his army of the Imperial Order had been kept at bay, unable to cross that barrier. But Richard had destroyed those towers in order to be able to return to the New World after having been held at the Palace of the Prophets, and as a result the Imperial Order had been loosed on the New World. The war was not Richard's fault, but it could not have been rekindled without that act.

Richard and Cara were standing, waiting, on the wall of the great well of the sliph, the creature that had been walled away along with the Old World for all the time that the great barrier had stood.

Behind Richard and Cara the quicksilver face of the sliph watched Nicci as she hurried into the room. "Do you wish to travel?" the sliph asked in that eerie voice that echoed around the room.

"Yes, I wish to travel," Nicci said breathlessly as she scooped up her pack. Cara must have put it there for her. "Thanks," she said to the Mord-Sith.

Richard held his hand out as Nicci slipped an arm through a strap and lifted the pack onto her back. "Come on."

Nicci took his hand, letting him hoist her up onto the wall with one mighty pull. Nicci's heart felt as if it was coming up into her throat. She had traveled before so she knew the overwhelming ecstasy of the experience, and yet she could not help being afraid to breathe in the living quicksilver of the sliph. Such a concept just went against the very idea of the breath of life.

"You will be pleased," the sliph said as Nicci joined the others. Nicci didn't argue.

"Let's go," Richard said. "I wish to travel."

A shiny arm lifted out of the pool to surround Richard and Cara, but not Nicci.

"Wait!" Nicci said. "I must go with them." The sliph stilled. "Listen to me, Richard. You have to take Cara and my hands. Don't let go for anything."

"Nicci, you've done this before. It will be—"

"Listen! Cara and I are trusting you, and you have to trust us. You can't get separated from us. Not for anything. Not for so much as an instant. If that happens then you are lost to us. If that happens then whatever you have planned won't happen."

Richard studied her face silently for a moment. "Did Jebra have a vision of something happening?"

"Only if you get separated from us. Only if you are alone."

"What did she see?"

"The witch woman, Six. Jebra called her 'the dark witch.'"

Richard studied her face a moment. "Shota is going after Six."

"That may be, but Six has already usurped Shota's authority in her own territory."

"Maybe for the moment. But I'd not want to be her when Shota catches her. Shota covered her throne with the hide of the last person who came to take her home, and he was a wizard."

"I don't doubt how dangerous Shota is, but we don't know how dangerous Six is. The gift is different in different individuals. Shota could in the end turn out to be no match for Six's ability. I do know that the Sisters of the Dark were afraid of her. Jebra had a terrible vision and says that you must not be allowed to be alone. I don't intend to allow her vision any chance to come to pass."

He must have read the resolve in Nicci's face, because he nodded. "All right." He took her hand and then took Cara's. "Don't let go, then, and then we won't have to worry about it."

Nicci squeezed his hand in agreement. She leaned past him to address

Cara. "Do you understand? We can't let him out of our sight. Not for an instant."

Cara's brow drew down in a dark frown. "Since when have I ever wanted to allow him out of my sight?"

"Where do you wish to travel?" the sliph asked.

Nicci glanced to Richard and Cara and realized that the question was directed to her.

"To where they are going."

The silver face turned sly. "I cannot reveal what my other clients do when they are in me. Tell me what you wish and I will please you."

Nicci twitched a frown at Richard.

"She never reveals anything about anyone else; it's a kind of professional confidence. We're going to the People's Palace."

"The People's Palace," Nicci said. "I wish to travel to the People's Palace."

"She's going with Cara and me," Richard told the sliph. "To the same place. Do you understand? She is to stay with us as we travel there."

"Yes, Master. We will travel." The face, looking like a highly polished statue, smiled. "You will be pleased."

The liquid silver arm tightened around all three of them, drawing them off the wall. Nicci's hand tightened on Richard's.

As they plunged into the total darkness of the sliph, Nicci held her breath. She knew she had to breathe, but the very idea of breathing the silvery liquid terrified her.

Breathe.

At last she did, a desperate gasp drawing the sliph into her lungs. Colors, light, and shapes melted together all around her in a spectacular display. Nicci tightly held Richard's hand as they glided into the silken distance. It was a glorious, lazy, floating sensation of a headlong rush at impossible speed.

She drew in another dizzying breath of the sliph's essence. It was a glorious release from everything that haunted her, from the crushing weight on her soul. She was left with only that connection to Richard. There was nothing else. There was no one else.

It was rapture.

She never wanted it to end.

Kahlan watched as the three Sisters peered into the distance, watching for any movement. With the sun going down, the shadows were beginning to melt together into a gloomy haze. At the horizon to the south a sliver of fading daylight shone beneath menacing gray clouds that towered into a dark violet sky. The cloud tops were touched by a wash of red light that lent the evening an odd, dreamlike quality.

The sky in this place, so often filled with monumental, billowing clouds, seemed overpoweringly immense, leaving Kahlan feeling tiny and insignificant. The flat plains to the south stretched endlessly to the lonely horizon. Little vegetation grew in such a desolate place, and what did grow was found mostly in the low-lying places.

The clouds sweeping across the landscape dragged columns of rain but, as vast as the place was, the rains never seemed any more than a distant, isolated phenomenon. Kahlan suspected that if one were to stand in the same spot for a year waiting for one of those random showers to pass over-head, it would likely not happen. The barren landscape made life seem fragile and forlorn. Only the mountains to the north and east seemed able to comb rain from the parade of clouds. As a result, the trees didn't venture down from their mountain refuge.

When the horses snorted and stamped their hooves, Kahlan pulled the reins tighter and absently rubbed one of the animals under its jaw to reas-sure it that all was well. The horse gently nudged her, wanting more. As she waited, Kahlan turned away from the haunting desolation and gave the horse a more attentive scratch.

In the distance she could see where the wall of mountains dwindled into a massive headland. That headland, like the tail of some sleeping beast, looked to be the southern tip of the mountains they had been following south. Kahlan wished she were back in those mountains. The mountains gave her a sense of sanctuary, probably because, unlike the open plains, she didn't feel like anyone for miles around could see her. Out on the plain she felt naked and exposed. She realized that she didn't really know why she should feel that way, since she could hardly be in a worse circumstance than being a forgotten slave to the Sisters.

Kahlan thought that she could see what looked like buildings up on the distant headland. If her eyes weren't tricking her, the buildings looked like they were probably no more than ruins. If they really were buildings, then few of the structures appeared to have roofs. What at first made no sense finally began to when she considered if what might have been walls had actually crumbled long ago; that would explain the odd shapes. She didn't see any sign of people. They, too, were probably long forgotten.

Even if they really were abandoned buildings, long deserted places made the Sisters no less wary than everything else did. Their wariness seemed to be born of a sense of complete and total dominion nearly within their grasp. In this place, though, Kahlan shared their edginess.

The three Sisters had been silent for most of the day, speaking only when necessary. The back of Kahlan's shoulder still throbbed in pain where Sister Ulicia had unexpectedly struck her. It had not been punishment for any transgression—real or imagined—but rather had been delivered with a stern warning not to cause any trouble. The Sisters sometimes sought to express their superiority over others, even if it was by showing that they could hurt Kahlan just because they wanted to. She had to school her thoughts lest one of the Sisters pick up on what Kahlan thought of her treatment. She'd swallowed her dignity along with her thoughts and simply said, "Yes, Sister."

Kahlan didn't think that it was a good idea to go stumbling around in the dark, especially when they were beginning to come upon a landscape deeply rutted and eroded in places by runoff from the high ground. The horses could easily break a leg in such conditions. But, in their ambition to get to Caska, the Sisters hadn't wanted to stop when evening had begun to engulf them. What the Sisters wanted, the Sisters got. Kahlan wasn't looking forward to eventually setting up camp in the dark.

"I think there's someone out there," Sister Armina said in a quiet voice as she stared out into the darkness.

"I sense something, too," Sister Cecilia murmured.

Sister Armina glanced over, expectantly. "Maybe it's Tovi."

"Could be nothing more than a wild mule." Sister Ulicia didn't appear to be in a mood to stand around speculating. "Come on." She glanced back at Kahlan. "Stay close."

"Yes, Sister," Kahlan said. She handed the Sisters the reins to their horses.

Sister Cecilia, older than the rest of them, grunted with the effort of swinging her tired muscles up into her saddle. "My memories of the rare maps down in the vaults at the Palace of the Prophets tell me that we should be getting close to the place."

"I recall seeing that ancient map," Sister Ulicia said, once seated atop her horse. "It called this place the Deep Nothing. That would mean that it has to be Caska up on that distant headland."

Sister Armina heaved an impatient sigh as she urged her horse on after the others. "Then we will at last find Tovi here."

"And when we finally join up with her," Sister Cecilia said, "she is going to have some explaining to do."

Sister Armina gestured off toward the distant headland. "You know Tovi—always ignoring what she's supposed to do because she thinks she knows best. She's the most obstinate woman I've ever met."

As far as Kahlan was concerned, Armina had little room to talk.

"We'll see how obstinate she is when I have my fingers around her throat," Sister Cecilia said.

Sister Armina urged her horse up beside Sister Ulicia. "You don't think she could be up to no good, do you, Ulicia?"

"Tovi?" Sister Ulicia glanced back over her shoulder. "No, not really. She may be exasperating at times, but she has the same goal as do the rest of us. Besides, she knows as well as we do that we need all three of the boxes. She knows what's involved and what's at stake.

"We will soon have the three boxes all back together again—that's all that really matters—and we will already be in Caska, so I suppose it wouldn't really have done us any good to catch up with Tovi before now. We still would have had to come here anyway."

"But why would she have taken off the way she did?" Sister Cecilia pressed.

Sister Ulicia shrugged. Unlike the other two, she seemed to be somewhat at ease, now that Caska was in sight. "It could be nothing more than that she discovered Imperial Order troops nearby and she simply wanted to avoid any possibility of trouble so she left the area. She probably was using her head, that's all. She knew we had to come here. She probably saw a chance to slip away and took it. We're better served by such caution.

She was, in the end, going to where we planned on going all along, so I don't really see what mischief she could be up to."

"I suppose." Sister Cecilia seemed somewhat disappointed not to have a villain upon whom to fixate her anger.

They rode in silence for nearly an hour more before it became apparent to the Sisters that riding over such ground in the dark might not only risk breaking a horse's leg, but one of their necks as well. As far as Kahlan could tell, they weren't much closer to the headland than they had been for most of the day. Out on the plain, distances were far greater than they appeared to be. What at first seemed to be a place only a couple of miles distant could turn out to take days to reach. The Sisters, despite their eagerness to get to Caska and Tovi, were tired and ready to stop for the night.

Sister Ulicia dismounted, handing the reins to Kahlan. "Get camp set up. We're all hungry."

Kahlan dipped her head. "Yes, Sister."

She immediately hobbled all the horses so they couldn't wander off, then made her way around to the side of the pack animals to start getting out their gear. She was dead tired but knew that it would probably be hours before she would have a chance to get any sleep. The camp had to be set up, food had to be prepared, and then the horses had to be fed, watered, and groomed for the night.

Sister Ulicia took hold of Sister Armina's arm and pulled her close. "While we're making camp, I want you to go out there and check the area. I want to know if it's just a mule."

Sister Armina nodded and immediately set out on foot into the darkness.

Sister Cecilia watched Sister Armina dissolve into the night. "Do you really think it's a mule?"

Sister Ulicia cast her a dark look. "If it is a mule, it's staying the same distance away as we travel. If it's someone watching us, then Armina will find them."

Kahlan pulled out the bedrolls when the Sisters asked for something softer to sit on other than the barren ground. She then pulled out one of the pots so she could get some dinner started.

"No fire tonight," Sister Ulicia said when she saw Kahlan with the pot.

Kahlan stared at her a moment. "What would you like for dinner, then, Sister?"

"There is bannock left over. We can have that and some dried meats. We have pine nuts as well." She gazed out into the night. "I don't want a fire out here in the open, where anyone from horizon to horizon could see us. Just get out one of the smaller lanterns."

Kahlan could not imagine what the Sisters had to worry about. She handed Sister Armina the lantern. The sister lit it with a flick of a finger, then set it on the ground before her and Sister Ulicia. It wasn't much light to see by as Kahlan finished unpacking, but at least it was better than nothing.

There had been times in the past when patrols of soldiers happened on them. The Sisters had never been especially spooked by such unexpected encounters with hostile forces. The Sisters had dispatched the soldiers without any problem—or mercy.

When they had run into patrols the Sisters were careful not to allow any witnesses to get away, apparently so that there wouldn't be any chance of reports getting back to the army. Kahlan supposed that it was possible that such reports could result in great numbers of angry men coming after them. The Sisters didn't appear especially concerned about that possibility; it seemed more likely that they simply had business and they didn't want to be slowed for anything.

Getting to Tovi and the last box was of paramount importance to them and they had driven hard to get this far this quickly. Kahlan was somewhat surprised that they had not caught Tovi before now, especially since nothing seemed anywhere near as important to the Sisters as their precious boxes.

Except that they were Lord Rahl's boxes. The Sisters had stolen them from Richard Rahl's palace.

On one occasion, in their rush, they had come across a large detachment of the big Imperial Order brutes. The Sisters had been impatient to get past the soldiers, to get on with their business with the boxes, but the men appeared in no hurry to move on out of the way. The Sisters waited until the middle of the night and then walked through the encampment of sleeping men. Any time a man saw them, one of the Sisters cast out a silent spell that dispatched the man without any ado. The Sisters had shown no compunction about killing any man who happened to be in their way. They moved through the camp quietly, fearlessly, and deliberately. Kahlan saw a lot of men die that night. To the Sisters, it had been no more eventful than stepping on ants pestering them at camp.

But that had been a long time ago and they had not seen any troops since. The Imperial Order army was now far distant behind them and for quite some time had no longer been a consideration. That didn't mean, however, that there couldn't be other hazards, and so the Sisters were frequently as nervous as cats. Without warning, however, they could easily turn as dangerous as vipers.

Long after Sister Armina returned without finding anyone about, and the three Sisters had eaten, Kahlan still worked to finish her chores before she was allowed to eat. She was currying the horses when she thought that she heard the soft sound of footsteps on the hardscrabble ground. The sound brought her out of her thoughts about the soldiers. Her hand with the curry brush paused.

She looked over her shoulder and was startled to see a slender girl with short, dark hair standing timidly just at the edge of the faint lanternlight.

With the moon only occasionally peeking out from between the passing clouds, the camp was mostly left to the light of the single lantern back by the Sisters, so it was hard to see, but Kahlan could see well enough to see the young woman's pale eyes staring at her.

In those eyes was the clear look of cognition. The girl saw Kahlan.

"Please—" the girl said. Kahlan crossed her lips with a finger, lest the Sisters hear the girl. Just like the man back at the inn, this girl saw and remembered Kahlan. Kahlan was astonished, and at the same time fearful that the same thing would happen to the girl as had happened to the man.

"Please," the girl repeated in a low whisper, "may I have something to eat? I'm so hungry."

Kahlan glanced at the Sisters. They were busy talking among themselves. Kahlan reached into her saddlebag in the pile near her feet and pulled out a strip of dried venison. She again crossed her lips with one finger and handed the girl the meat. The girl nodded her understanding and didn't make a sound. Taking the meat eagerly in both hand, she immediately used her teeth to rip off a bite.

"Go, now," Kahlan whispered, "before they see you. Hurry."

The girl glanced up at Kahlan, then looked past her. Her eyes went wide. Her chewing halted.

"Well, well," came a menacing voice over Kahlan's shoulder, "if it isn't our little mule come to steal from us."

"Please, she was hungry," Kahlan said, hoping to douse Sister Ulicia's anger before it flared. "She asked for a bite to eat. She didn't steal it. I gave her my food, not any of yours."

Sister Ulicia was joined by the other two, so that it looked like three vultures all in a row. Sister Armina lifted the lantern to have a better look. All three looked like they intended to pick the girl's bones clean.

"Probably waiting till we went to sleep," Sister Ulicia said as she leaned closer, "so she could cut our throats."

Copper-colored eyes shown in the lamplight as the frightened young woman gazed up at them. "I wasn't lying in wait. I was hungry. I thought I might be able to get a little food, that's all. I asked, I did not steal."

The young woman reminded Kahlan a little of the girl back at the White Horse Inn, the girl Kahlan had promised to protect, the girl that Sister Ulicia had so brutally murdered. At night, before she fell asleep, the memory of that girl's terror still haunted Kahlan. Her failure to keep her promise of protection still burned in Kahlan's soul. Even if the girl hadn't been able to remember Kahlan's words long enough to comprehend them, Kahlan hated that she had made such a promise and then failed to keep it.

This girl was a little older, a little taller. Kahlan could see in her eyes, too, a kind of quiet comprehension of the true dimension of the threat before her. There was a kind of knowing caution in her copper eyes. But she was still a girl. Womanhood was still a mystery that lay just over her life's horizon.

Sister Armina suddenly smacked the girl. The blow spun her around, knocking her to the ground. The Sister pounced on her. The girl covered her head with her arms as she tried her best to get out an apology for asking for food. Sister Armina pawed at the girl's clothes between striking her.

When the Sister rose she held a knife that Kahlan didn't recognize. She waggled it in the lanternlight, then tossed it to the ground at Sister Ulicia's feet. "She was carrying this. Like you said, she probably intended to cut our throats after we'd gone to sleep."

"I intended no harm!" the girl cried out as Sister Ulicia raised her oak rod.

Kahlan knew all too well what was coming and dove over the frightened girl, covering her, protecting her.

Sister Ulicia's rod came crashing down across Kahlan's back instead, right over the spot where she had been hit earlier. The girl flinched at the crack of oak against bone. Kahlan cried out with the pain of the blow.

With all her effort she pushed the young woman farther away from the Sisters, trying to keep her protected from harm.

"Leave her be!" Kahlan yelled. "She's just a child! She's hungry, that's all! She can't hurt any of you!"

In the grip of panic, the girl's spindly arms clung to Kahlan's neck, as if it were the lone root hanging at the edge of a cliff. If Kahlan could have killed the Sisters right then, she would have, but instead she did no more than protectively shield the girl; she knew that if she tried to fight them, the Sisters would pull her away for retaliation and then she could be no protection at all. This was the most Kahlan could do for the girl.

Again, Sister Ulicia struck Kahlan across the back. Kahlan gritted her teeth against the pain. Again and again the woman landed blows with the rod.

"Let the brat go!" Sister Ulicia yelled as she beat Kahlan.

The girl panted in terror.

"It's all right," Kahlan managed between gasps for breath, "I'll protect you. I promise."

The young woman whispered back a "thank you" in Kahlan's ear.

Besides her desperate desire to protect such an innocent child, Kahlan desperately didn't want to lose this connection to the world. The girl knew that Kahlan existed. She could see her, hear her, remember her. Kahlan needed that lifeline back to the world of people.

Sister Ulicia took a stride closer as she swung away at Kahlan, putting all her muscle into the beating. Kahlan knew she was in grievous trouble, but she was not going to willingly allow them to harm this girl as they had the last one. The girl had done nothing to deserve what Kahlan knew they would do to her.

"How dare you—"

"If you wish to kill someone," Kahlan yelled up at Sister Ulicia, "then kill me, but leave her be! She's no threat to you."

Sister Ulicia seemed content to do just that, growling with the effort of clubbing Kahlan, striking over and over in a frenzy. Kahlan was getting dizzy with the pain but she would not move to allow the Sister to get at the girl.

The young woman hid under the protection of Kahlan's larger frame, crying out with fright, not at what the Sisters might do to her, but in anguish for what they were doing to Kahlan. The rod made a sickening sound as it struck the back of Kahlan's skull. It stunned her nearly sense-less. Still, she would not let go of the young woman. Blood matted her hair and ran down her face.

And then the rod broke against Kahlan's back. The larger piece spun out into the night. Sister Ulicia stood panting, in a blind rage, holding a useless stub. Kahlan expected to be killed, but in a way she no longer cared. There was no possibility of escape. There was no future for her. If she couldn't fight for the life of an innocent young woman then life was of no value to her.

"Ulicia," Armina whispered as she caught Ulicia's wrist. "She sees Kahlan. Just like that man at the inn."

Sister Ulicia stared at her companion, seemingly startled by the idea.

Sister Armina lifted an eyebrow. "We need to find out what's going on."

Sister Cecilia, a sinister glare twisting her features, not having heard what Sister Armina had said, stepped closer and stood over Kahlan. "How dare you defy a Sister? We're going to skin this brat alive and make you watch the whole thing to teach you a lesson."

"Sister?" The girl asked. "Are you all sisters?"

The night suddenly seemed impossibly quiet. Kahlan's world spun sickeningly. Each breath felt like knives twisting between her ribs. Tears from the pain of the blows ran down her face. She couldn't stop trembling, but still she would not abandon the girl.

Sister Ulicia tossed the end of the broken oak rod aside. "We are Sis-ters. What of it?" she asked, suspiciously.

"Tovi told me to watch for you, although you don't look to me much like Tovi's sisters."

Everyone paused.

"Tovi?" Sister Ulicia cautiously asked.

The girl nodded. She peeked out past Kahlan's shoulder. "She's an older woman. She's big, bigger than any of you, and she doesn't really look like your sister, but she told me to go out and watch for her sisters. She said that the three of you had another woman with you."

"And why would a girl like you agree to do as Tovi asked?"

The girl brushed her dark hair back from her face. She hesitated, then answered. "She is holding my grandfather captive. She said that if I didn't do as she said, then she would kill him."

Ulicia smiled the way Kahlan imagined a snake would smile, if a snake could smile. "Well, well. I guess you really do know Tovi. Where is she, then?"

Kahlan pushed herself up on an arm. The girl pointed toward the headland. "There. She is in a place with old books. She made me show her where the books were kept. She told me to guide you to her."

Sister Ulicia shared a look with the other two. "Perhaps she's already located the central site in Caska."

Sister Armina cackled with relief as she jovially clapped Sister Cecilia on the back of the shoulder. Sister Cecilia returned the gesture in kind.

"How far is it?" Sister Ulicia asked, suddenly eager.

"It will take all of two days, maybe three, if we leave at first light in the morning."

Sister Ulicia peered off into the darkness for a moment. "Two or three days . . ." She turned back. "What's your name?"

"Jillian."

Sister Ulicia kicked Kahlan in the side, the unexpected blow rolling her off the girl. "Well, Jillian, you can have Kahlan's bedroll. She won't be needing it. She's going to stand for the night as punishment."

"Please," Jillian said as she laid a hand on Kahlan's arm, "if not for her, you would now be without a guide to the place where Tovi is. Please don't punish her. She did you a favor."

Sister Ulicia considered a moment. "I'll tell you what, Jillian. Since you spoke up for our disobedient slave, I'll let you make sure that she doesn't sit down during the night. If she does disobey us, I will give her a beating that will leave her with a painful limp for the rest of her life. But you can prevent that by making sure she stands the entire night. What do you think of that?"

Jillian swallowed, but didn't answer.

Sister Ulicia snatched Kahlan by the hair and hauled her to her feet. "Make sure she stays on her feet, or what we do to her will be your fault for not making sure that she did as she was told. Understand?"

Jillian, her copper-colored eyes wide, nodded.

Sister Ulicia smiled a sly smile. "Good." She turned to the other two. "Come on. Let's get some sleep."

After they had gone, Kahlan gently laid a hand on the top of the head of the girl sitting at her feet.

"Glad to meet you, Jillian," Kahlan whispered so that the Sisters wouldn't hear.

Jillian smiled up at her, and whispered. "Thank you for protecting me. Your promise was true." She gently took Kahlan's hand and held it to her cheek for a moment. "You are the bravest person I've seen since Richard."

"Richard?"

"Richard Rahl. He was here before. He saved my grandfather, before, but now . . ."

Jillian's voice trailed off as she looked away from Kahlan's gaze. Kahlan gently stroked the girl's head, hoping to comfort her heartache for her grandfather. She gestured, pointing with her chin.

"Go in that saddlebag, there, Jillian, and get yourself something to eat." She was trembling from the pain, and wanted very much to lie down, but Kahlan knew that Sister Ulicia had not made an empty threat. "Then if you would, please . . . just sit with me for the night? I could use a friend tonight."

Jillian smiled up at her. It warmed Kahlan's heart to see such a sincere smile.

"In the morning you will have another friend to join us." When Kahlan twitched a frown, Jillian pointed up at the sky. "I have a raven, named Lokey. In the day he will come and entertain us with some of his tricks."

Kahlan smiled at the very idea of having a raven for a friend.

The girl squeezed Kahlan's hand. "I won't leave you tonight, Kahlan. I promise."

As much agony as she was in, as bleak as her future seemed, Kahlan was joyous. Jillian was alive. Kahlan had just won her first battle, and that accomplishment was exhilarating.

As he walked among the gathered soldiers, Richard acknowledged their greetings with a smile and a nod. He was in no mood to smile, but he feared that the men would misunderstand it if he didn't. Their eyes were filled with expectation and hope as they watched him make his way among them. Many a man stood silently with a fist over his heart, not just in salute but in pride. Richard could not begin to explain to each of these men the horrific things Shota had shown him, and so he smiled as warmly as he was able.

Beyond the encampment, lightning flickered at the horizon. Even over the sounds of camp life, the thousands of men and horses, of the ring of blacksmiths' hammers, the unloading of supplies, the provisions being distributed, the orders being shouted, Richard could hear the lightning's ominous rumble rolling along the Azrith Plain. Angry thunderclouds gathered an ever-growing charge of black shadows under their skirts. The still, humid air was occasionally aroused by gusts that lifted flags and pennants to flapping attention. Almost as soon as it arrived, the wind would suddenly vanish, like an advance guard racing back to report to the gathering storm.

No one seemed to care about the threatening sky, though. They all wanted to get a glimpse of Richard as he made his way through the encampment. There was a time when this very army was bound and determined to kill or capture him. But that was before Richard had become the Lord Rahl.

Once he had taken on that responsibility, he had given these men the chance to stand for a worthy cause, rather than carry arms in service to tyranny. There had been some who had viewed that offer with open hatred. They turned instead to the cause of the Order and swept across the land with blind brutality, seeking to exterminate the very idea that any man had a right to his own life.

But the rest of them, most of them in fact, had not just taken up Richard's challenge, they had embraced it with the kind of fervor that only men who had lived under repression could. These men, the first in generations to be offered real freedom, truly grasped its meaning for their lives. They held on tenaciously to the chance to live in the kind of world Richard had shown them was possible. There was no greater nor more meaningful a gift these men could in turn give their families and loved ones than that chance to live life free, to live for themselves. Many had died in that noble effort.

Much the same as the Mord-Sith, these men followed him now because they chose to, not because they were forced to. When they called him "Lord Rahl" it had meaning to them that it had never carried before.

But these men now faced the edged steel that enforced a belief that said they and their loved ones had no right to their own lives. Richard did not doubt the hearts of these men, but he knew that they could not prevail in a battle against the vast numbers of Imperial Order invaders. This day of all days, he had to be the Lord Rahl. If there was to be a chance at a future worth living, Richard had to be the Lord Rahl in the purest sense, the Lord Rahl who cared about those he led. He had to make them see what he saw.

Verna, hurrying along beside him, tightened her grip on his arm as she leaned a little closer. "You can't imagine how uplifting it is for these men to see you before the battle they will be facing, Richard, the battle that prophecy has been foretelling for thousands of years. You just can't imagine."

Richard doubted that the men could imagine what he was about to ask of them.

He glanced over at Verna's smile. "I know, Prelate."

Because they were steadily making headway south to meet the threat from the Imperial Order, the ride from the People's Palace to catch up with them had taken considerably longer than the last time he had come to see these soldiers. Once the Order turned north up into D'Hara, this army was all that stood against them. These men were the last hope of the D'Haran Empire. That was their calling, their duty.

And Richard knew without doubt that they would lose that battle.

Richard's task was to convince them of the certainty of their impending defeat and death.

Cara and Nicci, right behind him, were practically walking on his heels. He didn't think they needed to be that close to protect him, but he also knew that neither woman would likely take his word for it. When he glanced back over his shoulder, Nicci gave him a tight smile.

He wondered what she would say once she heard what he was about to tell the soldiers. He supposed that she would understand. Of all those who would hear what he had to say, she was the one person he believed would understand. In fact, he was counting on it. Her understanding and support were sometimes all that kept him going. There were times when he had been ready to give up and Nicci had given him the strength to go on.

Richard knew that Cara, on the other had, would welcome what he was about to say, if for entirely different reasons.

Although Cara looked as grim as ever, as if she might have to kill the entire army should they suddenly turn to treason and attack Richard, he could tell by the way her fingers worked at a seam of her red leather outfit that she was eager to at last see General Meiffert—Benjamin—again. Since the last time they had been with these men she was a little less reticent about letting her feelings for the handsome D'Haran general be known. Richard suspected that Nicci had something to do with that.

As overwhelmed as he felt about a world that seemed to be coming down around him, he was inwardly gratified that a Mord-Sith could ever come to have such feelings, and even more so that she would finally be willing to let them be known, at least to him. It was confirmation that, beyond the brutal training of these women, they were individuals who each had long-suppressed desires and aspirations that had not withered and died, and that the true person inside could again blossom. It was an affirmation of his belief in a better future, that there could be a better future, like finding a beautiful flower in a vast wasteland.

As Richard marched past rows of tents, wagons, picketed horses, blacksmith stations, and supply areas, he could see men approaching from all directions, abandoning their evening chores of caring for animals, repairing gear, tending to supplies, cooking, and setting up yet more tents. A glance to the thick overcast told him that they would be smart to at least finish setting up their tents.

Richard spotted General Meiffert among the sea of men in dark uniforms. He stood tall among officers outside a large command area. When Richard glanced back over his shoulder, he could see by Cara's smile that she saw him as well.

The assembled officers and men of rank were too many to fit into a tent, so they had gathered among a scattered boulder field. Awnings had been strung together over the area, anchored to the massive boulders, so that the men in the command center would be protected should the rain start. It didn't look to Richard like it would protect them from any wind, but it would at least keep them mostly dry as they worked on the details of directing an army this large.

Richard leaned a little toward Verna as thunder shook the ground. "Your Sisters will be there?"

Verna nodded. "Yes. I sent runners to tell them that you wanted them there along with all the officers. There are a few on distant reconnaissance, but the rest will be there."

"Lord Rahl," General Meiffert said as he clapped a fist to his heart.

Richard bowed his head. "General. Glad to see you well. The men all look in order, as always."

"Thank you, Lord Rahl." His blue eyes were already taking in Cara. He bowed at the waist to her. "Mistress Cara."

Cara actually smiled. "You are a happy sight for my eyes, Benjamin."

Had Richard not been so distressed about the things that had brought him to be there, he would have derived great pleasure from seeing them gaze into each other's eyes. Richard remembered looking at Kahlan that way, remembered his inner joy at seeing her.

Captain Zimmer, his shaped leather armor serving to accentuate his powerful build, stood not far behind the general. Some of the other officers, in similar if less simple uniforms, waited in a cluster nearby, while most were already assembled under the awning. The groups of men, engaged in earnest conversation, all fell quiet and turned to see Lord Rahl, the leader of the D'Haran Empire. Richard didn't have time for pleasantries, so he dove right in. Likewise, the regular soldiers who had gathered all around stood silently watching.

"Are all the officers and men of rank here, General?" Richard asked.

The man nodded. "Yes, Lord Rahl. Every one of them in camp, anyway. There are some out on long-range patrol. Had we known of your arrival and wishes I would have recalled them, but as it is we would need some time to get them back here. If you wish, I will send word at once for them to return."

Richard lifted a hand to forestall the suggestion. "No, that's not necessary. As long as most of them are assembled that will do. The rest can be briefed later."

There were far too many men in the encampment for Richard to be heard and understood by them all. His intent was to speak in detail to the officers and men of rank, and then have them spread the word among their own men. There were enough officers gathered for that task.

The general, in a casual but clearly commanding manner, gestured to the men surrounding the command area, watching the great event. They immediately began to disperse, going back to their own work, while their commanders learned of their fate.

General Meiffert held out an arm, inviting Richard and his escort in under the shelter. Richard first glanced at the sky, judging the chances to be good that the rain would soon start in earnest. In under the expansive tarp, hundreds of men were gathered tightly together. Richard tapped his fist to his heart, returning the collective, muffled thump of their sharp salutes.

"I am here today," Richard began as he scanned all the eyes watching him, "about the gravest of issues . . . the coming final battle with the advancing army of the Imperial Order.

"There must be no confusion about what I will have to say. I need every one of you to understand what is at stake, what I am going to ask of you, and why. This is about all of our lives; I will not hold back anything from you and I will answer honestly and to the best of my ability anything you want to know. Please feel free to ask your questions, voice your objections, or even to disagree with certain points as I lay out what I've decided. I value your vast collective knowledge and skill. I trust in your ability and experience.

"But I have had to weigh and consider matters outside your purview and on everything put together I have made my decision. I can appreciate that, absent such information, you many not entirely understand my reasoning, so I will do my best to explain it, but there will be no dissent about my conclusion."

Richard's voice took on an edge of absolute resolve. "You will follow my orders."

The men all shared looks. This was as stern a command as any Richard had ever given them.

In the afternoon hush, Richard began to slowly pace back and forth, choosing his words carefully. He finally gestured out to the crowd before him.

"As officers, as men of command, what is it that preoccupies your minds the most?"

After a moment's confused silence, an officer to the side spoke up. "I suppose that we're all thinking about what you've already mentioned, Lord Rahl: the final battle."

"That's right, the final battle," Richard said as he came to a halt and turned to the men. "That's the common way we all think, that everything will come down to that defining moment, the climax of everyone's effort, and that there will be a final, grand battle to decide it all—who wins, who loses, who rules, who serves, who lives, who dies. This is the way Jagang thinks as well."

"He wouldn't be their leader if he didn't," an older officer said.

Sporadic chuckles rippled through the assembled men.

"True enough," Richard said in a solemn voice. "Especially in the case of Emperor Jagang. His objective is to carry his cause to that final battle and in that concluding contest crush us once and for all. He is a very intelligent foe. He has gotten us to focus on that final battle. His strategy is working."

The laughter had died out. The men looked a little displeased that Richard would give the man so much credit. Soldiers like these didn't like to grant their enemy too much mastery lest their own men suffer a failing of courage at fighting him.

Richard had no interest in making Jagang seem less of a threat than he was. Quite the opposite; he wanted to give these men an accurate glimpse of what they were up against, and the true dimensions of the menace.

"Jagang is a devotee of a game called Ja'La dh Jin." Seeing some of the men nod, Richard knew that they had become at least somewhat familiar with the game. "He has his own Ja'La team, much like the Fellowship of Order has its own army. Jagang's overriding concern, when he sends his team in to play, is to win at Ja'La. To that end he collected the biggest, toughest players for his team. He does not view it as a contest, a competition, as some do. He intends not merely to be victorious in any Ja'La match, but to overwhelm the opposition.

"Jagang's team once lost. His solution was not to try harder the next time, to train and coach his players, to do better the next time. He instead went out and got other players. He created a team of the biggest, strongest, fastest men. The translation of Ja'La dh Jin, by the way, is 'the game of life.'

"In the beginning, when he was joining all the various kingdoms and lands of the Old World into one nation, Jagang lost battles. He learned the lessons of life. He got the biggest, meanest army he could and in the end he united the entire Old World under the banner of the Order. When he embarked on this war, at the behest of the Fellowship of Order, Jagang made sure that he would have at his disposal the resources necessary to insure that he would have a force large enough to do the job. You men would do no less.

"Jagang occasionally still lost battles. Again he learned. He responded by calling upon those resources to see to it that he had more men. That's how he approaches the goal of winning the war on behalf of the Order. The result is that today he has a force so overwhelming that he can crush all opposition. He knows that he will win. So, he looks forward to the final battle.

"In addition, Emperor Jagang was a dream walker, a man with powers handed down to him through ancient magic. He used that ability to invade the minds of others not only to gain knowledge, but to control them. Today, as you know, he controls a number of gifted people, Sisters of the Light and the Dark among them. He thus commands both forces of steel and magic."

"Lord Rahl," one of the older officers said, interrupting Richard's pacing speech, "you dismiss our men too easily. Most of our army is made up of D'Haran forces and the rest we have trained. These men know what is at stake. They are not green recruits. They are experienced soldiers who know how to fight. We also have Verna and her Sisters, who had proven themselves. Along with these skilled soldiers and Sisters of the Light, we have right on our side."

"The Imperial Order is not predestined to lose just because they are evil. In the long run evil will turn in on itself, but for our lives and the lives of those we protect that is little comfort. Evil can still dominate mankind for a thousand years, two thousand, or even more before it eventually dies of its own poison."

Richard started pacing again as he spoke with great passion. "There are times in history when things might have gone either way but for the valiant efforts of some individuals, I grant you that. In fact, I am counting on it. This is the time when we decide what will be our future. This is the time when we must do what must be done, despite how painful it will be, if we and our children are to have a future. Our future, freedom's future, hinges on us and what we do, on whether or not we succeed."

"Lord Rahl," the older officer said with quiet assurance, "the men know that our backs are to the wall. They will fight, if that's what you're suggesting."

Richard realized that the men weren't understanding what he was getting at. He stopped and faced the men as he clasped his hands behind his back. In the back of his mind he could see the ghostly image that Shota had shown him of the bloody end of it all. It was like a weight trying to drag him under.

Richard finally spoke. "I've always said that I can't lead us into a final battle with the Order or we would lose. Things have happened since last I was with you men that make me believe that now more than ever before."

Rumblings of discontent matched the rumblings of thunder filling the gloomy afternoon air. Before they could object or take him off on a tangent, Richard went on.

"The army of the Order is very soon going to be advancing up into D'Hara from the south on their way to the People's Palace. You men are advancing south to meet them. They know that. They expect that. They want that. We are marching to Jagang's orders. He is controlling our tactics. He is drawing us into a battle he knows we can't win and that he can't lose."

Voices of protest erupted, all shouting that the future wasn't fixed, that they could prevail.

Richard held up a hand to halt the voices. "While the future isn't fixed, reality is what it is. As soldiers you plan your tactics according to what you know, not what you wish.

"Even if by some miracle we were able to win this looming battle, it would turn out not to be decisive. Such a battle would end up merely being a fight we won at a great cost, while the Order would simply come right back at us again with an even larger force. Even if we were to win the impending battle—which I know we can't—we would then have to fight another battle against even more men, and then another.

"Why? Because each time we fight them we lose men and get weaker. We have little reserves to call upon. Each time Jagang needs them, he gets a steady stream of nearly limitless reinforcements and only gets stronger.

"We would lose in the end for one very simple reason: no war is ever won defensively. While a defensive battle can be won, a war cannot be won defensively."

"So," an officer asked, "what do you propose? That we sue for peace?"

Richard dismissed the idea with a casual, if irritated, gesture. "The Order would grant no peace terms. Maybe long ago, in the beginning, they would have accepted our surrender, allowed us to bow and kiss their boots, allowed us to put on the chains of slavery, but not now. Now they want only a victory bought and paid for with our blood. But what difference would it have made? Either way, the end result would be the same: the murder and subjugation of us and our people. How we lose, for the most part, is irrelevant. Surrender or defeat ends with the same result. One way or the other all is lost."

"Then . . . what?" the man stammered in a heated voice. "Fight on until we are finally killed or captured?"

The men stared at the red-faced officer who had spoken. These men had been fighting the Order for a long time. They were not hearing anything they didn't already know. Still, fighting the invaders was all they could do. It was their duty. It was the only thing they knew.

Richard turned and took in Cara. Standing there in her red leather, her feet spread, her hands clasped behind her back, she looked like she believed she could take on the Order all by herself.

Richard gestured to the woman standing beside Cara. "Nicci, here, once served on their side." When he heard the whispers about an enemy among them, he added, "Much the same as all of you were once in the service of tyranny when you served Darken Rahl, and some of you even his father, Panis Rahl. You had no choice. Darken Rahl did not care what you wanted to do with your lives. He only cared that you followed his orders. Now, when given a choice, you have committed to our cause. Nicci has as well.

"The men of the Order are different. You were fighting because you were made to under threat of violence or even death. They are fighting because they believe in a cause. They hunger to fight. They want to be a part of their war effort.

"Since she was there, with Jagang, Nicci has firsthand knowledge. She has seen things that may help put it into perspective for you."

Richard turned again to Nicci. She looked like a statue, her skin smooth and fair, her blond hair tumbled down over her shoulders. There was nothing about her face, her figure, that Richard would have changed if he were the one to carve a statue of her. She was a picture of beauty, who had seen ugliness beyond imagining.

"Nicci, please tell these men what will happen to them if they are captured by the Imperial Order."

Richard had no idea what she would say, what she knew, but he did know, especially from the things Jebra had told them, that the Order had only contempt for life.

"The Order does not execute their captives immediately." With deadly calm, Nicci glided one step closer to all the men staring at her. She waited at Richard's side until the silence was painful and she had the undivided attention of every man before her. "First," she said, "every man captured is castrated."

A collective gasp went up from the assembled men.

"After that, after they have suffered unendurable agony and humiliation, the ones still alive are put to torture. The ones who survive the torture are finally put to death in one brutal fashion or another.

"Those who surrender to the Order without a fight are spared such treatment. That is the design behind the cruelty toward captives—to strike fear into a potential adversary so that they will surrender without a fight. Their treatment of civilians in captured cities is just as brutal and it has the same goal in mind. As a result, many cities have fallen to the Order without a fight.

"You men have fought them long and hard. You would not be spared any of it. If you are caught by Jagang's forces there is no hope for you. You will be made to wish with all your hearts that you had never been born. Death will be your only release.

"Not that it matters. Life under the Order is not much different than waiting for death at the hands of the Order. Life under the Order is a slow, grinding death in itself. It just takes longer; the misery of it stretches out over years.

"Only those who hate life, and everything good, prosper. The Order, in fact, fosters and encourages those who hate the good aspects of life. Their teachings are, after all, formed from a bitter hatred for the good. The environment such beliefs create is one of universal misery. The haters relish the misery of others, since the good angers them. If captured, these haters would be your masters."

The men stood in stunned silence. In that silence, Richard heard the gentle patter of rain on the awning stretched overhead. The storm was rolling in on them.

Nicci spoke offhandedly into the silence. "The fried testicles of their enemies are a prized treat for the soldiers of the Imperial Order. The camp followers will scour a battlefield after a battle, looking for loot and any wounded enemy still alive that they can castrate. Those precious, bloody gems harvested from a living enemy are a valuable and sought-after commodity during the drunken celebration after a victory. The soldiers believe that such a delicacy gives them greater strength and virility. Afterwards, they turn their attention to their women captives."

Richard pinched the bridge of his nose between a thumb and first finger. "Anything else?"

Nicci raised an eyebrow. "Isn't that enough?"

Richard heaved a sigh as he let his hand drop. "I guess so."

He turned back to the men. "The simple truth is that there is no way you can win the coming battle. You are going to lose."

Richard took a deep breath and finally uttered the unspeakable words he had come to say.

"That is why there will be no final battle. We will not fight Emperor Jagang and his army of the Imperial Order. As Lord Rahl, leader of the D'Haran Empire, I refuse to allow such an act of pointless self-destruction. We will not fight them.

"Instead, I have come to disperse our army. There will be no final battle. Jagang will have the New World unopposed."

Richard saw tears filling the eyes of many a man.

Richard's words were received like a slap.

An angry officer shouted, "Then why should we fight?" He swept an arm around at his fellows. "We've been at this war for years. Many of our fellow soldiers are no longer here, with us, because they have sacrificed their lives to preserve our cause and loved ones. If there is no chance, if we are just going to lose in the end, then why have we bothered to fight? Why should we bother to continue in this struggle?"

Richard smiled bitterly. "That's the whole point."

"What point?" the man growled.

"If people see no chance for triumph, no chance to win, and see instead that they face only ruin and death, then they begin to lose their will to fight. If they see that they have no chance to spread their beliefs, that they face only death if they continue to try to do so, then they will begin to want to forget all about such a war."

If anything, the man was only getting angrier, as were many of the other officers. "So you're telling us to forget about the war? That we can't win against the will of the Order? That since we can't win there is nothing to fight for?"

Richard clasped his hands behind his back as he lifted his chin with resolve. He waited until he was sure that he had every ear.

"No. I'm telling you that I want to make the people of the Old World feel that way."

The men frowned in confusion, muttering questions among themselves. They quickly quieted down as Richard went on.

"Jagang is bringing his army up into D'Hara. He wants to meet us in battle. Why? Because he believes he can defeat us. I believe he is right. I don't believe this because you men lack anything in bravery, training, strength, or skill, but simply because I know how vast his resources are. I've spent time down in the Old World. I know how vast the place is. To an extent, because I have traveled through the Old World, I know how many people they have, how much livestock, crops, and other assets. I've seen these things on a scale I've never seen before. They have reserves you cannot even begin to imagine.

"Jagang has amassed an enormous force of savage men who are devoted to their beliefs. They intend to crush everyone and everything opposing them. They lust to be conquering heroes, to spread their faith. Jagang has been provided with everything his experience tells him he will need, and then he doubled it. Just to be certain, he then doubled it again.

"Jagang does not hold perverse moral notions of warfare fought by employing no more assets than an opponent possesses—of some kind of fabricated fairness imposed on the act of mortal combat. He has no interest in an equal contest—nor should he. He is interested only in mastering us. That is his task.

"To that end, they want us to defend from the position of our greatest vulnerability, fight from our weakest footing—on the battlefield, in a traditional final battle. That is what all of Jagang's efforts have been dedicated to because it's what everyone expects. They want to meet us this way because we don't stand a chance against their numbers. There is simply no way that we have enough forces to prevail. They will then crush us.

"Afterwards, they will celebrate their great victory—as if the accomplishment was ever in doubt—by frying up all your testicles and then in a drunken orgy they will rape your wives and sisters and daughters!"

Richard leaned toward the men and jabbed a finger at his temple. "Think! Are you so mired on the concept of a traditional final battle that you have forgotten its purpose? Are you putting the 'the way it's always been done' ahead of the reason for doing it? The sole reason for such a battle is to prevail over the enemy, to settle the matter once and for all. That concept of a final battle has evolved into thinking that it's the way it must be done because that is the way it has always been done.

"Stop being pointlessly tied to that idea. Think. Stop being blinded by what you have done before. Stop throwing yourselves into your graves as if by rote. Think—*think*—about how to accomplish our objective."

"You mean to say that you have a better idea than fighting them?" a younger officer asked. Like most of the men, he looked truly puzzled.

Richard took a breath in an effort to get a grip on his temper. He lowered his voice and looked among all the sober faces as he went on.

"Yes. Instead of doing the expected and throwing ourselves into a final battle, I simply want to destroy them. That is, after all, the root objective of a grand final battle. If such a battle will not accomplish that objective, then we must find another way.

"Unlike those who fight for the beliefs of the Order, none of us needs to brag about a glorious victory on the field of battle. There is no glory in such things. There is simply success or failure. Failure means a new dark age. Success means we live free. Civilization hangs in the balance. It's as simple as that.

"There is no narrowly defined field of battle in such a struggle for life, such a struggle for our very survival against men driven by a desire to murder us because they think we have no right to exist. Such a struggle is not a fight over a plot of ground, a war over turf, but is based in the minds of men, based in the very ideas that motivate them.

"Our loved ones will not be better served by a victory on a battlefield; they will only be served if we prevail in this struggle of ideas."

General Meiffert finally lifted a hand to speak. "Lord Rahl, if not by meeting them in combat, then how do you propose we accomplish such a task against a foe that you have just explained is so vast that it is unbeatable? After all, even if it is their beliefs that drive them, it is their swords that we must deal with."

Men nodded, happy that their general had asked the question they all had in mind. It was also the question Richard had been waiting for. He had discouraged their hope of a victory in a traditional battle by throwing out their mindset. Now he had to show them how to win the war.

As the drumbeat of rain on the tarp overhead increased, Richard, hands clasped behind his back, appraised all the faces watching him. "You must be the thunder and lightning of freedom. You must be vengeance unleashed against a people with corrupt ideas that have not just allowed evil to dwell in their hearts, but authorized and advocated it.

"We must fight the war our way. We must fight it for what it really is— not armies on a field of battle acting as surrogates for ideas, but a war for the future of mankind.

"As such, it is a war in which the Old World is totally committed, in which everyone on their side has dedicated themselves to the struggle. They are passionate about their cause. They *believe* in what they are doing. They think they have right on their side, that they are acting morally, that they are fulfilling the Creator's wishes, and so they are justified in murdering whoever they wish in order to define how mankind will live.

"They are all investing their property, their labor, their wealth, and their lives in the struggle. Their people—not just their army—want to subjugate us and make us bend to their beliefs. They want us to be slaves to their faith, just as they are. They encourage their army to attack innocent people here, in the New World, in order to force their beliefs on us. They want us, as followers of the same faith as they, to sacrifice our lives to that faith, to live the lives they wish us to live, to dictate what our children will believe . . . by force if necessary.

"All the people who believe in the ways of the Order, who contribute, who encourage, who support, who pray for their soldiers to crush us, are part of their war effort. Each of those people adds something to their cause. As such, they are just as much the enemy as the soldiers swinging the swords for them. They are the ones who feed their blades with a supply of young men and everything they need to come after us, from food to moral support and encouragement."

Richard pointed south. "In fact, those people who make this war possible are perhaps even more of an enemy because each one is a silent enabler who wishes us harm from afar, who hates by choice, who believes that there is no consequence for them forcing their will on us.

"Loot and plunder goes back to reward their support. Slaves are sent back to labor for them. Blood and tears are extracted to enforce their demands for faith.

"These people have made the choice to believe, made the choice to think that they have a right to our lives, made the choice to do anything necessary to rule us. There must be consequences to the choices they have made, especially when their choices ruin the lives of others who have done them no harm."

Richard opened his hands. "And how are we to accomplish this?"

He drew his hands into fists. "We must bring this war home to the people who support and encourage it. It must not simply be the lives of our friends, our families, our loved ones who are thrown into the bloody cauldron these people of the Old World stoke. It must now be their lives as well.

"They see this as a struggle for the future of mankind. I intend to see that it is. I want them to fully understand that if they set out to murder and subjugate us—for whatever reason—then there will be consequences.

"From this day forward, we will fight a real war, a total war, a war without mercy. We will not impose pointless rules on ourselves about what is 'fair.' Our only mandate is to win. That is the only way we, our loved ones, our freedom will survive. Our victory is all that is moral. I want any supporter of the Order to pay the price for their aggression. I want them to pay with their fortunes, their future, their very lives.

"The time has come to go after these people with nothing but cold black rage in our hearts."

Richard lifted a fist. "Crush their bones to blood and dust!"

There was a moment of silence as everyone took a collective breath, and then a thunderous cheer erupted, as if they had all secretly known that they had no chance to succeed and that they were doomed to face only death and failure in the end, but now they had been shown that there was a way. There was, at last, a real chance to save their homes and loved ones, to save the future.

Richard let the revelry go on for a time, then held up a hand to make them listen as he went on.

"The army of the Order has the support of the people of their homeland. The soldiers of the Order each know that their families, friends, and neighbors support them. The men of the Order need to hear from those back in the Old World. What I want the men of the Order to hear are wails of agony. I want them to know that their homes are being gutted, their cities and towns leveled, their businesses and crops destroyed, and their loved ones left with nothing.

"The Order preaches that life in this world is nothing but misery. Make it so. Strip away the thin veneer of civilization they so despise."

Richard looked to Verna and the women with her, Sisters of the Light, all. "They hate magic; make them terrified of it. They think those with magic must be destroyed; make them believe that they can't be. They want a world without magic; make them wish only not to anger us ever again. They want to conquer; make them want only to surrender."

As the lightning crackled through the gloomy afternoon air, and the wind-driven rain beat against the awning overhead, Richard turned his attention back to the men. When the latest crackle of thunder died out, he went on.

"To accomplish our purpose, we must have a coordinated plan aimed at every facet of the threat. To this end, some of our forces must be devoted to the important goal of hunting and killing their supply trains. Those trains are essential to the Order's survival. They not only get the reinforcements they need, but those trains send a steady stream of supplies that they must have in order to survive. The Imperial Order forces plunder as they go, but it's nowhere near enough to sustain them. Their overwhelming size is also a vulnerability. We must deny them those supplies they need to survive here in such numbers. We must cut that vital link. If the Imperial Order's soldiers starve to death they are just as dead. Any Order soldier who dies of starvation is one less we have to worry about. That's all that matters to us.

"Also, the recruits coming up from the south will be much more vulnerable since they will not yet have joined up with experienced men, or be in massive numbers. They are poorly trained and little more than young thugs going off to rape and pillage. Slaughter them before they go north and have the chance. It will be ever more difficult to enlist new recruits if they are being killed on their own soil before they can ever go off to kill helpless strangers. Even better if they are small units just assembling in their home towns. Bring the war to them. Kill them before they have a chance to bring it to us. If young men know that if they volunteer they will never get to be heroes, never get their hands on plunder and young captive women, and see that they will not make it far before they are set upon by men who don't fight as they expected, don't throw themselves into a futile final battle against impossible odds, their passion for joining the fight will turn icy cold. If it doesn't, then they can die, too, before they ever have a chance to join the army to the north. Seeing the bodies of these young heroes-to-be rotting on their doorsteps will help us crush the spirit of the people of the Old World."

Richard appraised the intent gazes before going on. "The idea of a final battle dies here, dies today. Today we dissolve into thin air. After today there will be no D'Haran Empire army that the Imperial Order can engage in a final battle and destroy. They want to do this, after all, in order to strip our people of our protection, leaving them naked and vulnerable. We are not going to allow that. Today we start fighting this war a new way—our way—a way rationally thought out, a way that will win.

"I want everyone in the Old World to fear you as if you were avenging spirits. Beginning today, you will become the phantom D'Haran legions.

"No one will know where you are. No one will know when you will strike. No one will know where you will strike next. But I want everyone in the Old World to know without any doubt whatsoever that you will come after them and you will strike as if the underworld itself were about to open up and annihilate them. I want them to fear the phantom D'Haran legions as if you are death itself.

"They wish to die so that they may enter the everlasting glory of the afterlife . . . deliver them their wish."

One of the men toward the back cleared his throat, then spoke up. "Lord Rahl, innocent people down there are going to die. These aren't soldiers we will be attacking. A lot of children are going to die in this kind of thing."

"Yes, that is unfortunately true, but don't let your mind be clouded or your determination turned aside by such a spurious and irrelevant charge. The Order is responsible for conducting a war of aggression against innocent people who have done them no harm—including women and children. We seek only to end the aggression as swiftly as possible.

"It's true that innocent people—including children—will be hurt or killed. What is the alternative? Continuing to sacrifice good people out of fear of harming someone innocent? We are all innocent. Our children are all innocent. They are being harmed, now. The Order's rule will eventually harm everyone, including all those children in the Old World. The Order will turn many of them into monsters. Many more people will die in the end if the Order wins.

"Moreover, the lives of the people in the Old World are not our responsibility, they are the Order's responsibility. We did not start this war and attack them—they attacked us. Our only proper course of action is to end the war as swiftly as possible. This is the only way to do that. In the end, this is the most humane thing we can do because in the end this will mean the least loss of life.

"Whenever possible you should of course avoid harming innocent people, but that is not your overriding objective. Ending the war is your objective. To do that, we must destroy their ability to wage war. As soldiers, that is the responsibility.

"We are defending our right to exist. If we succeed we will, as a consequence, help countless others to live free as well. But it is not our aim to free their people. If they wish to be free then they can join with us in our efforts.

"As a matter of fact, I know people in the Old World who have already revolted against the Order and are with us in this struggle. A simple blacksmith named Victor and his forces in Altur'Rang, for example, have lit the flame of freedom in the Old World and already fight with us. Wherever you can find these people who hunger to be free you should encourage them and enlist their support. They will willingly see their towns and cities burn if those blazes destroy the vermin who eat away at their lives.

"In all you do, never forget that your aim is to stop the Order from killing us and to do that we must make them lose their will to fight. To do that, we must take the war to them.

"I grieve for innocent lives lost, but their loss is a direct result of the immoral actions of the Order. We have no responsibility to sacrifice our lives to prevent innocent people on their side being harmed. We cannot be responsible for their lives in such a struggle not of our making.

"We have every right to defend our right to exist. Don't let anyone ever tell you otherwise. The threat must be eliminated. Anything else is just whistling on your way to your grave."

The men all stood somber and still under the billowing awning protecting them from the downpour. None had any argument to offer. They had been fighting a losing battle for a long time. They had seen thousands die. They understood that there was now no other way.

Richard gestured to Captain Zimmer, a young, square-jawed, bull-necked man who stood with his arms folded across his massive chest. He was immersed in total concentration as he'd listened to Richard. The man had become the head of the special forces when Kahlan had promoted Captain Meiffert to commanding general of the D'Haran forces. Kahlan had also told Richard that Captain Zimmer and his men were very good at what they did, that they were experienced, businesslike under stress, tireless, fearless, and coolly efficient at killing. What made most soldiers blanch made them grin. Kahlan had also told him that they collected the ears of the enemy.

"Captain Zimmer, as part of our new, coordinated operation, I have a special job for you."

The man beamed with an infectious smile as he dropped his arms and stood up straighter. "Yes, Lord Rahl?"

"Of primary importance is the elimination of anyone—anyone—who preaches the tenets of the Order. These people are the fount of hate, the source of the corrupt beliefs that poison life.

"The Fellowship of Order has set their goal on the conquest of all of mankind for the purpose of bringing all people under their strict teachings.

They advocate the killing of all those who don't bow to their beliefs. The ideas of these men are the spark that ignites murder. Were it not for those teachings, they would not be here killing people.

"The Order is a viper that exists because of their beliefs, their ideas, their teachings. That viper stretches here all the way from the heart of the Old World. From this moment on, your objective is to behead this snake. Kill every man who preaches their beliefs. If they give a speech, the next morning I want their body found in the middle of a very public place, and I want it to be clear to all that they did not die of natural causes. I want it known that professing the beliefs of the Order is asking for a swift death.

"How you kill them is irrelevant, but kill them we must. When they are dead they can no longer spread their poison and raise the passions of other men to kill us. That is your job: kill them. The less time you take killing one, the sooner you can kill others.

"Keep in mind, though, that the high priests of the Fellowship of Order are gifted. While you must be cautious and aware that these men are wizards, also keep in mind that even such wizards still have hearts that pump blood through their veins. An arrow will kill them as surely as any other man.

"I know, because not long ago I was nearly killed by an arrow fired in a surprise attack on my camp." Richard gestured to the two woman behind him. "I was fortunate in that Cara and Nicci were there to save my life. The point is that, despite their power, these men are vulnerable. You can eliminate them.

"After all, how often have I heard you men say that you will be the steel against steel so that I can be the magic against magic? Implicit in that maxim is the fundamental truth that the gifted are mortal and vulnerable to the same perils as all men.

"I know that you and your men will find ways to eliminate these men. I want every man who preaches the hate of the Order's beliefs to find that death is the consequence. There must be no doubt of the hard truth that they are not going to escape that fate just because they are gifted. You and your men are to deliver that truth to them.

"This is, after all, about truth and illusion, a battle over which of those concepts mankind will serve. They preach an illusion of beliefs in things that are not real, of faith and fantasy, of kingdoms in other worlds, of punishments and rewards after we no longer exist. They kill to force people to bow to that faith.

"The counter to that is the reality of our promise of the consequence of harming us. That promise must be kept. That promise must be true. If we fail in this struggle, then mankind will slip into a long, dark age."

Richard looked out over the silent men and spoke quietly, but in a tone that every man heard. "I am counting on the experience and judgment of you men to accomplish what we must. If you see something you think is useful to them, destroy it. If anyone tries to get in your way, kill them. I want their crops, homes, towns, and cities burned to the ground. I want to see the Old World burning all the way from here. I don't want one brick left standing atop another. I want the Old World to suffer such ruin that they no longer possess the ability to extend their murderous intent to others. I want their will to fight broken. I want their spirits crushed.

"I trust that you men will be able to come up with ways to accomplish all this. Don't be limited by what I tell you. Think about what is a valuable resource to them and what would make it a good target for us. Think of how best to carry out your new orders."

He watched the eyes of men who were being called upon to do what they had never expected would be their job. "There will be no final battle with the army of the Order. We will not face them in the way they wish. Instead, we will haunt them into their graves."

The gathered officers all clapped fists to their hearts.

Richard turned again to Captain Zimmer. "You have my orders as to your specific objective. Be ruthless. There is to be no alternative allowed for these men. Their death is the only result that is acceptable. Make it swift, sure, and without mercy."

Captain Zimmer stood tall. "Thank you, Lord Rahl, for allowing me and my men to rid the world of those who preach this poison."

"There's one other thing I'd like you and your men to do for me."

"Yes, Lord Rahl?"

"Bring me their ears."

Captain Zimmer smiled as he put a fist to his heart. "There will be no escape or mercy for them, Lord Rahl. I will bring you proof."

As they put their minds to their new goal, the officers all began coming forward with suggestions for both targets and methods of destroying them. Their enthusiasm enlivened their faces, as if they had gotten so used to the idea that there was no choice but to be worn down by an implacable enemy, that their faces had taken on creases as they sagged with the burden. Now Richard could see a new vigor in them, an excitement that there was a solution, an end in sight.

Men offered ideas of salting fields, poisoning water supplies with rotting, infected carcasses and corpses, destroying dams, cutting down orchards, slaughtering livestock, and torching mills. Nicci discouraged some suggestions, explaining why they wouldn't work or would involve too much effort, and offered alternatives in their place. She refined other ideas to make them more devastating.

To a degree, Richard was sickened by the things he heard and the knowledge that he was the architect of such mayhem, but then he thought about the vision Shota had given him of Kahlan, of how those very horrors and more were real for uncounted innocent people, and he was gratified that they were at last striking back in a way that had a chance to end such horrors. The Order, after all, had brought this on themselves.

"Time is of the essence," Richard told the officers and gathered Sisters. "Every day that passes the Order captures more places, subjugates, tortures, rapes, and murders yet more people."

"I agree," General Meiffert said. "This can't be a march south."

"No, it can't," Richard said. "I want you to ride fast and strike hard. The Order has a huge army and everywhere they go in the New World falls to their swords. But, because of their size, they are ponderous. It takes them a long time to move across the land. Jagang uses his slow speed as a tactic; it makes each city that lies in his path suffer the agony of waiting, imagining what will become of them. It gives fear time to build until it is unendurable.

"We actually have an advantage in that if we use cavalry and keep the units small and nimble, we can strike like lightning in one place after another. They seek to roll in on cities, envelop, and occupy them. We must not be drawn into that kind of drain on manpower and effort. We must simply lay waste to everything we can and then immediately move on to the next target. We must make everyone in the Old World feel fear, feel that there is no safety from our vengeance."

A bearded officer gestured out at the camp. "There's not nearly enough horses to turn the whole army into cavalry."

"Then you need to quickly find horses for all the men," Cara said. "Get them wherever you can."

The officer scratched his beard as he considered. He smiled at Cara. "Don't you worry, we'll find a way to do just that."

Another man spoke up. "I know of a number of places in D'Hara where horses are raised. I think we can gather what we'll need in relatively short order." When Richard nodded his approval, he tapped a fist to his heart. "I'll see to it immediately," he said before making his way out into the rain.

"The army needs to be broken into smaller units," Richard said to General Meiffert after the officer hurried past. "We don't want them to stay together in a large force."

The general stared off as he considered. "We'll form them into a number of strike-forces and send them south immediately. They will have to depend on their own resources, make do for themselves. They can't rely on command to direct all the details of their actions or supply them with anything."

"We'll need to set up some communication," one of the older officers said, "but you're right, I don't think that it will be possible to coordinate everyone. We need to give everyone clear instructions and then let them do their job. There is plenty of Old World to attack."

"It would be best if they didn't keep in communication," Nicci said. When a number of men stared at her she went on. "Any messengers who are captured will be tortured. The Order has experts in torture. Any man who is captured will tell what he knows. If all the units keep in communication, then they can be betrayed. If anyone captured doesn't know where other units are, then they can't betray that information."

"Sounds like wise advice," Richard said.

"Lord Rahl," General Meiffert said in a cautious tone, "our entire army unleashed on the Old World, without an opposing force to check them, will wreak unprecedented devastation. Set loose with such a goal, all of them cavalry, well, they will lay waste to the Old World on a scale never previously known."

The man was giving Richard one last chance to change his mind, and a last chance to make it clear that he would not lose his sense of purpose at their expense. Richard didn't shy away from the implied question. He instead took a deep breath as he clasped his hands behind his back.

"You know, Benjamin, I remember a time when the mere mention of D'Haran soldiers struck fear into my heart."

The men nearby nodded in regret for an edge lost.

"By drawing us into a final battle that we can't possibly win," Richard told them, "Jagang has succeeded in making D'Haran soldiers look weak and vulnerable. We are no longer feared. Because they now see us as weak, they think they can do as they will with us.

"I believe that this is our last chance to win the war. If we let it slip away, we are lost.

"I don't want this chance wasted. Nothing is to be spared. I want Jagang to receive word from messenger after messenger that all of the Old World is burning. I want them to think that the underworld itself has opened up to swallow them.

"I want to again make people tremble in paralyzing fear at the very idea of avenging D'Haran soldiers coming after them. I want every man, woman, and child from the Old World to fear the phantom legions of D'Harans from the north. I want everyone in the Old World to come to hate the Order for bringing such suffering down upon them. I want a howl to raise from the Old World to end the war.

"That's all I have to say, gentlemen. I don't think we have a moment to lose, so let's get to it."

Men filled with a new resolve saluted as they filed past Richard, thanking him and saying that they would get the job done. Richard watched them dashing out into the steady rain toward their troops.

"Lord Rahl," General Meiffert said as he stepped closer, "I just want you to know that even if you aren't with us, you have led us in the coming battle. While it may not be one big battle like everyone was expecting, you have given the men something they would not have had without you. If this works, then your leadership is what will have reversed the course of the war."

Richard watched the rain dripping off the edge of the canvas awning in a curtain of beaded water. The ground was turning muddy beneath the boots of the soldiers as they dashed in every direction. The sight reminded Richard of the vision of kneeling in the mud, his wrists bound behind his back, a knife at his throat. In his mind he could hear Kahlan screaming his name. He remembered his helplessness, his sense of his world ending. He had to swallow back the unbidden, rising terror. The sound of Kahlan's screams made his very marrow ache.

Verna stepped up beside the general. "He's right, Richard. I don't like the idea of pulling people other than soldiers into the fight, but everything you said is true. They are the ones who brought this about. This is about survival of civilization itself and in that, they have made themselves part of the battle. There is no other way. The Sisters will do as you have asked, you have my word as Prelate."

Richard had feared that she would hold out against the plan. He was too grateful for words that she had not. He embraced her tightly and whispered, "Thank you."

He had always believed that those on his side had to not only understand the reasons they were fighting, but to do so with or without him, do so for themselves. He now believed that they did grasp the truth of everything at stake, and would fight not just because it was their duty, but for themselves.

Verna held Richard out at arm's length and peered into his eyes. "What's wrong?"

Richard shook his head. "I'm just so sick of the terrible things that are happening to people. I just want this nightmare to end."

Verna showed him a small smile. "You have shown us the way to make that come about, Richard."

"What part do you plan to play in this, Lord Rahl?" the general asked when Richard turned away from Verna. "If I might ask, that is."

Richard sighed as he put his mind back to the matter at hand. As he did, the terrible vision faded. "I'm afraid that there is serious trouble with magic. The Imperial Order army is only one of the threats that must be dealt with."

General Meiffert frowned. "What sort of trouble?"

Richard didn't think he could explain the whole story again, so he kept it short and to the point. "The woman who made you a general is missing. She is in the hands of some of the Sisters of the Dark."

The man looked completely puzzled. "Made me general?" He squinted off into the haze of his memory. "I can't recall . . ."

"It's all wrapped up in the trouble that has developed with magic."

The general and Verna shared a look.

"It was Lord Rahl's wife, Kahlan," Cara said. "She's the one, Benjamin, who named you general." His expression turned to astonishment. Cara shrugged. "It's a long story for another time," she added as she laid a hand on his shoulder. "None of us but Lord Rahl remembers her. It was a spell called Chainfire."

"Chainfire?" Verna grew yet more suspicious. "What Sisters?"

"Sister Ulicia and her other teachers," Nicci said. "They found an ancient spell called Chainfire and initiated it."

Verna regarded Nicci rather coolly. "I guess you would know what kind of trouble those women are, since you were one of them."

"Yes," Nicci said, wearily, "and you captured Richard and took him to the Palace of the Prophets. Had you not, he would not have destroyed the great barrier and the Imperial Order would be back in the Old World right now, not the New. If you want to start assigning blame, the Sisters of the Dark would never have encountered Richard had you not captured him in the first place and taken him back across the barrier to the Old World."

Verna pressed her lips tight. Richard knew the look, and what was coming.

"All right," he said in a low voice before they could start going at it. "We all did what we had to at the time, what we thought best. I've made my share of mistakes as well. We can only shape the future, not the past."

Verna's mouth twisted with a look that said she would like nothing more than to continue the argument, but she knew better. "You're right."

"Of course he is," Cara said. "He is the Lord Rahl."

In spite of herself, Verna smiled. "I guess he is, Cara. He has come to fulfill prophecy even if he didn't intend to."

"No," Richard said, "I have come to try to help us save ourselves. This isn't over yet, and prophecy, in the case of what you're talking about, has a different meaning."

Verna's suspicion returned in a flash. "What meaning?"

"I don't have time to go into it right now. I need to get back and see if Zedd and the others have come up with anything."

"You mean about finding your wife, Lord Rahl?"

"Yes, General, but it gets worse. Other things are happening. There is fundamental trouble with magic."

"Such as?" Verna pressed.

Richard appraised her eyes. "You need to know that the chimes have contaminated the world of life. Magic itself has been corrupted. Parts of it have already failed. There is no telling when yet more of it will fail, or how soon. We have to get back and see what can be done—if anything. Ann is there, along with Nathan, and they are working with Zedd to find some answers."

Before Verna could launch into a barrage of questions, Richard turned his attention to the general. "One last thing. With no army here to stand in their way, I'm sure that Jagang will try to take the People's Palace."

General Meiffert scratched his head of blond hair as he thought it over. "I suppose." He looked up. "But the palace is high on a huge plateau. There are only two ways up: the small road with the drawbridge, or through the great inner doors. If the great doors were closed there's not going to be any assault up that way, and the road is pretty useless for an armed attack.

"Still," the general said, "just to be on the safe side, I would advise that we send some of our best men up to the palace as reinforcements. With all of us heading south, Commander General Trimack and the First File will be facing Jagang's entire army all alone. But still, an assault on the palace?" He shook his head skeptically. "The palace is impenetrable."

"Jagang has gifted with him," Cara reminded him. "And don't forget, Lord Rahl, those Sisters made it into the palace before, way back in the beginning. Remember?"

Before Richard could answer, Verna caught his arm and turned him back to her frown. "Why would those Sisters ignite this spell you mentioned, this Chainfire spell?"

"To make people forget that Kahlan exists."

"But why would they want to do such a thing?"

Richard sighed. "Sister Ulicia wanted to get Kahlan into the People's Palace to steal the boxes of Orden. The Chainfire spell was designed to make a person the same thing as invisible. With the Chainfire spell ignited on Kahlan, no one remembers her. No one remembers that she walked right in and took the boxes out of the garden of life."

"Took the boxes . . ." Verna blinked in astonishment. "What in the world for?"

"Sister Ulicia put them in play," Nicci said.

"Dear Creator," Verna said as she pressed a hand to her forehead. "I will leave some Sisters there with a stern warning."

"Maybe you ought to be one of them," Richard said as he glanced out and saw the wind come up to carry the rain sideways at times. "We can't allow the palace to fall. Causing havoc down in the Old World is relatively simple conjuring for the Sisters. Defending the palace from Jagang's horde and his gifted may be a much greater challenge."

"Perhaps you're right," she admitted as she pulled a lock of wind-borne, wavy hair back off her face.

"Meanwhile, I'll see what I can do to stop Ulicia and her Sisters of the Dark." Richard glanced around at Nicci and Cara, then out at all the men rushing about through the rain to carry out their new mission. "I need to get back."

General Meiffert clapped his fist over his heart. "We will be the steel against steel, Lord Rahl, so that you can be the magic against magic."

Verna touched Richard's cheek, her brown eyes welling up. "Take care, Richard. We all need you."

He nodded and gave her a warm smile, putting more than words could say into it.

General Meiffert slipped an arm around Cara's waist. "Could I escort you to your horses?"

Cara smiled up at him in a very feminine way. "I think we would like that."

Nicci pulled the hood of her cloak up as they ducked out into the down-pour. She looked over at Richard and frowned suspiciously.

"Where did you get such an idea as the 'phantom legion'?"

He put a hand on the small of her back and guided her into the down-pour. "Shota gave me the thought when she said I needed to stop chasing phantoms. She implied that a phantom can't be found, can't be caught. I want these men to be phantoms."

She gently circled an arm around his shoulders as they sprinted for their horses. "You did the right thing, Richard."

She must have read the sorrow in his eyes.

Rachel yawned. Seemingly out of nowhere, Violet spun around and clouted her hard enough to knock her off the rock she'd been sitting on.

Stunned, Rachel pushed herself up on an arm. She cradled her cheek in one hand, waiting for the stupefying pain to loosen its grip, waiting for everything around her to come back into focus. Satisfied, Violet turned back to her work.

Rachel had been so groggy from not sleeping that she hadn't been paying attention, allowing Violet's blow to take her completely by surprise. Rachel's eyes watered with the tingling hurt but she knew better than to say anything or to make a show of the pain.

"Yawning is impolite, at best, disrespectful at worst," Violet's plump face peered back over her shoulder. "If you don't behave, then the next time I'll use the whip."

"Yes, Queen Violet," Rachel answered in a meek voice. She knew all too well that Violet wasn't making an empty threat.

Rachel was so tired she could hardly keep her eyes open. She had once been Violet's "playmate" but now she seemed to be nothing more than an object of abuse.

Violet had become preoccupied with extracting revenge. At night she had an iron device fastened in Rachel's mouth. It was a terrifying process. Rachel was made to stick her tongue into a beaklike clamp made of two flat, scored pieces of iron. The jaws were then tightened down hard enough to grip her tongue.

Resisting, Rachel had learned, earned her a whipping followed by guards prying her mouth open and then using painful tongs on her tender tongue to help accomplish the task of getting it placed in the clamp. They always won in the end; her tongue had nowhere to hide. Once the clamp was on her tongue, then the iron mask that was a part of it was locked around her head to kept her tongue immobile.

Once it was on, Rachel couldn't speak. It was hard even to swallow.

After that, Violet locked her in her old iron box for the night. She said she wanted Rachel to know what it was like to be mute and in pain.

And it was painful. Being locked in her iron cage all night with that terrible device clamped down on her tongue had nearly driven her crazy. At first, terrified out of her mind by the feeling of being trapped and alone, unable to get out, unable to get that painful thing off, she had screamed and screamed. Chuckling, Violet merely threw a heavy rug over the box to mute Rachel's cries. Crying and screaming, though, only made the iron jaws pinching her tongue hurt all the more and leave her bloody.

But what finally made her stop crying and screaming was that Violet came and put her face right up to the little window and said that if Rachel didn't be quiet, she would have Six cut Rachel's tongue out for real. Rachel knew that Six would do it if Violet asked.

After that she didn't scream or carry on. She instead curled up in a ball in her little iron prison and tried to remember all the things Chase had taught her. That, in the end, was what had calmed her.

Chase would have told her not to think of her present predicament, but to keep watching for the time when she could get herself out of it. Chase had taught her how to watch for patterns in the way people behaved, and openings where they weren't paying attention. So, that was what she did as she lay in the iron box every night, unable to sleep as she waited for morning to come, waited for the men who would pull her out of the box and remove the terrible device for the day.

Rachel could hardly eat because her tongue was so raw and scraped—not that they gave her much to eat anyway. Each morning her tongue throbbed painfully for hours after the clamp was removed. Her jaws hurt, too, from her mouth being held open all night by the device. Eating hurt. But then, when she did eat, everything tasted like dirty metal. Talking hurt, too, so she only spoke when Violet asked her something. Violet, seeing how Rachel would avoid speaking, would sometimes smile in a contemptuous manner and call Rachel her little mute.

Rachel was completely dispirited by once again being in the clutches of such a wicked person, and sad beyond anything she had ever known because Chase was gone. She couldn't get the memory of him being so brutally hurt out of her mind. She grieved endlessly for him. Her heartache, misery, and utter loneliness seemed unendurable. When Violet wasn't at her drawing lessons, or ordering people to do things, or eating, or trying on jewels, or being fitted for dresses, then she amused herself by hurting Rachel. Sometimes, reminding Rachel of how she had once threatened her with a fire stick, Violet would hold Rachel by the wrist and put a little white-hot ember from the fire on her arm. Still, Rachel's sorrow for Chase hurt her worse than anything Violet could ever do to her. With Chase gone, it almost didn't matter what happened to her.

Violet needed to "discipline" Rachel, as she'd put it, for all the terrible things Rachel had done. Violet had decided that losing her tongue had in large part somehow been Rachel's fault. Violet had said that it was going to take a long time for Rachel to earn forgiveness for such a serious transgression, and also for showing disrespect by escaping the castle. Violet viewed Rachel's escape as a shameful rejection of what she called their "generosity" to a worthless orphan. She often went on and on at great length about all the trouble she and her mother had gone to for Rachel only to have her turn out to be an ungrateful waif.

When Violet eventually tired of hurting her, Rachel suspected that she would be put to death. She'd heard Violet ordering the deaths of prisoners accused of "high crimes." If someone displeased her enough, or if Six told her that the person was a threat to the crown, then Violet would order their execution. If the person had made the grave mistake of openly questioning Violet's authority, or rule, then Violet would tell her guards to make it slow, and make it painful. She sometimes went to watch, just to make sure that it was.

Rachel remembered back when Queen Milena had ordered executions and Violet had first begun to go watch. As her playmate, Rachel had to go along with her. Rachel always averted her eyes from the ghastly sight; Violet never did.

Six had set up a whole system whereby people could secretly report the names of those people who said things against the queen. Six had told Violet that people who made such secret reports had to be rewarded for their loyalty. Violet paid handsomely for the names of traitors.

Since the time when Rachel had been with her before, Violet had acquired a new fondness for inflicting pain. Six often commented that pain was a good teacher. Violet had become exceedingly fond of the notion that she controlled the lives of others, that on her word other people could be made to suffer.

She had also become acutely suspicious of everyone. Everyone but Six, that was, who she'd come to rely on as the only person who could be trusted. Violet greatly distrusted most of her "loyal subjects," frequently referring to them as nobodies. Rachel remembered that Violet used to call her a nobody.

When Rachel had lived at the castle before, people had been careful to watch themselves lest they cross the wrong people, but it was more a sense that they were just being on their toes. People had been afraid of Queen Milena, and with good reason, but they still would smile and laugh at times. The wash women would gossip, the cooks would now and then make funny faces in the food, the cleaning staff would whistle as they went about their chores, and the soldiers would sometimes tell jokes to one another as they walked the halls of the castle during guard duty.

Now there was quiet quaking whenever Queen Violet or Six were around. None of the cleaning staff, the washwomen, the seamstresses, the cooks, or the soldiers ever smiled or laughed. They all looked afraid all the time as they hurried to do their work. The atmosphere at the castle now was always charged with terror that, at any time, anyone might be pointed out. Everyone went out of their way to openly show respect for the queen, especially in front of her tall, grim advisor. People seemed to fear Six just as much as they feared Violet. When Six smiled with that strange, empty, snakelike smile she had, people would stand frozen in place, wide-eyed, sweat breaking out across their brows, and then swallow in relief after she had glided out of sight.

"Right here," Six said.

"Right here, what?" Violet asked as she gnawed on a bread stick.

Rachel eased herself back up on the rock where she had been sitting. She reminded herself to pay more attention. The slap was her own fault for getting bored and not paying attention.

No, it wasn't, she told herself. It was Violet's fault. Chase had told her not to take on blame that belonged to others.

Chase. Her heart sank yet again thinking about him. She had to put her mind to other things lest she end up being so sad thinking about him that she start to weep. Violet was not at all tolerant of anything Rachel did without permission. That included crying.

"Right there," Six said again with exaggerated patience. When Violet only stared at her, Six drew a long finger across the face of the torchlit rock wall. "What is missing?"

Violet leaned in, peering at the wall. "Umm . . ."

"Where is the sun?"

"Well," Violet said in a snippy voice as she stood up straight again and waggled a finger at the yellow disc, "right there. Surely you can see that this is the sun."

Six glared at her a moment. "Yes, of course I see that it's the sun, my queen." Her empty smile returned. "But where is it in the sky?"

Violet tapped the chalk against her chin. "The sky?"

"Yes. Where is it in the sky? Straight up?" Six pointed her finger skyward. "Are we meant to understand that we are looking straight up at the sun in the sky? Is it high noon?"

"Well, no, of course it's not high noon—you know it can't be. It's supposed to be late in the day. You know that, too."

"Really? And how are we to know that? After all, it makes no difference what I know it must be. The drawing must say what is. It can't elicit comment from me, now, can it?"

"I guess not," Violet admitted.

Six again drew her finger across the wall beneath the sun. "What's missing, then?"

"Missing, missing . . ." Violet muttered. "Oh!" She quickly drew a straight line right where Six had indicated with her finger. "The horizon. We need to fix the time of day with the horizon. You told me that before. I guess it slipped my mind." She glared over at Six. "It's a lot to remember, you know. All this stuff is hard to keep straight."

Six held the cold smile frozen in place. "Yes, my queen, of course it is. I apologize for forgetting how hard it was for me to learn all these things way back when I was your age."

The drawing that Violet was working on was complex beyond anything else in the cave, but Six was always there to remind Violet of the right thing to draw at the right time.

Violet shook the chalk at Six. "You would be well advised to keep that in mind."

Six carefully knitted her fingers together. "Yes, my queen, of course." She pursed her lips and finally drew her glare away from Violet as she turned back to the wall. "Now, at this point we need the star chart for this domain. I can give you the lesson in the specific reasons later, if you want, but for now why don't I just show you what's necessary?"

Violet glanced to where Six was pointing and shrugged. "Sure." She went back to sucking on the bread stick as she waited.

Six opened a small book. Violet leaned in, squinting in the flickering light. Six tapped the page with a long nail as Violet finally bit through the crunchy bread stick.

"See the azimuth? Remember the lesson about the referent angle to the horizon for this star, here?"

"Yes . . ." Violet drawled, looking like she actually did know what Six was talking about. "That would involve this angular reference, here, then. Right?"

"Yes, that's right. It's an aspect of the binding agent that ties it all together."

Violet nodded. "In turn tying it to him . . ." she said, thoughtfully.

"That's right. The link is one element of what is necessary to lock it in place at the time of the concluding connection. That, in turn, makes the horizon you just drew necessary to fix this angle. Otherwise it would be a floating correlation."

Violet was nodding again. "I think I see, now, why they have to connect. If the interrelationship is not fixed"—she straightened and gestured to an arc of symbols—"then these could happen any time. Today, tomorrow, or, or, I don't know, a dozen years from now."

Six smiled in a sly manner. "Correct."

Violet smiled in triumph at her accomplishment. "But where do we get all these symbols, and how do we know where to use them in the drawing? For that matter, how do we know that they are needed at the precise points that you had me draw them?"

Six took a patient breath. "Well, I could teach it all to you first, but that will take about twenty years of study. Are you willing to wait that long for vengeance?"

Violet's frown darkened. "No."

Six shrugged. "Then I suggest that the shortcut of me helping direct the design is the shortest route to the result."

Violet screwed up her mouth. "I suppose."

"You have the basics, my queen. You are doing quite well for this stage of developing your talent. I assure you, even though I am helping you with some of the complexities, none of this would function without your considerable talent added in. I couldn't make this work without your ability."

Violet smiled like a prize pupil. Taking another careful look in the volume Six was holding open, Violet finally went back to the wall, carefully drawing the elements she needed from the book.

Rachel was amazed at how well Violet actually could draw. All the walls of the cave, from the entrance all the way back into the deep place where they were working, were covered with drawings. They were stuck in every available space. In places it looked like they had been squeezed into small spots left between older drawings. Some of the drawings were very good, with details like shading. Most, though, were simple drawings of bones, crops, snakes, or other animals. There were pictures of people drinking from mugs with skulls and crossed bones on them. In one place a woman, looking like she was made of sticks, was running out of a house that was on fire; the woman, too, was covered in the flames. In another spot a man was in the water beside a sinking boat. In another scene a snake was biting a man's ankle. The walls were also covered with pictures of caskets and graves of all sorts. All the pictures had one thing in common, though: they were of terrible things.

But there was not one single drawing in the entire cave that began to approach the complexity of the thing Violet was drawing.

Other drawings were only infrequently life-size pictures of people and even those only had a few things added, like rocks falling on them, or them being trampled beneath a horse. Most of the drawings showed the same sorts of things but were only a few hands' widths across. Violet's drawing, though, went on and on for dozens of feet, from the ground to as high as she could reach, working its way deeper into the cave. Violet had drawn the entire thing all by herself, with Six guiding her along the way, of course.

What alarmed Rachel the most, though, was that after Violet had been working on the drawing for quite some time, after she had drawn in stars and formulas and diagrams and strange, complex symbols, she had in the center of it all finally drawn a figure of a person.

The figure was Richard.

Violet's drawing was unlike anything else in the cave. It made them all look simple and crude by comparison. The other drawings all had easy, obvious things in them, like maybe a thundercloud with angled lines for rain, or a wolf baring its teeth, or a man simply clutching his chest as he fell back. There was little else on the walls but a few simple things around the figures.

Violet's drawing was covered with things that were completely different. There were numbers and designs, words in strange languages, some written along the lines of diagrams, numbers carefully placed where angles came together, and there were strange geometric symbols cast everywhere throughout the illustration. Whenever Violet drew any of those symbols Six would stand close, concentrating, whispering guidance for every single line, sometimes correcting where Violet was about to place the chalk, preventing her from even touching it to the wall for the next line lest it be out of sequence or out of place. Once Six even became alarmed and snatched Violet's wrist before she could touch the chalk to the wall. Sighing in relief, Six then moved Violet's hand and helped her begin in the correct place.

Unlike every other drawing in the cave, Violet's was done in different colors. The other drawings all along the way deep into the cave, to where Violet had started hers, were simple chalk drawings. Violet's drawing had green trees in one spot, blue water in another, a yellow sun, and red clouds. Some of the designs were done entirely in white, while others were multicolored yet in an orderly manner of colors.

And, unlike every other drawing, when they left the cave and Rachel looked back she could see elements of the drawing glowing in the dark. It was not the chalk that made it glow, because the same chalk in other places in the drawing did not glow in the dark.

There was also a part of one symbol that glowed when left to the darkness. It was a strange face glowing out from an otherwise dark drawing made entirely of complex designs. Whenever the torch was near, the face wasn't visible and it only looked like a network of lines. Rachel could never see what aspects of the design could possibly make up the face. But in the dark it stared out at her, the eyes following her, watching her leave.

The thing that really gave Rachel goose bumps, though, was the picture of Richard. It was a drawing done so well that Rachel could actually recognize him by his face alone.

It amazed Rachel to see how well Violet could draw. There were other things to tell who Richard was, though, even if the drawing hadn't been so good. His black outfit was depicted accurately, just the way Rachel remembered it. It even had some of the mysterious symbols drawn around the edge of his tunic. Six had been very careful in her guidance of precisely how Violet was to draw those designs. In Violet's picture, Richard also wore the flowing cape that looked to be made of spun gold.

The way Violet had drawn it made it look almost like he was in water.

All around him, too, were wavy colored areas that Six called "auras." Each color had complex formulas and designs lying between them and Richard. Six had said that at the end, as the final step, those interposing elements between him and his essence would be connected to form an intervening barrier. Whatever that meant, Rachel didn't know, but it was obvious that it was important to Violet.

Six seemed especially proud of that part, of the intervening barrier elements. She would sometimes stand for long periods of time and just stare at them.

In the picture, Richard had the Sword of Truth, but it was drawn faintly, as if it was there with him, but not. It almost seemed part of him, the way Violet had drawn it with Richard holding it so that it crossed his chest, yet Rachel couldn't tell for sure if he really was meant to be holding it because it was drawn so faintly. Violet had worked hard to make it that way. Six had her do it over several times because she said that it was too "substantive."

Rachel was puzzled by the sword being drawn with Richard, since Samuel had Richard's sword now. Still, it somehow only seemed right for Richard to be drawn with the sword. Maybe Six felt that way, too.

Violet stood back, cocking her head, appraising her work. Six stood transfixed, staring at it as if no one else were there with her. She reached out, tentatively, and lightly touched the designs around Richard.

"How long until we make the final connection of elements?" Violet asked.

As Six's fingers moved slowly, lightly, along the designs, some of the interposing elements responded to her touch, sparkling and glowing in the dim light.

"Soon," she whispered. "Soon."

Lord Rahl!"

Richard turned just in time to see Berdine, in a dead run, leap toward him. She landed against his chest, throwing her arms and legs around him. The impact drove the wind from his lungs. Her long, single braid of wavy brown hair whipped around him. Richard staggered back a step as he put his arms around her to help keep her from falling. With her arms and legs clinging to him, though, she didn't appear to need his help.

Richard had rarely seen even a flying squirrel make a better leap. Despite everything on his mind, he could not help but to smile at Berdine's exuberance. Who would have thought that a Mord-Sith would ever again come to be as spontaneously joyful as a little girl.

She sat back, gripping his shoulders, legs locked around his middle, grinning at him. She looked over at Cara's scowl. "He still likes me best—I can tell."

Cara simply rolled her eyes.

With his hands on Berdine's waist, Richard lifted her and set her down. She was shorter than most of the other Mord-Sith Richard knew. She was also more voluptuous, and far more vivacious. Richard had always found her to be a rather disarming combination of guileless sensuality combined with a mischievous, playful nature. Like any of the Mord-Sith, though, she also possessed the potential for instantaneous, ruthless violence lying hidden just below the sparkling surface of her childlike wonder. She also loved Richard passionately and openly, but in an honest, innocent, filial sort of manner.

"You are a sight to warm my heart, Berdine. How are you?"

She puzzled at him. "Lord Rahl, I am Mord-Sith. How do you think I am?"

"As much trouble as ever," he said under his breath.

She smiled, pleased by the comment. "We heard that you were here earlier, but I just missed you. That's twice I've missed you recently. I wasn't going to let you vanish again without seeing you. We have so much to talk about that I don't even know where to begin."

Richard looked down the broad corridor, across the expanse of richly veined golden marble set in a diagonal pattern within a border of black granite, and saw a knot of soldiers marching toward him at a brisk pace. High overhead rain beat steadily against skylights that let in flat gray light. Somehow, that dull light managed to gather and reflect brightly off the polished breastplates of the soldiers.

All of them had crescent axes hooked at their belts, along with the swords and long knives they also carried. Some of the men were armed with crossbows that were cocked and ready to fire. Those men, given ample clearance by the others, wore black gloves. Their crossbows were loaded with deadly-looking red-fletched arrows.

The halls were crowded with people of every sort, from those who lived and worked there to people who had come to trade or sell goods. All of them gave the approaching soldiers ample space. At the same time, they watched Richard while trying not to look like they were watching him. When Richard met their gazes or caught them looking, some tipped their heads in a bow while others fell to one knee. Richard smiled, trying to put them at ease.

It was a rare event, in recent years anyway, when the Lord Rahl was home in his palace. Richard could hardly expect people not to be curious to see him. In his black war wizard's outfit, along with the flowing golden cape, he was hard to miss. He still couldn't think of such a place as his home, though; in his own heart he thought of the Hartland woods as home. He had grown up walking among towering trees, not lofty stone pillars.

Commander General Trimack of the First File at the People's Palace came to a smart halt and in salute thumped a fist against the shaped leather armor over his chest. The soft metallic rattle of gear died out after the dozen men with him all saluted together. These men, constantly scanning the halls and appraising each of the people moving past, were the Lord Rahl's personal guards when he was at his palace. They each took in Cara and swiftly assessed Nicci, standing just beside Richard. These men were the ring of steel that kept harm from getting a look at the Lord Rahl. They served in the First File because they were the most skilled and loyal of all the D'Haran troops.

After the salute, the commander added a bow to Cara and then Richard. "Lord Rahl, we're pleased to have you home, at last."

"I'm afraid, General Trimack, that it's only a brief visit. I can't stay." Richard gestured to Cara and Nicci. "We've got urgent business and have to leave at once."

General Trimack, looking sincerely disappointed but not entirely surprised, sighed. He then appeared to have a thought and brightened a bit. "Did you find the woman—your wife—who had been up in the garden of life and left that statue you found there?"

Richard felt a pang of anguish for Kahlan. He felt guilty for not doing more to find her. How could he let other matters keep him from finding Kahlan? How could there be anything important enough to distract him from finding her? He tried not to think of the vision of her that Shota had given him. It seemed like with everything going on he had pushed aside his search for the one person who meant the most to him. He knew that was not the way it really was, that it couldn't be helped, but still, he needed to get back to the Keep and back to working on a way to find her.

Even while working on other things, she was never really out of his thoughts. He kept trying to think of where Sister Ulicia would have taken Kahlan. Now that they had the boxes of Orden—or at least two of them— where would the Sisters go? What could they be up to? If he could figure that out then maybe he could go after them.

It had also occurred to him that they still needed *The Book of Counted Shadows* in order to open the right box of Orden, so it was possible that if he simply sat still in one place long enough they would have to come to him, since the book only existed now in his memory. The simple fact was, unless they were willing to guess and risk being wrong, they needed *The Book of Counted Shadows* to open the right box, and Richard could not imagine that they would risk the loss of what they believed would be their immortality on chance. They needed the key that only he had to unlock the solution to opening the correct box. Kahlan was part of the key to that solution, but they still needed what only Richard had.

The only method he could think of to find her was to learn everything he could about Chainfire and the boxes of Orden, and somewhere in that mix maybe there would be a clue as to what the Sisters would do next. The books he needed to study to that end, along with the people who understood them best and had by far the most experience at such things, were at the Keep. He needed to get back there.

Richard looked to the general's waiting eyes. "Not yet, I'm afraid. We're still looking for her, but thank you for your concern."

No one but Richard even remembered her, remembered her smile, the shadow of her soul showing in her green eyes. At times Kahlan didn't even seem real to him, either. She seemed impossible, like no one who could be all that he remembered, like she could only be an invention of his deepest desires in life. He could understand the difficulty those closest to him had in dealing with the situation.

"Sorry to hear that, Lord Rahl." The general scanned the throngs moving down the hallway. "I trust that at least you are not here this time in the middle of a mess of trouble?"

It was Richard's turn to sigh. How to begin?

"In a way, I am."

"The Imperial Order army is continuing to advance on D'Hara?" the general guessed.

Richard nodded. "I'm afraid so. The long and the short of it is, General, I've given our forces orders that they are not to engage Emperor Jagang's army in battle because they don't have the numbers to stand a chance. It would be a slaughter for no purpose and Jagang would still end up having the New World all to himself."

General Trimack scratched a scar that stood out white against the ruddy skin at the back of his jaw. "What other option is there, Lord Rahl, but to meet the enemy in battle?"

His quiet, simple words had the sound of advice, of caution born of experience, of hope balanced on a razor's edge of despair. For a moment, Richard listened to the cathedral whisper of feet against stone as the crowds moved steadily through the hallway.

"I've ordered our forces to set out at once to lay waste to the Old World." Richard turned his glare back to the general. "They wanted war; I intend to jam their wish down their throats and see them choke to death on it."

At the startling news, the mouths of some of the men dropped open. Commander General Trimack stared in surprise for a moment, then he thoughtfully stroked the scar with a single finger. A sly look finally showed that, despite his initial surprise, he was beginning to like the idea.

"I guess this means that the First File will be called upon to keep the bastards out of the palace."

Richard marked the man's steady gaze. "Do you think you can do it?"

A crooked smile curled across the general's mouth. "Lord Rahl, my humble talent will hardly be the margin of safety for the palace. Your ancestors built this place as they did specifically to prevent anyone from taking it." He gestured at the soaring columns, walls, and balconies all around them. "Besides the natural defenses, this place is invested with powers that weaken any of the encmy gifted."

Richard knew that the palace was built in the shape of a spell that strengthened the power of any Rahl within the palace, and sapped the strength of any other gifted person. The whole palace itself was constructed in the form of an emblem. To an extent, Richard understood its shape and the general nature of its meaning. He could read the motif of strength inherent in the pattern.

Unfortunately, that spell would weaken even those with the gift who were on his side, such as Verna. He needed Verna to be able to help protect the palace, but if she and the Sisters with her were weakened by that spell, then she would have a harder time defending the palace. The balance to that, he supposed, was that anyone attacking would have the same problem, so they would not have an advantage over Verna and her Sisters. There was no alternative but to count on Verna to do her best.

"Besides reinforcements, I'm sending some Sisters here, along with Verna, their prelate."

General Trimack nodded. "I know the woman. She's a stubborn one when she's happy and impossible when she's not. I'll be glad she'll be on our side, Lord Rahl, and not the other way round."

Richard had to smile. The man did indeed know Verna.

"I'll return when I can, General. In the meantime, I'll count on you to safeguard the People's Palace."

"The great inner doors will have to be sealed."

"Do what you think best, General."

"The great doors are invested with the same power as the rest of the palace, so they are not a weak link that will provide any opportunity for attack. The only problem with closing the doors is that it puts an end to commerce, which is the lifeblood of the palace . . . in peacetime, any-way."

Richard watched the throngs of people making their way through the passageway and along the balconies above. "With what's coming, com-merce is not going to be possible at the palace anyway. No one is going to be able to travel the Azrith Plain—or anywhere else in the New World, for that matter. Trade everywhere is being disrupted. Prepare for a long siege."

The man shrugged. "That's what enemy armies historically do, sit out there and hope to starve us out. Can't be done; out on the Azrith Plain they'll starve first. Will you be coming back, Lord Rahl, to help in the pro-tection of the palace?"

Richard swiped a hand across his mouth. "I don't know when I'll be able to return. But I will if I can, I promise. For now, I have to put my mind to this new effort.

"We're going to try to kill the Order by cutting out its heart, rather than trying to fight its muscle."

"And if they lay siege to the palace in the meantime and you need to re-turn? How will you be able to get back in?"

"Well, I don't have a dragon, so I can't fly in." When the man only stared blankly at him, Richard cleared his throat and said, "If need be I can come back the way I came today, with the aid of magic—through the sliph."

The general didn't look like he understood, but he accepted Richard's word without question.

"I'm on my way back there now, General. If you want, you can escort us and see it for yourself."

He looked somewhat relieved to be invited to be allowed to do his job of protecting the Lord Rahl. Richard took Berdine's arm and started walk-ing her down the hall as all the soldiers fanned out to form a protective perimeter.

Berdine was considerably shorter than Richard, so he leaned down a bit to speak without raising his voice. "I need to know some things. Have you been translating any more of Kolo's journal?"

She grinned like a maid full of gossip. "I'll say I have. Because of some of the things Kolo had to say, though, I've had to start researching other books as well—so that I could better understand how it all fits together." She leaned closer. "There were things going on that we didn't even realize, before, when we worked on it together. We had only scratched the surface."

Richard didn't think that she knew the half of it. "Do any of those things have to do with First Wizard Baraccus?"

Berdine abruptly halted and stared at him. "How did you know that?"

Richard reached back, took Berdine by the arm, and pulled her along with him. "I'll explain it later, when I have more time. What did Kolo write about Baraccus in his journal?"

"Well, what Kolo wrote is only part of the story. Kolo just hinted at some of what was going on so, to fill in the blanks, I started reading the books in your restricted, private libraries."

It never failed to amaze Richard that, being the Lord Rahl, he now had access to such restricted libraries. He could not begin to imagine the wealth of knowledge contained in all those volumes.

"What kinds of books?"

Berdine pointed. "One of them is on the way, not in the common areas but deeper in the private sections of the palace—places where almost no one is ever allowed. I'll show you. Part of it has to do with something called central sites."

Keeping pace on the other side of him, Nicci leaned in. "Nathan told me that he read some things about places called central sites."

"Like what?" Richard asked.

Nicci pulled her blond hair away from the side of her face and back over her shoulder. "The central sites are top-secret libraries. Back sometime near or after the great war the central sites were established as a safe, secure, and hidden place to keep books there that were considered too dangerous to be known except by a very restricted, select group of a few people. Nathan said that he thinks there were maybe a half-dozen of these sites."

"That's right," Berdine said. She looked around to make sure that none of the soldiers following them were close enough to hear. "Lord Rahl, I found a reference where it implied that at least some of these sites were marked with the names of a Lord Rahl from prophecy."

Richard halted. "You mean they put his name on a gravestone?"

Berdine's brow lifted. "That's right. It mentioned that these places, these libraries, were kept with the bones. They thought, from what they knew of prophecy, that a future Lord Rahl would need to find books that were kept there and so, in at least one instance that I found mentioned, it said they put his name on a grave marker."

"In Caska."

Berdine snapped her finger, then shook it at him. "That's the place I saw named. How did you know?"

"I've been there. My name is on a big monument in the graveyard."

"You were there? Why? What were you looking for? What did you find?"

"I found a book—*Chainfire*—that helped prove what happened to my wife."

Berdine glanced to Cara and the Nicci before looking back at Richard. "I've been hearing rumors about you having a wife. At first I thought it had to be just crazy gossip. So, it's really true, then?"

Richard took a deep breath as he marched through the corridor, surrounded by guards and watched by the passing crowds. He didn't feel up to explaining to Berdine that she knew Kahlan, and had in fact spent a great deal of time with her.

"It's true," he said, simply.

"Lord Rahl, what's this all about?"

Richard waved off the question. "It's a long story and I don't have the time to tell it right now. What is it about these central sites that has you so worked up?"

"Well," Berdine said as she leaned in again while they rushed down the broad hallway, "you remember how Baraccus killed himself after he came back from the Temple of the Winds?"

Richard glanced over at her. "Yes."

"There was something behind it."

"Behind it. What do you mean?"

Berdine came to a side passageway guarded by two men with lances. As they took in Richard and his entourage, they clapped fists to their hearts and stepped aside. Berdine pulled open one of the double doors clad in metal. It had a picture of a courtyard garden meticulously embossed in the polished surface. Beyond the door the smaller hallway of rich mahogany paneling was empty of people. It was the entrance into the private areas of the palace.

"I haven't been able to figure out what, but I believe that Baraccus did something while he was at the Temple of the Winds." Berdine glanced back at him to make sure he was paying attention. "Something big. Something significant."

Richard nodded as he followed Berdine down the empty hallway. "When Baraccus was at the Temple of the Winds he somehow insured that I would be born with Subtractive Magic."

This time it was Nicci who snatched Richard's arm and yanked him to a halt, spinning him around to face her. "What! Where did you ever get an idea like that?"

Richard blinked at her shocked expression. "Shota told me."

"And how would Shota know such a thing?"

Richard shrugged. "You know witch women, they see things in the flow of time. Some of it I put together from the pieces of history that I know."

Nicci looked anything but convinced. "Why in the world would Baraccus ever do such a thing? Shota tries to tell you that, out of the blue, this ancient wizard just happened to travel to the underworld and while he was there he thought . . . what? As long as he was already there he might as well see to it that when some fellow named Richard Rahl is born three thousand years from then he might as well be born with Subtractive Magic?"

Richard gave her a look. "It's a little more complicated than that, Nicci. I'm pretty sure that he did it to counter what another wizard had done when he'd been there before. That wizard was Lothain. Remember him, Berdine?"

"Of course."

"Lothain was a spy."

Berdine gasped. "That's what Kolo thought—that he had been a spy all along—planted there to lie in wait for an opportunity to strike. Kolo didn't believe that Lothain had just gone crazy or something like everyone assumed. That was the common story at the time—that the stress and danger of his job had just gotten to Lothain and he couldn't handle it anymore, that he simply lost his mind. Kolo never made a point of telling other people what he thought because he didn't think that they would believe him, and also because people had started to think that it was Baraccus who was the spy."

Richard frowned as he started out again. "Baraccus! That's crazy."

"That's what Kolo thought, too."

"What did this wizard Lothain supposedly do?" Nicci asked in a forceful voice meant to bring him back to the subject at hand and to underline the seriousness of her question.

Richard gazed into her blue eyes a moment and saw there not just Nicci, but the powerful sorceress she in fact was. Because of her stunning features, her intent blue eyes, and the way she treated him with such regard, to say nothing of her steadfast friendship, it was easy to forget that this was a sorceress who had seen and done things he could hardly begin to imagine. She was probably one of the most powerful sorceresses ever born, and she was a force to be reckoned with.

More than that, Nicci, of all people, deserved to know the truth. It wasn't that he'd been trying to keep it from her—he just hadn't had the time to discuss it. In fact, he wished that he had already told her about it, that he had had her thoughts on the whole thing, especially the part about the secret library that Baraccus kept, and the book meant for Richard that he'd sent there with his wife for safekeeping . . . until the day a war wizard was again born into the world to take up their cause.

Richard sighed. There just hadn't been any time, yet. As much as he did want to tell it all to her, he wanted to tell her the entire story when he could discuss it, along with some of the questions he had, so he decided for the moment to leave out most of the details and kept it to the pertinent point.

"Lothain was a spy for the forces of the Old World. Maybe he could see that they were not going to be able to win the war. Maybe he was just taking extra precautions. Anyway, when he went to the Temple of the Winds he sowed the seeds for their cause to rise again at some future time. He did something, at the least, to see to it that a dream walker would again be born into the world.

"Baraccus was unable to reverse the sabotage, so he did the next best thing. He saw to it that there would be a counter born into the world: me."

Nicci, speechless, could only stare at him.

Richard turned back to Berdine. "So, what does this business with Baraccus have to do with these central sites?"

Berdine glanced around again, checking how close the soldiers were. "Kolo wrote in his journal that there were whispers among a group of influential people that Baraccus may have been a traitor, and if he was, then he could have done something ruinous while he was at the Temple of the Winds."

Richard shook his head in frustration. "What did they suspect him of doing?"

Berdine shrugged. "I haven't been able to figure it out yet. It as all very hush-hush. They were all being very careful. No one wanted to come right out and say anything or accuse Baraccus of being a traitor. They didn't want to anger the wrong people. He was still widely revered by many people, like Kolo.

"It could even be that they didn't have any specific accusation, but just held a suspicion that he may have done something. Don't forget, no one was ever able to get back into the Temple after Baraccus, until you did it. Apparently, they were also afraid of that woman, Magda Searus. You know, the one who was made into a Confessor."

"Yes, I remember," Richard said. "Seems odd, though, that something that supposedly had the potential to be so disastrous wouldn't be more out in the open."

"No," Berdine said under her breath, almost as if the ghosts of the past would hear her. "That's the thing. They feared that if people found out about their suspicions, then it might cause a panic or something—cause people to give up. Don't forget, the war was still going on and it was still in question if they would even survive, much less triumph. Everyone was worried about the morale of the people as they fought on and at the same time worked to find a way to win. In the middle of all that, this small circle of high-ranking people were all worried that Baraccus might have done something terrible at the Temple of the Winds that was never supposed to be done."

Richard threw up his hands. "Like what?"

Berdine's face screwed up in an expression of exasperation. "Don't know. Kolo only hinted at it. He believed in Baraccus. And he was angry that these people were doing whatever it was that they were doing, but at the same time he wasn't in any position to argue with them. He was not among those in command, or a high-enough-ranking wizard.

"But there was one passage, one mention in his journal, that kind of gave me goose bumps when I read it. I don't know if it was about the Baraccus dispute or not—I mean I can't point to anything specifically to connect it, not so as—"

"What did this passage say?"

Along with Richard, Nicci and Cara both leaned in a little.

Berdine heaved a sigh. "He was writing in his journal, talking about the foul weather and how sick everyone was getting of rain, and he made this offhanded comment that he was upset because he'd learned through his sources that 'they' had made five copies of 'the book that was never to be copied.' "

That gave Richard pause, and goose bumps.

"Not far after that," Berdine said, "his entry started wandering back to talking about the central sites."

"So you think . . . what? That maybe they hid these copies they weren't supposed to make in the secret central sites?"

Berdine smiled as she tapped her temple with a finger. "Now you're starting to ask the same questions I've been asking myself."

"And he didn't make any mention at all of what book they copied?" Nicci asked. "Not even an indication?"

Berdine shook her head. "That's the part that gave me the goose bumps. But there was more there than his words."

"What do you mean?" Nicci asked, impatiently.

"You know how when you work forever at translating someone's writing, you come to be able to see their mood, see their meaning, see their train of thought even if they didn't write it down? Well"—she pulled her brown braid over her shoulder, twiddling with the end of it—"I could tell by the way he said it that he was afraid to even write down the name of a book so secret, so important, that it was never to be copied. It was like he was walking on eggshells even mentioning it in his journal."

Richard thought that she certainly had a good point.

Berdine came to a halt before a tall iron door that was painted black. "Here's where I found the books that mention the cental sites being with the bones—whatever that means."

"The place I found was in catacombs," Richard said.

Berdine frowned as she considered. "That might explain that much of it."

"Nathan told me," Nicci said in a low voice, looking between Richard and Berdine, "that he believes that there were catacombs beneath the Palace of the Prophets, and that the palace itself was built there in part to conceal what was buried."

The soldiers slowed to a halt, collecting in a knot a short distance back up the hall. Richard noticed Berdine watching them.

"Why don't you wait out here with your men?" Berdine called back to

General Trimack. "I have to go in the library and show Lord Rahl some books. I think maybe you should guard the hall and make sure that no one is sneaking about."

The general nodded and started ordering his men to take up stations throughout the passages. Berdine pulled a key out of the top of her outfit.

"In here I found a book that gave me nightmares."

She looked back at Richard and then unlocked the door.

Nicci leaned close to Richard's ear. "This place is shielded." Her tone was tight with suspicion.

"But she's not gifted," Richard whispered back. "She can't get through shields. If it's shielded, then how is she able to get in?"

Berdine, hearing them, waggled the key after she pulled it back out of the lock. "I have the key. I knew where Darken Rahl kept it hidden."

Nicci lifted an eyebrow as she looked back at Richard. "The key just shut down the shields to the door. I've never seen such a thing before."

"It must have been designed to give access to trusted aides or scholars who weren't gifted," Richard guessed. He turned back to Berdine as she worked at opening the lever on the heavy door.

"By the way, did you learn anything else about Baraccus?"

"Not much," she said, looking back over her shoulder. "Except that Magda Searus, the woman who became the first Confessor, had once been married to him."

Richard could only stare at her. "How *does* she know these things?" he muttered to himself.

"What?" Berdine asked.

"Nothing," he said, dismissing it with a wave before flicking the hand at the door. "So what is it that you found in here?"

"Something that connected with what Kolo said."

"You mean about this book that wasn't supposed to be copied."

Berdine merely gave Richard a sly smile as she tucked the key down into a pocket inside the top of her outfit, then pushed open the black door.

Inside, three tall windows that made up most of the far wall lit the room with the gloomy late-afternoon light. Rain pattered against the glass and ran down in snaking rivulets. The walls of the small room were lined with bookshelves made of golden oak. There was only enough space in the center of the room for one simple oak table that was in turn only large enough for the four wooden chairs, one on each side. In the center of the table sat an unusual four-lobed lamp, offering each empty chair its own light from a silvered reflector.

With a sweep of her arm, Nicci sent a spark of her gift into the four wicks. The flames swelled, lending golden warmth to the small room. Richard noticed that, despite the way the palace spell diminished the power of any but a Rahl, she seemed to have had no trouble lighting the lamps.

Berdine went to the shelves to the right of the door. "Near the part of Kolo's journal where he mentioned the book that wasn't supposed to be copied, I think he might have been implying that the men who didn't trust Baraccus were the ones who made the copies. I think that's who he meant, anyway, but I'm not sure; he refers to them as 'the half-wits from *Yanklee's Yarns.*' "

Nicci spun around to Berdine. "*Yanklee's Yarns!*"

Richard looked from Nicci's astounded expression to Berdine's. "What's *Yanklee's Yarns*?" he asked.

"A book," Berdine said.

Richard turned a questioning look on Nicci.

Nicci huffed in exasperation. "It's more than just a book, Richard. *Yanklee's Yarns* is a book of prophecy. A very, very peculiar book of prophecy. It predates the great war by seven centuries. The vaults at the Palace of the Prophets had an early copy of it. It was a curiosity that every Sister studied in the course of her education about prophecy."

Richard peered around at the books lining the shelves. "What was so peculiar about it?"

"It's a book of prophecy that is nothing but gossip and hearsay."

Richard turned back to her. "I don't get it."

"Well," Nicci said, pausing to find the right words, "it wasn't believed to be prophecy about future events . . . exactly. It's, it's, well, it's actually believed to be prophecy about future gossip, so to speak."

Richard rubbed his tired eyes as he sighed. He looked up at Nicci again. "You mean to say that this Yanklee fellow wrote predictions about gossip?" When Nicci nodded, all he could do was ask, "Why?"

Nicci leaned in a little. "That's the very question to which everyone wanted an answer."

Richard shook his head, as if to clear the cobwebs.

"You see, there are many things that are secret"—Nicci gestured toward Berdine—"like this business with the book that wasn't supposed to be copied. Those kinds of secrets often remain secret because people go to their graves without ever revealing them. That's why when we study historical records we sometimes are not able to solve mysteries—there just isn't any information to be had.

"But, sometimes, there are little tidbits of information floating around, things people saw or overheard, and the people who saw or overheard them start to gossip about those tasty tidbits. There were Sisters at the Palace of the Prophets who believed that hidden within this prophetic book of gossip there would be hints of what those future secrets would turn out to be."

Richard arched an eyebrow. "You mean these Sisters were, in essence, listening to gossip in order to overhear something?"

Nicci nodded. "Something like that.

"You see, there were a few Sisters who considered this simple book of seeming nonsense to be one of the most important books of prophecy in existence. It was kept under tight security. It was never allowed to leave the vaults for study, as some other volumes of prophecy were.

"There were Sisters who devoted a lot of their spare time to studying this seemingly silly book. Because people don't generally go to the trouble to record gossip, *Yanklee's Yarns* is thought to be the only book of its kind—the only written account of gossip, even if it hadn't happened yet. These Sisters believed that there were events that couldn't be discovered or studied in any other way except through this book, which predated such events. In essence, they believed that they were eavesdropping on whispered gossip about things that would happen in the future, gossip about secret things. They believed that *Yanklee's Yarns* held invaluable clues to secrets unknown to anyone else or in any other way."

Richard pressed his fingertips to his forehead as he tried to take it all in. "You said that there were Sisters devoted to studying this book. Do you happen to know who any of these Sisters were?"

Nicci nodded slowly. "Sister Ulicia."

"Oh, great," Richard muttered.

Berdine opened a glassed door to one of the bookshelves and pulled a volume off the shelf. She turned back and showed the book's cover to Richard and Nicci.

The title was *Yanklee's Yarns*.

"When I read in Kolo's journal about 'the half-wits from *Yanklee's Yarns*,' that name was so odd that it kind of stuck in the back of my mind. You know what I mean? Then, one day, I was in here doing research and this book's title jumped out at me. I didn't realize it was a book of prophecy, like you said, Nicci."

Nicci shrugged with one shoulder. "Some books of prophecy are hard to recognize as prophecy—especially for someone not trained in such things. Such important volumes can appear to be simply boring records or, in the case of *Yanklee's Yarns*, nothing more than trivial nonsense."

Berdine indicated the bookshelves lining the small room. "Except there would hardly be anything trivial in this room."

"Good point," Richard said.

Berdine smiled, pleased that he recognized the value of her reasoning. She set the book down on the table that occupied the center of the small library and carefully opened the cover. She leafed through the fragile pages until she found the place she wanted. She looked up at each of them in turn.

"Since Kolo had mentioned this book, I thought I ought to read it. It was really boring. Nearly put me to sleep. It didn't appear of any importance at all"—she tapped a page—"until I spotted this, here. This really woke me up."

Richard twisted his head to read the words above her finger. He had to work at it a moment to figure out the meaning of the passage written in High D'Haran. He scratched his temple as he translated aloud.

" 'So nervous will be the meddling half-wits to copy the key that should never be copied, that they will tremble in fear at what they have done and cast the shadow of the key among the bones, never to reveal that only one key was cut true.' "

The hair at the back of Richard's neck stood on end.

Cara folded her arms across her breasts. "So you mean to say that you think that when it came right down to the deed itself and they made the copies, they turned chicken and made all but one copy a fake?"

Berdine drew her hand down her long braid of glossy brown hair. "It would appear so."

Richard was still lost in the words. "Cast the shadow of the key among the bones . . ." He looked up at Berdine. "Hid them in the central sites. Buried them with the bones."

Berdine smiled. "It's so good to have you back, Lord Rahl. You and I think just alike. I've missed you so much. There have been so many things like this I've wanted to go over with you."

Richard laid an arm gently around her shoulders, revealing a similar sentiment without using the words.

Berdine turned over more pages in the book, finally stopping at a place that was blank. "A number of the books seem to have text missing, like this place, here."

"Prophecy," Nicci said. "It's part of the Chainfire spell that the Sisters of the Dark used on Richard's wife. The spell also eliminated prophecy related to her existence."

Berdine considered Nicci's words. "That certainly is going to make it all more difficult. It takes away a lot of information that might be useful. Verna had mentioned that there was copy missing from the books of prophecy, but she didn't know the reason."

Nicci glanced around at the shelves. "Show me all the books you know of with text missing."

Richard wondered why Nicci looked so suspicious.

Berdine opened several of the glass doors and pulled out volumes, handing them each in turn to Nicci. Nicci scanned them briefly, then dismissively set them on the table. "Prophecy," she pronounced yet again as she tossed the last one Berdine handed her on the pile.

"What are you getting at?" Richard asked.

Instead of answering him, she looked at Berdine. "Any more with missing text?"

Berdine nodded. "There is one more."

She glanced briefly at Richard, then pushed a row of books out of her way. At the back of a shelf she drew a panel aside. A small section of the wall opened to reveal a gilded niche with a small book sitting on a dark green velvet pillow with a golden fringe. The leather cover looked to once have been red, but was now so faded and worn that the bits of faint color only hinted at its past glory. It was a delicately beautiful book, intriguing partly because of its small size, and partly because of the ornate decorative leatherwork.

"I used to help Lord Rahl—I mean Darken Rahl—work on translations of books in High D'Haran," Berdine explained. "This room was one of the places he would study his private books—that's how I knew where to find the key and about this secret compartment in the back of the bookcase. I really thought it might be something useful."

"And was it?" Richard asked.

"I thought it would be, but I'm afraid not. It, too, is missing text. Except, unlike those other books, this one isn't just missing some of the text here and there, or missing whole sections. Instead, this book is missing every single word. It's completely empty."

"It's missing every word?" Nicci asked suspiciously. "Let me see it."

Berdine handed the little book over to Nicci. "It's completely blank, I'm telling you. See for yourself. It's useless."

Nicci opened the ancient, worn leather cover and scanned the first page. Her finger followed along as if she were reading. She flipped the page and studied the next, then did the same thing yet again.

"Dear spirits," she whispered as she appeared to read.

"What is it?" Richard asked.

Berdine stretched up on her tiptoes and peeked over the top of the book. "It can't be anything. See—it's blank."

"No, it's not," Nicci murmured as she read. "This is a book of magic." She looked up. "It only appears blank to those without the gift. And, in the case of this particular work, even they must possess the gift in sufficient strength to be able to read this. This is a profoundly important volume."

Berdine wrinkled her nose. "What?"

"Books of magic are dangerous, some exceedingly dangerous. Some, such as this one, are beyond even that." Nicci waggled the book at the Mord-Sith. "This one is far more than profoundly dangerous.

"As a form of protection such books are usually shielded in some way. If they are considered dangerous enough, then they are protected with spells that make the text vanish from a person's mind so quickly that they don't recall seeing it. It makes them think the pages are blank. A person without the gift simply can't hold the words of a book of magic in their mind. You actually do see the words in this book, but you forget seeing them so fast that you aren't cognizant that there was anything on the pages—the words vanish from your mind before you actually perceive them.

"That particular spell is, in part, the basis for the concept of the Chain-fire spell. The wizards in ancient times—who often used such spells to protect dangerous books they wrote—began to wonder if such a thing could be done with a person, in effect making them vanish, just as the words in some books of magic can seem to vanish."

Nicci gestured vaguely as her attention drifted back to the book. "Of course, when a soul is involved it complicates the whole matter beyond words."

Richard had long ago learned that he had been able to memorize *The Book of Counted Shadows* only because he was gifted. Zedd had told him that if he hadn't had the gift, he wouldn't have been able to hold the words in his mind long enough to have remembered a single one.

"So, what is this book about?" he asked.

Nicci finally pulled her gaze away from the pages and looked up. "This is a book of magic instruction."

"I know, you said that already," he said, patiently. "Instruction for what?"

Nicci checked the page again, and swallowed as she again gazed into his eyes. "I think this is the original instruction book for putting the boxes of Orden in play."

Richard felt goose bumps, yet again, tingle up his arms and legs.

He gently lifted the book from Nicci's hands. Sure enough, it was not blank at all. Every page was packed with small written words, diagrams, charts, and formulas.

"This is in High D'Haran." He looked up at Nicci. "You mean to say you can read High D'Haran?"

"Of course."

Richard shared a look with Berdine.

He could see immediately that the book was profoundly complex. He had learned High D'Haran, but this book was something only on the brink of his understanding.

"This is far more technical than the High D'Haran I'm used to reading," he said as he scanned the pages.

Nicci leaned close and pointed to a place on the page he was staring at. "This here is all reference material to formulas needed in incantations. You have to know the formulas and spells to really understand it."

Richard looked up into her blue eyes. "And do you?"

She twisted her mouth as she frowned at the page. "I don't know. I'd have to study it at length to know if I can be of any help in translating it."

Berdine again stretched up on her tiptoes and peered into the book, as if checking to see if maybe the words might now appear to her. "Why can't you tell right away? I mean, either you can read and understand it, or you can't."

Nicci raked the fingers of one hand back through her blond hair as she took a deep breath. "It's not that simple with books of magic. It's kind of like doing complex mathematical equations. You may know the numbers and at first think you know what it's about, that you can work the equation, but if you then discover unknown symbols buried in the equation—symbols that refer to things unfamiliar to you—then the entire equation is pretty much unworkable. Just knowing some of the numbers isn't enough. You have to know what every element means, or at least how to find the value or quantity it represents.

"This is much the same, although I'm simplifying it so that you can understand my point. In this there are not just symbols, but obsolete references to spells, making it all the more difficult to understand. Being in High D'Haran makes it worse yet because over time High D'Haran words and their meaning have changed. Added to that, this text is an ancient, argot form."

Richard gripped her arm, drawing her attention. "Nicci, this is important; do you think you can manage to do it?"

She looked hesitantly at the book. "It will take some time before I can translate enough to be able to tell you if I have a chance of being successful."

Richard took the book out of her hands, closed it, and handed it back to her. "Then you'd better take it with you. When we have more time you can study it and see if you can figure it out."

She frowned suspiciously. "Why? What are you thinking?"

"Nicci, don't you see? This could be our answer. If you can translate it, understand it, then what's in here might provide us with a way to counter, reverse, or dismantle what Sister Ulicia did. With this, maybe we can take the boxes of Orden back out of play."

Nicci gently rubbed her thumb over the cover of the little book. "That sounds like it makes sense, Richard, but knowing how to do something doesn't mean that you can undo it."

"Kind of like trying to get yourself unpregnant?" Cara asked.

Nicci smiled. "Something like that."

Cara's unexpected analogy threw Richard's mind back to Kahlan, and when she had been pregnant. A gang of men had caught her alone and beaten her nearly to death. She lost her and Richard's child. Her pregnancy ended before he'd even known about it.

The memory of seeing Kahlan so grievously hurt nearly buckled his knees. He had to force the ghastly thoughts back into the blackness from where they'd come.

Nicci's brow twitched with a frown, apparently at seeing the anguish in his face. He ignored her unspoken worry for him.

"I don't need to remind you how important this is," he said.

She held him in her gaze for a long moment, as if wanting to tell him that it was impossible, but desperately not wanting to say no to him. She finally pressed her lips tight and nodded.

"I'll do my best, Richard."

Her expression suddenly brightened. She flipped to the end of the book and hurriedly turned back the last page. She stood absorbed for a moment as she scrutinized the final page.

"This is interesting," she murmured.

"What?" Richard asked.

Nicci looked up from the middle of what she was reading. "Well, at the end of some books of magic, as a precaution against unauthorized use, they will occasionally have some final step that's essential but not included. If so, then, even if the boxes are already in play, we might be able to interrupt the series of specific actions required. Do you see what I mean? Sometimes, if the book is dangerous enough, it won't be complete in and of itself, but will require something else to complete it."

"Something else? Like what?"

"I don't know. That's what I'm checking." She held up a finger. "Let me read just a little of this part. . . ."

After a moment she looked up as she tapped the page. "Yes, I was right. This warns that to use this book, the key must be used. Otherwise, without the key, everything that has come before will not only be sterile, but fatal. It says that within one full year the key must complete what has been wrought with this book."

"Key," Richard repeated in a flat tone.

He glanced to Berdine.

" 'They will tremble in fear at what they have done and cast the shadow of the key among the bones,' " she quoted from *Yanklee's Yarns*. "You think that could be the key this book is talking about?"

Something stirred in the dark fringes of his consciousness.

With a lightning-swift spark of comprehension, Richard understood.

His whole body flashed icy cold. His arms and legs went numb.

"Dear spirits . . ." he whispered.

Nicci frowned at him. "Richard, what's wrong. You've gone as pale as chalk."

Richard had trouble making his voice work. Finally, he heard himself say "I've got to get back to Zedd."

Nicci reached out and laid a hand on his arm. "What's wrong?"

"I think I know what the key is."

Richard began to pant as his heart pounded out of control. Everything he knew was turning upside down and all the pieces were coming apart. It felt like he couldn't get his breath.

They will tremble in fear at what they have done and cast the shadow of the key among the bones.

"Well, what do you think—"

"I'll explain when we get there. We have to go—now."

Worried, Nicci slipped the book into a pocket in the black skirt of her dress. "I'll do my best, Richard. I'll figure this out—I promise."

He nodded absently as his mind raced to try to fit all the pieces back together. He felt as if he were only watching himself begin to move.

He seized Berdine by the arm. "Baraccus had a secret place—a library. I need you to try to find out where it was."

Berdine nodded at his urgency. "All right, Lord Rahl. I'll see what I can learn. I'll do my best."

She glanced down at the white knuckles on his hand gripping her arm. Richard realized that he must be hurting her and let go.

"Thank you, Berdine. I know I can count on you." The others were all staring at him. "I've got to get back to Zedd. I've got to talk to him right away. I've got to know where he got it."

"Got what?" Nicci pressed a hand to his chest, stopping him before he went through the door. "Richard, what's so important that—"

"Look, I'll explain it when we get back there," he said, cutting her off. "Right now I need to think this through."

Nicci shared a troubled look with Cara. "All right, Richard. Calm down. We'll be back to the Keep soon enough."

He snatched a fistful of Cara's red leather outfit and pushed her through the doorway ahead of him. "Get us back to the sliph—the shortest route."

All business, now, Cara spun her Agiel up into her fist. "Come on, then."

He turned back to Berdine, trotting backward after Cara. "I need you to find out everything you possibly can about Baraccus. Everything!"

Berdine raced along just ahead of Nicci. "I will, Lord Rahl."

He pointed back at her. "Verna will be here soon. Tell her that I said I need her to help you. Have her Sisters help you, too. Go through every book in the entire palace if you have to, but find out everything you can about Baraccus—where he was born, where he grew up, what he liked, what he didn't. He was First Wizard, so there should be information of some kind. I want to know who cut his hair, who made his clothes, what his favorite color was. Everything, no matter how trivial you think it is. While you're at it, see if you can find out anything more about what the half-wits from *Yanklee's Yarns* did."

"Don't worry, Lord Rahl, if there is any information to be had, I will have it. I'll figure it out and have an answer when you return."

Richard snatched Nicci's hand to make sure she kept up and then turned toward Cara. "Hurry."

Berdine, Agiel in her fist, ran after them, guarding the rear. Richard was only dimly aware of the flashes of light off polished armor and weapons, and the jangle of gear, as the soldiers took up the chase as if the Keeper himself were after the Lord Rahl.

As his mind raced as fast as his feet, Richard resolved that he had better go to Caska first.

The more he considered that idea, and as pieces of the puzzle started fitting together, he reconsidered the idea. With the sliph, he could travel swiftly back to Caska from the Keep.

It was more urgent that he get to Zedd.

As they ran through the labyrinth of halls, rooms, and passageways, Richard heard the distant toll of the bell, calling people to the devotion to the Lord Rahl.

He wondered if they would all soon be kneeling before the Keeper of the underworld, and saying their devotions to him.

Six abruptly stood. Without a word she took three long strides to the wall of the cave that held Violet's expansive drawing. The woman carefully pressed her bony hands against the chalk symbols that Violet had drawn there days before. Those symbols had suddenly begun to glow, the yellow chalk glowing with yellow light, the red chalk with red light, and the blue with blue light. The eerie illumination from the flaring colors shimmered over the walls of the cave the way light reflected off rippling water.

Rachel glanced over at Violet, sitting on a squat, purple-tufted stool she'd had Rachel carry in for her days before. The bored queen picked with her fingernail at flaking stone on the wall behind her. Rachel had come to think of Violet as the queen of the cave, since that was where they spent more and more of their time.

Violet didn't like sitting on rock when she wasn't drawing. A filthy old rock, she'd said, was more than good enough for Rachel, but not for a queen. Six hadn't cared at all about the stool. She appeared to always have more consequential matters on her mind than cushions for sitting. Violet, though, got tired of waiting while Six thought about those consequential matters, and so she'd had Rachel lug the heavy stool to the cave.

Now, the queen of the cave, under the flickering light of torches and glowing symbols, sat upon her tufted purple throne waiting for her advisor to advise her as to what needed to be done next.

"He comes," Six hissed. "Again he comes through the void."

It was clear to Rachel that the woman wasn't really talking to Violet, but to herself. The queen might as well not have been there.

Violet glanced up. She didn't look inclined to bother to stand unless Six told her that it was necessary that she do more drawings, but it was clear that her interest had been roused. This was, after all what she wanted and the whole reason she bothered to go to all the work of making such complex drawings down in a dank and dingy cave when she could just as well be trying on dresses and jewels or attending grand feasts where guests fawned over the young queen.

Six seemed in a world of her own as her hands glided over the drawing. She put the side of her face against the stone and at the same time reached an arm back.

"Come, my child."

A scowl creased Violet's round features. "You mean, 'my queen.' "

Six either didn't hear her, or didn't care to correct herself. "Hurry. It is time to begin the links."

Violet stood. "Now? It's long past dinnertime. I'm starving."

Six, stroking her cheek against the chalk drawing of Richard like a cat rubbing the side of its face against a person's legs, didn't seem at all interested in dinner.

She rolled her long fingers, beckoning Violet. "It must be now. Hurry. We must not waste such a rare opportunity. Such links as we need will take time and there is no telling how much time we may have."

"Well then why didn't we begin earlier, when there—"

"It must be started now, when he is in the void." Six clawed the air with one hand. "Easier to scratch his eyes out when he's blind," she said in her hissy voice.

"I don't see why—"

"The way is the way. Do you wish this or not?"

Violet's folded arms, along with her defiance, came undone. Her expression took on a dark set. "I do."

A sinuous smile slipped across Six's features. "Then let it begin. You must now complete the links."

Looking suddenly resolute, Violet plucked the sticks of colored chalk off a little ledge in the stone wall behind her royal stool. As she strode up beside Six, the woman tapped a long, thin finger to the stone.

"Begin at the sign of the dagger, as I've taught you, just as you've practiced, to insure that, at the initiation of the link, what you have wrought will be ready to slice swift and sure."

"I know, I know," Violet said as she boldly touched the tip of the yellow chalk to the point of one of the elaborate glowing symbols off to the side of Richard.

Six snatched Violet's wrist, pulling her hand back just enough to lift the chalk away from the wall. She moved Violet's hand over a few inches, then let the chalk again touch the symbol, but at the next apex in a design with a perimeter comprised of dozens of points.

"I told you," Six said with strained civility as she helped Violet begin the line, "a mistake here will last us for eternity."

"I know—I just got the wrong apex point, that's all," Violet huffed. "I've got it, now."

Six, ignoring the queen, her gaze fixed on the drawing, nodded approvingly as she watched the chalk begin to move across the stone.

"Change to red," Six prompted in a low voice after Violet had pulled the chalk a few inches across the open distance.

Without argument or hesitation, Violet changed the chalk for the red one and started it moving at an angle from the yellow line she had already drawn. After bringing it half the remaining distance toward the drawing of Richard, she stopped without needing to be told and switched to the blue chalk.

She hesitated, then, and glanced up at Six. "This is the node? Right?"

Six was already nodding. "That's right," she murmured, pleased with what she was seeing. "That's right, take it around and back now to complete the first ligature."

Violet drew a blue circle at the end of the red line before crossing the empty place on the smooth, dark stone wall. When the blue chalk reached one of the points on the next symbol, she went back and drew a line from the circle to connect to Richard. The completed triad of lines Violet had just drawn began to glow. The blue circle ignited with a beam of light, as if it were a beacon coming through a window in the dark stone.

Six abruptly held up a hand, commanding that Violet stop before she could put the chalk to the next point in the sequence.

"What's wrong?" Violet asked.

"Something . . . is not right. . . ."

Six pressed the side of her face to the drawing, this time laying her cheek right atop Richard's face.

"Not right at all. . . ."

Richard drew another silvered breath of the ecstasy but, with his urgent worries overriding the experience, it was something short of the remarkable essence of rapture that he usually experienced within the sliph.

He realized, though, that when he traveled in the sliph he was usually gravely troubled by something; after all, trouble of one sort or another was why he traveled in the sliph in the first place. Still, it had never before felt this way. This feeling was not dread so much as it was a sense of the great, but intangible, weight of foreboding. With every breath, that phantom weight pressed in on him ever more.

Within the sliph there was no real sense of vision, as such, just as there was no real sense of time, or up, or down. Even so, there was a semblance of sight; there were colors and, on occasion, obscure shapes that seemed to loom up and just as quickly vanish. There was also a visual perception of the phenomenon of mind-bending speed that made him feel as if he were nothing more than an arrow fired from a powerful bow. At the same time, there was a feeling of almost floating motionless within the thick void of the sliph. Those different sensations mixed together created a heady mix of the whole of the experience that suspended his urge to separate them into constituent parts.

As he raced through the quicksilver essence of the sliph, he began to discount his anxiety. It was then that Richard felt the faint brush of an odd sensation against his skin, a stealthy pressure that he instantly recognized as a sensation he had never before experienced as he traveled. Tingling apprehension rippling through him.

Forboding, he realized, was not tangible in the way that this touch had been.

As he drifted, held in the embrace of the vast silver emptiness, he tried to separate the perception of having been touched from everything else. Richard felt the placid isolation of the sliph surrounding him, caressing him, insulating him from the terrible, headlong rush of speed that otherwise seemed as if it would surely have to tear a person apart. He still felt the balm of serenity quelling his fear of breathing into his lungs the liquid in which he floated.

But Richard felt something else, even if he was not yet able to set the troubling sensation apart from all others enough to define it.

With growing conviction, though, he was sure that something was wrong. Frighteningly wrong. It was all the more disturbing because he couldn't understand how he knew that something was imperfect. He worked to comprehend why he would think such a thing.

It had to have been, he decided, that furtive touch. He briefly wondered if he could have imagined it, but then discounted the notion. He had felt it.

It seemed almost as if he were in the presence of an unholy taint, like lying in a warm, sunlit meadow on a beautiful day, surrounded by the cascade of colors and balmy aroma of wildflowers, watching cottony clouds slowly drift through a bright blue sky, and then catching the first faint whiff of a decomposing carcass while at the same time realizing that the vague sound you heard was the buzzing of flies.

What ordinarily seemed like a timeless spell spent racing through the smoothly silver sliph had begun to drag out into an agonizing suspension of headway.

Cara already had his right hand in an iron grip, but Nicci gripped his left hand even more tightly. He could tell in that urgent squeeze that she sensed something as well. He wished that he could ask her what she felt, but talking within the sliph was not possible.

Richard opened his eyes wider, trying to see more of what was around him, but it was a muted, murky world where there was little to be seen, other than the shimmering shafts of light—yellow, red, blue—piercing the gloom through which they raced. Richard didn't think that those shafts of light were moving as they once had been. It was hard to tell such things for sure within the sliph, though. It was generally a hazy sense of events, rather than actual perception.

There was something out ahead of him, Richard realized, something maneuvering fluidly through the silver obscurity. At first it looked like long, slender petals just beginning to blossom open. As it came closer, Richard saw that it looked more like numerous arms—tapered, long, undulating objects—fanning open from a central element that for some reason he could not quite figure out.

It was disorienting to watch because it was so incomprehensible. As it came ever closer, it began to appear to Richard as if whatever it was was made up of segments of glass, all assembled into something orderly, something billowing open before him. He could see through the transparent, expanding arms, see the shafts of color and light shimmering beyond.

It was the oddest thing he had ever seen. As hard as he tried, he simply could not make sense of it. It was like it was there, but not there.

And then, with icy dread, comprehension washed through him.

At the same time, Nicci pulled his hand so hard that it nearly wrenched his arm right out of its socket. The yank must have pulled him back, because Cara, still holding his other hand, sailed around him as if falling through midair. Richard ducked. The translucent shape whipped past his face, just missing him.

Nicci had pulled him back just in time.

Richard knew now what it was.

It was the beast.

The sense of being in the presence of evil was suddenly so strong that it engulfed him with suffocating panic. As the beast, like some temporal vision, skimmed past him, it twisted around. The glassy arms fanned open as they reached out and again tried to snatch him.

With a sharp tug Nicci again drew him back from the star-shaped net of tentacles spread wide before him. Again they tried to close around him.

Richard pulled his hand away from Cara's and drew his knife. With her now free hand, she immediately snatched a fistful of his shirt to hold on to him.

Richard did his best to slash at the ever-reaching arms trying to embrace him in their deadly grasp. It didn't take long to realize that fighting with a knife within the sliph was close to impossible. It was too fluid an environment for Richard to be able to strike with any speed. It was like trying to maneuver in honey. He changed his tactics and instead waited for the arms to draw in around him, waited for whatever was at the glassy center to come to him.

When they did, he drove the blade toward that aware center of the translucent threat. Rather than be impaled on the blade, though, the creature only seemed to fold around Richard's knife and twist effortlessly away.

And then it again came in to attack, now with a kind of abrupt, intent fury that Richard could sense. The thing moved with a fluid grace that didn't seem to be hindered at all by the fluid world surrounding them.

To one side Richard saw the shimmering shape of Cara, still gripping his shirt as she tried to attack the beast with her free hand. To the other side, he knew, Nicci was trying to work magic. It didn't seem that her magic was working in the environment of the sliph.

One of the beast's arms coiled around Richard's arm, another lashed around Cara's. She seized his wrist with her other hand. The beast fastened onto her other arm as well and effortlessly ripped the two of them apart. In an instant, Cara was gone. In the murky darkness Richard couldn't tell where she was, or how close she might be. Worse, he didn't know if she was all right, or if the creature had her.

Nicci tightened her arm protectively around Richard's waist, holding on for dear life, as more of the undulating, transparent arms came out of the gloom and coiled around them. It was like getting tangled in a nest of snakes, all entwining themselves and constricting with great force once attached. The one around Richard's leg drew so tight that he thought it would surely rip his flesh from the bone.

Even though Richard could not hear Nicci in the conventional sense, he could perceive her muffled cries of fury as she fought the thing that had snared them. An odd, muted form of lightning flickered madly around Nicci. Richard knew she was trying to use her power, but it wasn't having any effect on the beast.

Richard ignored the pain of the glassy tentacles that already had him and stabbed over and over, cutting into thick arms that looked to be only partly there. With determined and focused rage he slashed with the knife and was able to cleave some of the arms away from the core of the thing. Once severed, they writhed wildly as they fell away into the void around them, as if sinking into a bottomless sea.

It seemed to do no good; ever more of the twisting tentacles came at him from out of the darkness. It was like finding himself at the bottom of a dark pit full of angry vipers. Richard fought on with all his strength, cutting, stabbing, slashing. His arms ached with the effort. Nicci grappled with the thick tentacles with one hand, her other arm still refusing to let him go. He could tell by the way she arched and twisted that she was in agony. Richard abandoned the coils around himself and with all his fury hacked at the arms of the beast hurting Nicci as they tried to pull her away from him.

But then she was violently torn away from him.

Richard was suddenly alone in the middle of nowhere with a glassy, slippery, powerful creature trying to wrestle him in toward its center, toward something he could hear snarling, snapping, clacking.

There was no way to fight such a thing, no way to get an advantage over its power, no way to escape its multi-armed grasp. Ever more of the arms whipped in to capture him.

With all his strength, before his arm was captured, he thrust the knife toward the center mass that he couldn't clearly see.

He made solid contact. The beast howled with a sound that hurt his ears. The arms loosened just a bit—not letting go of him, but loosed just enough for Richard to give a mighty twist of his body that succeeded in spinning him out of the creature's grip. It an instant, like a pumpkin seed squeezed between wet fingers, he squirted away from the deadly grip.

Richard tried to swim away, to somehow escape the thrashing, translucent arms coming for him, but it was faster than he was, more powerful, and tireless.

"Here!" Six urged as she rapped her knuckles against the center of an emblem.

Violet raced with the chalk to the spot her advisor was urging her toward. Her fingers flew with swift and sure movements. With the back of her other hand, Violet swiped sweat off her face, then with her fingers wiped it from her eyes. Rachel had never seen Violet work so hard, or so fast.

Rachel didn't know what was happening, but it was obvious that something was not going the way Six had expected. She was in a state balancing precariously between panic and rage. Rachel feared whichever way it fell.

While Violet swiftly completed links, switching chalk and moving to each successive point, Six went back to softly chanting her incantations. The corrosive sound of those whispered words felt as if they were searing Rachel's soul. While she could not understand the words or their meaning, they were spoken with a sinister intent that terrified her.

She glanced toward the distant cave entrance, but with it being dark outside, Rachel couldn't see anything. She wanted to run but dared not. She knew that if she caused Violet or Six to have to stop what they were doing and come after her, it would go very badly for her.

Chase had taught her to bridle her impulses, as he'd called it, and to watch for true openings. He had cautioned her that if she wasn't in immediate mortal danger, she should act only when she had a deliberate plan that she had thought out ahead of time. He said that she shouldn't act out of blind fear, but work to find ways to increase the odds of success.

Despite how busy the other two were, Rachel knew that with both of them together and both in such a frantic state, they both would react to any misdeed by Rachel with swift and unrestrained violence. This was not the right opportunity; getting up right then and running was not a good plan, and she knew it.

As Rachel sat still and quiet, trying to keep from being noticed, Six gently tapped the side of her fist against several of the flaring nodes in the links Violet had already drawn. Each bright circle she tapped went dark with a low growling sound that ran a shiver up Rachel's spine. The cave seemed to hum with the rise and fall of Six's rhythmic conjuring.

Violet, drawing with bold, slashing strokes, glanced to the side, checking on Six's progress. Six, extinguishing the beacons in sequence, was catching the queen. Violet, as if in a trance, drew faster. The chalk made a clack, clack, clacking sound with each line that Violet threw down against the stone. The sound of the chalk matched the rhythm of Six's chant.

All around the figure of Richard, Six, conjuring with murmured verses spoken in a rising, singsong chant that gradually brought a howling wind swirling down into the cave, rapped the side of her fist against points in the links Violet had been drawing without pause for hours. Rachel had thought that Violet might soon collapse from exhaustion but, far from it, she seemed to be working herself into a fever pitch of effort trying to stay ahead of Six. Despite how swiftly her hand moved, each line Violet drew looked true, each intersection met accurately and completely. Six had made Violet practice endlessly drawing the symbols and now it seemed to be paying off.

The drawing of Richard was almost completely encased in the web of symbols and connecting lines.

With a strange word, shouted in order to be heard over the howling wind, Six extinguished the final beacon around the figure of Richard. The wind abruptly died. Little pieces of leaves and other debris fluttered down through the abruptly still air.

Six paused in her chanting. Her brow twitched. With her fingertips she touched several of the symbols, as if feeling their pulse. Shimmers of colored light flickered through the cave.

"It has him," Six whispered to herself.

Violet paused, swallowing as she caught her breath. "What?"

"Apogee to inferior apex." She turned a venomous look on a startled Violet. "Do it!"

Without hesitation Violet turned back to the wall and reached up, drawing coiled lines downward from one of the central elements above Richard's head.

Six lifted a hand. "Be ready, but don't touch the primary invocation points until I tell you."

Violet nodded. Six's eyes rolled back in her head as she leaned in on her fingertips over the figure of Richard. As Violet and Rachel watched, Six breathed a low murmur of strange words.

Nicci broke above the quicksilver surface of the sliph. The weight of the leaden liquid rolled from her hair and face. Colors and light seemed to explode out of the quiet, mellow darkness.

Breathe.

With all her effort Nicci immediately forced the silver fluid from her lungs.

Breathe.

With her need overwhelming her dread, she gasped a desperate breath. It burned like drawing in acidic vapors.

The room spun sickeningly in her vision. Nicci saw a smear of red. She floundered woodenly as she again gasped. She managed to reach the edge and throw an arm over the sliph's stone wall to hold herself up. Panic threatened to swamp her.

A hand seized her arm. Nicci managed to heave her pack up and over the wall. Another hand reached down and helped to haul her up enough for her to get both arms over the wall of the sliph. The red she had seen was Cara.

"Where's Lord Rahl!"

Nicci blinked up at the Mord-Sith's intense blue eyes. She had never known blue to hurt so much. She closed her eyes and shook her head, still trying to clear her mind of the experience, of the confusion, of the ringing sound of Cara's voice echoing through the marrow of her bones.

"Richard . . ."

If felt as if her insides twisted with the anguish of wanting nothing so much as to help him.

"Richard . . ."

Cara grunted with the effort of lifting Nicci's dead weight and pulling the top half of her body the rest of the way up and out of the well. Nicci, feeling like the survivor of a shipwreck in a stormy sea, slid out over the top of the stone wall, unable to do much to contribute to her own rescue. Cara put one knee to the floor, catching Nicci before her limp body hit the stone.

Once Cara had lowered her down onto the stone floor, Nicci gathered all her strength and pushed herself up on trembling arms. She couldn't seem to muster her usual strength. It was a frightful feeling, not being able to make her body do her bidding. With great effort she finally managed to tip herself upright and sit heavily back against the wall of the sliph's well. She still gasped, trying to catch her breath. She still hurt everywhere. For a moment she slumped against the stone well, trying to gather her strength.

Cara seized her by the collar of her dress and shook her.

"Nicci—where's Lord Rahl?"

Nicci blinked, looking around, trying to make sense of everything. She hurt so much. The pain reminded her of one of Jagang's beatings, the way during his rage she would start to feel the pain through a half-numb fog of confusion. But this had not been the emperor's doing. This was pain from something that had happened in the sliph. Traveling had never hurt before. It had never been a painful experience.

"Where's Lord Rahl!"

Nicci winced at the ache of the shout echoing around the room. She swallowed past the raw pain in her throat.

"I don't know." She put her elbows on her knees and ran her fingers back into her hair, holding her pounding head in both hands. "Dear spirits, I don't know."

Cara leaned over the well so fast and so hard that Nicci thought she might topple in. Instinctively, she reached out to catch the Mord-Sith's legs, thinking that she would surely fall in, but she didn't.

"Sliph!" Cara's shout again echoed around the ancient, dusty stone room. Nicci shared the emotion, but knew that the intensity would not accomplish anything.

Ignoring the searing pain in her joints, she staggered to her feet. The spinning feeling was slowing a little. She saw the quicksilver form of the sliph's face partly emerge from the well, her features forming in the glossy surface to look up at them.

"Where's Lord Rahl?" Cara asked.

The sliph chose to ignore Cara's question. Instead she peered over at Nicci.

"You must not ever do that when you are within me." The eerie voice echoed softly around the room.

"You mean magic?" Nicci guessed.

"I have great difficulty being able to endure such power being unleashed within me, but such a thing could be worse for you and anyone else traveling at the same time. You must not ever try to use your ability when you travel. It will make you sick at the least. It could easily turn out far worse. It is dangerous to all."

"She's right about that," Cara said, confidentially. "When you started doing that it hurt like an Agiel was being used on me. My legs still don't work right."

"Mine either," Nicci admitted. "But I couldn't very well just let the beast have Richard without trying to protect him, now, could I?"

Ill at ease for even giving the hint of an impression that she wouldn't have done anything to protect Richard, Cara shook her head. "I would have taken far worse than that to protect Lord Rahl. You did the right thing—I don't care what the sliph says."

"Me too," Nicci said. At that moment, though, she wasn't concerned about herself or Cara. She turned to the sliph. "Where is Richard? What happened to him? Where is he?"

"I cannot—"

Cara's patience, if she'd had any, was gone. She lunged for the sliph as if she was going to try to strangle the silver neck. "Where is he!"

The face glided out of reach. Nicci snatched Cara's outfit and pulled the woman back, standing her up on the floor beside her. Her face, red with rage, nearly matched her leather outfit.

"Sliph, this is vital," Nicci said, trying to sound reasonable. "We were with Richard—with Lord Rahl, your master—when we were attacked. That's why I had to use my power. I was trying to protect him. That beast is extremely dangerous."

The flawless silver face distorted into a fearful cast. "I know, it hurt me."

Nicci paused in astonishment. "The beast hurt you?"

The sliph nodded. Reflections of the room bent and flowed in twisting shapes over the smooth contours of the statuesque, silver features. Nicci stared in wonder as shimmering quicksilver tears formed along the lower lid of the sliph's eyes and rolled down the glossy surface of her cheeks.

"It hurt. It did not want to travel." The silver brow wrinkled with what looked like indignation layered atop torment. "It had no right to use me in that way. It hurt me."

Nicci shared a look with Cara.

Cara may have looked surprised, but she did not look sympathetic. The truth be told, at that moment Nicci's worry for Richard took precedence over any other concern.

"Sliph, I'm sorry," Nicci said, "but—"

"Where is he?" Cara growled. "Just tell us where Lord Rahl is."

The sliph hesitated. "He no longer travels."

"Where is he, then?" Cara repeated.

The sliph's voice turned cold and distant. "I never reveal information about others who have been with me."

"He's not just a traveler!" Cara screamed in rage. "It's Lord Rahl!"

The sliph backed to the far wall of her well.

Nicci held a hand up toward Cara, urging a little restraint and for her to be quiet a moment. "We were attacked by something evil when we were traveling together. You know that." Nicci tried to calm some of the menace in her voice. She knew, though, that she wasn't being altogether successful. Her rising panic about Richard was making it difficult to think—that and Jebra's frantic warning that they must not allow Richard to be alone, even for an instant. "Sliph, that evil thing was after your master, after Richard. We're Richard's friends—you know that, too. He needs our help."

"Lord Rahl may be hurt," Cara added.

Nicci nodded her confirmation to Cara's words. "We need to get to him."

The quiet in the stone room felt painful. Nicci was still trying to accustom herself to being back, still struggling to suppress the agony of pain twisting through her while trying to think what to do next.

"We need to get to Richard," she repeated.

The silver face rose up a little farther, drawing a neck of silver fluid up out of the well with it. The sliph puzzled at Nicci.

"You wish to travel?"

Nicci kept a tight rein on her rage. "Yes. That's right. We wish to travel."

Cara, taking the cue from Nicci, gestured down into the well. "Yes, that's right. We wish to travel."

"I won't use my magic in you again, I promise." Nicci motioned the sliph closer. "We wish to travel—right away. Right now."

The sliph brightened, as if all was forgiven. "You will be pleased." She seemed eager to satisfy. "Come, we will travel."

Nicci put a knee up on the wall. Her thighs ached with the effort. She ignored the fiery agony burning through her muscles and joints and worked to climb up atop the broad stone wall. She was relieved that they had at last found a way to get the sliph to comply—if not by telling them where Richard was, then by taking them to him.

"Yes, we will travel," Nicci said, still trying to catch her breath.

The sliph formed an arm, slipping it around Nicci's waist, helping to pull her up onto the wall. "Come, then. Where do you wish to travel?"

"To where Lord Rahl is." Cara clambered up onto the wall beside Nicci. "Take us there," she said, putting on a smile for the sliph's benefit, "and we will be pleased."

The sliph paused and gazed at her. The arm drew back, melting into the slowly sloshing surface. The silver face looked suddenly impersonal, even forbidding.

"I cannot reveal information about other clients."

Nicci fisted her hands. "He's not just any client! He's your master and he's in trouble! He's our friend! You have to take us to him!"

The sliph's reflective face moved away. "I cannot do such a thing."

Nicci and Cara stood mute for a moment, both at their wits' end, unable to think of how to convince the sliph to cooperate. Nicci felt like screaming, or crying, or unleashing enough magic to boil the sliph into talking.

"If you don't help us," she finally said in an even tone, "then you will feel more pain than you did from the beast. I will see to that. Please don't make me resort to that. We know you want to protect Richard. That's what we're trying to do, too."

The sliph stared in silence, like a silver statue, as if trying to assess the threat.

Cara pressed her fingers to her temples. "It's like trying to reason with a bucket of water," she muttered.

Nicci glared at the sliph. "You will take us to your master. That's an order."

"You'd better do as she says," Cara said, "or when she's done with you, then you will have to answer to me."

The Mord-Sith spun her Agiel up into her fist to make her point.

But when she did she suddenly froze stiff, staring at the weapon. The blood drained from her face. Even her hands stood out white against the red leather of her outfit.

Nicci leaned closer and laid a hand on Cara's shoulder. "What's wrong?"

Cara's hanging jaw finally moved. "It's dead."

"What are you talking about?"

Cara's blue eyes were filled with unbridled panic. "My Agiel is dead in my hand. I can't feel it."

While Nicci could clearly read the startled dismay in the Mord-Sith's voice, she didn't understand its source. Having an Agiel not give her pain hardly seemed like cause for panic. Even so, such naked terror was infectious.

"Does that mean something?" Nicci asked, fearing the answer.

The sliph watched from the far side of the well.

"The Agiel is powered through our bond to Lord Rahl—by his gift." She held the weapon out, as if in evidence. "If the Agiel is dead, then so is the Lord Rahl."

"Listen, I'll use my power if I have to to make the sliph take us to him. But Cara, don't start jumping to conclusions. We can't know—"

"He's not there."

"He's not where?"

"Anywhere." Still, Cara stared at her slender weapon held up in her trembling fingers. "I can no longer feel the bond." Her liquid blue-eyed gaze turned up to Nicci. "The bond always tells us where the Lord Rahl is. I no longer can feel him. I no longer feel where he is. He's not there. He's not anywhere."

A wave of nausea washed through Nicci. She felt faint. Her fingers and toes were going numb.

She turned back to the sliph.

It was gone.

Nicci leaned over the wall, peering down into the well. In the darkness below she saw a faint silver glimmer just as it vanished, leaving behind only blackness.

She turned back to Cara and seized a fistful of leather at her shoulder. She hopped down off the wall, pulling Cara with her.

"Come on. I know someone who can tell us where Richard is."

With Cara at her side, Nicci raced down the torchlit hallway, over elaborately designed carpets that muted their footfalls, past doorways into darkness, past rooms with oil lamps warmly lighting only vacant furniture. The Keep, nearly as vast as the mountain that sheltered it beneath its stoic stone shoulders, felt empty and haunted. Nicci had spent decades in the vast complex known as the Palace of the Prophets, which in some ways was reminiscent of the Keep, but the palace had been alive with hundreds of people of all kinds living there, from the Prelate to the boys who tended the stables. It, too, had been a place of wizards—wizards in training, anyway. The Keep existed for the purposes of man, and yet it stood silent and absent of those who would give it life. If a place could be said to be forlorn, the immense structure of the Keep was such a place.

Cara ran with all her strength, driven by her loyalty and love for Richard, by dread that the worst had happened to him. Nicci ran just as fast, driven by fear of even considering the possibility that he was dead, as if trying to outrun death itself. She couldn't allow herself to even entertain such a concept, lest she collapse in despair. A world without Richard in it would be a dead world to her.

Cara slid across the polished gray marble floor to slow herself enough to make the turn when Nicci hooked a hand on a cold, black marble newel post and charged up the wide, black, granite steps. The windows far above were dark, making them look like black voids in the world. The stairwell, lit by a few glass proximity spheres, rose up through a soaring tower to seemingly impossible heights above them, making Nicci feel as if she were at the very bottom of a very deep stone well.

The sounds of their footsteps echoed through the Keep, like the haunting whispers of those long-dead souls who had once walked these very halls, climbed these very steps, laughed and loved and lived in this place. At the top of the third run of stairs, Nicci, her legs aching with the frantic effort, led them into a broad passageway. As she ran past the warm reddish brown cherry pilasters separating expanses of brightly colored, leaded glass, she pointed ahead, letting Cara know that they would be turning at the next hallway to the right.

Finally into the network of smaller halls leading to the quarters where they had been staying, Nicci spotted Zedd in the distance, marching toward them. Rikka followed close on his heels. The old wizard, looking grim as he drew to a halt, waited for them to close the last bit of distance.

"What is it?" he asked, apparently knowing by the looks on their faces that something was awry.

"Where's Lord Rahl?" Rikka demanded as she came to an abrupt halt right behind him.

Nicci recognized the anxious look on her face. It was the same look that Cara had worn ever since she'd discovered that her Agiel didn't work. Nicci glanced down and saw that Rikka was gripping her Agiel in a white-knuckled fist, the same as Cara. Those talismans of their connection to the Lord Rahl were now dead.

"Where's my grandson?" Zedd asked, framing it in an anguished, personal tone. "Why isn't he with you?"

The last of it sounded like an accusation, as if reminding them of the warning Jebra had given them before they left, and of the promise Nicci had made.

"Zedd," Nicci began, "we can't say for sure."

The wizard cocked his head, his white hair sticking out in disarray. The look he gave her was very much that of a wizard taking charge of the disquieted man.

"Don't give me the runaround, child."

Had the situation not been so deadly serious, Nicci might have laughed at the characterization.

"We were all together in the sliph, returning to the Keep," Nicci told him, "and somewhere along the way—it's impossible to tell where you are while you're traveling—we were attacked by the beast."

Zedd glanced to Cara. "The beast."

Cara nodded confirmation.

"Then what?"

"I don't know." Nicci lifted her arms in frustration at trying to find the words to describe the experience. "We tried to fight it off. It had all these snakelike arms. We were grappling with it. I tried to use my Han against it—"

"In the sliph?"

"Yes, but it was of little or no help. I was trying everything I could think of. Then, the beast just ripped both Cara and me away from Richard. We couldn't find him in the darkness. We tried, but we couldn't find anything—not even each other. Like I said, it's impossible to tell where you are when you're in the sliph. You can't see, you can't really hear. It's a confusing kind of place and, try as we might, we just couldn't find Richard."

He was looking more angry by the moment. "Then why are you here, instead of in the sliph looking for him?"

"The sliph spit us out," Cara said. "We found ourselves here, back at the Keep. Nicci and I were each trying in our own way to find Lord Rahl, but . . . there was nothing. No Beast, no Lord Rahl. Then the sliph dumped us out here, at the place where we had all been headed when we were attacked."

"What are you doing up here, then?" he asked again in a menacing voice. "Why aren't you back in the sliph searching or, better yet, making the sliph tell you where he is?"

Nicci saw his hands fisted at his sides. She knew how he felt. She gently grasped his arm.

"Zedd, the sliph wouldn't tell us where he is. Believe me, we tried. It might be possible to get her to do so, I just don't know, but I think I know a better way—someone who might be able to tell us where Richard is: Jebra. I don't want to waste any more time, and I think Jebra might be able to provide an answer sooner than the sliph would."

Zedd pressed his thin lips tight as he considered. "It's worth a try," he said at last, "but you need to understand that the woman has been in quite a state since you left. She's been inconsolable at best and at times in the iron grip of something akin to hysteria. We've tried to calm her down, but to no avail. I'm afraid that, with all she's been through, it's all the more daunting for her to have to face the sudden return of her unique kind of visions. It's obviously difficult for her to come to grips with having them again, to say nothing of the nature of this particular one.

"We finally put her to bed, hoping that if she got some rest she would gain her strength back and be better able to sort out the confusion of her visions. At least she's not in a state like Queen Cyrilla; she's fighting not to allow herself to fall into that madness. She is aware that she needs to be able to help us, but at the moment her despair is simply overpowering her common sense. I'm sure, too, that her complete exhaustion is playing a role in her difficulty. We're hoping that after some rest she can add more to what she's already told us."

"And what has she said?" Nicci asked, hoping the answer might provide a clue.

Zedd studied her eyes a moment. "She said that you would come back without Richard."

Nicci stared at the man. "And what has become of him?"

Zedd's gaze fell away. "That's the part we're trying to get out of her."

"My Agiel has gone dead," Rikka said. "I can't feel the bond. I can't feel Lord Rahl. What if he's dead?"

Zedd turned a little and lifted a hand, as if urging her to calm down. "Let's not jump to conclusions. There could be any number of explanations."

Cara did not look at all cheered by his suggestion. "Such as?" she asked.

Zedd turned his hazel eyes toward her, studying the Mord-Sith for a moment as he considered his answer. "I don't know, Cara. I just don't know. I've been running every possibility through my mind ever since Jebra told me that he wouldn't return with you. There are any number of possibilities but at this moment scant evidence to go on. We will not leave a single rock unturned, I can promise you that."

Nicci swallowed back the lump rising in her throat. "Right now, our best chance is to see if we can find out from Jebra where Richard is. If we can get that much out of her then we can act. If we can act, then we have a chance to help him."

"If he's still alive," Rikka said.

Nicci gritted her teeth as she turned a glare on the woman. "He's alive."

Rikka swallowed. "I was just saying . . ."

"Nicci is right," Cara insisted. "This is Lord Rahl we're talking about. He's alive." A tear rolled down her cheek. "He's alive."

"Nonetheless," the wizard said in a pained voice, "we have to be prepared should the worst turn out to be true." When he saw the look on Cara's face, he offered a small smile. "Saying it out loud will not make it so. What is, is. I'm only saying that we must be prepared for any eventuality, that's all. It's the wise thing to do. It's what Richard himself would do if he lost one of us, and what he would want us to do should anything happen to him. Wouldn't you expect him to fight on if something happened to you? We simply cannot ignore the things we are facing. Richard would want us to fight on, to fight for ourselves."

Nicci thought, perhaps more than ever before, that she was hearing the First Wizard himself speaking. She could see where Richard got some of his remarkable resolve.

Cara glared at the man. "You're talking like he's dead. He's not."

Zedd offered her a smile and nodded his agreement. He was not able to make it look convincing.

"I need to talk to Jebra," Nicci said. "Right now that's the best place to start. What else has she had to say about her vision?"

Zedd sighed. "Not much. It's been years since she has had a vision and this one was not only a complete surprise but apparently overpoweringly appalling. I have begun to fear that the reason she hasn't had visions is because of what Richard had to say about magic failing. If so, then for this one to break through her failing ability speaks volumes. While she was conscious and during the periods when she's been coherent, her ability to grasp the entirety of her vision, the events in it seemed to have been fragmented and incomplete."

"Maybe we can help her to piece it together," Nicci said as gently as possible, despite how powerfully determined she was to make the woman do what was needed.

Zedd obviously didn't think it was going to do any good, but he apparently would rather invest his effort in the attempt than surrender to the unimaginable.

"This way," he said as he turned in a flourish and rushed off down the dimly lit hall.

At a rather small, round-topped door with intricate vines and overlapping leaves carved into the mahogany panels, Zedd, with Nicci and the two Mord-Sith flanking him, gently knocked. While he waited for an answer, he turned to Rikka.

"Go and get Nathan. Tell him it's urgent, and that he will need to pack. He is going to have to leave at once."

Nicci suspected what Zedd was going to ask Nathan to do, but she forced the thought from her mind. It would require her to think of the unthinkable.

She instead concentrated on the task at hand. She had to get Jebra to tell her where Richard was, tell her what was happening to him. If necessary, Nicci intended to use her gift to accomplish the task.

As Rikka raced off down the hall, Zedd rapped again, a little louder. When there was no response, he looked back over his shoulder at Nicci.

He fidgeted with the cuff of his simple robes. "Do you sense any-thing . . . odd?"

Nicci was so filled with frantic thoughts and emotions that she hadn't been paying any attention. They were in the Keep, after all. There were alarms everywhere that should protect them from any unwanted visitors.

She set aside her thoughts as her senses went into a heightened state of awareness.

"Now that you mention it, something does feel . . . odd."

"Odd like what?" Cara asked as she spun her Agiel back up into her hand. She looked startled for just an instant before realization cut off the surprise.

Nicci gently lifted the wizard's hand from the lever before he could open the door. "There isn't anyone in there with her, is there? Maybe Tom, or Friedrich?"

Zedd frowned at her. "Not that I know of. Those two are out on patrol. I was sitting with Jebra when I sensed you and Cara coming. She was asleep. I had wanted to be near if she awoke and was able to tell me any more about her vision. I left her and came to meet you, hoping to see that she had been wrong about Richard. Ann and Nathan have already gone to bed. I suppose it's possible that it could be one of them."

Nicci, her inner senses now fully alert, shook her head. "It's not either of them. Something else."

Zedd stared off as he puzzled at the question, the way one would listen for any sound, but Nicci knew that he wasn't exactly listening for a tell-tale sound. He was doing the same thing she was doing, using his gift to probe what they couldn't see or hear, to try to sense the presence of life. As far as Nicci could sense, though, there were only the three of them close by: her and Zedd and Cara, and more faintly on the other side of the door, Jebra.

But there was something else as well. The feeling, though, made no sense. It was a presence, but not the kind of sensation she would have were there another person lurking beyond the door.

It did seem, though, as if she might have had a very similar sensation just recently. She frowned, trying to remember.

"I have extra alarms set all over this area," Zedd told her.

Nicci nodded. "I know. I felt them."

"There isn't any way someone could have gotten past them. I would know. Bags, there's no way even a mouse could get by the snares I set."

"Could it be because of what Lord Rahl told us?" Cara asked in a low voice. "I mean, about there being something wrong with magic? Could it be that there's something wrong with your gift and that's why you feel what you feel?"

Zedd gave the woman a sour look. "You mean you think our gift is . . . is what? Scrambled?"

Cara shrugged and then added to the idea. "I don't know much about magic, but maybe that's what's wrong with my Agiel. Maybe that's all it is. Lord Rahl was pretty insistent that he knew that magic was corrupted. Maybe your gifted senses are corrupted in that same way. Maybe the conclusion I was jumping to is all wrong. Maybe that's why—the corruption."

Zedd huffed, scoffing at the idea. He lifted an arm to the side and the oil lamps on the tables flanking the door went dark. "Well, that much of my power works, so that means it works," he whispered. He laid a hand back on the lever as he gave Nicci a resolute look. "Be ready for anything."

"Wait," Nicci said.

Zedd looked back over his shoulder. His features were hard to see in the dim light, but his eyes were not. She saw in them some of Richard's eyes.

"What is it?" he asked.

"I just remembered something I've been trying to figure out."

Nicci steepled her fingers as she hurriedly tried to recall the details. She finally shook a finger as she spoke. "When the beast attacked us while we were traveling, I felt an odd sensation. I discounted it because being in the sliph is so strange to begin with that it's hard to tell if anything you're feeling is important, much less really out of the ordinary. Everyday sensations can seem wondrous—even miraculous. You don't know if it's all just the culmination of all the unfamiliar perceptions or something more."

"Exactly when did you have this feeling?" Zedd asked, suddenly acutely interested in what she had to say. "All the time you were traveling, or at one specific time?"

"No, like I said, it was after the beast attacked us."

"Be more specific. Think. Was it when the beast attacked? Maybe when it grabbed Richard? Or when it grabbed you?"

Nicci pressed her fingertips to her temples as she squeezed her eyes shut, desperately trying to recall it accurately. "No . . . no, it was after I was pulled away from Richard. Not immediately after, but shortly."

"What was the sequence in which these events took place?"

"The beast attacked. We were fighting it. I tried to use my gift but it didn't help. The beast was hurting me. Richard used his knife to cut away some of the tentacles. He saved me from being crushed.

"Then the beast pulled Cara away from him. Not long after that it pulled me away from him as well. It was then, after that—not immediately after, but it was only a short time later. I know because it was when I was frantically searching for Richard that I felt the odd sensation."

Nicci looked up at the wizard. "The thing is, right after I felt that sensation, I could no longer sense the presence of the beast. I searched, trying to find Richard, but couldn't. As the sliph swept us back to the Keep the feeling swiftly faded and I forgot all about it."

"What did it feel like—this sensation?"

Nicci gestured. "It felt exactly the same as what is beyond that door."

Zedd stared at her for a long moment. "What is beyond feels the same? A kind of . . . humming flow of power?"

Nicci nodded. "A charge of magic that somehow is baseless."

"Magic frequently seems to be free-floating," Cara said. "What's so odd about that?"

Zedd shook his head. "Magic isn't something that just floats around by itself. Magic has no consciousness, but this feeling in some way mimics that kind of conscious intent."

"Yes," Nicci said. "That's my sense of it. That's why it feels so odd, because magic with this kind of bearing cannot be baseless. This is domination generating its characteristic controlling fields of presence, but without the life necessary to generate it."

Zedd straightened. "That's a very good description of what I feel." He peered suspiciously at the door. "I think that if we get closer we might be able to sense it better and find out what it is. If we can get close enough, perhaps we can analyze it." He gave them both a look. "Let's be careful, shall we?"

The three of them huddled close in the dim hallway as the wizard carefully turned the lever and slowly pushed open the door. Nicci sensed no more with the door partly opened than she had with it closed. Zedd stuck his head inside for a moment, then pushed the door the rest of the way open. The room was dark, with only the dim light from the hall revealing shapes and shadows of what was inside.

At the far wall on their left Nicci could see an empty chair with a comforter folded neatly and draped over the back. Not too far from the doorway on the same side of the room sat a short, round table with a lamp that wasn't lit. Beyond the table the bed lay empty. The rumpled sheets had been pushed off the side of the bed and puddled on the floor. Nicci peered around along with Zedd and Cara but she didn't see Jebra. If she was somewhere else in the room it was too dark to spot her. With the odd sensation even stronger inside the room, Nicci's inner perception wasn't much help.

Zedd sent a flicker of his Han into the lamp. The wick was turned low, so the light wasn't strong enough to chase the heavy shadows from the corners, or the far side of the wardrobe on the other side of the room. Still, there was no sign of Jebra.

Nicci, detached from her emotions and focused instead on perception governed by her Han, stepped past Zedd to stand tense and still in the center of the room, listening. With her gift she tried to open herself to the sensation of another presence lurking in the darkness, but she felt none.

A faint breeze rustled the curtains. The double doors, made of small glass panes, both stood open to a small balcony. Nicci knew from the balcony in her own room nearby that this balcony also overlooked the dark city far below at the base of the mountain.

Atop the balcony railing, a dark silhouette blotted out the moonlit countryside beyond.

Behind Nicci, Zedd turned up the wick on the oil lamp. When the light came up, Nicci saw that it was Jebra out on that balcony. Her back toward them, she was standing barefoot atop the fat stone railing.

"Dear spirits," Cara whispered, "she's going to jump."

The three of them stood frozen, fearing to do anything that might startle the woman and cause her to jump before they could reach her. She didn't seem to know yet that they were there.

"Jebra," Zedd said in a soft, cautious voice, "we've come to see you."

If Jebra heard him, she didn't show any reaction. Nicci didn't think that Jebra heard anything, though, except the haunting whisper of magic.

Nicci could feel the faint waves of that alien power rushing past her, humming toward the seer standing like a stone statue on the railing of the balcony. She stared out over the city of Aydindril far below. A gentle breeze ruffled her short hair.

The balcony, Nicci knew, while facing the valley below, was not right out over the edge of the Keep. Still, Jebra was confronting a drop of hundreds of feet to one of the inner courtyards, walkways, ramparts, or slate roofs of the Keep. At this height it didn't matter that she wouldn't be falling down the mountain were she to fall or jump; she would just as surely be killed against the stone of the Keep far below.

"Stars," Jebra said in a low, thin voice to the empty space before her.

Zedd seized Nicci's arm and pulled her close. He put his mouth by her ear. "I think someone is seeking the same answers we are. I think someone is probing her mind. That's what we feel. It's a thief, a thief of thoughts."

"Jagang," Cara breathed.

Nicci knew that that would be the logical assumption. With the bond to Richard somehow broken, Jagang could in theory do such a thing. Without Richard filling the role of the Lord Rahl, all of them were suddenly vulnerable to the dream walker.

A sickening ripple of icy dread coursed through Nicci at the memory of Jagang possessing her mind, her will. Without the Lord Rahl, the bond protecting them all was broken. If the emperor was riding the night he very well might discover them unprotected. The dream walker could, at any moment, without warning, drift unseen, unfelt, right into their minds and invest himself in their thoughts.

But Nicci knew Jagang. She knew what it was like when he possessed a person's mind. He had at one time, after all, possessed her mind, controlled her, ruled her through that terrible presence. This was different.

"No," she said, "it's not Jagang. What I sense is something else."

"How do you know for sure?" Zedd whispered.

Nicci finally took her gaze off of Jebra and looked at the frowning wizard.

"Well, for one thing," she whispered back, "if it was Jagang, you would sense nothing. The dream walker leaves no trace. There is no way to tell he is there. This is entirely different."

Zedd rubbed his clean-shaven chin. "It still seems somehow familiar," he murmured to himself.

"Stars," Jebra said again to the night beyond the balcony.

Zedd started for the open doorway through the double doors, but Nicci seized his arm and held him back. "Wait," she whispered.

"Stars fallen to ground," Jebra said in a haunting voice.

Zedd and Nicci shared a look.

"Stars among the grass," Jebra said in that same dead voice.

Zedd stiffened. "Dear spirits. I recognize it now."

Nicci leaned closer. "The presence?"

The wizard nodded slowly. "That's the feeling of a witch woman plying her power."

Jebra lifted her arms to the side.

"She's going to jump!" Nicci shouted as Jebra began to topple forward out into the night.

Richard coughed violently.

The pain of the involuntary upheaval jolted him to consciousness. He heard himself trying unsuccessfully to groan. He had no breath with which to make a groan. With consciousness came a growing, confused panic of suffocation, as if he were somehow drowning.

He coughed again, wincing in pain as he did so. He tried to cry out in agony as he curled up into a ball on the ground, arms pressed tight across his middle, trying to prevent another fit of convulsive coughing.

"Breathe."

Richard regarded the haunting voice that seemingly came from some netherworld place as the voice of insanity. He was doing everything he could *not* to breathe. He took careful, shallow, thimbleful breaths, trying to prevent another racking bout of coughing.

"Breathe."

He didn't know where he was and at the moment he didn't really care. All that mattered was the feeling of suffocating. He didn't want to breathe, despite how desperately he needed a breath. That sensation was so oppressive, so sickening, that in his mind it was not only completely debilitating, but all-powerful. Dying seemed preferable to the feeling continuing. He couldn't endure it continuing.

Richard didn't want to move because, with each passing moment, it was becoming easier not to breathe. It seemed that if he could just manage to keep from breathing a little longer, then over the crest of that dark hill out there somewhere ahead of him the pain and suffering would lift. He fought to lie perfectly still, hoping the spinning world would stop before he vomited. He could not imagine how much that would hurt. If he could just lie still a little longer, then it would all become easier. If he could just lie still a little longer, then it would all go away.

"Breathe."

He ignored the distant, silken voice. His mind drifted to a time in the past when he had hurt this much. It had been when Denna had him chained and helpless, when she had him at her mercy, when she hurt him until he was delirious from being tortured.

Denna had taught him to endure pain, though. He envisioned her standing there, watching him, waiting to see if would tip over the edge into death. There had been times with her when he had reached the crest of that distant, dark hill, and started down the other side.

When that happened Denna would be right there to put her mouth over his, forcefully breathing her life into him. She had not only controlled his life, she had controlled his death. She had taken everything. Not even his own death belonged to him; it belonged to her.

She watched him now. Her silver face came close, waiting to see what he would do. He wondered if he would be granted death, or if she would again put her mouth over his and . . .

"*Breathe.*"

Richard puzzled at her. Denna didn't look at all like a silver statue.

"You must breathe," the silken voice told him. "If you do not, you will die."

Richard blinked at the beautiful face softly lit by the cold moonlight. He tried to pull a little more air into his lungs.

He squeezed his eyes shut. "Hurts," he whispered with the entirety of that shallow breath.

"You must. It is life."

Life. Richard didn't know if he wanted life. He was so tired, so exhausted. Death seemed so inviting. No more struggle. No more pain. No more despair. No more loneliness. No more tears. No more agony of missing Kahlan.

Kahlan.

"*Breathe.*"

If he died, who would help her?

He drew a deeper breath, forcing it past the scalding agony it pulled down into his lungs. He thought of Kahlan's smile, instead of the pain.

He drew another breath. Deeper yet.

A silver hand gently glided over the back of his shoulder, as if to comfort him in his agony of struggling to hold on to life. The face looked sadly sympathetic as it watched his struggle.

"*Breathe.*"

Richard nodded as he tightened his fists and gasped in the cold fire of the night air.

He coughed up thin red fluid and clots of blood that tasted metallic. He pulled in another breath, giving him the power to cough out more of the liquid burning his lungs. For a time he lay on his side, alternating between gasping in air and coughing out fluid.

When he was breathing again, if raggedly, he flopped onto his back, hoping to make the spinning stop. He closed his eyes, but that only made it worse, adding a kind of tilting, rolling movement to the spinning. His stomach roiled, on the brink of upheaval.

He opened his eyes and in the darkness stared up at the leaves above him. He saw mostly maple leaves in the canopy of tree limbs above him. Looking at leaves—talismans of the familiar—felt good. In the moonlight, he saw other kinds of trees as well. To take his mind off the pain and nausea, he made himself identify all the trees that he could make out. There were a smattering of heart-shaped linden leaves and, towering farther above, a bough or two of what looked to be white pine. There were some clusters of oak in the distance to the sides, along with spruce and balsam. Close by, though, there were mostly maples. With every breath of breeze he could hear the distinctive, soft rattle of cottonwood leaves.

Beside the pain associated with the difficulty of breathing, Richard clearly recognized that there was something wrong within himself. Something far more basic, more elemental.

It wasn't an injury, in the conventional sense, but he knew that there was something dreadfully wrong. He tried to identify the perception, but he couldn't pinpoint it. It was a hollow, empty, desolate feeling unrelated to the familiar emotions of his life, things like his need to find Kahlan, or what he had done with setting the D'Haran army loose on the Old World. He considered the troubling things Shota had told him, but that wasn't it, either.

It was more a sense of a disturbing void within himself that he knew he had never felt before. That's why he had so much trouble identifying it: it was a completely unfamiliar condition. There had been something there, some sense of himself, that he realized he had never thought about, never identified as a distinct element, a discrete part of his makeup, that was now missing.

Richard felt as if he was no longer himself.

The story Shota had told him of Baraccus and the book he had written, *Secrets of a War Wizard's Power,* came to mind. Richard wondered if his inner voice was trying to suggest that such a book might help him in just such a situation. He had to admit that the problem did feel connected in some way to his gift.

Thinking about that book caused his mind to wander to what Shota had told him about his mother, that she had not died alone in that fire. Zedd was insistent that he'd looked through the charred remains of the house and he had found no other bones. How could that be? Either Zedd or Shota had to be wrong. For some reason, he could not believe that either of them were.

Somewhere deep in the back of his mind the answer ticked at him. Try as he might, though, he could not coax it out.

Richard felt a pang of loneliness for his mother, a feeling that had visited him from time to time throughout his life. He wondered what she would have to say about all that had happened to him. She'd never had a chance to see him grow up, to see him as a man. She'd only known him as a boy.

He knew his mother would love Kahlan. She would be so happy for him, so proud to have a daughter-in-law like Kahlan. She always wanted him to have a good life. There could be no better life than a life with Kahlan.

But he no longer had a life with Kahlan.

He guessed that he had life and, all things considered, that was about as much as could be expected at the moment. At least he could work toward his dreams. Dead men had no dreams.

Richard lay on his back, letting the air saturate his burning muscles, letting himself regain his senses, his composure. He was so weak he could hardly move, so he didn't try to. Instead, as long as he was lying there recovering, he focused on everything that had happened, trying to put it all back together in his mind.

He had been traveling back to the Keep with Nicci and Cara when they had been attacked. It had been the beast. He had sensed its aura of evil. It appeared in a form different from any he had ever seen before, but it was the beast's nature to assume different forms. The only thing he could count on to be consistent was that the beast would continue to come after him until it killed him.

He remembered fighting it. His hand went to a place on his leg where one of the tentacles had squeezed until he thought his leg would be stripped of flesh. His thigh was swollen and painful to the touch but, fortunately, not torn open. He remembered slicing through some of the creature's arms. He remembered Nicci trying to use her power, and wishing that she would stop because it was somehow conducting right through the sliph so that some of the power she had unleashed against the beast had ripped through him. He suspected that were it not for the substance of the sliph, Nicci's magic could have killed him. It certainly didn't harm the beast—at least, not enough to slow it down. It, too, must have been insulated, at least to some extent, by the sliph.

He remembered Cara being pulled away from him. He remembered Nicci likewise being violently separated from him. He remembered the beast trying to rip him apart. And he remembered managing to abruptly break free.

But then something had happened that he did not understand.

While he was separated from the beast, he had been jolted by an unfamiliar, painful sensation that ripped right down into the core of his being. It had been distinctly different from the pain caused by Nicci's power—or that of any magic he had ever felt.

Magic.

Once he had formed the thought, he realized that he was right; it had been magic of some sort.

Even if it was the touch of a kind of conjuring completely unlike anything he had ever felt, he recognized that it had been the touch of magic. Even though he'd been free of the beast—he hadn't even known where the beast was at that particular moment—that was when everything had suddenly changed.

As he'd gasped in pain from the abrupt assault of the strange charge of power, the sliph's essence again filled his lungs. That breath had brought a shock of panic.

Richard remembered a similar feeling when he had been young. He'd been with several other boys, diving down to the bottom of a pond in a contest to retrieve pebbles. Their afternoon of swimming and diving from branches overhanging the small but deep pond had churned up the muddy bottom. Under the murky water, while diving for pebbles, Richard lost his sense of direction. He was out of air when he bumped his head on a thick branch. Being disoriented, he thought that bumping into the low branch meant that he'd broken the surface and run into one of the low-lying limbs hanging out over the edge of the pond. He hadn't. It had been a sub-merged branch. Before realizing what he had really done, he breathed in some of the muddy water.

He'd been close to the surface, to the shore, and to his friends. It had been a terrifying experience, but it had ended quickly and he'd recovered soon enough, learning a lesson to have more respect for water.

That memory of breathing in water as a boy, in addition to the natural unwillingness to inhale water, had made it all the more difficult to breathe in the sliph the first time. He overcame that fear, though, and it turned out to be a rapturous experience.

But in the sliph, when he suddenly found himself drowning, there was no surface, no shore, no help at hand. Such a thing had never happened in the sliph before. There had been no way for him to escape, no way to get to the surface, and no one to help him.

Richard looked over in the moonlight. The sliph was close by, watching him. He realized that she was not in a well, the way he had always seen her before. They were on the ground in a sparsely wooded place. He could hear no sounds but the sounds of nature. He could detect nothing but for-est smells.

Beneath leaves, pine needles, forest debris, and roots Richard felt a rough stone floor. The grout joints were fat, more than a finger wide. These were not tight joints like those in finely crafted palaces, but they were with-out a doubt man-made.

And the silver face of the sliph, rather than looking out from within her well, had risen slightly from a rather small and irregular opening in the ancient stone floor. Ragged pieces from that stone floor now lay about on top of the dried leaves and rubble of branches, as if they had just been bro-ken open from underneath—as if the sliph has broken up through them.

Richard sat up. "Sliph, are you all right?"

"Yes, Master."

"Do you know what happened? It felt like I was drowning."

"You were."

Richard stared at the face in the moonlight. "But how can that be? What went wrong?"

A silver hand reached up from the ground to trail quicksilver fingers across his brow, testing him.

"You do not have the required magic to travel."

Richard blinked in confusion. "I don't understand. I've traveled many times before."

"Before you had what was required."

"And now I don't?"

The sliph watched him a moment. "Now you do not," she confirmed.

Richard felt like he must be hallucinating. "But I have both sides of the gift. I can travel."

The sliph cautiously reached out and again felt his face. The hand slipped down to his chest, pausing for a moment to put light pressure against him. Her arm drew back into the dark hole in the broken stone.

"You do not have the required magic."

"You already said that. It makes no sense. I was already traveling."

"While you were traveling, you lost what is required."

Richard's eyes widened. "You mean to say that I lost one side of the gift?"

"No, I mean to say that you do not have the gift. You have no magic at all. You may not travel."

Richard had to run the words through his head again to be sure he'd heard correctly. He didn't see how he could have mistaken what the sliph had said. His mind raced through fragments of jumbled thoughts as he tried to grasp how such a thing was possible.

A terrible realization came to him. Could it be that the corruption caused by the chimes might be responsible? Had that corruption finally caught up with him and undone his gift? Rotted it away without his knowing it until it had finally failed?

But that would not explain the sensation he'd felt back in the sliph, just after he'd escaped the grip of the beast and just before he'd started drowning—the sudden sensation of some dark and furtive magic reaching out when he was most vulnerable and touching him.

Richard looked around but saw nothing other than the trees. They were dense enough that he couldn't see beyond them in the moonlight. As a guide, he hated the feeling of not knowing where he was.

"Where are we, anyway? How did we get here?"

"When it happened, when you lost what is needed to travel, I had to bring you here."

"And where is 'here'?"

"I am sorry but I don't know, exactly."

Master. They are safe. I took them to the Keep, where they had
to travel. They had what was required to travel."

nd you told them where I was. You told them what had happened."
e looked surprised by what had sounded more like a mandate than a
stion. "No, Master. I would never reveal what I do with another."

"Oh, great," he muttered. He worked to keep his exasperation in check.
ut you've told me about others."

"You are my master. I do things with you that I would not do with anyone else."

"Sliph, they are my friends. They're probably frantic with worry for
me. You must tell them what they need to know."

The silver head tilted toward him. "Master, I cannot betray you. I
would not."

"It's not a betrayal. I'm telling you that it's all right to tell them what
happened."

The sliph looked like she thought this was just about the strangest request she had ever had. "Master, you wish me to tell others about us, about
what we do when we are together?"

"Sliph, try to understand. You are no longer a whore."

"But people use me for their pleasure."

"It's not the same thing." Richard raked his fingers back through his
hair, trying not to sound angry. "Listen, wizards in ancient times changed
you from who you were, from what you were."

The sliph nodded solemnly. "I know, Master. I remember. I was the one
it happened to, after all."

"You're different now. It's not the same. You can't equate the two
things. They're different."

"I have been given a duty to serve others in this capacity. My nature is
still within me."

"But there are some of us who use you who greatly value your help."

"I have always been valued for what I do."

"This is different from what you did before." Richard didn't want to be
having this argument. He had more important matters to worry about.
"Sliph, when you travel with us you are often helping to save lives. When
you traveled with us to the People's Palace, you were helping me to end
the war. You are doing a good thing."

"If you say so, Master. But you must understand that those who created

"How can you bring me here, and not know where you are? You always
know where you are and the places to which you can travel."

"I already told you, I have never been to this place before. This place is
an emergency passage. I knew of it, of course, but I have never been here
before. There has never been an emergency within me before."

"That terrible beast hurt me. I was struggling to keep all of you alive.
And then, there was something else that came within me. I could not stop
it. Like the beast, it entered me without my permission. It violated me."

That confirmed Richard's sense of events, that just after the beast lost
its grip on him, something else, some kind of power, had reached out and
touched him with its dominion.

"I'm sorry that you were hurt, sliph. What happened to the beast?"

"After this other power came into me, the beast became no more."

"You mean that this other power destroyed it?"

"No. The power did not touch the beast. It touched only you with its full
force. After it did, then you no longer had what is required to travel. After
that, the beast cast around in me for a brief time, and then vanished. I
could no longer sustain you within me, so I had to find the nearest emergency portal."

"What about Nicci and Cara? Were they hurt? Are they safe?"

"They, too, felt the pain of what happened to me, and one of them tried
to use her power in me—something that is wrong to do. After I brought
you here, I took them to the Keep where they had wished to travel. I told
the one that used her power that it was dangerous to do so, and she must
not do such a thing."

"I think I understand," Richard said. "It hurt me, too. Were they hurt
badly?"

"They are safe at the Keep."

"Then we must be somewhere between the People's Palace and the
Keep," Richard said, half to himself.

"No."

He looked over at the liquid silver face. "I don't understand. We were going from the palace to the Keep. If you let me out, then this place here, this
emergency passage out, would have to be between the palace and the Keep."

"While I don't know this place, I do know its general area. We are at a
place a little more than halfway across the Midlands from the Keep, past
Agaden Reach, almost to the wilds."

Richard felt as if the world had just lurched and slid him far from where he had been. "But, but, that's much, much farther from the People's Palace than the Keep is. Why didn't you take me to the closest place—to the Keep?"

"I do not function in that way. What to you may seem like the shortest distance between two places is not the shortest way for me. I am in many places at once."

Richard leaned toward the sliph. "How can you be in many places at once?"

"You have one foot on that dark stone, and one on a stone that is lighter. You are in two places at once."

Richard sighed. "I guess I get your point."

"I travel in a way that is different from your way of traveling. This place, here, even though it is halfway across the Midlands for you, was the closest place for me. I had to get you out into your world again so that you could breathe.

"You no longer had what was needed to travel. Your lungs were filled with me. For those without the gift, breathing me is poison. It will kill them. But for you, since you were in me and breathing me already, there was a brief period when you were going through a transition, so having me in you was not instantly fatal. You would have died soon, but there was a brief time before that would happen. I knew that the time you had before you would die was not very long at all. I thought to do my best to save you, to get you to a place where you could be back in your world and hopefully recover.

"I brought you here, broke the seal, and placed you out in your world again. You were hurt, but I knew that the essence of me still within you would help sustain your life for a short time."

"If I could no longer travel, because I don't have the required gift, then what made you think that?"

"I was made to have properties to assist in emergencies. Those properties are within me—and thereby they were within you. They help to start the process of recovering. It is only intended for a crisis and even then I was warned that it could not be certain that it would work because there are variables that cannot be controlled.

"While you slept between worlds, and my magic that you still had within you was working to extract what had now become poison to you, I

finished taking the others to the Keep. Wh. until you were recovered enough to be re helped to remind you what you must to do to ι.

"For a time I did not know if it would work. I ι a thing before. It was terrible to have to wait whι there, not knowing if you would ever again breathe failed you, and that I would be the cause of your death.

Richard stared at the silver face for a long moment. F. her a smile. "Thank you, sliph. You saved my life. You did t. You did good."

"You are my master. I would do anything for you."

"Your master. A master who can't travel."

"It is as puzzling to me as it is to you."

Richard tried to think it through, tried to make sense of it, but with pain of breathing after nearly drowning in the sliph still feeling like it w. pressing heavily on his chest, he was having trouble making his mind fo- cus on thinking.

Richard rested his forearms across his knees. "I don't suppose there is any way for you to take me back to the Keep?"

"Yes, Master. If you wish to travel, I can take you."

Richard sat up straighter. "You can? How?"

"You must simply acquire the required magic, and then I can take you again. Then we will travel. You will be pleased."

Acquire the required magic. He didn't even know how to use the magic he had—or used to have. He couldn't imagine what had happened to his gift, and he had absolutely no idea how to get it back. There had been any number of times he'd wanted to be rid if it, but now that it had actually happened all he could think about was getting it back.

When his gift had failed, the beast had apparently lost him in the sliph. As consolation to losing his gift, it seemed the beast would be one less prob- lem he had to face at the moment—his gift, after all, had been the mecha- nism by which the beast was keyed to him, the way in which it hunted him. There was supposed to be balance in magic; perhaps that was the balance to losing it.

Richard raked his fingers back through his hair. "At least Nicci and Cara made it through and are safe." He looked up at the sliph. "You're sure that they're all right?"

me made me the way I am. They used what I once was to create me as I am now. I can be no way other than the way I am. I cannot wish myself to be different, any more than you can travel now simply by wishing it."

Richard sighed. "I suppose not."

With one hand he snapped dry twigs in half as he thought it over. He shared a long look with the beautiful face watching him, hanging on his every word. Finally, he spoke softly.

"There are times when there is no other way, and you must trust others. This is one of those times."

Something about his words clearly struck home. The beautiful, liquid face came a little closer.

"You are the one," the sliph whispered.

"The one? Which one?"

"The one Baraccus told me would come."

The hair on the back of Richard's neck stood on end.

"You knew Baraccus?"

"He was once my master, like you are, now."

"Of course," Richard whispered to himself. "He was First Wizard."

"He is the one who insisted that I possess the emergency elements I told you about. He also directed that there be this emergency portal. Had he not done those things, you would have died. He was very wise."

"Very wise," Richard agreed as he stared wide-eyed at the sliph. "You said that Baraccus told you something about one who would come?"

The sliph nodded. "He was kind to me. His wife hated me, but Baraccus was kind to me."

"You knew his wife, too?"

"Magda."

"Why would she hate you?"

"Because Baraccus was kind to me. And because I took him away from her."

"You mean, you took him away when he wished to travel."

"Of course. When I would tell him that he would be pleased, she would fold her arms and glare at me."

Richard smiled a little. "She was jealous."

"She loved him and did not want him to leave her. When I would return with him after we traveled, she would often be there, waiting for him. He would always smile when he saw her, and she would smile in turn."

"And what was it that Baraccus said about me?"

"He told me the same thing that you just did, that there are times when there is no other way, and you must trust others. Those were his words, just as they were yours. He said that one day another master would say those exact same words, and then add exactly the same words you did: 'This is one of those times.'

"He told me that if a master ever said these words, that meant that they were the right one and I was to tell them some things."

Richard could feel every hair on his arms stand on end.

"You took Magda Searus somewhere, didn't you?"

"Yes, Master. After that I never saw Baraccus again. But before, when he told me that someday someone would say those words, he told me to tell them his message."

"He left a message?" When she nodded, he rolled his hand. "So what is it?"

" 'I am sorry. I don't know the answers that would save you. If I did, please believe that I would give them eagerly. But I know the good in you. I believe in you. I do know that you have within you what you must to succeed. There will be times when you doubt yourself. Do not give up. Remember then that I believe in you, that I know you can accomplish what you must. You are a rare person. Believe in yourself.

" 'Know that I believe you are the one who can do it.' "

Richard sat frozen. The words echoed around in his head. They were oddly familiar.

"I've heard almost those exact words before."

The sliph glided a little closer, her features tightening. "You have?"

Richard concentrated as he ran the words through his mind again, trying to recall . . .

And then he did. It was right after Shota had told him about Baraccus. Just before she left, she'd said those very words to him. There was something about those words, spoken by Shota, that had aroused an indistinct memory.

"It was Shota, the witch woman," Richard said as he frowned in recollection. "She told me those words."

The sliph retreated. "I am sorry, Master. You have failed the test."

Richard looked up at her. "What test?"

"The test Baraccus just gave you. I am sorry, but you have failed his test. I can tell you nothing more."

Without further word, the sliph abruptly vanished into the black hole in the stone.

Richard threw himself down on his stomach, leaning down into the hole. "No! Wait! Don't leave!"

His own voice echoed up out of the empty, black shaft.

The sliph was gone. Without his gift, he had no way to call her back.

Nicci heard a soft knock at the door. Zedd looked up but he didn't stand. Cara, hands clasped behind her back, gazing out the window, looked back over her shoulder. Nicci, standing closest to the door, pulled it open. The small flame in the lamp on the table was not up to the task of chasing the gloom from the room, but it cast what warm light it could across the face of the tall prophet.

"What's going on?" Nathan asked in his deep voice. He cast a suspicious look around at those in the room. "Rikka wouldn't say much other than that you and Cara were back and Zedd wanted to see me immediately."

"That's right," Zedd said. "Come in, please."

Nathan glanced around the somber room as he strode in. "Where's Richard."

Nicci swallowed. "He didn't make it back with us."

"Didn't make it back?" He paused to take in the bleak look on Nicci's face. "Dear spirits . . ."

Zedd, sitting at Jebra's side at the bed, didn't look up. Jebra was unconscious. When they tried to close her eyes her lids would pop open again. They finally quit trying and let her stare up at the ceiling.

Zedd had already tended to her broken leg as best he could. She was very fortunate that Cara was not only quick but strong, and that she had been able to catch Jebra's ankle just in time as her dead weight had toppled outward from the balcony. Still, her momentum had whipped the seer down around and under the balcony, where her leg smacked a support strut that broke her leg. Nicci suspected that the woman had been unconscious the moment she started falling.

It had been a bad break. Zedd had set to work immediately on her injury, but because of the unusual state Jebra was in he had not been able to heal the break. All he had been able to do was set it, splint it, and add enough of his gift to help it begin to mend. When she finally awoke he would be able to finish the healing. If she awoke. Nicci had her doubts.

Nicci knew that Jebra's broken leg was the least of the woman's problems. Despite everything they had tried, they had been unable to arouse her from her catatonic state. Zedd had tried. Nicci had tried. She had even tried dangerous conjuring involving Subtractive Magic. Zedd had been against it at first, but when Nicci confronted him with the stark nature of their choices he grudgingly agreed.

Unfortunately, even that hadn't helped. Jebra's mind was locked away from them. Whatever magic the witch woman had used on her was something they were unable to break. Whatever had been done didn't appear to Nicci to be intended to be reversible. If they knew its nature perhaps they might stand a chance of breaking the spell, but they didn't know its makeup.

Nathan bent and touched two fingers to the unconscious woman's temple. He straightened and helplessly shook his head at Zedd's questioning expression.

Nicci had never seen anything like it. Zedd, on the other hand, had in the beginning rubbed his chin as he brooded. He'd muttered that there was something oddly familiar about its nature. What, he couldn't say. Despite how insistent Nicci had been, and despite his own desperate desire to do something, Zedd was at his wits' end that he could not pinpoint why he felt that he had seen some aspect of such conjuring before.

He was, after all, he had reminded them, the First Wizard, and he had spent a good portion of his life studying such things. He believed that he should be able to identify what kind of web had been spun around the woman. Nicci knew that if Jebra had been conscious it would have made the job a great deal easier, but Zedd wasn't willing to use an excuse for his own failure to identify what the conjuring involved.

Nicci heard a commotion out in the hallway. Nathan stuck his head out the doorway for a look.

"What is it?" a voice in the distance called out. It was Ann, rushing up the hall, escorted by Rikka. She finally reached the door. "What's going on?"

As she came into the room, laboring to catch her breath, Nathan laid a big hand on her shoulder. "Something has happened to Richard."

Strands of gray hair stuck out from the loose bun at the back of her head like a plume of ruffled feathers. Her calculating gaze swept over those in the room, assessing the degree of seriousness she saw in each of them. It was the kind of swift, lean evaluation Nicci associated with Ann.

As the Prelate of the Sisters of the Light, she had always had a commanding presence that could strike fear into just about anyone, from high-ranking Sister to stableboys. Even though Nicci was no longer a Sister of the Light, her guard always went up whenever the former prelate came into the room. The woman's short stature in no way diminished the air of looming menace that seemed to surround her.

Ann turned an intent look up at Nathan. "What happened? Is the boy hurt—"

"I don't know, yet," Nathan said, holding up a hand to forestall a flood of questions before they could landslide in on him. "Let the woman explain."

"All we know for sure," Nicci said when Ann turned a hot glare on her, "is that while we were traveling in the sliph back here from the People's Palace, the beast attacked us. Cara and I tried to help Richard fight it off, then we were separated from him. As soon as that happened I felt some kind of extrinsic magic. Next thing we knew, Cara and I were back at the Keep. Richard wasn't with us. We have no idea what happened to him after he was touched by the strange power I sensed. We never saw the beast again, either.

"After we got back here, Jebra was attacked by a web that I could discern had been cast by the same person who cast the power that touched Richard in the sliph. Because Zedd recognized its unique composition, we know now that it was power conjured by a witch woman."

"And my Agiel doesn't work," Cara said, holding the weapon up. "Our bond to Lord Rahl is broken. We can no longer sense him."

"Dear Creator," Ann whispered as her gaze dropped away.

Zedd gestured to the woman lying in the bed before him. "Whatever power it is that this witch woman cast, it left Jebra unconscious. We can't rouse her. Although I know that it was a witch woman's spell that somehow took her, I can't figure out how a witch woman could do such a thing—cast such webs from afar. From my experience they not only keep to themselves but can't accomplish things of this nature. It's beyond their ability."

"Are you are certain that it was a witch woman?" Ann asked.

Zedd took a deep breath as he considered the question seriously. "I've had dealings with a witch woman before. Once a cat has had its claws in

"How can you bring me here, and not know where you are? You always know where you are and the places to which you can travel."

"I already told you, I have never been to this place before. This place is an emergency passage. I knew of it, of course, but I have never been here before. There has never been an emergency within me before.

"That terrible beast hurt me. I was struggling to keep all of you alive. And then, there was something else that came within me. I could not stop it. Like the beast, it entered me without my permission. It violated me."

That confirmed Richard's sense of events, that just after the beast lost its grip on him, something else, some kind of power, had reached out and touched him with its dominion.

"I'm sorry that you were hurt, sliph. What happened to the beast?"

"After this other power came into me, the beast became no more."

"You mean that this other power destroyed it?"

"No. The power did not touch the beast. It touched only you with its full force. After it did, then you no longer had what is required to travel. After that, the beast cast around in me for a brief time, and then vanished. I could no longer sustain you within me, so I had to find the nearest emergency portal."

"What about Nicci and Cara? Were they hurt? Are they safe?"

"They, too, felt the pain of what happened to me, and one of them tried to use her power in me—something that is wrong to do. After I brought you here, I took them to the Keep where they had wished to travel. I told the one that used her power that it was dangerous to do so, and she must not do such a thing."

"I think I understand," Richard said. "It hurt me, too. Were they hurt badly?"

"They are safe at the Keep."

"Then we must be somewhere between the People's Palace and the Keep," Richard said, half to himself.

"No."

He looked over at the liquid silver face. "I don't understand. We were going from the palace to the Keep. If you let me out, then this place here, this emergency passage out, would have to be between the palace and the Keep."

"While I don't know this place, I do know its general area. We are at a place a little more than halfway across the Midlands from the Keep, past Agaden Reach, almost to the wilds."

Richard felt as if the world had just lurched and slid him far from where he had been. "But, but, that's much, much farther from the People's Palace than the Keep is. Why didn't you take me to the closest place—to the Keep?"

"I do not function in that way. What to you may seem like the shortest distance between two places is not the shortest way for me. I am in many places at once."

Richard leaned toward the sliph. "How can you be in many places at once?"

"You have one foot on that dark stone, and one on a stone that is lighter. You are in two places at once."

Richard sighed. "I guess I get your point."

"I travel in a way that is different from your way of traveling. This place, here, even though it is halfway across the Midlands for you, was the closest place for me. I had to get you out into your world again so that you could breathe.

"You no longer had what was needed to travel. Your lungs were filled with me. For those without the gift, breathing me is poison. It will kill them. But for you, since you were in me and breathing me already, there was a brief period when you were going through a transition, so having me in you was not instantly fatal. You would have died soon, but there was a brief time before that would happen. I knew that the time you had before you would die was not very long at all. I thought to do my best to save you, to get you to a place where you could be back in your world and hopefully recover.

"I brought you here, broke the seal, and placed you out in your world again. You were hurt, but I knew that the essence of me still within you would help sustain your life for a short time."

"If I could no longer travel, because I don't have the required gift, then what made you think that?"

"I was made to have properties to assist in emergencies. Those properties are within me—and thereby they were within you. They help to start the process of recovering. It is only intended for a crisis and even then I was warned that it could not be certain that it would work because there are variables that cannot be controlled.

"While you slept between worlds, and my magic that you still had within you was working to extract what had now become poison to you, I finished taking the others to the Keep. When I returned, I waited with you until you were recovered enough to be ready to breathe again, then I helped to remind you what you must to do to live.

"For a time I did not know if it would work. I have never had to do such a thing before. It was terrible to have to wait while I watched you lying there, not knowing if you would ever again breathe. I feared that I had failed you, and that I would be the cause of your death."

Richard stared at the silver face for a long moment. Finally he offered her a smile. "Thank you, sliph. You saved my life. You did the right things. You did good."

"You are my master. I would do anything for you."

"Your master. A master who can't travel."

"It is as puzzling to me as it is to you."

Richard tried to think it through, tried to make sense of it, but with the pain of breathing after nearly drowning in the sliph still feeling like it was pressing heavily on his chest, he was having trouble making his mind focus on thinking.

Richard rested his forearms across his knees. "I don't suppose there is any way for you to take me back to the Keep?"

"Yes, Master. If you wish to travel, I can take you."

Richard sat up straighter. "You can? How?"

"You must simply acquire the required magic, and then I can take you again. Then we will travel. You will be pleased."

Acquire the required magic. He didn't even know how to use the magic he had—or used to have. He couldn't imagine what had happened to his gift, and he had absolutely no idea how to get it back. There had been any number of times he'd wanted to be rid if it, but now that it had actually happened all he could think about was getting it back.

When his gift had failed, the beast had apparently lost him in the sliph. As consolation to losing his gift, it seemed the beast would be one less problem he had to face at the moment—his gift, after all, had been the mechanism by which the beast was keyed to him, the way in which it hunted him. There was supposed to be balance in magic; perhaps that was the balance to losing it.

Richard raked his fingers back through his hair. "At least Nicci and Cara made it through and are safe." He looked up at the sliph. "You're sure that they're all right?"

"Yes, Master. They are safe. I took them to the Keep, where they had wished to travel. They had what was required to travel."

"And you told them where I was. You told them what had happened."

She looked surprised by what had sounded more like a mandate than a question. "No, Master. I would never reveal what I do with another."

"Oh, great," he muttered. He worked to keep his exasperation in check. "But you've told me about others."

"You are my master. I do things with you that I would not do with any-one else."

"Sliph, they are my friends. They're probably frantic with worry for me. You must tell them what they need to know."

The silver head tilted toward him. "Master, I cannot betray you. I would not."

"It's not a betrayal. I'm telling you that it's all right to tell them what happened."

The sliph looked like she thought this was just about the strangest re-quest she had ever had. "Master, you wish me to tell others about us, about what we do when we are together?"

"Sliph, try to understand. You are no longer a whore."

"But people use me for their pleasure."

"It's not the same thing." Richard raked his fingers back through his hair, trying not to sound angry. "Listen, wizards in ancient times changed you from who you were, from what you were."

The sliph nodded solemnly. "I know, Master. I remember. I was the one it happened to, after all."

"You're different now. It's not the same. You can't equate the two things. They're different."

"I have been given a duty to serve others in this capacity. My nature is still within me."

"But there are some of us who use you who greatly value your help."

"I have always been valued for what I do."

"This is different from what you did before." Richard didn't want to be having this argument. He had more important matters to worry about. "Sliph, when you travel with us you are often helping to save lives. When you traveled with us to the People's Palace, you were helping me to end the war. You are doing a good thing."

"If you say so, Master. But you must understand that those who created me made me the way I am. They used what I once was to create me as I am now. I can be no way other than the way I am. I cannot wish myself to be different, any more than you can travel now simply by wishing it."

Richard sighed. "I suppose not."

With one hand he snapped dry twigs in half as he thought it over. He shared a long look with the beautiful face watching him, hanging on his every word. Finally, he spoke softly.

"There are times when there is no other way, and you must trust others. This is one of those times."

Something about his words clearly struck home. The beautiful, liquid face came a little closer.

"You are the one," the sliph whispered.

"The one? Which one?"

"The one Baraccus told me would come."

The hair on the back of Richard's neck stood on end.

"You knew Baraccus?"

"He was once my master, like you are, now."

"Of course," Richard whispered to himself. "He was First Wizard."

"He is the one who insisted that I possess the emergency elements I told you about. He also directed that there be this emergency portal. Had he not done those things, you would have died. He was very wise."

"Very wise," Richard agreed as he stared wide-eyed at the sliph. "You said that Baraccus told you something about one who would come?"

The sliph nodded. "He was kind to me. His wife hated me, but Baraccus was kind to me."

"You knew his wife, too?"

"Magda."

"Why would she hate you?"

"Because Baraccus was kind to me. And because I took him away from her."

"You mean, you took him away when he wished to travel."

"Of course. When I would tell him that he would be pleased, she would fold her arms and glare at me."

Richard smiled a little. "She was jealous."

"She loved him and did not want him to leave her. When I would return with him after we traveled, she would often be there, waiting for him. He would always smile when he saw her, and she would smile in turn."

"And what was it that Baraccus said about me?"

"He told me the same thing that you just did, that there are times when there is no other way, and you must trust others. Those were his words, just as they were yours. He said that one day another master would say those exact same words, and then add exactly the same words you did: 'This is one of those times.'

"He told me that if a master ever said these words, that meant that they were the right one and I was to tell them some things."

Richard could feel every hair on his arms stand on end.

"You took Magda Searus somewhere, didn't you?"

"Yes, Master. After that I never saw Baraccus again. But before, when he told me that someday someone would say those words, he told me to tell them his message."

"He left a message?" When she nodded, he rolled his hand. "So what is it?"

" 'I am sorry. I don't know the answers that would save you. If I did, please believe that I would give them eagerly. But I know the good in you. I believe in you. I do know that you have within you what you must to succeed. There will be times when you doubt yourself. Do not give up. Remember then that I believe in you, that I know you can accomplish what you must. You are a rare person. Believe in yourself.

" 'Know that I believe you are the one who can do it.' "

Richard sat frozen. The words echoed around in his head. They were oddly familiar.

"I've heard almost those exact words before."

The sliph glided a little closer, her features tightening. "You have?"

Richard concentrated as he ran the words through his mind again, trying to recall . . .

And then he did. It was right after Shota had told him about Baraccus. Just before she left, she'd said those very words to him. There was something about those words, spoken by Shota, that had aroused an indistinct memory.

"It was Shota, the witch woman," Richard said as he frowned in recollection. "She told me those words."

The sliph retreated. "I am sorry, Master. You have failed the test."

Richard looked up at her. "What test?"

"The test Baraccus just gave you. I am sorry, but you have failed his test. I can tell you nothing more."

Without further word, the sliph abruptly vanished into the black hole in the stone.

Richard threw himself down on his stomach, leaning down into the hole. "No! Wait! Don't leave!"

His own voice echoed up out of the empty, black shaft.

The sliph was gone. Without his gift, he had no way to call her back.

Nicci heard a soft knock at the door. Zedd looked up but he didn't stand. Cara, hands clasped behind her back, gazing out the window, looked back over her shoulder. Nicci, standing closest to the door, pulled it open. The small flame in the lamp on the table was not up to the task of chasing the gloom from the room, but it cast what warm light it could across the face of the tall prophet.

"What's going on?" Nathan asked in his deep voice. He cast a suspicious look around at those in the room. "Rikka wouldn't say much other than that you and Cara were back and Zedd wanted to see me immediately."

"That's right," Zedd said. "Come in, please."

Nathan glanced around the somber room as he strode in. "Where's Richard."

Nicci swallowed. "He didn't make it back with us."

"Didn't make it back?" He paused to take in the bleak look on Nicci's face. "Dear spirits . . ."

Zedd, sitting at Jebra's side at the bed, didn't look up. Jebra was unconscious. When they tried to close her eyes her lids would pop open again. They finally quit trying and let her stare up at the ceiling.

Zedd had already tended to her broken leg as best he could. She was very fortunate that Cara was not only quick but strong, and that she had been able to catch Jebra's ankle just in time as her dead weight had toppled outward from the balcony. Still, her momentum had whipped the seer down around and under the balcony, where her leg smacked a support strut that broke her leg. Nicci suspected that the woman had been unconscious the moment she started falling.

It had been a bad break. Zedd had set to work immediately on her injury, but because of the unusual state Jebra was in he had not been able to heal the break. All he had been able to do was set it, splint it, and add enough of his gift to help it begin to mend. When she finally awoke he would be able to finish the healing. If she awoke. Nicci had her doubts.

Nicci knew that Jebra's broken leg was the least of the woman's problems. Despite everything they had tried, they had been unable to arouse her from her catatonic state. Zedd had tried. Nicci had tried. She had even tried dangerous conjuring involving Subtractive Magic. Zedd had been against it at first, but when Nicci confronted him with the stark nature of their choices he grudgingly agreed.

Unfortunately, even that hadn't helped. Jebra's mind was locked away from them. Whatever magic the witch woman had used on her was something they were unable to break. Whatever had been done didn't appear to Nicci to be intended to be reversible. If they knew its nature perhaps they might stand a chance of breaking the spell, but they didn't know its makeup.

Nathan bent and touched two fingers to the unconscious woman's temple. He straightened and helplessly shook his head at Zedd's questioning expression.

Nicci had never seen anything like it. Zedd, on the other hand, had in the beginning rubbed his chin as he brooded. He'd muttered that there was something oddly familiar about its nature. What, he couldn't say. Despite how insistent Nicci had been, and despite his own desperate desire to do something, Zedd was at his wits' end that he could not pinpoint why he felt that he had seen some aspect of such conjuring before.

He was, after all, he had reminded them, the First Wizard, and he had spent a good portion of his life studying such things. He believed that he should be able to identify what kind of web had been spun around the woman. Nicci knew that if Jebra had been conscious it would have made the job a great deal easier, but Zedd wasn't willing to use an excuse for his own failure to identify what the conjuring involved.

Nicci heard a commotion out in the hallway. Nathan stuck his head out the doorway for a look.

"What is it?" a voice in the distance called out. It was Ann, rushing up the hall, escorted by Rikka. She finally reached the door. "What's going on?"

As she came into the room, laboring to catch her breath, Nathan laid a big hand on her shoulder. "Something has happened to Richard."

Strands of gray hair stuck out from the loose bun at the back of her head like a plume of ruffled feathers. Her calculating gaze swept over those in the room, assessing the degree of seriousness she saw in each of them. It was the kind of swift, lean evaluation Nicci associated with Ann.

As the Prelate of the Sisters of the Light, she had always had a commanding presence that could strike fear into just about anyone, from high-ranking Sister to stableboys. Even though Nicci was no longer a Sister of the Light, her guard always went up whenever the former prelate came into the room. The woman's short stature in no way diminished the air of looming menace that seemed to surround her.

Ann turned an intent look up at Nathan. "What happened? Is the boy hurt—"

"I don't know, yet," Nathan said, holding up a hand to forestall a flood of questions before they could landslide in on him. "Let the woman explain."

"All we know for sure," Nicci said when Ann turned a hot glare on her, "is that while we were traveling in the sliph back here from the People's Palace, the beast attacked us. Cara and I tried to help Richard fight it off, then we were separated from him. As soon as that happened I felt some kind of extrinsic magic. Next thing we knew, Cara and I were back at the Keep. Richard wasn't with us. We have no idea what happened to him after he was touched by the strange power I sensed. We never saw the beast again, either.

"After we got back here, Jebra was attacked by a web that I could discern had been cast by the same person who cast the power that touched Richard in the sliph. Because Zedd recognized its unique composition, we know now that it was power conjured by a witch woman."

"And my Agiel doesn't work," Cara said, holding the weapon up. "Our bond to Lord Rahl is broken. We can no longer sense him."

"Dear Creator," Ann whispered as her gaze dropped away.

Zedd gestured to the woman lying in the bed before him. "Whatever power it is that this witch woman cast, it left Jebra unconscious. We can't rouse her. Although I know that it was a witch woman's spell that somehow took her, I can't figure out how a witch woman could do such a thing—cast such webs from afar. From my experience they not only keep to themselves but can't accomplish things of this nature. It's beyond their ability."

"Are you are certain that it was a witch woman?" Ann asked.

Zedd took a deep breath as he considered the question seriously. "I've had dealings with a witch woman before. Once a cat has had its claws in

you, you don't soon forget what it feels like. I don't know the specific person who did this, but I know the feel of this. It was a witch woman."

Nicci folded her arms. "I think we have a pretty good idea who the
witch woman was: Six. And don't forget, just because you recognize the
signature of a witch woman's power, that doesn't mean that the same limits necessarily apply to the individual who did this. After all, for someone
to recognize your power as that of a wizard doesn't mean that they know
your limits or would know your real potential."

"True enough," Zedd admitted with a sigh.

Nathan waved off the topic of witch women. "Did Jebra say anything
else about the vision she had? Anything at all?"

Zedd shared a look with Nicci. "Well, not until this spell took her. Just
before she went into this state, we heard her say, 'Stars. Stars fallen to
ground. Stars among the grass.'"

"Stars . . ." Nathan repeated as he paced in the small room, holding an
elbow with one hand and tapping the tips of the fingers of the other to his
chin. He finally turned toward Zedd. "I'm afraid that such a prophecy
means nothing to me. It's probable that she only spoke a fragment aloud.
In that case, it could easily be that there isn't enough for me to go on."

Nicci's heart sank. She had been hoping that the prophet would be able
to decipher the seer's prophecy.

Ann scratched the side of her nose, searching for words. "So it is possible, then, that we . . ." She cleared her throat. ". . . that we have lost
Richard. That this witch woman killed him."

Cara took an aggressive step forward. "Lord Rahl is not dead!"

In the echoing silence, Zedd rose from the chair. He cast Cara a cautionary glance before addressing Ann. "I don't think so, either."

Ann looked from Cara's heated expression to Zedd. "I know why she
doesn't believe it is so. Why don't you?"

He gestured down at Jebra. "Because of this woman lying here in
this bed."

Ann frowned. "What do you mean?"

"Well, the first vision Jebra has had in several years is about Richard."

"That's right," Nicci put in. "Her vision was about what was going to
happen to him. She told me—specifically—not to let him be alone, not for
an instant."

Ann arched an eyebrow. "And yet you did."

Nicci ignored the affront. "Yes. Not deliberately, but because of the beast. The beast was an unforeseeable factor, a random event."

When Ann only looked more perplexed, Zedd explained. "We believe that it was this witch woman's plan to touch Richard with her power. But the beast dropped in at just the wrong moment, spoiling up her carefully constructed plan."

Ann's frown deepened. "In what way?"

"The beast caused her to miss getting Richard, as she had planned," Nicci said. "Because of the beast, she lost Richard in the sliph, just as we did. Now she has a problem. She has to find him."

"So she did the same thing we did," Zedd said. "She came here, or at least she sent her power here, to find out from the seer where he will be."

"She was seeking prophecy?" Ann asked. "Witch women see things in the flow of time. Why would she need the seer?"

Zedd spread his hands. "Yes, they see things but, as I'm sure Nathan can explain better than I could, they can't see exactly what they want to see, when they want to see it."

Nathan was nodding his agreement. "There is a random element to prophecy. It comes when it comes, not when you wish it to come. Perhaps the wizards of ancient times knew the keys to using prophecy at will, but if they did, they did not pass such knowledge on. It is seldom that you can pick and choose with prophecy what events you want to see."

Zedd lifted a finger, stressing his point. "Six probably saw, either through her ability or her conjuring having to do with the events, that Jebra had already had a vision revealing what would happen to Richard and where he would be next, so she simply stole into Jebra's mind to steal the answer."

"I think that's why we can't wake Jebra," Nicci said. "I don't think that Six wants anyone else to be able to get the information that she already got. While Jebra spoke only a few words aloud, I would bet that Six extracted all of it—the entire vision—from Jebra's mind. I believe that Six then compelled Jebra to jump from that balcony to kill herself so that she couldn't reveal her vision to anyone else. Failing that, the spell rendered Jebra unconscious—like suicide, it's a whole lot easier than killing from afar, and just as good for her purpose."

Nathan's brow had drawn down as he listened. He rolled a hand as if turning over the event in his mind. "So you think that in her prophecy, Jebra was revealing that Richard is going to find stars that have fallen to the ground? That he will be at a place with stars among the grass? Like a place where meteorites are found?"

Zedd clasped his hands behind his back and nodded. "It rather seems that way."

Nathan stared off as he considered, nodding to himself from time to time. Ann didn't look so convinced.

"So you think that Richard is alive," she asked, "and that this witch woman, Six, somehow spelled him?"

Nicci gave the former prelate a single, firm nod. "That's the conclusion Zedd and I have reached."

Ann leaned closer to her former charge. "For what purpose? I can fathom reasons for Six murdering Richard, but why would she want to get her hands on him?"

Nicci didn't shy from the woman's steady gaze. "Six usurped the witch woman who lived up here—Shota. Why? Well, what did Six take? Shota's companion, Samuel," she said in answer to her own question. "And Samuel has the Sword of Truth, the sword he once carried."

Ann looked like she had just lost the thread of the story. "What does that have to do with anything?"

"What did Samuel use the sword for? What did he steal?" Nicci asked.

Ann's eyes went wide. "One of the boxes of Orden."

"From a Sister of the Dark," Nicci said, "with the help of the Sword of Truth."

Ann turned a flustered look on Zedd. "But why would this woman, Six, want Richard?"

Zedd's gaze sank to the floor as he rubbed the tips of his fingers across the furrows of his brow. "To open the correct box of Orden, one has to have a very important book. I think you two, of all people, should be quite familiar with that particular volume."

Nathan's jaw fell open with realization.

"The Book of Counted Shadows," Ann breathed.

Zedd nodded. "The only copy of that book now resides in Richard's head. He burned the original after he had memorized it."

"We have to find him first," Ann said.

Zedd grunted derisively at the very suggestion, lifting his eyebrows in mock wonder, as if he could never have divined such an idea without her help.

"We have a more immediate problem," Nicci said.

Cara, across the small room, waggled her Agiel. "Until we find Lord Rahl, there is no bond."

"Without the bond," Nicci said, "we are all at the mercy of the dream walker."

The realization seemed to hit Ann like a clap of thunder.

"Something must be done immediately," Zedd added. "The threat is dire and there is little time. If we don't act, we could lose this war at any moment."

"What are you getting at?" Nathan asked, suspiciously.

Zedd looked up at the scowling prophet. "We need you to become the Lord Rahl. We dare not risk our people being without the bond for another moment. You must then leave at once for the People's Palace."

Nathan stood silently, looking grim. He was a tall man, with broad shoulders. With his white hair brushing those shoulders he cut an imposing figure. It made Nicci sick at heart to think of anyone else taking Richard's place as Lord Rahl.

The alternative, though, was to allow the dream walker to ravage their minds. She knew all too well what that was like. She knew how her bond to Richard had not merely saved her life, but shown her the joy of living. Her bond to Richard hadn't been the formal acquiescence to the rule of the Lord Rahl, as it was with the people of D'Hara; rather, it had been a deeper commitment to Richard, the man. The man she had loved from almost the first moment she had seen the spark of life in his gray eyes. Richard had shown her not just how to live again, but how to love.

She swallowed back the pain of it, of knowing that she could never have him—worse, of knowing that his heart belonged to another, belonged to someone she didn't even remember. It would be better if Nicci could remember this Kahlan, know that she was smart, loving, beautiful, because then she could be happy for Richard. It was hard to be happy for him when he loved a phantom.

"I understand," Nathan said at last in a deep voice.

Ann looked like she had close to a thousand objections, one to match each year of the prophet's age, but she managed to bottle them up under the cork of her realization of the consequences of not having a Lord Rahl.

"The D'Haran army is not far from the palace," Nathan said. "They will soon have to face Jagang's horde. I think you're right that I would best help our cause if I were there."

Nicci hadn't told any of them yet. She cleared her throat to make sure that her voice would not fail her. "Richard spoke to the army. That's why he went to D'Hara. He told them that they could not fight the Imperial Order and hope to win."

Ann's face went crimson. "So what does he expect them to do! If not fight the army of the Order, then . . . what?"

"Lay waste to the Old World," Nicci said with grim resolve.

Zedd, Nathan, and Ann stared silently at her.

"He told them to do what?" Zedd asked incredulously.

"It's the only way," Nicci said. "We have no hope of destroying their army. Richard intends the D'Haran army to instead destroy their will to fight. It's the only chance we have."

"Dear spirits," Zedd whispered as he turned away. He went to the window and stood staring out into the night. He finally turned back, his eyes brimming with tears.

"I have been in his position. I have had to direct our side to do things that had to be done." He shook his head again. "The poor boy. I'm afraid he's right. I should have seen it myself. I guess I didn't want to. Sometimes, it takes lonely courage to do what must be done."

Cara stepped forward and went to one knee before Nathan. She bowed her head.

"Master Rahl guide us. Master Rahl teach us. Master Rahl protect us. In your light we thrive. In your mercy we are sheltered. In your wisdom we are humbled. We live only to serve. Our lives are yours."

Zedd dropped to one knee, as did Rikka. Nicci did the same. Finally, reluctantly, Ann followed.

"Master Rahl guide us," they all said in unison. "Master Rahl teach us. Master Rahl protect us. In your light we thrive. In your mercy we are sheltered. In your wisdom we are humbled. We live only to serve. Our lives are yours."

Nathan stood tall and silent, hands clasped, looking down at the bowed heads, looking very much like the Lord Rahl. When they had finished the

devotion, they all stood, somewhat disquieted by the unspoken significance of what they had just done, of what it meant, that Richard was no
longer the Lord Rahl.

"It is done," Cara said. She tested the feel of her slender red weapon in
her fingers, gazing at it with liquid blue eyes. "My Agiel is alive again."
She smiled in a distant, sad way. "The link of the bond is whole once more.
All D'Harans will recognize it and know that we again have a Lord Rahl."

Nathan let out a deep breath. "At least we have that on our side."

"Nathan," Zedd said to the prophet, "you must get to D'Hara at once.
There are Imperial Order troops at the larger passes east of here into
D'Hara, still trying to find a way in the back door. I will show you some
ways around them.

"It would be best to have a Lord Rahl, the guardian of the bond, standing with those now standing alone at the palace."

"What about Jagang's army?" Ann asked, looking concerned after
Nathan nodded his agreement. "What do you think Jagang will do once he
discovers that the D'Haran army has evaporated right before he could
close his fist around them?"

Zedd shrugged. "He will lay siege to the People's Palace. Verna and
some of her Sisters will be there to help defend the place, but the People's
Palace is built in the form of a spell that amplifies the power of a Rahl and
suppresses it in others. Verna and the Sisters will not be able to wield the
full force of their ability. Right now Nathan is the only Rahl we have to
help defend the palace and its people."

"That's why we need Nathan to leave at once for the palace," Nicci said.

"Tonight," Zedd added.

Nathan's gaze moved from Zedd's eyes to Nicci's. "I understand. I will
do my best. Let us hope that Richard will one day be able to take his place
back from me."

At that moment, his words lifted at least a little of the weight from
Nicci's heart.

"We will be working on that," Zedd assured him.

"You can count on it," Nicci said.

Cara pointed her Agiel at the prophet. "And you had better not get any
crazy notion in your head that you will be keeping the post. It belongs to
Lord Rahl."

Nathan arched an eyebrow. "I am the Lord Rahl, now."

Cara made a sour face. "You know what I mean."

Nathan smiled a slow smile.

Ann jabbed Nathan in the ribs with a finger. "And don't you get any grand ideas, *Lord Rahl*. I'm going with you to make sure you stay out of trouble."

Nathan shrugged. "I guess that the Lord Rahl could use an attendant. You'll do."

After lying on the ancient, cold stone floor in the depths of a lonely forest for what seemed like an eternity, staring down into the black abyss, not knowing what else to do, Richard finally sat back up. He had called to the sliph until he was nearly hoarse, but there was no answer. The sliph was gone.

Richard put his elbows on his knees. As his head sank, he clasped his hands behind his neck. He felt like he had lost his way and didn't know what to do next. How many times, since he'd left his Hartland woods, had he felt just this way, had he thought that he was at the end of his rope? He'd always found a way. He didn't know if, this time, he could.

As he was growing up, Richard had never known that he had been born with the gift. He'd never known anything at all about magic. Once he discovered that he'd been born with the gift, he didn't want it. He wanted only to be rid of it, as if it was a sickness that had been passed down to him. He just wanted to be himself. But he had finally come to accept the value of his abilities and understand that they were part of who he was. They had on many occasions, after all, helped him save not only his own life, but Kahlan's and many others along the way. His gift was a part of him, something that couldn't be separated from him any more than his heart or lungs could be taken away.

Now, though, he'd somehow lost the gift.

At first, when the sliph had told him that he no longer had the magic required to travel, he'd had a hard time believing that such a thing was possible, that his gift could really be gone. He'd thought it must be a magical malfunction, an anomaly of some sort. Back when he'd wanted to be rid of it, he had inquired as to how he could shed his gift and had learned that such a thing simply wasn't possible.

While it didn't seem conceivable to him, Richard knew that it was true. He knew because along with his gift, he had lost his ability to remember

The Book of Counted Shadows. He might as well have never memorized it, because, along with his gift, that memory was suddenly lost.

The Book of Counted Shadows had been a book of magic. The gift was required to be able to read it, and required to remember even so much as a single word of the text. Without the gift, Richard couldn't read books of magic or, more accurately, recall the words long enough to know that there had been anything there to read. Without the gift, books of magic appeared blank. Now his memory of *The Book of Counted Shadows* had gone dark.

And now he had failed a test he hadn't even known he was taking. He wasn't even at all clear as to what the test had been. Somehow, though, he had failed it.

He felt as if he had failed Kahlan.

He couldn't imagine how those words could have been a test from Baraccus. How could they possibly test him? Test him at what? He didn't know what test the sliph could be talking about, so he had no way to figure out how he had failed it.

He wished he had Zedd to help him figure it out, or Nicci, or Nathan— someone, anyone. He stopped and asked himself how many times that night he had wished for answers, for help, for salvation to come save him. None of the wishes had been answered. Wishes, he knew, never were.

He reminded himself that he was wasting valuable time feeling sorry for himself. He had to think, not sit around hoping that someone else would come along and think for him.

He lay back on the stone and stared up at the canopy of limbs and leaves above and, beyond them, the stars. He smiled, mocking himself, thinking that maybe a falling star would answer his wishes. He pushed aside the thoughts of wishes and put his mind to the task at hand.

He'd run the whole thing through his mind a hundred times and it still made no sense. Baraccus said, through the message left with the sliph, that he didn't have the answers that would save Richard. Baraccus believed, though, that Richard had within him what was needed to succeed. Baraccus told Richard to believe in himself, and wanted him to know that he believed in Richard, although he hadn't used Richard's name, specifically.

The message, Richard reasoned, had been meant for the one who would be born with the Subtractive side of the gift that Baraccus had seen to it was released from the Temple of the Winds, but Baraccus didn't know that person's name, didn't know, specifically, who that person would be. At least, Richard didn't think he did. It made more sense that Baraccus simply spoke directly, personally, without using names. The message had been clear enough without having to use the name of the person who would eventually hear it. That gave it the sound of a direct address.

How could that be a test? How could Richard fail it?

He sighed in frustration as he pulled a long stalk of grass growing from one of the missing mortar joints off to the side. As he considered the issue, he flattened the soft base of the stalk of grass with his front teeth.

Could it be that the sliph somehow had been given some power by Baraccus, like the power he'd given her to act in an emergency, so that she could see whether or not Richard had what it took to succeed? Could it be that this insight given the sliph told her that Richard fell short in some way?

The source. As he stared up at the stars, Richard mulled that over in his mind. He'd told the sliph that he had heard those words before from Shota and then, all of a sudden, the sliph had been done with him.

Could the sliph know Shota? Maybe, in Baraccus's view, Richard should not be associating with a witch woman. Maybe that was the reason Richard had failed—because he hadn't been doing things on his own, by himself. He made a face. He had difficulty imagining that Baraccus wouldn't want him to work with people, to find answers, to solve problems.

He ran over the words in his mind, as best as he could recall them, anyway.

I am sorry. I don't know the answers that would save you. If I did, please believe that I would give them eagerly. But I know the good in you. I believe in you. I do know that you have within you what you must to succeed. There will be times when you doubt yourself. Do not give up. Remember then that I believe in you, that I know you can accomplish what you must. You are a rare person. Believe in yourself.

Know that I believe you are the one who can do it.

That was what the sliph had said was the message from Baraccus. Richard recalled, though, that those had been the same words Shota had told him not very long ago, the last time he had seen her, just before she left.

Richard didn't really believe in coincidence. In this case, he certainly didn't. Shota could not have said by chance the same words that Baraccus had told the sliph to say. The message was too long and too detailed, with characteristics that were far too idiosyncratic.

If that was the case, that it had not been coincidence, and Richard was sure it wasn't, then why would Shota have used the exact same words that Baraccus had? Was it a message of some kind? Was she trying to tell him something? Warn him about something?

If the witch woman had wanted to help him, then why didn't she warn him about the test, and tell him? If she could not tell him the answer, she could at least have told him what the test would be. Zedd had often said, though, that a witch woman never told you what you wanted to know without telling you something you didn't. Could that be it? He doubted it, since she had told him a great many terrible things that day—things, it turned out, that had helped him finally grasp what he had to do with the army, rather than allowing them to fight Jagang in a final battle.

The thing that was itching at him, though, was that there were phrases in the message that were unique: *answers that would save you; give them eagerly; know the good in you; you have within you what you must to succeed; know that I believe you are the one.* Those were all slightly uncommon patterns in the way people spoke. They were not drastically different, but they were a bit eccentric, almost childlike, and yet rather formal in a simplistic way. Richard sighed. He couldn't seem to put his finger on it, but there was something distinctly unconventional in the use of language within that message.

With an icy shock of realization, he remembered.

He remembered why those words had sounded unsettlingly familiar when Shota had said them. It was because he had heard those exact words before.

Those were the exact words that had been spoken by the night wisp the evening of the first day Richard had met Kahlan.

They had been in the wayward pine. Kahlan asked if he was afraid of magic and then, after approving of his answer, she brought out a little striped bottle that held the wisp. The night wisp, Shar, had guided Kahlan across the boundary, but by then it was dying. The wisp was unable to live away from its home place and those of its kind. It didn't have enough strength to cross the boundary again.

Richard remembered Kahlan saying, *"Shar has sacrificed her life to help me because if Darken Rahl succeeds, all her kind, among others, will perish."*

The wisp had been the one who told Richard for the first time that Darken Rahl was after him. Shar had warned that if Richard ran he would be caught and killed. Richard had thanked the wisp for helping Kahlan. He told Shar that his life had been made longer because she had saved him from doing something foolish that day. He told Shar that his life was better for knowing her, and thanked the wisp for helping bring her safely through the boundary.

Shar had then told him that she believed in him, and the rest of it, exactly as Baraccus had related through the sliph. At the time he had thought that the slightly odd speech characteristics were simply idiosyncratic of wisps—and perhaps they really were, but Baraccus had used those exact words for a reason.

Shota had used the same words, too—either deliberately or in innocent unawareness of their source—no doubt in order to help him by reminding him of those words from Shar. She probably didn't realize the real reason for saying those exact words, but through her ability they were intended to make him think. To make him remember. It was probably only because of the terrible vision Richard had had of Kahlan witnessing his execution that he hadn't connected Shota's words with the same words he'd heard years before from the night wisp. That vision had simply overpowered everything else.

Richard listened to the night sounds off in the woods, of bugs chirping, the leaves rustling in the wind, and a distant mockingbird, as another memory began seeping back into his consciousness.

Shar, the wisp, had used his name without being introduced. He supposed that the wisp could simply have overheard it while in the little bottle in the pouch at Kahlan's belt.

Or she might have already known his name.

Richard's eyes were opened as wide as they would go as he recalled something else. He had asked the wisp why Darken Rahl was trying to kill him, if it was because he helped Kahlan or if there was another reason.

Shar had come close and asked, *"Other reason? Secrets?"*

Secrets.

Richard jumped to his feet and cried out aloud with the shock of understanding.

He pressed his wrists to the sides of his head, unable to suppress another shout.

"I understand! Dear spirits, I understand!"

Secrets.

Richard had thought at the time that the wisp knew about the tooth that Richard kept hidden under his shirt, but that wasn't it at all. It had nothing to do with that tooth. Shar was asking him something entirely different. She was offering him his first chance at recovering the secret book Baraccus had left for him.

But it had been too soon. Richard hadn't yet been ready.

Richard had failed Baraccus's test back then, too. Failed it for the first time that night with the wisp. Baraccus, though, probably had no way to know when Richard would be ready. He had to have a way to test him from time to time. Shota had said that just because Baraccus had seen to it that Richard had been born with the ability, that didn't mean he would do the right things.

Baraccus hadn't taken his free will—and so, from time to time, Baraccus needed to test the one born with that ability to see if he had learned to use it to accomplish those things along the way that needed to be accomplished. Richard wondered how many other things put in his path had been the doing of Baraccus. At the moment, he had no way to know the answer to that question.

He did know that when the sliph said he failed the test, that was at least the second time he had failed it. The sliph's test was a reserve test, a repeat test, for after Richard had learned more. After he'd had a chance to know who he really was.

Secrets.

Richard felt as if his head might explode with the power of comprehension. Every emotion he had ever had seemed to collide together, twisting his insides with the excitement and anxiety of it all.

He threw himself down on the stone floor, hands gripping the edge until his knuckles were white.

"Sliph! Come back! I know what Baraccus meant! I understand! Sliph!"

Mere inches away, liquid metal rose up into the cold, silvery moonlight, forming into the flawless features of the sliph. It was an impossibly beautiful vision, reflecting the swaying trees and his own face in flowing distortions of reality.

The sliph slowly smiled. "Do you wish to change your answer, Master?"

Richard wanted to kiss the quicksilver face. "Yes."

The sliph cocked her head to one side. "What is it you wish to confide in me, Master?"

"A night wisp told me that before. Not just Shota." Richard gestured with the frustration of trying to get it all out at once before the sliph could say that he had not passed the test. "Shota was second. It was a night wisp who first told me those same words—the words Baraccus used. That's where I heard it first. That's what Baraccus wanted me to know—that it's the night wisps."

Richard half expected silver arms to slip around his neck and draw him closer. "Anything else, Master?" the sliph whispered intimately.

"Yes. With that message, Baraccus wanted me to realize that what he left—left for me alone—is hidden with the night wisps."

The sliph came closer yet, still showing the gentle curve of a knowing smile. Her gaze drank him in. For the first time ever, her lips moved with her words, her voice coming in the breathy whisper of surrender. "You have passed the test, Master. I am pleased."

"Now, there's a first," Richard said.

The sliph laughed, a sound as clear and pleasant as the moonlight.

"Do you know the place of the wisps, Master?"

Richard shook his head. "No, but Kahlan told me a little about them, about their homeplace. Kahlan is my wife. She has traveled in you before and was pleased, but you don't remember her because she was captured by some very bad people who released a spell to make everyone forget her—something a little like what was done to you. I'm trying to find her before those same bad people can hurt everyone.

"That's what this is all about. That's why Baraccus left something for me—something to help me in my efforts."

"I see. I am happy for you, Master."

"Anyway, Kahlan told me about the place where the night wisps live. She said that it's beautiful."

"So Baraccus told me, too."

"Kahlan said that you can't see the wisps in the daytime, only at night. I guess that's why they're called night wisps.

"Kahlan said they're like stars, like stars fallen from the sky. She said that it's like seeing stars among the grass."

The sliph nodded at his excitement. "I am happy that you are pleased, Master."

"Can you go there? To the place of the night wisps—this place of stars fallen to the ground?"

"Even if you could travel, I'm afraid not," the sliph said. "Baraccus directed that this emergency portal be built here for a reason. He did not want me to be able to go to the home place of the night wisps because he did not want anyone to know that he went there. He did not want it to become a destination, either, but rather to remain a remote and secret place of stars fallen to the ground.

"Baraccus told me that this portal is not a great distance from the wisps, but it is the closest I can get to them. He did not want me to give any hint that this place existed, or to ever divulge anything involving my future masters. It was his way of protecting you. That is why I could not tell your friends where you were. That secrecy and security was also meant to be part of what would bring forth the right words, from the right person. That protection not only protected you, but denying you the help of your friends prompted you into thinking for yourself. Thinking is what Baraccus said would turn the key for you."

Richard's head spun with everything he was learning. He leaned closer, seeking to confirm what he already knew. "You brought Baraccus's wife, Magda, here, didn't you? And she was carrying something with her."

"Yes. This is the place I brought Magda after the last time I saw master Baraccus. She repaired the stone, here, before going back. That was the last time I saw her. No one has been through to this place ever since then.

"You have passed the test, Master. This is the way to the secret library Baraccus left for you."

Kahlan stepped carefully among the rubble of ancient buildings that had over the millennia crumbled and eventually toppled, sending sections tumbling down the steep hillside. Dusty pieces of brick and stone lay scattered everywhere among the dry, decomposing dirt of the slope. It would be easy to stumble and fall in the dark, and it was a long way down. Jillian, a shadowy, lithe shape just ahead of them, climbed the scrabble as effortlessly as a mountain goat. Sister Ulicia, ahead of Kahlan, and the other two Sisters, behind her, huffed and puffed with the effort of the arduous ascent. As eager as they were to press on, the Sisters were getting tired. They frequently lost their footing and slipped, nearly falling from the bluff.

Kahlan thought that they would be well advised to wait until daylight to finish climbing up into the ruins of the city of Caska. She wasn't about to give them that advice, though. The Sisters did what the Sisters wanted to do and there was nothing Kahlan could do about it. In the end, the only result of any suggestion she might offer would be a beating for interfering.

Kahlan would have been happy to see any one of the Sisters fall and break her neck, but she knew that the other two would be no less trouble than all three. For that matter, one of the Sisters was more than capable of making Kahlan's life a torturous nightmare. Any of them could easily use her power through the iron collar around Kahlan's neck to put her in a state of unendurable agony. So, she climbed without commenting on the wisdom of doing such a thing by the light of the moon alone.

Since Jillian's trail was so treacherous, they'd had to leave the horses at the base of the headlands. There were certain items, though, that the Sisters would not let out of their sight, much less leave behind, and so Kahlan was made to carry them, along with what other packs she could lift. It was a grueling effort to lug the heavy load up the precipitous trail. Jillian had wanted to help with some of the packs, but the Sisters refused to allow it, saying that Kahlan was a slave and meant for a slave's work. They told Jillian to worry about guiding them to Tovi. Kahlan signaled Jillian with her eyes to do as the Sisters wanted and move out. She silently reminded herself that such work would only make her stronger, while the Sisters, shunning any effort, would only grow weaker.

Kahlan wanted to remain strong. Someday she was going to need her strength. But it had been a long day and that strength was flagging.

At least they were nearing the end of the lengthy, headlong journey. Soon enough the Sisters would all be reunited and then maybe they would settle in for a time, be a little less tense, a little slower to anger. While Kahlan looked forward to a respite of a day or two, she was troubled by what it would mean.

The Sisters had given the clear impression that this was to be the end of the journey, the end of their struggle, and the beginning of a new era. Kahlan could not imagine what that could mean, but it worried her greatly. The Sisters often talked among themselves of the reward that awaited them being nearly in their grasp. More than once, Sister Ulicia had remarked, in answer to the others' impatience, "It won't be long, now."

Kahlan had no idea what their plan was, what great event was about to take place, but she was certain that it involved the boxes she carried on her back—Lord Rahl's boxes. The two Sisters following behind kept a careful watch on those boxes. The night before, Kahlan had overheard the Sisters say that when they reached Tovi, and the third box, the preparations would begin.

Kahlan sighed in relief when they at last reached the top of the steep incline, finding themselves standing at the base of a decomposing wall. In places gullies had undermined and washed out sections of the wall. Kahlan took one last look out over the moonlit plain far below before following Jillian through one of the dark gaps in the wall. Once into the breach in under the wall still remaining overhead, Kahlan discovered that the wall was as thick as a small house. Whatever people built such a wall must have been decidedly worried about what might come to attack them.

The steep trail leveled out on the other side of the wall and led them among buildings set close together. Many places near to the edge had crumbled or were leaning and about to fall. The massive wall had held much of the decaying rubble back, but in places parts of falling buildings had gone over the top. Over time, broken bricks, blocks, and mortar had also been washed down through the gullies.

They soon found themselves on a narrow street among buildings that were in better shape. The outer fringe of structures had seemed to take the brunt of the weather and as a result were the most deteriorated. From the confinement of buildings they made their way out into a graveyard. In the moonlight it was a haunting sight. Statues stood here and there like phantoms among the dead.

Making their way among the graves, Kahlan saw that higher up the buildings lay like an endless carpet over the rolling landscape. In the clear sky she spotted Jillian's raven, Lokey. The girl had never pointed it out, apparently hoping the Sisters would think it just a wild bird, but when Kahlan glanced her way Jillian would sometimes signal with her eyes to look up. Lokey would do aerial tricks that would make Jillian, if the Sisters were looking the other way, smile. She seemed a girl searching for some small reason for joy among the desolation of what had befallen her and her grandfather because of the Sisters. When Sister Armina once noticed the raven, she thought that it was a vulture following them across the desolate landscape. Kahlan didn't correct her.

"How much farther?" Sister Ulicia asked as she paused among the grave markers. For some reason, Kahlan thought that she sounded suspicious of Jillian.

Jillian pointed. "Not far. Up there, through that building. It's the passageway to the dead."

Sister Cecilia snorted. "Passageway to the dead. Tovi always did have quite the sense of drama."

Sister Armina shrugged. "Seems pretty appropriate to me."

"Go on, then," Sister Ulicia said as she gestured for the girl to get moving again.

Jillian started out at once, leading them out of the maze of the graveyard and up into the empty city. Kahlan couldn't tell for sure by the light of the moon alone, but it seemed that everything—every wall, roof, street, every part of everything—was the same color of dust and death. The ghostly silence in among the buildings shrouded the night with an eerie sense of stillness. Kahlan felt as if she were walking through the immense skeleton of a city, as if every bit of tissue and life had been stripped away and all that was left was crumbling beige bones.

Along a broad thoroughfare that, by the look of the decorative, curving stone walls to each side, must once have been beautiful, Jillian slipped like a shadow through the arches fronting one of the larger buildings. Inside, it was hard to see. Kahlan heard the girl's feet crunching across bits of crumbled mortar. The Sisters didn't seem to notice the mosaic underfoot. Where moonlight fell across the floor Kahlan could see faded little tiles that made up a picture of trees, paths, and a wall surrounding a graveyard. There were even mosaic people.

Looking at the sweep of the picture across the floor as she lugged her heavy load, Kahlan tripped on a missing section of tile and fell to her knees. Sister Ulicia immediately struck her across the back of her head, knocking Kahlan sprawling on her face.

"Get up, you clumsy ox!" Sister Ulicia shouted as she kicked Kahlan in the ribs.

Kahlan was trying, but with the weight of the load on her back it was easier said than done. "Yes, Sister," she said, gasping between the kicks, hoping to gain time to stand.

Jillian stepped between them. "Leave her be!"

Sister Ulicia straightened with a glower. "How dare you interfere. I'll wring your scrawny neck."

"I think we ought to skin her alive," Sister Armina said, "and leave her bleeding corpse out there for the vultures."

Sister Ulicia snatched Jillian's collar. "Get out of the way so I can teach this lazy ox a lesson."

"Leave her be," Jillian repeated, refusing to back down.

"Let's just cut the little brat's throat and be done with her," Sister Cecilia complained. "We don't have time for this. We can find Tovi on our own, now."

Knowing that she had to pacify the Sisters before they carried out their threats to harm the girl, Kahlan finally managed to regain her feet. She immediately took Jillian's arm and pulled her back out of harm's way.

"I'm sorry—it's my fault," Kahlan said. "We can go now."

Kahlan half turned to start out, but she didn't take a step. She knew better than to do so without permission. Sister Ulicia didn't move. She had murder in her eyes.

"Not until she sees you get the kind of lesson we've owed you for quite a while now," she said. "You're getting far too used to being treated lightly at your every transgression."

"You will leave Kahlan be," Jillian said from halfway behind Kahlan, trying not to be pushed any farther into the background.

Sister Ulicia planted her fists on her hips. "Or what?"

"Or I'll not show you where Tovi is."

"You foolish child," Sister Ulicia growled. "We already know where Tovi is. She's in here. You've already led us to her."

Jillian slowly shook her head. "There are miles of passageways down there. You'll get yourselves lost among the bones. You leave Kahlan be or I'll not show you the way."

"I can sense Tovi," Sister Cecilia said with a dismissive sigh. "Cut the girl's throat. We're close enough that I can find Tovi, now, with my gift alone."

"I, too, can sense her," Sister Armina said.

"Sensing that she is near," Jillian said, "doesn't mean that you will be able to find the correct passageway to get to her. Down there, down with the bones, you may be only a short distance from her but if you take one wrong turn among many you must make, you will go for miles and never reach her. People have gone down there and died because they couldn't find their way back out."

Sister Ulicia clasped her hands, considering, as she peered down her nose at the girl.

"We don't have time for this right now," she finally announced. "Get going," she told Jillian. She turned a meaningful look on the other two Sisters. "Soon enough we will even this score—along with others."

She turned back with a menacing expression that widened Jillian's eyes. "You get us to Tovi or she's liable to get impatient and start breaking your grandfather's bones . . . one at a time."

Jillian's face registered sudden alarm. She immediately led them into a labyrinth of passages and rooms through the back of the building. There were places where the passageways were open to the moonlight. In other places it was cramped and black as death. The Sisters lit small flames that hovered above their palms so that they could see. Jillian looked startled to learn that the women could do such a thing.

They emerged from the building into another graveyard. Without slowing, Jillian led them through the place of the dead, among hillocks covered with gnarled olive trees and rows of graves mottled with wildflowers. She finally brought them to a halt above a gravestone standing on its side beside a black hole in the ground.

"Down this rat hole?" Sister Armina asked.

"If you want to get to Tovi." Jillian grabbed a lantern from beside the cover stone and, after a Sister lit it, started down.

They all funneled into the narrow stairway, following Jillian down. The ancient stone steps were irregular, with their leading edges rounded over and worn smooth. For Kahlan, with all the weight she was carrying on her back, the descent was treacherous. The sisters held out wavering flames to help them see. At landings they all turned with the stairs and continued ever deeper into the realm of graves.

When they finally reached the bottom the passage opened into wider corridors that were carved from the solid but soft rock of the ground itself. All around were niches carved in the rock walls. Kahlan noticed that all those recesses held bones.

"Watch your heads," Jillian said over her shoulder as she went through one of the doorways to the side.

They all ducked as they went through after her and into a room with a ceiling just as low as the doorway. At intersections Jillian took turns without any hesitation, as if she were following a trail painted on the floor. Kahlan noticed that there were a few footprints in the dust, but she also saw footprints going off down many of the different corridors. The prints were bigger than would have been made by the girl's small feet.

The cramped corridor finally opened into larger chambers. They passed through seemingly endless rooms stacked with orderly piles of bones. Other, narrow rooms were lined with niches stacked full of bones, as if they had begun to run out of places to put all the dead.

There was a series of several rooms filled only with skulls. Kahlan estimated that there had to be thousands of them. They had all been carefully fitted together into large niches, each skull facing out. Each niche was filled right up to the top. Kahlan gazed at all the hollow eyes staring back at her, watching her pass. She reminded herself that these things had once been people. They all had once been alive. Each had once been a living, breathing, thinking individual. They had once lived lives filled with fears and longings. It reminded her of how precious and brief life was, how important it was because once it was gone, for that person it was gone for good. It reminded her yet again of why she wanted her life back.

With Jillian, Kahlan felt that she now had a link back to the world, to who she was. When Jillian saw and remembered her, Kahlan felt just a little more alive, as if she really was somebody, and her life had meaning.

They passed through rooms with leg bones stacked in their own niches, arm bones in yet others. Long stone bins carved at the base of the side walls lined some of the rooms. These bins held smaller bones, all laid in neatly.

Separating the bones of skeletons in such a way seemed to Kahlan a strange thing to do. She thought that, surely, it would be more respectful of the dead to leave the bones of the deceased together. It was possible, she supposed, that they didn't have the luxury of space, since stacking them this way did save a great deal of space. Maybe it was simply too much work to carve a niche for just one body, or one family, when there were so many dead to bury. Maybe there had been a great sickness that claimed a large portion of the population and they couldn't be burdened with such niceties.

The city within the walls looked pretty cramped. Space must have been at a premium. If the people, and their dead, were to remain within the walls of the city, the living would have had to make concessions.

It seemed an odd problem, since the land around the city stretched empty from horizon to the horizon. She wondered if it could have been a time of war, when sentimental considerations for the dead had to be abandoned in favor of the needs of the living. The headland did seem the most defensible place around. While parts of the walls were at the edge of the sheer bluffs, they could always have enlarged the city farther back on the headland. She supposed that it could be that expanding such massive city walls was considered too difficult.

She wondered if it could be, too, that the people who had once lived here simply didn't have the same sentiment for the dead that other peoples did. After all, what real significance was there in bones? The life was gone from them. The individual they once had been was no more. It was life, after all, that really mattered. Their world had ended with their death.

But the people here must have had an attachment to these bones, to the people they had been, considering how difficult it would have been to construct such an underground city for the dead. Kahlan noticed, too, the faded, carefully drawn and carved decorations around the niches. No, those alive cared. They mourned for those who had died.

She wondered if, when she died, anyone would remember who she had been, or ever even know that this person, Kahlan, once had lived, had loved life. She felt an odd jealousy for all these bones. Friends and family of each set of bones down in this place had known the person they had been, grieved for them, and put these talismans of that valued individual to rest in a way that the living would remember those who had passed.

Kahlan wondered what had happened to all the people who had lived in this place, to the people who buried these bones. She wondered who had buried them. After all, the empty buildings bore silent testament that no one was left. Except Jillian. From what Kahlan had learned, Jillian lived with a small band of nomadic people who came to this place from time to time.

They abruptly arrived at a section of the passageway that looked like it had partially collapsed, leaving the floor strewn with rubble. Sister Armina snatched the girl's arm. "This tour of the catacombs is getting ridiculous. You had better not be leading us on some silly roundabout lark."

Jillian lifted an arm to point. "But we're almost there. Come on and you'll see."

"All right," Ulicia said, "get on with it, then."

Jillian stepped around a huge slab of stone that looked like it might have once sealed what was beyond. There were gouges on the floor where it had been slid aside to clear the passageway and allow access to what lay beyond. When Jillian went in, Kahlan could see that her lantern lit a chamber beyond with shelves carved from the solid rock. The shelves were all loaded with books. The colors of the leather spines were faded, but they looked to once have been mostly an assortment of rich reds and deep blues, with the rest being a variety of other colors from pale green to gold.

The Sisters marveled as they gazed at all the books. They were suddenly in good spirits. Sister Armina let out a low whistle as she slowed to peer around at the shelves. Sister Cecilia laughed out loud. Even Sister Ulicia smiled as she ran her fingers over the dusty spines.

"This way," Jillian said to move them along.

They happily followed the girl as she went through a series of rooms, mostly small and cramped, with shelves all stuffed full of books. Jillian wound her way through a warren of passageways carved though the soft rock, taking them ever deeper into the underground library. The Sisters' heads swiveled, seemingly lost in reading what titles they could make out as they shuffled along behind Jillian and Kahlan. The light of the lantern fell into dark rooms they passed, revealing yet more books.

"Curse the Light," Sister Ulicia whispered to herself in delight. "We have found the central site in Caska. This is the place where the book will be. I bet that Tovi has been spending her time searching for it."

"I bet she's already found it," Sister Cecilia said, excitement animating her voice.

Sister Ulicia grinned. "I have a feeling you're right."

Through a more finely carved, barrel-ceilinged hallway adorned with a vineyard mural that had long ago faded to a ghost of what it once had been, they rounded a corner and arrived at a set of double doors. The two doors, carved with simple designs of grape vines and leaves, were each narrow enough that they could easily have been one wide door. Kahlan supposed that the two doors made the entrance a little grander, for some reason.

"I sense Tovi beyond—at last," Sister Cecilia said with a sigh of relief.

"I think we should start the rituals tonight," Sister Armina said in a bubbly voice.

Sister Ulicia nodded as she laid a hand on the bronze lever. "If Tovi has managed to find the book—and I bet that by now she has—then, with the three boxes finally back together, I don't see why it can't begin at once." She smiled distantly. "The sooner the Keeper is freed from his prison, the sooner we will have our reward."

Kahlan wondered if there was any way she could ruin their plans. She was sure that once they accomplished whatever it was they intended to do, there would be no going back—for anyone. She considered the boxes she was carrying, and wondered what would happen if, when the Sisters were distracted with finally seeing Tovi again, she were to smash at least one of the boxes. She might even have time to smash both.

Kahlan knew that such an act would do more than incur the full wrath of the Sisters; she expected that they would probably kill her. But then, Kahlan had come to believe that if the Sisters succeeded, she would be as good as dead anyway.

Sister Armina leaned in. "And, as our first act, I think we should settle an old score." Her expression turned venomous. "I remember all too well being sent to the tents by that arrogant brute. I'll never forget what his soldiers were allowed to do to us."

Sister Ulicia's brow drew down with a murderous glare. "Oh, I think that is one score we will all relish settling." A baleful smile spread through the glare. She twisted the bronze lever. "Let's get on with it."

Sister Ulicia threw open the doors and marched into the pitch black room beyond. "Tovi? What are you doing in the dark—sleeping?" Annoyance took control of her tone. "Wake up. It's us. We finally made it here."

With the Sisters in the lead, carrying small flames above their upturned palms, there was just enough light to make out nearby torches in brackets on the walls to each side, but not much else. The Sisters sent those small flames into the cold torches, igniting them with a hot whoosh. As the torches flared to life, light flooded a room that wasn't very large, with bookshelves carved into the straw-colored rock of the walls.

On the other side of the small room sat a heavy iron and plank table. In the tall, decoratively carved chair behind the table sat a burly man, his chin resting on a thumb as he watched them.

He was the fiercest-looking man Kahlan had ever seen.

The three Sisters froze in midstride, their eyes opened wide, reflecting their confused, disbelieving shock at what they were seeing before them.

The powerfully built man sat calmly behind the table, watching the three Sisters. That he didn't speak, didn't move, didn't seem to be in the least bit of a hurry only increased the palpable sense of danger in the room. The only sound was the hissing torches.

The man, with massive, muscled arms and a bull neck, was the embodiment of pure menace. Without a shirt, his brawny shoulders bulged from a lambskin vest that lay open in the middle, displaying his naked, powerful chest. Silver bands encircled his arms above bulky biceps. Each of his thick fingers bore a gold or silver ring, as if brazenly proclaiming them plunder rather than decoration. His shaved head reflected glimmers of the fluttering torchlight. Kahlan couldn't imagine him with hair; it would have diminished his intimidating presence. A gold ring in his left nostril held one end of a thin gold chain that ran to another ring at mid-height in his left ear. He was clean-shaven except for a two-inch braid of mustache growing downward from the corners of his smirk, and another braid in the center under his lower lip.

As frightening, as formidable, as remorseless as the man looked, it was his eyes that were the true nightmare. There were no whites to them at all. Instead, they were clouded over with sullen, dusky shapes that shifted in a field of inky obscurity. Even so, there was no doubt whatsoever in Kahlan's mind when his gaze settled on her. That gaze made her feel naked. She thought her knees might buckle under the weight of her galloping panic.

When his grim gaze moved to the Sisters, Kahlan reached out blindly, finding Jillian, and pulled her protectively under an arm. She could feel the girl trembling. Kahlan noticed, though, that Jillian didn't seem surprised to find the man in the room.

Kahlan couldn't understand the Sisters' silence, or their inaction. By the overt look of threat presented by the man, she expected that they would have incinerated him by now, just to be on the safe side. The Sisters had never before been the least bit shy about killing anyone they even suspected might be trouble. This man was clearly far more than trouble. He looked capable of crushing their skulls in his fist. The look in his eyes said that he was used to seeing such deeds done.

Behind Kahlan, two burly men stepped out of the dark corners and closed the double doors. They, too, were fierce-looking, with wild tattoos in menacing swirls over their features. Their massive muscles were sweat-slicked and sooty, as if they never washed off the smoke of oily fires. As they stepped together before the closed doors, Kahlan could smell their sour sweat through the stench of the burning pitch.

These two looked more than ready for any eventuality. Heavy, studded leather straps holding a variety of knives crisscrossed their chests. Axes and flanged maces hanging on their weapons belts glinted in the light of the hissing torches. Their faces were also studded with metal spikes—in their ears, eyebrows, and through the bridges of their noses. It almost appeared that they had hammered nails through parts of their faces. They, too, were shaved bald. The two men didn't look entirely human, much less civilized, but rather a deliberate corruption of the notion of mankind, embracing instead steel, soot, and elements of a beast.

Even though they carried short swords, they didn't draw them. They didn't appear the least little bit afraid of the Sisters.

"Emperor Jagang . . ." Sister Ulicia's watery, weak voice trailed off in abject terror.

Emperor Jagang!

The shock of those two words jolted Kahlan down to her soul.

There was something about her concept of this man, formed from seeing his army from a distance and from having been through some of the places they had attacked, that made Kahlan fear him even more than the Sisters. In contrast to the Sisters, masculinity added an alien dimension to the nature of the threat he projected.

For as far back as she could remember, they had done everything possible to stay away from Jagang, and yet here he sat, right in front of them. He looked relaxed, like a man who had everything well in hand. He appeared to have no worries. Not even Sisters of the Dark appeared to concern him.

Kahlan knew that this was no accidental encounter. It had been staged.

More than Kahlan's fear of Jagang engendered by the Sisters' overheard conversations and their dogged avoidance of the man, there was something else, something deeper, a dark dread rooted in her very soul, almost like a memory beyond her reach betrayed only by its indistinct but sinister shadow.

When Kahlan stole a glance to the side, she saw that the Sisters appeared frozen in place, as if they had been turned to stone. They had also gone ashen.

Sister Ulicia was wearing her blue dress, chosen especially for the reunion with Tovi. It was now dusty not only from the climb up onto the headland, but from the descent down into the interior of it. Sister Armina wore a dress with white ruffles at the wrists and at the low neckline. Under the circumstances, in a dusty grave and standing before leering brutes, the ruffles looked naively ridiculous. Sister Cecilia, older, tightly controlled, and habitually tidy with curly gray hair, now looked on the ragged rim of a leap into the refuge of madness.

Jagang's sullen eyes watched the three Sisters. He was savoring the moment, Kahlan knew, savoring their startled horror. If the Sisters had been able to do anything about the situation, Kahlan was sure that they would already have done it.

Sister Armina's tongue darted out to moistened her lips. "Excellency," she said in a small, strained voice. Kahlan thought it a pitiful attempt at a respectful greeting, conspicuously born of panic, not respect.

"Excellency," Sister Cecilia added in a voice no more steady.

Kahlan had on rare occasions seen the Sisters cautious, even wary, but she had never seen them afraid. She had never even been able to imagine them being frightened. They had always seemed in utter and complete control. Now their habitual, haughty dispositions were nowhere in evidence.

All three Sisters bowed in halting movements, like three puppets on strings.

When she straightened, Sister Ulicia swallowed in trembling terror. As frightened as she obviously was, confused curiosity, as well as the unendurable silence, drove her to speak.

"Excellency, what are you doing here?"

Jagang's treacherous glare again melted into a smirk at the gentle, innocent, feminine tone of her question.

"Ulicia, Ulicia, Ulicia . . ." He sighed heavily. "You really are one monumentally stupid bitch."

All three women went to a knee as if they had been slammed down by an invisible fist. Small, whining whimpers escaped their throats.

"Please, Excellency, we meant no—"

"I know exactly what you meant. I know every last dirty little detail of everything in your minds."

Kahlan had never seen Sister Ulicia cowed, much less so badly shaken. "Excellency . . . I don't understand . . ."

"Of course you don't," he said with a sneer as her words dwindled away to silence. "That is why you are on your knees before me, and not the other way around, which is just what you were wishing, isn't it, Armina?"

When his gaze slid to Sister Armina she let out a small, startled cry. Blood oozed from her ears, running in a little red trail down the snow white flesh of her neck. Other than her slight trembling, she didn't move.

Jillian's arms clutched at Kahlan. Kahlan put a hand protectively to the side of the girl's face, pressing her close, trying to comfort her when there was no real comfort to be had before such a man.

"You also have Tovi, then?" Sister Ulicia asked, still so surprised by the turn of events that she couldn't come to grips with it.

"Tovi!" Jagang burst into a fit of gruff laughter. "Tovi! Why, Tovi has been dead for ages."

Sister Ulicia stared in horror. "She's dead?"

He lifted his arm with a dismissive wave. "Finally sent to the afterlife by a mutual friend, a very unfaithful and traitorous friend. I imagine that the Keeper of the underworld is quite angry with Tovi's failure in her service to him. You will have all of eternity to find out just how angry." His smirk returned as he glared at the woman. "But not until I am finished with you in this life."

Sister Ulicia bowed her head. "Of course, Excellency."

Kahlan noticed that Sister Armina had wet herself. Sister Cecilia looked like she was ready to collapse into tears—or screams.

"Excellency," Sister Ulicia ventured, "how could you . . . I mean, with our bond."

"Your bond!" Jagang roared with laughter again, slapping the table. "Ah yes, your bond to Lord Rahl. Your touching loyalty to Lord Rahl that 'protects' you from my talents as a dream walker."

Kahlan's heart sank to hear that the Sisters were in some kind of alliance with Lord Rahl. For some reason, she had thought more of the man. It hurt to find she was wrong.

" 'We're not the ones attacking Richard Rahl,' " he said in a falsetto voice, clasping his hands in a mocking manner, apparently quoting some statement from Ulicia's past. " 'Jagang is the one going after him, seeking to destroy him, not us. We are the ones who will wield the power of Orden and then we will grant Richard Rahl what only we will have the power to grant. That is enough to preserve our bond and protect us from the dream walker.' "

He lost the effeminate pretense. "Your loyalty and devotion to Lord Rahl is touching."

His fist slammed down on the table. His face went red with rage. "Do you stupid bitches actually believe that such a bond to Lord Rahl as you dreamed up would hold you free of harm?"

Kahlan remembered the Sisters talking about the same thing, and she hadn't been able to understand it back then, either. Why would Richard Rahl have anything to do with these evil women, much less enter into a pact with them? Could such a thing really be true? Could it be that he was really no better than they?

One thing about it all didn't seem to make any sense, though. If they were sworn to him, then why would they steal the boxes from his palace?

"But the bond's magic . . ." Sister Ulicia's voice trailed off into silence.

Jagang stood—a move that made the three gasp and tremble all the more. Kahlan was sure that, had they been able to, they would have backed up at least a step and likely more.

He shook his head, as if he could not believe that they could be so ignorant as not to understand. "Ulicia, I was there in your mind watching the whole sorry event. I was there the day, years ago, that you proposed the scheme to Richard Rahl. I have to tell you, I didn't really believe that you were serious. I had difficulty believing that you could be so stupid as to believe that you could strike such a bargain to gain your freedom from me."

"But it should have worked."

"No, there was no way such a thing could work. It was nothing more than an irrational idea. You wanted to believe it was true, so you did."

"You were in our minds that day?" Sister Cecilia asked. "Why would you allow us to believe we had succeeded?"

His inky gaze fixed on her. "Don't you remember what I told you all in the very beginning, on the first day you stood before me? Control, I told you, is more important than killing. I told you then that I could have killed you six, but what good would you be to me then? As long as you're under my dominion, you're no threat to me, and of use in oh so many ways.

"No, of course you don't remember because you chose instead to think that you were smart enough to trick me with your convoluted, illogical notion of the bond. You think you are too clever to be outwitted, and so here you stand before me again, never having left my dominion."

"And yet, you just let us . . . go about our business?" Sister Cecilia asked.

Jagang shrugged as he stepped around the table. "I could have stopped you at any moment, if I chose. I knew I had you under my thumb. But what would I have had to gain, then? Just a few more Sisters of the Dark, and I already had plenty of those—although their numbers are seriously diminished by now." He leaned down toward them with an aside. "Your kind has a tendency to do a lot of dying on the behalf of the cause of the Fellowship of Order.

"But with you," Jagang said as he straightened, "I had something highly interesting. I had Sisters of the Dark who were up to things." He tapped a thick finger to his temple. "Who had devious plans, and the knowledge to pursue them.

"You have a lifetime of experience from the vaults at the Palace of the

Prophets, vaults holding thousands of books that are now gone. No matter how irrational your plans sometimes become—witness your present condition—that does not negate your reserve of knowledge gained through decades of study, or mean that every one of your plans was unworkable."

"So, you knew our plans all along? From that day with Richard Rahl?"

Jagang glared at Sister Ulicia. "Of course I knew. I knew your plan the instant you concocted it." His voice lowered with menace. "You thought I only came into people's dreams. I don't. You thought I wasn't there, in your mind, when you were awake. I was. Once I enter into your mind, Ulicia, I am there, in your mind, always.

"Whatever you think, whenever you think it, I witness it. Every dirty little thing you conceive, I see. Every thought, every action, every vile wish, I know as if it were spoken aloud the instant you conceive it. Because I wasn't making you aware of my presence, though, you ignorantly believed I wasn't there, but I was." He waggled a thick finger. "Oh, Ulicia, I was there.

"When you told Richard Rahl your plan, that you wanted to swear loyalty to him in exchange for someone he cared deeply about, well, I could hardly believe that you just assumed it would work."

For some reason, Kahlan felt a pang of sadness to hear that Richard Rahl had someone he cared deeply about. She guessed that ever since that day she had been in his beautiful garden, she had come to feel a connection to him on some deeply personal level, even if it was only a shared appreciation for the beauty of growing things, an appreciation of nature, and thus the world around them, the world of life. But now she was hearing that he was dealing with Sisters of the Dark, and that he had someone he cared deeply about. It made her feel all the more like a forgotten nobody. She wondered what she could have been thinking.

"But . . . but," Sister Ulicia stammered, "it worked . . ."

Jagang shook his head. "Fidelity on your terms, fidelity even though you would continue to work for his destruction, even though you would continue to work for everything he stands against, fidelity even though you would continue to be sworn to the Keeper of the underworld, fidelity concocted of your selected, selfish wishes is just that—wishes. Wishing doesn't turn your desires into reality just because you want it to."

Kahlan felt at least a small level of relief to hear that the Sisters were continuing to work for Lord Rahl's destruction. Maybe that meant that he wasn't really an ally of the Sisters. Maybe, in some way, he was like her, being used against his will.

"I could hardly believe it as I listened to you dictating the terms of your loyalty to him," Jagang was saying, gesturing in a grand fashion, "claiming that such fidelity was subject to the moral filter you, not he, would apply. I mean, if you were going to contrive beliefs out of thin air, Ulicia, why didn't you just save yourselves some trouble and decide that by sheer willpower alone your mind had been rendered impenetrable to a dream walker? That would have been just as effective a shield."

He shook his head. "My, my, Ulicia. How cruel of the nature of existence not to allow you your irrational desires."

He swept an arm out. "And, just as amazing, the rest of your Sisters believed it too. I know; I was there in their minds as well, watching as they were overcome with glee that they were to be free of my ability just because you claimed you could tap into the bond to the Lord Rahl with your own form of loyalty."

"But you allowed us to do it," Sister Ulicia said, still overwhelmed with astonishment. "Why would you not strike us down then?"

Jagang shrugged. "I had plenty of Sisters under my thumb. This was an interesting opportunity. I learn a great deal from the knowledge others possess. Learning things gives one power one would not otherwise have.

"I decided to see just what you could accomplish if left to your own devices, see what you could learn for me. After all, I could have dropped any of you at any time if I grew weary of my little experiment. There were times when I was greatly tempted, such as the time not long ago when Armina said 'I'd love to string Jagang up and have my way with him.'"

He arched an eyebrow. "Remember that, Armina? Not to worry if it has slipped your mind. I will be reminding you of it from time to time, just to refresh your memory."

Sister Armina lifted a hand, as if in supplication. "I, I was only . . ."

He glared at her until she fell silent, unable to conjure an excuse, and then went on.

"Yes, I was there all along. Yes, I saw everything. Yes, I could have struck you down at any time. But I have something you don't have, Ulicia. I have patience. With patience you can move mountains—or go around them, or climb over them."

"But you could have had Richard Rahl right there, when we offered him our terms. Or you could have had him at his camp."

"You could have had him at camp as well. You spelled him, and had him down. You could have ended it. Then why didn't you? Because you had a grander plan, so you left him be, thinking that your bond to him was your protection, while you went on to pursue something of greater worth to you."

"But you didn't need him," she pressed. "You could have taken him."

"Ah, but while killing people as punishment is useful, it's not nearly as beneficial as what you can do with them when they are alive. Take you three, for example. Death brings no great punishment, only the reward of the afterlife if you have served the Creator in this one. You three, however, will be denied the Creator's Light. What use is that to me? But if a person is alive I can make them suffer." He leaned closer. "Don't you agree?"

"Yes, Excellency," Sister Ulicia managed to say in a strangled voice as blood began to trickle from her ear.

"I liked parts of your plan," he said as he straightened. "I find them very useful for my own purpose—things such as the boxes of Orden. Why should I kill Richard Rahl; I have the opportunity to do so much more than simply kill him. I want him to be alive to endure inconceivable suffering.

"By letting him live that day at his camp, the same as you did when you ignited your Chainfire spell, I knew that I would be able to use this new opportunity to take everything from him. Since I was in your minds, I, too, was protected from the Chainfire spell, the same as you.

"Now, with everything you have given me, I can strip Richard Rahl of his power, his land, his people, his friends, his loved ones. I can take everything from him in the name of the Fellowship of Order."

Jagang drew his hand into a tight fist before him as he gritted his teeth. "For opposing our rightful cause, I intend to crush him down to his soul, and then, when I have wrung everything out of him, given him every kind of pain there is in this world, I will extinguish the flame of that soul. And you have made it all possible."

Sister Ulicia nodded tearfully at all that was lost to her. She seemed resigned to her new duty.

"Excellency, we can accomplish none of it without the book we came here for."

Jagang lifted a volume off the table and held it up for them to see. "*The*

Book of Counted Shadows. The book you came here to find. I thought to search for it while I waited for you to complete your journey here."

He tossed the book back on the table. "An exceedingly rare book. This, of course, is one of the few copies that were never supposed to be made and so it was hidden in this place. Of course I was there, in your mind, when you found all of this out.

"You even brought me the means of verification." His unsettling gaze moved to Kahlan. "And you have a collar around her neck by which I can control her." He turned a condescending smile on Sister Ulicia. "You see, since I'm in your mind I have but to command it and through you I control her every move—just as easily as you do."

Kahlan's hope for a chance to escape evaporated. If the Sisters were cruel masters, this man was something far worse. Kahlan didn't yet know what his intentions were, but she held no illusions that they were anything but vile.

An inkling of something else began to well up in her. For some reason she was of value to the Sisters and now just as valuable to Jagang. How could she be the means of verification of some ancient book hidden away for thousands of years? She had always been told that she was a nobody, a slave, and nothing more. She was beginning to understand that the Sisters had been lying to her. They only wanted her to think she was a nobody. It appeared, instead, that she was, somehow, pivotally important to all of them.

Jagang flicked a hand at Jillian. "Besides the collar, I have her to help me convince Kahlan here to do as she is told. Tell me, my dear, have you ever been with a man?"

Jillian pushed up against Kahlan. "You said you would free my grandfather. You said that if I did exactly as you said, and brought the Sisters here, you would set him and the others free. I did what you told me to do."

"Yes, you did. And you really were quite convincing. I was there, in their minds, the whole time, watching your performance. You followed my instructions flawlessly." His voice turned as threatening as his glare. "Now answer the question or your grandfather and the others will be vulture food by morning. Have you ever been with a man?"

"I'm not sure what you mean," she said in a small voice.

"I see. Well, if Kahlan doesn't do everything I tell her to do, you will be given over to my soldiers for their amusement. They like getting their hands on young things like you who haven't before experienced . . . de-sires such as theirs."

Jillian's fingers tightened on Kahlan's shirt. She pressed her face against Kahlan's arm as she stifled a sob. Kahlan squeezed the girl's shoulder, trying to comfort her, trying to let her know that she wouldn't let anything bad happen to her if she could help it.

"You have me," Kahlan said. "Leave her be."

"Tovi has the third box," Sister Ulicia said. It was clear to Kahlan that she was trying to stall, to buy time, as well as ingratiate herself with Jagang.

He glared at her. "It was stolen from her."

"Stolen? Well . . . I can help you find it."

Jagang leaned his backside on the table as he folded his massive arms. "Ulicia, when are you going to learn that not only do I stand in front of you, but I am in your mind as well. I know everything you're thinking. But do keep coming up with your schemes. They're quite inventive.

"And did you ever conceive some grand plans," he said with a satisfied sigh as he strolled closer. "You got farther with them than I thought you would ever be able to."

His voice took on an edge that ran shivers up Kahlan's spine. "And look at what my patience has netted me," he said as he turned to her, fixing her in the gaze of his terrible, inky eyes. "You wanted to know why I let you wander around free, doing as you wished? Here is the answer. Letting you cast about on your own, Ulicia, has netted me the prize of prizes."

Kahlan knew now that she had been correct. She was for some reason valuable. She wished she knew why. She wished she knew who she re-ally was.

Kahlan could do nothing but watch as Jagang closed the distance to her. There was nowhere to run. Just in case she might have had that thought, though, she felt a shock of pain blaze down her spine and burn through her legs, locking them in place. She knew it was the collar causing the painful paralysis, because the Sisters had done that very thing before. He, of course, would know that, because he had been in their minds all along to see it done. She could see in his merciless expression that, this time, he was the cause of the pain.

Jagang reached out and ran his thick fingers through Kahlan's hair. She didn't want him touching her, but she could do nothing to prevent it. He seemed to forget everyone else in the room as he stared at her.

"Yes, Ulicia, you surely did bring me the prize of prizes. You brought me Kahlan Amnell."

Amnell.

So now she knew her last name. She had detected the slightest hesitation after her name, almost as if a title should have been added to her name.

Jagang leaned close with an obscene smile that carried meaning she didn't want to consider. Kahlan stood her ground by her own will, even if she had no real choice. Jagang's powerful, muscled body pressed up against her. It was like feeling the weight of a bull leaning against her.

With one finger, the man lifted her hair away from her neck. His stubble scraped her cheek as he put his mouth by her ear.

"But Kahlan doesn't know who she is, doesn't even know the true nature of the prize that she truly is."

For the first time, Kahlan wished that she were invisible, that this man could not see her just as everyone but the Sisters and Jillian could not see her. This was not a man she wanted to recognize her. This was a man she didn't want anywhere near her.

"You cannot begin to imagine," he whispered intimately in a voice that seared her with hot dread, "just how extraordinarily unpleasant this is going to be for you.

"You were worth my patience, worth everything I've had to put up with from Ulicia. We are going to become quite close, you and I. If you think I intend the worst for Lord Rahl, then you cannot even begin to imagine what I have in mind for you, darlin."

Kahlan had never felt so alone, so helpless, in her life. Against her will, she felt a tear run down her cheek even as she managed to hold back a sob deep in her throat.

Once Jagang turned away and was no longer looking at her, Kahlan at last allowed herself to swallow with silent relief to have his hands off of her, even if he had only touched her hair. Helpless dread shivered through her at him having been that close to her. She fully understood the meaningful look he'd given her. She knew that he could do anything he wanted to her, and she was completely at his mercy.

No. There was still breath in her lungs. She couldn't give in to such a belief. She couldn't allow herself to think she was helpless.

She had to think, instead of simply surrendering to panic. Panic could not help her accomplish anything. Maybe it would turn out to be true that she had no control of her own life, but she knew that she was lost to his will if she resigned herself to the blind guidance of panic. That's what he wanted her to do.

Across the room, at the heavy table, Jagang pulled the book closer. He opened the front cover and then leaned on both hands as he silently peered down at it. The rounded brawn of his broad shoulders, heavily muscled back, and thick neck looked more like that of a bull than a man. The things he wore only served to enhance his less than human appearance. He, and his men, appeared to deliberately shun the mantle of the noblest ideals of mankind and instead embrace a base, animalistic aspect. The aspiration toward the lower form of existence, rather than a higher one, revealed an elemental dimension of the overt threat these men represented; they aspired to be not men, but something less.

Back not far in front of the doors, the two huge guards stood silently with their feet spread and their hands clasped behind their backs. Kahlan rested a hand on Jillian's shoulder when the girl looked up in silent anxiety at being in the presence of such men, who, from time to time, cast dark gazes her way.

The two guards didn't see Kahlan. At least, she didn't think they did. She had minded their behavior and noticed that from time to time, besides

Jillian, they eyed the Sisters, but without much interest. When Jagang spoke to Kahlan the guards looked a bit confused. They said nothing, but Kahlan knew that, to them, it must have appeared that their leader was talking to himself. Like everyone but Jillian, the Sisters, and Jagang through his link to the Sisters, the guards forgot Kahlan before they knew they had seen her. She wished she could be just as invisible to their leader.

"What of your army, Excellency?" Sister Ulicia asked, still plainly trying to buy time by engaging him in conversation. She, too, was trying not to give in to panic.

Jagang looked over his shoulder with a wicked grin. "They are close."

Bewildered, Sister Ulicia blinked. "Close?"

He nodded, still grinning. "Just over the horizon to the north, up into D'Hara."

"The north—into D'Hara!" Sister Armina blurted out. "But that's not possible, Excellency."

He lifted an eyebrow, clearly enjoying their surprise.

"They must be wrong in their reports about their location," Sister Armina said, sounding like she was grasping at an opportunity to ingratiate herself with the emperor. She licked her lips. "What I mean, Excellency, is that, we, well, we passed them long ago. They were still back up in the Midlands, still on their way south to get around the intervening mountains. They could not possibly have gotten . . ."

Her quavering words dwindled to nothing, as if looking upon Jagang drained her of all courage, even the courage to speak, until she was left a silent shell of dread.

"Oh but they have already rounded the mountains down here and turned north up into D'Hara," Jagang said. "You see, I influenced your minds to direct you to go where I wanted you to go, when I wanted you to go there. It was my aim to have you think you were safe, to think you knew where I was. You never even heard my whispers, but those whispers still guided you without you even being aware of it."

"But we saw your troops," Sister Cecilia said. "We saw them and went around them. We left them far behind."

"You saw what I wanted you to see," Jagang said with a dismissive gesture. "You thought you were going where you wanted, but you were in fact going where I guided you—right to me and my main force.

"I sent you past a number of rear-guard divisions and then some units going south to other areas in the Midlands. I was making you believe what I wanted you to believe, seeing to it that you all felt confident in your plans, while I saw to it that the main army proceeded with my plans.

"Our forces have made it a great deal farther than you thought. I want to finish this war and I can see that such a goal is finally within sight, so I adjusted my tactics accordingly. Marching the main force at such a grueling pace is something that I usually don't do because it wears an army down and costs us a number of men, usually to no purpose, but the end is now in sight so it is worth the losses. Besides, they are there to serve the cause of the Order, not the other way around."

"I see," Armina said in a small voice, disheartened to learn yet more of their complete deception and of their helpless plight.

"Now, we have work."

The three Sisters suddenly sprang forward, as if yanked closer by invisible leashes around their necks. "Yes, Excellency," they all said as one. Apparently, Jagang had growled a silent order that only they could hear, probably just to remind them that he was there, in their minds.

It occurred to Kahlan that he could control her by the collar around her neck, through his control of the minds of the Sisters, but it didn't appear that he was able to control her directly. Besides merely having some basic hatred for her, he also seemed to be trying to paralyze her with fear as one aspect of controlling her behavior by stopping her from thinking—in addition to using the collar and the Sisters. It would seem that while he was somehow within the minds of the Sisters, he was not in Kahlan's mind.

Of course, she couldn't be sure of that. After all, the Sisters had been deluded into thinking the same thing—that the dream walker was not there, in their minds, watching their every thought. So, while she had to assume that it was a possibility, she just didn't think it was true that he was in her mind as well. There was more to it, though; he was treating her in a different way than he treated the Sisters. They were treacherous captives; Kahlan was a prize.

He had deceived them for a purpose. In essence he was spying on their thoughts. They were up to things and he wanted to surreptitiously eavesdrop on those plans so that he could turn them to his own advantage. He knew that Kahlan was not up to anything other than wanting to escape from the Sisters. She had no more plans beyond that. She didn't even have a memory of who she really was. There was nothing for Jagang to spy on within her mind. It had to be obvious that she didn't want to be his captive, either, that she wanted her life back. So, there was nothing that he could really learn by secretly spying on her thoughts—at least, not yet, not unless she began to think rather than be blinded by panic.

But if he really wasn't in her mind, then why not? He was a dream walker, after all, a man of such power that the Sisters had been trying to stay away from him—unsuccessfully, as it turned out, precisely because of his ability and power. He very much wanted Kahlan as his prize of prizes, as he'd called her. If he was in her mind he could have controlled her with the same invisible leash he used to control the Sisters and not have to go through their ability to do it. He didn't seem like the sort of man who would resort to such a secondhand method of control if he didn't have to. He wouldn't need the Sisters to control her if he could enter her mind.

What would be the point, now, of not making his presence in her mind known, if he really could do it? Even more material, if she was that important to him, he would surely want to have that manner of control if it was possible, so why wasn't he able to get into her mind and control her directly?

There was something more going on. She got the distinct impression that there were things he was being careful not to say.

"This is it, then," he said to the Sisters. "This is *The Book of Counted Shadows*. This is what you came here for, what you needed. I want to get started right away."

"But Excellency," Sister Ulicia said, looking startled by the very idea, "we only have two of the boxes. We would need all three."

"No you don't. You only need to use this book to discover if one of the two boxes we have here is the one you really need. If the missing box is the one that would destroy us, or destroy all that exists, then why would we need it?"

Sister Ulicia looked like she had very good reasons why they would need it but she really didn't want to argue the point.

"Well," she said, searching for the right words, "I suppose that very well might be true. After all, we haven't actually had the chance to study *The Book of Counted Shadows* yet, so we can't know for sure. The other references could have been wrong. That's why we were coming here, after all. We needed the book. It could be as you say, Excellency, that we don't actually need the third box."

It was obvious to Kahlan that Sister Ulicia didn't believe such a thing. Jagang didn't seem concerned by her doubt.

"And here it sits, waiting." He gestured to the book lying on the heavy table. "Once you study this book, then you can tell which box is which— which one is the one we need. If it turns out that these two are the wrong boxes, perhaps by then the third will turn up."

The Sisters hesitated at agreeing to his idea, but didn't seem willing to offer an argument.

Finally, after glancing to the others, Sister Ulicia conceded the value of his suggestion. "None of us has seen this book before, so we will need to . . . to learn from it what we can. I think you are correct, Excellency. Studying the book would be in order."

Jagang tilted his head toward the book lying on the table. "Then get to it."

The Sisters crowded close and leaned over, reverently gazing for the first time upon the book they had so long sought. They read in silence, with Jagang keeping an eye on them as well as the book.

"Excellency," Sister Ulicia said after only a brief examination, "it would appear that we can't just . . . start, as you put it."

"Why not?"

"Well, look here." She tapped the page. "Right in the beginning, this confirms what we previously had reason to suspect, that there are safe-guards against any eventuality. It says that you need . . ."

She fell silent as she glanced over her shoulder at Kahlan.

"Well," she went on, "right here in the very beginning it says, '*Verification of the truth of* The Book of Counted Shadows, *if spoken by another, rather than read by the one who commands the boxes, can only be insured by the use of* . . . ' Well, Excellency, you can see yourself what it says."

It was clear to Kahlan that the woman was avoiding saying something aloud. Jagang likewise read it in silence.

"So what?" he argued. "It *is* being read by the one who commands the boxes. It's being read by me, through you. I control the boxes now."

Sister Ulicia cleared her throat. "Excellency, I want to be perfectly honest with you—"

"I'm in your mind, Ulicia. It would be impossible for you to be anything but perfectly honest. I know you doubt my idea, but are unwilling to express such thoughts aloud. So, as you know, I would be aware if you were trying to deceive me."

"Yes, Excellency." She gestured to the book. "But you see, this is a very technical issue."

"What is?"

"The verification issue, Excellency. This is an instructional book on implementation of profoundly complex matters. These things are not only profoundly complex, but profoundly dangerous—to all of us. So, for that reason, it is critical to pay strict attention to what this book says. This is not a matter to be approached casually. You can't assume anything. The things this book says are exceptionally specific for good reasons. You have to think about every word, every sentence, every formula in it. You have to consider every possibility. Our lives all depend on the utmost caution in these matters."

"What's so technical about this? It says quite plainly 'Verification, if spoken by another.' It's not spoken by another. We're reading it directly."

"That's the precise point, Excellency. We are not reading it directly."

Jagang's face went red with rage. "What do you think we're standing here doing, then!"

Sister Ulicia gulped air, as if an invisible hand had her by the throat. "Excellency, you command the boxes now. But you are not really reading *The Book of Counted Shadows.*"

He leaned toward her in a menacing fashion. "Then what is it I'm reading?"

"A copy," she said.

He paused. "So?"

"So, in this case, you are not, technically, reading *The Book of Counted Shadows.* You are reading a copy of it. You are, in essence, reading something spoken by another."

His frown deepened. "Who is the one reading it, then?"

"The one who made the copy."

Jagang straightened as comprehension dawned in his expression. "Yes . . . this isn't the original. In a sense I'm hearing it from the one who made the copy." He scratched his stubble. "So it must be verified."

"Exactly, Excellency," Sister Ulicia, visibly relieved.

Jagang looked back over his shoulder at Kahlan. "Come here."

Kahlan hurried to do as he ordered, not wanting to be given any pain in a fight she knew he would easily win. Jillian stuck close to her side, apparently not wanting to be left standing alone back closer to the two fierce guards.

Jagang's big hand grasped the back of Kahlan's neck. He forcibly pulled her forward and bent her down toward the book.

"Look at this and tell me if it is genuine."

After he released her, Kahlan could still feel the painful, lingering impression of his powerful fingers where they had squeezed her neck. She resisted the urge to rub her throbbing flesh and instead picked up the book.

Kahlan didn't have the slightest idea how to tell if a book that she had never seen before was genuine or not. She didn't have any idea what would constitute authenticity. She knew, though, that Jagang would not accept such an excuse. He only cared about getting an answer; he wouldn't want to hear that she didn't know that answer.

Deciding that she at the least had to try, she began leafing through the pages, trying to make it look like she was putting in an honest effort when she was really doing nothing more than flipping over blank pages of a book lying open on the table before her.

"I'm sorry," she said at last, unable to think of anything to tell him other than the truth, "but this is all blank. There is nothing for me to verify."

"She can't see the words, Excellency," Sister Ulicia said under her breath, as if it were hardly a surprise to her. "This is a book of magic. An intact link to specific kinds of Han is required to read it."

Jagang glanced at the collar around Kahlan's neck. "Intact." He peered suspiciously into her eyes. "Maybe she's lying. Maybe she just doesn't want to tell us what she sees."

Kahlan wondered if this was confirmation that he was not in her mind, or if for some reason he was still carrying out a carefully crafted ruse. It didn't seem to her that at this point such reticence to reveal a presence in her mind, if there really was one, would serve any purpose. After all, the boxes, and the book, were the central reason for the entire deception of the Sisters. He had used his secret presence specifically to bring them here, to this book.

Jagang abruptly snatched Jillian by her hair. Jillian let out a surprised but brief, clipped cry. He was obviously hurting her. She did her best not to pull against the hand holding her hair, lest he rip her scalp off.

"I'm going to gouge out one of this girl's eyes," Jagang told Kahlan. "I will then ask again if the book is genuine or not. If I don't get an answer— for whatever reason—then I will gouge out her other eye. I will ask one last time, and if you again don't give me the answer, then I will gouge out her heart. What do you have to say about that?"

The Sisters stood mute as they watched, making no move to interfere. Jagang pulled a knife from a sheath at his belt. Jillian began panting in terror as he jerked her around, drawing his arm up tight across her throat, holding her against his chest to render her helpless and keep her still as he brought the point of a knife perilously close to her face.

"Let me see the book," Kahlan said, hoping to avert the irrevocable.

With a thumb and a free finger of the hand holding the knife, he picked up the book and handed it to her. Kahlan thumbed through the pages more carefully, making sure she wasn't missing any page that might say anything at all, but she still saw nothing. Every single page was blank. There was nothing to see, no way to tell if it was real or not.

She closed the cover and smoothed the flat of her hand over it. She didn't know what to do. She had no idea what to look for. She flipped the book over, checking the back cover. She looked at the deckle edges of the pages. She turned the book, looking down at the title embossed in gold letters on the spine.

Jillian let out a strangled cry as Jagang tightened his grip across her throat, lifting her feet clear of the ground. He brought the point of the knife right up to the girl's right eye. She blinked, unable to turn away from the threat, her lashes brushing the blade's point.

"Time to go blind," Jagang growled.

"It's fake," Kahlan said.

He looked up. "What?"

Kahlan held the book out to him. "This book is a false copy. It's fake."

Sister Ulicia took a step forward. "How can you possibly know that?" She looked clearly confused that Kahlan could pronounce the book a fraud without being able to read a single word in it.

Kahlan ignored her. Instead, she continued to look into the dream walker's nightmare eyes. Cloudy shapes shifted like angry thunderstorms on a midnight horizon. It took all of her willpower not to look away.

"Are you sure?" Jagang asked.

"Yes," she said with all the confidence she could muster. "It's a fake."

Now acutely focused on Kahlan, Jagang released Jillian. Once free, the girl fled around behind Kahlan, using her for cover.

Jagang watched Kahlan's eyes. "How do you know that it's not *The Book of Counted Shadows*?"

Kahlan, still holding the book out to him, turned it so that he could see the spine. "You are all looking for *The Book of Counted Shadows*. This says *The Book of Counted Shadow*."

His glare heated. "What?"

"You asked how I know it's not genuine. That's how. It says 'Shadow,' not 'Shadows.' It's a fake."

Sister Cecilia wearily wiped a hand across her face. Sister Armina rolled her eyes.

Sister Ulicia, though, frowned at the book, reading the spine for herself. "She's right."

"So what?" Jagang threw up his hands. "So the word 'Shadow' is missing a letter. It's shadow, singular instead of plural. So what?"

"Simple," Kahlan said. "One is real, one is not."

"Simple?" he asked. "You think it's that simple?"

"How much more simple can it get?"

"It probably means nothing," Sister Cecilia said, eager to side with her ill-tempered master. "Singular, plural, what difference could it make? It's just the cover; it's what's inside that counts."

"It could just be a mistake," Jagang said. "Maybe the person who bound the copy made a mistake. The book itself would likely have been bound by someone else, so the book itself is no doubt fine."

"That's right," Sister Armina said, wanting to join in with the emperor as well. "The person who made the binding is the one who made the error, not the one who made the copy. It's highly unlikely they would be the same person. The binder was probably an incompetent oaf. The one writing the words in the book would have had to be gifted. Those words written inside the book are what matters. That's the information that must be true, not what it's wrapped in. There is no doubt that it's a simple error made by a binding artisan and it means nothing."

"We brought her here for this reason," Sister Ulicia reminded them under her breath. "It is irrelevant how simple it might appear. The book itself, before anything else, cautions that in this very circumstance it must be verified . . . by her."

"This is a highly dangerous matter. Such an answer is too simple," Sister Cecilia proclaimed.

Sister Ulicia cocked her head at the woman. "And if an assassin is coming at you with a knife, is that blade too simple for you to believe it a danger?"

Sister Cecilia did not look amused. "This matter is too complex to be decided by something so simple."

"Oh?" Sister Ulicia leveled a condescending glare on the woman. "And where does it say that the verification must be complex? It says only that she must make it. None of us noticed the error. She did. She has satisfied the instruction."

Sister Cecilia looked down her nose at the woman who used to be her leader but was no more. Now Sister Ulicia was no longer the one in charge, no longer the one they had to please.

"I don't think it means anything," Jagang said, still staring into Kahlan's unflinching eyes. "I doubt that she really knows that this is a fake. She's just trying to save her own neck."

Kahlan shrugged. "If that's what you want to think, fine. But maybe there is an absence of doubt in your mind because you *want* to believe that this copy is real"—she lifted an eyebrow—"not because it is."

Jagang stared at her a moment. He suddenly snatched the book out of her hands and turned back to the Sisters.

"We need to take a careful look at what's inside. That's what matters in finding and opening the right box. We need to make sure it's not flawed in any way."

"Excellency," Sister Ulicia began, "there may be no way to tell if something written in here is—"

Jagang tossed the book on the table, cutting her off. "I want you three to go over everything in this book. See if you can find any reason at all to think that this might be a fake."

Sister Ulicia cleared her throat. "Well, we can try—"

"Now!" His booming voice echoed around the room. "Or would you rather go to the tents and entertain my men? The choice of service is up to you. Pick one."

The three Sisters jumped to the table. They all leaned in as they began studying the book. Jagang pushed between Sisters Ulicia and Cecilia, apparently to watch over what they were reading and make sure that they were not overlooking anything.

Once she was sure that the four of them were busy, Kahlan quietly ushered Jillian back to the far end of the room, off to the side of the two big guards.

"I want you to listen to me very carefully and do exactly as I say," Kahlan told her in a low voice that Jagang and the Sisters couldn't hear.

Jillian frowned up at her, waiting.

"I need to be sure of something. I'm going to go walk over to those two guards—"

"What!"

Kahlan pressed her hand over the girl's mouth. "Shhh."

Jillian glanced to their captors, now worried that she had caught their attention. She hadn't.

Satisfied that she had made her point, Kahlan took her hand away. "I've come to suspect that I've been spelled by those three sorceresses. I think that's why I don't remember who I am—it's magic of some sort. Almost no one but them and Jagang can ever remember seeing me. Almost no one does. I have no idea why you can. They also put this collar around my neck and they can use it to hurt me.

"Now, I don't think the guards can see me, but I need to find out for sure. I want you to stay right here. Don't watch me or you will make them suspicious of you."

"But—"

Kahlan crossed her lips with a finger. "Listen to me. Do as I ask."

Jillian finally nodded her agreement.

Without waiting to see if the girl would change her mind and decide to argue, Kahlan again checked to make sure that Jagang and the Sisters were busy reading. Once seeing that they were, she immediately started across the floor. She moved as silently as she could; the guards may not know she was there, but if Jagang or the Sisters heard her, she would lose her chance before she could begin.

The two guards stared ahead, watching their emperor. Occasionally, the one closest to Jillian would glance over at the girl. Kahlan could tell by his lingering gaze what he was thinking: he was hoping that Jagang would give Jillian to him. Kahlan imagined that with a man like Jagang, such occasional rewards were a benefit of having earned such a trusted position as personal guard to an emperor. Jillian had no idea of the fate that was in store for her. Kahlan had to do something to change the headlong course of those looming events.

Once in front of the guards, she was careful to stay out of the line of sight between them and the four people at the table. She also had to be careful not to draw the attention of the Sisters, or Jagang, either. Even if the two guards couldn't remember Kahlan long enough to be aware that she was there, she didn't want to find out what would happen if they were mysteriously blocked from seeing their leader. These two were wary men, no doubt of exceptional talents, and there was no telling how small a thing could alert them to trouble, and Kahlan intended on being a great deal of trouble—but not until she was ready.

Standing directly in front of the two huge men, she realized that she came up only to the tops of their shoulders, so she wouldn't likely block their view. They didn't look at her, or in any way acknowledge her presence. She gently touched the metal post through one man's nose. He wrinkled his nose and then casually reached up and scratched, but he did not grab her hand.

Satisfied that he would do no more, Kahlan reached out and smoothly drew a knife from a sheath on the leather strap crossing the men's chest. As the blade came out into the torchlight, she was very careful to draw it evenly, without putting any twisting pressure on the sheath or strap. He didn't notice anything as it came completely free.

It felt good to have the weapon in her hand. The emotion of it caused her to remember being back at the White Horse Inn when the Sisters had killed the husband and wife who had run the place. She remembered picking up a heavy cleaver to try to stop them from harming the daughter.

She remembered the deep inner satisfaction at having a weapon in her hand because it represented a sense of having the means to control her own life, to help her to survive. A weapon meant not being at the mercy of evil people who respected no law, whether of man or reason, of not being a helpless prey of those who were stronger and would use that strength to dominate others.

Kahlan twirled the knife across her hand, weaving it through her fingers, watching it reflect the flickering light from the torches as it spun. She caught the handle and for a moment stared at the well-honed, polished blade.

It represented salvation. If not for her, at least for Jillian.

Remembering where she was and what she was doing, Kahlan quickly slipped the weapon down inside her boot. She looked over to make sure that Jillian was quiet and staying put. The girl's eyes had gone wide. Kahlan turned back to her task and carefully drew a second knife from a sheath on the other guard's chest strap. The blade was a little thinner, the weapon a little better balanced. Like the first, she pierced the blade through the leather of her boot, near the top, and slid it down into her boot, being careful to position it as she did, so that the blade would be behind the bone of her ankle. She then pushed the point securely into the bottom of the boot. In the makeshift sheath the knife couldn't move around and cut her when she walked.

As silently as possible, walking lightly on the balls of her feet, Kahlan quickly returned to a startled Jillian. The Sisters and their master were involved in an animated conversation about the relevance of star positions, weather, and time of year to the formation and concentration of power needed for specific spells. The Sisters were explaining the meaning of passages and Jagang was asking questions every few minutes, challenging their assumptions at every turn.

Kahlan was a bit surprised to hear how well versed the man was. The Sisters sometimes found that he had learned more than they knew on certain subjects to do with the boxes of Orden. Jagang didn't look like a man who would be the kind to value knowledge from books, but Kahlan was wrong. While she didn't understand most of what they were talking about, it was obvious that Jagang was well read and more than up to the task of conversing intelligently with the Sisters—especially about subjects that they said were found only in the rarest of books.

He wasn't just a brute. He was worse than that. He was a very smart brute.

"All right," Kahlan said in a voice low enough that she was sure the others couldn't hear her. "I want you to listen to me. We may not have much time."

Jillian's eyes were still wide. "How did you do that?"

"I was right, they can't see me."

"And twirling the knife like you did?"

Kahlan shrugged, dismissing a question she couldn't answer to address more important matters. "Look, I need to get you out of here. This may be our only chance."

Jillian looked horrified at the notion. "But if I escape he will kill my grandfather, and probably the others as well. I can't leave."

"That is the power he holds over you. But if you don't get away, the truth is that you all very well may be killed anyway. You need to understand that this could be the only chance you have, or will ever have, for your freedom."

"Are you really sure of that? How can I risk my grandfather's life on what you think might happen?"

Kahlan took a deep breath. She hadn't wanted to have to explain it. "I don't have time to put it to you nicely, to persuade you in gentle ways. I only have time to give you the bare bones of the truth, so that's what I'm going to do, so listen carefully.

"I know what these men are like. I've seen what they do to young women like you and me—seen it with my own eyes. I've seen their naked broken bodies left sprawled where they lay when Imperial Order soldiers are finished using them, or dumped in ditches like refuse.

"If you don't get away, very bad things are going to happen to you, at best. You will spend the rest of your short life as a slave, being used by soldiers for their sick pleasure and amusement in ways you don't want to learn about. You will spend the rest of your life alternating between terror and sobbing. That's at best. You will live, but wish every moment that you were dead. At worst, you are going to be killed when Jagang leaves.

"Either way, it's a fool's wish to think he's going to let you go. No matter what happens, whether you escape or stay, he might let your grandfather and the others go simply because they may not want to take the time and trouble to kill them. Jagang has more important things he's interested in.

"But you are plunder that has value to him. If nothing else, he will give you to those two guards as a bonus for their service. That's how men such as Jagang draw ruthless brutes like those two into loyal service—by giving them tasty little scraps like you. Do you have any idea what they will do with you—before they cut your throat? Do you?"

Jillian was silent for a moment. She swallowed before speaking. "I know what Jagang meant, before, when he asked if I've ever been with a man—but I pretended I didn't. I know what he meant when he said that he would give me over to his soldiers. I know what he meant when he said they would like getting their hands on a young woman like me. I know what he meant about their desires.

"My family has warned me about the dangers from strangers like these. My mother has explained it. I think that she did not tell me everything, though, so that I wouldn't have nightmares. I think the parts you know would give me nightmares. Before, I only pretended I didn't know what Jagang was talking about so that he wouldn't know how afraid I was of him doing that to me."

Kahlan couldn't help smiling. "That was a very wise thing you did, keeping such knowledge to yourself."

Jillian twisted her mouth, fighting back tears at the grim fate she had just admitted understanding. "You have a plan?"

"Yes. You have long legs, but I still doubt that you can outrun them. There's another way, though, a way that uses what you know and they don't. You said that one wrong turn out there and people get lost in the maze of tunnels and rooms. If you get even a small head start you will be able to quickly lose them in all the twists and turns. As complex as this place is, I don't think that even the powers of the Sisters would help them get you, and I don't think that Jagang would waste the time trying."

She still looked dubious. "But I—"

"Jillian, this is a chance for you to escape. Another may never come along. I don't want anything terrible to happen to you. If you stay, it will. I want you to understand that you must take this chance. I want you out of here. This is all I can do for you."

Jillian was overcome with a look of horror. "You mean . . . you're not going with me?"

Kahlan pressed her lips tight and shook her head. She tapped the metal collar around her neck. "They can stop me with this. It's magic of some sort. They will be able to put me down. But I think that before they do I'll be able to help slow them enough so that you can get away."

"But they will hurt you, or even kill you, for helping me get away."

"They are going to hurt me anyway—Jagang has already promised me the worst he can dream up. He can do no more than he already intends. As for killing me, I don't think they would do that, for now at least. They still need me.

"I'm helping you get away and that's all there is to it. My mind is made up. It's my choice. It's the only thing I can do, the only thing that I have a choice about. If I help you, then it makes my own life, no matter what will become of me, mean more to me. I will at least have done something to fight back. I will at least have this victory over them."

Jillian stared at her. "You're as brave as Lord Rahl."

Kahlan's eyebrows lifted. "You mean Richard Rahl? You know Richard Rahl?"

Jillian nodded. "He helped me, too."

Kahlan shook her head in wonder. "For living out here in the middle of nowhere, you sure seem to have met a lot of important people. What was he doing here?"

"He came back from the dead."

Kahlan frowned. "What?"

"Well, not exactly the dead, really. At least that's what he told me. But he came up from the well of the dead in the graveyard, just as the tellings said he would. I am the priestess of the bones. I am his servant, a dream-caster. He is my master. There have been many priestesses of the bones before me, but he never came for them. I never knew that it would turn out that he would come back in my lifetime.

"He came to find books, too. He is the one who found this place—I never even knew it was down here. None of my people knew. Even my grandfather never knew this place of bones was here.

"Richard was looking for a book to help him find someone important to him. The book was called *Chainfire*. Once he discovered this place and brought me down here, I'm the one who found the book for him. He was really excited. I was so happy that I was the one who helped him find what he needed.

"Since coming down here with him, I've spent all my time exploring this place, learning every turn and tunnel and room. I hope Richard will return one day, as he said he might, and then I will be able to show him everything. I very much want to make him proud of me."

Kahlan could see the longing in Jillian's eyes to satisfy the man, to do something he would value, to have him recognize her effort and ability.

Kahlan wanted to ask a thousand questions, but she didn't have the time. She couldn't resist one, though.

"What's he like?"

"Master Rahl saved my life. I've never met anyone else like him." Jillian smiled in a distant way. "He was, well, I don't know . . ." She sighed, unable to find the words.

"I see," Kahlan said at the dreamy look in the girl's copper-colored eyes.

"He saved my life from soldiers sent by Jagang, before. They were looking for these books. I was so afraid the man who had me was going to cut my throat, but Richard killed him. Then, he held me in his arms and quieted my tears." She looked up from gazing into her memories. "And he saved my grandfather, too. Well, not exactly him, but the woman with him."

"Woman?"

Jillian nodded. "Nicci. She said that she was a sorceress. She was so beautiful. I couldn't stop staring at her. I'd never before seen a woman that beautiful. She was like a good spirit standing there before me, with hair like sunlight, and eyes like the sky itself."

Kahlan sighed. Why wouldn't a man like that have a beautiful woman with him. After hearing it, she didn't know why she hadn't ever considered such a likelihood before now.

Kahlan didn't know why, but she felt as if something, some hope she had never dared define, or maybe an unfathomable longing she still clung to for something profoundly valuable hidden beneath the black shroud that had been drawn over her past . . . had just slipped away from her.

She had to look away from Jillian's gaze lest she lose control at the thought of the forlorn situation she found herself trapped in. She used the excuse of looking over her shoulder, checking to make sure that the emperor and his Sisters were still busy, as she wiped an unexpected, solitary tear from her cheek.

The Sisters looked more involved than ever in a discussion of the technicalities in the book. Jagang was demanding to know how they could be sure that certain parts were correct.

When Kahlan looked back, Jillian was staring at her. "But she wasn't as beautiful as you."

Kahlan smiled. "Diplomacy must be a requirement of being a priestess of the bones."

"No," Jillian said, looking suddenly worried that Kahlan might not believe she was telling the truth. "Really. There's something about you."

Kahlan frowned. "What do you mean?"

Jillian's nose scrunched up with the struggle of searching for words. "I don't know how to explain it. You're beautiful, and smart, and you know the right thing to do. But there's something else."

Kahlan wondered if this could be some link to who she really was. She had been looking for someone who would be able to see her, and remember her, and maybe give her a clue.

"Like what?"

"I don't know. Something noble."

"Noble?"

Jillian nodded. "You remind me of Lord Rahl in a way. He saved my life without hesitation, just like you want to do. It wasn't just that, though. I don't know how to explain it. There was just something about him . . . and you have that same quality about you, too."

"Good. At least he and I have something in common, then, because I'm about to save your life, too."

Kahlan took a steadying breath as she checked over her shoulder again. The others were still engaged in their heated conversation. She turned back to Jillian and gave her a dead serious look.

"We have to do this now."

"But, I'm still worried about my grandfather. . . ."

Kahlan looked into the girl's eyes for a long moment.

"Now, you listen to me, Jillian. You're fighting for your life. It's the only life you will ever have. They will show you no mercy for staying. I know that your grandfather would want you to take this chance."

Jillian nodded. "I understand. Lord Rahl told me much the same thing about the importance of my life."

For some reason, that lifted Kahlan's heart and made her smile. The smile quickly vanished, though, as she put her mind back to the task at hand. She didn't know if Jagang and the Sisters would be finished soon, or if they would be at it for the rest of the night, but she couldn't afford to miss the opportunity.

"We have to do this now, before I lose my nerve. I want you to do exactly as I say."

"I will," Jillian said.

"Here's what we're going to do. You will stay right here. I'm going to go over there and kill these two men."

Jillian's eyes went wide. "You're going to do what?"

"Kill them."

"How? You're just a woman, and they're big. And there's two of them."

"It's not impossible if you know how."

"You're going to cut their throats?" Jillian guessed.

"No. They would make noise if I did that. Besides, I couldn't do that to both of them at the same time. So, I'm going to take two more of their knives and then I'm going to slip up behind them and I'm going to stab them right . . . here."

Kahlan jabbed a finger in Jillian's back, a little to the side, right in the soft spot of her kidney. Even the small jab made the girl grunt with the pain of how sensitive that place was.

"Stabbing a man right there, in his kidney, is so painful that it makes it impossible for him to cry out."

"You can't be serious. Surely they will scream."

Kahlan shook her head. "The pain is so great when you're stabbed in the kidney that your throat clamps shut. Your scream is locked in your lungs. That will be our chance. Before they collapse and hit the floor as they're dying, we have to get through that door behind them. We have to slip through as quietly as possible to buy as much time as we can. We'll probably only have a brief moment before we're discovered, but that moment is all we need for you to get away.

"You stand right here. As soon as I drive the knives in their backs, you head for the door—fast as you can. But don't make any noise. I'll be there with you at the doors."

Jillian was panting in fear of such a task. Her eyes were brimming with tears. "But I want you to go with me."

Kahlan squatted down and hugged the girl.

"I know. This is all I can do to protect you, Jillian. But I think it will be enough to get away."

She wiped at her eyes. "But what will they do to you?"

"You just worry about getting away. If I get a chance to escape, I promise you I will. Tell Lokey to watch for me in case I ever do get away."

"All right."

Kahlan knew that it was a false hope. She squeezed Jillian's shoulder and stood. She checked the four at the table one last time. She did so just in time.

Jagang glanced over his shoulder to see what Kahlan was doing. She stood silently beside Jillian, watching him and the Sisters working, as if she had been there the whole time, doing nothing but awaiting her fate. He turned his attention to the heated words between Sister Ulicia and Sister Cecilia. Sister Ulicia was being her obstinate self, while Sister Cecilia was trying to find a way to appease Jagang by telling him whatever he wanted to hear.

Once she was sure that Jagang's attention was back on the book, Kahlan immediately started for the guards. As one was again eyeing Jillian with increasingly open lust, Kahlan carefully pulled a long knife from his weapons belt. Without delay, she moved to the far guard and did the same, taking his long knife as well.

Standing behind them, she glanced to the Sisters and Jagang and, seeing them still busy, she looked over at Jillian. The girl, wiping her palms on her hips, nodded that she was ready.

Kahlan reached to the man on the right and drew a knife he carried in a sheath hanging from a strap on his side. She placed the blade sideways between her teeth.

Without lingering any longer, she scrutinized the lower backs of the guards, selecting the precise spots she needed to hit. She chose the right side of the man on her left, and the left side of the man on her right, so that she would have targets closest together and she would be able to put her full strength into the thrust.

She looked back and forth between the men, making sure that she would hit the right spot with each knife. If she missed, it would be fatal, but not necessarily for the men. It would be Jillian who paid the price of an error. It had to be right, and it had to be right the first time.

Kahlan took a deep breath, holding it only briefly, then she exhaled hard, adding that power to the force she put into her thrust. With all her strength, she plunged both knives into the men's backs. The blades went in up to the hilts.

Both men stiffened at the jolting shock.

Kahlan had already drawn another breath. This time, as quickly as she could, she forced out the breath and used all her considerable strength to pull the handles together toward one another so that the blades would pivot and rip through the men's kidneys.

The men stood frozen stiff and slightly twisted, backs arched with the intense wallop of excruciating pain. Their eyes bulged, their mouths opened, but they made no sound. They stood in mortal trauma, unable to draw in a gasp or let out a cry.

When Kahlan looked up, Jillian was already on her way. Kahlan turned and swiftly opened one of the narrow doors. She didn't want to give their pursuers a clear path by opening both.

Jillian was there. The men's knees began buckling. Kahlan put her hand on Jillian's back, between her shoulders, and pushed her through the doorway, propelling her out into the hallway.

Kahlan took the knife from her teeth. "Run. Don't stop for anything."

Jillian nodded back. She looked as if the Keeper himself were on her heels.

Kahlan turned to close the door, but just then the men hit the floor.

Four startled faces spun around toward her. Kahlan pulled the door closed and ran as if the Keeper were after her, too.

She saw Jillian in the dim distance just as she reached an intersection where a juncture of branches of passages went off in different directions. The girl paused, looking back at Kahlan. They shared a brief look filled with meaning, and then she was gone, vanished down one of the passages. It was so dark in the distance that Kahlan wasn't sure which one Jillian had taken.

Behind came an explosive splintering of wood, as if the doors had been blown apart. Torchlight suddenly spilled through the hall, surrounding Kahlan. She immediately stopped and spun back. She gripped the knife by the point. She saw shadows in the room rushing toward the gaping doorway.

With all her strength she heaved the knife without there even being anyone there, yet, in that doorway.

An enraged Sister Cecilia burst through first. The knife slammed into her chest. Kahlan had hoped it would be Jagang first through, but she had been pretty sure it would be a Sister, so she had aimed accordingly. The blade had flown true, and plunged right through Sister Cecilia's heart.

The Sister went down hard. Kahlan turned and ran with all her strength. Just as she had turned, she had seen the others fall over the body of Sister Cecilia.

Kahlan ran as she had never run before. She took the first corner to the left. She didn't know which turns Jillian had taken, but she didn't see her. The girl was gone.

A flush of pure exhilaration washed through Kahlan, filling her very soul with the thrill of success. It had worked. She had kept her promise to Jillian, and to herself. She had at least beaten them in this much of it.

She was giddy with the victory even as she ran like a madwoman. She had not only killed the two guards but taken out Sister Cecilia. Images of the pain that woman had given her, and the satisfaction she had derived from it, flashed through Kahlan's mind, and she savored her vengeance.

Now that it had worked, and Jillian was away, terror flooded up through her. She knew she wouldn't get away. All she could do was run, taking random turns, and wait for the end.

It came with a sudden shock of pain she thought must be something like what the two men had felt.

She knew she hit the ground, but she didn't really feel it.

And then it felt as if the entire ceiling and dead city above all caved in on top of her.

The world went as black as a grave.

Richard was winded by the time he had finally crested the rise. It wasn't just that he was out of breath, though; he was out of strength as well. He knew that he hadn't taken the time to eat as much as he should have along the way, and now he was paying the price for it. His legs felt like lead. His stomach ached with hunger. He felt weak and just wanted to lie down, but he couldn't, not now, not when he was this close. Not when there was so much at stake.

He'd eaten some pine nuts and a few handfuls of huckleberries he'd come across as he went along, but he hadn't gone out of his way to collect any more. He just hadn't wanted to take the time.

At least he had his pack with him, so the night before he had been able to set out a fishing line in a small lake just at sunset. He then collected an armload of dry wood and started a fire with a flint and steel. By the time the fire was hot he had three trout on his setline. He had been so hungry that he'd been tempted to eat them raw, but fish cooked quickly, so he waited.

Not wanting to stop any longer than necessary, he'd gotten little sleep on the short journey from the sliph. He reasoned that the sooner he got his hands on the book that Baraccus had left for him, the better off he would be. The book had already been waiting there for him for three thousand years. He didn't want it to wait another night. He thought about how, if he had been smart enough to find the book sooner, he might have avoided the problems he now faced. He was hoping that it could somehow help him in finding Kahlan, maybe even help him find a way to reverse the tainted Chainfire spell.

He'd reasoned that the best plan would be to recover the book as soon as possible; then he could do some reading while he took the time to eat. He would worry then about sleeping and getting back to the Keep.

The Keep was a long way off. He didn't know exactly where he was, except that he was a good distance south of Agaden Reach in what appeared to be an uninhabited area either near or in the wilds, so he was concerned about how he was going to find some horses. One problem at a time, he reminded himself, one problem at a time.

As difficult as it had been to undertake the climb up the steep, rocky rise in the dark, he couldn't bring himself to stop when he knew that he was close. Besides, if he wanted to see the night wisps, it could only be at night, so he didn't want to wait until morning to make the climb and then have to wait around all the next day for it to get dark again.

Finally reaching the top, Richard scanned the area to get his bearings. Above the edge of the steep slope the ground leveled off into a sparsely wooded oak grove. The breeze from earlier in the day had died hours ago, at sunset, and it was now dead calm. The silence felt like an oppressive weight lying over him. For some reason, the typical night sounds of small animals, insects, and such that were common in the lowlands stretching out endlessly behind him were silent up at the top of the long climb.

In the moonlight, Richard immediately noticed that there was something wrong with the trees. It looked as if they were all dead. The fat, squat trunks were twisted and gnarled. The bark had started to come away in ragged strips. The bent and distorted branches looked like claws reaching out to snatch anyone who dared enter the place.

Richard had been focused at the trek and the climb, but he suddenly switched to being on guard, his attention riveted as he listened for any sound in the eerie silence. He moved carefully beneath the trees, trying to make as little noise as possible. It was difficult, though, since the ground was littered with dry sticks and leaves. The branches looming overhead cast grotesque shadows in the moonlight, and the air had a chill to it that ran a shiver up his back.

With the next step, something underfoot broke with an odd, bony pop. In all the years he'd spent in the woods, Richard had never heard a sound like that.

He froze in place, listening, waiting. His mind raced as he went over the memory of the sound, trying to come up with its cause. Try as he might, he couldn't place it. When he heard nothing more, and saw nothing move, he carefully backed up, lifting his foot off whatever it was that had broken.

After checking in every direction, appraising every shadow, he squatted down to see what it was that he had stepped on. Whatever it was, it was covered in leaves. He cautiously pushed the decaying leaves aside.

There, half-buried in the forest loam, dark with age, was a broken human skull staring up at him. The weight of his foot had broken in the rounded top of the skull. The eye sockets, which seemed to be watching him, were still intact.

Richard scanned the forest floor and saw other humps under the leaves. He also saw something else: more skulls that weren't buried beneath the forest litter. Just from where he crouched, he could see a good half-dozen skulls lying at least partially atop leaves, and even more rounded shapes below them. Beneath the leaves he found the rest of the bones that belonged to the skull he had stepped on.

He stood slowly and began moving again, scrutinizing the ground, the fat, twisted tree trunks, as well as the limbs overhead as he went. He saw no one and heard nothing.

Now that he knew what he was looking for, he was able to spot skulls seemingly everywhere. He stopped counting once he'd reached thirty. The bones appeared scattered, not bunched together as if people had all died together or in groups. With a few exceptions, they appeared to have been individuals who had died at those particular places. He supposed that the bodies might have been placed there; he had no way of really knowing. The few exceptions were skulls close together, but he reasoned that might have been chance—people who had happened to have fallen near another body.

Richard crouched down to inspect a number of the skulls, both those lying exposed and those buried beneath the litter. His initial thought was that it was possibly the site of a battle, but as near as he could tell in the moonlight these people had not died at the same time. There were some bones that were sound, while others were moldering away. Some appeared so ancient that they fell apart when he touched them. The place was like a graveyard, but with all of the bodies above ground, rather than being buried.

The other thing that he noticed was that no predators looked to have disturbed the dead. Richard had come across remains in the woods when he had been a guide. Animals always got at the dead, human or otherwise. It looked as if each one of these bodies, though, had rotted away over time, leaving the bones lying in the exact same position in which the person had fallen—on their sides, or with arms sprawled, or facedown. None had been laid out as if in burial, with arms neatly crossed on their chests, or at their sides. They looked simply to have fallen dead. It still might not have seemed quite so peculiar except that not one of the corpses looked to have been touched by any predator.

As Richard walked endlessly through the oak grove, he wondered if it would ever end. On a moonless, cloudy night, or even a cloudy day for that matter, it was the kind of place where it would have been easy to get lost. Everything looked the same. The trees were spaced evenly, and there was nothing to indicate if he was going in the right direction, except the moon and stars.

For what seemed like half the night, Richard moved ever onward through the forest of the dead. He was sure that he had followed the directions the sliph had given him. The sliph, however, had no way to know exactly what he would find; she had only been given directions from Baraccus, and that had been three thousand years before. The landscape could have changed a great deal since the time of Baraccus. The bones, though, didn't look to be anywhere near that old. Of course, it could be that lying in the oak grove there were bones thousands of years old, but by now those would have all crumbled to dust.

As Richard continued on, the woods began growing murkier, until he found himself entering the black shadows of a dark forest of immense pines, their trunks standing close together and each nearly as big as his house back in the Hartland woods had been. It was like encountering a wall of mountains that rose up into the sky. The trunks, like pillars, were clear of branches until somewhere up out of sight. But those branches completely closed off the sky and left the forest floor below a dark and confusing maze among the massive trunks.

Richard paused, considering how he would keep to a direction in the pitch blackness that lay ahead while being unable to move in anything resembling a straight line.

That was when he heard the whispers.

He cocked his head, listening, trying to make out the words. He couldn't, so he carefully stepped deeper into the gloom, letting his eyes adjust to the darkness before taking a few more steps. Before long he began to be able to make out the shapes of the trees ahead, so he moved forward, ever deeper into the close canyons among the trunks of the monumental pines.

"Go back," came a whisper.

"Who's there?" he whispered back.

"Go back," said a faint little voice, "or stay forever with the bones of those who have come before you."

"I've come to speak with the night wisps," Richard said.

"Then you have come for nothing. Go, now," the voice repeated with more strength.

Richard tried to lay the sound of the words over his memory of what a wisp sounded like. While it wasn't the same, it did have qualities in common.

"Please come forward so that I may talk with you."

Only silence surrounded him. Richard moved ahead a dozen paces into the darkness.

"Last time warned," came the eerie voice. "Go, now."

"I have come a long way. I'm not going back without speaking with the wisps. This is important."

"Not to us."

Richard stood with one hand on a hip as he tried to conceive of what to do next. He was far from clearheaded. His weariness was hampering his thinking.

"Yes, this is important to you, too."

"How?"

"I have come for what Baraccus left for me."

"So did those whose bones you have passed."

"Look, this is important. Your lives ultimately depend upon this as well. In this struggle there will be no uninvolved bystanders. All will be drawn into the storm."

"The stories you have heard about a treasure are empty lies. There is nothing here."

"Treasure? No—you don't understand. That's not what this is about at all. I think you misunderstand me. I've already passed the tests Baraccus left for me—that's why I'm here. I'm Richard Rahl. I'm married to Kahlan Amnell, the Mother Confessor."

"We don't know this person you speak of. Go back to her while you still can."

"No, that's the point, I can't. I'm trying to find her." Frustrated, Richard ran his fingers back into his hair. He didn't know how much time he might have to say what he needed to say, or how much he should leave out, if he was to convince the wisps of his true reason for being there—to convince them to help him.

"You once knew her. Magic was used against Kahlan to make everyone forget her. You knew her, too, but you forgot her like everyone else. Kahlan used to come here. In her role as the Mother Confessor she fought to protect the land of the night wisps and to keep others out.

"She told me about the beautiful land of the night wisps. She told me about the open fields in ancient, remote forests. She has been among the wisps as they gather at twilight to dance together in the grasses and wildflowers.

"She told me that she spent many a night lying on her back in the grass as the wisps gathered around her, speaking with her of things common to both of your lives: of dreams and hopes, of loves.

"Please, the wisps knew her. She was your friend."

Richard saw, then, a tiny light come out from behind a tree. "Go, or your bones will remain out there, with the others who seek treasure, and no one will ever see you again or know what became of you."

"If I need gold I earn it. I have no interest in treasure."

The tiny spark of light started away. "Not all treasure is gold."

As it glided into the distance, the shafts of spinning light played over the trunks of trees it passed.

"I knew Shar," Richard called out.

The light paused. It stopped spinning.

For a moment, Richard watched as the spark of light hung there, in the distance, faintly illuminating the closely gathered monarchs of the forest standing like sentries for what lay beyond.

"You did not come because of the legends that there was treasure to be found here?"

"No."

"What do you know of the name you spoke?"

"I was with Shar after she went through the boundary. Shar crossed that boundary to help stop the threat from Darken Rahl. Shar crossed the boundary to help in the effort to find me so that I, too, could help in that struggle. Before she died, Shar said that if I ever needed the help of the night wisps, then I should say her name and they would help me, for no enemy may know it."

Richard pointed back toward the grove of dead oaks, where the forgotten, moldering remains reposed. "I have a feeling that none of the people whose bones lie back there knew her name, or the name of any wisp."

The light slowly returned through the trees, finally coming to a stop not far from him. He could feel the softly glowing shafts of light gliding over the contours of his face. They almost felt like the faint touch of a spider's web.

Richard took a small step closer. "I spoke with Shar before she died. She said that she could not live away from those of her kind any longer, and she did not have the strength to return to her home place.

"She gave me my first test from Baraccus. She said that she believed in me, believed that I had inside me what it takes to prevail. It was a message from him. She asked me about secrets."

The tiny light turned a warm, rosy color as it spun in silence for a moment.

"And you passed her test?"

"No," Richard admitted. "It was too soon for me to understand it all. Later, I finally came to understand. The sliph said that I have now passed the test that Baraccus left for me."

"What is your name?"

"I grew up named Richard Cypher. Since then I've come to learn that I am Richard Rahl. I have been called by other names as well: the Seeker; the one born true; the bringer of death; Richard with the Temper; the Pebble in the Pond; and *Caharin*. Does one of those names mean anything to you?"

"Does the name Ghazi mean anything to you?"

"Ghazi?" Richard thought a moment. "No. Should it?"

"It means 'fire.' Ghazi was given that name by prophecy. If you were the one, you would know that name, too."

"I'm sorry, but I don't. I don't know why, but I can tell you that I don't hold much with prophecy."

"I am very sorry, but misery has come to this land. The wisps are in a time of suffering. We cannot help you. You should go now."

The wisp began leaving again, spinning as it floated off into the towering trees.

Richard took a step forward. "Shar said that if I needed the help of the wisps, they would help me! I need your help!"

The little point of light paused again. Richard got the distinct impression by the way it hovered motionless that it was considering something. After a moment, it slowly began rotating, casting off shimmering beams of light. It came partway back.

The wisp then spoke a name that Richard had not heard spoken aloud in many years.

His blood turned to ice.

"And does *this* name mean anything to you?" the wisp asked.

"How do you know my mother's name?" Richard whispered.

The wisp slowly drew closer. "Many, many seasons ago, Ghazi went through a dark boundary to find her, to help her, to tell her of her son, to tell her many things she needed to know, many things her son would need to know. Ghazi never returned."

Richard stared, his eyes wide. "What do the wisps do in the day? When it's light?"

The wisp, like nothing more than a glowing silver ember, slowly spun, throwing shafts of light across Richard's face. "We go where it is dark. We do not like being in the light."

"Does fire hurt you?"

The shafts of light dimmed. "Fire can kill us."

"Dear spirits . . ." Richard whispered.

The wisp came closer, the shimmering light brightening again, as it seemed to study his face. "What is it?"

"What was the prophecy about Ghazi?" Richard asked.

The slowly spinning light paused. "The prophecy was about Ghazi's death. It said he would die in fire."

Richard's eyes closed for a moment. "Many seasons ago, when I was but a boy, my mother died in a fire."

The wisp remained silent.

"I'm sorry," Richard said in a small voice as Shota's words rang through his head. "I think Ghazi died in my home. Our house caught on fire. After my mother brought my brother and me safely out, she went back in for something—we never knew what. She was probably overcome by the smoke. She never came out. I never saw her again. She died in the blaze.

"I think she went back for Ghazi. I think my mother and Ghazi died together in that fire, without him ever completing his purpose."

The wisp seemed to watch him for a time. "I am sorry for what happened to your mother. After all this time, tears still come to you."

Richard had run out of words and could only nod.

The wisp again started spinning faster. "The name Richard Cypher is the name we know you as. Come, Richard Cypher, and we will tell you what Ghazi went to tell your mother."

Richard followed the sparkling point of light into the ancient stand of timber, a place of quiet and peace. He had never seen trees this big. It struck him as odd that creatures so tiny would live among trees so big.

It seemed like they walked for hours, though Richard knew that it only felt that way because he was so drained. When they at last emerged from the trees into a vast clearing, Richard could hardly believe his eyes. It was just as Kahlan had described it. The grassy meadow sparkled with hundreds of night wisps gliding among the tall blades of grasses and wildflowers. The swath of stars above, through the gap in the towering pines, seemed lifeless and dead compared with the stars in the grass.

It was a beautiful sight, but it brought pain into Richard's heart because it reminded him of Kahlan, of the first day he had met her, when she had introduced him to Shar, of the time she'd told him about the wisps. Kahlan and the wisps were forever linked in his mind.

And now, after all this time, he knew that it was a night wisp that his mother had run back into the burning house to save. She had not died alone.

All because a man thousands of years before had gone to the Temple of the Winds and done something that would result in Richard being born with both sides of the gift, both sides that the sliph said he no longer had.

As Richard stepped into the grass, some of the night wisps came closer, curious to see the stranger among them. The wisps flashed brighter and dimmer, as if in conversation among themselves.

"What are you called?" Richard asked the wisp who had escorted him.

"I am Tam."

Richard watched wisps gliding closer, rising up the length of him, before shooting away.

"Our numbers dwindle," Tam said. "Such a thing has never happened before. It is a time of suffering for us. We don't know the cause."

"The cause is in part why I am here," Richard told him. "I'm hoping to find help so that I can stop what is causing this sickness among the wisps. If I don't succeed, you will all vanish from the world."

Tam considered in silence for a time. Others who had heard Richard's words drifted away, sinking into the dark places in the grass, as if seeking a quiet place to weep. Some, though, came closer.

"Many here knew Ghazi," Tam said. "They miss him. Can you tell us any of what he said before his life was gone? The way you have spoken of Shar's words?"

"I'm sorry, Tam, but I never saw Ghazi. I never knew that he had come to see my mother. Ghazi and my mother must have died before he had a chance to tell us anything of his reason for being there."

Richard wondered if that had been the reason for the fire.

Many of the wisps dimmed, as if in disappointment that he could tell them none of Ghazi's last words.

Richard remembered his purpose and turned to his guide.

"Please, Tam, I have come for an important reason that, as I said, may in the end help the wisps with what they suffer. I have come because Baraccus left something here for me. His library is here. He sent his wife with a book for me."

"Magda," one of the nearby wisps said. He wasn't sure which one was speaking, but it sounded decidedly more feminine than Tam.

"That's right."

"This was long before our time," she said. "but the words of Baraccus have been passed down to us. We still hold the secrets he asked us to keep. I am Jass. Come. Tam and I will show you."

Tam and Jass led Richard off through the silky grass, toward the towering trees to his left. Among the trees, away from the open meadow, it was again like descending into a dark world. Only the two wisps gave him enough light to see his way.

"How far?" Richard asked.

"Not far," said Jass.

"It is a place within our realm," said Tam, "a place where we can watch over and protect it. Over the millennia the seed of stories planted in the fertile soil of bits and scraps of facts was watered by wishes and began to take root and grow. Eventually, a bountiful fruit of rumors burst forth, to be spread on the wind of whispers that said we hid a fabled hoard of gold.

Nothing could convince the believers that it was not true. The truth does not glitter for these people like gold does. Their dream of reaping unearned wealth was so strong for them that they would rather sacrifice everything truly precious to them than accept the truth that it was an empty belief."

"What we hide is not a treasure," Jass said, "but a promise made by our ancestors."

"It is a treasure, of a sort," Richard told them. "To the right person, anyway."

What seemed not far to them seemed quite far to Richard. It was getting ever more exhausting for him to put one leg in front of the other. His stomach growled with hunger as they moved through the silent wood.

It had to be somewhere deep in the middle of the night when the trees opened up and Richard could see at last, illuminated by the silvered moonlight, a valley spread out far below. Lush forests carpeted the bowl of the valley, with the mat of trees ascending the slopes of mountain close in on each side. The place where he stood overlooking the length of the valley was not only a commanding spot, but a place with hauntingly beautiful views of the things that Richard had always loved. He ached to be able to explore such a place, to be down in those woods . . . but to be there with Kahlan. Without her, beauty was only a word. Without Kahlan smiling at him, the world was empty and dead.

"This is the place of the library that Master Baraccus left with us for safekeeping," Tam said.

Richard looked around. He saw only ferns, some vines trailing down from the darkness above, and the massive trunks of the pines standing with him at the rim of the overlook.

"Where?" he asked. "I don't see a building anywhere."

"Here," Jass said as she drifted down to a small boulder, coming to rest atop it. "Under here is the library."

Richard scratched his scalp. It seemed an odd place for a library. But then he recalled finding the entrance to the library in Caska under a gravestone. In light of that, this made more sense. A building might have long ago been discovered and raided.

He bent and put his shoulder against the rock, in a curved niche that wasn't sharp. He was sure that he wasn't strong enough to move such a huge slab of stone, but he put all his weight against the stone socket anyway. With great effort it slowly began to pivot to the side.

The wisps came close, looking with Richard at what lay below. The stone had rested on a small, carefully smoothed lip. There was no hole, no stairway down into the ground within that lip.

Richard knelt and dug at what was under the rock, inside the stone lip. It was soft, and dry.

"This is just sand."

"Yes," Jass said. "When Magda came, she followed her husband's instructions, using magic, and filled what was below."

Richard was incredulous. "With sand?"

"Yes," Jass said.

"How much sand?" Richard asked. He wasn't looking forward to digging out a sand-filled hole, no matter how small it turned out to be.

"You see that small river down in the valley?" Jass asked.

Richard squinted in the dim moonlight. He saw the sparkling reflections off the water wandering among sandbars.

"Yes, I see it."

"The words passed down to us," Jass said, "say that Magda brought with her a powerful spell from Baraccus. She used it to create a whirlwind that drew the sand up from the riverbanks, and funneled it into this hole, here, filling up the place below to protect it."

"Protect it?" Richard asked. "From what?"

"From any who might make it this far. This sand is meant to foil anyone who might come for what is down there."

"Well, I suppose that if there was enough sand that would certainly slow them down." Richard looked over suspiciously at the two wisps spinning slowly in the moonlight. "How much sand is down there, anyway?"

Tam floated out past the edge of the drop-off. "You see that ledge down there?"

Richard carefully leaned over the edge of the cliff and looked. It had to be several hundred feet down to the narrow stone shelf.

"I see it."

"That is how far down the rooms of the library are to be found."

"The rooms of the library are buried under all this sand—down there, at the bottom?"

"Yes," Tam said.

Richard was dumbfounded. There had to be a palace-worth of sand.

"How am I to dig such a thing out? It would take forever to accomplish such a thing."

Tam returned, coming close to his face. "Maybe. But Baraccus said that if you were the one, you would know what to do."

"If I'm the one?" Richard felt the weight of discouragement, like a mountain of sand on top of him. "Why do I always have to be the one?"

Tam spun for a moment. "That is not for us to say."

Richard groaned with the disappointment of being so close but so far. "If I'm the one, then why couldn't he just leave a message for me so that I would know what to do?"

Tam and Jass were silent for a moment, as if thinking.

"Well, there was one other thing passed down," Jass finally said.

"What would that be?"

"Baraccus said that the wisps would have to guard this for ages and ages, but when the sands of time had finally run out, the one who was meant to have the book would be here and take it with him." Jass spun closer. "Does that help, Richard Cypher?"

Richard wiped a hand across his face. Why couldn't Baraccus simply tell him how to recover *Secrets of a War Wizard's Power*? Maybe Baraccus thought that the man who was meant to have the book must already have mastered his power to the point where this would present no obstacle. Maybe he thought that Richard should know how to spin a magical whirlwind and suck out the sand. If that was so, then Richard was not the one. Not only did he not know how to use his power but, since being in the sliph, he no longer had his gift.

As far as Richard was concerned, the sands of time had already run out for him. The Sisters of the Dark had put the boxes of Orden in play; the chimes had contaminated the world of life, beginning the destruction of magic, which was probably the great misery the wisps were suffering; and the army of the Imperial Order was rampaging unchecked through the New World. But worst of all for him, personally, Kahlan had been abducted, was under the influence of the Chainfire spell, and desperately needed his help.

And here he stood, waiting for the sands of time to run out.

Richard took his hand away from his face as he frowned. He leaned out over the edge of the cliff, looking down at the ledge far below. The sands of time.

He looked to the left side and studied the rock. He didn't see anything he could use there, but on the right he thought he saw a way to use the rocks to climb down. He swung his pack off his back and set it on the ground while he dug out his camp shovel and hastily assembled it.

" 'When the sands of time had finally run out, the one who was meant to have the book would be here and take it with him,' " he quoted. "Isn't that what you said?"

"Yes," Jass said, "That is what we were told."

Richard gazed out over the cliff again. "I have to go down there, to that ledge," he told the wisps.

"We will come and light the way," Tam said.

Richard wasted no time climbing down the side of the rock precipice. It turned out to be just as difficult as he had judged it would be, but it didn't take long and he was soon standing on the narrow shelf far below the top where he had pivoted the boulder out of the way.

He searched around, picking at the face of the rock wall, until he found what he was looking for. He immediately started digging, chipping, and prying out rocks that had been so tightly jammed in that it was hard to tell for sure in the poor light of the moon and two wisps if it really was what he thought it was. When rock began coming out, his confidence level rose. The more rock fragments he pulled out, the easier it was to get out more.

He had to work carefully to free some of the larger stones; one wrong step and he could slip and fall off the narrow ledge. Some of the boulders back in the growing hole were larger than he could have lifted, so he had to roll and walk them out of the ever-expanding opening. Fortunately, he was able to loosen the rock beneath most of them and then roll them out. He stood to the side on the narrow ledge and let the rocks and boulders tumble out past him. He watched them sail out into the night air, falling soundlessly until they finally crashed down into the forest far below.

Suddenly, when the shovel broke through to something soft, the rest of the rock plug began to let go with a grating sound and abruptly burst out in a cascade of fragments. Richard had to duck out of the way. With a rumbling roar, the sand followed in a column pouring far out into space before beginning to arc downward.

Richard stood with his back pressed against the rock wall, his heart pounding from the surprise of the sudden explosive clearing of the opening into the hollow interior of the cliff. The two wisps spun as they watched the amazing sight. One of them, Richard wasn't sure which one, followed the column of sand out and down for a ways before returning.

It seemed to go on forever, but the last of the sand finally dwindled away as it poured out of the hole, leaving only small amounts to drizzle out in fits.

Richard wasted no time climbing into the hole. "Come on," he called back to the wisps. "I need light."

The two wisps obliged, passing over the tops of his shoulders to enter first. Once past him they lit the chamber beyond. Richard stood up inside, brushing himself off as he gazed around at shelves filled with books. It was astounding to think that he was the first person who had stood in this place since Magda Searus, the woman who would become the first Confessor.

That reminded him of Kahlan, and his need to find her, so he immediately started looking around. It appeared a rather simple library, with a doorway at the far side that he could see led deeper into the interior of the cliff. He saw shadows of doorways, and circular stairs. Despite the sand pouring out of the hole, there was still a lot of sand covering everything. It would take some time to clean the place and really tell what was there.

To the right, though, on a stone pedestal against a blank stone wall, sat a book all by itself. Richard lifted it off the stand and blew the sand and dust off of it.

On the cover it said *Secrets of a War Wizard's Power.*

His fingers gently glided over the gilt letters on the cover as he again read the words meant for him.

It was an awe-inspiring feeling to realize that a war wizard, First Wizard Baraccus himself, had made this very book for the person who would be born with the power that he saw to it would be released from the Temple of the Winds. Richard had at last found the treasure that Baraccus had left for him.

A night wisp hovered over each shoulder, watching him as he reverently stared at the book that would finally answer his questions, that would finally help him master his gift.

Finally, his heart pounding, Richard opened the cover to see what Baraccus wanted him to know.

The first page was blank.

Richard turned over more pages, but they were all blank. He thumbed through the entire book and, other than the words on the cover, he found that the entire book was completely blank.

Richard squeezed his temples between the fingers and thumb of one hand. He thought he might be sick.

"Can either of you see anything on the pages?"

"No," Jass said. "Sorry."

"I see no marks of writing at all," Tam added.

Richard realized, then, what the problem was. His heart sank.

Secrets of a War Wizard's Power was an instruction book on the use of a specific form of the gift. The book involved magic. For some reason, Richard had been cut off from his gift. Without that gift to assist him, whatever was written on the pages would not stay in his mind. He would forget the words before he could remember reading them.

Just as he no longer remembered a single word of *The Book of Counted Shadows*, he could not remember the words of *Secrets of a War Wizard's Power* long enough to remember having seen any words. Without the gift, it would appear blank to him.

Until he could figure out what was wrong with his gift, he wouldn't be able to read this book.

"I'll have to take this with me," Richard told the wisps.

"Just as Baraccus said you would, Richard Cypher," Tam said.

Richard wondered if Baraccus somehow knew this, as well. Whether he did or not, Richard didn't have time to ponder it. He climbed back out of the hole and up the rock face of the cliff.

He noticed that the rock jutted out over the opening into the library, probably so that water wouldn't eat away at the plug over time or work its way inside. The sand had to be dry not only so that the books inside wouldn't be ruined, but so that it would pour out. Richard decided that for the time being the library was relatively safe from rain.

At the top of the cliff, he stored the valuable blank book away in his pack. He saw that inside the stone rim, where there had been sand before, there was now a spiral stairway down into the darkness below. To make sure that no one discovered the library, he struggled mightily against the boulder until he managed to pivot it into place.

Panting from the exertion, he swung his pack up onto his back. His mind was racing with a thousand different thoughts. On the way back through the dark wood, Richard spoke little to the wisps, other than to thank them for their help.

Once they had reached the meadow again, he gazed out over the sight of all the night wisps gliding through the grass and wildflowers, some spinning in an intricate dance as they moved together in pairs. He wondered how many more wisps there had been when Kahlan had been here.

Richard missed Kahlan so much that it brought a lump to his throat. She was his world. The whole world, in so many ways, seemed to be slipping away.

"I have to go," he told Tam and Jass. "I hope to use what I found here to help stop the suffering of the wisps, and others."

"You will come back?" Jass asked.

Thinking briefly about the hidden library, Richard nodded. "Yes. And I hope to bring Kahlan with me, and that by then you will remember her. I know she will be overjoyed to see you all again."

"When we remember her," Jass said, "then we will be filled with joy, too."

Unwilling to test his voice again, Richard nodded and then started out.

Tam escorted him through the ancient forest, helping him find the way. At the edge of the ancient trees, the wisp came to a halt.

"Baraccus was wise to choose you, Richard Cypher. I believe that you have it in you to succeed. I wish you well."

Richard smiled sadly. He wished he was as sure. He no longer had access to the gift within him—if it was still even there—and he had no idea how he would succeed. Maybe Zedd could help.

"Thank you, Tam. You and the wisps have been good protectors of those things Baraccus left with you. I will do my best to protect you, and the other innocents who are in so much danger."

"If you fail, Richard Cypher, I know that it will not be from lack of effort on your part. If you ever need our help again, as Shar told you, say one of our names and we will try to help you."

Richard nodded and started away, turning once to wave. The wisp spun a rose color for a moment and then vanished back into the trees. He suddenly felt awfully forlorn by the light of the moon alone.

The dead oaks seemed to go on forever. He plodded along in a numb daze. He needed to get some food and rest, but he wanted to get out of the strange wood and back down into the forest first. He saw bones among the roots of the oaks, as if the trees were trying to gather in the dead to hug them to their bosoms.

Somewhere in the dead wood, after walking endlessly, absorbed in his troubled thoughts, Richard felt a sudden chill to the air that made him shudder and gasp the sharp cold into his lungs.

It felt as if he had walked into the fangs of winter.

When he looked up, he spotted what at first looked like an upright shadow among the skulls. When he saw at last what it really was, another shudder shivered up his spine.

It was a tall woman with black, wiry hair. She wore inky black robes. Her skin was as pale as the moon, making her gaunt face seem to float in the darkness. Her desiccated flesh was stretched tight over her bony features, the way he imagined the dead would have looked for a time as they lay lifeless in this forsaken forest, waiting for the worms to do their work.

Her thin, menacing smile marked her unmistakably as the sort to leave the bones of used-up people to rot in just such a place, among the moldering dead.

Richard felt so cold he couldn't move. He realized that he was shivering, but he couldn't seem to make himself stop. He couldn't feel his fingers or toes. He wanted to move, to run, but he couldn't force his legs to move.

He had no gift to summon. He had no sword to draw.

He felt helpless in the beguiling gaze of her blanched blue eyes.

Richard wondered if his lifeless remains would end up discarded in this desolate place to rot, forgotten, along with all the other anonymous bones of those who had come with lofty dreams.

The woman's arms swept up, like a raven's wings lifting, and the night swallowed him.

Kahlan ever so gradually became aware of the bewildering drone of voices, both near and far. She was so dazed, though, that she wasn't sure if it was real or if she was only imagining it. She knew that some of the thoughts streaming endlessly through her mind had to be her imagination, despite how real they seemed. She knew that she wasn't one moment in a flowered field among the stars, the next moment in the middle of a pitched battle with desiccated corpses atop horseback, and the next instant flying through the clouds atop a red dragon's back. It all seemed real, but she knew that it couldn't be.

After all, there weren't any such things as dragons. That was only myth.

But if it really was voices that she was hearing, she couldn't understand the words. They came to her more as disembodied, raw sounds, each tonal pulse resonating painfully with something deep inside her.

What she was sure of was that her head throbbed in a slow rhythm and each time the agonizing beat squeezed, it felt as if her skull would split open from the pressure. As each intermittent cycle subsided, nausea oozed up inside her, only to be forced back into relative insignificance once again by the next, overwhelmingly torturous compression.

Try as she might to open her eyes, Kahlan couldn't lift her heavy lids. It would have taken more strength than she could call forth right then. Besides, she feared that there might be light, and she was sure that light would hurt like long needles stabbing into her defenseless eyes.

It felt as if some unknown, thick pressure were suspending her, keeping her immobile, while a hidden force tortured her under the throbbing pressure. Trying desperately to escape the grip of it, she attempted to bend her arms, but they were too stiff. She tried to move her legs, or even to lift a knee, but her legs were tightly encased in the cocooning, dense darkness.

A sound, possibly a harsh word, startled her, bringing her closer to the brink of wakening awareness, lifting her up through the numb confusion toward the world of life. This time she was sure that the sounds were voices. She began to be able to make out the occasional word.

She mentally seized those words like a lifeline and used them to help pull herself up out of the dark dregs of unconsciousness. She breathed evenly, concentrating on the words, forcing the throbbing to the background as she listened carefully for each word, trying to string them together into meaningful concepts. She recognized women's voices, and a man's voice. A surly man.

The pain of being awake, though, was even more debilitating than the dreamlike suffering she had felt while unconscious. Reality had a way of adding an agonizing dimension to the pain, an inescapable misery, a relentless torment throbbing through her body.

In an effort to get her mind off the pain she was in, Kahlan opened her eyes just enough to peek out and take a careful look around. She was inside some kind of structure. It looked something like a tent made of a pale tan canvas, but if it really was a tent it was much larger than any tent she remembered ever seeing before. Rich carpets hung to one side, looking to serve the purpose of double doors.

She was lying on thick furs that were atop something slightly elevated rather than being spread out on the floor. In the hot, muggy air the furs were making her sweat. At least she wasn't covered with blankets. She thought that maybe she had been placed there to keep her out from underfoot. There was a chair, with a carved back, opposite where she lay, but no one sat in it.

Several lamps were set around the room on chests while others hung from chains. They did little to chase away the gloomy atmosphere inside the tent, but at least the smell of the burning oil helped cover the heavy stench of sweat, animals, and manure. Kahlan was relieved that the light didn't hurt her eyes as she'd feared it would.

One of the Sisters paced in the dim light, like a phantom who couldn't find her grave.

Jumbled, muffled noises from outside drifted through the heavy canvas and carpeted walls of the tent. It sounded like a whole city surrounded the muted sanctuary. Kahlan could hear the murmured drone of men in the thousands along with the clop of hooves, the rattle of wagons, the braying of mules, and the metallic jangle of weapons and armor. Men in the distance shouted orders, or laughed, or cursed, while those closer told stories she couldn't quite make out.

Kahlan knew what this army was like. She had seen glimpses of it from afar, been through places where they had been, and had seen those that they'd tortured, raped, and murdered. She didn't want to ever have to go out there, among such savages as she knew these men were.

When she noticed Jagang glance her way, she pretended to still be unconscious, breathing evenly, lying perfectly still, and keeping her eyes almost closed. Apparently thinking she wasn't yet awake, he let his gaze drift back to the pacing Sister Ulicia.

"It can't be that simple," Sister Armina insisted from where she stood beside a table. She lifted her nose in a haughty manner.

Kahlan could just make out the edge of a book on that table. Sister Armina's extended fingers rested on the book's leather cover.

"Armina," Jagang asked in a calm, almost pleasant voice, "can you even begin to imagine how entertaining it is for me to be in the mind of a troublesome Sister that I send out to the tents to be passed around among my men?"

The woman paled as she backed up a step until her back met the tent wall. "No, Excellency."

"To be there, witnessing their dread? To be in their mind, seeing how completely helpless they are as powerful hands rip their clothes off and grope their bodies, as they are pushed to the bare ground, their legs forced open, and they are mounted by men who consider them of no value except as a bit of lustful entertainment? Men who have absolutely no sympathy for them at all, who don't care in the least what suffering they inflict in their heedless pursuit of what they want? Can you imagine how satisfying it is for me to be there, in the minds of such vexatious Sisters, to be an eyewitness, so to speak, of their well-deserved punishment?"

Her eyes wide in panic, Sister Armina spoke in a barely audible voice. "No, Excellency."

"Then I suggest that you stop protesting based not on what you think, but on what you think I want to hear. I'm not interested in your bootlicking. In my bed you may flatter me if you think it will gain you favor, which it won't, but in this I'm only interested in the truth. Your obsequious arguments will not make us successful. Only the truth will. If you have something worthwhile to say, then say it, but stop interrupting Ulicia to criticize her opinion with what you think I want to hear, or you will again be sent out to the tents sooner rather than later. Do you understand?"

Sister Armina's gaze dropped away. "Yes, Excellency."

Sister Ulicia took a settling breath as Jagang turned his attention on her. Her pacing came to a halt. She lifted an arm toward the book on the table.

"The problem is, Excellency, there is no way for us to confirm if the copy inside is true or not. I know that's what you want us to do, and believe me we've tried, but the truth is we can't find anything that could settle the matter."

"Why not?"

"Well, if it says 'position the boxes facing north,' how are we supposed to be able to detect if that is a true or false instruction just from reading it? For all we know, facing them north could be an accurate copy of the original manuscript, in which case not doing as it says would prove fatal—or it could be a corruption of the true direction and doing as it says would be fatal. How are we to know? You may wish us to be able to come to a conclusion as to the book's validity just from reading it, but we have no way of doing that. I know you don't want me to lie to satisfy your request. I'm serving you best by being truthful."

Jagang eyed her suspiciously. "Be careful, Ulicia, not to cross the line into fawning. I'm not in the mood."

Sister Ulicia bowed her head. "Of course, Excellency."

Jagang folded his husky arms across his massive chest and returned to the matter at hand. "So you think that for this reason the ones who made the copies left us this other way to tell the false from true?"

"Yes, Excellency," Sister Ulicia said, despite looking anxious to be taking a stand that she knew would not please him. Since the emperor could read her thoughts, he would know the truth of what she honestly believed. Kahlan imagined that Sister Ulicia reasoned that her best chance of not incurring his wrath was to be true to her belief. Sister Ulicia was nothing if not smart.

"You believe that this is the real explanation, then, that it isn't a mistake, but that it was calculated and deliberate."

"Yes, Excellency. There has to be some way to tell. Otherwise, the successful use of the book would only be the result of chance. The boxes of Orden were made as a counter . . ."

She paused as she glanced briefly Kahlan's way. Kahlan kept her eyes almost closed into the narrowest of slits so that the woman wouldn't know she was awake. Sister Ulicia turned her attention back to Jagang.

"They would have reasoned that if it ever became necessary to use that counter it could only be because the situation was desperate, so they would need very badly to know that the book was true or else they risked losing everything they believed in. They would, after all, be using the book to save everything they believed in. If the ones using the counter of the boxes were wrong about the copy they were referring to, then they stood to lose more than just their lives—they risked losing the world of life itself."

"Unless those who made the copies wanted the false copies to foil a greedy thief," Jagang said.

"But Excellency," Sister Ulicia said, "to stop any treacherous plans, those in charge of the boxes would need to have a way to know the true copies from the false. If they didn't leave such a method to those who would come after them, then they would have abandoned their descendants to survival by chance. Their whole reason for making the copies in the first place was because they were worried about the risks that might develop in the future with having only the original text. After all, the only book in existence would be subject to any number of threats, from fire, to water, to worms, and that isn't even including the array of deliberate threats. They were trying to make sure that there would be an accurate copy if it ever came to be necessary to use the boxes and the original book was unavailable for reasons they might not even be able to imagine. Risking that future on chance would be counter to their purpose for making the copies in the first place.

"Do you see what I mean? Since they made only one true copy, and the rest false, they were attempting to discourage the wrongful use of the boxes—putting another obstacle in the path of them being used—but at the same time, if the boxes were ever truly needed, they most certainly would not have wanted that call to have been answered by chance. They would have left those coming after them a way to confirm the truth.

"Since the text inside the book is not contradictory in and of itself, it seems to me that those who made the copies would unquestionably have devised another means to determine the true from the false."

Jagang turned to the other Sister. "Ah, Armina has had a thought. Do speak up, darlin."

Sister Armina cleared her throat. "We are being asked to believe that a singular rather than a plural word served as their only indication of validity?" Sister Armina shook her head. "While I grant the general point, I believe that this is just too simple an answer, if not far too opaque a message. This means of telling true from false in and of itself becomes chance, too, unless they gave us a way to confirm it."

"And they have, now, haven't they?" Sister Ulicia arched an eyebrow as she leaned a little toward the woman. "It's right there, right in the beginning, where it tells us precisely how to detect if the book is true or not. It says that *she* must verify it. She has."

Armina folded her arms. "Like I said, I think that's just too simple to be the answer."

"If it's so simple, Armina, then why didn't you see it?" Sister Ulicia asked.

Kahlan closed her eyes a little more when Sister Ulicia pointed at her. "She found the flaw. Why did none of us see it? Only she saw it. Without her we probably would not have noticed it or, if we had, we probably would have thought that it couldn't be important and we would have ignored it. She has done what the book said she must. She found it. She said that it means the copy is a false copy. That is precisely the purpose for which the book itself said she must be used.

"Some of us may not consider that flaw complex enough to be the determining element, but that's irrelevant. The fact remains that she must verify the veracity of this book and, because of a flaw that only she noticed, she claims it is a false copy. That's what matters. We have to take that pronouncement as valid."

Considering the words of each woman, Jagang rubbed a meaty hand back over his bull neck as he paced before the table. He stared down at the book for a time, then spoke.

"There is one way to be sure." He glared at each Sister in turn. "We find the other copies and compare them. If they all, or only a few, have this exact same flaw in the title, then it would point to it being meaningless. On the other hand, if all but one has this same flaw, then the one that doesn't would likely be the true copy. We can then compare all the versions of the text and if the one without the flawed title is different from all the others, we will have confirmed that it's the one true copy."

"Excellency," Sister Armina said with a deferential bow of her head, "that is an excellent idea. If we can locate the others, and this is the only one with this flaw, then it would prove my point that it is nothing but a simple, isolated mistake by an ignorant bookbinder."

Jagang stared at her for a moment before finally breaking eye contact and going to a chest to the side. He opened the top and pulled out a book. He tossed it on the table so that it slid across the top toward the two Sisters.

Sister Armina picked it up and read the cover. Even in the dim light of the oil lamps, Kahlan could see the woman's face going a deep shade of red.

"*The Book of Counted Shadow*," she said in an incredulous whisper.

"*Shadow*?" Sister Ulicia asked, peering down over Sister Armina's shoulder. "Not *Shadows*?"

"No," Jagang said. "It is *The Book of Counted Shadow*, the same as the one from Caska."

"But, but," Sister Armina stammered, "I don't understand. Where is this copy from?"

A condescending smile joined his glare. "The Palace of the Prophets."

Sister Armina's jaw dropped in speechless shock.

Sister Ulicia frowned. "What? That can't be. Are you sure?"

"Am I sure?" He grunted in derision. "Oh, yes, I'm sure. You see, I've had this book for quite some time. That is part of the reason why I allowed you fools to continue in your quest. I needed the same woman you were after in order to find out if this is a true copy or not.

"All the time I had this book I never noticed the word 'shadow' in the title as being anything other than what it should be. I just assumed it said what it was supposed to say. But our unconscious friend over there noticed it immediately."

"But how could you have gotten this from the Palace of the Prophets?" Sister Ulicia asked. "From what we've learned, these copies were buried with bones, like in Caska, in hidden catacombs. No catacombs were ever discovered at the palace before it was destroyed."

Jagang smiled to himself, as if he were explaining things to children. "You think you are so clever, Ulicia, finding out about the boxes, about the book needed to open them, about the catacombs, and about the one person needed to verify the text of the book. But I have known for decades what you have only recently discovered.

"I have been visiting minds for a very, very long time to aid our cause. You would be surprised at all the things I learned long ago. While you Sisters were engaged in palace politics, in battles for power on your own little island, in courting either the Creator or the Keeper, seeking favors in return for loyalty to one or the other, I have been working to unite the Old

World in the cause of the Fellowship of Order, which is the true cause of the Creator and therefore the only righteous cause of mankind.

"While you were teaching young men to be wizards, I was showing those same young men the true Light. Without the Sisters even being aware of it, many of those young wizards had already devoted themselves to the future salvation of mankind by becoming disciples of the Order. They spent decades walking the halls of the Palace of the Prophets, right under the noses of the Sisters, while working as brothers of the Fellowship of Order. And I was there in their minds as they read all those restricted books down in the vaults of the palace.

"As a dream walker, I gave them direction and purpose in their studies. I knew what was needed. I had them search for me. As brothers of the Order they long ago found the secret entrance down into the catacombs—it was hidden under an unused and long-forgotten storage area in the older section of the stables. They spirited this book, as well as other valuable volumes, out of the catacombs, and then when I finally arrived at the palace after triumphantly unifying the Old World, they delivered them to me. I have had this particular copy for decades.

"The only thing I didn't have was a way through the great barrier so that I could get at both the boxes and the means of verification. But then, through their meddling, the Sisters obliged me by doing things that resulted in the destruction of that barrier.

"Now that the Palace of the Prophets has been destroyed, I'm afraid that the catacombs and the books they held have been lost for all time, but those young men searched through most of those hidden volumes, and through their eyes I've read most of them. The palace and the catacombs are now gone, but not all the knowledge contained there has been lost. Those young men grew up to become brothers, many still alive and serving in our struggle.

"When I witnessed you hatch your plan to capture the Mother Confessor, I realized I could use that plan to finally get my hands on her and use her for my purposes, so I allowed you to think you were accomplishing exactly what you wanted, while you were, in fact, accomplishing what I wanted. I now have the book, and the Mother Confessor that the book says must be used to confirm their validity."

Both Sisters could only stare.

Kahlan's mind spun in confusion. Mother Confessor. She was the Mother Confessor.

What in the world was a Mother Confessor?

Jagang flashed the Sisters a cunning smile. "You have been the perfect fools, don't you think?"

"Yes, Excellency," they both conceded as one in small voices.

"So, you see," he went on, "we now have two copies of *The Book of Counted Shadows*, and both have the same mistake—the word 'shadow' instead of 'shadows' on the cover."

"But this is still only two," Sister Armina said. "What if all the other copies have the same flaw?"

"I don't think that's going to happen," Sister Ulicia said.

"Well, if they did, it would certainly prove something, now, wouldn't it?" Jagang arched a questioning eyebrow over one dark eye. "I now have two, and they have the exact same error. We will need to have the rest to confirm the theory that one will have the title written correctly, as 'shadows.' So, as it turns out we will need to keep the Mother Confessor alive until we can see if she has really found the flaw that will verify the true copy."

"And if all the copies have the same flaw, Excellency?" Sister Armina asked.

"Then we will have learned that the error in the title isn't the method for verifying *The Book of Counted Shadows*. It may turn out that we need to give her access to the copy itself so that she can have a broader basis for making the verification—for making it on things that for now she isn't able to see."

Sister Armina lifted a hand. "But Excellency, I don't know that such a thing is even possible."

Jagang didn't answer Armina's concern, but instead took the book from her and set it beside the one on the table. "The Mother Confessor is still vital to us. She is the only way to verify the one, true copy. We can't yet be certain that she has done that. So far she made a judgment on the only information available to her. For now, we need her alive."

"Yes, Excellency," Sister Armina said.

"I think she might be waking," Sister Ulicia said.

Kahlan realized that she had been listening so intently that she had failed to completely close her eyes when Sister Ulicia looked her way. The Sister came closer, peering down at her.

Kahlan didn't want them to know she had heard them call her by the title Mother Confessor. She stretched a little, as if trying to escape the bounds of unconsciousness while she tried to imagine what such a title could possibly mean.

"Where are we?" she mumbled, feigning a groggy voice.

"I am confident that it will soon enough become all too clear to you." Sister Ulicia forcefully jabbed Kahlan's shoulder. "Now, wake up."

"What is it? Do you wish something, Sister?" Kahlan rubbed her eyes with the backs of her knuckles, trying to look uncoordinated and dazed. "Where are we?"

Sister Ulicia hooked a finger through the collar around Kahlan's neck and jerked her upright.

Before Sister Ulicia could say anything more, Jagang's meaty hand grabbed her arm and drew her back out of his way. He was intent on Kahlan. His fists seized her shirt at her throat. He lifted her clear of the ground.

"You killed two trusted guards," he said through gritted teeth. "You killed Sister Cecilia." His face was going red with rapidly building rage. His brow drew down over his dark eyes. It seemed that lightning might flicker in the cloudy shapes drifting through those black eyes. "What made you think that you could get away with killing them?"

"I didn't think I could get away with it," Kahlan said as calmly as she could manage. As she had suspected, her calm only served to provoke his fury.

He roared in unleashed anger and shook her so violently that it felt like it might have torn muscles in her neck. It was obvious that he was a man who at the slightest provocation flew into fits of uncontrollable rage. He was on the brink of murder.

Kahlan didn't want to die, but she knew that a swift death might be preferable to what he had promised her for later. She couldn't really do anything to stop it, anyway.

"If you didn't think you could get away with it, then why would you dare to do such a thing!"

"What difference does it make?" Kahlan asked with calm indifference as his fists on her shirt held her up so that her boots were clear of the ground.

"What are you talking about!"

"Well, you've already told me that your treatment of me will be terrible beyond anything I have ever experienced. I believe you; that's the only way people like you can ever win—by threats and brutality. Because you are such a pompous fool, you made the mistake of telling me that I could not begin to imagine all the terrible things you intend to do to me. That was your big mistake."

"Mistake? What are you talking about?" He drew her up against his muscled body. "What mistake?"

"You've made a tactical error, *Emperor*," Kahlan said, managing to stress his title in a way that made it sound like a mocking insult. She wanted him angry, and she could see that it was working.

Despite hanging from his white-knuckled fists, Kahlan tried to sound composed, even aloof. "You see, you have made it clear to me that no matter what I do I have nothing to lose. You've made it clear that you can't be reasoned with. You said that you are going to do your worst to me. That empowers me because I am no longer bound by any hope for mercy from you. In revealing that I have no hope whatsoever for any mercy, you have given me an advantage I didn't previously have.

"You see, by making that mistake, you showed me that I had nothing to lose by killing your guards and, since I'm to be subjected to your worst anyway, I might as well have my revenge on Sister Cecilia. By making such a tactical mistake, you have shown me that you are not so smart after all, that you are just a brute and can be bested."

He relaxed his grip just enough for Kahlan to touch the toes of her boots to the ground so that she could gain some leverage.

"You really are something," he said as a slow, cunning smile overcame his rage. "I'm going to enjoy what I have planned for you."

"I've already told you your mistake, and you repeat it? Apparently, you don't learn very well, either, do you?"

Before, when he'd pulled her up against him in a rage and had brought her face close to his, when his hands had been firmly occupied holding her in a threatening manner, Kahlan had used the distraction to gingerly slip his knife from the sheath on his belt. With two fingers she'd worked it up into her hand. He had been so angry he hadn't noticed.

Rather than get worked up into another fit of rage at her latest insult, he began to laugh.

Kahlan already had his knife gripped tightly in her fist.

Without ceremony or warning, she thrust it at him as hard as she could.

Her intention had been to drive the blade up under his ribs, to cut open vital organs, maybe even his heart if she could get it in that far. The way he was holding her, though, hampered her movement just enough so that she missed her mark by a fraction of an inch and instead struck his lowest rib. The point stuck in bone.

Before she had time to yank it back and stab him again, he seized her wrist and wrenched her arm over, spinning her around. Her back slammed against his chest. He had the knife out of her grip before she had a chance to do anything about it. His arm across her throat cut off her air as he held her against his massive muscles. His chest heaved in anger against her back.

Rather than admitting defeat, and before she blacked out from lack of air, she used all her muscle to drive the heel of her boot into his shin. By his cry she knew it hurt. She struck sharply with her elbow directly into the fresh wound. He flinched. As her elbow rebounded from the blow she cocked it forward to gain momentum and then smashed back into his jaw. He was so big, though, so strong, that it didn't have a disabling effect. It had been rather like punching a bull. And, like a bull, he was only enraged further.

Looking no worse for her attack, Jagang seized a fistful of her shirt before she could slip out of his reach. He punched her in the middle hard enough to double her over and drive her breath from her lungs. She gasped, trying to draw a breath against the stunning pain.

Kahlan realized that she was on her knees only when he lifted her by her hair and placed her back on her feet. Her knees wobbled unsteadily.

Jagang was grinning. His flash of anger had been washed away by an unexpected, dangerous, but one-sided brawl, and an opportunity to inflict pain. He was beginning to enjoy the game.

"Why don't you just kill me?" Kahlan managed to get out as he stood watching her.

"Kill you? Why would I want to kill you? Then you would just be dead. I want you alive so that I can make you suffer."

The two Sisters made no move to rein in their master. Kahlan knew that they would not have objected to anything he did to her. As long as his attention was on Kahlan, it wasn't on them. Before he could strike her again, light abruptly flooded the tent, drawing his attention.

"Excellency," a deep voice said. It had come from the side. One of the big brutes held the carpet aside as he waited. The man looked similar to the two guards she had killed before. Kahlan supposed that Jagang had an endless supply of such men.

"What is it?"

"We're ready to strike your camp, Excellency. I am sorry for interrupting, but you asked to be told as soon as we were ready. You said that you wanted us to make haste."

Jagang released Kahlan's hair. "All right, get started then."

He swung around unexpectedly, backhanding her across the face hard enough to send her tumbling across the floor.

While she lay on the floor recovering her senses, he pressed a hand to the wound over his rib. He pulled the hand away to see how much he was bleeding. He wiped his hand on his trousers, apparently deciding that it was a relatively minor wound and nothing to be concerned about. From what Kahlan could see of him, he bore a number of scars, most testifying to injuries far worse than the one she had given him.

"See to it that she doesn't get any more ideas," he told the Sisters as he headed for the carpet that the guard was holding aside for him.

Kahlan felt fire race down from the collar, through her nerves all the way to her toes. The burning pain pulled an involuntary gasp.

She wanted to scream in rage at having that hot pain yet again ripping through her. She hated the way the Sisters used the collar to control her. She hated the helpless agony they could put her in.

Sister Ulicia stepped closer and stood over her. "That was a pretty stupid thing to do, now, wasn't it?"

Kahlan couldn't answer through the stunning pain. What she would have told the Sister was that it wasn't stupid at all, that it had been worth it.

As long as she had breath in her lungs, she would fight them. With her last breath, if need be, she would fight.

At the opening out of Emperor Jagang's tent, Kahlan recoiled at seeing the army of the Imperial Order up close for the first time. Distance had taken off a bit of the rougher edges. Even though she had a pretty good sense of them, it was still an unnerving sight.

The dense mass of men spread unbroken to the horizon. With everyone in motion and moving about—bending, standing, turning, lifting gear, joining into ranks, saddling horses, loading wagons, with different groups on horseback moving like waves through the mass of men—it looked like an endless, churning, treacherous black sea.

There was not a single man in sight—and she could see thousands upon endless thousands—who looked kindly or harmless. Every single man looked grim and grisly, as if there was nothing he looked forward to in life as much as the prospect of doing violence. These men looked driven by the singular prospect of an unrestrained rampage. Kahlan feared to think of those who might find themselves in these mens' path.

As she took it all in, she began to notice that there were differences among the men. The closest group to the emperor were more disciplined, orderly, and measured in everything they did. They were more attentive to their weapons. All the men in closest around the emperor's tents looked much the same as the two Kahlan had killed.

Out past them were other men dressed in different kinds of uniforms made of chain mail and leather. They all looked to be nearly as big and well trained as the men closest to the emperor, but their primary weapons appeared to be crescent axes. Beyond were more encircling layers of men, including men with loaded crossbows, swordsmen, and ranks of pikemen forming up in close formations, preparing for the long march ahead.

While each of the layers of men around the emperor were outfitted in their own distinctive uniforms that matched the rest of their group, they were all big, muscled, armored, and heavily armed with well-made weapons. This was the core of the emperor's force of the deadliest, the most fearsome and formidable, of his army.

In among the inner circles were men who looked to be officers. Some gave orders to messengers, some gave orders to lower-ranking men, while others assembled in groups, making plans over maps. Yet others came from time to time to speak briefly with Jagang.

Out beyond the barriers of career soldiers were the rabble who made up by far the largest mass of the army. The weapons carried by those men— swords, axes, pikes, lances, maces, clubs, and knives—were inelegantly made, and looked all the more deadly for it. These were coarse men who looked to be out for a riot. They shared one thing with the men in closer to the emperor: they all looked like wide-eyed idealists intent on enforcing their beliefs under the heel of their boot. Kahlan felt as if she were stranded on a treacherous island, surrounded by monsters in a wild sea.

Kahlan saw something else different in among the inner circle. There were women. At first she hadn't noticed them, because their dress was so drab that they blended in with all the men. Given the way these women watched everyone, she began to suspect that they were Sisters who served to guard the emperor. There were also men who were largely unarmed, but who had a look to them that in a way reminded Kahlan of the Sisters. They were probably gifted as well. None of the men or the Sisters so much as glanced Kahlan's way. No one but Sister Ulicia, Sister Armina, and Jagang knew she was there.

There were also young men who, by their simple, loose trousers and to- tal lack of any weapons, appeared to be slaves taking care of the menial tasks. From some of the other tents in the emperor's compound, Kahlan saw young women emerge to be herded into wagons before the tents were taken down. By the way the men openly stared at these women and by their scanty clothes, their purpose among the men of rank was obvious to Kahlan. The hollow, dead look in the women's eyes told her that they must have been captives pressed into service as whores.

The mob out beyond made a ceaseless, noisy ruckus, while most of the men in closer were silent as they went about preparations to strike camp. Most of the men close by had studs, rings, chains, and tattooed faces with unique designs that made them look not just savage, but deliberately less than human, as if they were rejecting a higher value in favor of a lower one. Their chosen purpose in life was clearly brutality. As they went about

their work they talked little and payed attention to orders shouted by officers riding through their midst. They worked with practiced precision as
they packed gear, readied weapons, and saddled horses.

The great masses of men out beyond, though, were nowhere near as orderly or careful. They threw together their gear in a haphazard fashion. As
they departed they left behind mounds of refuse and broken plunder. They
couldn't be bothered with such concerns; their calling in life was bringing
to task those who didn't believe in their superior ways.

At seeing Kahlan's reaction to all the fierce men, Sister Ulicia gestured
with a nod out to the men and then leaned a little closer to Kahlan. "I
know how you feel."

Kahlan doubted it. She didn't want to say anything because she was
pretty sure that Jagang was in the Sister's mind, watching for what Kahlan
might have to say when he wasn't around.

"It doesn't really matter how I feel, now, does it?" She said to the two
Sisters watching her. "He will do what he wants to me." She checked the
cut on her cheek from one of Jagang's rings. It had finally stopped bleeding. "He's made that clear enough."

"I suppose he will," Sister Ulicia said.

"He will do what he wants to all of us," Sister Armina added. "I can't
believe we were so foolish."

A group of officers returned with Jagang. Soldiers behind them pulled
already saddled horses along with them. Other men were already taking
chests, chairs, tables, and smaller items out of the emperor's tent and loading it all into crates in the waiting wagons. As soon as the tent had been
emptied, the lines came down, followed by the poles, and at last the tent itself. In a matter of moments what had looked like a small town of tents,
with the emperor's large tent at the center, was just an empty field.

Jagang gestured for a man to hand Kahlan the reins to a horse. "Today
you will ride with me."

Kahlan wondered what she would be doing the next day, but she didn't
ask. It sounded like he had plans for her. She couldn't begin to guess at
them but she feared what was in store for her.

She stuffed a boot in a stirrup and swung up into the saddle, then
scanned the sea of men, estimating her chances if she made a run for freedom. She might be able to make it past the men, because, with the exception of the two Sisters and Jagang, the men couldn't remember her long

enough to recall that they saw her. Out among those men, as daunting as such a thought was, she was as good as invisible. To them it would appear as if a riderless horse was running away, and they probably wouldn't want to get trampled for no good reason.

The Sisters, watching her carefully, mounted up as well, one to each side of her to make sure that she didn't get a chance to bolt. Even if she was invisible to the soldiers, Kahlan knew that the Sisters could use the collar to drop her where she was. They didn't need to be close, either; she had learned that the hard way. Her legs still ached from what they had done a little earlier. It was a good thing that she was to ride, because right then she didn't think she would make it far on foot.

The sea of men had already begun moving away in a dark, surging tide. The dawn light sparkled off millions of weapons, making the army look liquid. As if floating in the tightly formed raft of the emperor's personal guards and retinue of Sisters, servants, and slaves, they began to drift out into the vast churning ocean of men moving north toward the horizon.

They rode with the hot, rising sun to their right. Kahlan, between the Sisters, in among the emperor's personal guards, moved along in the mass of men streaming northward. She had a good view of it all from high in her saddle. At least she didn't have to carry the Sisters' things on her back, as she had always had to do before.

The early chatter among the soldiers soon died out with the monotonous effort of the march. Talking became too difficult for them. It wasn't long before Kahlan was sweating in the heat. Men carrying heavy packs plodded onward, eyes to the ground in front of them. To stop would probably mean being trampled. There had to be a force of millions that she could see behind them, driving north with them.

Throughout the day wagons, or men on horses, worked their way through the men, passing out food. Wagons dispersed throughout the army at intervals carried water. There was soon a line of men, marching along, waiting their turn to get some water from each of the wagons rolling among them.

Near midday a small wagon arrived in the center of the emperor's people. It had hot food that was passed out to all the officers. The Sisters passed Kahlan the same as what the rest of them were offered—flat bread wrapped around some kind of salty, mushy meat. It didn't taste very good, but Kahlan was starving and glad to have it.

By nightfall everyone was exhausted from the arduous march. They had eaten on the move and had stopped for nothing. They were covering more ground than she thought an army of this size capable of doing in a day. She felt as if she were coated with much of the ground they had covered. She didn't know if she would be any happier for rain that would knock down the dust, because then they would have to contend with mud.

Kahlan was surprised when she saw out ahead of them what looked like the emperor's compound. Flags atop tents flapped in the hot wind as if to welcome the emperor home. She realized that the wagons with all the emperor's equipment must have ridden on ahead and set up camp. The army was so vast and covered so much area that it took hours, if not days, for them all to pass the same spot, so the wagons would not have had to ride out ahead of the protection of the army. Men would merely have opened a path for them to race ahead through the marching men and before dark start setting up camp so that by the time the emperor arrived everything would be ready.

Kahlan saw meat roasting on spits over a series of fires. The aromas made her stomach ache with hunger. Other fires held steaming cauldrons on iron cranes. Slaves scurried here and there carrying a variety of supplies, working at tables, turning spits, stirring what was in the cauldrons and adding ingredients as they prepared the evening meal. Platters with breads, meats, and fruits were already being readied.

Jagang, riding directly in front of Kahlan, dismounted before his large tent. A man rushed in to take the reins. When the Sisters and Kahlan dismounted, more young men ran in to take their horses as well. The Sisters, as if directed by wordless commands, ushered Kahlan along with them as they followed Jagang in under the large, ornate hanging covering the tent's opening that was being held aside by a muscled soldier without a shirt. He was slick with sweat, probably from the work of erecting the tents, and had a sour stink about him.

Inside, it looked just like it had that morning when they had left. Just by looking at it, it was hard to tell that they had gone anywhere. The lamps were already lit. Kahlan was glad for the smell of the burning oil because it covered some of the stench of urine, manure, and sweat. There were a number of slaves inside, all rushing about the task of preparing the emperor's meal being set out on the table.

Jagang abruptly turned and seized Sister Ulicia by her hair and yanked her forward. She let out a small cry of pain and surprise at first, but quickly cut off the whimper and offered no resistance as he pulled her close. The slaves only briefly glanced over at Sister Ulicia's cry, and then immediately went back to their work as if they saw nothing.

"Why does no one else see her?" Jagang asked.

Kahlan knew what he was talking about.

"The spell, Excellency. The Chainfire spell." Sister Ulicia was being held in an awkward and uncomfortable position, bent halfway over and standing off balance. "That was the whole purpose of the spell—so that no one would see her. It was created specifically to make a person appear to vanish. I think it may have been envisioned as a method of creating a spy who couldn't be detected. We used the spell for that purpose—so we could get the boxes of Orden out of the People's Palace without anyone knowing what we had done."

Kahlan felt as if her heart had come up into her throat at hearing how she had been used, at how her life and her memory had been stripped from her. A lump swelled in her throat at hearing the arrogant disregard the Sisters had for her precious life. What gave these women the right to steal anyone's life in such a way?

Only a short time ago, she had thought she was a nobody without a memory, a slave to the Sisters. Now, in a short time, she had found out that she was Kahlan Amnell, and that she was the Mother Confessor—whatever that was. Now she knew that she hadn't known her name was Amnell, or that she was this Mother Confessor person, because the Sisters had spelled her.

"That's the way it's supposed to work," Jagang said. "So why did that innkeeper see her? Why did that little rock rat back in Caska see her?"

"I, I, don't know," Sister Ulicia stammered.

He jerked her a little closer. She began to reach up to grasp his wrists to try to keep from having her scalp torn off, but she thought better of trying to resist anything he did and let her arms drop to dangle from her stooped shoulders.

"Let me rephrase the question so that even a stupid bitch like you can understand it. What did you do wrong?"

"But Excellency—"

"You must have done something wrong or those two would not have been able to see her!" Sister Ulicia trembled but didn't answer as he lectured her. "You and Armina can see her because you were controlling the spell. I can see her because I was in your minds and so I was protected by the same process. But no one else should be able to see her.

"Now," he said after a pause to grit his teeth, "I will ask again. What did you do wrong?"

"Excellency, we did nothing wrong. I swear."

Jagang crooked a finger at Armina. She meekly came forward in mincing steps.

"Would you like to answer my question and tell me what you did wrong? Or would you also like to be sent to the tents along with Ulicia?"

Sister Armina swallowed back her terror as she spread her hands. "Excellency, if I could spare myself by confessing, I would, but Ulicia is right. We did nothing wrong."

He turned his glare back on the Sister he had by the hair. "It seems pretty obvious to me that you two are wrong—the spell should make her invisible but others can see her. And yet you continue to stick to a story when that's obviously a lie? You had to do something wrong or those two people would not have seen her."

Sister Ulicia, tears dripping from her cheeks from the pain she was in, tried to shake her head. "No, Excellency—it doesn't work that way."

"What doesn't work that way?"

"The Chainfire spell. Once ignited, it runs its course. The spell does the work. It's self-directing; we didn't guide it or control it in any way. In fact, no intervention is possible during the process. It is ignited and then the spell runs through its predetermined routines. We don't even know what those routines are. In some aspects they function similarly to a constructed spell. We wouldn't dare try to tamper with any of it. The power unleashed in Chainfire is far more than we know how to regulate—and we have no way to alter such a spell even if we wanted to."

"She's right, Excellency. We knew what it was supposed to do, what the result was supposed to be, but we don't know how it works. What would we change? Our goal was for it to work, to do what it was designed to do. We had no reason to try to tamper with it, so there is nothing we could have done wrong."

"All we did was ignite it," Sister Ulicia insisted, tears starting to weep through her words. "We ran the verification webs to make sure that everything was as it should be, and then we ignited it. The spell did the rest. We have no idea why those two people can see her. We were completely surprised by it."

He turned his glare on Sister Armina. "Can you fix whatever is wrong?"

"We have no idea what the problem is," Sister Armina said, "so there is no way we can fix it. We don't even know for sure that there really is something wrong. For all we know, it could be that this is simply the way the spell works—that there will be a few people who, for some reason unknown to us, can still see her. The spell is far more complex than anything we've ever encountered before. We have no idea what is wrong—if there really is something wrong—or how to correct it."

"I think that maybe it was a random anomaly," Sister Ulicia suggested when the silence in the tent became ominous. "Those things sometimes happen with magic. Small little issues that aren't anticipated by the spell's creator slip through and aren't affected. It might be nothing more than that.

"After all, the spell is thousands of years old. Those who created it never tested it, so there might have been unresolved issues they weren't aware of."

Jagang did not look convinced. "There must have been something you did wrong."

"No, Excellency. Not even those ancient wizards could do anything with the spell once it had been ignited. After all, the magic of Orden was created to deal with the spell if it was ever unleashed. Nothing less can alter its course."

Kahlan's ears perked up. She wondered why the Sisters would have used a spell to steal the boxes of Orden that were designed to counter the spell. Maybe their intent had been to make sure that no one could use that counter.

Jagang finally released Sister Ulicia by tossing her to the ground with a grunt of disgust. Her hands covered her scalp, comforting the hurt.

Emperor Jagang paced as he thought about what he'd been told. Seeing someone peeking into the tent, he stopped and signaled. Several women entered with pitchers and poured red wine in mugs set out on the table. Serving boys began spilling into the room carrying platters and trays filled with a variety of steaming-hot food. Jagang paced, paying the slaves little attention as they went about their work.

When the table was finally filled, Jagang took a seat at the carved chair behind the table. He brooded as he watched the two Sisters. The slaves all silently lined up behind him, ready to do his bidding or bring him anything he requested.

He finally turned his attention to dinner and dug his fingers into the ham. He squeezed off a fistful of the hot meat. With his other hand he tore long strips off the large chunk and ate them as he watched the Sisters and Kahlan, as if judging whether they should live or die.

When he had finished the ham, he pulled the knife from his belt and used it to slice off a piece of roast beef. He stabbed the red slab of meat and held it up, waiting. Blood ran down the blade and down the length of his arm to his elbow resting on the tabletop.

He paused and smiled up at Kahlan. "A better use for my knife than the use you had for it, don't you think?"

Kahlan considered keeping silent, but she couldn't resist speaking. "I liked my use better. I only wish my aim had been true. Had it been, we would not be having this conversation."

He smiled to himself. "Maybe." He took a gulp of wine from a mug before using his teeth to pull a chunk of the beef off the slab stuck on the knife.

As he watched Kahlan, and while he chewed, he said, "Take off your clothes."

Kahlan blinked. "What?"

"Take off your clothes." He gestured with the knife. "All of them."

Kahlan clenched her jaw. "No. If you want them off, you will have to rip them off me."

He shrugged. "I will do that later, just for the satisfaction of it, but for now, take them off."

"Why?"

He lifted an eyebrow. "Because I said so."

"No," she repeated.

The gaze of his nightmare eyes glided to Sister Ulicia. "Tell Kahlan about the torture tents."

"Excellency?"

"Tell her about the extensive experience we have in convincing people to do as we wish. Tell her what tortures we employ."

Before Sister Ulicia could speak, Kahlan spoke first. "Just get on with it and torture me. No one is interested in hearing you gossip about it like an old hen. I'm sure that you'd rather make me suffer—so get on with it."

"Oh, the torture isn't for you, darlin.'" He twisted a leg off a roasted goose and used it to gesture to a young woman behind him. "The torture is for her."

Kahlan glanced at the suddenly panicked woman and then frowned at Jagang. "What?"

He bit off some of the dark goose meat. Grease ran down his fingers. He sucked the grease off the rings.

"Well," he said as he picked at the meat hanging from the leg, "perhaps I should be the one to explain. You see, we have this torture where the inquisitor makes a small incision in a lower abdomen of the person in question." He turned and poked the goose leg at the young woman's belly, just below her navel. The goose leg left a greasy spot on her bare flesh. "Right about there.

"Then," he said, turning back, "the inquisitor pushes the jaws of a pair of tongs deep into the belly and gropes around until he is able to grab hold of a bit of the small intestine. It's all quite slippery in there, and the person being subjected to this treatment is not just lying still for it, if you know what I mean, so it usually takes a bit of doing to snag the proper bit of their insides. Once he has it, he slowly begins to pull a few feet of it out. Quite an ordeal."

He leaned over and pulled off another strip of ham. "Now, if you don't do as I say, then we are all going to go over to the torture tents"—he gestured with the limp strip of ham off to his left—"and we're going to let one of our experienced inquisitors do that to this girl behind me."

He turned an icy look up at Kahlan. "All because you refuse to do as you are told. You will get to watch the whole agonizing thing. You will get to listen to her screams, listen to her begging for her life, watch her bleed, see her vital insides being drawn out of her. After the man has pulled a few feet free, he then begins winding it around a stick, like spare yarn—just to keep the mess all neat and tidy. After that, he will pause and look to me.

"At that time, I will again politely ask you to do as I have instructed. If you again refuse, then we will slowly pull out a few more feet of her tender, delicate, bloody gut, winding it around the stick, while we all listen to her scream and cry and beg to die. This whole process can go on for quite a long time. It's an excruciatingly slow and painful ordeal." Jagang gave

Kahlan a cheerful smile. "And then, near the end, you will get to see her convulse in her death."

Kahlan looked up at the girl. She hadn't moved, but she had gone as white as the sugar mounded in the bowl to the side of the table.

Jagang slowly chewed and then washed the mouthful down with a swig of wine. "After that, you can watch us throw her lifeless carcass on the dead cart, with other ruined bodies of people who have been questioned.

"Then, I will offer Ulicia and Armina the choice of either being sent to the tents to entertain my men, who have quite the lustier desires, or, if they would rather, think of ways to use that collar around your neck to give you more pain than you have so far experienced from it. The stipulation will be that they must not allow you to pass out. I will, of course, want you to feel it all."

Outside, the din of the army carried on without letup, but inside the tent it was dead quiet. Jagang sawed off another slab of the bloody beef as he went on.

"After the Sisters have exhausted their imaginations, and I believe that the incentive will spark some inventive ideas, then I will personally beat you to within an inch of your death. After all of that, I will rip your clothes off of you and you will be standing there naked before me."

His nightmare eyes fixed on her. "Your choice, darlin. Either way, in the end, you are going to comply with my order and end up standing there naked before me. What method do you choose? Make it quick. I'll not offer you the choice again."

Kahlan had no choice. Resisting in this was pointless. She swallowed and immediately started unbuttoning her shirt.

Jagang scooped a handful of pecans from a silver bowl and popped a few in his mouth. He smiled at his triumph as he watched Kahlan begin removing her clothes. His self-satisfied expression made her feel all the more forlorn and powerless.

She was certain that her face had gone crimson. She made no further attempt to fight his order. She knew that she had to pick her battles, and this was not one she could win. She wondered if she would ever win another. She began to doubt that it was really possible. There would be no salvation for her. This was her life, her future, all there would ever be for her. She had nothing to look forward to, no reason to aspire to anything good.

As unceremoniously as possible, she dropped her clothes in a pile as she removed them, not bothering to stall by folding them. When she was done and had removed every stitch, she stood hunched in the dead-silent room, not looking up at Jagang because she didn't want to face his gloating, leering triumph. She tried her best to keep her trembling from being evident.

"Stand up straighter," Jagang said.

Kahlan did as she was told. She suddenly felt weary. Not weary of physical effort, but weary of all effort. What was she struggling for? What life could she ever have? She stood no chance of ever being free, of ever experiencing love, of ever feeling safe. What chance had she of ever achieving any happiness in life?

None.

At that moment she wanted nothing so much as to curl up into a ball and cry—or just stop breathing and be done with it. Everything seemed hopeless. Her efforts were futile against such strength, such numbers, such abilities.

She ceased to be embarrassed. She didn't care if he stared at her. She was sure that it wouldn't be long until he was finished with his dinner and then did a lot more than merely stare. She had no choice in that, either.

She had no choice in any of it. She had only an imitation of life. Without the ability to control even this much of her life, control if she would have to submit to any indignation, she didn't really have life. Life was something that others had. She breathed, she saw, she felt, she heard, she tasted, she even thought, but she did not live in a meaningful sense.

"There is a rock formation straight out from the opening to my tent," Jagang said as he leaned back in his chair. "Do you remember seeing it when we arrived?"

Kahlan looked up at him, feeling dead inside. She went through the task of doing as instructed, like a good slave. She thought about his question; she remembered seeing it. It was a long way off, but she remembered the way the dark river of men poured around the rock outcropping.

"Yes, I remember it," she said in a dull voice.

"Good." He took a swig and set the mug down. "I want you to walk to that rock. Don't go straight there, but go around in a circular route." He lifted an eyebrow. "No need to go all red, darlin. The men can't see you—remember?"

Kahlan stared at him. "Then why do you want me to do this?"

He shrugged. "Well, you killed my two guards. I need some more."

"There are plenty of your men right outside."

He smiled. "Yes, but they can't see you. I want men who can see you."

Kahlan began to grasp his meaning. She suddenly began feeling very naked again.

"The way I figure it, there is probably no better way to ferret out men who can see you than to have you walk by them showing them all you have to offer." His gaze roamed the length of her before returning to her eyes. "Believe me, if they can see you, there is no chance they will fail to make themselves known. I have no doubt whatsoever that if they can see you, like that innkeeper or that girl could see you, and they see you like this, then they will drop whatever they're doing and come out to pay you a kindly greeting."

He laughed heartily at his own joke. No one else in the tent so much as cracked a smile, but he didn't seem to care. Finally his fit of laughter died out.

"With all the men we have, I would bet that we are bound to net us a few who can see you. Among this many men, there are bound to be more 'anomalies,' as Ulicia put it." He cocked his head toward her. "Then, we will have guards that you can't sneak up on, or sneak past, the way you did the others.

"You see, darlin, you made a tactical mistake. You should have kept that trick for a better chance to escape. Now you wasted it."

She hadn't wasted it. She had done what she had done to save Jillian's life. Kahlan knew that she had no chance at freedom for herself, but at least she had given that gift to Jillian. There was no benefit to saying so, though, so she didn't dispute what he thought had gained him an advantage in the game he was playing with her.

Kahlan could think of nothing to say that would talk him out of such a plan. Her only hope now was to remain invisible. But she didn't feel at all invisible. She suddenly felt as if, when she walked out of the emperor's tent, every man in camp would be able to see her. She could already feel millions of lewd men leering at her.

Jagang gestured. "Ulicia, Armina, you will go along, but hang back a goodly distance. If any man can see her I don't want them to notice you two and go all shy before they have a good chance to make themselves known to us. I want any men who can see her to be eager enough and bold enough to drop whatever they're doing to come and investigate our fine young lady, here."

They both bowed and as one said, "Yes, Excellency."

Jagang lost his cheerful pretense and turned menacing. "Now, get going. Make a big circle to the right, through the camp, to that rock formation, and then continue the circle on around back to here. Move, woman!"

Kahlan padded across the soft rugs to the carpet hanging over the doorway. She could feel his leering gaze on her. She pushed the carpet aside and slipped through the opening.

Outside, facing the sprawling camp, she went stiff with dread. She forced herself, trembling every step, to walk among the hulking brutes near the emperor's tent. Tears stung her eyes. She felt humiliated and completely naked to all the men in camp.

She paused at the first defending ring of soldiers, terrified to go out among the men beyond. She wanted to scream with fury, with mortified embarrassment. She felt trapped by those who controlled her. She couldn't make her legs take another step. She looked back over her shoulder.

Emperor Jagang was standing just outside his tent, holding by the hair the woman he had threatened to torture. She was in helpless tears.

Kahlan had done something hard to save Jillian's life. She decided that she would devote herself to doing this to save the life of the woman Jagang now held under such terrible threat. She, too, was a slave who had no choice in her life. Only Kahlan could make a choice that would spare the woman terrible suffering.

Kahlan turned back to the pandemonium of the camp and started out. The ground was rough and she had to step carefully to avoid not only rocks and bits of broken gear, but fresh manure as well.

She reminded herself that none of these men could see her. She paused at another defensive line where big brutes stood guard. She peeked up at the man beside her. He didn't notice her, but instead watched those out beyond. So far, none of the men could see her. She looked back and saw the Sisters waiting for her to get farther away. Jagang was still holding the woman by the hair. Kahlan understood the message and without wasting a moment started moving again.

She saw horses nearby and briefly contemplated making a run for them. In her mind she envisioned jumping up onto the back of a horse and galloping away, escaping out of the camp altogether. She knew it was only a fantasy. The Sisters would unleash a torrent of pain through the collar and bring her down. What's more, the woman Jagang held would die. He was not a man to make idle threats. He carried them out lest anyone ever think he was the kind to bluff.

Kahlan knew such an escape was impossible, but thinking about it took her mind off all the men so close all around her, off all the filthy hands she couldn't help staring at. She felt completely vulnerable and exposed. She stood out among the sprawling encampment like an alabaster water-lily blossom stranded in the middle of a vast, reeking mudflat.

She moved quickly, reasoning that the sooner she made the circuit, the sooner she would be back in the sheltering protection of the tent. It was a terrible thought, Jagang's tent being her protection, that terrible man her security. At least she would be out of sight again and right then that was all she wanted. It became the focus of her thoughts. Make the distance to the rocks and make it back. The sooner she did it, the sooner she would be back inside.

Unless there were men out in this mass of soldiers who could see her. It only made sense. She had run across two people who could see her and that was among a small sampling of people. There were millions of men in this army. The chances were that she would run across men who would see her only too well.

What would she do then? She glanced back over her shoulder. The Sisters looked like they were way back across a river of men. What if a man grabbed her and pulled her down, dragged her away? The Sisters finally started following after, but they were a long way back. Kahlan worried about what would happen if men could see her, and grabbed her. What if a whole group of men all could see her? Would the Sisters be able to pull a whole mob off her? Besides, the Sisters were a long way back. Kahlan worried how far a rape would go before the Sisters showed up.

But the Sisters could cast magic. Surely, they would not allow men to ravish her.

She wondered what made her have any such confidence.

Jagang. He wanted her for himself. He was not the kind of man to let underlings have his prize of prizes. He would want to take her himself. The thought of him on top of her ran a shiver of icy dread through her.

The immediate problem, though, was not Jagang, it was these men. In one fluid movement, as she passed a soldier with his back to her, she lifted a knife from the sheath at his hip. She made the motion fit in with the swing of her arms, so that if the Sisters were looking they wouldn't have seen what she had done. The man glanced around, having felt something. Even though he looked directly at her for an instant, his gaze moved on and he went back to his conversation.

The men she had been moving among were all still the outer rings of the many layers around the emperor's compound, but she was now moving out beyond, in among the regular soldiers. They were drinking, laughing, gambling, and telling stories around fires. Horses were picketed among them. Wagons stood about at various places. Some men had already pitched crude tents, while others were content to cook over fires, or sleep.

She saw, too, women being taken into the tents. None went cheerfully. She saw other women emerge only to be snatched up by waiting men and dragged to the next tent. Kahlan remembered Jagang mentioning sending the Sisters out to the tents as punishment. Hearing the women in those tents weeping made Kahlan sweat in dread of her own fate when she finally returned to Jagang's tent. As terrifying a circumstance as being taken into those tents with those men would be, Kahlan could not feel sorry for the Sisters. If they ended up being raped by these men it was not enough punishment to Kahlan's mind. They deserved far worse.

One of the nearby men glanced up at her. Kahlan could see recognition flash in his eyes—eyes that fixed on her. He saw her. His mouth fell open, thrilled with his luck at what sort of woman had just stumbled into his arms, so to speak.

As he rose up, before he was fully erect, Kahlan sliced his belly open from one side to the other as she swiftly continued to move past, as if nothing had happened. The man, his face registering the shock of it, weakly tried to catch his guts as they spilled out in a heavy mass. He toppled over and crashed to the ground while making panicked grunts that weren't noticed as anything more than the other raucous noise all around. When he hit the ground, his insides spilled out. Men turned to look, some shocked, some laughing, all of them thinking the man had just lost a knife fight.

Kahlan didn't slow or look back. She kept moving, without breaking her stride, reminding herself of her task: get to the rock, get back to the tent. Make the circuit. Do as she had been told.

As a man appeared out of the crowd and rushed up to her, she tightened her muscles and used his momentum to drive the knife up under his ribs, ripping his vital organs apart. The lifting cut, like a punch, along with his descending weight, drove her fist through the gash and into his warm insides. By the way he went down like a sack of sand without so much as a word, she was pretty sure that she had managed to cut open his heart. As a memento of the brief encounter, she now wore a glove of his blood.

She wondered where she had learned to do such things. It felt like they came instinctively to her, the way emotions just came naturally, without the need to summon them. She couldn't remember anything about herself, but she remembered how to use a weapon. She supposed that she should just be glad she could.

In making her way out into the sea of men, she came to a dense island of activity. Men had all drawn back to leave an open field in the center of a low area, and teams of men were playing Ja'La there. Soldiers gathered all around in the tens of thousands cheered on one team or the other. The game was a violent affair, with the point man encountering the worst of it from the other team. When he went down, bloodied, half the men surrounding the field cheered wildly.

"Well, well," a man to her left said. "Looks like a fine whore come to pay me a visit."

As she began to turn toward him, another man to the right seized her wrist, twisted, and had her knife. In an instant, both men were on her, grabbing at her, pulling her back away from the crowd gathered to watch the Ja'La game.

Kahlan fought to get free, but they were a lot stronger, and had taken her by surprise. She silently raged at herself for being caught unawares like that. None of the men around noticed anything at all. They couldn't see her; she was invisible to them, but not to these two, who pressed in tight to hide her from their fellow soldiers lest they have to fight for their fresh prize. She might as well have been alone with these two.

One of them shoved his hand between her legs. She gasped at the sudden violation. As he leaned in to grope her, she managed to get her wrist free. In an instant she whipped her arm around and slammed her elbow into the center of his face, breaking his nose. He fell back screaming, blood gushing across his cheeks and eyes. The other man laughed, seeing it as his opportunity to have her for himself. He changed direction, pulling her along, holding both of her wrists together in one of his powerful hands as he used the other to explore the spoils.

Kahlan struggled and twisted, but he was far too big and husky for her. She couldn't get any leverage to break free of his grip.

"You're a feisty one," he said into her ear. "What did you think—that you could avoid your sacred duty to the soldiers of the Order? Think you're too good to serve in the tents? Well, you're not. Here's my tent, so it's time to do your duty."

Kahlan twisted around to try to bite him as he dragged her toward an empty tent not far away. He backhanded her. The blow stunned her. The noise of the encampment seemed to fade away. She couldn't make her muscles do as she wished, couldn't make them resist the grimy soldier as he pulled her toward the tent.

Suddenly, Kahlan saw Sister Ulicia's face. She had never before been glad to see one of the Sisters, but she was now.

The Sister distracted the man's attention from Kahlan for an instant, then pressed her fingers to the side of his forehead. Finally free, Kahlan jumped back as her captor dropped to his knees, clutching his fists to his head as he cried out in pain.

"Get up," Sister Ulicia told him. "Or I'll do worse by far." He stood on wobbly legs. "You are ordered immediately to the emperor's tent to serve as a special guard."

The man looked confused. "Special guard?"

"That's right. You will be guarding this troublesome young lady for His Excellency."

The man gave Kahlan a dangerous look. "It would be my pleasure."

"Pleasure or not, get moving. That's an order from Emperor Jagang himself." She pointed a thumb back over her shoulder. "That way."

The soldier dipped his head in a bow, obviously fearful of her ability with magic. He regarded the Sister with a kind of wary, if unspoken, loathing. These men obviously did not hold those with the gift in high regard.

"I'll be seeing more of you, soon," the man promised Kahlan before he ran off to do as he'd been ordered.

Kahlan saw Sister Armina giving the man with the broken nose the same instructions. She spoke in a voice that Kahlan couldn't hear over the riot of cheering, but the man clearly heard her because he stiffened with fear, bowed to her, and ran off after the first man.

Sister Ulicia turned her attention back to Kahlan. "Tears won't do you any good. Now get going."

Kahlan didn't argue. The sooner it was over, the better. She started out at once, counting herself fortunate to have eliminated two of the four who had so far been able to see her. She had to skirt the Ja'La game that was working the crowd of men to a fever pitch of excitement. She paused at one point to rise up on her tiptoes and make sure where the rock was; then she headed for it.

By the time she had made it back to Jagang's tent, they had collected five men. All of them stood outside the tent, awaiting orders, including the one nursing his broken nose. He glared at her as she walked past him, ushered through the tent's opening by the two Sisters.

Kahlan had managed to quickly arm herself after Sister Ulicia had rescued her the first time. This time, though, Kahlan had seen to it that she secured two knives, one for each hand. She held the hilts in her fists, with the blades lying up against the insides of her wrists so that the Sisters, following her at a good distance, hadn't been able to see them.

Kahlan had managed to kill another six men who could see her, without the Sisters realizing what she had done. It hadn't been hard; they saw no threat coming from a naked woman. They were dead wrong. With their guard down she had been able to thrust her weapons home quickly and without a fuss. There was so much noise, confusion, drinking, yelling, and fighting in the camp that the Sisters never noticed the men Kahlan had taken out.

When she hadn't been able to dispatch the men who could see her, either because Sister Ulicia or Armina were too close or because they were watching closely and rushed in to rescue her and give the soldiers their new assignments as special guards, Kahlan always let her knives slip to the ground and vanish under the throng of soldiers so that the Sisters wouldn't suspect what she had been up to. Being invisible to almost all the men, it had been easy enough to get more knives throughout the long, nerve-racking walk among the soldiers.

Once she was inside the tent, Jagang threw Kahlan's clothes at her. "Get dressed."

Rather than questioning his reasons for a command she hadn't expected, she wasted no time in complying with his orders. Under the unwavering dark gaze of the man, it was a huge relief to finally have her clothes back on. It didn't seem to lessen his obvious interest in what he had seen, though.

His attention finally turned to the two Sisters. "I've instructed our new guards in their duties." He smiled in a way that made both Sisters swallow in dread. "What with some guards to take the load off your backs, you will have some free time to spend in the tents, being on your backs for a different duty."

"But Excellency . . ." Sister Armina said in a trembling voice, "we have done everything you requested. We got the men—"

"You think that because you do as you're told for a short time I will forget the years you have been running around plotting and scheming to do me in? You think I will so easily forget your neglect of your duty to others, your obligations to the cause of the Order, your moral responsibility to sacrifice your worldly wishes to the good of others?"

"It wasn't that way, Excellency." Sister Armina dry-washed her hands as she searched for words that might save her. "Yes, we were shamefully selfish, I admit, but we had no direct thought to harm you."

He snorted a laugh. "You don't think freeing the Keeper of the underworld would harm me? You don't think turning mankind over to the

Keeper of the dead would be against me, against the ways of the Order, against the Creator?"

Sister Armina fell silent. She knew she had no argument. Kahlan had always thought of the Sisters as vipers. But now they were writhing before someone with hide too tough to sink their fangs into.

Sister Ulicia and Armina were attractive women. Kahlan had the feeling that their looks were only going to make it worse for them out among the animals that were the Imperial Order army.

"I have control of the . . ." Jagang caught himself almost using her title. ". . . of Kahlan, through the collar, through your ability. You don't need to be present for me to call upon that power if necessary—just alive. I will instruct the men that I don't want you two murdered while they are enjoying your feminine charms."

"Thank you, Excellency," Sister Ulicia managed in a small voice. She was gripping her skirts in white-knuckled fists.

"Now, there are two men waiting outside who have been instructed in what they are to do with you both. Go with them." He grinned at them like death itself. "Have a good night, ladies. You deserve it—and many more."

As they left the tent, Kahlan stood in the center, awaiting a similar fate.

Jagang stepped closer to her. Kahlan thought she might either faint from dread, or be sick at the thought of what was about to happen to her.

Kahlan stared at the pattern in the carpet on the ground at her feet. She didn't want to look defiantly into Jagang's black eyes. A show of bravery at the moment, she knew, would serve little purpose.

When she had been made to walk while the Sisters rode, she had always told herself that it would make her stronger for a time when she would need strength. In much the same way, she wouldn't now use her resolve for a useless show of defiance. Railing against her captor and what he was about to do to her when she knew that she could do nothing to stop it would only be squandering her strength.

She wanted to save her hot rage until the time was right.

And that time would come. She promised herself that such a time would come. Even if it was when she threw herself into the teeth of death itself, she would unleash her smoldering anger at those who did this to her and all the other innocent victims of the Imperial Order.

She saw Jagang's boots appear right in front of her. She held her breath, expecting him to seize her. She didn't know what she would do when it actually happened, how she would be able to endure what she knew he was going to do. Her gaze lifted just a little, just enough to see where his knife was on his belt. He rested the heel of his hand on the knife handle.

"We're going out," he said.

Kahlan looked up with a frown. "Out? For what purpose?"

"Tonight is a night of Ja'La dh Jin tournaments. Different units of our soldiers have teams. There are nights devoted to the tournaments. It lifts the hearts of our forces to have their emperor there to witness how they play the game.

"Men are also gathered from all over the conquered parts of the New World and given the chance to join in challenging other teams. It is a great opportunity for them to begin to fit into the new culture we bring to defeated lands, to become part of the fabric of the Order, to participate in our ways.

"The best players can sometimes become heroes. Women fight over such men. The men of my team are all such men—heroes who never lose. Crowds of women wait for these men after the games, eager to open their legs for them. Ja'La players have their pick of any woman."

Kahlan noted that while, as emperor, Jagang probably had the pick of many women who would want to be close to such a man of authority and power, he would rather force himself on her. He would rather take what was not offered, have what he had not won as a result of merit.

"Tonight some of those teams play for ranking. They all hope that one day they might have the chance to play my team in a grand contest for top honors. My team plays the best of the best once or twice a month. They never lose. There is always a burning hope among each new group of challengers that they will be the ones to defeat the best—the emperor's team—and be crowned champions of the games. There would be many rewards for such a team, not the least of which would be the most beautiful of the women who now are eager only to be with the men of my team."

He seemed to enjoy telling her about the habits of such women, as if he were generalizing about all women and in so doing telling her that he thought she was at heart the same. She would rather open a vein. She ignored the innuendo and asked him something else instead.

"If your team is not playing, why do you wish to watch? Surely a man such as you would not bestow your precious presence on the faithful on such a regular basis just to be generous."

He peered at her with a puzzled look, as if it were a strange question. "To see their strategy, of course, to learn the strengths, the weaknesses, of those who will become the opponents of my team."

His sly smile returned. "That is what you do—size up those who might be your opponents—and don't try to tell me that you don't. I see your gaze go to weapons, to the layout of rooms, to the position of men, cover, and escape routes. You are always searching for an opportunity, always watching, always thinking of how to defeat those who stand in your way.

"Ja'La dh Jin is much the same way. It is a game of strategy."

"I've seen it played. I'd say that the strategy is secondary, that it's primarily a game of brutality."

"Well, if you don't enjoy the strategy," he said with a smirk, "then you will no doubt enjoy watching men sweat, strain, and struggle against one another. That's why most women like to watch Ja'La. Men enjoy it for the strategy, the give and take of the contest, the chance to cheer their team to victory, and to imagine being such men themselves; the women like to watch half-naked bodies and sweat-slicked muscles. They like to watch the strongest men prevail, dream of being the desire of conquering heroes, and then scheme of ways to make themselves available to such men."

"Both sound pointless to me. Either brutality, or meaningless rutting."

He shrugged. "In my tongue, Ja'La dh Jin means 'the game of life.' Is not life a struggle—a brutal contest? A contest of men, and of sexes? Life, like Ja'La, is a brutal struggle."

Kahlan knew that life could be brutal, but that such brutality did not define life or its purpose, and that the sexes were not rivals, but meant to share together in the work and joys of life.

"To those like you it is," she said. "That's one difference between you and me. I use violence only as a last resort, only when it's necessary to defend my life—my right to exist. You use brutality as a tool of fulfilling your desires, even your ordinary desires, because, except by force, you have nothing worthwhile to offer to exchange for what you want or need—and that includes women. You take, you do not earn.

"I'm better than that. You don't value life or anything in it. I do. That's why you must crush anything good—because it puts the lie to your nothing of a life, shows by contrast how you do nothing but waste your existence.

"That's why you and those like you hate those like me—because I'm better than you and you know it."

"Such a belief is the mark of a sinner. To consider your own life meaningful is a crime against the Creator as well as your fellow man."

When she only glared at him, he arched an eyebrow with an admonishing look as he leaned a little closer. He held up a thick finger—adorned with a plundered gold ring—before her face to mark an important point, as if lecturing a selfish, headstrong child who was within an inch of getting a well-deserved thrashing.

"The Fellowship of Order teaches us that to be better than someone is to be worse than everyone."

Kahlan could only stare at such a vulgar ideology. That pious statement of hollow conviction gave her a sudden, true insight into the abyss of his savage nature, and the vindictive character of the Order itself. It was a concept that had abandoned the distant foundation upon which it had been built—that all life equally had the right to exist for its own sake—in order to justify taking life for the Order's own contrived notion of the common good.

Within that simple-sounding framework of an irrational tenet, he had just unwittingly revealed everything.

It explained the depravity of his whole cause and the determinant emotions driving the nature of those monstrous men massed outside, ready to kill anyone who would not submit to their creed. It was a dogma that shrank from civilization, praised savagery as a way of existence, and required constant brutality to crush any noble idea and the man who had it. It was a movement that drew to it thieves who wanted to think themselves righteous, murderers who wanted holy absolution for the blood of innocent victims that drenched their souls.

It assigned any achievement not to the one who had created it, but instead to those who had not earned it and did not deserve it, precisely because they did not earn it and did not deserve it. It valued thievery, not accomplishment.

It was anathema to individuality.

At the same time, it was a frighteningly sad admission of a rotting core of weakness in the face of life, an inability to exist on any level except that of a primitive beast, always cowering in fear that someone else would be better. It was not simply a rejection of all that was good, a resentment of accomplishment—it was, in fact, far worse. It was an expression of a gnawing hatred for anything good, grown out of an inner unwillingness to strive for anything worthwhile.

Like all irrational beliefs, it was also unworkable. To live, those beliefs had to be ignored to accomplish goals of domination, which in themselves were a violation of the belief for which they were fighting. There were no equals among those of the Order, the torchbearers of enforced equality. Whether a Ja'La player, the most professional of the soldiers, or an emperor, the best were not simply needed but sought after and highly valued, and so as a body they harbored an inner hatred of their failure to live up to their own teachings and a fear that they would be unmasked for it. As punishment for their inability to fulfill their sanctified beliefs through adherence to those teachings, they instead turned to the self-flagellation of proclaiming how unworthy all men were and vented their self-hatred on scapegoats: they blamed the victims.

In the end, the belief was nothing more than fabricated divinity—unthinking nonsense repeated in a mantra in an attempt to give it credibility, to make it sound sacred.

"I've already seen the Ja'La games," Kahlan said. She turned away from him. "I have no desire to see more of it."

He seized her upper arm, pulling her back around to face him. "I know you're eager to have me bed you, but you can wait. Right now we are going to watch the Ja'La games."

A lecherous smile oozed onto his face, like greasy muck bubbling up from his festering soul. "If you don't enjoy watching the games for their strategy and competition, then you can let your eyes roam over the naked flesh of the rivals. I'm sure that such sights will make you eager for what comes later tonight. Try not to be too impatient."

Kahlan suddenly felt foolish for protesting any reason to avoid his bed. But the Ja'La game was out among the men, and she had no desire to go out there again. She also had no choice. She hated being among those vile men. She reminded herself to get a grip on her feelings. The soldiers couldn't see her. She was being silly.

He pulled her toward the passageway out of the tent. She went without resisting. This was not a time to resist.

Outside, the five special guards waited. They all noticed that Kahlan was dressed, but none of them spoke. They stood tall, straight, and attentive, looking ready to jump if told to do so. They were obviously on their best behavior before their emperor, wanting to impress him.

Kahlan guessed that to be better than someone was all right if you were the emperor, and that it wouldn't make him worse than everyone. He fought for a doctrine from which he exempted himself, as did each and every one of his men. Kahlan knew better than to point it out.

"These are your new guards," Jagang told her. "We'll not have a repeat of the last incident, since these men can see you."

The men all looked pretty content with themselves, and the apparently harmless nature of the woman they were to guard.

Kahlan took a quick but good look at the first man the Sisters had brought to task, the partner of the one with the broken nose. With a glance she evaluated the weapons he carried, a knife, and a crudely made sword with two halves of a wooden hilt wired onto the tang, and how graceless he appeared in the way he wore them. In that glance she knew that they were implements he no doubt used with bravado when slaughtering innocent women and children. She doubted that he had ever used them in combat with other men. He was a thug, nothing more. Intimidation was his weapon of choice.

By his self-satisfied smile, he looked unimpressed with her. After all, he had already, by himself, nearly brought her to task, and to his tent. In his mind he had been only a few steps away from having her under him.

"You," she said, pointing right between his eyes. "You I will kill first."

The men all snickered. She swept an appraising gaze over them and their weapons, learning what there was to learn.

She pointed at the man with the broken nose. "You die second, after him."

"What about us three?" one of the others asked, unable to suppress a chuckle. "What order will you kill us in?"

Kahlan shrugged. "You will know just before I cut your throat."

The men all laughed. Jagang didn't.

"You would be well advised to take her seriously," the emperor told them. "The last time she got her hands on a knife she killed my two most trusted bodyguards—men a lot better at soldiering than you—and a Sister of the Dark. All by herself, and all in a matter of a few brief moments."

The laughter died away.

"You all will stay on your toes," Jagang said in a low growl, "or I will gut you myself if I even think you are being inattentive to your duty. If she gets away under your watch, I will send you to the torture tents and command that your death take a month and a day, that your flesh rot and die before you do."

There was no longer any doubt in the men's minds as to the seriousness of Jagang's orders, or the value of his prize.

A vast escort of hundreds, if not thousands, of the inner and most expert of the emperor's guards formed up around their leader as he strode purposefully away from his tent. The five special guards surrounded Kahlan on every side except the side Jagang was on. They all moved out into the camp in a wedge of armor and drawn weapons. Kahlan supposed that, as a leader, Jagang was just taking normal precautions against spies, but she thought that it was more than that.

He was better than everyone else.

By the time they returned to the emperor's compound and his large tent after the Ja'La contests, Kahlan's level of worry had risen. It wasn't just the obvious dread of being alone with such an unpredictable and dangerous man—or even her near panic over what she knew he intended to do to her.

It was all of that, with a sinister undercurrent to his cruelty churning just beneath the surface. There was a flush to his face, a more assertive nature to his movements, an edgy quality to his short comments, a fierce intensity in his inky eyes. Watching the games had put Jagang in an even more violent mood than what she believed was his norm. The games had worked him up. They had excited him—in every way.

Back at the games he'd felt that one of the teams had not played to their full potential, had not given it everything they had. He'd thought they were holding back and not putting their all into the contest.

When they lost, he had them executed on the field.

The crowd had cheered more at that than at the rather tedious play of the game itself. Jagang was hailed for putting the losers to death. The games that followed were played with considerably more passion, and on ground soggy from the blood of the beheadings. Ja'La was a game in which men ran, dodged, and darted past one another, or blocked, or chased the man with the heavy ball—the broc—trying to capture it, or attack with it, or score with it. Men often fell or were knocked from their feet. When they did they rolled across the ground. In the summer heat, without shirts, they were soon slick not just with sweat but with blood. From what Kahlan could see of the female camp followers watching from the sidelines, they weren't in the least put off by the blood. If anything, it made them only more eager to catch the attention of the players who were now whipping the crowd into a frenzy with their fast-paced, aggressive tactics.

In all the rest of the games after the one resulting in executions, as in the ones previous, the losing teams, since they had at least played with wild determination, were not put to death but flogged. A terrible whip, made up of a number of knotted cords bound together, was used for the penalty. Each of those cords was tipped with heavy nuggets of metal. The men were given one lash for each point by which they lost. Most losing teams lost by several points, but even one lash from that whip ripped open the naked flesh of a man's back.

The crowd enthusiastically counted out each lash to each man on the losing team kneeling in the center of the field. The winners often cavorted around the perimeter of the field, showing off for the crowd, while the losers, with bowed heads, received their whipping.

It had made Kahlan sick to witness such a thing. It had excited Jagang.

Kahlan was relieved that the games were at last over, but now that she was back inside the emperor's compound and about to enter his tent, a gnawing sense of dread was eating away at her insides. Jagang was in a temper provoked by violence and aroused by blood. Kahlan could see in his eyes that he was in no mood to be denied anything.

And the only thing left for him that night was her.

As the special guards were just about to be posted outside the tent, she spotted a man running into the compound, being followed by a small group of men. Jagang paused in his instructions to Kahlan's special guards as the rings of defenders parted to let the man and a gaggle of officers through. When the man came to a breathless halt, he announced himself as a messenger.

"What is it, then?" Jagang asked the messenger, scrutinizing the half-dozen men of rank with him. Jagang was not at all pleased to be bothered when he had his mind set on other things.

Kahlan knew that she was the focus of his brooding thoughts, and that he wanted to get her inside, and alone. The time had come and he was impatient to get at her.

He had so far not touched her in any improper manner. He was saving it all up. In much the same way that any city in the path of his army had to wait in agonizing dread for the impending assault, she, too, felt the stranglehold of overpowering fear as she waited for what she knew was coming. She tried not to imagine what he was going to do to her and what it would be like, but she could not think of anything else, any more than she could slow her galloping heart.

The messenger handed over a leather tube. It made a hollow thunk when Jagang popped the lid off. With two fingers he extracted a rolled piece of paper. He broke the wax seal, unrolled it, and held it up to read it in the light of the torches flanking the entrance to his tent. The rings he wore on each finger sparkled in the flickering torchlight.

At first frowning, the emperor began to smile as he read. He finally laughed aloud as he looked up at his officers. "The army of the D'Haran Empire has fled the field of battle. Scouts and Sisters alike have all reported the same thing, that the D'Harans were so terrified of the prospect of facing Jagang the Just and the army of the Order that they all deserted and have scattered in every direction, proving what faithless cowards they really are.

"The forces of the D'Haran Empire are no more. There is nothing standing between us and the People's Palace."

The officers cheered their emperor. Everyone was suddenly in a jovial mood. Jagang bestowed his congratulations on the officers for being a part of putting the enemy on the run.

As she listened, standing off to the side while the others all watched Jagang waving the paper and speaking of the end of the long war being at hand, Kahlan slowly, carefully, lifted a leg until her fingers found the hilt of the knife tucked into her right boot.

Making as little movement as possible so as not to draw the attention of the five men who could see her, or Jagang himself, she worked the weapon up out of the boot and into her fist. As soon as it was securely in hand, she retrieved the second knife from the other boot.

She tightly grasped the leather-wrapped handle of each well-made weapon, working her fingers to get a secure grip on the hilts. Having weapons in hand filled her with a sense of purpose, banishing her helpless dread at what was in store for her that night. She now had a way to strike at them. She knew that she might not be able to stop Jagang from what he would do to her, but it would not be without a fight. This was her chance to extract a price.

She didn't move her head, only her eyes, as she took stock of where each man was standing. Jagang, unfortunately, was not close to her. He had stepped to the messenger, and then closer to his officers. Kahlan knew that he was far from stupid. If she were to walk up to his side he would instantly be suspicious. He would know that she would not do such a thing willingly. She also knew that he was an experienced fighter. He would react before she could lunge at him. Having him closer probably wouldn't have done her much good anyway.

There were better targets, a better chance for surprise. The five special guards were close to her left, the officers a little farther away to her right. The officers couldn't see her. Beyond was a camp of men who couldn't see her. But even though the officers couldn't see her, the five could and as soon as she moved she would have only an instant before they reacted.

She knew that she could draw a lot of blood, but there was little chance she would escape.

The alternative was to submit meekly to her impending rape.

Kahlan summoned her rage. She gripped the hilts of the knives tighter. This was a chance to strike back against her captors.

With a straight-in, direct, and mighty thrust she slammed the long knife in her left hand into the center of the chest of the special guard she had promised to kill first. Some dim part of her mind noted his stiff surprise.

Just beyond him, the eyes of the man with the broken nose went wide as he, too, stiffened with shocked surprise. Kahlan used the knife planted in the chest of the first man as an anchor, for leverage. With that grip to help her, she spun around the man already stabbed. At the same time, she brought the knife in her right hand around with her, in an arc. The blade slashed open the throat of the man with the broken nose. In two beats of her hammering heart she had killed them both.

Kahlan drove her left boot into the first man as he fell, in order to pull free the embedded knife and to spring herself in the opposite direction—toward the officers. On the third beat of her heart she hit the first officer like a Ja'La tackle. As she flew into him, she plunged the knife in her right hand deep into his belly, jerking up as she did so to rip him open.

At the same time she stabbed the other knife square into the throat of the man immediately to the side and a little behind the first officer. He had been the ranking officer and the one she was really targeting. She hit him with such force that the blade not only drove through the man's throat but, hitting the space between the vertebrae, pierced all the way through his neck. His spinal cord cut, his entire dead weight dropped straight down so fast that Kahlan's grip on the knife twisted her off balance and pulled her with him.

At the same time, before she could catch herself or yank the knife back, the power from the collar hit Kahlan like a lightning bolt.

At the same time, the other three special guards tackled her, taking her the rest of the way off her feet and ramming her face-first into the soft ground. With the collar making her arms numb and useless, and her legs unable to respond to her wishes, the men had no trouble disarming her.

When Jagang shrieked the order, they hauled her to her feet. Kahlan panted from the effort of the brief battle. Her heart still raced. Even if she had failed to escape, she wasn't entirely disappointed. She hadn't really thought that her chances of making it were that good to begin with. She had expected, though, to at least kill a couple of officers, and she had accomplished that. She was disappointed only that the special guards had not killed her rather than capture her.

Jagang dismissed the confused officers, explaining that it was a bit of magic that had gotten loose. He assured them that he had everything well in hand. They were men used to violence and seemed to take the sudden death of two fellow officers by an invisible hand, if not in stride, at least with a level of self-control, reassured by the demeanor of their emperor.

As they made their way out of the emperor's compound, they collected a number of men who rushed in to remove the bodies. The guards who came to see what the commotion was all about were dismayed to see such a murder within their layers of defenses. They all glanced to Jagang to gauge his mood and, seeing him calm, swiftly went about the business of carrying off the four dead men.

Once they had departed, Jagang finally turned a glare on Kahlan. "I see that you were closely watching the games. You appear to have been paying more attention to the strategy than the bare flesh of muscular men."

Kahlan met the gazes of the three special guards holding her. "Just keeping a promise."

Jagang slowly let out a deep breath, as if trying to keep from murder himself. "You are quite a remarkable woman—and a formidable opponent."

"I'm the bringer of death," she told him.

He glanced at the four bodies being carried out into the night. "So you are."

He turned his intense attention to the three men holding Kahlan. "Is there a reason that I should not send you three off to be tortured?"

The men, who had been smug about having taken her down, suddenly didn't seem so smug. They glanced nervously at one another.

"But Excellency," one of them said, "The two men who failed you paid with their lives. The three of us stopped her. We didn't let her escape."

"I am the one who stopped her," he said through barely restrained rage. "I stopped her with the collar she wears around her neck." He considered them silently for a moment, letting his flash of rage calm down a little. "But I am called Jagang the Just for good reason. I will allow you three to live for the time being, but let this be a lesson to you. I warned you that she was dangerous. Now, perhaps, you can see that I know what I'm talking about."

"Yes, Excellency," the three said over one another.

Jagang clasped his hands behind his back. "Release her."

He passed a withering glare over each man before taking Kahlan's arm and leading her back toward the opening of the tent. She was still reeling from the shock of the collar. Her joints ached, her legs and arms burned from inside.

She had wondered if Jagang had been telling the truth that he could use the collar without the Sisters needing to be present. Now she knew. Without that collar she might have stood a good chance of breaking free; with it, she didn't. She dared not take Jagang's ability lightly from now on. At least now she knew. Sometimes, it was worse to wonder if something would have been possible.

"I want you three to guard outside my tent tonight. If she comes out without me, you had better stop her."

The three soldiers bowed. "Yes, Excellency."

They no longer looked at all smug. They looked like what they were— men who had just escaped a death sentence.

As the men took up their posts, Jagang turned a grim look on Kahlan. "The last time you only went for a walk among the men. It was a short walk. You saw only a small sampling of my army. Tomorrow, you are going to have a much better chance to see a great many more of my men. And a lot more of those men are bound to see you.

"I don't know what the anomaly is that Ulicia spoke of, or its cause, but it doesn't really matter to me. What matters is that, like in all things, I intend to use it to my advantage. I intend to see to it that you are well guarded. You will ride again tomorrow and we will take a tour through the troops, but you are going to do it without your clothes. In that way, you will help find us a goodly supply of new special guards. It should be quite an exciting day."

Kahlan didn't offer an argument—none would have done any good. She could tell by the careful way in which he explained it that he meant for it to make her uncomfortable. She suspected that her humiliation was only just beginning.

Emperor Jagang ushered her in through the opening of his tent as if she were royalty. He was mocking her, she knew. As she moved inside she could feel the power of the collar release its grip on her. She could at last move her feet and arms on her own. The pain, thankfully, began to fade as well.

Inside the tent it was nearly dark, lit only by candles. They gave the tent a warm glow, making it feel cozy and safe, almost like a sacred place. It was anything but.

She felt as if she were being led to her execution.

The slaves who had prepared a late-night sampling of light foods for the emperor were all dismissed. At seeing the look in his eyes, and after having heard the screams of dying men, everyone was only too happy to leave when he growled at them to get out.

He watched as they all rushed out and then, with a thick finger pressed into the center of her back, Jagang silently steered Kahlan past the table with mugs of wine, platters of meats, loaves of dark bread, bowls of nuts, and arrangements of fruits and sweets, escorting her beyond another tapestry hanging before an opening into an inner bedroom within the tent.

The bedroom was isolated from the rest of the tent and from the outside by what looked to be padded panels, probably to make it quieter. The walls were also covered with hides and fabric hangings of material woven into muted patterns. The room was warmly decorated with exquisite carpets, a few small pieces of fine furniture, glass-fronted bookcases filled with books, and ornate silver and gold lamps. The bed, covered in furs and satin, had spiraled, dark wooden posts at each corner.

Kahlan hid her trembling fingers behind her back as she watched Jagang cross the room and remove his lamb's-wool vest. He tossed it over a chair at a small writing desk. His naked chest and back were covered in dark, curly hair. He looked like a bear of a man in more ways than one. He looked like anything but a man who would have satin bed coverings. She suspected that he didn't really appreciate such things, but wanted them as a mark of his station. She guessed that he must have forgotten that no one was supposed to be better than anyone else in the Order. She guessed that he never considered whether or not the men out in the grimy tents had satin blankets to sleep under.

Jagang looked up at her. "Well, woman, take off your clothes. Or would you rather I tear them off you. Your choice."

"Whether I take them off, or you rip them off, it is still rape."

He straightened and peered at her for a time in the silence within the tent. The camp outside had quieted down considerably, leaving only the muted sounds of distant words to melt together into a dull hum. The men were tired from the day's long march, as well as the excitement of the Ja'La games, and Jagang had decreed that each day's march would be equally swift until they reached the People's Palace, so most of the men were no doubt in their tents sleeping.

The only one not quieted down for the night was Jagang. If he was in an excited state after the games, then after her killing the four men he was on the edge of a rampage. Kahlan didn't really care. If he beat her senseless, then she wouldn't have to be conscious for what else he was going to do to her.

"You are mine, now," he said in a low, dangerous tone. "You belong to me—to no one else. To me alone. I can do whatever I wish with you. If I choose to cut your throat, then it is your duty to bleed to death for me. If I give you to those three men who can see you, then you will submit to them, whether you like it or not, whether you do so willingly or not.

"You belong to me, now. Your fate is what I choose for you. You have no choice in what happens to you. None. Everything that happens to you is by my choice alone."

"It's still rape."

He crossed the room in three angry strides and backhanded her, knocking her sprawling. He pulled her up by the hair and heaved her at the bed. The world spun as Kahlan tumbled through the air. She only missed the wooden post by inches.

"Of course it's rape! That's what I want it to be! That's what you have coming!"

He charged to the bed like an enraged bull. His black eyes were filled with wild storms of shapes. Before she knew it, he was above her. Kahlan had it all planned out. She wasn't going to try to stop him, to give him the satisfaction of having to use force to have her. But with him right there, on top of her, straddling her hips, those thoughts were lost in the sudden panic of events that she desperately didn't want to happen. She forgot all her plans and desperately tried to push his hands away, but in such a mood there was no stopping him. She had no strength to begin to match him. He didn't even bother to slap her to make her stop resisting. With one yank, he ripped her shirt open.

Kahlan went still as he stopped, her chest heaving from the effort. He stared down at her breasts.

She used the sudden quiet to school herself. She had just killed four brutes. She could do this. This was nothing compared with having a collar around her neck, having her memory stripped away from her, losing her identity, losing who she was, becoming the helpless slave to Sisters of the Dark and an emperor of a mob of thugs.

This was nothing. She was better than to fight him in such a foolish manner, like a schoolgirl trying to slap away the hands of a bully. She didn't fight like that. She wouldn't. She knew better. Yes, she was terrified, but she didn't have to surrender to panic. She was afraid when she'd killed those four men, but she had controlled her fear and acted.

She was better than he was. He was only stronger. He could only have her by force. That knowledge gave her a thread of power over him, and he knew it. He could never have her willingly because she was better than he was, and she deserved better by far. He could never have a woman like her except by force because he was weak and worthless as a man.

"Is your prize of prizes satisfactory, Excellency?" she mocked.

"Oh, yes." Jagang's wicked smile widened. "Now take off those traveling pants."

When she made no move to comply, he did it for her, opening the buttons one at time as if opening something valuable. She lay with her hands at her sides. He hooked his fingers over the waist of her pants, drew them down her legs, and pulled them inside out getting them off over her feet. He threw them aside as he paused to take in the length of her nearly bare body.

Kahlan silently bit the inside of her cheek to keep from pushing his hand away in a panic as he glided his hand up her leg, feeling the softness of her thigh. Kahlan fought back her tears. She would have given anything not to be there, to be anywhere else but at the mercy of this monster.

"Now, the rest of it," he said in a thick whisper. "Take off those underthings."

She could tell that pulling her clothes off had only excited him even more, so she did as he told her to do, trying to make it look anything but seductive as she did so.

As he watched her following his orders, he sat on the edge of the bed and pulled off his boots. He dropped his pants and kicked them off. As sickened as she was terrified by the sight of him naked, Kahlan gave in to weakness and turned her eyes away from him.

She wondered how she would ever be able to fall in love and let a man touch her after this. She reproached herself. She was never going to have the chance to fall in love. She was fretting over a problem she would never have.

The bed moved under his weight as he climbed up beside her and lay down. He paused to stare at her, to run his hand over her belly. She'd expected it to be a rough touch, a harsh grabbing of her, but instead it was a furtive touch, a slow, measured evaluation of something quite valuable. She didn't expect his gentle approach to last much longer.

"You really are quite extraordinary," he said in a husky voice, almost more to himself than to her. "Perceiving you through the eyes of others just wasn't the same—I can see that now."

His tone had changed. The anger had melted away under the heat of his desire for her. He was on the brink of surrendering to uninhibited lust.

"It's not at all the same. . . . I always knew you were exceptional, but now that I see you, like this . . . you are a remarkable creature. Just . . . remarkable."

Kahlan wondered what he meant when he'd said that he had perceived her through the eyes of others. She wondered if he meant that he had watched her through the eyes of the Sisters. She was struck by an unexpected thought that rattled her: it was the thought of him having watched her undressing when she had thought that only a Sister was there. It filled her with an icy rage at such a violation.

He had been there, then, watching her, planning this. But at the same time she got the feeling that he was talking about something else, too. There was more to his words, more meaning in them, something hidden. Something in the way he'd said it made her think that he was talking about something in her life before the Sisters, back before she had lost who she was. She was angry thinking about him watching her through the Sisters, but thinking about him seeing her before, in her life that she couldn't remember, rattled her.

He abruptly rolled over onto her. "You can't imagine how long I've waited to do this to you."

Her breathing, and her heartbeat, had only just started to settle down. Now, it was happening too fast. Her heart was again thumping against her ribs. She wanted to slow him down, to give herself time to think of a way to prevent him from doing this to her. At the feel of his flesh against hers, though, her mind went blank. She couldn't think of any way to stop him. She could only fixate on how badly she didn't want him to do this.

She reminded herself of the promises she had made to herself. She was better than him; she should act like it.

She said nothing. She stared past him up at the roof of the tent illuminated softly in the lamplight.

"You can't imagine how much I've wanted to do this to you," he said in a suddenly menacing voice. "You can't imagine how much you have this coming to you."

She shifted her gaze to meet his nightmare eyes. "No, I can't. So just get on with it and spare me a speech that means nothing to me, since I have no idea what you're talking about."

She turned her eyes away to stare off once more. She wanted to show him only indifference. She freed her mind to wander. It wasn't easy with him pressing against her, about to have his way with her, but she did her best to ignore him, to think about other things. She didn't want to give him the satisfaction of a struggle she would only lose. She thought about the Ja'La game, not because it was something she wished to think about, but because it was fresh enough in her mind to be easy to recall in detail.

He abruptly hooked his arms behind her knees and pulled her legs up almost to her chest. It was hard to breathe. It hurt her hip joints to be bent like that, with her legs spread that way, but she swallowed back the scream and tried to ignore the way he was trying to control her, to dominate her as he took her.

"If he knew . . . this would kill him."

Kahlan's eyes turned to him. She could only pull in half a breath against the weight of him. "Who are you talking about?"

She thought that maybe it was her father—a father she didn't remember. Perhaps she had a father who was a commander in the army, and that was why she seemed to know how to fight with a knife. She couldn't imagine who else he could be talking about.

She wanted to say something to deflate him, but she thought better of it and remained silent, indifferent.

Jagang's mouth was on her ear. His rough stubble scraped painfully against her cheek and neck. His breathing was fast and ragged. He was lost to the lust he was about to unleash on her.

"If only you knew . . . this would kill you," he said, obviously and profoundly pleased with the thought.

Even more puzzled, she remained silent, her worry building about what he could possibly mean.

She thought he was about to resume his obviously lecherous need, but he rested there, holding her legs open, staring down at her. The length of his hairy body pressed against her, on the brink of his intent. With his weight on her, she could hardly get a breath, but she knew that any protest would only be met with disinterest in what discomfort he might be causing her.

In a way, she wished he would just hurry up and get it over with. The waiting was making her crazy. She wanted to scream, but she refused to allow herself to. She couldn't help dreading how much he would hurt her, how long it might last—how it would undoubtedly be repeated not just this night but in the nights to come. Had not his bull-weight been pressing her down into the bed she would have been trembling in terrible anticipation.

"No," he said to himself. "No, this is not what I want."

Kahlan was bewildered. She wasn't sure she had heard what she thought she'd heard.

He let go of her legs, letting them slip down onto the bed as he pushed himself up on his hands. She wished he weren't lying between her legs so that she could draw them together.

"No," he repeated. "Not like this. You don't want this, but it would only be onerous. You would not like it, but nothing more.

"I want you to know who you are when I do this. I want you to know what I mean to you when I do this. I want you to hate this more than you have ever hated anything in your entire life. I want to be the one to do this to you both. I want to plant the memory of what it means to you in your mind when I plant my seed in you. I want that memory to haunt you for however long you might live, to haunt him forever, every time he looks at you. I want him to learn to hate you for it, to hate what you have come to represent to him. To hate your child, the child that I will give you.

"To do that, you have to know who you are, first. If I do this to you now, it will only dull you to it, spoil the exquisite suffering it would cause you if you knew who you were when it happens to you."

"So then tell me," she said, almost willing to endure rape to know.

A slow, sly smile came to him. "Telling you is no good. Words would be hollow, without meaning, without emotion. You have to know. You have to remember who you are, you have to know everything, if this is to truly be rape . . . and I intend it to be the worst rape you can suffer, a rape that will give you a child that he will see as a reminder, as a monster."

Staring down at her, he slowly shook his head with the self-satisfaction of the dimension of his intent. "To be that, you have to be fully aware of who you are, and everything this will mean to you, everything it will touch, everything it will harm, everything it will taint for all time."

He abruptly rolled off her to the side. Kahlan drew in a breath that was almost a gasp.

He gritted his teeth, and his big hand seized her right breast. "Don't think you've escaped anything, darlin. You'll not be going anywhere. I'm only seeing to it that it's a lot worse for you than this would have been, tonight." He chuckled as he squeezed her breast. "Worse for him as well."

Kahlan could not imagine how anything could make it worse than it would have been. She could only imagine that to him, rape cast guilt on the victim. That was the way he thought, the way the Order thought, that the victim was to blame.

He abruptly shoved her out of the bed. She landed painfully on the floor, but at least her fall was broken by somewhat soft carpets.

He looked down at her. "You will sleep on the floor, right there, beside the bed. Later, I will have you in my bed." He grinned. "When your memory returns, when this will destroy you. Then I will give you what you deserve, what only I can give you, what only I can do to ruin your life . . . and his."

Kahlan lay on the floor, fearing to move, fearing that he might change his mind. She felt heady relief that this night she would not have to endure it.

He leaned over the edge of the bed, closer to her, peering down at her with his disturbing black eyes. He shoved his big hand between her legs so unexpectedly that she cried out.

He grinned at her. "And if you get the idea of trying to think of a way to sneak away, or worse, to do me in while I sleep, you had better forget it right now. It won't work. All it will get you is time in the tents, later on, after I've ruined everything for you. I'll see to it that all those men will have you, right there where my fingers are. Do you understand?"

Kahlan nodded, feeling a tear run down her cheek.

"If you move off those carpets beside the bed tonight, then the power of that collar will stop you. Do you wish to test it?"

Kahlan shook her head, fearing her voice might fail her.

He withdrew his hand. "Good."

She heard him turn over on his side, facing away from her. Kahlan lay perfectly still. She could hardly breathe. She wasn't sure what had happened this night, or what it could all mean. She only knew that she felt more lonely than she had ever felt in her life—at least, the part of her life that she could remember.

In a strange way she almost wished he had raped her. If he had, she would not now be trembling in fear of what he'd said, wondering what he'd meant. Now she would have to wake each morning not knowing if that was the day she recovered her memory. When she did, it was somehow going to make that rape all the worse, make everything worse, far worse.

Kahlan believed him. As eager as he had been to have her, and she knew very well how eager he had been, he would not have stopped at that point unless everything he'd said was true.

Kahlan realized that she no longer wanted to know who she was. Her past had just become too dangerous to her for her to want to ever know who she was. If she knew, he would do the worst to her. Better that she remain in oblivion, and safe from that.

When she heard his even breathing, and then his low, rumbling snore, she reached out and with trembling fingers pulled on her underthings and then the rest of her clothes.

Despite it being summer, she was shaking with icy dread. She pulled a nearby carpet over her as she lay beside the bed, knowing better than to test his word about the consequences of any attempt to escape. There was no escape. This was her life.

She now only hoped to keep the rest of it buried and forgotten.

If she ever remembered who she was, then her life would get infinitely worse. She wouldn't let that happen. She would stay behind the dark shroud. This night she was a new person, separated from who she had been. That person had to remain forever dead.

She wondered who the man could be that Jagang had talked about. She feared to imagine what Jagang was going to do to him, through her, that would so destroy him.

She forced those thoughts away. That was the old her. That person was gone forever, and would remain so.

In the depths of loneliness and despair, Kahlan curled up in a ball and wept silently in racking sobs.

Richard walked in a daze, watching the ground before him lit by moonlight. Through that dark, hazy state, only one spark of anything seemed able to burn through.

Kahlan.

He missed her so much. He was so tired of the struggle. He was so tired of trying. He was so tired of failing.

He ached to have her back. To have his life with her back. To hold her . . . just to hold her.

He remembered the time, years before, in the spirit house, when he had not known that she was the Mother Confessor and she had been feeling desperately lonely and overwhelmed by the crushing secrets she had to keep. She had asked him to hold her, just to hold her. He remembered the pain in her voice, the pain of needing to be held, comforted.

He would give anything to do that now.

"Stop," a voice hissed at him. "Wait."

Richard halted. He had trouble trying to care what was going on, even though he knew he should. He could read the tension in her posture; she was like a bird of prey cocking its head, lifting its wings the slightest bit.

He couldn't seem to escape the thick lethargy that weighed him down so that he could think it through. Her deportment appeared to be the coiled potential for aggression, but underlying that he saw a hint of fear.

He finally managed to summon the concern to try to understand. Then, in the moonlight, he saw what Six was watching: what looked like a vast encampment spread across a valley. Because it was the middle of the night, things were relatively quiet down below. Even through the numb miasma of her presence, Richard felt his level of concern rising.

He saw something else, too. Past the valley encampment, he saw, up on the high ground beyond, a castle that he thought he recognized.

"Come on," Six hissed as she glided past him.

Richard trudged after her, once more sinking back into the indifferent haze where all he could think about was Kahlan.

They walked for what seemed like hours through the countryside in the dead of night. Six was as quiet as a snake, moving, pausing, then moving again as she made her way along minor trails through thick woods. Richard felt comforted by the smell of balsam and fir trees. The moss and ferns delighted him with childhood memories.

The delight of the woods evaporated when they walked along cobbled streets, among closed shops, past dark buildings. There were men in the shadows, pairs of them, carrying pikes. Richard felt as if he were in a dream watching it all pass before his mind's eye. He half expected that all he would have to do was imagine the woods again and they would appear.

He imagined Kahlan. She did not appear.

Two men in polished metal armor rushed out of a side street. They fell to their knees before Six, kissing the hem of her black dress. She slowed only slightly for their groveling supplication. They followed along as she continued up the streets, becoming escorts for the night's shadow trailing darkness behind her.

It all felt so dreamy. Richard knew that he should fight it, but he couldn't make himself care. He cared only about doing as Six told him. He couldn't help himself. Seeing the flowing form of her charmed him, looking into her eyes captivated him, hearing her voice bewitched him. Without his gift, she filled that empty void within his soul.

Her presence somehow completed him, filled him with purpose.

The two guards with them gently rapped on an iron door in a great stone wall. A small door on the inside over a small slit in the iron door opened. Eyes peered out. They widened a little at seeing the pale shadow before them. Richard could hear men on the other side rushing to draw back a heavy bar.

The door opened and Six slipped through with Richard in tow. He saw great stone walls in the moonlight, but paid them little heed. He was more fascinated by the snaking shape leading him through the silky night.

Once they passed through great doors, men rushed about, opening yet more doors, shouting orders, and bringing torches.

"This way," one man said as he led them into a stone stairwell.

Down they went, spiraling and turning, ever deeper. Richard felt as if they were being swallowed down the gullet of some great stone beast. As long as Six was taking him, though, he was content to be swallowed. At lower levels, in a dank corridor, the men led her into a gloomy place. Hay was scattered over the slimy floor. Water echoed as it dripped in the distance.

"Here is the place you requested," a guard told her.

The heavy door squealed in rusty protest as he pulled it open. Inside, on a small table, he lit a candle with the torch.

"Your room for the night," Six told Richard. "It will be light soon. I will be back, then."

"Yes, Mistress," he said.

She leaned toward him a little, a thin smile slitting her bloodless face. "If I know the queen, she will want to begin immediately. She's quite impatient, to say nothing of being impulsive. She will no doubt bring the big men with whips. I expect that before the morning is over she will have the flesh torn from your back."

Richard stared. He couldn't make his mind grasp it all. "Mistress?"

"The queen is not only vicious, but vindictive. You are going to be the object of her venom. But not to worry; I still need you alive. You may suffer excruciating agony, but you will live."

She turned with a billowing flourish and swept out the door, a shadow swallowed into the darkness. Men funneled out the door after her. The door banged closed. Richard heard the lock click home. Before he knew it, he was suddenly standing alone in a stone room, deserted, forsaken, forgotten.

In the silence, terror began to seep into his bones. Why would a queen want to hurt him? What did Six need him alive for?

Richard blinked. As the moments passed, he felt his mind working to understand. It felt as if the farther away Six went, the better he could think.

After the torches were gone, it was a while before his eyes adjusted to the light of a single candle. He looked around at the stone room. There was only a chair and a table. The floor was stone. The walls were stone. The ceiling had heavy beams.

It hit him like a thunderclap.

Denna.

This was the room where he had been taken when he had first been captured by Denna. He recognized the table. He remembered Denna sitting in that very chair. He looked up and there, right where he remembered it being, he saw the iron peg.

His wrists had been in iron manacles. Denna had hung the chain holding them together over that iron peg. He had hung from it as Denna tortured him with her Agiel. Horrifying images of the night Denna had broken him flashed through his mind. The night she had thought she had broken him, anyway. He had partitioned his mind. But he remembered the things she had done to him that night.

And he remembered what had prompted her to such violence.

He had been hanging there when Princess Violet had come in to watch. The princess had decided that she wanted to participate, to join in his torture. Denna gave the little monster her Agiel and showed her how to use it on him.

Richard remembered Violet bragging about how she was going to have Kahlan raped, tortured, and finally killed.

Richard had kicked Violet hard enough to shatter her jaw and sever her tongue.

This was that room.

Richard leaned back against the stone wall and slid down to sit and rest. He needed to think, to figure it out, to understand what was going on.

He was leaning against his pack, so he pulled it off and set it in his lap. A thought struck him and he looked through the pack, pushing his war-wizard outfit and gold cape aside until he found the book Baraccus had left for him. He thumbed through the pages. They were still blank. If only he hadn't lost his gift, he would have been able to read the book. If he knew how to use his ability he would have been able to save himself. If only.

He suddenly had a thought. He couldn't let them find this book. Six had the gift. Some form of it, anyway. He couldn't let her see this. Baraccus had hidden it for three thousand years. It was meant for no eyes but his. He couldn't fail such a trust. He couldn't let anyone know about this book.

He got up and paced around the room, searching for any place he could hide the book. There was no place. It was a simple stone room. There were no cubbyholes, no niches, no loose stones. There was nowhere to hide anything.

As Richard stood in the center of the room, thinking, he looked up and saw the iron peg. He moved through the room, inspecting the beams. There was one beam, running parallel to one wall, without much room between the beam and the wall. The beam, like most in the ceiling, had long cracks from when the freshly cut beam had been hewn and then dried. An idea struck him.

He immediately pulled the chair over and climbed up on top of it. It wasn't high enough. He pushed the chair out of the way and dragged over the table. After stepping from the chair to the top of the table, he at last was able to reach the iron peg. He wiggled it, but it was stuck tight. He needed that iron peg if he was to hide the book.

He hooked his hands over the peg and used all his weight to spring up and down. At last the peg began to loosen. Working swiftly and using all his muscle, he finally managed to get the peg to wiggle. He wiggled it back and forth until he was able to pull it free.

Richard dragged the table over to the side of the room near the dark corner, and got up on top. He inspected the crack in the beam, finding a place where it wandered toward the top, near the cross-planks overhead. He wedged the iron peg into the split in the beam, working it in until it was stuck fast.

He retrieved the pack and crammed it up in the tight space between the beam and the wall. Once he had it as high and as flat as he could get it, he shoved it along the beam until it wedged above the iron peg. He tested the pack by tugging on it but it was stuck tightly in place. It wasn't going anywhere.

He hopped down and put the table and chair back where they had been. The pack was a color similar to the aged oak of the beam, and it was in the shadows. Unless a person was looking for it, he didn't think anyone would notice the pack lodged up where he had put it. Besides, it was the best he could do.

Satisfied that he had done everything he could to keep the book, and the war-wizard outfit, from falling into the wrong hands, he lay down on the cold stone floor against the opposite wall and tried to get some sleep.

He found it impossible to sleep thinking about what Six had promised him for the next day. Fear gnawed at him, making his mind race. He knew he needed to get some rest, but he just couldn't calm himself.

He did feel a sense of relief to be away from Six. He'd lost all track of time since he had been with the wisps and Six had been there as he left the ancient trees. He couldn't think when he was with her, couldn't do anything. She consumed his entire mind.

His entire mind.

He remembered being in this room before, with Denna. She had told him that he was to be her pet, and that he would be broken to her will. He remembered telling himself that he would let her do what she would, but that he would save a piece of himself, put it away, and not allow anyone into that part, not even himself, until he needed to unlock that safe place and be himself again.

He had to do that again. He couldn't allow Six to have all of his mind, the way she had since she had captured him. He could still feel the weight of her influence, the pull of her will, but now that he wasn't in her immediate presence it seemed so much less by comparison that he felt free of her and able to think. Able to decide, to a degree, what he wanted.

What he wanted was to be free of the witch woman.

He created a place in his mind, as he had done so long ago in this very room, and he locked a part of himself away, a part of his strength, the core of his will, in much the same way he had hidden his pack away in a hidden corner where no one would find it.

With his new ability to think, and a plan, he felt a sense of relief. Even though he could still feel the witch woman's fangs in him, he felt that she no longer had the control she thought she did. He at last was able to relax a little.

He thought then of Kahlan. Her memory brought a sad smile. He made himself think of happy times with her. He thought about what it felt like to hold her, to kiss her, to be alone in the night with her whispering to him how much he meant to her.

Thinking about Kahlan, he drifted off to sleep.

Richard woke with a start when he heard the door being unlocked. It was a rude awakening, because Kahlan had visited him in his dreams. He didn't remember his dreams, but he did know that those dreams involved her. He felt suffused with her presence, as if he had really been with her, only to be pulled away by being awake. Once he was awake, her essence immediately began draining away. The loss of even her dream presence to cold, empty consciousness was disheartening. The world seemed to have been much richer in his dreams. Even though he didn't remember them, those dreams seemed sweet, like music in the distance. Just the feel of them was enough for him to know that he would rather not be in the waking world.

Richard started to sit up only to realize how much he ached from sleeping on the stone floor. Given how foggy his head felt, he doubted that he had more than a few hours' sleep. When he saw guards spilling into the stone room, Richard staggered to his feet, trying to stretch his cramped muscles as he did so.

Six swept into the room like an ill wind. Against her wiry black hair and flowing black robes, her skin looked ghostlike. Her blanched blue eyes fixed on him as if there was nothing else in her world but him. Richard felt that look come down on him as if it were the weight of a mountain. That look, her presence, crushed his will.

He swam in the feeling inundating him. As she came closer, he fought to keep his head above the dark waters of abdication of his will. It felt like fighting for his life in a raging river whose powerful current was pulling him under.

"Come along, we have to get to the caves. We don't have much time."

Rather than ask what she meant by not having much time—a question he doubted he would have been able to summon the strength to ask—he instead asked something else, something for which he had the strength, something still strong in his thoughts.

"Do you know where Kahlan is?"

Six stopped and turned halfway back to peer at him. "Of course. She is with Jagang."

Jagang. Richard was stunned senseless. Six not only remembered Kahlan, but knew where she was. She seemed pleased by the pain she had so obviously just caused him.

Six turned and marched for the door. "Now, come on. Hurry."

Something was wrong. He didn't know what, but he could feel it in her power over him. She held him under her spell of seductive influence, like a balmy leash of iron strength, yet it was not the same as before. He could feel that something was different. There was a trace of distress in her demeanor.

But that was hardly what concerned him. Jagang had Kahlan. He could not imagine how Six even knew who Kahlan was because he was so stunned by the meaning of those words: *She is with Jagang.*

If not for the pull of Six dragging him along in her wake, Richard would surely have collapsed to the floor. He could not conceive of a worse nightmare than Jagang having Kahlan. His thoughts tumbled in blind panic as he followed the witch woman through the dark twists and turns of the stone passageways. He had to do something. He had to help Kahlan. Not only was she in the hands of Sisters of the Dark, but they were in collusion with Richard and Kahlan's worst enemy.

The thought uppermost in Richard's mind—other than his fear for Kahlan—was that he knew where Jagang was. The emperor was on his way up into D'Hara, toward the People's Palace. And now Kahlan was with him.

So deep was he in thought that he found that they were outside before he even realized it. He understood at once what had Six so agitated. There were troops pouring into the grounds from every direction. These were the troops they had seen camped in the valley the night before.

Six cursed under her breath as she looked for a way to escape the courtyard. At every entrance soldiers flooded in. The passageway back into the castle, back to the stone room, was already closed off by a wall of men marching into the castle grounds.

These were all grimy men, some wearing plate armor, some chain mail, but most wore dark leather for protection. Studded leather straps crossing their chests held leather pouches with supplies, or sheathed knives at the ready. Hung on heavy leather belts they carried axes, maces, flails, and swords. They were as menacing as any men Richard had ever seen. The guards, in chain-mail shirts covered with red tunics, were not foolish enough to make an attempt to stop such men, especially not in such numbers.

Richard knew without a doubt that these men pouring onto the grounds of the castle were Imperial Order troops.

"By agreement," a muscular man said as he strode up to Six, "we have come to see that Tamarang is secure for the cause of the Imperial Order."

"Yes, of course," Six said. "But . . . this is considerably earlier than you were supposed to arrive."

The man rested a hand on the hilt of his sword as his dark eyes scrutinized the layout of the place. Richard recognized the quality of the weapons the man carried, how well made his armor was, and the way he immediately took charge. This was the commander of all these men.

"We made good time," he said. "Some of the towns and cities along the way offered no resistance, so we were able to get here now, rather than after winter, as we had thought."

"Well . . . please accept our welcome on behalf of the queen," Six said. "I, well, I was just going to go look for her."

The commander wore shoulder plates of formed leather, along with a pressed-leather breastplate embellished with designs. Looking to have served him well, the leather plate had cuts and scrapes from fending off weapons. He had rings lining the back of his left ear and a tattoo of scales down over the right half of his face, as if he were half man, half reptile.

"The Order operates for the good of the Order and our cause. Tamarang is now part of the Imperial Order. I trust all here are pleased to now be people of the Order?"

The sound of boots on stone covered the sound of birds singing at the impending sunrise. Men closed in all around, flowing into the courtyard walkway right up to Richard.

"Yes, of course," Six said to the commander. She seemed to be regaining her composure. "The queen and I trust that you will honor the agreements made, that the castle is not to be entered by anyone from the Order, that the castle itself is to be left to Her Majesty, her advisors, and servants."

The man stared into her eyes for a moment. "Makes no difference to me. The castle is of no use to us." He blinked, as if somewhat surprised to hear himself agreeing to such a thing. He puffed up his chest, regaining some of his fire. "But by our agreement, the rest of Tamarang is now a province of the empire of the Imperial Order."

Six bowed her head in acknowledgment. Her thin smile was back. "By agreement."

Richard noted but hardly heard the conversation. He had been using the loosened grip Six had on him to slip out of it. He used her distraction like an iron bar to pry her invisible claws off of him. He had managed to pry open that grip just enough to let his mind slip out.

It was time he did something for himself, for Kahlan.

Even though he had lost the gift, and had lost the Sword of Truth, he had not lost the lessons mastered from that weapon, much less the lessons learned throughout his life. He might not have had the gift, but he remembered the meaning of the symbols. He knew the rhythm of the dance with death.

He was still one with a blade.

Now he needed only to get his hands on a blade.

While Six and the officer decided the limits of where the men would go on the grounds, where they would stay out of, and what was theirs within the city itself, Richard glanced behind, noticing the wooden handles on the swords of the soldiers, and the leather handle on the sword of the subordinate officer right behind, just a little to Richard's right.

He smiled at the man as he pulled a copper penny from his pocket and casually rolled it across his knuckles. He let the penny slip and fall, as if he were clumsy. He squatted down to pick it up, pressing one hand to the sandy dirt beside the path for balance as he reached out for the coin, letting grit stick to his palms and fingers. He scooped up the penny, getting as well a small amount of sandy dirt. The officer behind, watching his superior speaking to Six, glanced Richard's way only as Richard wiped the dirt off the penny and then returned it to a pocket. Six presented a much more captivating subject than an awkward nobody. Richard acted like he was idly brushing his hands, but he was really covering his palms and fingers with the grit.

Once he began, he didn't want his hands slipping on leather.

Without turning, he leaned back toward the lesser officer standing behind him. The man was intent on the bewitching figure of Six as she spun her web, telling the men what she would like them to do. Out of his peripheral vision, Richard could see the hilt of the weapon hanging at the man's hip. It was better made than the weapons carried by most of the men.

As Six and the commander were talking, Richard turned a little, feigning a stretch. In an instant, his hand was on the sword. In another instant the blade was free.

Having a weapon, a sword, in his hand, instantly flooded Richard with memories, forms, and skills he had spent long hours learning. The lessons might have in part come from otherworldly sources, but the knowledge was not magic. It was the experience of countless Seekers before Richard. Even though he didn't have that weapon with him, he still had that knowledge.

The officer, apparently half thinking Richard was just being foolish, made a move to recover his weapon. Richard spun the sword and with a backward thrust ran him through.

Other men sprang into action. Swords came free in the cool dawn air. Big men freed huge crescent battle-axes from their belts, along with maces and flails.

Richard was suddenly in his element. The haze was gone from his mind. He had not expected the part of his mind that he had locked away for safekeeping to be called upon this soon, but the time had come and he had to act. This was his chance.

He knew where Kahlan was, and he had to get to her.

These men were in his way.

Richard swung, taking off an arm wielding an axe. The cry, the spray of blood, made the men nearby flinch. In that sliver of an instant, Richard made his move. He brought his sword up through another man lifting his sword. The man died before he even had his arm fully cocked back. Richard spun out of the way of weapons coming for him.

Despite the sudden cacophony of metal clanging, of men yelling, Richard was already in a silent world of purpose. He was in control. These men might have thought that they had an army against him, but in a way that was his advantage. He didn't fight an army. He fought individuals. They thought like a collective mass, a collective element, allowing one another to move, as if the soldiers were trying to be one big fighting centipede.

That was a mistake. Richard used it to cut into them. While they hesitated, waiting for others to act, waiting for an opening, Richard was already moving through their lines, cutting them down. He let them swing and lunge, using strength and effort, while he floated through the onslaught of steel. Every time he thrust, he made contact. Every time he swung his weapon, he cut. It was like going through thick brush, slashing aside the branches that reached out at him. He let the momentum of the sword power the next strike, keeping it in continuous motion rather than using effort, and precious time, to draw it back. If he brought the blade down, slicing through the side of a man's neck, he continued the movement, bringing the weapon up behind to run a man through as he rushed in, and then, as he pulled the blade out, he spun away as swords, axes, and flails came down where he had been only a moment before. It was a fluid dance, moving through the grunting, diving, jumping men. Slice, slice, slice, letting the screams fill the morning air, letting the alarm of not being able to stop him cause others to hesitate in fear of what could be happening.

At all times, Richard kept his objective in sight. He was heading for the opening out of the wall. Even though he charged, wove, and feigned his way through the onslaught of men, he headed relentlessly for that opening, and his freedom. He had to get through, and then he could get to Kahlan.

Richard scythed down some of the men in his way while he spun past others. His object was not to kill as many as he could, but to get to his goal of that open doorway.

Even though orders were being shouted, soldiers were screaming in rage for a chance to get at him, and men were shrieking in pain as they were slashed open, disemboweled, or stabbed, there was quiet purpose in Richard's mind. He cut from that void. He selected targets swiftly, and cut them down just as swiftly. He didn't waste effort swinging, but cut with certainty. When he saw a leader among the men, a man who moved with more skill, a man others looked to in the attack, Richard cut into that strength. As he moved toward the opening in the wall, he slipped through gaps in their guard, all the time cutting. He didn't allow himself to pause for an instant in his relentless advance. He didn't allow the enemy to catch their breath as he cut into them. He cut without mercy, taking any man he could. Whether he looked fierce or afraid, Richard cut him down. They had expected him to be intimidated by their numbers, by their battle cries as they rushed him; he was not. He cut them down mercilessly.

At last he made the door, beheading the man just to the left and then the one to the right. The opening was at last free of Imperial Order soldiers. Richard dashed through.

Everything came to an abrupt halt. Beyond was a wall of archers, all with bows drawn, all aiming their arrows at him. Men with bows and men with crossbows were formed into a semicircle beyond the doorway, trapping him in that pocket of razor-sharp, steel-tipped arrows all aimed at him. Richard knew all too well that he didn't stand a chance against the hundreds of arrows aimed at him, especially not at this close range.

The commander appeared in the doorway. "Very impressive. I've never seen the like of it."

The man truly did sound amazed, but it was over. Richard heaved a sigh and tossed his sword down.

The commander stepped closer, frowning as he appraised Richard, looking him up and down. Behind, Six appeared in the opening through the wall, a black silhouette against the sunrise.

The commander folded his muscled arms. "Do you know how to play Ja'La dh Jin?"

Richard thought it the oddest question he could imagine at that moment. In the background, beyond the rather small opening in the wall he had made it through, grievously injured men screamed, cried, and begged for help.

Richard didn't shy away from the commander. "Yes, I know how to play the game of life."

The man smiled at Richard using the translation of Ja'La dh Jin from the emperor's tongue.

The commander, looking far from concerned about the numbers of his men Richard had cut down, smiled to himself as he shook his head in wonder. Richard wasn't concerned for the dead and injured, either. They had chosen to be a part of a conquering army, to plunder, rape, and murder people who had done them no wrong, people who had committed the sin of not believing in the ways of the Order, people who had wished to live their own lives free.

Six stalked up beside the commander. "I appreciate your valiant efforts to apprehend this dangerous man. He is a condemned prisoner and my responsibility. His punishment is to be directed by the queen herself."

The commander glanced over at her. "He just killed a number of my men. He is my prisoner now."

Six looked ready to spit fire. "I'll not allow—"

Hundreds of arrows all lifted as one to point right at the woman. She froze still and silent, appraising the threat. Like Richard, she obviously knew that her talent was no match for this many massed men with weapons that could be released with a twitch. It would take only one twitch to end her life.

"This man is my prisoner," Six said to the commander in a quiet but firm voice. "I was just taking him to the queen for—"

"He's my prisoner now. Go back to the castle. The grounds belong to the Order now. This is no longer the queen's—or your—dominion. This man is ours now."

"But I—"

"You are dismissed. Or do you wish to break our agreement, and have us slaughter the whole lot of you?"

Six's blanched blue eyes swept the hundreds of men aiming arrows at her. "Of course our agreement stands, Commander." She turned her intense eyes on the man. "I have honored it, as agreed, and so will you."

He tipped his head in a slight bow. "Very well. Now, leave us to our duty. As agreed, you, as well as those in charge here, may go about your business, go where you wish, and my men will not accost you, them, or the castle staff."

With one final murderous look at Richard, she turned and stalked away. Along with the commander and all his men, Richard watched the witch woman glide through the opening in the wall and up the bloody path among the dead and dying, not giving them so much as a second look as she headed for the entrance to the castle. Men parted for her, letting her through.

The commander turned back to Richard. "What is your name?"

Richard knew that he couldn't give his real name. He couldn't even give the name he grew up with, Richard Cypher. If he did, he was liable to be recognized for who he really was. His mind raced as he tried to think of another name he could use. The name Zedd liked to use when he needed to disguise his identity popped into his head.

"I'm Ruben Rybnik."

"Well, Ruben, I will give you a choice. We could skin you alive, stake you out, slit open your belly, and let you watch as the vultures pull your intestines out and fight over them."

Richard knew he wouldn't have to face such a fate, because all he would have to do was attack and the archers would kill him. Still, he didn't want to die. He couldn't help Kahlan if he was dead.

"I don't much like that choice. You have another?"

A sly smile spread on the man's face, befitting the reptilian half with the scale tattoos. "Yes, as a matter of fact I do. You see, the different divisions of the army have Ja'La teams. Ours is made up of a mix of my men and the very best of those we have come across—men blessed by the Creator with exceptional talent.

"It was quite impressive the way you made your way through all those men and to the opening in the wall, like you were making your way toward a goal. You continued on toward that goal without allowing yourself to be stopped no matter what the men threw at you . . . well, you're a natural point man."

"Dangerous position, being the point man."

The commander shrugged. "That is the game of life. We are absent a point man right now. He died in the last game. As he was evading a blocking man he missed a catch and the broc stove in his ribs. They punctured his lungs. It was a messy, painful death."

"That doesn't sound like a very tempting job."

The commander's eyes gleamed with menace. "If you would rather, you can take your chances without your skin, watching the vultures fight over your bowels."

"Would I get the chance to play the emperor's team?"

"The emperor's team," the commander repeated. He stared at Richard for a moment, interested that he would have asked such a question. "You really are a competitive sort." He finally nodded. "All sanctioned Ja'La teams dream of having a chance to face the emperor's team. If you show your worth, and help us win tournaments with your skill as point man, then, yes, you might very well get the chance to play the emperor's team. If you survive that long."

"Then I'd like to join."

The commander smiled. "You are thinking of being a hero? Is that it? A Ja'La player who is cheered? A player of renown?"

"Perhaps."

The commander leaned a little closer. "I think you are dreaming of the women such a victory would earn you. The looks in the eyes of beautiful females. The smiles of attractive women."

Richard thought of Kahlan's beautiful green eyes, her smile.

"Yes, that thought had crossed my mind."

"Crossed your mind!" The man snorted a laugh. "Well, Ruben, banish the thought. You are not a player who has come to join. You are a captive, and a dangerous one at that. We have provisions for players of your kind. You will be put in a cage and taken by wagon. You will be let out to play, or to practice, but otherwise you will be no more than a caged animal. During practice sessions you will have to work hard to learn to work with the rest of the team, to learn their strengths and weaknesses—after all, you are the point man. But even so, you will not be one man alone."

Richard didn't see an alternative. "I understand."

The commander took a deep breath as he hooked his thumbs in his weapons belt. "Good. If you play well, if you do your best in every game, and if we should happen to beat the emperor's team, I will allow you to have your choice of the women who will be gathered, eager to lie with the players."

"With the victors," Richard corrected.

The commander nodded. "With the victors." He lifted a finger. "Make one wrong step in the meantime, and you will be killed."

"Bargain struck," Richard said. "You have your new point man."

The commander lifted an arm, signaling other officers closer. They came to attention before the commander.

"Have the wagon brought up—the one with the iron box—for our new point man, here. I think you already know how dangerous he is. Handle him as such. I want to unleash his talent against our opponents."

The officer gave Richard an appraising glance. "It would be nice to win more than on occasion."

The commander nodded as he started reeling off orders. "Post guards near the castle and in town, enough to insure that there will be no trouble from the people of Tamarang. Then have all the laborers start setting up the stations for our supply trains. You'll first have to find a place big enough. Look just outside the city, near the river.

"Summer is waning. Winter will be here before you know it, and the supply trains soon coming up through here will be large and often. All our troops in the New World will be needing supplies to last them the coming winter.

"The city of Tamarang will provide what our men will need for the construction. There is a port on the river where the lumber is to be brought in, so you will need to make provisions for roads to the new site, and for the barracks for all the men who will eventually be billeted here."

One of the officers nodded. "We have all the plans ready."

Richard could only assume that the Order intended to use the city of Tamarang for help in all the construction for the depot. He had seen them do such things before. It was easier to deal with places that were eager to join in the Order than to destroy everything and then just have to build it up again.

"I will be leaving at once with our troops and this supply train," the commander told the officers. "Jagang wants all the men he can get for the assault on the D'Haran Empire."

The leader of the D'Haran Empire stood quietly listening to the plans for the final assault on the people of the New World, for the slaughter of those who believed in freedom, for the battle that he had made sure would never happen.

Rachel woke when she heard Violet padding around the bedroom. Through the little slit in the door of her iron box, Rachel could see the tall window across the room. Even though the heavy royal blue drapes were drawn, she could tell by the color of the light coming in the narrow gap between them that it was just dawn.

Queen Violet did not ordinarily get up this early.

Rachel listened, trying to hear what Violet was doing. She heard a long yawn, and then the sounds of the cave queen getting dressed.

Rachel's legs were cramped from being in the box all night. She wanted to get out and stretch. That was not a desire she dared to voice, though. At least they hadn't put the tongue clamp on her the night before; sometimes Violet didn't feel like bothering.

All of a sudden there was a BANG, BANG, BANG that made Rachel jump, made her heart race. It was Violet beating the heel of her shoe on the top of the iron box.

"Wake up," Violet said. "Big day. A messenger slipped a note under the door in the night. Six returned—a few hours before dawn."

The queen whistled as she went about dressing. That in itself was a little unusual, because the queen usually called in her attendants to get out her clothes and dress her. Now she was dressing herself, and whistling while she did it. Rachel had rarely heard Violet whistle. It was pretty clear that she was in a good mood because of Six returning.

Rachel's heart sank at all that meant.

What little light came into the sleeping box darkened as Violet's eyes appeared just outside the slit in the door. "She has Richard with her. The spells I drew all worked. Today is going to be the worst day of his life. I will see to that. Today, he begins to pay for his crimes against me."

Violet's face vanished. The whistling started in again as the queen crossed the room, finished getting dressed, and drew on stockings and laced boots. In a few moments she returned and leaned close again.

"I'm going to let you watch while the men whip him." She cocked her head. "What do you have to say?"

In the back corner of her box, Rachel swallowed. "Thank you, Queen Violet."

Violet snickered as she straightened. "He won't have an inch of flesh left on his back by the time the sun sets today." She went a short distance to the desk in the corner and then returned. Rachel heard the key turn in the lock. The lock made a metallic clang as it popped open, banging against the iron door. Violet pulled the lock off the hasp. "And that's only the beginning of what I will have done to him. I'll—"

There was an urgent knock at the door. A muffled voice demanded that the door be opened. It was Six's voice.

"Hold on, I'm coming," Violet shouted across the room.

Rachel moved a little closer to the slit and saw Violet hurriedly hook the lock back through the hasp. She pushed it to lock it again just as Six banged on the door.

"All right, all right," Violet said as she let go of the lock and rushed across the room. She turned the latch on the big, heavy door and almost immediately it burst open. Six swept into the room, all dark and towering like a thunderhead.

"You have him, right? He's here, locked up where I told you to put him?" Violet asked, her voice filled with trembling excitement as Six closed the big door. "We can start punishing him immediately. I will have the guards assemble—"

"The army took him."

Rachel moved closer to the iron door and cautiously peered out the slit. Six was standing just inside the door. The queen's back was to Rachel. Violet stood in a white satin dress with a deep blue belt and laced boots over her white stockings, staring up at the stark figure of the witch woman.

"What?"

"Imperial Order troops appeared right before dawn. They're flooding into the city as I speak, into the grounds of the castle. There are thousands of them—tens of thousands of them—maybe hundreds of thousands of them for all I know."

Violet looked confused, not wanting to believe what she was hearing as she searched for words. "But that can't be. The message you sent said that he was locked up, just as I instructed, locked up in the cell where he hurt me."

" 'Was' is the operative word. We arrived in the night and I locked him up just as you wished. Then I sent you the message and saw to a few things, waiting for morning.

"I was bringing him with me, just now. I was bringing him to face you when we encountered the occupying soldiers. It's one of those massive advance columns of reinforcements. Their purpose is not a slaughter and rampage; they want to establish a staging area in Tamarang for other supply trains coming up from the Old World. They were open to my offers of—"

"What about Richard!"

Six heaved a sigh. "I was too late. There was nothing I could do. The troops were pouring in from every direction. Our men had no chance to stop them. Those who tried were swept aside. I thought that it was best to deal with the Order's men myself, to try to find a way to secure safety for you, and your staff, while I had the chance.

"While I was speaking to the commander, insuring favorable terms for us in return for help in what they want to do with establishing supply routes, all of a sudden Richard came up with a sword."

Violet planted her fists on her hips. "What do you mean, he 'came up with a sword'?" Her temper, along with her voice, was rising by the moment. "You saw to it that he doesn't have his sword."

"No, it wasn't the Sword of Truth. It was another sword. Just a plain sword. He must have grabbed it from a soldier when no one was looking. Plain though it may have been, he knew how to use it. All of a sudden a war broke out. Richard was like death itself unleashed. He was killing Imperial Order troops by the dozens. It was madness. The men thought they were facing a major battle. Everyone went into combat without even knowing what they were up against. Things just went crazy in an instant.

"I can't control pandemonium on that level. There were too many men, there was too much violence. I would have needed some time to gain control and there was no time. Richard made it out through the wall—"

"He escaped! After all this, he escaped!"

"No. Outside the wall waited hundreds of archers. They had him trapped. He was captured."

Violet sighed in relief. "Good. For a moment I thought—"

"No, not good. The commander would not release him. Because Richard had killed so many of his men, the commander wanted Richard as a prisoner. They probably intend to execute him. I doubt he will live to see tomorrow.

"Once in the castle, on the way up here, I looked out a window and saw them put Richard in an iron box in a wagon. They took him away with the column of troops heading north."

Violet blinked indignation. "You let him get away? You let those filthy nobodies take him—take my prize?"

In the sudden quiet, Rachel saw Six's glare darken. She had never seen the witch woman give the queen such a look before, and she thought that Violet would do well to be a little more prudent.

"I had no choice," Six said with an icy inflection to her words. "There were hundreds of archers pointing arrows at me. They left me no choice in the matter. It's not like I wanted to give Richard over to them. A lot of work has gone into this."

"You should have stopped it! You have powers!"

"Not enough for—"

"You boneheaded moron! You stupid, stupid, worthless, no-good dim-witted jackass! I trust you with an important task and you don't even see it through for me! I'll have you whipped to within an inch of your life for this! You're no better than the rest of my worthless, no-good advisors! I'll have you whipped in Richard's place to teach you yours!"

Rachel flinched at the resounding sound of the slap. It knocked Violet from her feet. She landed on her bottom on the floor.

"How dare you touch me in that way," Violet said, comforting her cheek. "I'll have you beheaded for this. Guards! I need you!"

Almost immediately there was a knock at the double doors.

Six opened one of them. Two men with pikes looked at the queen sitting on the floor, and then up into the blanched blue eyes of the woman holding the door handle.

"If you dare to knock on this door again," Six hissed, "I will eat your raw livers for my breakfast and wash it down with your blood."

The two men turned as white as Six. "Sorry to bother you, Mistress," one said. "Yes, sorry," the other said as they turned tail and ran off down the hall.

With a growl of rage Six grabbed Violet by her hair and lifted her to her feet. The witch woman unleashed a blow that sent Violet tumbling across the floor, leaving strings of blood across the carpets in her wake.

"You ungrateful little brat. I've had about all I can stomach of you. I've endured it long enough. From now on, you will keep that tongue still or I will rip out what I gave you back."

Her long, bony fingers seized Violet by the hair and pulled her up again, then slammed the queen against the wall. Rachel could see Violet's arms hanging limp. She made no move to defend herself as Six struck her time after time. Blood ran from Violet's nose, from her mouth, and was splattered across the wall. A bib of blood stood out against the white satin of Violet's dress.

When the tall witch woman released the queen, she dropped into a heap on the floor and fell to helpless sobbing.

"Shut up!" Six roared, her anger building. "Stand! Stand up this instant or never stand again!"

Violet struggled to her feet, finally standing before Six, looking up at her, her eyes filled not only with tears, but terror.

Violet lifted her chin. She visibly pushed her fear aside and grasped at indignation, instead. "How dare you touch your queen in such a fashion. I will—"

"Queen?" Six sneered. "You were never anything more than a puppet queen. Now, you are no longer even that. You are no longer queen. As of this moment, you resign.

"I am the queen, now. Not like you, a pompous little twit who thinks herself important because of the extravagance of her tantrums, but a real queen. A queen with real power. Queen Six. Got it?"

When Violet started crying in angry resentment, Six slapped her hard enough to toss her head aside and throw yet more blood against the lacy, powder blue designs stenciled on the wall. Again, faced with an angry witch woman, Violet didn't respond, even to ward the assault.

Six rested her fists on her knobby hips as she leaned down toward Violet. "I asked if you got it."

Violet, on the edge of ragged panic at hearing the deadly threat in Six's voice, nodded.

"Say it!" Six slapped her again. "Answer your queen properly!"

Violet's sobs grew louder, as if that alone would save her throne.

"Say it or I'll have you boiled alive, chopped up, and fed to the hogs."

"Yes . . . Queen Six."

"Very good," Six hissed with a venomous smile. She straightened. "Now, what good can you be to me?" She looked up at the ceiling, touching a finger to her chin in royal contemplation. "Should I even bother to keep you alive? Yes, I know—you will be the court artist. A petty member of my staff. Do your job properly and you live. Fail me in any way, and you will be boiled and fed to the hogs. Got it?"

Violet nodded at the glare that focused on her. "Yes, Queen Six."

Six smiled with grim pride at how quickly she had brought Violet to task. She seized the former queen's collar behind her neck.

"Now, we have urgent business. We can still save this mess."

"But how?" Violet whined. "Without Richard—"

"I've clipped his fangs. His gift is mine for now and he will remain cut off from it. I will decide when the time is right to deal with him.

"As for the rest of it, there is another way, but it is, unfortunately, more difficult. I only used Richard in the first place because certain aspects of it were less complicated. It also kept you quiet and working without complaint while I pulled your strings. The other way is far more complex because, unlike Richard, a number of other people are involved, so we must get started at once."

"What other way?"

Six flashed an affected smile. "You will draw some more pictures for me." She opened the door with one hand and with the other dragged Violet out into the hall. "I need you to draw a woman. A woman with an iron collar around her neck."

"What woman are you talking about?" Violet asked in a trembling voice.

Rachel could just barely see them out in the hallway as Six reached for the doorknob. "You don't remember her. It will be harder to do because of that, but I can instruct you in how to accomplish the elements that I will need. Still, it will be more difficult than anything you've done before. I'm afraid that it will test not only your ability, but your strength and endurance. If you don't want to end up in the trough as hog slop, you will put your all into it. Got it?"

"Yes, Queen Six," Violet said in a voice choked with tears.

As Six started to march away, dragging Violet along, she slammed the bedroom door closed behind her.

In the sudden silence, Rachel held her breath, wondering if they would remember her and return. She waited, but then finally had to let the breath out. Violet had replaced the lock, so she probably wouldn't give Rachel a second thought. Violet had a lot bigger problems, now, than worrying about letting Rachel out.

Rachel feared that she was going to die in the cursed box. Would anyone ever let her out? Would Six return and put Rachel to death? After all, Rachel had only been kept around for Violet's amusement. There was no longer any reason for Six to keep up the pretense.

Six was in charge, now.

Rachel knew most of the people who worked in the castle. She knew that none of them would dare to say a word when Six told them that she was now the queen. Everyone was afraid of Violet, because she had people punished and put to death, but everyone was more afraid of Six because she was the one who enforced Violet's whims. Besides, when Six said things to people, they just seemed to lose their ability to do anything but what she'd told them to do. Those who crossed Six seemed to vanish. It occurred to Rachel that the hogs looked well fed.

Rachel thought again about how when Six was slapping Violet, Violet didn't even make an attempt to protect herself with her hands. Rachel knew that Six was a witch woman. Witch women had a way of making people forget how to fight against what was happening. They just did as she said, no matter how much they didn't want to. Like the two guards. They saw the queen on the floor with a bloody nose, calling for help, but they quickly chose to do as Six told them, not Violet.

Rachel sat in her iron box for a while, thinking, worrying, wondering what would become of her.

And then she had a thought.

Carefully, quietly, even though there was no one in the room and the door was closed, she pressed herself tight up against the door. She put one eye right up to the slit. First, she looked around, fearful that the witch woman might somehow be watching her. The witch woman sometimes came to her in the night . . . in her dreams. If Six had materialized in the center of the room, Rachel wouldn't have been at all shocked. There were plenty of whispers among the staff of the strange things that had been happening at the castle since the woman had arrived.

But the room was empty. There was no one there, no tall figure in black robes.

Confident that she was alone, Rachel peered over at the lock. She had to stare awhile, because she wasn't sure that what she was seeing was real.

The lock, hanging in the hasp, wasn't locked.

Rachel remembered Violet pushing at it as Six knocked on the door, but in her haste she must not have gotten it locked. If Rachel could get the lock out of the hasp, she could open the door. She could get out.

Six had taken Violet to the cave. Violet and Six were gone.

Rachel tried to reach through the slit to pull the lock off, but it was too far. She needed a stick, or something to reach it. She cast about inside her sleeping box, but there was nothing. There was no stick just lying around. There were plenty of things outside the box that she could have used, but they were outside the box.

As long as that lock was hooked through the loop of steel sticking out through the slot in the hasp, there was no way Rachel could push open the door. The lock might as well have been locked.

She flopped back down on her blanket, dejected, her hope gone. She missed Chase. For a time her life had been a dream. She had a family, a wonderful father who watched over her and taught her so many things.

Rachel idly pulled on the loose end of the coarse thread that had been used to sew the edging on the blanket. Chase would be disappointed to see her giving up so easily, to see her moping, but what was she to do? There was nothing she had in her box that she could use to get the lock off. She had on a dress, and boots. Her boots wouldn't fit through the slit. The only other thing she had was her sleeping blanket. Violet had taken everything away from her. She had nothing.

As she pulled, more of the heavy thread unraveled. As Rachel looked down at the thread looped around the end of her finger, inspiration struck.

She started pulling at the thread, pulling out the stitches, pulling more of it free. She soon had the entire end of the blanket undone and she had a long length of thread. She doubled it over and rolled it between her palm and leg, twisting it into a heavier thread. It was long enough to make several layers, all rolled together into a sturdy string. She made a loop in the end and then went to the slit.

Carefully, she cast out the string, trying to get the loop over the lock so that she could hook it and pull it up, out of the hasp. It sounded a lot easier than it was. The string wasn't heavy enough to throw with any accuracy. Rachel tried several different ways of doing it, but it always fell short or, if it did get over the top loop of the lock, it just slid off over the side. It just didn't want to go down over the far side to hook the lock's shank. The string was too light to throw well, but at the same time it was too stiff to drape over the lock those times when it did land where she wanted it.

Yet again, she managed to get the end of the string to land over the lock. The end, though, dangled out at an angle rather than lying down where she could slip it over the open shank of the lock.

She brought the string back in and wet it with spit, then tried again. The wet string was a little heavier. She was able to throw it with a little more accuracy. Her hand was getting sore and tired from trying because she had to twist it sideways to cast the string. It seemed she had been at it all morning. The string kept getting dry.

Rachel brought the string back in and wet it in her mouth, getting it good and soaked. She went to the slit and cast it. The first time it landed over the lock. The loop of the string was just below the end of the lock's shank.

Rachel froze. This was as close as she'd ever gotten it. It was difficult to have her hand out of the slit and then to be able to see through the little space that was left over. She could see, though, that if she pulled, the string would be pulled up and not hook over the shank where she needed it to hook.

The string, as wet as it was, was adhering to the long bar that latched when it was locked. Rachel had an idea. She carefully began to roll the string between her finger and thumb. With the string stuck with her spit to the metal, it rolled, sticking, until the end flopped over. Rachel blinked as she stared. It looked like the loop was right where she needed it to be. She was afraid to move, afraid to make a mistake, afraid to lose her chance, afraid to make the wrong move because she hadn't thought it through well enough.

Chase had always told her that she had to use her head—her judgment, he called it—and then act on that judgment.

By every measure she could judge, the loop was in the right place. If she pulled, and the string stayed stuck with her spit to the shank of the lock, the loop would hook over the end of the bar. Her heart pounded in her chest. She realized that she was panting.

Holding her breath, Rachel began ever so carefully to pull the string. The flat end of the metal caught the loop. If she pulled too hard, it might just pop off.

She lowered her fingers to change the angle of the pull, to help it pull the loop over the end, rather than slip off.

The loop stretched tight and then slipped over the end of the lock's shank. She could hardly believe it. Carefully, steadily, she pulled the string upward, sliding the lock up out of the hasp. When it was almost out of the loop of metal, the notched end of the bar on the lock caught the hasp. She tried pulling just a little harder, but with the way it was caught it only made the lock twist at an angle, rather than lift. Rachel feared to pull too hard. She was afraid that the string would break.

She had doubled the thread over several times, making the string several layers thick. She figured that it was probably pretty strong. The question she couldn't answer was how strong it was, and if it was strong enough if she pulled harder. She released some of the tension and let the lock lower, then jerked it a little, twitching it rapidly up and down, trying to jiggle the shaft of the metal bar up through the hoop.

Suddenly, the lock jumped up out of the hasp and fell. It dangled from the string, swinging back and forth beneath Rachel's hand sticking out of the slit.

She pushed, and the door squeaked open. With the backs of her hands, Rachel wiped the tears of relief from her cheeks. She had gotten herself free. If only Chase could have seen what she had accomplished.

Now she had to escape the castle before Violet or Six returned. Rachel didn't know if Violet was aware that she hadn't latched the lock. If she knew she hadn't locked it, and she mentioned it to Six, they would be back.

Rachel immediately headed for the big door, but then she remembered something important. She turned and ran to the desk in the corner. She pulled the angled lid down into the position Violet used when she wrote notes on who was to be punished or put to death. Rachel grabbed the gold knob on the bottom, center drawer and pulled the drawer out. She set it aside, then reached her hand way into the back and felt around. Her fingers touched something metal.

She brought it out. It was the key. Violet hadn't taken it out yet. It was still there, where she kept it for the night.

Relieved, Rachel slipped the key down into her boot and then replaced the door and shut the lid of the desk.

Remembering her sleeping box, she closed the door and put the lock through the hasp. She pushed the lock, making sure it latched closed. She tugged just to make sure that it was secure—something Violet had failed to do. If anyone came in the room they might suspect that Rachel was still safely locked in her box. If she was lucky, Six or Violet wouldn't even look and by then Rachel would be long gone.

She ran to the big double doors and opened one just a sliver to peek out. She didn't see anyone in the hall. She slipped out the door, closing it quietly behind her.

Checking around again, she made for the stairs, then raced up as quietly as she could. On the next floor, in a hallway of wood paneling without windows, Rachel headed for the room that would be locked. There were reflector lights still lit. They were kept lit throughout the night in case the queen ever wanted to go to her jewel room. As she hurried down the hall, she hopped on one foot as she reached down into her boot to retrieve the key.

Key in hand, Rachel looked over her shoulder as she arrived at the door she was looking for. Just then she saw a man in the distance coming down the hall. He was one of the butlers. Rachel knew him by his face, but she didn't know his name.

"Mistress Rachel?" he said, frowning as he reached her.

Rachel nodded. "Yes, what is it?"

"Exactly." He glanced to the door. "What is it?"

Chase had taught her to turn things around on people asking questions she didn't want to answer. He had also taught her how to turn suspicions around to make it look like the other person was up to no good. They'd often made it into a game at camp. She knew that she had to do that now. This time, though, it was not a game. It was deadly serious.

She put on her best scowl. Chase had taught her how to do that, too. He'd said for her to just imagine that a boy wanted to kiss her.

"What does it look like it is?"

The man arched an eyebrow at her. "It looks like you're about to go into the queen's jewel room."

"Do you intend to rob me of the queen's jewels I've been sent to get for her? Is that why you were lurking around the corner, waiting for someone to be sent to the queen's jewel room? So you can rob them?"

"Lurking—rob you—why no, of course not. I merely want to know—"

"You want to know?" Rachel put her hands on her hips. "*You* want to know? Are *you* in charge of the jewels? Why don't *you* go ask Queen Violet what *you* want to know? I'm sure she won't mind a butler questioning her. Maybe she will only have you whipped and not beheaded.

"I'm on her business, getting something for her. Do I need to go get some guards to protect me and the queen's jewels I'm to take back to her?"

"Guards? Why of course not—"

"Then what business have *you* with this business?" She looked one way and then another, but saw no one. "Guards!" she yelled, but not too loudly. "Guards! A thief is after the queen's jewels!"

The man panicked, trying to get her to be quiet, but then abandoned the attempt and rushed off without another word. He never even looked back. Rachel quickly unlocked the door, checked the hall again, and then slipped inside. She didn't think anyone had heard her, but she didn't want to take any more time than necessary.

She didn't give the shiny, polished wall of little wooden drawers a second look. The dozens and dozens of little drawers were filled with necklaces, bracelets, brooches, tiaras, and rings. She immediately went instead to the fancy white marble pedestal that stood by itself in the opposite corner of the jewel room. Atop it had once stood Queen Milena's favorite object, the jeweled box she fawned over at every opportunity.

Now in its place was a box that looked like it was made of the Keeper's blackest thoughts. It was so black that the room filled with precious jewels seemed trivial in the presence of something so monumentally sinister.

Rachel had hated touching Queen Milena's jeweled box of Orden. She hated the thought of touching this even more.

She had to do it, though.

She knew she had to hurry if she was to have any chance of getting away. There was no telling if Violet would remember that the iron sleeping box in her room hadn't been locked. She might tell Six—or Six might just read her thoughts. Rachel suspected that Six was capable of doing such things. If they knew Rachel wasn't locked in that box, they would come back.

Rachel took the black box down off the white marble pedestal and stuffed it into the leather bag that was sitting against the wall. It was the same bag that Samuel had used to bring Six the box.

On the way to the door, Rachel paused before the tall, wood-framed mirror. She hated looking at herself in the mirror, hated seeing her hair, the way that Violet had chopped it all off. When she had lived at the castle before, back when she had been Princess Violet's playmate, Rachel hadn't been allowed to let her hair grow because she was a nobody. As soon as Violet had Rachel back, one of the first things she did was take a big pair of shears and chop off Rachel's long, beautiful blond hair. This was the first time she had really had a chance to get a good look at it, though, an up-close look.

She wiped tears from her cheek.

Chase had told her, when she first went with him, that if she wanted to be his daughter she would have to let her hair grow. Her hair had grown long and lustrous over the last couple of years, and she felt as if she really had grown to be his daughter. She didn't look the same in the mirror, now, as she had the last time she had stood in this room, looking at herself in the mirror when she had been helping Wizard Giller steal the jeweled box of Orden. Her features were different now. Less childlike, less . . . cute.

Now she was starting the gangly phase, as Chase called it, before she would bloom into the beauty of being a woman that he promised she would one day. That day seemed an impossibly long way off. Besides, without Chase, no one would be there to see her grow up, or care.

Now Chase was dead and her hair was chopped off again. Violet had not simply chopped it off, either, but had cut it in ragged cuts, bits and pieces, chunks and wads. It made her look like a cur dog that slept beside the midden heap. There was something else, though, that Rachel saw in that mirror. She saw the woman she would be one day, the woman Chase promised she would be.

What would Chase think if he could see her now, with her hair all chopped up?

Rachel pushed her thoughts to the back of her mind and swung the leather bag held closed with a drawstring over her shoulder. She opened the door just enough to look down the hall, then opened it a little more to look the other way. Still all clear. She hurriedly went out into the hall, and closed and locked the door.

She remembered the halls and passageways of the castle as well as she remembered the curve of Chase's smile when she made him smile when he tried not to. She always like that best when he laughed when he was trying to scowl at her.

She took the servants' stairs so as to avoid the most guards. They stayed mostly to the main halls and such. People were going about their duties without pause. None of them yet knew that there was a new queen. She didn't know what people would think of such a thing. Rachel knew that people hated Violet, but they were terrified of Six.

Washwomen carrying bundles turned as they gossiped, watching Rachel run past. Men carrying supplies didn't pay her any attention. Rachel didn't meet the eyes of any of them lest they ask her something.

She reached the door out into a side hall that had a way out of the castle. She went around a corner and came face-to-face with two guards. They wore the red tunics over their chain mail and carried pikes with gleaming points. Swords hung from their belts.

Rachel could clearly see that they had no intention of letting her pass without finding out what she was doing there and where she was going.

"You must get away!" Rachel cried out at them. "Hurry!" She turned and pointed behind her. "The Imperial Order troops are entering the castle—back that way!"

One of the men gripped his pike with both hands and rested his weight on it. "We have nothing to fear from those men. They're our allies."

"They intend to behead all the queen's guards! I heard the commander giving them their orders! Behead them all, he said! More for us, he said. The soldiers all drew their big battle-axes. They were told they could keep anything on the men they behead. Hurry! They're coming! Save yourselves!"

Both men's mouths fell open.

"That way!" Rachel shouted, pointing toward the servants' stairs. "They won't think to look there. Hurry! I'll warn the others!"

The men nodded their thanks and headed for the door to the servants' stairs. When they had vanished, Rachel started out once more, quickly making the door out of the castle. She took to the pathway that the servants used when going to town to get things they needed for the running of the castle. There were big soldiers, fearsome-looking men, who were patrolling everywhere, but they didn't seem to be bothering the servants, so Rachel fell in with some carpenters and walked along beside the tall wheel of their handcart. She hid her face behind the load of boards.

The soldiers paid only casual interest to the servants going about their work, mostly watching the prettier women. Rachel kept her head down and kept walking. With her hair all chopped off she looked like a nobody, and none of the soldiers stopped her.

Once beyond the big stone wall, she kept walking along with the servants until they went through a patch of woods that was right up close to the path. She glanced back over her shoulder and didn't see any soldiers looking her way.

Quick as a cat, Rachel slipped into the trees. As soon as she was in among the thick balsams and pines, she started running. She took deer paths through the bramble, following any she could find that went west or north. Once she was running, panic came out of nowhere and took control of her legs. All she could think about was getting away. This was her chance. She had to run.

If the Imperial Order soldiers caught her out here, she knew that she would be in trouble. She wasn't sure what they would do to her, but she had a pretty good general idea. Chase had given her those lessons one dark night by the campfire. He told her something of what men like that would do to her.

He told her not to let herself get caught by men like that. He told her that if she was facing such men, and capture, she had to fight them with everything she had. Chase said that he hadn't meant to scare her, but hoped to keep her safe. Still, it made her cry and she only felt better when he sheltered her under his big arm.

She realized that she had nothing with which to fight. Her knives had all been taken away. She wished she had been smarter and before she left the castle had taken a quick look in Violet's room to see if she could find any of her knives. She was so eager to get away that she never thought of it. She should have at least gone through the kitchens when she'd been down in the service areas and gotten a knife. She was so busy congratulating herself over a piece of string, and that she had gotten away, that she had never thought about getting a weapon. Chase was probably angry enough to come back to life and scold her for being so thoughtless. Her face burned with shame.

She stopped when she saw a stout branch lying on the ground. She picked it up and tested its strength. It seemed sound. She whacked it against a fir tree and it made a solid sound. It was a little heavier than she would have wanted to carry, but at least she had something.

She slowed to a trot and kept moving, trying to put as much distance between her and the castle as she could. She didn't know when they would discover her missing, and she didn't know if Six could track as well as she could do everything else. Rachel wondered if Six might be able to gaze into a bowl of water and see where Rachel was. That made her run faster again.

By early afternoon she came across a trail. It looked like it headed roughly north. She knew that Aydindril was somewhere to the north. She didn't know if she could find something that far away, but she couldn't think of anywhere else to go. If she could get back to the Keep, back to Zedd, he would help her.

She was so deep in thought that she didn't even see the man until she almost ran into him. She looked up and realized that it was an Imperial Order soldier.

"Well, well, what have we here?"

As he started to reach down for her, Rachel swung the club with all her strength, whacking him across the knee. The man cried out and fell to the ground, clutching his knee, shouting curses at her.

Rachel tore off running. She took to the deer paths again because she was smaller and it was easier for her to negotiate them than it would be for big men. It sounded like there were suddenly a dozen men after her, crashing through the brush. She could hear the man she had clubbed far back, still cursing up a storm, yelling at his fellows to get her.

As she burst into a clearing, winded and nearly out of strength, she saw that there were men blocking the path ahead. They all started for her.

Rachel ducked to the side and ran. It seemed like there were soldiers all around. She was in a panic, not knowing how to get away from them.

She heard one man fall. She didn't look back, but kept running. She heard another fall, crying out briefly, then going silent. She wondered if, when running at breakneck speed, they were catching their feet in holes, or twisting ankles on low vines.

Another man let out a grunt. This time Rachel stopped and turned just long enough for a quick look. It had not been a fall, or a twisted ankle. It had been a sound released in death. Rachel's eyes were wide as she stared. Another man shrieked like he was being skinned alive.

Rachel wondered what kind of woods she was in, and what monsters were loose in them.

She turned and ran. She had no chance if the men got her. She didn't know what else was about, but she first had to keep from getting caught or they were liable to slit her throat for giving them a difficult time.

Suddenly, three men charged out of the brush, roaring in rage. A little cry squeaked out as Rachel ran with all her strength and fear. The men, though, had longer legs and were catching her.

One of them stopped suddenly. Rachel glanced back over a shoulder and saw the man arching his back, as if in pain. She saw, then, a foot of steel jutting from his chest. The other two turned to the unexpected attack from behind.

As the man who had been run through with a sword started to fall, Rachel's jaw fell open at what she saw behind him.

It was Chase, big as life.

She couldn't make sense of it.

The two men charged him. Chase fought them with swift, powerful strikes, taking them both down as if doing no more than brushing aside pests, but at the same time more men poured out of the woods around them. She saw at least a half dozen of the big Imperial Order soldiers to one side alone charging the even bigger boundary warden.

Rachel ran back as Chase fought all the men at once. When he killed a man to his side, a man to the other side used the opening to go for him. Rachel whacked the backs of his knees. His legs folded under him. Chase swung around and ran the man though, then met the fierce charge of yet more men, all of them grunting with the effort of trying to take down this one big man. They gritted their teeth as they growled and tried to grapple Chase's arms so other men could stab him. Rachel waled away at them with all her strength, but to no avail.

When one of the men fell dead, Rachel snatched the knife in a sheath at his belt and immediately stabbed the legs of a man going for Chase's back. He cried out and turned. Chase took him in an instant.

All of a sudden it was quiet, except for Rachel and Chase's labored breathing. All the men lay dead.

Rachel stood staring up at Chase. She couldn't believe what she was seeing, couldn't believe her eyes. She feared that he might vanish, like a phantom.

He looked down at her, and that wonderful grin of his came over his face.

"Chase, what are you doing here?"

"I came to see if you were all right."

"All right? I was held captive in the castle. I thought you were dead. I had to rescue myself. What took you so long?"

He shrugged. "I wouldn't have wanted to spoil your accomplishment. Isn't it better that you did it on your own?"

"Well," she said, a bit perplexed, "I could have used some help."

"Is that so?" He appeared unmoved by her complaint. "You look to have managed."

"But you don't know. It was terrible. They locked me up in the box again, and they locked my tongue so that I couldn't talk."

Chase eyed her askance. "I don't suppose you brought that tongue lock with you, did you? It sounds like a useful device."

Rachel grinned and hugged him around his waist. When she had first met him she had to hug his leg because that was all she could reach. She basked in the comfort of his big hand on her back. It felt like everything in the world was right again.

"I thought you were dead," she said as she started to cry.

He ruffled her chopped-off hair. "I wouldn't do that to you, little one. I promised to take care of you, and I meant it."

"I guess that I'm stuck with being your daughter."

"Guess so. Your hair is ugly, though. You'll have to grow it back if you want to stay with me. You can't keep chopping it off like that if you want to be my daughter. I told you that before."

Rachel grinned through her tears.

Chase was alive.

With Cara right on her heels, Nicci strode through the immense brass-clad doors covered in elaborate, engraved symbols. A flickering flash of lightning came in through the dozen round-topped windows between the towering mahogany columns to illuminate row upon row of shelves all around the cavernous room. They had managed to patch only the worst of the damage to the two-story-tall windows—enough, they hoped, that the room could be used for its intended purpose as a containment field. Some of the heavy dark green velvet draperies with gold fringe were getting wet as rain blew in the remaining holes on some of the stronger gusts.

Seeing what was in the center of the room, floating above the large table Nicci had once floated above herself, she hoped that a bit of errant rain would be all that came in through those missing parts of the windows.

Rushing to meet her, Zedd gripped her shoulders. Desperation was clearly evident in his eyes.

"Did you find him? He's alive, isn't he? Is he all right?"

Nicci took a breath. "Zedd, he survived the events in the sliph—I at least found out that much."

The sliph had also already told them that much. Rikka had been there, guarding the well, when the sliph had unexpectedly returned. They were all surprised that the sliph had returned at all, much less returned to tell them what had happened.

The silver creature had abruptly been eager to talk—up to a point—to tell them what had happened to Richard. It wasn't because the sliph wanted to tell where she had been with one of her travelers, but rather that Richard, her master, had told the sliph to tell them that he was safe and where he had gone. She was eager to do his bidding.

Unfortunately, the sliph's nature was to be secretive, and they weren't able to get straight answers from her on much more of it. Zedd had said that the sliph wasn't being perverse; she simply couldn't help the way others had created her. She was being true to her nature. He said that they would just have to go along with the sliph's way of revealing information and do their best to learn what they could from her.

Zedd had also detected on the sliph the trace residue power left by a witch woman. They were pretty sure that it had to be Six. They weren't sure what Six was up to, but at least they knew from the sliph that Richard had somehow escaped her clutches.

"But where is he? Did the sliph take you there? Take you where she said she left him?"

"She did." Nicci glanced at the Mord-Sith and then laid a hand on Zedd's shoulder. "After we got to the place where the sliph had taken him, she then told us where he had gone: to the land of the night wisps. We still had to travel some distance to get there."

Zedd stared in astonishment. "The night wisps?"

"Yes. But Richard wasn't there."

"At least he's alive. It sounds like he was acting on his own volition, and not that of a witch woman," Zedd said, sounding a little relieved. "What did they say? What were the wisps able to tell you?"

Nicci heaved a sigh. "I wish you could travel so that you could have gone there, Zedd. Maybe they would have told you more than they would tell us. They wouldn't even allow us to enter beyond this strange, dead forest."

"Dead forest? What dead forest?"

Nicci lifted her hands. "I don't know, Zedd. I'm no expert in the out-doors. There was this vast area of oaks but they were all dead—"

"The oak wood is dead?" Zedd leaned closer to her. "Are you serious? The oaks are dead?"

Nicci shrugged. "I guess. They were oak trees. Richard taught me what an oak was. These were all dead, though."

Zedd glanced away as he scratched an eyebrow. "Were there bones among these oaks?"

"Yes, that's right," Cara said, nodding. "There were bones scattered everywhere among those dead trees."

"Bags," Zedd cursed under his breath.

"Why?" Nicci asked. "What is it?"

Zedd looked up. "But you talked to the wisps?"

Nicci nodded. "Tam, he said his name was."

Zedd rubbed his chin as he stared off in thought. "Tam . . . don't know him."

"There was another, named Jass," Nicci added.

Zedd's mouth twisted as he considered the name. "I'm afraid I don't know that one, either."

"Jass said that Richard was looking for a woman that the wisps should know."

"That would have to be Kahlan," Zedd said with a knowing nod.

"That's what we figured, too," Cara said.

"But why would he go to the wisps to look for her?" His question sounded more for himself than for Nicci, but she answered it anyway.

"The sliph wouldn't tell us about any of that part, only where she took him. Apparently, Richard wasn't specific enough about what he instructed the sliph to tell us. She won't go beyond her explicit instructions. Like you said, it's her nature.

"The wisps wouldn't tell us why he had been there, either. They said that his reasons for being there were his own and were not necessarily for others to know. They said that they couldn't reveal such things on his behalf."

"Not for others—but, but . . ." His voice ended in sputtering agitation. Zedd looked back at both of them. "But didn't they tell you anything about what Richard was doing there? Anything at all? We have to know why he would go to the wisps. He was on his way here, and then something happened to cost him his gift while traveling—probably something involving Six—so he went to the wisps? Why? What did they tell him? What happened when he was there?"

"I'm sorry, Zedd," Nicci said. "We really weren't able to find out much. The sliph did tell us some of it—what happened to Richard, where she took him, and that he went to the wisps—but she either doesn't know anything more, or she simply doesn't want to tell us the rest of it for some reason. Richard never returned to the sliph, but because he can no longer travel that only makes sense. It could be that the sliph really doesn't know any more.

"Richard would probably have started out on foot. I imagine he would head back here, to the Keep. After all, that's where he was going when something went wrong in the sliph. For some reason he went to the wisps, but that may have had more to do with geography than anything else—he was much closer to them than coming all the way back here, so he may have decided to make a quick stop there before heading back to us. It may be nothing more than that.

"As far as the wisps, they wouldn't tell us much either. They wouldn't let us go beyond the dead trees, into those huge, ancient trees beyond. But there is some good news in it. We at least know for sure that Richard is alive, and that he went to the land of the wisps. That's what matters—Richard is alive. Knowing Richard, he will try to find a horse as soon as possible and will probably show up here before we know it."

Zedd squeezed her arm. "You're right, my dear." It was a gesture that Nicci found comforting, almost as if it were a connection to Richard himself. It was the kind of reassurance Richard himself would have offered at such a troubling moment.

Zedd suddenly frowned. "You said the wisps wouldn't let you into the big pines?"

Nicci nodded. "That's right. They wouldn't let us proceed any farther than the dead oak woods, or allow us to see the other wisps."

"In a way it makes sense." Zedd ran a finger up along his temple as he considered. "The wisps are secretive creatures, and don't generally allow anyone into their land, but it seems odd under the circumstances—and with word from me—that they wouldn't welcome you in."

"They're dying."

Zedd's eyes turned up at her. "What?"

"Tam said that the wisps were dying out and that was why they didn't want us to enter. He said that it's a time of great strife among the wisps, great sadness and worry. They didn't want strangers among them right now."

"Dear spirits," Zedd whispered. "Richard was right."

Nicci's insides tightened with anxiety. "What are you talking about? Richard is right about what?"

"The oaks dying. They protect the land of the wisps. The wisps are dying, too. It's part of a cascade of events. Richard already told us why, in this very room. As if I needed yet more reason to believe him."

"Yet more reason? What do you mean by that?"

He took Nicci's elbow and turned her toward the spell-forms floating above the table. "Look here."

"Zedd," Nicci said in admonition, "that's the Chainfire verification web—and it looks suspiciously like an interior perspective."

"That's right."

"I know I'm right. The question is, what's going on? What are you up to?"

"I found a way to ignite a kind of simulation of an interior perspective—one without you needing to be in it. It isn't the same in every respect," he said with a dismissive gesture, "but for the purpose I had in mind it was good enough."

Nicci was astonished that he had been able to do such a thing. It was also somewhat disquieting to again see the very thing that had almost taken her life. But that wasn't at all what she found most disturbing.

"Why are there two of them?" she asked. "There is only one Chainfire spell. Why are there two spell-forms here?"

Zedd flashed her a wry smile. "Ah, there is the trick of it. You see, Richard claimed that the chimes had been present in the world of life. If that were true, their presence would have contaminated the world of life, would have contaminated magic. And yet none of us has seen any evidence of it. That is the paradox of such contamination; it erodes your ability to detect its presence. I wanted to find a way to see if Richard was right—"

"Richard Rahl is right."

Zedd shrugged one bony shoulder at her emphatic declaration. "But I needed to see if I could actually find any evidence. I didn't understand all that emblem business Richard was going on about. I believe in him too, Nicci, but I don't understand how he can see language in symbols the way he does, how he was able to come to the conclusions that he does. I need to see proof I understand."

Nicci folded her arms as she stared at the twin spell-forms. "I guess I know how you feel. I believe in him, and he makes sense, but I sometimes feel lost, like I used to as a novice when there would be a test on things that were taught when I hadn't been in class. When Richard . . ."

Nicci fell silent. Her arms came unfolded.

"Zedd, those two spell-forms aren't the same."

His smile grew sly. "I know that."

Nicci stepped closer to the table, closer to the two forms made of glowing lines. She inspected them more carefully. She pointed at one.

"That one is the Chainfire spell. I recognize it. This other is identical, but it's not the same. It's a mirror image of the real spell."

"I know." He looked rather proud of himself.

"That's impossible."

"I thought so too, but then I remembered a book named *The Book of Inversion and Duplex*—"

Nicci rounded on the old wizard. "You know where *The Book of Inversion and Duplex* is?"

Zedd gestured vaguely. "Well, yes, I managed to lay my hands on a copy."

Nicci eyed him suspiciously. "Lay your hands on a copy?"

Zedd cleared his throat. "The point is," he said, taking her arm and turning her back to the glowing lines and the subject at hand, "I remembered from reading that book many, many years ago that it talked about techniques to duplex spell-forms. It never made any sense to me at the time. Why would anyone want to duplex a spell-form?

"But there was more. The book went on to give instructions on how to invert the spell-form that had first been duplexed. Craziest thing I'd ever heard of. At the time I dismissed the book and its obscure procedures. What could be the purpose of such a thing? Who would ever need to do such a thing? No one, I thought."

He held up a finger. "And then, when thinking about the possibility of contamination left by the chimes, and trying to think of a way to prove Richard's theory, I suddenly remembered reading that book once, and it hit me. I knew why someone would want to duplicate and invert a spell-form."

Nicci was getting lost. "All right, I give up. Why?"

Zedd gestured excitedly to the two spell-forms. "This is why. Look. This one is the original, much like the one you were in, but without some of the more complex and unstable elements." Zedd waved a hand, stressing that it was beside the point. "We don't need them for this purpose. This one, here, is the exact same spell, duplicated, and then inverted. It's a copy."

"I understand that much of it," Nicci said, "but I still don't see what purpose it could serve to perform such a strange analysis."

Smiling knowingly, Zedd touched his fingers to the side of her shoulder. "Flaws."

"Flaws? What about—" Nicci gasped with comprehension. "When you turn a spell inside out and backward, the flaw won't invert!"

"That's right," Zedd said with an impish twinkle and an instructive shake of his first finger. "The flaw won't invert. It can't. The spell-form is just a demonstration of the spell, a surrogate for something real. Therefore it can be manipulated—inverted. It's not the real spell; you couldn't invert a real spell. But flaws are not subject to the influence of the magic in books of instruction—only the specific, target magic is. The flaw is real. The flaw resides whole."

Zedd turned solemn with the deadly serious nature of the material issue. "When the spell-form is activated, it carries with it the flaw, which is already embedded. When you duplicate the spell-form it carries the same flaw, but then when you invert it, the flaw can't invert because it's real, not a stand-in for something real like spell-forms are. Don't forget, that contamination was what nearly killed you."

Nicci looked from Zedd's intense hazel eyes to the two glowing spell-forms. They were mirrored. She started searching the structure, seeing each line, each element, looking to the other spell-form that was the same, but flipped.

And then she saw it.

"There," She breathed, pointing. "That part there is identical in both. It's not flipped. It's not a mirror image like everything else. It's the same in both of these while everything else is inverted."

"Exactly," Zedd said in triumph. "Hence, the purpose of *The Book of Inversion and Duplex*—to discover flaws that can't otherwise be seen or detected."

Nicci stared at the old man, seeing him in a new light. She had known of *The Book of Inversion and Duplex*, but, like everyone else who had studied it, she had never understood its purpose. There had been debate about it, of course, but no one could ever offer a purpose for such an esoteric book of magic. It defied the conventional wisdom on the functioning and purpose of magic. In the end it had been dismissed as a mere curiosity from a time past. In fact, it had been presented in lectures as just that, an oddity, a relic of ancient times, useless, but nonetheless an object of note simply because it had survived.

Zedd, like Richard, never dismissed any bit of knowledge. Like all knowledge collected, he kept it cataloged somewhere in the back of his mind in case it ever came up again. When he had trouble finding an answer he would check his memory of forgotten things residing in an index in some dusty corner of his mind.

Richard did the same thing. Knowledge, once acquired, remained in his arsenal. It enabled him to put things together in new ways, to come up with surprising solutions that often challenged old, established ways of doing things. Many people found such a way of thinking, especially when it had to do with magic, treading dangerously close to heresy.

Nicci saw its true value. Real answers to problems came from just such a process of thought, logic, and reason—all based on what was known. It was the essence of a Seeker, the foundation of what he did in his search for truth. It was also one of the central qualities about Richard that so captivated Nicci. He was a student without formal training who was able to intuitively grasp the most complex issues in a way no one else could.

Zedd leaned in, pulling Nicci with him. "Look here. See this? Do you recognize it?"

"The part that didn't invert?" Nicci shook her head. "No. What is it?"

"It's the contamination left by the chimes. This, I recognize. This is the spider in the web of magic."

Nicci straightened. "This proves that Richard was right, then."

"The boy got it right," Zedd agreed. "I don't really understand how, but he had it exactly right. Once it's isolated like this, I recognize the corrosion left by the chimes, the same as I recognize the reddish brown scale of rust. He was able to see it in the language of the lines, and he was right. The spell is contaminated; the source of that contamination was the chimes. This is the mechanism by which the chimes erode and destroy magic. If it has infected this spell, it has to have infected other things of magic as well."

"Is that what's killing the night wisps?" Cara asked.

"I'm afraid it would seem that way," Zedd told her. "The oaks around their home place are also invested with protective magic. That both the oaks and the wisps are dying out together is suspicious in the extreme."

Nicci walked to the windows, watching the indistinct fits of lightning through the opaque glass. "Creatures of magic are dying out. Just as Richard told us."

She missed him so much that mournful anguish passed through her like the shadow of death itself darkening her soul. She felt like she would shrivel and die if they didn't find him soon. She felt like she could not survive if she never got the chance to see him again, see the life in his gray eyes.

"Zedd, do you think he was right about the rest of it? Do you think that there really were dragons, and we've all forgotten that there were such things in the world? Do you think Richard was right that the world we knew is passing out of existence, vanishing into the realm of legend?"

Zedd sighed. "I don't know, my dear, I really don't. I'd like to think the boy is wrong in that much of it, but I learned a long time ago not to bet against Richard."

Nicci smiled to herself. She had learned the same thing.

Nicci," Zedd said, hesitating as he gestured vaguely, seeming to search for words, "you are . . . well, someone who holds Richard in the same regard as I do, feels a similar passion and loyalty for him. In many ways you almost seem like . . ." He threw his hands up and let them flop back down at his sides. "I don't know."

"Zedd, you, Cara, me—we all love Richard, if that's what you're trying to say."

"I guess that's the core of it. I don't have any recollection at all of Kahlan, but I imagine I must think of you in much the same way I can only imagine I must have thought of her, as more than just his confidante sharing the same struggle."

Nicci felt as if she had just been hit by lightning. She dared not allow herself to even begin to consider the emotional charge in his words. With the greatest of difficulty, she managed to keep her composure and merely twitch her brow, finally asking, "What are you getting at?"

"Like Cara and Richard, I've come to think a great deal of you, especially considering what I thought of you in the beginning. I've come to trust you, like I say, as I would trust a daughter-in-law."

Nicci swallowed but didn't meet his gaze. "Thank you, Zedd. Considering where I came from, and what I thought of myself in the beginning, that means more to me than you could know. To have people actually, sincerely . . ."

She cleared her throat and finally looked up at him. Despite how his words hit her, she didn't think that he meant them to have any meaning, but merely to preface something important. "You want to tell me something?"

He nodded. "I've learned some other things. Greatly disturbing things. I would not tell anyone else such things, but, well, other than Richard himself there is no one I would trust more than you and Cara. You two have become more than friends in all of this. I'm only trying to find a way to express to you how much . . ."

When his words trailed away and he stared off into the distance, Nicci gently laid a hand on his shoulder. "We'll get him back, Zedd, I promise you that. But you're right in how we feel about him. Richard completely changed my life. If there's something you need to talk about, I would like to think that you can trust Cara and me almost as much as you would trust Richard. I think that's what you're getting at? We all feel the same about him, and about our cause. I . . . well"—she tapped her fingertips together— "you know what I mean."

Fearing she'd already said too much, Nicci felt her face turning red.

"What I'm trying to say," Zedd finally said, "is that I need your help, and I want you to know what you both mean to me—that I do not now re- veal these things lightly or capriciously. All my life I've kept secrets be- cause they had to be kept. It's not the easiest thing to do, but that's just the way it was. Things have changed, though, and I can no longer keep certain knowledge to myself. There is so much more involved now than there ever was before."

Nicci nodded and turned her full attention to the wizard. "I understand. I'll do what I can to be worthy of your trust."

Zedd pursed his lips. "That book, *The Book of Inversion and Duplex*, was hidden in a place no one but me knows exists. It was in the catacombs beneath the Keep."

Nicci shared a look with Cara. "Zedd," she asked, "are you saying that there are bones beneath the Keep? And there are books there as well?"

Zedd nodded. "A lot of books. That was where I found *The Book of In- version and Duplex*."

He took a few steps away to stare at the windows flickering with light from the storm beyond the containment field. "No one that I'm aware of ever knew the place of the bones was down there. I found it when I was a boy. I knew that no other person had been in there for ages. Not a single footprint had marred the dust on the floors in thousands of years. I was the first to make a mark in that dust of ages. I did not need to be told the sig- nificance of that fact.

"As a boy it rather frightened me to find those ancient catacombs. I was already spooked because I was trying to find a way to sneak back into the Keep. When I found the catacombs I knew instinctively that it would not be hidden as it was unless there was a good reason, so, as much as I wanted to at times, I never told anyone about it. I almost felt as if the place had allowed me entry, but in return required my silence. I not only took my attitude of responsibility seriously, I felt genuinely protective of such an undiscovered place. It contained, after all, the remains of a great many people—perhaps even my own ancestors. I knew that there were always those who would exploit such a find and I didn't want that to happen to a place so clearly held in sacred regard by those who had hidden it.

"Added to that, I felt rather guilty for having disturbed such a burial place for the feeble reason of trying to sneak back in to avoid getting in trouble for having gone out without permission in the first place. I had slipped out of the Keep to go to the market down in Aydindril to look at all the exciting baubles being hawked there. It seemed so much more fascinating than the dry studies to which I was supposed to be devoting my time.

"After my chance discovery, I quietly asked veiled questions and found that not even the old wizards I knew had any knowledge of the place beneath the Keep. Over time, I came to realize that such a place was not even suspected, much less rumored to exist.

"As a boy, I had a lot of studies that took up nearly all my time. Back then, there were many people living in the Keep, and with my assignments I never had a chance to spend—in total—more than a couple of hours down there. I quickly found that there were many of the same books that we had up in the Keep, so, as a boy, I came to believe that it wasn't as important a find as I had at first believed it to be."

He smiled distantly. "I fancied myself a great explorer, discovering ancient treasures. This treasure was mostly bones and books. There were endless dry books up here in the Keep that I had to study, so yet more books wasn't exactly as exciting as thoughts of constructed spells encased in amber, or jewel-encrusted curses. But there was none of that down there. Just crumbling bones and old books.

"There are rooms upon rooms down in the catacombs filled with dusty old books. I never had much time to explore those rooms. I can't even begin to guess at the numbers of books hidden down there. I never had time to do more than look at a small sampling. As I said, many I'd seen before up in the Keep and of the ones I hadn't, at such a young age, none of them impressed me enough to remember, except a few, such as *The Book of Inversion and Duplex.*

"When I grew up I fell in love with the most wonderful woman and soon she was my wife. She gave birth to the other light in my life, a daughter—who grew up to be Richard's mother. As a young wizard working at the Keep, there was always more to do than there were hours in the day. There was no time to spend down among old bones.

"And then the world was cast into a terrible war with D'Hara. It was a dark time of terrible struggle. I had become First Wizard. The battles were gruesome as battles always are. I had to send men to die. I had to look into the eyes of wizards, young and old, that I knew were not up to the challenges, and tell them to do their best when I knew their best would not be good enough, and they would likely die in the effort. I knew in my heart that if I were to do it myself it would get done and I could make it work, but there were a lot of those kinds of tasks that needed to be done, and only one of me.

"At times, I found responsibility, knowledge, and ability were a curse. To look at all the innocent people counting on me as First Wizard, and know that if I failed they would die, was almost more than I could endure.

"In that respect, I know exactly what Richard is going through. I have been in his place. I have carried the world on my shoulders."

He gestured to dismiss his melancholy departure from the subject at hand. "Anyway, with all my other responsibilities, the catacombs lay mostly forgotten, as they had for thousands of years before I ever came along. I simply had no time to look into what might be down there. From my limited search as a boy I believed that there was nothing to be found but old and comparatively unimportant books buried along with forgotten bones. There seemed to be so many more pressing matters of life and death.

"To me, the most important thing about the catacombs was that they provided a secret passage for me to enter the Keep. That passage came to be invaluable when the Sisters of the Dark took the Wizard's Keep.

"Back when I was younger, after the war in which my wife had died, the council and I had a bitter dispute over the boxes of Orden. And then . . . Darken Rahl raped my daughter. So I left the Midlands—quit it for good—taking my daughter with me through the boundary to Westland. She was all I had left and all that mattered to me. I thought I would live out all my days beyond the boundary in Westland.

"Then Richard was born. I watched him grow. My daughter was so proud of him. I secretly worried that he had the gift, and fretted that forces from beyond the boundaries would one day come for him. And then, there was a fire and all of a sudden my daughter, Richard's mother, was gone from my life, from Richard's life.

"I turned to Richard for solace. I gave him everything I could that would help him be all he could be. I had some of the best times of my life with him.

"Unbeknownst to me as I did my best to forget the outside world, Ann and Nathan, driven by prophecy, had helped George Cypher recover *The Book of Counted Shadows* from the Wizard's Keep. It had been stored in the First Wizard's private enclave, where I had left it for safekeeping."

"Wait a minute," Nicci said, stopping his story. "You mean to tell me that *The Book of Counted Shadows*, one of the most important books in existence, was just lying around in the Keep?"

"Well," he said, "not exactly 'lying around.' Like I said, it was in the First Wizard's enclave. That's more secure than the Keep in general and not exactly an easy place to breach."

"If it's so secure," Nicci reminded him, "then how did Ann and Nathan and George Cypher get in to take the book?"

Zedd sighed as he looked up at her from under his bushy eyebrows. "Therein lies what has come to trouble me—the only copy of a book that important being that vulnerable—"

"That's what Richard was going to tell you," Nicci said with a sudden flash of comprehension. "That's why he was in such a hurry to get back here—he said he had to get to you right away. That was the reason!"

Zedd frowned. "What are you talking about?"

She stepped closer to the wizard and pulled the small book from her pocket. "This is the book that Darken Rahl used to put the boxes of Orden in play—"

"It's what!"

"This is the book that Darken Rahl used to put the boxes of Orden in play," she repeated to the astonished wizard. "We found it at the People's Palace. I promised Richard that I would study it and see if there was a way to undo what Sister Ulicia had done, see if there was a way to perhaps take the boxes of Orden back out of play. I tried to explain to Richard that magic doesn't work that way, but you know Richard, he doesn't so easily accept that something can't be done."

Zedd stared at the book she was holding up as if it were a viper that might bite someone. "That boy has a way of turning over rocks and finding trouble."

"Zedd, this warns that to use this book, the key must be used. Otherwise, without the key, everything that has come before, meaning what has been used from this book, will not only be sterile, but fatal. It says that within one full year the key must be used to complete what has been wrought with this book."

"The key," Zedd whispered, as if it were the end of the world. "The boxes must be opened within one year of being put into play. You need *The Book of Counted Shadows* to open the boxes. That book has to be the key."

"I think so, too," Nicci said. "The thing is, we found information from back at the time of the great war saying that some wizards had made five copies of 'the book that was never to be copied.' "

"And you think that 'the book that was never to be copied' was *The Book of Counted Shadows*?"

"Yes. There is a book of prophecy that says 'They will tremble in fear at what they have done and cast the shadow of the key among the bones.' "

Zedd was staring at her as if his world were crumbling apart. "Dear spirits. That sounds like it's from *Yanklee's Yarns*."

"That's right. The thing is," Nicci said, "all the copies but one were false copies. Five copies—four false, one true copy."

Zedd pressed a hand to his forehead. Nicci noticed that his breathing was faster than normal. He looked on the verge of passing out.

"Zedd, what is it?"

His fingers were trembling. "You know what you said about *The Book of Counted Shadows* being too easy to steal? That was always my thought too, but not something I consciously dwelled on. It was more one of those thoughts in the back of your mind that never fully surfaces."

"Yes," Nicci said, waiting patiently until he went on.

"Well, when I remembered *The Book of Inversion and Duplex*, I finally remembered where I had seen it as a boy: the catacombs. I needed it to test this spell, so while you were gone with Richard to the People's Palace I went back into the catacombs and looked for *The Book of Inversion and Duplex*."

Nicci knew what he was going to say before he said it.

"And while I was searching for *The Book of Inversion and Duplex*, I found a copy of *The Book of Counted Shadows*."

" 'They will tremble in fear at what they have done and cast the shadow of the key among the bones,' " Nicci quoted again.

Zedd nodded. "All my life, I never knew there was a copy of that book. I had been taught that there were no other copies. I had been taught that there was only one copy. That alone told me how important that book was. But if it's so important, then why was it not in a safer place? That question was what always stuck in the back of my mind.

"That was one of the reasons I was so angry with the council for giving the boxes of Orden away as gifts or favors. I knew how dangerous those boxes were, but no one would believe me. They all thought that the things I told them were only ancient superstitions, or children's tales.

"Part of the reason that no one believed the truth of the danger that the boxes represented was that the book that was needed to put the boxes in play had never been found. Without the book, the boxes were only a fanciful tale." He pointed at the book in Nicci's hand. "In fact, no one ever even knew the name of that book. The title looks to be in High D'Haran. We'll need someone to translate it."

"I can read High D'Haran," Nicci said.

"Of course you can," Zedd said as if nothing could surprise him anymore. "What is its name, then?"

"*The Book of Life.*"

Zedd turned nearly as white as his wavy hair. Apparently, he was not yet beyond shock. "*The Book of Life,*" he repeated as he wiped a hand wearily across his face.

"What an appropriate name," he said. "The power of Orden is spawned from life itself. Open the correct box, and one gains the power of Orden—the essence of life itself, power over all things living and dead. They would have unchallenged power. Open the wrong box, and the magic would claim them—they're dead. But open the other wrong box, and every living thing in existence is incinerated into nothingness. It would be the end of all life.

"The magic of Orden is twin to the magic of life itself, and death is part of everything that lives, so the magic of Orden is tied to death as well as to life. And the key is the means to know which box is which. The person opening them can take a chance, but they would be foolish to do so without using the key first, to be sure of which is which."

"Foolish," Nicci said, "like Sisters of the Dark who don't necessarily care if they open the wrong box?"

Zedd could only stare at her.

"So, you were saying that you found one of the copies," Cara finally said when Zedd had fallen silent for a time, lost in thought.

Nicci was relieved that Cara was the one to prompt him when he looked so stricken by contemplation of events so terrible she probably couldn't even begin to imagine them.

"I'm afraid that's not even the worst of it," he said. "You see, Richard memorized *The Book of Counted Shadows* as a boy. George Cypher feared that the book would fall into the wrong hands, but he was wise enough that he didn't dare destroy the knowledge the book contained, so he had Richard memorize it. After Richard had learned every word, he and George Cypher, the man who had raised him and who at the time Richard believed was his father, burned *The Book of Counted Shadows*.

"When Darken Rahl captured Richard, and was opening the boxes, he made Richard read out the instructions from *The Book of Counted Shadows*. I don't recall how—probably as a result of the Chainfire spell.

"The point is, I was there. I remember that part quite well because I was so shocked—for two reasons. First, to learn that the book had been stolen from my enclave at the Keep for Richard to memorize and, secondly, because it was a book of magic and that fact meant that Richard could only memorize and speak the words because he was gifted.

"When I found the copy of *The Book of Counted Shadows* down in the catacombs, I was shaken to my core. I read it and sure enough it was word for word exactly what Richard had memorized."

Nicci cocked her head. "It was the same? Are you sure?"

"Positive," Zedd said, emphatically. "The two were identical."

Nicci was beginning to feel sick herself. "That can mean only one of two things. Either one was the original, and the other the one true copy of that key . . . or else they were both false keys, false copies."

"No, they couldn't be false," Zedd insisted. "When Richard read the book out, he left out an important element at the very end. It was by leaving out that one piece of the book that he defeated Darken Rahl. He, in essence, turned it into a false copy, thus tricking Darken Rahl to defeat him. As I often told Richard, sometimes a trick is the best magic."

Nicci laid the book on the table. "That doesn't necessarily mean it's the true key and not the false. Look at this." She laid *The Book of Life* open and tapped a page in the very beginning that had only one thing all by itself on the page to emphasize how important—how central—it was.

"This is the introductory statement to *The Book of Life*. I already translated it. It's a warning to anyone who would read this book.

"It says, '*Those who have come here to hate should leave now, for in their hatred they only betray themselves.*'"

Zedd squinted at the words in High D'Haran all by themselves on the page. "So you are saying, what . . . that because Darken Rahl turned to the boxes of Orden out of hate, he would have been destroyed by the true *Book of Counted Shadows* just the same as by a false one?"

"That's one possibility," Nicci said.

Zedd shook his head. "I don't believe that. Some magic works by reading intent. The Sword of Truth works that way. People who hate don't usually recognize that vile taint within themselves. They spew their hatred as righteous. That corruption is what makes them so evil—and so dangerous. They are able to do the most despicable things and think themselves heroes for having done them."

"Then you are going to tell me that you believe that it was coincidence, luck, that both those books just happen to be the only true keys? And they just happened to be that close together? You think that the wizards who made the copies, sending them to distant, hidden places, would have put the one true copy right here, right near the only other true key? What would be the purpose of scattering the copies?"

Zedd rubbed his chin with his fingertips as he thought it over. "I see what you mean."

"With books like this, there has to be a way to confirm the copies—to validate them."

"There is," Zedd told her. "In the beginning of *The Book of Counted Shadows*, it says, '*Verification of the truth of the words of The Book of Counted Shadows, if spoken by another, rather than read by the one who commands the boxes, can only be insured by the use of a Confessor. . . .*'

"A copy constitutes 'spoken by another,'" he said. "The person making the copy is, in essence, speaking it; the reader is not actually reading the original. Unless it's the original key, and that original key is actually being read by the one who put the boxes in play, this forewarning invokes the necessity of verification."

"Kahlan," Nicci said.

The other two looked at her, and by the looks on their faces, they understood her meaning.

"Zedd," Nicci finally asked into the silence, "None of us remembers Kahlan. If we could find her, and if we could somehow fix this Chainfire spell, or something . . . is there a way to make her remember what she right now would not recall?"

Zedd's gaze wandered to the glowing spell-forms above the table. "No."

Nicci hadn't expected such certainty. "Are you sure?"

"About as sure as I can be. The spell destroys memory. It doesn't cover it over, or block it from access, it destroys it. It doesn't make people forget, it actually erases the memory. To the person upon whom such a terrible thing was unleashed, their memory is gone."

"But there must be some way," Cara insisted, "some magic this-or-that that will restore her mind."

"Restore it with what? What none of us can recall? Memory is the stuff of life. Magic functions in specific ways, as do all things that exist. Magic is not some super-intelligent consciousness behind a veil that knows what we want to accomplish and can pull a person's entire memory—their entire life—out of a pocket and hand it back just because we wish it."

Cara didn't look convinced. "But can't—"

"Look at it this way. If I push that book off the table, it will fall to the floor. The invisible force of gravity makes it happen. Gravity functions in a specific way. I can't wave my arms and by my wish command gravity to go make me dinner.

"Same with magic and memory. The Chainfire spell destroyed her memory. It can't be brought back. You can't restore what was and is no longer there. You just can't. What's gone is gone."

Cara drew her hand down her long blond braid. "Then it sounds like we're in a lot of trouble."

"Trouble indeed," the wizard conceded.

Nicci wanted to say that Richard's heart was in a lot of trouble, but she dared not say such a thing out loud. She felt despondent for him, for what he would one day have to face. But she didn't want to be the one to point it out.

"Then, if Richard finds her," Nicci asked in a weak voice, "what is he to do?"

Zedd, hands clasped behind his back, stared at her a moment before looking away.

"There's another way to confirm the true copy," Cara said.

Zedd and Nicci both frowned at her, both relieved to have a diversion.

"You just find the other copies," she said, "and compare them. The one Richard memorized is gone. So, if you find the others you can compare them. The one that's different has to be the one true copy. The other four that are all the same have to be the false keys."

Zedd arched an eyebrow. "And what if the people who made the false keys were worried that one day a clever Mord-Sith would think of that and so they made all the copies different from one another, so that they couldn't be compared?"

Cara made a face. "Oh."

Nicci threw up her arms. "How would he even go about finding the others, anyway? I mean, they've been hidden for three thousand years."

"Not only that," Zedd said, "but Nathan told us that there were catacombs under the Palace of the Prophets, and that place was destroyed. I know, I set the light spell myself. There would be nothing left, and even if somehow a pocket of the catacombs survived, the palace was built on an island. After the island was destroyed water would have flooded any underground room that hadn't already been ruined.

"That one copy, if one of them was there, has already been destroyed. Was it a true or a false key? What if, over all this time, others have been destroyed? The question remains, how to tell if the one Richard knows, and the one I found, are the only two true keys."

Nicci stared off. "I'm afraid they might be false copies—the one Richard memorized, and the one you found down in the catacombs."

Zedd began pacing. "I don't know any way to be sure."

"There might be two ways," she said. "The first, I can't swear to, yet. I've only just started translating *The Book of Life*. But there is material having to do with the mention of using the key. It says that if the person who put the boxes in play fails to use the key properly, the boxes will be destroyed along with the one who put them in play."

"Use the key properly . . ." Zedd said, deep in thought.

"That seems to me to say that if Darken Rahl would have failed to use the true key properly, such as by leaving off the last part—as you said Richard did when reciting it back to him—he would have been destroyed, but so would the boxes of Orden. As we know, the boxes of Orden weren't destroyed, so that tells me Richard may very well have read him the false key and Darken Rahl simply opened the wrong box and it destroyed him.

"It doesn't say that the boxes will be destroyed if a false key is used because at the time this was written there were no false keys yet, so that problem hadn't been taken into consideration when this material was all created."

Zedd frowned in thought. "Are you sure of this?"

"No," Nicci admitted. "It's complex and I've only just started to translate it. I scanned that part because it pertained to using the key to complete the required steps. It also has formulas that have to be taken into account. I'm only giving you my preliminary impression."

Nicci ran her fingers back into her hair with one hand. She stood before the table with the open book on it, with her other hand on a hip.

"Do you see what I mean, though?" She gestured down at the book. "If Richard had corrupted the true key, making Darken Rahl pick the wrong box, this seems to indicate that the boxes would have been destroyed along with Darken Rahl. That seems to support the idea that Richard memorized a false key."

"Maybe. You said you weren't sure of that, yet." Zedd rubbed the back of his neck as he paced. "Let's not make the error of jumping to conclusions."

Nicci nodded.

"You say there was something else you were going on?" Zedd asked.

Nicci nodded and then quoted the central prophecy, the one Nathan had told them. " 'In the year of the cicadas, when the champion of sacrifice and suffering, under the banner of both mankind and the Light, finally splits his swarm, thus shall be the sign that prophecy has been awakened and the final and deciding battle is upon us. Be cautioned, for all true forks and their derivatives are tangled in this mantic root. Only one trunk branches from this conjoined primal origin. If *fuer grissa ost drauka* does not lead this final battle, then the world, already standing at the brink of darkness, will fall under that terrible shadow.'

"Do you see?" Nicci asked. "The 'champion of sacrifice and suffering under the banner of both mankind and the Light' is Jagang and the Imperial Order. The next words say that when he 'finally splits his swarm, thus shall be the sign that prophecy has been awakened and the final and deciding battle is upon us.' He has split his army. Half is holding the passes, while the other half has gone around to come up through D'Hara from the south. As it says, 'the final and deciding battle is upon us.' "

As if to confirm what she had said, a fit of lightning flickered through the windows, accompanied by thunder rumbling the Keep beneath their feet.

Zedd frowned. "I'm not following your reasoning."

"Why did Ann and Nathan steal the book in the first place for Richard? Because they misinterpreted prophecy—they thought the final battle was Darken Rahl. They thought that Richard needed *The Book of Counted Shadows* to fight Darken Rahl in the final battle. They found the only copy in existence—they thought.

"Don't you see? That was too easy. Richard was born to fight this battle, now, with Jagang and with what the Sisters of the Dark have done by putting the boxes of Orden in play. This, now, is an extension of the same final battle begun with Darken Rahl.

"I think the prophecies may hint that Richard learned the wrong key: 'Be cautioned, for all true forks and their derivatives are tangled in this mantic root.' All true forks—true keys?—are on the prophetic root of this final battle. It says that the other forks are false. Maybe other forks contain the false keys.

"Couldn't it be said that the battle against Darken Rahl was a false fork? Ann and Nathan didn't know enough at the time—not enough events had unfolded, so they went down that fork, preparing Richard to fight Darken Rahl, not Jagang. But this prophecy says, 'If *fuer grissa ost drauka* does not lead this final battle, then the world, already standing at the brink of darkness, will fall under that terrible shadow.'

"That terrible shadow is the power of Orden unleashed by the Sisters of the Dark. They want to darken the world of life. Ann, Nathan, and Richard were preparing for the wrong battle. This is the battle he was meant to fight."

Zedd paced, his face creased in thought. He halted, finally, and turned to her. "Maybe, Nicci. Maybe. You've spent a great deal more time studying prophecy than I have. Maybe you have something.

"But then, maybe you don't. Prophecy, as Nathan has explained, is not subject to study the way you have just explained. Prophecy is a means of communication between prophets. It can't necessarily be studied, analyzed, or understood by those without the gift for prophecy.

"Just like Ann and Nathan may have jumped to conclusions without sufficient information, I think it's also too early for you to draw such conclusions."

Nicci nodded, conceding his point. "I hope you're right, Zedd—I really do. This is not an argument I want to win. I'm only bringing it up because I think we need to consider the implications."

He nodded. "There is something else to consider. Richard doesn't take to prophecy. He is a creature of free will, and prophecy has a way of having to open up to accommodate him. In this case, with Darken Rahl, maybe Darken Rahl was a false fork, but had he won there are prophetic roots to cover that eventuality as well. Proponents of prophecy would have pointed to them to confirm that Darken Rahl was the true root. We would now find ourselves on one of those other branches, and this one would be false. You can find a prophecy to support just about any belief."

"I don't know," Nicci said as she ran her fingers back through her hair, "perhaps you're right."

She was so tired. She needed to get some sleep; maybe then she could think more clearly. Maybe her worry was causing her to race down false trails.

"There is no way we can say at this point if the copies of *The Book of Counted Shadows*, the one I found and the one Richard knows, are true keys or false."

"So, what are we going to do?" she asked.

Zedd halted his pacing and faced her. "We're going to get Richard back, and he is going to find a way to stop this threat."

Nicci smiled. He had a way of making her feel better in the darkest of times—just the way Richard did.

"But I'll tell you one thing," Zedd said. "Before that time comes, we had better find out if the key he memorized is the true or the false key."

Nicci closed the cover on *The Book of Life* and picked it up, holding it in the crook of her arm. "I need to learn this whole book, cover to cover. I need to find out if there is a way to do what Richard asked of me—take the boxes back out of play, or somehow annul the threat.

"Failing that, I had better know it inside and out so that I can hopefully be useful to Richard in finding an answer to it all."

Zedd appraised her eyes. "That's going to be a great deal of work. It's going to take a lot of time—a book that complex could take months to fully understand. I only hope we have that much time. I have to say, though, that I agree with you. I guess that you had better get started right away."

Nicci slipped the book back into a pocket in her dress. "I guess that I had better. There may be books here that would help. If there are any I can think of, or that are mentioned, I'll let you know. From what I've seen so far, there are technical matters I may need help with. If I get stuck, I could use the help of the First Wizard."

Zedd smiled. "You have it, my dear."

She shook a finger at him. "But if you come up with a way to find Richard, you had better tell me before you finish having the thought."

Zedd's smile widened. "Agreed."

"What if we don't find Lord Rahl?" Cara asked.

The other two stared at her. Thunder rumbled through the distant valley. Rain pattered steadily against the windows.

"Well get him back," Nicci insisted, refusing to consider the unthinkable.

"Nothing is ever easy," Zedd muttered.

Despite how weary she was of riding, Kahlan was awestruck by the sight rising up in the distance. Past a dark flood tide of men of the Imperial Order, across the purple-gray shadows settling across the vast plain, rose an enormous plateau, catching the last golden rays of the setting sun.

On that plateau stood a place as vast as any city. The high outer walls glowed in the waning evening light. White marble, stucco, and stone making up the vast array of buildings in an endless variety of sizes, shapes, and heights shimmered with the departing blush of daylight. Roofs sheltered the place from the coming cold night of the dying season as if gathering it all up under protective skirts.

It was like seeing something good, something noble, something beautiful, after all she had seen for endless weeks of travel had been grim, brooding men restless for someone upon whom to vent their vile nature.

It felt to Kahlan as if it were a desecration having these men in the shadow of such a place as this. She felt ashamed to be among the profane rabble gathered at the feet of such a shining accomplishment of man so proudly rising up before them. Just looking at the place for some reason made her heart sing. Though she couldn't recall ever having seen it before, she felt as if she should have.

All around them were grunting men, baying mules, snorting horses, creaking wagons, and the clang of armor and weapons—the sounds of the beast come to slay all that was good. The stench was like a toxic cloud that always followed along with them to serve to remind anyone they came upon just how unwholesome these men really were. As if anyone would need the additional clue.

All around Kahlan rode the special guards who for weeks now had kept a watchful eye on her. There were forty-three of them. Kahlan had counted so that she could keep track of them all. She had made it her business as they traveled to learn their faces, their habits. She knew which ones were clumsy, which were stupid, which were smart, and which were good with weapons. As a game while riding endless day after endless day, she studied their strengths and weaknesses, planning and visualizing how she could kill each and every last one of them.

So far, she had not killed any. She had decided that her best chance in the long run was to go along, for now, with whatever she was told to do, to be compliant, to be obedient. The men had all been warned that she belonged to Jagang, and they were not to lay a finger on her—except to keep her from escaping.

Kahlan wanted to blend into the monotony of daily life, to have the men guarding her become lulled into thinking of her as innocuous, harmless, even cowed, so that she became just another one of their tedious chores. She'd had a number of opportunities to kill several of the men. She never took that opportunity, no matter how easy it would have been, choosing instead to let them feel comfortable, safe, even bored with her. Such inattention to the danger she represented would one day serve her better than a useless attack that for now could not really accomplish anything. It would not help her escape, and would only cause Jagang to use the collar—if not his hands—to bring her pain. While he needed no excuse, she saw no purpose to giving him a good one.

The only one not lulled into indifference and carelessness was Jagang himself. He did not misjudge her, or her will. He seemed to enjoy watching her tactics, even tactics as uninteresting as doing nothing. Like her, he carried patience in his arsenal. He was the only one not to let his guard down for an instant. Kahlan thought that he knew precisely what she was doing.

She ignored him as well; even if he knew what she was doing, she reasoned that it still diminished the level of caution he could maintain when nothing ever happened. Waiting for something that never came was wearing, even if you knew it was inevitable. Even if he knew that she would eventually try something, weeks and weeks of her meek compliance would buy her the element of surprise, even if it was only a momentary surprise. That instant of advantage might be all that made the difference when the time came.

Sometimes, though, she could not ignore him. When he was in a foul mood and she angered him—usually by her mere presence, not anything that she did—he would beat her bloody. Twice she had had to be healed by a Sister lest she bleed to death. When he was in one of his truly vile moods, it usually ended up being a great deal worse than a simple beating. He was a very inventive man when it came to how to abuse a woman. When he was in an abusive mood, not simple pain but humiliation seemed to fascinate him. She had learned that he would not stop until he made her finally cry for one reason or another.

If she did cry, it was only when she could not help it, when she fell to depths of such pain, or humiliation, or despair, that she simply could not hold back her tears. Jagang enjoyed watching her cry, then. She did not do it just to give in, to make him stop what he was doing, but only because she was at a point where she could not help herself. And that was what he liked seeing.

At other times he would bring women to his tent while Kahlan had to stay on the carpet beside the bed, where she was always made to sleep, as if she were his dog. He usually brought some unfortunate, captive woman who was less than willing. He seemed to seek out captives who most feared his attention, and then gave them a violent introduction to being a slave to the emperor and his bed. When he fell asleep, Kahlan would hold the terrified woman, tell her that things would one day be better and comfort her as best she could.

He might have done it because he enjoyed such things, but that was only a side benefit. His real objective was to constantly remind Kahlan of what would happen to her once her memory returned.

Kahlan intended it never to return. Her memory would be her undoing.

Now that they had arrived at their destination, there would be more time for Ja'La games. Kahlan imagined that there would be tournaments. She hoped that they would divert Jagang's attention from her, keep him occupied. She would have to accompany him—she was made to stay close—but that was better than being alone with him.

As they arrived at the emperor's tents she was at first a little puzzled that the compound specifically, and the camp in general, was so far from their distant objective. He was so close. It seemed that it was only a matter of another hour's ride or two and they would be there.

Kahlan didn't ask why they had stopped short, but she soon found out when officers arrived for a nightly briefing.

"I want all the Sisters on watch tonight," Jagang told them. "This close, there is no telling what sorts of wicked powers the enemy up there might send down on us."

Kahlan noticed that Sisters Ulicia and Armina, not far away, were relieved to overhear such orders. It meant they wouldn't be sent to entertain the men. In the long march of weeks, after being sent to the tents almost nightly as punishment for their transgressions against Jagang, they both looked to have aged years.

They had both been rather attractive women, but no more. They both had lost whatever beauty they once possessed. Their eyes, heavy with dark bags, were rather hollow and distant. Sister Armina's sky blue eyes seemed to always look startled, as if she still couldn't believe her fate. Creases had come to their faces, giving them both a heavy, drained, downcast look. They were always dirty, their hair perpetually tangled and their clothes torn. They often showed up in the morning with lurid bruises.

Kahlan didn't like to see anyone suffer, but she could not work up any sympathy for these two. Were it not for them, she would not be in the clutches of a man who was only counting the moments until she recovered her memory and he could begin in earnest to make her suffer what he had promised to be insufferable agony, both physically and mentally. He had promised her, more than once, that when she had her memory back he was going to impregnate her and she was going to bear him a child—a male, he always claimed. He always added a cryptic message about how when she had her memory back, she would then truly understand just what a monster such a male child would be to her.

As far as Kahlan was concerned, whatever Jagang did to those two women was not enough.

Beyond what they had done to her, by hearing bits and pieces Kahlan had put together the nature of their plot and what those two had planned to do to everyone. That alone made it impossible to treat them too brutally. If it was Kahlan's choice, though, she would simply have put them to death. Kahlan held no favor with torture; she simply believed that they did not deserve to continue to live. They had forfeited their right to live by the harm they had already done to others, and by what they planned to do to deprive everyone of their lives. By that measure, the entire army deserved to die.

Kahlan only wished that Jagang could suffer a similar fate.

"At least their army has fled," one of the senior officers said to Jagang as the emperor's horse was led away. Another man took Kahlan's mare.

The officer was missing half his left ear. It had long since healed over in a lump, becoming a distraction that was hard to ignore. Men who didn't ignore it sometimes lost an ear.

"They have no defenders left," another officer said.

"I'm sure they have gifted up there," Jagang said, "but they shouldn't present an obstacle that can stop us."

"The reports of the scouts and spies say that the road up the side is narrow—too narrow for any kind of mass assault. There is also a draw-bridge that they have raised. Bringing building materials up that road, and then defending ourselves while we tried to span the chasm, would be hard to do.

"As for the great door leading to the interior way up into the plateau, it has been closed. No one entertains any faith in breaching that door. It has stood for thousands of years against any assault. Besides, the reports from the gifted say that their powers are weakened near the palace."

Jagang smiled. "I have some ideas."

The man missing part of his ear bowed his head. "Yes, Excellency."

As Jagang and his officers talked, Kahlan noticed a small cluster of men in the distance riding at breakneck speed through the camp. They were coming up from behind, from the south. At every checkpoint, the men brought their horses to a skidding halt, spoke briefly to sentries, and were ushered through.

Jagang had noticed the riders, too. His conversation with his officers dwindled away and soon all of them were watching with the emperor as the riders made it to the inner defenses and dismounted in a cloud of dust. They waited at the final ring of steel for permission to enter the emperor's compound.

When Jagang signaled, the men were brought forward. They came with haste, despite how tired they looked.

The man at their lead was a wiry fellow, older, with a hard look in his dark eyes. He saluted.

"Well," Jagang said, "what is it that's so urgent?"

"Excellency, cities in the Old World have come under attack."

"Is that so." Jagang heaved an impatient sigh. "It's those insurrection-ists, mostly from Altur'Rang. Haven't they been put down yet?"

"No, Excellency, it is not insurrectionists—although they are causing trouble as well, led by one called the blacksmith. Too many places have been attacked for it to be the doings of insurrectionists."

Jagang eyed the man suspiciously. "What places have come under attack?"

The man pulled a scroll out from inside his dusty shirt. "Here is a list we have collected, so far."

"So far?" Jagang asked, arching an eyebrow as he unfurled the scroll.

"Yes, Excellency. The information is that there is a wave of destruction sweeping across the land."

Jagang scanned the long list of places on the scroll. Kahlan tried not to appear obvious as she glanced at the report out of the corner of her eye. She saw two columns of towns and cities listed. There had to be more than thirty-five or forty places written on the scroll.

"I don't know what you mean by 'sweeping across the land,'" Jagang growled. "These places are all random. They're not located in a line, or cluster, or one area of the Old World. They're all over the place."

The man cleared his throat. "Yes, Excellency. That is the report."

"Some of this has to be overstated." To make his point, Jagang jabbed the paper with a fat finger. The silver rings on each finger flashed in the fading light. "Taka-Mar, for instance. Taka-Mar has been attacked? It couldn't have been very effective for a malcontent mob of fools to attack such a place. There are troop garrisons there. It's a transfer station for supply trains. There are ample defenses in place. There are even Brothers of the Fellowship of Order in charge of the place. They wouldn't have allowed a rabble to have their way in Taka-Mar. This report most likely is overstated by nervous fools who are afraid of their own shadow."

The man bowed apologetically. "Excellency, Taka-Mar was one of the places I saw with my own eyes."

"Well?" Jagang roared. "What did you see, then? Out with it!"

"The roads into the city from every direction are lined with stakes topped with charred skulls," the man began.

"How many skulls?" Jagang waved dismissively. "Dozens? As many as a hundred?"

"Excellency, there were numbers beyond counting, and I stopped counting at several thousand without having made much headway in a full tally. The city itself is no more."

"No more?" Jagang blinked in confusion. "What do you mean, no more? Such a thing is impossible."

"It has been burned to the ground, Excellency. There was not a single building left standing. The fires were so intense that the lumber cannot be salvaged. The orchards all the way out into the hills were all cut down. The fields of ripe crops for miles and miles in every direction have all been burned. The ground has been salted. Nothing will ever grow there again. A once fertile place will never support anything again. It looks like the Keeper himself destroyed the place."

"Well, where were the soldiers! What were they doing during all this!"

"The skulls on stakes were the soldiers garrisoned there. Every last one of them, I'm afraid."

Jagang cast a look at Kahlan, as if she were somehow responsible for the catastrophe. His glare told her that he somehow associated the trouble with her. He crushed the paper in his fist as he returned his attention to the messenger.

"What about the Brothers of the Order? Did they say what happened and why they weren't able to stop it?"

"There were six Brothers assigned to Taka-Mar, Excellency. They were impaled on posts placed in the middle of different roads into the city. Each had been skinned from the neck down. A cap of office was left on each man's head so that all could know who they were.

"The masses of people who fled the city say that the attack came at night. As terrified as they were, we weren't able to get much useful information from them, other than that the men who attacked them were soldiers of the D'Haran Empire. They were all sure of that much. Every one of these people has lost their home.

"The attackers made no move to slaughter the escaping refugees if they offered no armed resistance, but they made it quite clear to the fleeing people that they intended to lay waste to all of the Old World and anyone who supports the Imperial Order.

"The soldiers told the people that it is the Order and their beliefs that has brought this strife upon them, and who will bring them and their land to ruin. The soldiers vowed that they would haunt the people of the Old World into their graves and then into the darkest corners of the underworld if they did not give up the teachings of the Order and their belligerent ways that flowed from those teachings."

Kahlan only realized that she was smiling when Jagang rounded on her and backhanded her hard enough to knock her from her feet. She knew that he was going to beat her bloody that night.

She didn't care. It was worth it to hear what she had just heard. She couldn't stop smiling.

Nicci pulled her cloak tighter around herself as she leaned one shoulder up against the great stone merlon. She peered down through the crenellation to the road far below, watching the four riders making their way up the mountain toward the Keep. They were still quite a distance, but she thought she had a good idea who they were.

Nicci yawned as she looked out over the city of Aydindril below, and the vast carpet of forests all around. The vivid colors of autumn were beginning to fade. Looking at the trees spreading up onto the slopes of the surrounding mountains, and how they so boldly heralded the change of seasons, made her think about Richard. He loved the trees. Nicci had come to love them, too, because they reminded her of him.

She saw the trees in a different light for other reasons as well. They marked the turn of time, the passing of seasons, the change of patterns that were part of her world now, too, because of their connection to all the things she had been studying in *The Book of Life*. It was all intricately interconnected—how the power of Orden worked, and how that power functioned through its connection to the world of life. The world, the seasons, the stars, the position of the moon, were parts of the equation, all parts of what contributed to and governed the power of Orden. The more she studied and the more she learned, the more she felt that pulse of time and life that was all around her.

She had also come to recognize with complete clarity that Richard had memorized a false key.

She never made the point to Zedd. It seemed unimportant for the present. It was also a difficult case to make. It wasn't so much what *The Book of Life* said, but how it said it. The book was in another language, and not just High D'Haran. While it was written in High D'Haran, the true language of the book was its interconnection to the power invoked through it. The formulas, spells, and procedures were only one aspect.

In many ways it reminded her of how Richard spoke so convincingly of the language of symbols and emblems. She was coming to understand what he meant by seeing it for herself all laid out in *The Book of Life*. She was coming to see the lines and angles in certain formulas as a language all their own. She was beginning to truly grasp what Richard meant.

The Book of Life carried meaning that had forced Nicci to look at the world of life in a new way—in a way that very much reminded her of the way Richard had always looked at the world, through a prism of excitement, wonder, and love of life. In a way it was a profound recognition of the precise nature of things, an appreciation of things for what they were, not for what people imagined of them.

In part, that was because *The Book of Life* was not just Additive, but Subtractive Magic in the same way that death was part of the process of life. It dealt with the whole. For that reason, Nicci couldn't explain it to Zedd; he didn't possess the ability to use Subtractive Magic. Without that ability, a constituent part of what was needed to understand *The Book of Life* was missing. She could explain the formulas, lay out the procedures, show him the spells, but much of it he could only observe through the filter of his limited ability. While he could intellectually understand some of it, he couldn't actually perform what was involved.

It was something like the difference between hearing about love, understanding the depth of such feelings, grasping how it affected people, but never having actually experienced it. Without that experience, it was only academic, sterile.

Until you felt the magic, you didn't know it.

It was in that sense that Nicci had come to know that Richard had memorized a false key. She had been right, before, in that if the person who put the boxes in play failed to use the key properly, the boxes would be destroyed along with the one who put them in play. But it was more than that simple statement. There was the whole complex nature of the processes involved in using the boxes that demonstrated that concept in ways that the words only presented in a simplified, condensed manner.

Through the mechanisms in the book, she could glimpse how the power functioned. By understanding that function on a profound level, she could see how the magic, if invoked, needed and used the key for completion. Through grasping that process, she could see how if the key was used improperly the boxes themselves were inescapably destroyed along with the person making the fatal mistake. The magic simply would not allow such a breach to go uncompleted.

It would be like tossing a rock and without any outside influence or intervention having it float in midair rather than fall back to the ground. It simply would not happen. In the same way, the magic of Orden had laws of its identity. By the way it functioned, by those laws of its identity, it had to destroy the boxes if the key was not used properly. The rock has to fall.

When Richard used his memory of what he believed was *The Book of Counted Shadows*, he changed it in order to trick Darken Rahl into opening the wrong box. But it had only been the wrong box named in a clever simulation that seemed as if it had meaning to *The Book of Life*. In fact, such a book was only a shrewd fake, a false key. Had it been real, and misused in such a way, the boxes would no longer exist.

A false key, a clever fake, simply could not trigger the power of Orden to destroy the boxes, but the real key, if used in the fashion that Richard had used it, would have caused the entire structure of spell to collapse in on itself, taking the boxes with it.

The boxes of Orden, after all, had been created for the purpose of countering the Chainfire spell. To misuse the key meant that someone without the proper intention and knowledge was trying to gain access to Orden's power, in essence tampering with the purpose for which it had been created. *The Book of Life* made it all too clear within the structure of the spell-forms that, as a safeguard, if everything was not done correctly, namely completed with the key in the exact, prescribed manner, the formulas and spells would self-destruct—not altogether unlike the way in which Richard had shut down the verification web, collapsing it, to save Nicci.

Richard had memorized a false key, that was the truth of it.

"What is it?" came Zedd's voice.

Nicci looked back over her shoulder to see the old wizard marching across the vast rampart. She knew that she had to set aside the things she had been considering. Telling Zedd about the false key now would only cause him to want to argue. Arguing with Zedd would serve no purpose.

Richard was the one who really needed to know that the key he possessed was false.

"Four riders," Nicci told him.

Zedd came to a halt at the wall. He peered down at the road and grunted to indicate that he saw them.

"Looks like Tom and Friedrich to me," Cara said. "They must have found someone sneaking around."

"I don't think so," Nicci said. "They hardly look like prisoners. I can see the glint of steel. The man is carrying weapons. Tom would have disarmed anyone he thought was a threat. Besides, the other one looks like a little girl."

"Rachel?" Zedd asked, frowning as he leaned out farther, trying to see better between the trees far down the road. It would not be many more days until those golden-brown leaves were gone for the season. "Do you really think it could be her?"

"That's my guess," Nicci said.

He turned and appraised her critically. "You look terrible."

"Thank you," she said. "Just what a woman likes to hear from a gentleman."

He huffed a dismissal of his rude manners. "When's the last time you got any sleep?"

Nicci yawned again. "I don't know. Last summer, when I came back from the People's Palace with that book?"

He made a face at her rather poor attempt at humor. She didn't know why she tried to be funny with him. Zedd could make people laugh just by grunting. Whenever she said anything she thought was rather amusing, people just stared at her, the way Cara was doing.

"How is it coming?" he asked.

Nicci knew what he meant. She pulled some hair back off her face, holding it back from the grasp of the wind. "I could use your help with some star charts and angle calculations. It might speed things up if I didn't have to do those myself. I could go on to some of the other translations and problems."

Zedd laid a hand tenderly on her back, giving her a gentle rub that conveyed a personal, comforting warmth. "On one condition."

"What's that?" she asked as she yawned again.

"You get some sleep."

Nicci smiled as she nodded. "All right, Zedd." She gestured, pointing with her chin. "First I think we had better get down there to see who our guests are."

They were just coming out the big door of the Keep at the side entrance with the paddock when the riders came under the arched opening in the wall.

Tom and Friedrich were escorting Chase and Rachel. Rachel's hair was chopped short, rather than long the way it had been, and Chase looked to be in surprisingly good health for a man who had been stabbed with the Sword of Truth.

"Chase!" Zedd shouted. "You're alive!"

"Well, it's hard to ride a horse upright when you're dead."

Cara chuckled. Nicci glanced at her, wondering where the woman's sudden appreciation for humor had come from.

"Found them returning," Tom said. "First people we've seen out there in months."

"It was good to see Rachel back," Friedrich said. The older man regarded the girl with a grin, showing how much he really meant it.

Zedd caught Rachel as she slipped from the saddle while Cara took the reins of the horse.

"My, but you're getting heavy," Zedd told her.

"Chase rescued me," Rachel said. "He was so brave. You should have seen him. He killed a hundred men all by himself."

"A hundred! My, my, what an accomplishment."

"You stabbed one in the leg for me," Chase said as he swung down out of his saddle. "Otherwise I'd only have gotten ninety-nine."

Rachel kicked her legs, eager to be put down. "Zedd, I brought something important with me."

Once on the ground, she untied a leather bag hanging right behind her saddle. She brought it to the granite steps and set it down, then undid the drawstring.

When she pushed back the leather covering, darkness came out into the crisp late-autumn daylight. To Nicci, it felt like looking into the inky obscurity of Jagang's eyes.

"Rachel," Zedd said in astonishment, "where did you get this?"

"A man, Samuel, who had Richard's sword had it. He stabbed Chase and took me with him. Then he gave it to a witch woman named Six, and to Violet, the queen of Tamarang, though I don't think she's queen anymore.

"You can't believe how evil Six is."

"I think I can imagine," Zedd told her.

Having a little trouble following the story, he lifted the leather back a little for a better look inside.

Staring at one of the boxes of Orden sitting on the steps before her,

Nicci felt as if her heart were in her throat. After the weeks and weeks of study of the book that went with the boxes, to actually see one was startling. Theory was one thing, but to see the reality of what this object represented was altogether something else.

"I couldn't let them have it," Rachel told Zedd. "So when I got a chance to escape I stole it and took it with me."

Zedd ruffled her chopped-off blond hair. "You did good, little one. I always knew you were special."

Rachel hugged the wizard around the neck. "Six made Violet draw pictures of Richard. It scared me to see what they were doing."

"In a cave?" Zedd asked. When Rachel nodded, he glanced up at Nicci. "That explains a lot."

Nicci took a step closer. "Was Richard there? Did you see him?"

Rachel shook her head. "No. Six left one day. When she finally came back she told Violet that she had been bringing him back, but the Imperial Order captured him."

"The Imperial Order . . ." Zedd said.

Nicci tried to imagine what was worse, the witch woman having Richard in her clutches, or the Imperial Order capturing him.

She guessed that what was the worst was Richard stripped of his gift, his sword, and being in the hands of the Order.

Kahlan pulled her cloak tighter around herself as she walked beside the emperor, his constant, compliant companion. It was not by choice, of course, but by force, whether applied or implied. At night she slept on the carpet beside his bed, a constant reminder of where she would end up. During the day she remained always at his side, like his dog on a leash. Her leash, though, was an iron collar with which he could bring her to heel at any time.

She could not imagine what could engender such hatred for her, what could have given rise to his burning need to bring punishment down on her for the sins he saw in all his enemies. Whatever she had done to earn his hatred, he deserved it.

When a gust of bitter cold wind ripped through the encampment, Kahlan hid the side of her face behind her cloak. Men turned their faces away from the blast of grit carried in the wind. With autumn rapidly drawing to an end, winter would soon be upon them. Kahlan didn't think it was going to be at all pleasant out on the open plain around the plateau that held the People's Palace, but she also knew that with this bone in his teeth, Jagang wasn't going to let it go for anything. He was nothing if not tenacious.

There was supposed to be another copy of *The Book of Counted Shadows* hidden somewhere within that plateau, and Jagang meant to have it.

Out on the Azrith Plain, the construction ground onward. It had been going on throughout the autumn, and she knew it would go on into winter, all winter if necessary, until it was complete. If, that was, the ground beneath them didn't freeze solid. Kahlan suspected that he had plans if that were to happen—probably fires, if needed, to keep the dirt thawed. She supposed, too, that if it remained dry, the ground could still be dug even if it was freezing.

There was no way to breach the great inner door into the plateau, and the road up the outside had quickly proven worthless for an attack by such vast numbers of men.

Jagang had a solution to the predicament.

He intended to construct a great, ramped road which would allow his army to march right up to the walls of the palace atop the plateau. He had told his officers that once they reached the walls, siege machines could be used to batter their way through the walls. First, though, they had to get up there.

To that end, out beyond the vast encampment, closer to the plateau, the army was constructing the ramp. The width of the ramp was staggering. They needed it wide for two reasons, both equally important. They needed a ramp wide enough to eventually support an assault massive enough that it couldn't be turned back by the defenders. Just as important, the plateau towered above the Azrith Plain. For the ramp to reach that height, the base had to be monumental lest the whole thing collapse. They had to, in essence, build a small mountain up against the plateau in order to reach the top. Tenacious, indeed.

The distance they had to their goal, from where they had started, was daunting. Because of the height, it required great length so that men and equipment could eventually be marched and rolled up the roadway they were building up to the very walls of the People's Palace.

It seemed at first to be a crazy idea, an impossible project, but what could be accomplished with millions of men who had nothing else to do and a driven emperor who cared nothing about their well-being was nothing short of astonishing. Every moment there was light, and sometimes by torchlight, long, snaking files of men either carried containers of dirt and rock to the site of the ever-growing ramp or dug up great mounds of supplies. Rock was mixed with the finer soil to make it stable. Other men had simple, weighted tampers to pack the new dirt as it was dumped.

Nearly all the men in the camp were engaged in the enterprise. Though the task was daunting, the progress made by so many men was continual. Inexorably, the ramp continued to grow. Of course, the higher it got, the longer it was going to take, because it would require so much more material.

Kahlan thought it appropriate that such men would assault fine construction of marble with dirt. It befitted the philosophy of the Order to grub in the dirt in order to bring down some of man's finest work.

Kahlan couldn't imagine how long it was going to take to complete such a project, but Jagang had no intention of abandoning his plan until he was successful. The end was in sight, he often reminded his officers, and he expected complete devotion and sacrifice from all for their noble purpose. He was implacable in his determination to bring down the last bastion of freedom.

From the edge of the emperor's compound, as they observed the construction, Kahlan saw a messenger coming in on horseback. To the south, she could see the long plume of dust rising from an approaching supply train. She had been checking on it for hours, watching it draw ever closer, and now the lead wagons were just beginning to enter camp.

Jagang had been relieved to see the supply train finally arrive. An army as vast as this one required constant supplies of all sorts, but mainly food. Out on the Azrith Plain, there was nowhere for the army to scavenge food; there were no farms, no crops, no herds of livestock. It would take constant resupply from the Old World to keep the army alive and building the emperor's ramp up into the sky.

After dismounting, the messenger approached and waited patiently. Jagang finally signaled several officers forward along with the man who'd ridden in.

The man bowed. "Excellency, I come with the supplies the good people from our homeland have sent. Many sacrificed to see to it that our valiant troops have what they need to vanquish the enemy."

"We can use the supplies, no doubt of that. The men are all working hard and I need to keep up their strength."

"Our train also brings some of the Ja'La dh Jin teams that wish to join the tournaments in the hopes of having the chance to one day play His Excellency's renowned team."

"What teams are they?" Jagang asked, absently, as he scanned a manifest the messenger handed him.

"Most are teams of our soldiers from various divisions. One is the team belonging to the commander of our supply train. To supplement his own men, he has gathered men from the New World along our journey north. He thinks that, with such men from the New World on his team, he can provide quite a spectacle for His Excellency's enjoyment."

Jagang nodded as he continued to read the list. "It will do these heathens good to learn our ways. Ja'La dh Jin is a good way to bring other peoples into our culture and customs. It diverts simple minds from the barren existence we all endure in this meaningless life."

The man bowed. "Yes, Excellency."

Jagang finally finished and looked up. "I've been hearing rumors. Is this team with the captives as good as I've heard?"

"They seem to be formidable, Excellency. They have defeated teams that no one thought they could beat. At first it was thought to have been simple luck. No one still thinks it is luck. They have a point man who is said to be the best ever seen."

Jagang grunted his skepticism. "I have the best on my team."

The man bowed an apology. "Yes, Excellency. Of course you are correct."

"What word do you bring from our homeland?"

The man hesitated. "Excellency, I am afraid that I must report some unsettling news. As the next supply train that was to follow after ours was assembling down in the Old World, it was set upon and destroyed. All the recruits who were to be sent north with the train to reinforce our army . . . well, I'm afraid, Excellency, that they were all killed. Their heads were left on stakes beside the road. The line of stakes stretched from one town to the next—both towns burned to the ground. A number of cities, along with forests and croplands, are burning. The fires are intense and, when the wind is right, we can smell the smoke even this far north. It is difficult to pin down exactly what is going on, except that the attacks are all reliably reported to be New World soldiers."

Jagang glanced at Kahlan. She suspected he was looking to see if she would smile, like the last time. She didn't need to smile. She could maintain a stony face, and rejoice inwardly. She felt like cheering those unknown men far away who were beginning to vex Jagang with the damage they were causing.

Almost as bad as the damage, rumors were sweeping through the camp. The attacks in their homeland were unsettling the men, who had always considered the Old World not just invulnerable to such attack, but invincible as well. As the rumors spread, they grew in weight among the men. Jagang had already executed a number of men for spreading such rumors. Since she had little interaction with the men—most didn't even see her—she didn't know if the executions quelled the rumors but, somehow, she doubted it. If the rumors of such things unsettled the soldiers, Kahlan could only imagine the fear beginning to grip those in the Old World. While their army was away seeking conquest, she imagined that the people back there were largely defenseless.

"The reports are, Excellency, that these marauders are destroying every-thing in their path. They burn crops, kill livestock, destroy mills, break dams, ruin every sort of craft producing goods for our noble effort to spread the word of the Order.

"Particularly hard hit are those who give support to our people by teaching them the ways of the Order—those who instill the need to sacri-fice for our effort to crush the heathens to the north."

Jagang was remaining calm on the outside, but Kahlan, as well as the officers watching him, knew that inside he was boiling with rage.

"Any idea who is going after our teachers, our leaders? Any particular unit of the enemy?"

The man bowed another apology. "Excellency, I regret to report that all of our teachers and the Brothers who have been murdered trying to teach the ways of the Creator and the Order, well . . . every one of their corpses was found to be missing a right ear."

Jagang's face went red with rage. Kahlan could see the muscles in his jaw and temples flex as he gritted his teeth.

"Do you think it could be those same men who plagued us on our way up into the Midlands, Excellency?" one of the officers asked.

"Of course it is!" Jagang roared. "I want something done about this," he said, directing his orders to the officers. "Do you understand?"

"Yes, Excellency," they all said as one as they bowed their heads and kept them bowed down.

"I want a stop put to this nuisance. We need those supply trains to con-tinue coming. We're close to ending this war in a great victory. I will not allow our effort to fail. Do you understand!"

"Yes, Excellency," they all said together, again, bowing deeper.

"Then get to it—all of you!"

As the men all departed to see to their orders, Jagang started marching away, out of his compound. Kahlan felt the shock of pain from the collar prompting her to keep up with him. Armed men, as always, fell in around Jagang as his royal escort and guard.

Richard watched through the bars covering the small window in the side of his iron cage as the wagon bounced through the sprawling encampment.

"Ruben, would you take a look at that," Johnrock said. Hands gripping the bars, he was grinning like a man on holiday at what he saw.

Richard glanced over at his cagemate. "Quite the sight," he agreed.

"Think there's anyone here who can beat us?"

"I expect we'll find out sooner or later," Richard said.

"I'll tell you, Ruben, I'd like to get a crack at cracking some heads on the emperor's team." The man gave Richard a sidelong glance. "Think if we beat the emperor's team they'll let us go home?"

"Are you serious?"

The man huffed a laugh. "It was a joke, Ruben."

"A poor one," Richard said.

"I suppose," Johnrock said with a sigh. "Still, they say the emperor's team is the best. I'd not like to feel that whip again."

"Once was enough for me, too."

The two of them had shared the iron cage ever since Richard had been captured back in Tamarang. Johnrock had already been a captive, taken before Richard. He was a big man, a miller, from the southern reaches of the Midlands. Just before the supply train had moved through his little village, soldiers on lead patrol had arrived and thought that, because of his size, Johnrock might make a good addition to the team.

Richard didn't know Johnrock's real name. He'd said everyone just called him Johnrock because of his size and how hard his muscles were from carrying sacks of grain. He knew Richard as Ruben Rybnik. Even though Johnrock was a fellow captive, Richard didn't think it would be safe to let anyone know his real name.

Johnrock had told Richard that he'd broken the arms of three of the soldiers trying to capture him before they took him down. Richard said only that they had pointed arrows at him, and so he'd given up. Johnrock had appeared slightly embarrassed for what he saw as Richard's lack of mettle.

Despite his rather goofy, lopsided grin, which he wore often and despite his circumstances, Johnrock had a quick wit and an analytical mind. He had come to like Richard because Richard was the only one who didn't assume he was stupid and didn't treat him as such. Johnrock was anything but stupid.

He had eventually decided that he'd been wrong about Richard's lack of bravery and had asked to be his right wingman in the Ja'La games. Wingman was a rather thankless position that exposed him to charges and bruises from the opponents. Johnrock saw the value in such a position because it allowed him to break the heads of men from the Order and he was cheered for doing so. Even though he was a big man, Johnrock was quick—a combination that made him a perfect man for Richard's right wing. He loved being close to Richard during play so he could see Richard vent his rage on the Ja'La field in a way that the other teams didn't expect. Together, the two of them had become a formidable pair on the field. It was never spoken, but they both knew that the other valued the chance to extract a little bit of revenge on those who had captured them.

The camp beyond the iron bars seemed to go on endlessly. Richard was sickened to see where they were—out on the Azrith Plain around the People's Palace. He didn't want to look anymore, and sat back down, leaning up against the other side of the box, resting a wrist over his knee as the wagon swayed and bucked through the endless horde.

He was relieved that the D'Haran forces were long gone, or they would have by now been annihilated for nothing. Instead, those men would by now have had enough time to make it down to the Old World. They were probably already laying waste to the place.

Richard hoped they stuck to the plan—fast and fierce attacks, keep separated and hit everywhere in the Old World, sparing nothing. He didn't want anyone in the Old World to feel safe. There needed to be consequences to the actions that flowed from their beliefs.

The men in the camp all watched the wagon train passing among them. It looked to be welcome, probably for the food it brought. Richard hoped they got their fill. Knowing the orders he had given, it was likely to be one of the last supply trains to leave the Old World. Without supplies, out on the Azrith Plain, with winter about to descend upon them, Jagang's army was going to find itself unexpectedly falling on hard times.

Nearly all the men they passed near to stared into Richard's cage, trying to get a glimpse of him. He expected that there were already rumors spreading through the camp about him and his Ja'La team. He had learned when they stopped to play teams at army posts along the way that their reputation preceded them. These men were fans of the game and looked forward to the tournaments, especially since there would no doubt be heightened interest because of the arrival of Richard's team—or Ruben's team, as it was informally known. The team really belonged to the commander with the snake face. There was little else to entertain these soldiers, other than the women captives. Richard tried not to think about that, because it only made him angry, and there was nothing he could do about it in his cage.

One day, after a particularly violent game that they had won handily, Johnrock admitted to being confused as to why Richard would have allowed himself to so easily be captured. Richard finally told him the truth of what happened. Johnrock at first didn't believe him. Richard told him to ask snake-face some time. He did and found that Richard was telling the truth. Johnrock greatly valued liberty and thought it was worth fighting for. That was when Johnrock asked to be Richard's right wingman.

Where Richard had once channeled his rage through the Sword of Truth, he now channeled it through the broc and the play of the Ja'La game. Even his own team, as much as they liked him leading them, to a degree feared him. Except Johnrock. Johnrock didn't fear Richard. He shared Richard's way of playing—as if the game were life-or-death.

For some of their opponents made up of Imperial Order troops who thought too much of themselves, it had been. It was not at all unusual for players, especially opponents of Richard's team, to be seriously hurt, or even die during a match. One of the men on Richard's team had died during a game. He'd been hit in the head with the heavy broc when he wasn't looking. It snapped his neck.

Richard remembered walking the streets of Aydindril with Kahlan, watching children play Ja'La. He had given out official balls if they would trade in their heavy brocs for the lighter ones Richard had had made up. He didn't want them getting hurt just to play a game. Now all those children had fled Aydindril.

"This looks like a bad place for us to be, Ruben," Johnrock said in a quiet voice as he watched the camp roll past their little window. He sounded uncharacteristically gloomy. "A very bad place for us to be slaves."

"If you think you're a slave, then you are a slave," Richard said.

Johnrock stared back at Richard for a long moment. "Then I'm not a slave, either, Ruben."

Richard nodded. "Good for you, Johnrock."

The man went back to watching the endless camp pass before his eyes. He had probably never seen the likes of it in his life. Richard remembered his own wonder when he first left his Hartland woods to discover what was beyond.

"Would you look at that," Johnrock said in a low voice, staring out through the bars.

Richard didn't feel like looking. "What is it?"

"A lot of men—soldiers—but not like the rest of the soldiers. These all look the same. Better weapons, better organized. Bigger. They look fierce. Everyone is making way for them."

Johnrock looked back over his shoulder at Richard. "I bet it's the emperor come to watch us roll by—come to see the challengers to his team come to the tournaments. From the descriptions I've heard, I bet that fellow being guarded by all those big guards in chain mail is Jagang himself."

Richard went back to the small opening to have a look. He gripped the bars as he put his face close to see better as they passed close to the guards and their charge.

"That looks like it's probably Emperor Jagang, all right," Richard told Johnrock.

The emperor was looking the other way, watching some of the other Ja'La teams made up of Imperial Order soldiers. They weren't locked in iron boxes in wagons, of course. Jagang was watching them marching proudly in ranks, carrying banners of their team.

And then he saw her.

"Kahlan!"

She turned toward his voice, not knowing where it was coming from. Richard was gripping the bars hard enough to nearly bend them. Even though she wasn't far, he realized that she probably couldn't hear him over all the noise. Men all around were cheering for the parade of marching teams.

Her long hair was tumbled down over her cloak. Richard thought his heart would explode it hammered so hard in his chest.

"Kahlan!"

She turned more toward him.

Their eyes met. He was staring right into her green eyes.

When Jagang started to turn around, she immediately turned away, looking off where he was watching. He turned back with her.

And then she was gone, hidden behind men and wagons and horses and tents, disappearing into the distance.

Richard fell back against the wall, gasping.

Johnrock sat down beside him. "Ruben—what's wrong? You look like you've seen a phantom walking among all those men."

Richard could only stare, his eyes wide, as he panted.

"It was my wife."

Johnrock let out a hardy laugh. "You mean you saw the woman you want when we win? The commander says that if we beat the emperor's team, we'd get to pick one. You see the one you want?"

"It was her. . . ."

"Ruben, you look like a man who just fell in love."

Richard realized that his smile felt like it might break his face.

"It was her. She's alive. Johnrock—I wish you could see her. She's alive. She looks exactly the same. Dear spirits, it was Kahlan. It was her."

"I think you'd best slow down your breathing, Ruben, or you're going to pass out before we have a chance to break some heads."

"We're going to play the emperor's team, Johnrock."

"We got to win a lot of games, first, to have that chance."

Richard hardly heard the man. He laughed with glee, unable to stop himself. "It was her. She's alive." Richard threw his arms around John-rock, hugging him tightly. "She's alive!"

"If you say so, Ruben."

Kahlan carefully controlled her breathing, trying to get her galloping heart to slow down. She couldn't understand why she was so shaken. She didn't know the man in the cage. She had only seen his face briefly as the wagon rolled past, but for some reason it shook her down to her very soul.

The second time the man yelled her name, Jagang acted like he thought he'd heard something. Kahlan had turned back around so that he wouldn't suspect anything. She didn't know why that had seemed so desperately important.

That wasn't true. She did know why. The man was in a cage. If he knew her, Jagang might have hurt him, even killed him.

There was more to it, though. That man knew her. He had to be con-nected to her past. The past she wanted to forget.

But when she had looked into his gray eyes, everything had changed in a heartbeat. Her numb acceptance had shattered. She no longer wanted her past to be buried. She suddenly wanted to know everything.

The look in that man's eyes was so profoundly powerful—so filled with something important, something vital—that it drove home to her how im-portant her life was.

Seeing the look in his gray eyes, Kahlan realized that she had to know who she was. Whatever the consequences, whatever the cost, she had to know the truth. She had to have her life back. The truth was the only way.

Jagang's threats of what he would do to her might be a very real conse-quence, but she suddenly knew that the real danger was that he was in-timidating her into abdicating her life, her will, her existence . . . into giving herself over to his control. By his threats of what he would do to her once she again knew who she was, he was dictating her life, enslaving her. If she went along with his will, then it was only because she surren-dered hers.

She couldn't allow herself to think that way. Her life meant more than that. She may be his captive, but she was not his slave. A slave was a state of mind. She was not a slave.

She would not surrender her will to him. She would have her life back.

Her life was hers alone and she would have it back. Nothing Jagang could do, nothing he could threaten her with, could take that away from her.

Kahlan felt a tear of joy roll down her cheek.

That man she didn't even remember had just given her the will to take her life back, the fire to live. It felt like the first real breath she had taken since she had lost her memory.

She only wished she could thank him.

Nicci marched through the vast hall of the People's Palace trailing Cara, Nathan, and a gaggle of guards. Every time someone called Nathan "Lord Rahl," it set her nerves on edge. She knew it was necessary, but in her heart the only Lord Rahl was Richard.

She would have given just about anything to see his gray eyes again. Being in the palace made it seem she could almost feel his presence all around her. It was the spell the palace was built around, she supposed. The palace was built in the form of a spell for the Lord Rahl. Richard was the Lord Rahl. At least in her mind.

To be fair, she knew there were others—Cara, for one—who felt the same. When she was alone with Cara, which was often, the two of them seemed to share understanding without words being needed. Both shared the same anguish. Both of them wanted Richard back.

Cara stepped forward, leading them through a network of small service hallways to an iron stairway up a dark well. Reaching the top, she threw open the door. They were greeted with cold light as they stepped out onto the observation deck. Being right out at the edge of the outer wall, at the edge of the plateau, felt like standing on the edge of the world.

Down below, spread like a black taint almost to the distant horizon, was the army of the Imperial Order.

"See what I mean?" Nathan said as he stepped up beside her, pointing out the construction in the distance. It was hard to see at first, but it quickly began to make sense.

"You're right," she said. "It does look like a ramp. Do you think they can actually build a ramp all the way up here?"

Nathan gazed out at the site, studying it for a moment. "I don't know, but I would have to say that if Jagang is going to all the trouble of doing such a thing, it can only be because he has reason to believe that he can accomplish it."

"If they make it up here with a ramp that broad," Cara said, "we're in trouble."

"More like 'dead,' " Nathan said.

Nicci studied what the men of the Order were doing, and the distance to the site of the work. "Nathan, you're a Rahl. This place amplifies your power. You ought to be able to send some wizard's fire down there and blow that thing apart."

"My thought, too," he said. "I suspect that they have Sisters down there with shields to prevent anyone up here from doing just that. I've not probed for such defenses, and I've not tried anything yet. I want to wait until they've been at it for quite a while longer—to make them feel complacent. Then, when they have some more done, and they're closer, and when I finally do hit them, I'll have a better chance of doing some real damage. If I'm able to destroy it now, they won't have lost much. Better to wait until they've already put a great deal more time and work into it."

Nicci frowned up at the tall prophet. "Nathan, you are a very devious man."

He smiled a Rahl smile. "I prefer to think of myself as ingenious."

Nicci went back to surveying the camp out beyond the site of the construction. It was just far enough away to provide their gifted with plenty of time to react to an attack. Nicci had spent enough time with Jagang's army to know a great deal about the way they thought. She knew the layers of defenses that Jagang's officers and gifted would place around the army. And some of those gifted were Sisters of the Dark.

"Look at that," she said, pointing. "It looks like a supply train is just arriving."

Nathan nodded. "Winter will be here shortly. The army looks like they're not going anywhere, so they will need a lot of supplies to keep all those men alive over the winter."

Nicci considered what could be done, finally deciding that, from where they stood, very little. "Well, Richard sent the army south to the Old World to attack their supply trains, among other things. Let's hope they're effective and can accomplish the task. If all those men starve to death that would solve our problem. In the meantime, I'll devote some thought to what we might be able to do to help them die."

She turned away from the depressing view of the encampment, and the supply train bringing all those men what they needed to stay and lay siege to the palace.

"Come on," she said to Nathan. "I need to get back, but why don't you show me before I leave."

Nathan took them down through the palace by the smaller, staff areas, rather than the vast halls. It was a quick descent through the stone interior of the palace, taking them ever lower into the dark, inner regions beneath the palace that were what most people never saw. There were elegant if simple stone halls even in these unseen places. Without elaborate decoration, they were made of polished stone in places, and rich woods in others. These were the private corridors used by the Lord Rahl and his staff.

Nicci had come to the People's Palace to pay a visit to the Garden of Life. After that, she had checked to see how Berdine was doing in her search for information, and how Nathan was getting on. They had wanted to tell her details of their difficulties; she hadn't really wanted to take the time but she made herself listen patiently.

After having again seen the place where the boxes of Orden had been, she had been too distracted to be able to really focus on what they were telling her. This time she saw the deserted Garden of Life differently, getting a feel for where Darken Rahl had opened the boxes, for where they had sat. She had studied the position of the room, the amount of light, the angles to various known star charts in addition to how the sun and moon transverse the place, and the area where the spells had been invoked.

Since translating *The Book of Life*, Nicci viewed the Garden of Life in a different way. She saw it through the context of the magic of Orden and how the room had been used. It had given her a valuable insight into the last place the boxes had been used. Such practical reference had answered some questions she'd had, and confirmed some of the conclusions she'd come to.

At last Nathan reached a set of double doors with guards standing before them. He gestured and the men opened the pair of white doors. Beyond was a wall of white stone that looked as if it had partly melted.

"Have you been in there?" she asked the prophet.

"No," he admitted. "At my age I try to stay out of tombs as much as I can."

Nicci stepped over the low ledge at the same time as she ducked through the low opening. "Wait here," she said to Cara, who had been about to follow her in.

"Are you sure?"

"This involves magic."

Cara wrinkled her nose as if she had gotten a whiff of sour milk, and waited outside along with the prophet.

Nicci sent a spark of Han into a torch to the side. After all this time it still lit. She saw then that the huge vaulted room was constructed of pink granite. The floor was white marble. On the walls all around were dozens and dozens of gold vases, each set in the wall beneath a torch. Nicci absently counted them. Fifty-seven. It appeared to her to be a number that had meaning. Probably the vases and torches represented the age of the man in the coffin in the center of the room.

The place was troubling, and not just because it was a crypt. She trailed her fingers along the symbols cut into the granite walls just beneath the vases. The words that ran around the entire room and around the golden coffin were High D'Haran. The inscriptions were instructions from a father to a son on the process of going to the underworld and returning. Quite the legacy.

Such spells contained Subtractive Magic. That was what was causing the walls to melt. Containing them by walling the place over with special stone had slowed the process greatly, but had not halted it entirely.

"Well?" Nathan asked, poking his head in through the melted hole. "Any ideas?"

Nicci stepped out, brushing off her hands. "I don't know. I don't think there's any imminent danger, but this involves dark things so there's a chance I'm wrong. I think it would be best to shield it behind an invocation of threes."

Nathan nodded in thought. "You want to do it? Lace it with Subtractive?"

"It would be best if you did it. You're a Rahl. That would be more effective. Even if I used Subtractive, this in here already has both mixed in, and it was created by a Rahl. Such power could breach any invocation I could create in here under the limitations of the protective spell of the palace."

He considered only briefly. "I will see to it at once." Nathan cast a look back at the crypt. "Any idea what's causing this spell to burn through?"

"Off the top of my head I'd say it was activated by one of the boxes of Orden having been opened up in the Garden of Life. I suspect they created a sympathetic reaction of some sort. It's not yet active enough for me to tell the purpose of the Subtractive element, but the words inscribed on the coffin and walls indicate that the constituent composition in there was intended to be used to aid in the acquisition of the power of Orden, so they act in a harmonic response after having been in the vicinity of that specific power."

Nathan nodded in thought. "All right. I'll do an invocation of threes and keep my eye on it."

"I have to get back. I will check back later, just to see if you've had any word from Richard and to see how the Order is getting along out there."

"Tell Zedd that I have everything well in hand, and I have the enemy surrounded."

Nicci smiled. "I'll tell him."

On her way through the vast halls of the palace, with Cara at her side, Nicci was lost in thought. She was unsure of what to do next. There were troubling problems descending from every direction. Most felt shadowy and ill defined. There was no one with whom she could really discuss all the things going through her mind. Zedd was a help in some of it, while Cara was good to talk to for other things.

But Richard was the only one who would be able to grasp the ways in which she was beginning to understand fundamental issues. Richard, in fact, was the one to introduce her to the concept of creative magic. She still clearly remembered that talk with him, one night at camp. It was one of the many defining moments with Richard.

There were also things Richard needed to know. There were incidents involving him and the boxes of Orden that were troubling, to say the least. In a way, he had built a fire under ingredients that were not merely dangerous but were beginning to bubble and boil and could possibly combine on their own in the most insidious ways if action wasn't taken.

There were prophecies involved that, not being a prophet, she didn't trust herself to understand. There were other prophecies that she was beginning to think she understood all too well and could not avoid taking into consideration.

Primary among those was the prophecy that said, "In the year of the cicadas"—which this was—"when the champion of sacrifice and suffering, under the banner of both mankind and the Light, finally splits his swarm"—which Jagang had done—"thus shall be the sign that prophecy has been awakened and the final and deciding battle is upon us. Be cautioned, for all true forks and their derivatives are tangled in this mantic root. Only one trunk branches from this conjoined primal origin." This was the time, succeed or fail, all or nothing, the watershed moment, that would forever set the course for the future. "If *fuer grissa ost drauka* does not lead this final battle, then the world, already standing at the brink of darkness, will fall under that terrible shadow."

That prophecy, she was beginning to see, was tangled in the boxes of Orden, but she couldn't quite grasp how. From time to time she felt on the brink of understanding, but she could never quite break through to it. There was something just beneath the surface of that prophecy that she knew was key.

At the same time, she felt that events were cascading, unrestrained, and she had to do something before those events tumbled out of control. With each passing day, she knew that options would continue to close for them. The Sisters of the Dark having put the boxes in play had already cut off their ability to use the power of Orden for its intended purpose: to counteract the ignition of the Chainfire event. With Chainfire contaminated by the chimes, they were rapidly losing the ability to use their gift to correct the damage.

There was no telling how much longer any of them would have sufficient control of their gift necessary to be of any use in overcoming any of the obstacles they faced.

At the same time, *The Book of Life* had come to have meaning for her that she could never have imagined. She had also studied several very obscure books Zedd had found for her on Ordenic theory. They, too, had added depth to her understanding, but all of that only seemed to open other areas to bigger questions.

Startled, Nicci halted and looked up. "What was that?"

"The bell for devotion," Cara said, looking a little puzzled at Nicci's reaction.

Nicci watched people begin to gather before a nearby square with a pool in the center. The pool, with a large, dark rock set off center, was opened to the sky.

"Perhaps we should go to devotion," Cara said. "It sometimes helps when you're troubled, and I can tell that you are definitely troubled."

Nicci frowned at the Mord-Sith, wondering how she knew that something was troubling her. She supposed that it really wasn't all that hard to tell.

"I don't have time to go to devotion," Nicci said. "I have to get back and figure this out."

Cara didn't look like she thought that was a good idea. She held a hand out toward the square.

"Thinking about Lord Rahl might help."

"Thinking about Nathan is not going to do me any good. I don't care if everyone thinks that Nathan is the Lord Rahl. Richard is Lord Rahl."

Cara smiled. "I know. That's what I meant." She took Nicci by the arm, drawing her toward the pool. "Come on."

Nicci stared at the woman as she was being dragged along, and then said, "I suppose it couldn't hurt to stop for a short time to think about Richard."

Cara nodded, looking somehow very wise at that moment. People respectfully made way for the Mord-Sith as she strode up to a spot near the pond. Nicci saw that there were fish gliding through the dark waters. Before she knew it, she was kneeling with Cara, putting her forehead to the floor.

"*Master Rahl guide us,*" the crowd began chanting in one voice, "*Master Rahl teach us. Master Rahl protect us. In your light we thrive. In your mercy we are sheltered. In your wisdom we are humbled. We live only to serve. Our lives are yours.*"

Nicci added her voice to the others, and together they lifted to reverberate through the halls. The words "Master Rahl" and Richard seemed indistinguishable to her. They were one in the same.

Almost against her will, Nicci's turbulent thoughts quieted as she softly chanted the words along with everyone else.

"*Master Rahl guide us. Master Rahl teach us. Master Rahl protect us. In your light we thrive. In your mercy we are sheltered. In your wisdom we are humbled. We live only to serve. Our lives are yours.*"

She lost herself in the words. The sunlight was warm on her back. The next day was the first day of winter, but inside Lord Rahl's palace the sun was warm, much like up in the Garden of Life. It seemed odd in that Darken Rahl, and his father, Panis, were the Lord Rahl before, making this place the seat of evil.

She realized, though, that the place was only that—a place. The man was what mattered. The man made the defining difference. The man set the tone that others followed, either rightly or wrongly. In a way, the devotion was the formal statement of that concept.

"*Master Rahl guide us. Master Rahl teach us. Master Rahl protect us. In your light we thrive. In your mercy we are sheltered. In your wisdom we are humbled. We live only to serve. Our lives are yours.*"

Those words reverberated in Nicci's mind. She missed Richard so much. Even though his heart belonged to someone else, she just missed seeing him, seeing his smile, talking to him. If that was all she could ever have, that was enough to sustain her. Just his friendship, his value in her life, and hers in his.

Just Richard being happy, being alive, being . . . Richard.

Our lives are yours.

Nicci abruptly rose up on her knees.

She understood.

Puzzled, Cara frowned up at her as everyone else chanted. "What's wrong?"

Our lives are yours.

She knew what she had to do.

Nicci stood in a rush. "Come on. I have to get back to the Keep."

As they ran together through the halls, Nicci could hear the whispering sound of voices rising up together to echo reverently through the vast corridors.

"*Master Rahl guide us. Master Rahl teach us. Master Rahl protect us. In your light we thrive. In your mercy we are sheltered. In your wisdom we are humbled. We live only to serve. Our lives are yours.*"

Nicci felt herself lost in words that suddenly had meaning for her that they had never had before.

She understood how it all fit together, at last, and knew what she had to do.

Zedd rose from his chair at the desk in the little room when he saw Nicci standing in the doorway. The lamplight softened his familiar face.

"Nicci, you're back. How are things at the People's Palace?"

Nicci hardly heard the question. Answering it was beyond her.

Zedd stepped closer, concern settling in his hazel eyes.

"Nicci, what's wrong. You look like a phantom come to haunt the halls."

She had to force herself to speak. "Do you trust Richard?"

Zedd's brow drew down. "What kind of question is that?"

"Do you trust Richard with your life?"

Zedd gestured with one arm. "Of course. What's this about?"

"Do you trust Richard with everyone's life?"

Zedd gently gripped her arm. "Nicci, I love that boy."

"Please, Zedd, do you trust Richard with everyone's life?"

The concern in his eyes overspread his face, deepening the creases. He finally nodded. "Of course I do. If there was ever anyone I would trust with my life, or the life of anyone, it would be Richard. After all, I'm the one who named him to be Seeker."

Nicci nodded as she turned.

"Thank you, Zedd."

He lifted his robes a little as he hurried after her. "Do you need some help with something, Nicci?"

"No," she said. "Thank you. I'm fine."

Zedd at last nodded, taking her word for it, and returned to the book he was studying.

Nicci walked through the halls of the Keep without seeing them. She moved as if following an invisible glowing line to her destination, the way Richard said he could follow the glowing lines of a spell-form.

"Where are we going?" Cara asked, rushing to follow behind.

"Do you trust Richard? Trust him with your life?"

"Of course," Cara said without an instant of hesitation.

Nicci nodded as she continued on.

She passed corridors, intersections, rooms, and stairs without really seeing them. In a daze of purpose, she finally reached the hardened area of the Keep and the grand room where the verification web had nearly taken her life. She would have died had it not been for Richard. He insisted on finding a way to save her when no one else believed it could be done.

She trusted Richard with her life, and her life was very precious to her, thanks to him.

At the double doors, Nicci turned to Cara. "I need to be alone."

"But I—"

"This involves magic."

"Oh," Cara said. "Well, all right, then. I'll just wait out here in the hall in case you need anything."

"Thank you, Cara. You're a good friend."

"I never had any real friends—friends really worth having—until Lord Rahl came along."

Nicci smiled a little. "I never had anything worth living for until Richard came along."

Nicci closed the double doors. Behind her, the two-story windows flickered with lightning. Nicci didn't know if she had ever been in that room when there wasn't a storm.

Now the whole world was caught in a storm.

When the lightning flashed the room lit with the harsh glare. There was one thing in the room, however, that did not register the touch of even such intense light. It waited like death itself.

Nicci laid *The Book of Life* open on the table before the inky black box of Orden sitting in the center of the table. It seemed that every time the lightning tried to ignite, that black box swallowed the light before it could really get started. Staring at it was like looking into forever.

Nicci invoked the first spell, calling forth darkness to match the impossible blackness of the grim box sitting before her. She reminded herself that, like the People's Palace, it was the person who defined it. With a thunderclap of power filling the room, the door was barred. No one could enter. The containment field of the windows no longer mattered. She had conjured something more powerful. The room was silent and pitch black. Nicci's vision came from the powers she had called forth.

She spoke the words written on the next page, invoking the next spell that opened the pathway for the governing formulas. She used a sliver of Subtractive Magic to void a razor-thin piece of flesh at the tip of her finger, and used the blood that began to ooze to begin drawing the diagrams needed before the box of Orden. As more blood ran from the open wound, she drew a containment field around the box itself. It was something like the field of the room, but on a much more intense scale. Without being contained first, such power as was liberated from the box of Orden could unintentionally breach the veil, but in a way that would kill only the person attempting what Nicci was attempting.

Almost not needing to read the book that she had been studying for what seemed half her life, she went on to the equations involving the time of year: the first day of winter.

Once that was completed, she drew the two opposing symbols and the joint of the apex from the proper charts in blood.

It went on, one intense formula after another, for the next hour, with calculations bringing the resultant layer of magic forth to be folded into the next step. Each node in the book required that only the appropriate level of power be applied. At each spot, Nicci let it flow forth without reservation.

There was no other way.

As the night wore on, the lines of the spell built around the box—in some ways like the Chainfire verification web, with lines that glowed green. But others were a pure white, while yet others were constructed of Subtractive elements and they were blacker than black, looking like nothing so much as voids in the world where the lines belonged, like slits looking into the underworld.

When Nicci completed the last incantation, she finally heard the whisper of Orden itself, confirmation that she had done everything properly. Yet it was not so much a voice as a force that formed the concept in her mind.

The power is open, it whispered through the darkness, in words that felt like ice cracking.

"I call upon this time, this place, this world to turn with this play of the boxes of Orden."

Name the player.

Nicci placed her hands on the dead black box before her.

"The player is Richard Rahl," she said. "Heed his will. Do his bidding if he proves worthy, kill him if he does not, destroy us all if he fails us."

It is done. From this moment forward the power of Orden is in play by Richard Rahl.

Prophecy said, "If *fuer grissa ost drauka* does not lead this final battle, then the world, already standing at the brink of darkness, will fall under that terrible shadow."

Nicci had come to realize that if Richard was to win, he must be the one leading them in this final battle. The only way to lead was for him to have the boxes in play. In that way, he truly would be the fulfillment of prophecy: *fuer grissa ost drauka*—the bringer of death.

Prophecy said that they had to follow Richard, but it was more than prophecy. Prophecy only expressed the formality of what Nicci knew, that Richard embodied the values that promoted life.

They weren't really following prophecy; prophecy was following Richard.

This was the ultimate following of Richard, following him in what he did with the boxes of Orden, in what he did with life and death itself. This was the ultimate test of who he was, who he would be, who he would become.

Richard himself had named the terms of the engagement when he spoke to the D'Haran troops, telling them how the war would be fought from now on: all or nothing.

This could be no different.

It now truly was all or nothing.

Ulicia and her Sisters of the Dark had likewise opened the gateway to the power of Orden. The struggle was now truly in balance. If Nicci was right about Richard, and she knew she was, then two forces now properly were engaged in the struggle that would decide it all.

If fuer grissa ost drauka *does not lead this final battle, then the world, already standing at the brink of darkness, will fall under that terrible shadow.*

They had to trust in Richard in that struggle. For that reason Nicci had to put the boxes of Orden into play in Richard's name. The Sisters of the Dark no longer were the exclusive arbiters of the power of Orden. In that sense, Nicci had just put Richard into play, giving him the ability to win this struggle.

Without what she had just done, he could not win, much less survive.

Nicci seemed to drift in a world apart. When she finally opened her eyes, the storm had ended.

The first rays of light were just touching the windows.

It was dawn, on the first day of winter.

Richard had one year to open the correct box.

Everyone's life was now in his hands.

Nicci trusted Richard with her life. She had just entrusted everyone's life to him.

If she couldn't trust Richard, then life wasn't worth living.

BE SURE TO LOOK FOR THE NEXT AND CONCLUDING BOOK
IN THE SWORD OF TRUTH SERIES.

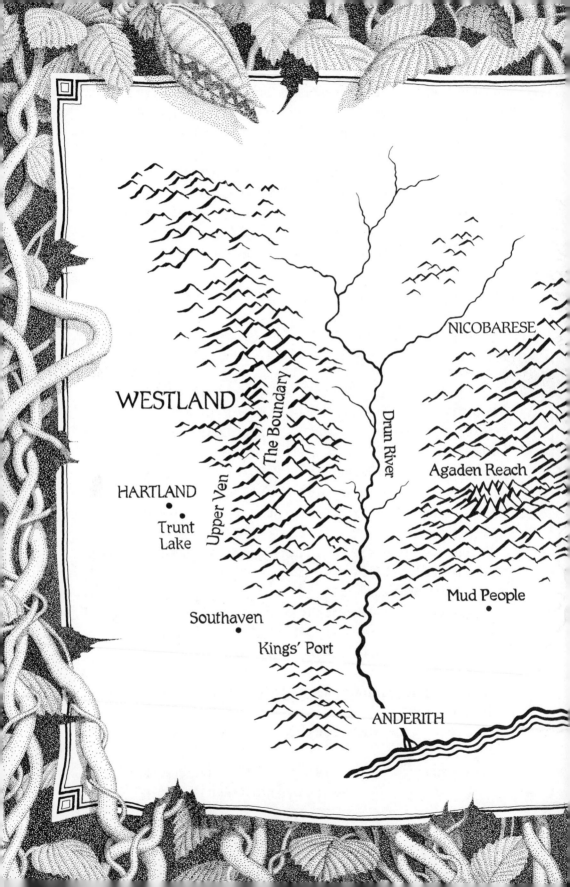

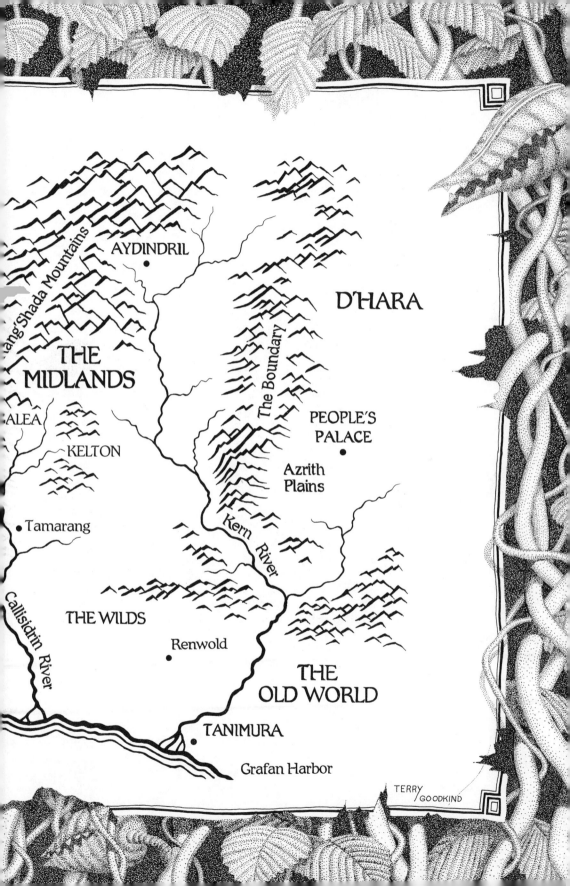